THE HIDDEN KINGDOM

L. ROSE

NOTE FROM THE AUTHOR

The Hidden Kingdom is the box set for previous published single titles:

A Torn Paige
A Lost Paige
A Final Paige

It also contains a bonus chapter of Paige and her guys in the future which was once shared on my website, and newer images of each character.

Happy reading!

Learn to love your inner monster.

PROLOGUE

I floated in the darkened sky looking below to the dirt mound surrounded by woods. I watched and waited for something to happen, as if I expected a situation. And when I saw the dirt shift, little rocks and soil tumbling to the side, I knew what I was waiting for.

I knew it as well as the next breath I needed.

Dirty hands popped through the earth. They clawed out of the ground, digging their way free.

Fear clenched my stomach, despite knowing I shouldn't be scared.

The scene was surreal.

A head broke free next and tipped back. A growl shuddered through the area. Wild red eyes took in everything. It was a woman. Her light-colored hair was either blonde or white, but filthy from the muck. She pushed at the dirt and then leaped from the hole she'd been buried in. As she landed in a crouch, her eyes frantically darted this way and that. Her head tipped again, her nostrils flaring. She scented her surroundings.

Another growl rumbled from her, tore from her. The sound almost animalistic.

The dress covering her small frame was in tatters.

My stomach tightened when I saw her clutch at her own gut as she slowly stood, as if I could feel the hunger eating away at her.

The wind brushed through the area, her hair and dress swaying in the breeze. Suddenly, she spun right and crouched again. A low, humming rumble echoed out of her mud-caked mouth and into the woods.

Again, fear bombarded me.

The woman looked crazed. Her body tensed when we heard a branch break close by. Her upper lip pulled back in a snarl, a warning, and I felt mine doing the same.

Into the small clearing stepped a….

Confusion swamped me. I should know what it was, but I couldn't place it in my mind. The animal looked like a dog, but it was different. Bigger. Four times bigger than any dog I'd seen. Its body was built like a tank, even under the thick fur I could see each muscle pull while it slowly took step after step toward the woman. Its bright red eyes glowed back at her.

The animal let loose its own growl, but the full force of it was obstructed by something it carried in its mouth.

The woman stayed perfectly still, but I could tell she was ready to pounce if she needed to. If a fight was to be had, she was ready. She hadn't survived being buried for nothing. There was a reason everything happened.

There had to be.

The animal went down on its legs as it drew closer and then belly crawled the rest of the way to her. The woman's head tilted to the side as if confused, and again she scented the air with a big breath in. Another growl erupted from within her when hunger stabbed her stomach once more.

How I knew it, I wasn't sure.

But I knew it with the clarity of my own hunger.

The animal dropped what was in its mouth, nosed it toward her, and then retreated a little. Sitting, it watched her, looking from the woman to what lay in front of her.

My focus landed on the item it dropped, and my eyes widened.

It was an arm.

An arm from a human body.

The woman dove at it, picking it up before the animal could withdraw the offering. She scooted back, and while keeping her eyes on the animal, she lifted the arm, sniffed it and….

Oh, God.

She opened her mouth wide before biting into the flesh. Blood ran down around her lips. The kill must have been fresh. She moaned as she swallowed the first bite. It had sated the hunger, but only a little, so she took off another chunk using her teeth, not caring it coated her mouth and clothes in more blood, or that she was eating human flesh in the first place.

The animal stood and edged closer to the woman. She watched it with wary eyes and growled once when it sat beside her.

I should have been disgusted.

Even scared.

But I wasn't.

I wasn't because I knew.

I knew the woman had been reborn into something else, and the animal at her side was there to help her.

I knew it all… because I was her.

CHAPTER ONE

I jolted awake, flying to sit upright on my bed. The sheets tumbled to my waist as I attempted to control the erratic rise and fall of my chest. Not exactly breathing, because I didn't need to.

That damn dream.

My sleeping pattern had also been altered. I didn't need much, only a few hours every couple of days, but when I did, that same dream played with my mind.

Six months had gone by since that night.

The night I found myself waking and starving for human flesh.

I didn't know how it happened, if I was attacked, kidnapped, or killed. It took me a few days to come back to my old self—my memories and life before that night finally clearing in my mind. Everything except what led to me being buried. It was as if that part of my memory was erased.

I hated not knowing who had done it or why.

I didn't even know exactly what I had become... but if I was to guess, it would be a ghoul. I'd read enough urban fantasy to take a stab in the dark at it, and besides, Google somewhat helped me narrow it down. I didn't want to suck someone's blood dry, I didn't turn hairy every full moon, I didn't have wings, and I didn't have a hunger for brains alone. I liked to consume human meat. If I didn't have it at least once a week, my moods changed when the gut-wrenching hunger started deep inside me. On top of the whole "human flesh" thing, was that my non-beating heart was pretty much a dead giveaway with the ghoul theory.

Hell, before I was reborn into whatever I was, I didn't even know there were *others* in the world. I'd always thought vampires, werewolves, witches, fae, and demons were the things of fairy tales and romance stories. Then again, I hadn't actually met any other species, but I took a big guess that there were more than just humans in the world or else, how was I created? I guess Mom had always been wrong when she used to say, "Paige, why do you read that nonsense? It'll never teach you anything."

The bonus side of being undead—an assumption made with the lack of a beating organ—was that I didn't get my period. In fact, I didn't need to visit the bathroom at all besides to shower. I worked out, I still sweated, which was weird, and I also... became wet when I was turned on. Found that out one night when I was out clubbing and was attracted to someone who took me home for the night. I blessed anyone who would listen for *that* part of me to still be working. If it hadn't, it would have been one uncomfortable experience for both of us. Not that I saw him ever again.

Needless to say, everything was different. I wasn't sure how my brain still functioned when just about the rest of my body wasn't. Though, I was grateful for having my memories.

Especially when I remembered who I was and who my family was.

Now, between working as a barista in a local coffee shop, I spent the rest of my time hunting for the person who'd changed me. I wanted to know with what purpose they'd done it.

There had to be a reason behind the act of ending my life, so I was reborn into what I was.

Sighing, a normal habit of mine, I slipped the sheet off the rest of my body and stretched. Ezra must have heard my movement as he came bounding into my room. I gave him a sleepy smile and bent to rub my hands over his body.

I would have been lost even more without the help of Ezra —the animal who had been at my side when I woke. I still didn't know exactly what he was, but I knew he was special and happy to stick by my side, helping me feed in those first few nights when I wasn't myself.

Since then, Ezra taught me how to hunt my own food.

Hunt.

I hunted humans to eat. *Warm human flesh, fresh from a kill is what I like best. However, if it's a couple of days old, I'm still good with it, but anything over that I can't stomach.* Usually a thought like that would have churned my gut, or I would have just thrown up. But the squeamishness was all behind me now.

It had to be done. I had to eat human flesh or I would slowly starve. I wouldn't say to death, because I wasn't sure what could kill me. But it was to a point where I worried I'd turn crazed and kill someone. Even loved ones, and I wouldn't risk that. So I made sure I hunted those who deserved it. Those who killed and raped.

Ezra helped me find them and take them down. I didn't know how he did it, but I was grateful to have him at my side.

Even though we couldn't talk to one another, we were still in sync. He knew how I was feeling, what I needed, and somehow understood what I said. I just couldn't speak animal. If he *was* an animal. I mean, he was. I just wasn't sure if he was any type that lived on Earth.

Still, I loved him no matter.

My life had changed, but I was still the same person on the inside—in my dead heart and soul. At first, because I didn't know what I was, I'd contemplated ending my life. What kept me going and not giving in to those dark thoughts were my family and Ezra.

Smiling down at him, I said, "Come on. I better get ready before we're late to meet Yasmin." He actually rolled his eyes at me. He didn't mind going to my sister's place because he loved playing with her kids. But that night my sister had wanted to go out for dinner to celebrate her husband's promotion, so Ezra was annoyed he wouldn't be getting the attention from them. Because even though Ezra could transform himself from his massive natural form—which I was yet to figure out exactly what he was in his real form since there were so many creatures he could resemble or ones I'd read up on without a picture for reference online—into a newfoundland breed of a dog, which, thanks to Google, I was able to recognize. The place we were going to didn't allow animals. That meant he would have to go unseen to the human eye.

Both of those talents I discovered within a few weeks of my return.

I'd been used to seeing him in his monstrous form, where his fur was wild and scruffy, his height reaching the top of my shoulders. He had glowing eyes and razor-sharp teeth. His mouth also revealed two long, sharp fangs jutting out and over his bottom lip, and then there were the spikes that ran down his spine. The night he first transformed his body into a canine form was when I'd told him I was going out, without him, to see my sister after finally feeling normal for the first time. He'd stood in front of the door and refused to move. I'd told him he couldn't go because everyone would have a fit at me for bringing him looking like he was—a scary beast. He'd huffed at me, and I'd tumbled back when his body altered, changed, and mutated to the newfoundland size.

The first time I'd discovered he could become invisible to humans was when we were out hunting. I was down at one end of the alley and Ezra at the other. I'd scented the fresh blood on my prey's hands, even though they seemed clean.

"Who did you kill?" I'd asked.

The man had sneered. "What are you talking about?"

"Wife?" I'd questioned and didn't get a reaction. "Sister?" I'd pressed and got nothing. "Employer?" Zilch. "Girlfriend?" He'd winced. I'd clicked my tongue, shaking my head. "Why?"

His face had contorted with rage. "She wouldn't give me money. Kept it all to herself, the greedy bitch."

"Seriously? You killed her over money?"

He'd kept backing up toward Ezra, as if he couldn't see the threat behind him each time he looked over his shoulder to see if he had a clear run.

I'd paused, tilted my head, and glanced behind him to Ezra. "He can't see you, can he?"

The guy had spun around, looking everywhere. I'd started laughing.

"What are you laughing at?" the man had screeched. His eyes wide in fear, finally.

I'd grinned. "Wow, I wish I could see your face if you saw what was behind you."

Fascinated, I'd watched as Ezra's body shimmered. He'd let out a snorted snuffle, and the man spun his way. He'd screamed, the scent of urine hitting my nose, and then he'd tried to run my way.

Of course, he hadn't expected my strength. He'd thought the gun in my grip was all I'd had to protect myself... well, besides Ezra. So he hadn't expected me to lower the gun, tuck it into the waist of my jeans, and then brace myself as he got closer. His chest had heaved with every breath he took; panic had him begging even before he'd reached me.

It was too late. He could beg all he wanted, but he'd taken a life, so his wasn't worth living either.

Ezra's nose burrowed under my hand, bringing me from my thoughts. "Eww, cooties," I complained with a laugh. He then, of course, got close and snorted into my hand on purpose. Just to be grosser, he licked all of my hand as I tried, while laughing still, to push him back. Wrapping my arms around his neck, I slid off my bed and tackled him to the ground. "You're a monster." His lips pulled back off his razor-sharp teeth, as if smiling. I groaned, laughing the word, "Whatever." I bounced up to my feet. "I'll get a quick shower in. Then we'd better move it."

After showering, I got ready. Since it was a fancy restaurant, where I would eat a little food since I still needed some type of sustenance between my "other" meals to help sedate my new side, I chose a black dress and heels to match my long dark hair and eyes. I'd even applied a little makeup to cover the paleness of my skin. I'd brought a long red jacket to go over the top since it was cold out. Not that the change in weather bothered me, but it made me look normal since others would have warmer clothing on.

The drive didn't take long. As I turned the corner to the restaurant, I slammed on the brakes. Ezra, in his canine form, went flying forward, only managing to brace at the end, so he didn't crash through the windshield. Thankfully no one was behind me. Then again, the streets were quiet in this area, something that I should have noticed already.

My heart would have taken off in flight if it could.

Instead, dread caused my hands to shake slightly. I quickly pulled my car off to the side of the road and parked. With Ezra at my heels, I climbed out. My hand went to the top of his head as he moved to my side. The street was usually a busy spot, bustling with people walking, driving, or heading into the numerous shops around. Instead, the place was quiet. No one was around except for three men dressed in black and armed to hell, who stood out the front of where my family was. They were barricaded by cars. Something had happened inside that restaurant, and I needed to find out what.

Something was wrong.

Very wrong.

I shivered in fear, a reaction I hadn't experienced in a long time.

Still, no matter what was happening, I was going in there to help my sister. My upper lip pulled back from my teeth in a silent snarl. No one hurt my sister.

With a purpose-filled stride, I made my way over, and as I stepped up to the back of the group of men, something caused my body to hum. Ignoring it, I kept going, stopping beside one of the men at the front.

Startled, the guy behind them tried to grab my arm with a surprised "Hey." But I dodged it.

The man I stood beside stopped talking to the guy next to him, noticing his other man calling out. He glanced over his shoulder to his man before doing a double take, his gaze landing on me. Actually, all of them were looking down at me, since they were damn tall, with wide eyes. The man at my side slowly slid his gaze all the way down my body and then back up. He looked about midthirties. His light blue eyes narrowed, and he jerkily ran a hand over his long black hair. With a quick glance, I took him in. His shoulders were wide, and I could see the definition his body held under his black Henley long-sleeve top. His jeans also sat snugly against his butt—one I wouldn't mind grabbing. *So wrong, Paige.*

"What's going on in there?" I asked, getting back on track to the situation.

He opened his mouth, snapped it closed, and then glowered. "Who are you?" Not waiting for an answer, he spun and demanded, "Smith, how did she get through your ward?"

Ward? That was a spell, right? Which meant I wasn't dealing with normal humans. An excited thrill ran up my spine. I hadn't yet met any *others.* Maybe I should have guessed they were different from the power that tingled over my skin. But I'd been distracted by the worry I held for my sister.

"I don't know, sir," Smith answered. I glanced at him, at his strange gray gaze and dark blond hair, which was buzzed at the sides and back, but longer and messy on top. He was built smaller in size than the other two, but still impressive, and I had a feeling his stamina would be good…. Why I even thought that I didn't know because it wasn't the time. It also wasn't time to get lost in his warm, soft eyes. He seemed like the nicer out of all of them. Smith, he'd been called. I had to remember it.

Ezra huffed from my side, and I caught Mr. In Charge's eyes lasered down on him.

No matter who or what they were, they were keeping me from helping my family. Since I was sick of waiting, I asked again, *"What's* going on in there?"

He pulled his piercing gaze back up to me. "You need to leave, little girl. Take your dog and go."

Little girl? I knew I looked young but being called a little girl was just an insult.

Annoyance dipped my brows. I hummed and tapped my chin, then shook my head. Behind us, Smith chuckled. "I don't think so. Now, are you going to answer *my* question?"

"No," he clipped, crossing his arms over his broad chest. "Smith?" he called.

"I would have guessed human, but she doesn't have a heartbeat. Then I'd have thought one of yours, but that's wrong. She feels different."

"You're right," he bit out, and I had a feeling he didn't like puzzles or that I'd just walked into his world. I swung my gaze around at them. They could tell I didn't have a heartbeat. Interesting. Now I was certain they were different like me.

"I can't pick it up either. Just make her leave," a guy growled out roughly.

Ezra snarled just as low.

I faced the man who'd spoken, the one on the other side of whoever "sir" was. His green, narrowed stare held mine when I told him, "I wouldn't try to make me leave, because I won't. My sister is in there with her family, and *I* want to know what's going on." The guy's upper lip raised. He was bigger than all of them, yet it looked good on him. Too good with his shaggy dark-brown hair. I tore my gaze away after I quickly coughed into my hand, "Dick." His eyes flashed wide for a second, but I saw it. I deemed his new name Mr. Arrogant.

Mr. In Charge said, "This isn't the time for hysterical family members—"

"Do I look hysterical?" Mimicking his stance, I crossed my arms over my chest. His gaze flicked down and then back up. Shit. I wished I'd worn my proper ass-kicking gear because I didn't think my black dress and heels were intimidating at all to these men. As well as my height and size. Sighing, I tried again, "Just please tell me what's going on in there, so I know what I'm walking into."

Mr. Arrogant man snorted. "You and your little doggie aren't going anywhere near there."

Ezra rumbled out another growl. I smiled. They would soon get a shock when they found out Ezra wasn't just a little doggie. The thought made me want to laugh. I didn't, of course. "Sure, okay. Guess I'm not going to get any answers anyway." I shrugged, turning. Smith moved aside for me with a pitying smile. I took one step by him and then spun back around, racing toward the entrance. The men shouted, cursed, and I even sensed one or two of them starting to come after me, until I called over my shoulder, "Ezra, keep them back."

Just before I walked through the front door, I glanced back

to see Ezra standing in the pathway, his body shaking with the change as he grew and grew to his full size.

Then I heard before the door closed, "Fuck me. She has a hellhound."

So that's what Ezra was.

CHAPTER TWO

Once the door closed fully, I straightened my dress and moved toward, then around the front closed-off section and into the restaurant. I stopped and took in what was before me.

A man, at least that was what I presumed it was since his body was misshaped, stood beside a table of three kids and a couple, a gun pointing down at them. His other hand, with a second gun, was already aimed my way. He must have heard me coming.

"You move, I'll shoot them all."

I quickly took in the rest of the room. A lot of the tables were filled with employees, couples, or families cringing and crying as they held one another. My family was off to the left of the man. Eric, my sister's husband, held Yasmin close. Their kids, my niece and nephew, were on their laps, silently crying.

I blinked. My hands shot up in front of me. "Whoa, hold on

a second. I just walked in here to meet my date. What's going on?"

The man scoffed. "Your date? And those guys out front didn't try to stop you?" His unbelieving gaze narrowed even more.

"Ah, yeah, they tried. But I wasn't listening to douches like that when I had a date to get to."

Loud snarling sounded from out the front. The ground shook a little. People screamed.

Dammit, they'd better not hurt Ezra, or I'd kill them myself. My thoughts drifted to Ezra being a hellhound. How did those men know? Though, I had a feeling they knew a lot of things, maybe even what I was for certain.

Shit. It wasn't the time to contemplate stuff. I had to bring forward my acting skills. "Holy hell," I cried, clutching my chest. "What could that be?" I glanced over my shoulder and then back to Mr. Dickhead.

"Probably them, but they won't come in here and risk the hostages." His head tilted, probably wondering why he'd just told me that. His face darkened. "If you're here on a date, where is he?"

I glanced around, pretending to search for someone. My sister looked like she wanted to scream at me for being in there and acting like an idiot. Terror shined in her eyes. Though I suspected she knew I was different, she definitely knew I was strong and fast. But she didn't know why. How could she since I didn't have the answers for her. Would I tell her if I ever found out? Probably. We'd usually tell each other everything; however, I felt the need to avoid the subject of how I dug my way out of a grave and the details of my new diet... for now at least. For most of our lives, we'd only had each other. After our parents had died on a safari, and since Yasmin had been twenty at the time it happened, she looked after my sixteen-year-old self. Though, she would always say we looked after each other.

"Hell, he's not here." I stamped my foot. "Do you think he stood me up?"

Mr. Dickhead eyed me skeptically. "Maybe. Too bad for you. Now you're involved." He gestured with his gun. "Sit down over there and shut the fuck up."

I made my way over to the chair he pointed to, where a man and woman already sat at the table. As soon as my butt was on the chair, I raised my hand like I was in school.

Mr. Dickhead sighed. "What?" he clipped.

"Can I ask what's all this about? I know I'm late to the game, but will this take long? I'd like to find the asshole who stood me up and give him a piece of my mind."

Dickhead's brows shot up. "Really?"

I rolled my eyes. "Yes. No one stands me up." I waved my hand around flippantly. "So, what's this about?"

His jaw clenched, and his eyes… they swirled, going from light brown to black and then back again. Something was on the inside peeking out. Did that mean his body wasn't his own, or was it a part of him? Was whatever in him the reason he was misshapen and the reason for his long arms? His bumpy face?

What was I facing?

Would it be something I could beat?

I had to. I couldn't let the worry seep in. I had to beat him —it—so my family was safe.

He shook his head back and forth over and over, then suddenly stopped. He focussed on me, his gaze fully black.

His teeth flashed at me. "Pretty, pretty pet." His head twitched to the side. A gun fired, people screamed and shrieked, and then the wailing came. I didn't move. I couldn't. I was frozen, waiting for the pain to come, thinking he'd fired the gun at me. He didn't. More screams rang around the room, those frantic with terror.

It was then I saw the man with his family slumped forward over the table. Blood poured from his head onto the white cloth.

He'd shot a father in front of his family.

A father.

The wife bellowed through her pain, gripping her children to her. The kids sobbed, hiding their faces against their mother's body.

"Shut up!" Dickhead yelled.

Everyone did. Even the noise from outside silenced.

Please, please let Ezra be okay.

Dickhead had been watching me the whole time. Another twitch of his head. His nose lifted without his face moving up. He drew in the scent around him. "Hmm." He licked his lips. "Soon. Soon. Soon. She's dying. You will change and be mine."

Confusion rolled through my mind, but I let it slide and asked the one question I needed to know. "Why?"

"Why?" he screeched. "Why? Why? Why? Why?" He laughed then. "Because I was called. He wanted help. I was called, and he had second thoughts of shooting his boss. His boss. His boss. No one backs out of a deal with me."

A demon.

I rolled my thoughts through the many Google searches. I concluded it had to be a demon because it was all I could think of.

Fuck.

I'd never dealt with one before. I didn't know if I could. Hell,

I'd never dealt with any other supernatural before, so no matter what, I was out of my element. Still, I had to try. I had to do something.

He licked his lips again, running his tongue slowly over his bottom lip. "I can taste your change. *Taste it.* Soon." He laughed gleefully and trained both weapons on me. "We leave. You come with me, and no one else gets hurt."

What did he mean by the change?

I'd already changed.

I stood and heard a yelp. I chanced a brief glance to my sister. Eric had a hand over her mouth. Tears filled her eyes. I closed my own. Turmoil sliced at my dead heart from the alarm I saw in her.

Because I knew, *knew* she would know I would do anything to stop people from dying.

Nodding, I straightened, opened my eyes, and stepped forward. "Okay. All right. I'll go." I walked toward him, and as soon as I was in grabbing distance, he reached forward with the gun still in his hand and took hold of my wrist. Spinning me, he placed me in front of him. His arm wound around my waist, drawing me back into his chest. I shuddered in disgust when I felt his warm breath on my neck.

"Yes. Soon, and then I will rule your people."

My people?

What did that mean?

I couldn't analyze his crazy words now, though.

"Everyone stay seated," he called out as he started backing toward the kitchen. I caught sight of Yasmin struggling within Eric's arms. I shook my head at her, and she slumped, defeated. Tears ran down her cheeks.

If I just got him outside, I could stop him. I would do something to make sure I was safe for my family. I couldn't let Yasmin lose me like we had our parents.

We were moving faster. I tripped, and he yanked me up. His grip was now painful around me.

A gun cocked from behind. The demon froze. "Where do you think you're going?" a deep voice, one I recognized as the Mr. In Charge out front, said.

The demon laughed. "You shoot me, she dies."

"She leaves with you, she dies" was his reply.

"We leave, we keep everyone else safe," I added my own tidbit.

The ground shook. Heavy pounding footfalls approached. Screams echoed around the room when the front of the building's glass shattered and Ezra came bounding in, skidding to a stop after he crashed through the divider from the front to the eating area.

I sighed in relief to see he was in one piece with a few scrapes and scratches.

"Shut up," the demon—as I was now convinced more than ever that was what he was—roared.

Fear stank up the room as people quieted down.

"Smith?" Mr. In Charge called.

A frazzled-looking Smith, with his hair sticking up all over the place, shuffled around Ezra's form. "Sorry, boss, he got away."

"Jesus," Mr. In Charge muttered. I really wish I knew his name because he certainly wasn't in charge of me.

"Any of you move, I will kill all the little humans," the demon growled.

Ezra snarled, just as Mr. Arrogant came to stand beside him. "Seems we have a standoff." The idiot smirked. "You only have your strength in that weak body. Leave now and you'll live to fight another day."

"She comes with me," he stated.

"She stays, demon," Mr. In Charge replied.

Ding, ding, ding, I was so right.

"Can we at least take this outside?" I asked.

"No," Mr. In Charge snapped.

"He gets you outside near his ley line, you're toast," Smith mentioned.

"Let her go," Mr. Arrogant demanded in a rough tone. A tone I kind of liked. At least my lady bits did, but it wasn't the time to be appreciating it.

"She comes—"

I groaned, loud and long. "How long are we going to do this? Just shoot him already."

Everyone blinked slowly at me.

But no one goddamn shot him.

The demon cackled. "They won't risk you."

Fine, if they wouldn't risk me, I had to.

"Yasmin, look away," I said, and then I reached up to place my hands at the back of the demon's neck.

"Don't!" Mr. Arrogant barked.

My body jolted from the demon's gun at my side. I dug my fingers into his neck as he dropped one gun and placed his fingers against my neck.

"You kill me, I take your life," he warned.

For a second, I froze. It was all of a second because anger flamed inside me. I would not let him take me. I wouldn't die a second time.

With all my strength, I twisted in his arms. He tried to hold me tightly, but I managed to spin in his hold, grip his head, and squeeze. My body shook as he loaded bullet after bullet into me.

I screamed into his face, just before I ripped his head clear off his body.

Silence.

Deafening silence. So much so, my ears started ringing. The body crumpled in a heap at my feet, and I stared down at the head in my hands.

More terrified yells grew around me.

"Smith," Mr. In Charge bellowed.

Then more silence.

Blinking, I looked up and around. The humans in the room were frozen in place. Some had already tried to make a run for it.

A hand touched my arm. I flinched and faced Mr. In Charge.

"What's your name?" he asked calmly.

"What's yours?" I countered.

His lips thinned in annoyance or humor. Either way, I didn't care. My family was safe. I was safe. "Asher Evans."

I nodded once. "Paige Alice," I replied. "I—" I gasped. Pain, agonizing pain sliced through my chest, as if there was a hot poker drilling into my heart slowly. I dropped the head to clutch the area. Crying out, I fell to my knees.

"Paige," Asher called. "What is it?" He got to his knees beside me but was knocked back when Ezra arrived to stand over me. "Move, beast. Let me help her."

Ezra growled from the back of his throat, a threat and warning. I rolled to my side, curling up, panting through the tearing, the ripping happening inside me. Clenching my jaw, I closed my eyes tightly.

"Move," someone else ordered.

Ezra let out a howl and scratched at the floor as he moved over my body more.

Fire.

Fire so hot burned from within.

My eyes sprung wide along with my mouth as I screamed. I yelled so loud and long it hurt my throat, but that was nothing compared to what I felt inside.

Male voices yelled, threatened, and roared around me. I couldn't focus on any.

A bright white light flashed and then nothing but blackness.

CHAPTER THREE

ASHER

The council for the supernatural community had been founded thousands of years ago. For five decades I had been working for them as one of their soldiers, or as they classed us, even in training, their elite enforcers.

Under orders, we went to war when needed. We eliminated any lawbreaking citizens or anyone who risked our existence to the human race. We protected those who couldn't protect themselves, and we hunted demons to send them back to where they came from. It was only moments ago when the council had received a call about a demon causing havoc, and they sent us for the job. Evicting a demon from Earth was a piece of cake. Especially with our mixed group, something that no other elite group had.

I was the one who had approached the council after being

there for a decade to see if they would accept a mixed-species group. At first, they quickly declined my idea, thinking it ridiculous. Four years after my first attempt, I asked again, and they allowed *one* group, my group, to try it. A test to see how things worked out. However, when they offered up a shifter for my first member, I was wary. I'd heard this shifter didn't work well with others. No matter how many shifter groups he'd teamed up with, he ended up on his own because of his asshole ways.

When I had seen Nate Felan, the shifter to our group, brutally fighting another shifter for intimidating a weaker opponent at the compound, I didn't second-guess the council's suggestion. I asked him if he would be interested in a position on the team. Nate and I had been working together for the last four decades.

Others had come into our group and either asked for a transfer, not liking Nate, or had died in battle.

The last and most recent addition to our small group was Alex Smith, a mage. He'd been with us for the last five years. Before he joined, I'd studied his file. He'd been top of his class and fresh out of magic school into the elite enforcers. He was full of power and intelligence, yet in many other ways, he was still young for his thirty years. Young in experience, but he was learning fast.

All of us aged differently, some not at all. Like Nate and me. We would stay at the age we appeared, in our late thirties, forever. Alex would age another ten years, but then his aging would stop there for him as well. We lived until we decided to leave this world, or died in war. We were the same in a lot of ways, yet we all thought and strategized differently, and worked well together. We'd seen a lot through our years. We were strong, feared and, at least Nate and I, had earned the respect of the council members for the work we'd done.

Nothing on this earth could surprise us anymore.

Until now.

I was good at blanking my expression, but when the shorter, sexy woman had stepped up beside me outside, I was shocked to the core, and I knew it showed. Then her quick wit and cool exterior impressed me, so I didn't notice everything there was about her. Not until Smith picked up she had no heartbeat. With my mind, I reached out to hers and tried to gain access, but it was impenetrable. What I did know was that she wasn't one of my kind. A vampire.

Which made me question what she could be.

As far as we knew, all other species that didn't contain a beating heart no longer existed.

There were demons, of course, but she didn't act like the soul-stealing monsters.

What made me more impressed was when she'd played us before she started for the front door. It was then my body reacted at the thought of the demon inside the restaurant getting his hands on her. My body woke from its decades of rest by fear creeping in, causing my gut to drop and my throat to thicken. I knew she'd entered the situation for her sister's sake, to make sure she'd be safe. I understood her reasoning because I'd do anything for my family and the team I worked with.

Still, I didn't think she understood the situation exactly or how much danger she was about to step into. Nate and I started to follow her. When she ordered her dog to keep us back, I wanted to throw my head back and laugh at the audacity the tiny woman showed. That was until her dog stepped in front of us and—I still couldn't believe it—changed into a goddamn hellhound.

If she wasn't a demon, then who else controlled hellhounds?

Would she be a danger to my crew?

What and who in the hell was she?

Christ, not even Nate could scent what she was, and he had the best damn nose in the business.

Nate shifted into his wolf form as my ears picked up on what was being said inside. Only what I heard, I couldn't believe. The woman's acting was questionable, and I wasn't sure the demon would go with it, but he seemed to want to.

The ground shook as Nate and the hellhound collided.

"Smith, detain the animal without harm while Nate distracts him," I ordered. It was a simple spell for Alex. Before I could see him work his magic, I made my way around the side of the building.

My heightened hearing picked up a gun being fired. People screamed and cried. All I could think about was that I hoped, whoever had been shot—since the scent of blood was in the air —wasn't the woman who'd just walked in.

Moving through the back door, I listened carefully. The demon's attention stayed on the walking and talking woman. He wanted her, but why? I was determined to have an answer to that question soon.

I slipped through the kitchen doors just as the demon backed closer my way.

Raising my gun higher, I aimed at the back of his head. I cocked it and smirked when the demon froze. "Where do you think you're going?"

The demon laughed. "You shoot me, she dies."

I rolled my eyes. I wasn't stupid, and this wasn't the first time we'd played with demons. "She leaves with you, she dies."

"We leave, we keep everyone else safe," the woman added. She was still trying to save everyone else but herself. Christ, it touched my cold, dead heart.

The ground shook. Heavily pounding footfalls approached. Screams echoed around the room when glass shattered up front. The damn hellhound, what she called Ezra, came bounding in. It skidded to a stop after he crashed through the divider from the front waiting area to where we all were.

"Shut up," the demon roared around the room.

People quieted straightaway out of fear.

"Smith?" I called.

He stood just to the side and behind Ezra, seeming exasperated. "Sorry, boss, he got away."

"Jesus," I muttered.

"Any of you move, I will kill all the little humans," the demon growled.

Ezra snarled back as Nate, in human form, came to stand beside him.

"Seems we have a standoff." Nate smirked. "You only have your strength in that weak body. Leave now and you'll live to fight another day."

"She comes with me," he stated.

"She stays, demon," I replied, growing bored, but I wouldn't risk killing him with her in his arms.

"Can we at least take this outside?" the woman asked, her tone full of irritation.

"No," I snapped, shocked she wasn't scared even a little.

"He gets you outside near his ley line, you're toast," Smith mentioned.

"Let her go," I demanded roughly.

"She comes—"

The little woman groaned in annoyance. Shit, I wanted to laugh at her, but refrained. She then said, "How long are we going to do this? Just shoot him already."

All I could do was blink at her audacity.

The demon laughed. "They won't risk you."

"Yasmin, look away," the woman called out. My eyes widened as she reached up to place her hands at the back of his neck.

"Don't!" Nate barked, worry appearing in his tone.

Goddamn, her beautiful body jolted from the demon's gun at her side being fired shot after shot into her.

For the first time in centuries, I was frozen in place, watching her push her fingers into the demon's neck. He dropped one gun and covered her neck with his free hand.

"You kill me, I take your life," he warned.

Her face contorted into anger. A silent snarl pulled her upper lip from her teeth.

With strength I didn't know she'd have, she twisted in his arms, gripped his head and squeezed. Her body spasmed as he unloaded more rounds into her. I made a dive forward to help, as did Nate and Smith.

She screamed into his face, causing us to all pause, and then, *fuck me*, she tore his head right off his body.

Silence.

Utter silence.

My body hummed with the adrenaline running through my veins, and I put it down to the panic I'd felt for the woman. Never had I reacted like this for a victim. Why her?

Her chest rose and fell, but I couldn't feel or scent her breath. Was she even breathing?

The body dropped to the floor at her feet. Only I didn't take my eyes off her.

The humans around us started to yell once again.

"Smith," I yelled over the noise.

Within seconds, there was more silence.

The woman blinked a few times before raising her head and gazing around, noting everyone but my team and her were frozen.

Gently, I reached out and touched her arm. She flinched but faced me with a calm, blank expression.

"What's your name?" I asked softly.

"What's yours?" she countered.

It was a struggle not to laugh. The woman was strong, and I needed answers. "Asher Evans."

She nodded once. "Paige Alice. I—" Paige's eyes widened as she gasped. The head slipped from her hands, and she clutched at her chest before falling to her knees.

"Paige," I called in alarm. "What is it?" I got to my knees beside her, only to be knocked on my ass when the hellhound barreled over to stand above her. "Move, beast," I snarled. "Let me help her."

"Move," Nate ordered, trying to shove Ezra off her.

He didn't budge; instead, he let out a howl and pawed at the floor as he stood more directly over her body.

Fuck.

I dug my hand into Ezra's neck and growled my own warning. If the beast didn't move, I would do it for him. Piece by piece.

I sensed Smith at my back, ready for my order.

To my surprise, Ezra backed off a little, his attention shifting to Paige, and ours followed. Her eyes popped wide, along with her mouth, and then she let out an ear-piercing scream. It was so damn loud and long, all of us had to cover our ears.

She stopped.

"Smith, calm her. Ezra, fucking move," I barked.

Nate shoved at him over and over, throwing threat after threat at the beast. Finally, he stepped back, one paw then the other. Smith and I reached her side at the same time, but before we could touch her, a bright white light flashed before us. Our bodies were thrown into the air, and we landed with a deafening crash onto the floor.

"What the hell was that?" I asked, my head spinning. Shit, I hadn't felt like that since I was a human and drunk. Slowly, I sat up. "Smith?"

"Magic of some sort, but I don't know what."

"Nate?" I called.

A mumbled response sounded from under the hellhound. It wasn't the time to laugh, but I had yet another urge to. As I rushed back to Paige's side, Ezra climbed to his feet, and I caught Nate shake his head as he sat up.

I stopped, hovering over Paige. She looked the same. Whatever happened hadn't caused her bodily harm. I tugged at a hole in her top. Even the wounds she'd had from the gunshots had healed quicker than any of us could have.

"Is she okay?" Smith asked, kneeling on the other side of her. Nate, who refused to go by his last name, stood by her feet.

"Stop," Nate shouted. We did. "Do you hear it?"

At his question, my ears picked up the extra, and loudest, heartbeat in the room. One I hadn't heard with all the others before. One that stood out more than the rest. We all glanced back down to Paige, knowing it was hers.

"But…." I didn't know what else to say.

"She didn't have one outside," Nate said.

"She didn't have one up until now," Smith added. "What is she?"

The hellhound came forward. It headbutted Nate out of the way and got close, sniffing Paige. He whimpered, then licked her face. I tried to shove his head away, but the bastard wouldn't move.

We all locked solid when she groaned.

"She's coming to," Smith muttered the obvious.

We all looked at each other. "You sure she's not one of your kind?" Nate asked.

I nodded. "She's not a vampire. I don't sense her as kin."

"So then what species doesn't have a beating heart one moment and then, in the next, does?" Nate asked.

"I—" Tensing, I felt a new pull in the room, as if something was drawing power. Ezra backed off Paige, whimpering. "Anyone?" I called roughly.

"Don't know," Smith replied.

"You all feel it?" Nate asked. He waved his hands above Paige. "I think it's coming from here."

"Nate, stop—" A surge of power pulsated out, sending us flying back once again, away from Paige. My head hit the wall as I crashed into it, causing my eyes to slam closed.

Opening them, I snarled at the figure standing over Paige.

"You'll not have her," I growled, my vampire side causing my voice to deepen, and I knew my eyes had bled to green.

Nate roared, shifting once more even as he stood and

moved closer. The man over Paige wore a bored expression and ignored us. He bent and slid his arms under her.

"Smith," I barked.

"It's not working on him," he called back, a tinge of panic in his voice.

The guy slowly straightened with her in his arms, and Paige let out a mew of protest. Nate was still midshift and hadn't reached them yet, so I charged them myself. I had to see what we were up against. Once I was close, I reached for his throat, only to skid to a stop.

Paige's eyes shot wide. Her pupils bled from dark blue to glowing red with a black ring around them. Her body arched in his hold so dramatically he had to drop her.

She landed in a crouch, her palms flat to the ground. With her upper lip raised over her teeth, she let out a low hiss.

Holy Christ. What was she?

CHAPTER FOUR

NATE

I forced the change back into my human body, my clothes torn and tattered, but still covering most of me. I couldn't believe what I was seeing. The annoying yet cute Paige, whose scent had appealed to a part of me and my wolf deep inside when I'd first seen her, was something else, and I didn't have a fucking clue what.

She looked wild.

Her head lifted more. Her nostrils flared. She was scenting the air like an animal.

"Too many humans," the naked guy beside her commented.

"What do you mean?" Asher asked harshly.

"She'll kill them all. She's not herself. Been changed." Worry seeped into his tone while his hands fisted at his sides.

"Fuck," I snapped. "Smith, it's your time to shine."

His lips thinned, but he nodded. His eyes shone purple, his hands moving around in the air. The barest of seconds later, all the humans stood and started for the front exit.

"Erase their minds," I added. Smith lifted his chin toward me as he led the people out.

Paige let out a low-sounding snarl, her gaze glued to the glass-eyed people shuffling out the door. Her head twitched to the side, toward the naked guy, then back again. Her whole body tensed; she was preparing to make a run.

Asher had already sensed it and dove. His arms circled her waist, and he rolled them both backward. She screamed as her nails raked over Asher's arms, causing him to curse. I rushed over to them. Asher curled his legs up and over hers to hold them down. I perched over both Asher and Paige to grab her wrists and drag them down to the floor.

Asher grunted when her elbow connected with his rib. The crunch of his bones shattering under her strength tore around the emptying room.

"Hold her," he snapped, pain lacing his voice. Though, I knew his body would quickly heal.

"I'm fucking trying," I yelled. Her teeth gnashed up at me, her eyes narrowing, and if I had to guess, she was picturing my death. "Where in the hell is her hellhound? He might be able to calm her."

"He's over there," the naked guy stated from Paige's side with a gesture of his chin. Then he bent down and—*holy motherfucking shit*—the guy shoved the dead man's arm into Paige's open mouth. When her teeth caught it, she paused. A low hum escaped her mouth around the hold on the arm. "Back off slowly," he ordered. Ezra dragged the rest of the body over to Paige, who growled from the back of her throat. He ignored her and sat protectively at her side. Paige's gaze never strayed from him, and when she let out a huff, Ezra responded with his own.

I slowly released her wrists and watched Paige's arms fly up to grip the arm in her mouth. She tore off a chunk of flesh, devouring it. Any human would have been sickened by the sight, the way the blood dripped down her mouth, her chin, and even the sides of her face. Only we wouldn't be. I hunted and ate animals in my other form. Asher drank blood to live, and it was obvious what Paige did was out of necessity—a need to survive.

My brows dipped. A sudden word rolled through my mind. "I thought they were extinct," I commented quietly.

Asher gently slid out from under Paige. She snarled at being disturbed, but other than that, she didn't care. Our boss sat on the ground beside her and stared on in astonishment.

He shook his head and replied to my comment, "That was what had been told centuries ago. The council implied they were bad, too powerful, and were trying to take over all of humanity. Before I even joined the elite, the council had wiped them out as a threat."

The naked guy grunted, and all eyes trained on him.

"Who are you?" I asked roughly.

"Thorn Jones. She is under my guard."

I crossed my arms over my chest and snorted. "We can't be sure of that."

"I was sent to her magically when her change hit. It occurred after I'd showered."

Huh, that explained why the guy was butt naked. Yet, he didn't seem to care.

Shaking my head, I told him, "We need to know everything you do."

We all tensed when Thorn narrowed his eyes. His upper lip raised, and he snarled, "None of you need to know anything. I will be taking her when she is self-aware."

In a blink, Asher stood in front of him with fangs showing. His vampire had come out to play. "You'll not take her."

Thorn moved closer, not caring he faced Asher's vampire. "I will. She is not your concern."

"Listen, dickhead," Asher bit out. "You might as well say we're the authority in this scenario, and we protect people. She looks all of seventeen, and my guess is, she doesn't know you at all. She's not going anywhere unless we deem it safe for her."

"She's twenty-five, and she *will* want to go with me."

"She's twenty-five?" Smith asked as he came to stand beside me. "She looks about sixteen."

Fuck, she really did, which was why I felt like a dick when, at first glance, I'd thought about how hot she was and how good she'd look under me.

I quickly pushed that thought aside. Even if she was of age, it didn't change the damn situation we were in.

"I think we're all getting off track here," I said snappishly. "How about we go back to her being a ghoul."

"What?" Smith yelled excitedly. "Are you serious? I mean, I can see she's eating an arm there, but it didn't cross my mind. I thought they were extinct. *This* isn't extinct." He ran his hands through his hair. He goddamn loved figuring new shit out. "Also, how is her heart beating now?"

"Asher," I called, ignoring Smith's rant. "We all agree he's not taking her until we can be assured she'll be all right and we know everything there is to know. Right?"

"Yes." Asher nodded curtly.

Paige flipped herself up to crouch over the dead body. The

arm no longer holding her interest, she bent and sniffed the body. We all watched and waited.

"Do you want some clothes?" I heard Smith ask, no doubt to the naked guy who was stepping up behind Paige. She turned her head to the side and hissed. I made a move toward them, but Ezra stood and let out a warning growl.

"You move again, I'll stop you, and you won't like how I do it," Asher clipped. He flashed to stand beside Paige, readying his body for a fight if need be.

Thorn's gaze narrowed more. "You have helped her this night, but I will fight you if I have to."

"Then be prepared to lose," I said. I barely held back my snort, wondering who the hell this fool thought he was. Asher by himself was no joking matter, but pitch the three of us elite enforcers together, and we were un-fucking-stoppable.

Thorn scoffed. "It'll not be me who loses."

"Uh, guys," Smith called.

"Do you know who we are?" Asher asked.

"I don't care. My priority is Paige, and nothing, nor no one, will stop me from keeping her safe."

"Guys."

"We can keep her safe as well. Hell, we'd do a better job than you. There's three of us after all," Asher pointed out. He was right. Whatever was going to happen to Paige—and the guy surely acted like something was going to happen—then there were three of us, and we'd have a better chance at keeping her safe if we had to. Thorn was one guy.

"She'll have her army once we get home."

I glanced to Asher. "Army?" I asked Thorn.

"Yes." Thorn nodded.

"Guys!" Smith snapped. Our attention went to him, and he pointed down at Paige. "I think she's coming to."

I darted my eyes to Paige. She swayed a little in her crouched form before resting her hands on the body to support herself. Blinking over and over, she shook her head and then closed her eyes, only to open them slowly, and her stunning dark blue eyes shone back up at me.

"You okay?" I asked roughly, annoyed I cared to even ask. I hadn't cared about short, hot women's feelings or pain before. Alex handled that shit after a job was done because he had the patience to.

She nodded hesitantly and glanced to each side of her. When she looked behind her, she gasped and squeaked, "Penis." Next, she landed on her butt and covered her eyes with her hands. Ezra snorted, and I was sure I saw the hellhound roll his eyes before he plopped himself down right next to her.

Asher's gaze hit me, so did Smith's. They were shocked by my reaction. Hell, I was as well, but I couldn't stop the laugh that fell from my mouth.

When my teammates wouldn't quit staring, I threw my hands up and muttered, "I've laughed before."

Smith shook his head. "I can't remember when."

"Cover him in clothes," I ordered, changing the subject.

Smith nodded. With a click of his fingers, Thorn was dressed in jeans, biker boots, and a plain black tee.

"Paige," Asher called in a gentle tone as he crouched beside her, but Thorn moved in and placed his body between Asher and Paige. She caught the situation between spread fingers.

"What's going on?" she asked, dropping her hands, one to her lap and the other around Ezra's neck. She spared a glance at the blood on her before her eyes trailed to the body and arm.

"I… ah, did I have a snack?" Confusion dipped her brows, and she gripped her hellhound tighter.

"You did, but something happened—"

"What?" she interrupted, her voice tight with fear.

"That's what we'd like to know." Asher smiled softly at her from around Thorn's legs.

"What do you mean?" She shook her head. "What happened after— Where is everyone? Is my sister okay? Did something else happen? Did I black out? Is my family all right?"

Thorn laid a hand on her shoulder. "Calm. Everyone is fine."

She lifted her gaze to him. "Who in the hell are you?"

I snorted when Paige shrugged off Thorn's hand and stood. She swayed a little. Without thinking, my body moved to help steady her. She brought her eyes to mine, gave me a nod, and moved her attention back to Thorn. "Who are you?"

"I'm your protector."

Since I was still holding her arm and, somehow, my other hand had slid to her waist, I felt her tense. What I hated most was how I could scent he spoke the truth.

"My protector? What does that mean?" She searched all our faces.

"He showed after a power surge shot out of your body," I answered.

She shook her head. "A power surge?"

"I'll explain everything when we're alone and safe," Thorn told her.

I stopped the growl rising in my throat by thinning my lips. My wolf and I didn't like the fact this cocksucker kept wanting to get her alone and away.

"As we've said, you'll not be taking her until we deem it safe," Asher replied.

Paige drew her hands up and waved them in front of herself as she stepped back and out of my grip. I didn't like it. "Hold up." She shook her head. "Ezra," she called. He stood, and I was sure he gave us a smirk as he made his way to her side. Paige reached out to run her hand over his head, as if for comfort.

Fucking hell, did the hellhound smile cockily for being the one she trusted most?

I'd easily wipe it from his smug face. I clenched my fists at my sides.

"Miss Alice," Smith started, asking for her attention.

Her nose screwed up. "Paige," she told him.

He smiled, red coating his cheeks. Guess I wasn't the only one attracted to Paige, which was strange. I was sure Smith was gay. Not that I'd ask. We didn't talk about our private lives. We worked well together, and that was all that mattered. He didn't cower when I was a prick, which happened a lot since my wolf was an alpha and a bastard in his own right. Alex had only been on our team five years. He'd joined us after we'd lost our last mage in battle. A guy who thought nothing and no one was as good as him. The dick deserved to die, especially after we found out he didn't take no for an answer and beat women he'd been with. Alex was ten times better than him anyway.

Shit, we were all protective to a certain point of innocents, but there was something about Paige where I felt the need to curl her in bubble wrap, tuck her under my arm, and run from everything and everyone to keep her safe.

That shit was fucked up.

Why her?

"Paige," he muttered. "Um, I'm sure we can get things sorted. We have questions, you have them, and that guy also has them. We just need to sit down calmly and talk things out."

"I don't have questions," Thorn stated.

"You have answers we want to know before you think you can take Paige anywhere." Asher glared.

"Wait, what? I'm not going anywhere with anyone." Ezra gently bumped his head into her shoulder. "Except for Ezra."

"My queen, you need to come with me. I'm your protector. Before others know of your existence, we need to get you to your fortress."

Queen? What the fuck? The queen of what and who? This cockhead needed to explain. My wolf wanted to reach down his throat for the answers.

Her eyes widened, then quickly narrowed. "Are you high? Drunk? On *something*?"

Smith laughed. When Thorn sent a snarl his way, Smith covered his laugh by coughing. I met Asher's amused stare with one of my own.

"No, my queen—"

"Stop with the queen stuff. I'm not a queen. I'll never be one, and really, I don't think I'd want to be one."

Thorn stepped toward her, his hands out, reaching. Asher slid in front of her, and I moved back to her side. Ezra huffed out in annoyance on her other side, and Smith took her back. Thorn's brows dipped, his lips thinning.

"I would never harm her," he growled low.

"We don't know that," I said. Paige's gaze shifted to me. Her head tilted, and I could scent she was confused by me, but she also smelled of fear and skepticism.

"I would only ever protect her." Thorn fumed through clenched teeth.

When Paige cleared her throat, the others glanced at her. "This is all fun and games, but I'm tired," she lied. "I just want to go home and sleep. We can revisit this weird trip tomorrow." More lies.

"Ah…," Smith started. She shifted to meet his eyes, and another blush sprang to his cheeks. Jesus, was the boy a virgin or something? "I'm not sure if you know, but we can tell you're lying."

Her head jerked back. "Bullshit."

He shook his head, a playful smile on his lips.

"Huh." She nodded. "Right." She glanced around at all of us. "Well, I guess I'll go for the truth."

CHAPTER FIVE

ALEX

y lips wanted to twitch. Actually, I just wanted
to laugh. Paige was too easy to read. The way
her gaze moved around us all quickly told me she was trying to
think of another way out of the situation. It wasn't only that,
though. I wasn't like Nate or Asher who could taste a lie. I could
feel one.

"Smith?" she asked my name.

"Alex, actually. I prefer only my teammates to call me Smith
when on the job," I told her, and when she smiled softly, I knew
my damn face heated. There was something about the woman
that sang to my desires. I wanted to reach out and touch her,
hold her, and tell her everything would be all right. I didn't
though, of course. I had a feeling she'd punch me.

I could tell I wasn't the only one affected by Paige. It seemed all of our protective instincts were lit for the woman. What was it about her that caused such a reaction?

"Right, Alex." My cock jerked behind my jeans when she said my name. She ran a hand through her hair, then looked at her hand, staring at the blood and no doubt becoming aware it was smeared in her beautiful hair. She cursed under her breath. "Right, ah, where was I?"

"The truth," I offered.

She clicked her fingers and pointed at me. "Yes." She nodded and moved away to face the four of us. Ezra, the hellhound, something I still couldn't believe, followed her like a well-trained dog and allowed her to pat him on his head. He leaned into her. "The truth of the matter is… I feel"—she touched her chest—"like I can trust you all. But all of this is strange. Up until now, I've never met someone else who's different like me. It's a lot to take in, and right now, all I want is a shower and to think."

"You can do both at the castle," Thorn offered.

She threw up her hands. "I don't even know your name."

He bent at the waist. "Thorn Jones, my queen."

Paige's eyes darkened. "You call me queen one more time and my fist is going up your ass," she threatened. Thorn straightened. His lips twitched, like all of ours were because Paige was just too damn cute when she tried to be menacing. Her face blanked, and she straightened. "Wait, did you say castle?"

Another lip twitch all around. "Yes, my—" He cleared his throat. "Yes."

Paige looked at me. I didn't know why she singled me out, but I liked that she had. Her smile was radiant. "I've always wanted to see a castle."

"Then you should." I wouldn't deny her something she'd

always wanted, even when Asher and Nate cursed at me. I shrugged at them. "She's always wanted to see one." I'd like to see them try and say no to her.

"Then we're accompanying her," Asher stated, crossing his arms over his chest. Thorn opened his mouth, probably to deny us, but Asher's hand shot up. "Since we work for the council on the elite enforcers team who governs the dangerous matters around the world, there isn't a chance in hell we would allow a woman to go to some castle on her own with a man she doesn't know."

Paige's eyes rounded, her mouth dropping open in surprise.

Though, what Asher had said was a crock of bullshit. It wasn't our job to escort a person somewhere. There was also the matter of how we could all sense that Thorn was speaking the truth.

"You're not allowed to accompany us. Having you know where we're situated is a risk to the queen. We don't know what your authorities would do with the information about the queen being reborn."

"Wait? Reborn?" Paige said, wide-eyed.

"Then we don't say anything," Nate growled. Everyone looked at him. "We're owed some time off. We take it now and go with them."

"I can't allow—" Thorn started.

"Wait, wait, wait," Paige called. "Can we please stop bickering? I don't understand why you all want to come, but I won't say no because I do believe none of you want to harm me, and I'm feeling Thorn thinks there'll be trouble for some reason, so it'll be safer in numbers." Her lips quickly thinned. I had a feeling she couldn't believe that she'd just said that. Unless…

could she feel the same connection to us, even though it was small, like we did for her?

"Agreed," Asher said.

Thorn studied Paige, and she stared him down until he eventually sighed. "Fine."

"Finally," Paige cheered. "Now I'm closer to getting my shower."

All the men froze, and I could imagine it was because all of our minds suddenly went to the gutter and thought of Paige and her naked, sweet, soft skin in the shower.

My dick throbbed.

With a click of my fingers, Paige stood before us clean and in fresh clothes of jeans and a tee that fit snuggly across her chest. I didn't even have to bring my full power forward to be able to do that for her.

Her gaze shifted down on herself slowly. Her mouth popped open, and then she sucked in a sharp breath. Her hands patted down her chest, stomach, and thighs. She looked over at me.

"That is amazing. I won't have to shower again."

I coughed. "It's nothing really."

"Oh, it's something. I wish I could do it."

And I wished she'd stop running her hands up and down herself; it wasn't helping the situation in my jeans since my dick had a mind of its own now and wanted to come out and play with Paige. She breathed hard. She smiled hard. She ran her hands over herself… hard.

Was I the only guy having the same problem?

I glanced to the others, mainly at their crotches. Nope. I wasn't the only one with the problem. A throat cleared. I ripped my gaze up from Asher's erection and straight into his eyes. His brow raised, and my face burned.

"Hang on," Paige said, bringing our attention back to her, thankfully. The only problem was, her hands were splayed over her breast. Panic shone in her eyes. "My heart's beating." She lifted her hand to point down at her organ. "It's beating. It hasn't done that since I woke and dug my way out of the ground."

"You what?" Nate snarled. He sounded like how I felt on the inside—angered by Paige having to go through that.

She fluttered her hand Nate's way, as if saying his words didn't matter.

Instead, she asked, "What's wrong with me? Am I human again? How? Why? Did the demon do something to me?" This woman amazed me with how she was taking everything in stride.

Thorn took a step forward. "We must leave this place, my queen, but please know there is nothing wrong with you. Your heart beats because you are Queen. I can explain more in detail when we're safely at the castle."

She nodded, her eyes staring at her chest. "Yes. All right. Let's go then."

"Nate, Smith, go with them while I organize our time off," Asher ordered. He turned to Thorn. "Are there sufficient feeding rooms provided? If not, I will make sure I'm catered for."

"It's strange to feel it beat after so long," Paige mumbled to herself, still touching her chest. I kept my lips tightly pressed together because I was close to moaning. Why did I react this way to her?

"There will be enough provided. We have plenty of people on the grounds. All types."

Nate snorted. "How do you know they're trustworthy?"

Thorn glared at him. "They have sworn their allegiance to the new queen before she was created."

"Does that mean other things in my body will work?" Paige asked, seemingly oblivious to the conversation going on around her. Her fingers pressed against her neck. "Hey, I have a pulse." Happiness rushed through my chest when she smiled.

"So because they've sworn their allegiance, they won't harm her in any way?" Nate asked with a smirk.

Thorn's jaw clenched. "If they break it, they die. They know this."

Nate scoffed. "Sometimes money and status can talk more than a threat."

"I feel like I need to go to the bathroom," Paige said, her eyes wide with wonderment. Then they narrowed. "Does this mean I'll get my period again?"

I palmed my face. We did not need to hear about her period. It was time to intervene. I clapped and said, "How about we take this conversation out of here so I can break the barrier on the restaurant and we can get things rolling."

"How far away is this place?" Paige asked Thorn.

"We fly for four hours, my—" Paige held up her fist, and Thorn altered to "Paige."

"Is it overseas? I don't have a passport."

"You won't need one, Paige. We have our own aircraft."

Asher turned to me. "Clean it up, Smith."

I nodded and stepped back a few paces. I caught Paige's gasp when my eye color changed. A spell dropped from my lips, and all the furniture swirled up into the air, fixed itself, and moved back to where it had been.

Asher stepped up to what remained of the body and pointed

down at the stained carpet. "Got it," I told him, adding it into the spell already created and activated.

Warmth touched my back, and I glanced over my shoulder to see a bug-eyed Paige there. "Hi," she said.

"Hey," I breathed and blushed. She rolled her head to the side, taking me in and looking cute. I actually wanted to press my lips against hers.

Her eyes hooded and darkened. "Do you know you smell wonderful?"

Holy motherchuck. What was going on? I didn't know, but I wanted to know badly. Only I couldn't because it would be a distraction. My cock strained in my jeans when her hands touched my waist and sent a zap throughout me. My heart ate at my ribs; it felt like it wanted out of my body to get to her.

What the hell?

"Nate," I called with a strained voice.

If it had been a short spell, I wouldn't have needed so much focus, but there'd been damage all over the place, even outside when Nate and the hellhound were at each other.

I caught Nate moving close, but then Paige shook her head and blinked. She said, "That's really damn cool how you do that. Your eyes are… wow."

I cleared my throat, then swirled my tongue around because it was suddenly dry. "Ah, thanks."

She stepped back, smiling. "I better go to the bathroom in case…. What a night, right?"

"Definitely different," I replied with my own smile. She turned and walked off toward the bathroom with Ezra following. Of course I watched her go, and I knew the other guys would be as well. Once she was through the door, with the hellhound standing outside of it glaring at us, I asked, "I'm not the only one feeling this pull toward her, right?"

"No," Asher said.

"Fuck. No," Nate replied, anger ever present in his tone. He was always pissed though, so I didn't wonder why he'd be angry about this.

"It shouldn't have happened," Thorn mumbled. All our gazes locked onto him.

"What do you mean?" I asked as the final chair slid into place. The spell was done.

He shook his head. "We need to get to the castle. I'll explain it all there."

"You can't just throw that out and not say shit," Nate clipped.

"Nate," Asher called. He shook his head and gestured toward the bathroom. Meaning Paige was probably listening in and he didn't think she'd want or need to know what Thorn meant just yet. She'd been through enough for one night.

Nate's jaw clenched, his hands fisting in frustration. Still, he nodded. The bathroom door opened, and Paige stepped out, saw all of us looking at her, and rolled her eyes. "So I don't need to use the bathroom still. But I was sure I needed to pee." She shrugged. "I can't figure it out."

"All will be answered soon, Paige," Thorn said.

"I know." She sighed. "Look, I need to check on my sister before we go anywhere. She'll freak if she can't contact me."

I glanced to Thorn. "Nate and I could take Paige and meet you at the airport," I suggested. Thorn seemed wary, but after looking at Paige, he finally agreed, stating he had things to prepare for our departure. He also probably knew he wouldn't get Paige to go if he didn't give her this.

"Come on then," Nate said and started for the door.

"I'll be in contact," Asher announced, and using his speed, he took the body and left the room.

Paige tried to track his movements, but it would be impossible. She then glanced to Thorn. "Thank you, and we won't be long. I just need to let her know I'll be safe."

"I understand." He bowed again before straightening. Paige and her hellhound, who was back in his canine form, followed Nate out while I hung back because Thorn's gaze came to me. "You'll have an hour. It's too risky for anything longer. Others may feel her power. Be at hanger twenty by then."

"We will."

"Be sure to keep her safe."

"You have my word."

He opened his mouth as if to say more, but then shook his head. As he went toward the back area, I made my way outside where Nate was already in the driver seat. Paige sat in the back with her hellhound.

I took the passenger seat in the front, even though I wanted to squeeze into the back with Paige. I didn't think the hellhound would appreciate it.

"Address?" Nate barked. He was probably still pissy because he'd laughed.

Paige rattled off the address. Nate started the car and pulled out onto the road. I wanted to turn around and say something, anything to get her attention, but I sat still like a moron, unsure what the best thing would be to say.

Never had I expected the night would lead us to be in a car with a woman who had somehow dug her claws into us. It was also something she'd never foreseen, but it had me wondering. Did she feel a connection to us?

CHAPTER SIX

PAIGE

I didn't know if this was one big, fat wet dream or not. I had to get real with myself. I knew supernatural people were out there; I was one of them for crying out loud. But seriously, had my mind conjured up four stunningly hot males and I was living out a fantasy? Not that I had a fantasy about four men at once. And if asked, I would deny, deny, deny.

So really, it was either a dream or I was tripping big-time.

Did Ezra spike my drink with an LSD?

I glanced at Ezra. He sat with his head hanging out the window, tongue lolled out to the side having the time of his life.

I quickly pinched myself.

Okay, it wasn't a dream.

Which meant everything that had happened did, well…

happen.

It all felt normal until I woke. It wasn't the sight of a dick staring me in the face that changed me. It was when I realized I had a heartbeat, a pulse. It was the fact I sensed I could trust the men around me. I didn't even know them, but deep within, there was a connection to them that I couldn't even begin to explain, let alone understand. And it started when I'd first saw them but deepened more once I knew they'd had my back in there. It was strange.

Then, when Alex used his magic, something came over me. I wanted to reach out to him, touch him… even lick him, nip at him, kiss him, and fuck him. Raw power shot to my stomach and groin.

It was something I had never felt before.

Which was why I'd fought it and used the excuse of going to the bathroom to see if I needed to pee. I hadn't, but I wanted time away to calm myself.

I still wanted to reach into the front of the car and rub my hands all over him. I even had a thought to sniff him. He, like all of them, was stunning.

Even Thorn.

Thorn who'd showed up after my power surge apparently. Whatever that meant.

If I didn't need answers, I would be running for the hills because my connection to them scared my panties off. I hoped my emotions were well hidden. I didn't want them to know they'd affected me so deeply, just in case I did have to run.

Alex cleared his throat. "Do you know what you are?" he asked, turning in his seat to look at me. I quickly sat on my hands, so they didn't betray me and grab him. It took every ounce of willpower to not haul him into the back seat with me.

I cleared my throat, not used to my heart's rhythm, and it liked Alex a whole lot, beating wildly at the sight of him. "Um, sort of, I think." He waited for me to continue. I didn't want to give my answer in case I was wrong and looked like a fool. However, I got lost staring into his soft gray eyes. Blue eyes that turned purple. I squeezed my legs together. Nate picked that moment to draw in the air; he shot me a dirty look in the rearview mirror. I gave him one back.

"Paige?" Alex said.

I shifted my gaze to his. "A ghoul."

Alex smiled. I sucked in a deep breath because I wanted to wipe that smile away with my own lips. He nodded. "That's right."

Gripping the seat, I added, "But I have a heartbeat now, so does that make me different again?"

"We're here," Nate clipped, which he seemed to do a lot. I had a feeling it was just his nature, but I worried it'd cause us to butt heads in time because I wouldn't take his shit. He pulled up out front of my sister's house and climbed out.

"Hey," Alex said, gaining my attention. "We don't know if it has changed you, but we'll find the answers out soon, and together."

Would kissing him really be out of the question?

Probably, so instead, I gave him a smile. Immediately, a blush spread across his cheeks. Maybe I wasn't the only one feeling this. "Thank you, Alex."

He nodded and quickly exited the car.

Ezra let out a huff. The dirty dog sniffed at my crotch and shot me a knowing look. I pushed him away. "You dick. It's not like I can help it. My body just reacts."

He let out a wheeze that sounded like a laugh. Grumbling, I

opened my door. Ezra jumped over me and out, landing perfectly on all fours. I got out slowly, thinking about what I would tell my sister. *"It's all right, Yasmin. I don't know them, but they set something off inside me where I know I can trust them, so I'm going with them. Also, my body seems to react to them in a carnal way."* Yeah, I wasn't sure that would work, but maybe if I told her what I'd figured out and how I needed answers, she would understand.

I walked up the path to her front door. Ezra was at my side, and I knew Nate was at my back, with Alex just behind him. "What can I tell her?" I asked.

"She's your blood, so anything as long as you know she'll not say anything to anyone," Alex replied.

"Unless you want to keep them safe. If so, say nothing," Nate added like an ass. But at least he was truthful. Would people come after Yasmin because of me? I didn't know, and I didn't want to risk it. But I also knew if the shoe were on the other foot, I'd want to know everything no matter what. She'd already seen my strength and speed when Oscar started to fall off a ladder. I'd gotten to him quickly, so he wouldn't hit the ground, taking his weight like it wasn't a problem for me. After her shock, she questioned me again and again, but in the end, she believed me when I told her I didn't have all the answers, but when I did, I promised her I would tell her. So really, I couldn't go back on that.

Before I could knock, the door swung open and Yasmin stood in it wearing winter pajamas with pigs all over it. "What's going on?" Her gaze flicked behind me. "Have you been arrested?"

Rolling my eyes, I asked, "Why do you think I've been arrested?"

"Because there're two men following you and they look professional."

My face screwed up. I stopped in the doorway and glanced behind me. I supposed they did look professional. I looked back at my sister. "Well, I'm not arrested."

She leaned in and whispered, "Are they from an asylum? I can vouch you're not crazy. They might believe me if they don't ask too many questions."

A muffled laugh sounded behind me. I knew it was Nate and his super hearing. "Yasmin, it's fine. Let's go inside and I'll explain. Are the kids in bed?"

"Yes." She stepped back and let us all in. Ezra made a beeline for the kids' room until Yasmin snapped, "Stop." Ezra glared over his shoulder at my sister. "If you go in there and wake them up, you have to stay the night to take care of them."

Ezra glanced up to me, then back to Yasmin. He huffed, turned, and walked back our way. Passing Yasmin, he let out a growl.

"I swear your dog is too smart to be normal."

A laugh escaped me. "Yeah."

We followed Yasmin into the living room. Eric was sitting on the couch but stood when we entered, taking us all in before his gaze snapped back to me. "What have you done now?"

I threw my hands in the air. "Why do you both think I've done something? Can't I just come to my sister's house with men you don't know and it be normal?"

"No," they said together.

"Fine, it's not, but still one day it will be. So stop assuming." I took a seat on the couch beside theirs. "However, I haven't done anything wrong." Ezra climbed onto the couch and plonked himself next to me, his head landing on my lap. I pat him absently, noticing Alex and Nate didn't sit; they chose to stand behind me, which was weird. I watched Eric's and Yasmin's gaze ping-pong back and forth between us all.

"Just introduce us and tell us what all this is about," Yasmin demanded.

"Do you need money?" Eric asked.

I scoffed. "No."

"Are they threatening you in any—"

Yasmin's hand slapped down on Eric's thigh. "Honey, how about we wait and see what all this is about?" It wasn't until I looked back at Alex and then Nate, who was glowering at Eric, that I realized why Yasmin interrupted.

Eric nodded.

Ezra groaned and rolled onto his back. I absently ran my hand up and down his chest. I'd decided to go for the truth. "Okay. Here's the thing. First, this here is Nate and Alex. Second, you know I've been different for a while, right?" Yasmin and Eric nodded. "Apparently I got changed into a ghoul somehow." Their faces morphed into ones of humor. My hand came up, hoping they'd hold off laughing. They did, so I went on, "Third. Tonight, I rocked up to the restaurant you were at for Eric's promotion."

I glanced at Alex. "Do they remember that?" He shook his head. "Right." I nodded and sent Yasmin and Eric a grimace, then an apology smile. "All right. It might be harder to believe because you guys don't remember, but you and all the other patrons in the place were being held hostage by a demon. I came in, saved the day, but then something happened to me. I passed out, and when I woke, my heart's beating again, so I don't know if I've changed again. Thorn, who magically appeared in the restaurant after I passed out, tells me I'm a

Queen, with a capital Q, and that I need to get to the safety of my castle where he'll answer all my questions. Asher, the boss of their group"—I thumbed behind me—"Nate, and Alex are tagging along to find out the answers as well because they don't trust Thorn."

They blinked slowly at me.

Yasmin patted Eric's thigh before she stood. "I'll start packing."

I shoved Ezra off me and also stood. "Wait, what?"

"Do you seriously think you can leave with men you don't know without me?" She threw a hand out. "They could be murderers for all we know."

It was my turn to blink slowly. "You believe me?"

Eric stood beside his wife, placing an arm around her shoulders. "Of course your sister does." Out of the corner of his mouth, he muttered, "Right?"

She elbowed him. "Yes! I know my sister, and I know when something's happened to her. You're stronger, faster, and I'm not sure you know this, but there's something up with your dog. I didn't know about the heartbeat part, but if you think you're a ghoul, then I'm not going to argue with you. I want answers as much as you do. We'll find them together."

My new heart skipped over a beat, and my eyes misted. I hadn't cried in forever because I couldn't shed a tear. It seemed, along with my heart, that had changed also.

I walked to my sister, shoved Eric out of the way, and hugged her tightly to me.

"Too much." She breathed the words out. I released my hold a little, then pulled back and shook her with my hands on her shoulders.

"You believe me."

"I believe you. To some extent."

"We wouldn't harm her. You don't have to travel with us," Alex said.

Yasmin was already shaking her head. "I'm coming. Eric, wake the kids and get your things ready."

"Hang on, *everyone?*" I asked.

"Yes, everyone," Eric stated.

"You're not dealing with life-altering situations without your family at your back."

"But Eric just got a promotion."

We both looked at him. He shrugged. "I can find another job. What I won't find is another wife. I go where Yasmin goes."

"But the kids—"

"They're coming," Yasmin informed.

A throat cleared, and we all faced Nate. "They'll see things that aren't normal."

"Their aunt isn't normal. They'll face it sooner or later. It just happens to be sooner." I wasn't sure if Yasmin was thinking clearly. She was being my older protective sister, and I loved her for it. But her family, her husband, and kids were important. I didn't want them risked because she felt it was her sisterly duty to help me.

"Their lives will be changed forever with the knowledge they find," Alex added.

Yasmin looked at Eric. They somehow silently conversed before tears brimmed in her eyes. "I'm rushing into things again."

I rubbed my hands up and down her arms. "You are, and it's always been in your nature to protect me. I don't need it, Yasmin. I can take care of myself. You don't have to uproot your lives for me."

She shook her head. "I can't have you not around. The kids will miss their crazy aunt. I'll miss my sister."

"And I'll be back to see you all. I just don't know when."

A knock sounded on the front door. Spinning around, I pushed Yasmin behind me. Ezra climbed to his feet, growling. Nate lifted his head and sniffed the air. "Shifter. Feline," he snarled.

A voiced shouted through the door. "Hello? It's May. Can I come in?"

"It's our neighbor," Eric said. He started for the door, but I grabbed his arm, shaking my head. I'd met twenty-year-old May before, but I'd never sensed anything from her. I hadn't known she was a shifter, but the question was if she was going to be trouble or not.

I looked to Nate and Alex. "Is she a threat?" I whispered. They shrugged.

The door opened and May slipped in. She quickly closed it and leaned against it. "You need to leave. Now. All of you. Demons are on the way." Her eyes locked on mine. "Your power is calling to them."

Nate stepped closer to her. "How do you know this?"

"I was on my way home when I caught a group of them. I overheard them saying just that and how they're planning to storm this house to get to her."

Over my shoulder, I told Yasmin. "Get the kids and anything important you need. Make sure they're dressed warm and be quick." Her eyes shone with fear, but she nodded and ran from the room with Eric following.

My stupid heart beat so fast it caused my ears to ring. I'd brought trouble to my sister's doorstep, and now she didn't have a choice but to run with us... if we could make it out.

CHAPTER SEVEN

PAIGE

*E*zra strode to my side still in his dog form. He headbutted my leg and whined. I ran my hand over his head; it calmed me a little.

I looked to the others. "Will we make it out?" I asked with a quiver to my voice. They didn't say anything, and it didn't bode well, having them unsure.

"I'll call Asher," Alex said.

"No. We'll leave now and outrun them to the airport," Nate clipped. "We have enough strength between us." He focussed on Alex.

I faced May, who'd been looking at Alex in a way I really didn't like. "Hey," I called rather harshly. Her eyes shot to me. "Why did you warn us?"

"I've been under a demon's rule. I'd never want that for another."

"You'll have to come with us," Alex said, and I hated he had. "They may have seen her come in, and if they see her leave, they'll gun for her."

May looked back to Alex with an appreciative smile. It rolled my stomach.

"Where can we dump her?" I asked and then slapped a hand over my mouth while everyone looked at me strangely. "Sorry, that, uh, came out wrong."

What was wrong with me?

Really, I should have been freaking out about demons over-running us, wanting to kidnap me for my power, whatever that meant. Instead, I worried Alex would enjoy May's attention. It was messed up.

Wait… why would the demons be out there waiting for us to come out? Why didn't they just attack?

I voiced my confusion. Nate and Alex shared a look. May took a step closer. "I know, I don't understand it myself, but I do know we'll have to risk it to get out."

"Lies," Nate growled.

May glared at Nate, "Shut it, dog."

Ezra growled low and took a step closer to May. "I don't think he likes you," I told her.

May jutted her hand out. Long, spiky claws grew. "I'll slice him open if he comes closer," she snarled.

"What happened to the nice, helpful May?" I asked.

"Nate," Alex said. Nate shook his head. "I have to."

All of a sudden, May ran at Alex. I yelled, "Ezra." He gave chase. May bounced off something in front of Alex and fell to the floor. Ezra stood close and started pacing back and forth in front of her.

"Do not fucking move," I bit out. May sneered up at me but didn't move. I wasn't above having Ezra ripping out her throat. I didn't like her going for Alex one single bit.

"What do you want with Alex?" I demanded.

May said nothing.

Yasmin and Eric raced into the room, a child in each of their arms, a bag slung over their shoulders. "What's going on?" Yasmin asked. "May, what are you doing on the floor?"

"Aunty Paige," Sophie cried. My six-year-old niece waved wildly at me while Oscar, my eight-year-old nephew in his dad's arms, took in the room silently.

"Hey, pumpkin." I waved back. "Hiya, little dude." I winked at Oscar. "May just had a fall. We don't want her to get up in case she hurt herself."

"Alex," Nate clipped. The kid's eyes turned on him and widened. I caught Alex's eyes change to purple, and my knees wobbled a little while my clit throbbed.

So not the time, body.

Nate's gaze shot to me and turned judgy.

"Hi, guys, my name's Alex, and I'm a friend of your aunt's."

Ignoring all the silent accusations in not only Nate's eyes but Ezra's, and even May's, I faced Alex, who had his back to me while he stood in front of my family.

"Your eyes are real pretty," Sophie whispered.

My chest burned in jealousy.

What the high waters was wrong with me?

"Thank you, sweetheart. I'm going to show you something. Look at my hands." When they did, I heard a click, as if Alex snapped his fingers, and I saw the kids' eyes close. Their heads fell back into their parents' shoulders. Alex straightened. "They'll sleep for a while."

"Thank you," Yasmin said with a smile, and I would not think of punching it off her face. I wouldn't.

"Now, let's throw this ho out of the house and get out of here," I suggested.

"What did May do?" Eric asked.

"She's with the demons outside," Alex explained.

"We can't," Nate said from the window. "They have the house surrounded." He stepped back and glanced to Alex. Then he nodded before gesturing to May. "You need to leave."

She glared up at him. "They'll find you. They won't stop until they have her." She leaped up, arms outstretched toward me. I heard Yasmin cry out as I braced, ready for her attack, but then Ezra was there. His body shook and morphed as his jaw circled her neck. The audible snap echoed in the otherwise still room.

Ezra dropped to the floor with May's neck and shoulder still in his mouth. We all watched as he released his grip and she fell to the floor, lifeless.

"Well, there goes that problem," I said. Everyone looked at me with widened eyes. I realized it sounded heartless, but I couldn't bring forth two fucks to give. I shrugged. "I'm sorry, but it was going to be her or me. I'm glad it was her. Good job, Ezra," I said, and I was sure he preened under my appraisal. "And let's not forget she was with the demons that are after me."

Nate snorted and shook his head, but I was sure I saw his mouth twitching. "We better get the fuck outta here."

"My way," Alex stated.

Nate shook his head. "No."

"Nate, we don't have a choice."

"You'll be knocked out from it."

"What's this?" I asked, glancing to my sister and her husband to see if they had an idea, but their eyes were glued to Ezra, who sat licking around his mouth. "Oh, yeah. I forgot to mention. Ezra's a hellhound. I found that out tonight too. I mean, I knew he was different, just not in what way."

"A hellhound?" Eric murmured.

"Yes."

"A hellhound was around our children?" Yasmin screeched, causing us to flinch. "They climbed over a hellhound?"

"Um... yes?"

"H-He just killed May."

"Ah, I didn't think you two were close?" I asked.

Yasmin shook her head. She seemed a little pale, but she was managing, like Eric. "We weren't. She kept on flirting with Eric. I never trusted her, but... death?"

"It's gonna come down to them or us," Nate said gruffly. Something crashed outside. Nate swore. He nodded to Alex, and then Alex called, "Everyone gather around me." His eyes bled to purple, and I was the first one to him, sliding my arms around his waist. His eyes bugged out as he looked down at me. His cheeks flamed with heat as he coughed and said, "Ah, yes, so, uh, grab onto me somehow. Nate, take hold of Ezra." Nate cursed, and I heard Ezra growl.

"Yasmin? Eric?"

"We're here and ready," Eric said.

The front door was blown open, and long-legged things crawled through the opening. Alex started chanting, and suddenly, a wind from nowhere picked up around us. Yasmin whimpered behind me. I reached my free arm out and gripped her to me.

As a white light shone through the room, I screwed my eyes closed, and then there was nothing but a tingle over my body. I opened my eyes in time to see Alex crumple and fall from my grip to the floor.

"Alex," I cried, dropping to my knees. Terrified, I rested a hand on his arm and chest. He was breathing.

"My queen," a voice came from beside me. Then arms circled around Alex, ready to drag him from my grip.

"No," I snarled and shoved the person away. They flew out to the side, slamming into the side of the plane and falling to the ground in a heap.

"Paige" was called roughly. I glanced up to see Thorn approaching. "What's wrong? What happened?"

I got to my hands and hovered over Alex's body, protecting him. He'd used his magic to get us out of there, but something had happened to him because of it. "Stop," I ordered, my voice cold and hard.

A breeze blew across my face, and then Asher stood in front of me, facing Thorn. "What happened?" His voice was hard. He glanced behind him and down at us. I caught the sight of his elongated teeth and vibrant, glowing green eyes. My body quivered.

No. Not now. Jesus, Paige, get a grip.

Men rushed at us. Asher snarled at them.

"Fuck's sake, stop," Nate called. He stood off to the side with Ezra sitting beside him.

"Stop," Thorn repeated, and the men did.

"Everyone cool it. No one here is going to harm anyone," Nate said, and then he waved a hand at me. "She overreacted. Didn't know Smith would pass out from teleporting a group of us. She panicked."

I cocked my head to the side. "Alex passed out? He's okay?" Relief washed through me, along with a mild case of embarrassment. Though I would totally do it again if it came down to protecting him. Strange, and yet it felt natural.

Nate snorted. "He's fine. Well, he will be. He's good to travel with one person, maybe two. More exhausts him."

Asher straightened, fixing his clothes before stepping up to our sides. I moved back to kneel beside Alex. My body settled, knowing Alex would be okay. Asher bent, picked Alex up in his arms, and started for the plane. I quickly got up, raced toward them, and grabbed Alex's hand. I couldn't leave his side just yet, not until I knew for certain he was okay. Asher glanced down at me and then forward. I wanted to bring his face down to mine. I wanted him to bring those pointy teeth out so I could lick them, suck them while his glowing eyes gazed into mine.

Wetness pooled between my legs. I ground my teeth together, and someone groaned behind us. Asher looked back down at me with surprise in his eyes. His step faltered for a fraction of a second before they smoothed out as if it didn't happen. A tick in his jaw told me that misstep annoyed him. He climbed the stairs with me close behind, my hand still clutching Alex's. Ezra, who'd at some time changed back into his canine form, let out a huff and came up behind me.

Whispers brushed by my ears, but I didn't take them in. Since I knew things were safer, I rested all my concentration on those close around me because my mind was already too full.

Then I remembered something at the top of the stairs and turned. "Yasmin," I called. How I forgot I didn't know, and guilt threaded through me.

She still stood where we'd teleported in. "He… you… the man… oh my God," she exclaimed and then stormed my way.

People I didn't know went to step in her way, until I called, "She's my sister. No one touches her." They moved back. Asher stepped inside the plane. I quickly followed with my hand still in Alex's. Since I knew Yasmin would catch up and that she'd be safe because it seemed the people around us listened to what I said, I didn't worry.

I released my hold on Alex when Asher lay him in a seat near the window. Then I sat next to Alex, taking his hand again. Asher shot me a puzzled look and sat across from us in another seat. Ezra plonked his backside next to me in the aisle—thankfully they were wide. Thorn, followed by Nate, entered before my sister and Eric barreled in. Nate sat next to Asher while Thorn took a seat opposite us. Yasmin and Eric, still holding the kids, sat in the group of four chairs with Thorn.

Other people climbed aboard. I noticed the man I'd thrown. When he looked at me, I said, "I'm sorry for throwing you."

He bowed. "I'm sorry for touching him, my queen." Before I could correct him on the queen part, he moved down the aisle.

Yasmin turned to me. "I knew you were strong, but not that strong. He shot straight over. I'm surprised the plane isn't dented. Then"—she leaned in to me—"his"—she gestured with her head Asher's way—"eyes glowed green, his teeth… did you see his teeth?" I nodded. Boy had I seen his teeth. "Who are these guys, Paige?" She looked down at my hand in Alex's.

I cleared my throat. It was going to sound weird no matter how I said it, so I just went for it. "You see, I met them tonight. Alex and Nate you already know. But what you don't know is that Alex is a mage. Nate is a shifter. Asher is a vampire, and Thorn is…" I stumbled a moment. "What are you?"

"A ghoul, like yourself."

My heart skipped a beat.

"Ah… right, there you go."

"Psst," my sister whispered, leaning in again. Rolling my eyes, I looked to her. "It doesn't explain that." Again she stared down at my hand.

"No, it doesn't because I can't really explain it myself. I just know I don't want to leave his side until he's awake and okay. It's freaking me out on the inside though."

Yasmin nodded. "I can see the crazy eyes coming out to play." Yes, she knew me well. I may not show how freaked I was, but on the inside, I cursed, sweated, curled into a ball, and sucked my thumb. The night was all too much and soon, if it didn't slow down—and I worried it wouldn't—I *would* be in a corner legit sucking my thumb and crying for a blanket.

"Also," I added to Yasmin, "there's no point in whispering. They hear everything." I drew the last words out like I was telling her a scary story.

She paled. "Right. Got it. Girl talk later in private."

The men chuckled. Except for Nate. Still, his lips were going crazy. I knew he was holding back.

"Does someone want to inform me what happened?" Asher asked.

"I'd also like to know," Thorn said.

"Can we take off first?" Nate mentioned. "Probably safer if we get away fast."

"I'll speak with the pilot." Thorn stood and stalked down the aisle.

I turned in my seat to check on Alex; he breathed easy. I shifted closer, and his warmth washed over me. I wished I could curl into it, but that would bring more questions from everyone, and I didn't have an answer to them. All I knew was that Alex sent my hormones alight the first time he used his power, and since then, I'd felt a sense of protectiveness and possessiveness toward him.

Out the corner of my eye, I saw Asher studying me with Alex. He was also on my list that sent my lady bits and organs crazy. Only I noticed, like with Alex, it had started when he'd first showed his power. His vampire side.

What was wrong with me?

Did it mean I'd be after every man if they had a power or a different side to them and used it in front of me?

I'd been with one man in the past. One man who'd been a dickhead in the end, but I'd been happy having just one guy. Then bam, all of a sudden I'd changed once more and was a horny slut.

Even worse, they could smell it.

Embarrassed didn't come close to describing how I felt.

Would I have to buy a chastity belt for myself, lock it, and then throw away the key?

I checked on Yasmin and Eric to drag my mind away from thinking of a straitjacket for myself. At least then I'd keep my hands to myself. They huddled together, holding their children. Regret for going to their place muddled my head. If I hadn't have shown, they wouldn't have needed to leave their house. They'd be safe. Free. Now they were mixed up in a world I was still learning to deal with myself.

Yasmin glanced at me. "Don't," she said. "I'm not sad or angry I'm here with you. We're family."

"But—"

She shook her head. "No buts, Paige. I have no regrets."

It wasn't the place to have this conversation, but I didn't hold back because of the people around us. "I do. I should have called you, not come by. Then you'd still be home, and your kids would still be safe in their beds. Eric would have gone to his job on Monday in his new position. It wasn't fair of me—"

"Paige, my life wouldn't be the same without you in it. We've already lost our parents. I can't lose you too. Family always." She smiled.

My chest swelled. "You're the best sister ever."

Her smile grew. "I know."

"And you have the best husband." I winked at Eric. He returned it with a grin. I thought I heard a sound across from me, but when I looked in the direction, both Nate and Asher were just watching me.

The door to the cockpit opened, then over the intercom came the announcement to prepare for takeoff. I heard seat belts click in, so I did mine up as Thorn sat down in his seat.

When the plane started moving down the airstrip, Thorn said, "Now, let's talk about what happened."

CHAPTER EIGHT

$\mathcal{I}$t was Nate who explained what happened at Yasmin and Eric's. By the end of it, we were high in the sky, and a frown marred Asher's and Thorn's lips. But it was Thorn who said, "I never should have left your side, my queen."

I shot him a look, annoyed at his "my queen" business, but chose to say, "It's not anyone's fault but my own."

He shook his head. "I knew you would be sensed, but I didn't realize how fast."

"What's done is done. There is no going back now," Asher said.

"I guess you got us time off?" Nate asked.

Asher nodded. "Yes."

Nate whistled. "How did you manage that?"

"They owed us."

"Bullshit. It's because Jessica wants in your pants."

My belly sank, twisted, and then it wanted to crawl up my chest. "Who's Jessica?" I demanded harshly.

All eyes turned to me. I caught Thorn's lips thinning, his brows dipping.

"Sorry?" Asher asked.

"Who is Jessica?"

"She's a member of the council, the one in charge of our group," Nate supplied, and there went his lips again. I wanted to rip them off. I didn't find my weird aggression funny.

Humming under my breath, I turned into Alex and looked out the window. Maybe I just needed some sleep. After all, it had been an eventful evening.

"We'll speak of everything once we land and we're in private," Thorn abruptly said.

I glanced to him and asked a question I'd been wondering just before. "So you can't say why this plane was strategically planned to be ready for tonight? How did you know something would happen tonight?"

"That I can tell you." Thorn smiled, and my heart fluttered. No, not him too. But I didn't feel the need to pee on his leg like I did with Alex and Asher. However, I wouldn't be surprised if it came sooner or later. I did feel a small connection to him. I could definitely trust him. I knew that. "From our former queen. We knew a rough time of the year to be prepared for your arrival. For the last couple of weeks, we've been ready. When our queen passed, a spell drew me to your side immediately. It happened to be after a shower at the time."

It was the truth. I sensed it.

Sometimes my new senses, or power—whatever—were really handy.

It still left me with more questions, but I held off on those and moved onto something else. With a quick glance around, I lowered my voice and leaned toward Thorn's way to ask, "Ghouls... what exactly can we do?"

He smiled. "From what I've gathered, your... dog has been around since you woke." I nodded and also noted he didn't refer to Ezra as a hellhound. I assumed in case the others in the back were listening and he didn't want them to know. "He has good instincts. Did he help?"

"Yes."

"So you would know by now what you need to eat." I nodded; he returned it. "Ghouls are strong, fast, and live forever, unless our heads are sliced from our bodies." Ezra let out a growl, and I reached down and patted him. Both Ezra and I didn't like to hear it, but it was information I needed to know. "With you being the queen, you'll have more strength and speed. Really, you'll be an unstoppable force."

An unstoppable force. I liked the idea of that. It meant I could protect my family more.

"Thank you," I told him. It was all the information I needed for that moment as there were too many ears for more.

"Anything," he replied.

Shifting in my seat, I looked behind us to the seats further back. I didn't know the other people on the plane. Even if they were called "my" people, I didn't trust them. Some looked at me in awe. Others I couldn't read whether they didn't like me being here or if they were just not showing anything until I proved myself somehow.

In total, there were seven other people I didn't know. Four men and three women. The man I'd pushed smiled at me. It was the women I wasn't sure about. One even looked like she sucked on a lemon as she stared back. But then her gaze flicked to Thorn and back to me. I got it; she wanted Thorn. There went that buzz of annoyance again. That pull. Her wanting Thorn didn't sit well with me.

I faced the front, but Asher's eyes met mine, looking into my soul. Unable to process everything, I rested my head against Alex's shoulder and closed my eyes. I did feel tired, but I was too wired to fall asleep. Instead, I listened to Yasmin and Eric talking about what they were going to tell the kids when they woke. Then I heard Nate calling for Asher's attention. They spoke about the demon in the restaurant, how it was a weak one, but there'd been more and more popping up over town.

It was listening to them all that surprisingly lulled me into sleep.

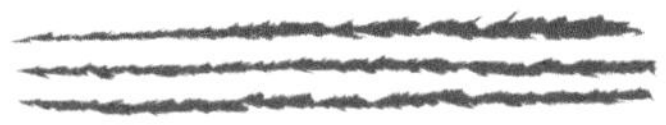

"She's been holding my hand the whole way?" Alex's voice drifted into my sleep, causing me to shiver. He was okay.

"Yep." Nate popped the *p* at the end.

"Why?" he asked. He didn't seem too fazed by it. He was still holding my hand. That was a good sign, right? He might be okay with me wrapping him in bubble wrap to keep him safe.

Wait… throw that thought out of my head; it was insane.

As I opened my eyes, I realized no sound was coming from the plane. We'd landed. I straightened in the seat and hoped I hadn't drooled. Discreetly, I wiped the side of my mouth on my shoulder, just in case.

"So, we're here." Being on the ground meant I had to release Alex's hand. I slowly unstuck one finger at a time from my vise grip as Thorn explained we'd landed on "our" own private airstrip. Apparently, the former queen, not that I was admitting to being the new one, had been rich.

Without looking at Alex, I moved my hand away from his and fisted it tightly at my side as I stood and stretched.

I pulled my gaze back down and caught four men watching me intently. A smirk played on my lips. They'd been checking me out.

The people from the back of the plane started down the aisle. They moved by, and each one bowed at me as they did. Only a couple of the women didn't bend far, and they kept their gaze on me with a slight glare in their eyes.

When I'd begun to stupidly curtsy with the first person, Thorn shook his head at me, and Asher stood, taking my arm and holding me up. Okay, so that had been wrong. The rest I felt like a fool just standing there as they bent at their waist in front of me.

When the last one left the cabin, Yasmin laughed her ass off. "They b-bowed to you." She tapped herself. "My sister."

"Shut up," I mumbled. If I wasn't weirded out, then I'd probably be laughing along with her.

Thorn stood. "Let's get you inside, my queen."

"Thorn," I warned.

"In private I will call you Paige. In public, it's better to show my allegiance and respect."

I sighed, a normal human reaction I still held. "Fine." I stilled and felt heat at my back. With a breath in, I knew it was Alex.

"What's wrong?" he asked.

If I could, I would have melted against him, but it seemed my emotions were catching up and mixing with my mind. Everything had changed. Again.

File it away, Paige. Have a breakdown in private.

I cleared my throat. "Nothing."

Yasmin gave me a sad, soft smile. She knew I was on the verge of crashing into a heap and not wanting to know more. More meant my brain would probably melt inside my head.

"Let us get you inside," Thorn said gently.

Nodding, I moved into the aisle. Ezra rose with a groan. His head thumped into my hand, and I patted him. Thorn started toward the door, and I gestured to Yasmin and Eric. They rose with the kids and moved into the space before me. I followed them, Ezra at my side, knowing the other men in our little group wouldn't be far behind.

Outside the plane, more people, at least over two hundred, stood gazing up at us. Thorn moved my family gently aside, and when the people saw me, they bowed, and all of them called, "My queen."

A tingle started in my lower spine and then spread all the way up. I straightened and tipped my head down slightly. The people went about whatever they had been doing. A lot kept glancing my way, but they still got busy.

"Well done," Thorn murmured.

I snorted softly. "What, for not freaking out?"

He smiled. "Yes."

I harrumphed and then shrugged. Glancing away from him to the opposite side, my jaw dropped open, my eyes widening. "Holy crap…. Yasmin?"

"I see it," she said, and I could tell she was smiling. Before Yasmin met Eric, we'd been planning to travel, to see the world and all the old castles we could.

Finally, I had one right in front of me, and it looked like the mother of all castles.

My chest filled with elation and warmed me all over. "It's so big," I whispered.

"That's what she said" came from Eric, who then huffed out a breath, and I knew it was from Yasmin elbowing him.

"Welcome home, my queen," Thorn said, stepping up to my side and ignoring Ezra's growl.

Home was definitely a castle.

It looked to be about the size of an extra-large football stadium long and at least five-stories high. But there were peaks all over the place, like little bell towers. My hands itched to explore the whole place, but I knew it would take me ages, maybe even a year, to see everything. There was even a moat out the front with a raised drawbridge.

A giddy light laugh dropped from my lips.

I would get to see inside a castle.

A *castle*.

My castle apparently.

At least I had the time on my hands to explore the whole place. That was unless I didn't like the answers I was hoping to get as soon as we settled. But still, I could stay a little longer. I hadn't had an adventure like this in… ever.

With a new spring in my step, I started down the stairs. At the bottom, I took another glance toward the castle, until Ezra growled at my side. I looked down at him and then over to the woods off the airstrip. Ezra took a step that way.

"Ezra," I called.

"Paige, stop." Nate's voice was strong and hard.

In the next second, I was surrounded by Asher, Nate, Thorn, and Ezra, who'd crept back closer to my side. Behind me, near the plane, Alex stood with my family, and I shot him an appreciative smile. He dipped his chin.

"Don't take another fucking step," Nate snarled.

Facing forward, I peeked over his shoulder and saw about twenty men and women of all shapes and sizes step from the woods. There were also wolves. At least fifty of them.

"Is she the new queen?" a man called. He was older, with gray tinting the sides of his dark hair. Built bigger than my men.

Hold up, my men?

Since when did they become my men?

Did I class Nate and Thorn as mine as well? I knew my lady bits were voting yes for Alex and Asher, but I wasn't sure Thorn and Nate were a part of the strong protectiveness and arousal my body felt. Well, besides the connection I sensed with them from the start.

"That's not your fucking business," Nate bit out.

"It is, pup. I'm the alpha of this territory. I pick if my wolves bow to the new queen or not, and as far as I can see, she doesn't look to be fit for the role of queen."

Thorn scoffed. "Tell me you don't feel her power, Jessup Falk."

Jessup shrugged. "A mild brush of it, but is it enough for what's to come?"

What's to come?

What did he mean?

"She needs to prove herself," a woman standing at Jessup's side yelled.

"Tell me why I need to do such a thing?" I asked.

"We follow the true queen only," someone shouted.

"I don't even know if I'm the true queen or if I'm a queen at all. I've had so much shit happen tonight I can't sort them all out in such a small span of time. I just want to go in there"—I pointed to the castle—"have a goddamn cup of coffee, and work out what in the hell is going on."

This shit was starting to piss me off.

"Not before you meet our son," Jessup said.

Is my hearing going?

"I'm sorry, what?"

Some of the men around me growled low. A man from behind Jessup stepped forward. He was tall, looked like his father, but a little younger, and a scar ran down the side of his face. He smirked, and even though I was behind Nate, it felt like his eyes were drinking me in and he liked what he saw. If the licking of lips was anything to go by.

"He wants to claim the new queen as a mate. He was promised a chance to prove his strength to her. To prove he would make a good king at her side."

The air thickened around me. My pulse ate at my throat. "I'm sorry, *what?*"

"Is she simple?" someone shouted.

Jessup stepped closer. Nate tensed, and his voice came out thicker, deeper. "Do not fucking move."

It shot a ting to my clit.

Not again.

Nate's body grew in height and width, and his chest rumbled with a snarl. His tee at the back lifted a little... it had me wondering why.

"She just grew into power and arrived *tonight,* Jessup," Thorn called. "My queen won't be taking on any mate or doing anything until she can get her mind around the change in her life."

I didn't listen to their back and forth words. It seemed my nose was too interested in Nate's new scent. My hands were too interested in wanting to touch Nate. Slowly, I reached out and lifted the back of his tee.

A tail sprang free.

"Oh my God, it's so cute," I cooed and then ran my hand up and down it.

I heard Nate suck in a quick breath, and he glanced over his shoulder. His facial hair had grown, and his eyes were dark brown now instead of green, and they were wide. His mouth, which had a full set of sharp teeth, opened.

"You have a tail." I smiled, still running my hand up and down it. I heard laughter behind me. As Asher scooped me up into his arms, he ordered, "Organize this shit. I'm taking her to the castle."

"I'll bring her family," I heard Alex say before Asher had us speeding through the night toward the castle.

Yet, I wanted to go back and pet Nate some more, ideally while rubbing myself against him.

CHAPTER NINE

NATE

She'd stroked my tail.

Stroked it like it was her new plaything.

"She rubbed your tail," Jessup said, shock marring his voice.

I let out a rough sound in the back of my throat. *Tell me about it.* I could still feel her hand running up and down the length of it. My dick throbbed goddamn hard. It wanted to be buried inside of her, and now.

"Does she know what that means?" the woman beside Jessup asked.

I didn't think Paige knew anything about werewolves and how, by touching a tail in half form, it meant she'd claimed me as her own.

What the fuck had she been thinking touching me like that?

It also goddamn meant....

"Fenris, are you backing down?" Jessup asked his son.

Fuck.

If he didn't back down from his so-called claim, I would have to challenge him. I glanced over to see Alex had already ushered Paige's family away. With their human hearing, I was grateful they wouldn't overhear anymore.

Fenris threw his head back and laughed. He shook his head. "Oh, I'll be claiming the so-called queen once I've shown no one will beat me. If I have to fight *him* to prove it, to have a chance at her side, I'll do it. Then I'll override her claim on the mutt and make her bend to my will as king."

Red-hot fury pulsed through me.

"I accept the challenge then," I said loudly.

Silence drifted through the tarmac.

Fenris grinned. "Then I'll be seeing you on the next full moon, mutt."

"So be it," I snarled.

The wolves disappeared. The people were slower to move off, except Fenris who strode over to a woman, picked her up and threw her over his shoulder, slapping her ass. She squealed.

As they drifted off, leaving their alpha behind, I waited to see what Jessup had to say. His thin lips told me nothing.

"Fenris is of our blood, but he is not the right person to be in charge of command. He's been filled with visions of winning and taking his place as king, ruling over all."

Holy fuck. He was warning me if his son won, shit would hit the fan.

"It won't happen," I told them.

"I feel your alpha strength. Why have you not claimed a pack?"

I shrugged. "It doesn't interest me."

It was his woman who spoke next. "I have a feeling that's going to change."

I crossed my arms over my chest and forced the shift back to my human state while staring them down.

Their gaze swung to Thorn. "Things have been altered."

Thorn nodded. "That they have."

"Let us pray it's for the better," Jessup said.

"Who filled your son's head with such lies to begin with?" Thorn asked.

Jessup shook his head. "That I can't say. It's not pack business, but I'm sure you'll find out soon enough. Learn who to trust within the walls."

He'd said enough to let us know it was someone on the grounds. Thorn nodded once, and they both moved off, back into the woods.

Sighing, I scrubbed a hand over my face. My life had changed in a goddamn blink of an eye because of Paige Alice. I didn't have a fucking clue if it was good or bad. Though I'd argue it leaned toward bad since I had to fight for my life on the next full moon.

But shit, I knew I'd put everything I had in it because it meant it'd keep Paige out of that fucker's hands.

She'd taken me by surprise. Had cemented herself inside me even before she'd unknowingly claimed me.

In over three decades, we'd never taken time off work. Yet, there we were, willing to step back from our work as council enforcers because Paige had walked into our lives.

We'd told Thorn our purpose was to make sure Paige would stay safe. That *was* the case, but something had tugged at our chests as soon as Paige had appeared.

It pissed me off. Not only was it unexpected, but I hadn't

wanted it… this connection.

However, that last part screamed bullshit, not only from my mind, but my wolf was happy with her claim over me, and that annoyed the fuck out of me as well.

"Come, let's see what mischief our queen has gotten up to." Thorn grinned.

A snort escaped. Yeah, Paige attracted trouble. She was tough and didn't seem to care what anyone thought. No doubt she'd be up to something.

I followed Thorn into the huge-ass castle. I couldn't blame Paige for being in awe with the place. It was monstrous. On the way, I noticed Thorn receiving his own bows, but just of the head, not a full waist one like Paige had received.

Who exactly was he to them?

It was curious. Not all of them shared the same scent as Paige or Thorn. There were other species as well—humans, vampires, witches, mages, and even shifters. I'd never seen so many in one place, and all seemed to be playing nicely. It didn't happen often. Not in big groups. Actually, never in large groups; they didn't mix well. Small groups, like how I worked with Asher and Alex, yes. We were together with a common goal: to make sure everyone played well by the law.

What was the reason they mixed well together?

"For the queen," Thorn replied to my unasked question. I snapped my gaze to his. "You're easy to read. However, I'll explain more when the others are around."

Clenching my hands so I didn't wrap them around his neck and squeeze the answers out of him, I grunted. We walked across the long drawbridge and in through the gate. I caught my eyes from widening and ground my teeth together instead. I didn't want Thorn to see I was impressed. The place was like something from medieval times. Carts, straw, stalls of food, clothing, and other shit jotted around the area. It wouldn't surprise me if the shopping area led all the way around the castle.

"This is how the people make their money and pay for their residence."

"How many people live in the castle?"

"Over two hundred. The people who work the market and the airstrip come from the village out behind the castle, and there are over one thousand people there."

Holy fuck.

"How did all this slip by the council?"

Considering the council's enforcers had never heard of this place, I could only assume it was hidden from the council. They didn't like large groups of mixed species to congregate because they were sometimes uncontrollable, and the council was all about control. Living by their rules only. If you didn't, we were sent in to deal with it.

"Our witches and mages keep us hidden. Others are repelled from the area unless they seek refuge and have sworn loyalty to the queen," he said, and added, "The old queen that was."

"It doesn't make sense. On the council there's some powerful mages and witches. They pick up on spikes of magic being used. A constant power surge would raise alarms. They would have sent a team to look into it."

Thorn smiled. "Our old queen knew that would occur. She made sure our people who designed the barrier put their work into devices she had made, which can be switched on and off only when we need to shut down the ward to allow people in. The devices are electrical and designed someplace else. The council," he sneered, the gesture prickling my skin, "doesn't detect anything from this area since the barrier also contains all magic inside."

My mind didn't want to wrap around the idea of such a place existing and how it was hiding from the council. The council had always ruled their people fairly. As far as my brothers and I knew, they were even-handed. I didn't understand why the old ghoul queen had hidden from them. We'd been following the council—their rules and all that entailed—forever. We followed them blindly, and it was drilled into me to inform the powers that be of such a place.

Yet, I couldn't.

Thorn led us through an entryway into the stone castle. Warmth radiated throughout the place. It didn't feel over-heated, just perfect. A grand staircase stood in front of us; Thorn ascended it, and as I made my way behind him, I glanced around, catching sight of people. With a sniff, I detected a few shifters, some humans, and a couple of magic users. Some looked my way, but they all showed Thorn some type of respect with either a bow of their head or a salute. Women smiled coyly at him.

He was popular among them all. It'd make it hard if we had to take him out in the end for being a threat to Paige.

Goddamn, there I went again. Wanting to protect her.

The place was mammoth; it'd be easy to get lost. Thank fuck I had my nose. I could easily scent Paige's sweet smell down the hall we walked. She was in a room with Asher, Alex, her family, and two others I didn't know. One was a human, the other a vampire.

My ears picked up the sound of someone pacing.

Thorn opened the door in front of us. It led to a large seating area. With a quick glance, I saw the hellhound wasn't around. Paige's sister and her man didn't hold the children any longer either, and they weren't in the room, but that's all I saw before I got distracted by someone trying to shove me, when I didn't move I received a jab to the gut.

With a growl in the back of my throat, I grabbed the wrist and dragged Paige close. She glared up at me.

"You were out there forever. I thought they were going to have you for dinner. What took so long?"

I jerked my head back in shock. She'd been worried about me.

Me.

What the fuck for?

Asher cleared his throat, and I lifted my gaze to his, seeing his lips twitch. "We got inside and then, when I refused to allow her to go back out to, as she put it, 'kick some ass' if they tried to screw you over, she started worrying."

I opened my mouth before snapping it closed. I didn't know what to say. No one had worried about me in decades. I knew I wasn't the nicest guy to get along with, which was why I stuck to one-night stands. And I'd definitely been a dick to Paige, yet she had been concerned on my behalf.

My chest expanded. It seemed my heart liked the thought of Paige caring.

Only, my mind won out. I flicked her hand away from mine and stalked by her. "I can take care of myself," I clipped. Alex winced, and Asher shook his head. Paige's family glared at me, and Thorn snorted. I ignored them all.

A vamp and human I didn't know stood off to the side, near a tray of food and drinks.

"Asshole," I heard Paige cough out.

Ignoring it, I made my way over to the table of food,

grabbed a small cut sandwich, and shoved it in my mouth. While chewing, I poured a glass of what looked like red wine.

I lifted my head to take a sip and found the vamp woman, with long red hair and cunning eyes, smiling at me. Heat hit my back. Paige's arm came around my waist and pointed at the woman.

"Don't you dare try it on him as well. You've made googly eyes at all the men in the room. *Even* my brother-in-law. I've had enough. There is no way any of them will be interested."

The woman smirked. "We'll see, won't we?"

With a snarl, Paige tried to move me out of the way to get to the taunting bitch. Anyone could see Paige was on edge, but of course, the vamp pressed her buttons. I curled an arm around her waist, twisted and lifted her off her feet enough to walk to Alex, who sat in a chair, and deposited her in his lap.

Alex grunted, his hands landing on her waist.

Leaning in, I snapped in her face, "Calm the fuck down."

"You calm down," she spat back like a toddler.

The vamp woman giggled. Paige tried to launch herself off Alex, but his arms wrapped around her waist tightly.

"Patrice, Mesilla, out," Thorn ordered.

Straightening, I stood beside the chair and crossed my arms over my chest. The human woman scampered out quickly. Asher followed her quietly; he must need a feed.

The stupid vamp woman slowly swayed her hips across the room with a satisfied smile pasted onto her red lips. "I'll be seeing you, gentlemen." She winked. Paige sent her the middle finger before the woman closed the door.

Paige immediately settled back into Alex like it was normal for her, and Alex's face reddened. Goddamn it was funny to see him nervous. I didn't get it. Yeah, Paige was stunning, but he had to learn to control his expressions. From the look of his widening eyes, Paige had set off his cock as she shifted around on his lap. Thinking of cocks, mine perked up at the memory of Paige stroking my tail. My wolf huffed in annoyance; he wanted me to spread her legs and slip my throbbing hardness inside, claiming her right back. I clenched my jaw and threw that thought aside for now.

"Can you believe her?" Paige asked her sister.

Yasmin shook her head, her own eyes narrowed like Paige's. "She just thought all the men in the room would kiss her feet." She paused a beat. "Why didn't she care Paige is this supposed queen?" Yasmin asked.

Thorn sighed. "Vampires come here seeking peace, but they find it hard not to mix up a little drama. She will bow if it comes down to it in the end or she'll be forced out."

"Vampires are very sexual creatures," I added, noting Paige's narrowing eyes. "She was probably hoping to start an orgy."

Paige's cute nose screwed up in disgust. Her gaze moved to where Asher had been. She stood. "Where is he?" she bit out.

Ah, fuck.

If she acted how she did with the vamp woman making eyes at us, I didn't think it'd be good when she found out Asher was feeding off someone.

"He's gone to eat," Thorn said, his lips twitching.

"What?" Paige roared, then stormed from the room. Alex ran after her.

I slowly made my way to the door after Thorn. "We'll bring her back shortly… after we save the person Asher is with," I told Paige's sister and her guy. They both nodded, seeming numb from the events or possibly over the fact Paige was acting crazy possessive of all of us.

CHAPTER TEN

ASHER

*I*f people looked closer, they would notice I wasn't myself. Pain radiated over my body from the lashings I'd received from the council. Informing them about our time off hadn't gone well. When they'd refused our request, I hadn't backed down, and they didn't like that.

It didn't matter I'd been loyal and worked decades without a break.

We were theirs to rule.

I'd had to fight my way out and had barely made it with my life. They hunted for me. I could feel them every time they'd grown close, but so far, I'd managed to escape their grasp. Since other things had happened at the airstrip, I'd yet to tell Nate and Smith, but I would have to soon.

They'd classed us as rogue.

I didn't understand why we weren't allowed our time off. Why they refused my request. Something was going on within the walls of the council. The certainty of that buzzed through me. Something rotten. Corrupt. Regardless, we would have to find out what as well as how to prevent them from searching for us.

Had I put the people here at risk? Possibly, but I couldn't see any other choice. The need inside me to get back to Paige crawled across my skin the more time I'd been away from her. I hoped Thorn would have answers about why we had a connection with Paige Alice.

Anger washed through me once more over the council and their actions. I ground my teeth together as I second-guessed every mission we'd been sent on. Right then, I couldn't see how any of our cases had been for an ulterior motive, but I didn't know what to trust and that singed my insides.

Who had we been working for?

At least I had trust in my brothers-in-arms. I knew, since the council had acted the way they had toward me, that Nate and Alex would have my back. They wouldn't want anything to do with them until we knew for certain they weren't as corrupt as I was now thinking. We needed to eliminate the leeches from within the walls, but it would take time, and our priority right then was Paige.

So I pushed away my fury because, for now, I had to feed. The humans I'd enthralled along the way to the airport hadn't fully sated me. I needed more to bring my full strength back. I'd need it for whatever was to come.

I'd slipped out of the room earlier to follow the human down the hall. It wasn't until the end that I gained her attention by calling out, "Excuse me, miss."

She jumped and spun my way. "Y-Yes?"

"May I have a word with you for a moment?"

She glanced around, then nodded.

Smiling, I gestured her ahead of me into the room across from us. She made her way in. I followed and closed the door behind us.

When she heard the door close, her heart skipped a beat and started at a faster pace.

"Relax," I ordered. My eyes bled to glow green. She opened her mouth, but I put my power behind the next words, "I won't hurt you. You can relax, Mesilla."

Her mouth snapped closed, her eyes glazing over, and a smile touched her lips. "Yes. Relax."

"That's right, Mesilla. I just need a nip of your blood. You'll let me, won't you?"

"Yes." She nodded and shifted her long dark hair over her shoulder.

Stepping forward, I caught her heaving chest. I could scent her arousal. Usually I would take her up on her offer, but I couldn't. She wasn't who I wanted to sink into.

Stepping close, I swept an arm around her waist, and she gasped, her eyes hooded. Leaning in, my mouth pooled with saliva at the sight of her pumping vein in her neck.

The door burst open behind us. Spinning, I snarled at being interrupted.

Paige's finger came up as she snapped, "Don't you hiss at me, Asher Evans. You." She clicked her fingers at Mesilla, who didn't move. Paige stomped across the room toward us. Alex shot through the door with Thorn and Nate following.

"Fuck, Paige," Nate clipped.

"Paige," Alex warned.

They both knew I wouldn't like being interrupted while feeding.

"My queen," Thorn called. Even he was smart enough to be cautious. They would be seeing my glowing eyes, my elongated fangs, my claws out and ready to fight for my food.

What they didn't understand was how I didn't have it in me to harm Paige.

Before Paige could reach my meal, I spun her into my arms and crowded into her space. "I need to feed," I bit out, low and harsh.

Paige's chin tipped up, her hard gaze meeting mine. There wasn't a flinch or look of worry. Instead, she demanded, "Not from her."

She didn't have a right to order me, to tell me. It infuriated me, and yet I wanted to listen to what she said. "Then who?"

"Lead her out of here, Thorn," Nate said. I tensed, ready to fight if he thought to take Paige away. I dug my claws into the rock behind Paige's head. Her sweet, intoxicating scent drilled into me. I wanted a taste, and it wasn't only her blood I wanted to have sliding into my mouth, pressing against my tongue.

Someone stepped closer. A dark growl rumbled out of me. I inched my head slightly to the side. Nate stood there. I sensed another at my other side and knew it was Smith. The hunger, my vampire side, snarled in my head to end them. But I wasn't lost yet. I knew they were brothers-in-arms.

"You never let yourself go so long without. What happened?" Smith asked.

I shuddered when tiny hands touched my stomach and slowly slid up to my chest. "Asher, you need to back off."

"You demanded me to feed on someone, Paige. Who then?"

"I-I don't know."

"Why do you think you can order us around?" I questioned, my voice as cold as steel.

"Because."

"Because isn't answer enough. Why do you get aroused? Why do you become possessive? Why do you think you own us?"

"Asher," Smith called.

Her jaw clenched. "I don't know!" she yelled in my face.

Anyone else I would have ripped their arms off for speaking to me that way.

But not Paige.

"I need to feed, Paige. I hunger, and yet you deny me what I had. Someone ready and willing. What do I do now?"

"Feed from me" came out quietly. Only it wasn't the woman I stared down at. No, she had a surprised look on her face, which I was sure matched my own. Hearing that whisper, though, had my claws and fangs retracting. My eyes dulled to my light blue color.

Slowly, I turned to face Smith. He stood, hands clasped in front of him, rocking back and forth on his feet while his cheeks shone pink.

"Smith?"

He rolled his eyes. "Alex. We're not working."

But we were supposed to have been. Working on figuring out Paige, making sure she was protected from Thorn or the people around her.

He was younger than Nate and me, by many decades, but was still valued on the team. Although, he was still very young in mind compared to us. Even in the mage world, he was a baby at thirty. A strong one, but still an infant. Hell, he had been with us for years, yet he had a lot of growing to do.

In all that time, even after battle when I needed blood, he had never offered me sustenance.

"Alex?" I questioned.

He shrugged, blew out a breath and mumbled, "Ah, Paige might be okay if you fed on one of us."

Paige's heart accelerated.

"Why not her?" Nate clipped.

"If she fed Asher, then the link between them both will be locked."

We all faced Thorn. Even as my stomach tightened in hunger, I ignored it because I wanted to hear the rest.

"Explain," Nate barked.

"Should we head back to the other room and relax there?"

"No. I want to know why my body reacts like I'm the cat and the men are catnip," Paige said. She straightened and crossed her arms over her chest. "Also, it might be good to hear it not in front of my sister and her husband. Especially Eric. He doesn't need to know my achy and needy vagina is starving for attention from three men."

The room quietened.

The heat from Alex's body hit mine. His jaw clenched. Nate fisted his hands, and I had to lock my body down. I knew all three of us were willing to satisfy her needs right in that moment. However, we had to find out why we reacted this way first.

"Speak," I snarled, my eyes locked onto Thorn's as power rushed through me.

"Things have changed. I didn't expect this to happen. But it seems when our old queen died and the power transferred to Paige, it connected us all in a way where we became her mates."

Paige made a noise in the back of her throat. "Do you mean

the Australian term mates? As in friends? As in this will pass and I *haven't* dragged you all into this without any of you agreeing? Tell me I haven't fucked up your lives because my vagina suddenly sees you all as hers?" she screeched. She bent at the waist and breathed in and out quickly. I grabbed Alex by the shirt and dragged him over, pushing him toward her.

He was the best of us to console the emotional woman. I knew I made the right choice when he started saying soothing things and rubbing her back.

Paige shook her head. "I don't even need to breathe and I'm hyperventilating." She flapped her hands up and down in front of her. "I can't breathe."

Nate snorted. "You don't need to, remember?"

She glared over at him. Her lips thinned and she stood tall, as tall as she could get, which wasn't much. "How are you all calm? I've messed up your lives. Wait." She looked at Thorn. "Have I messed everyone's lives up? Are they stuck…. Hang on. You said *all* of you. You mean you too?" Her eyes widened when he nodded. Her head jerked back, tilted to the side, and then straightened. She ran a hand through her hair. "But, I mean, I feel a connection to you. Like I had with them from the start, but I'm not a raging psycho when you're around other women."

"Just around other women or all the time?" Nate teased.

It really wasn't the time.

Her gaze, full of liquid fire, snapped to Nate. "I think I'll fire you and find another mate."

His upper lip lifted, and a growl dropped out.

"Ha!" she shouted, pointing at Nate. "Don't like the thought of that, do you?" She whipped her eyes back to Thorn. "Why don't you all go crazy with me around other men? Also, let's go back to the other thing before the douche gallery spoke. Why don't I react the same with you like I do them?"

"The link is not yet finalized until—" He cleared his throat. "—bodily fluids are shared in a sexual way. Or if Asher were to feed from you or if—"

"I got it," Paige shouted, and it was the first time a blush hit her cheeks.

Thorn nodded. "Also, once the process is completed, we will become as domineering as you are with us. Well, as you are with just them, for now."

"For now? So are you saying I'll become more attached to you as well? Jesus, am I a slut?"

Nate snorted out a laugh, Paige made a move his way, and Alex wrapped his arms around her. On contact, she seemed to calm a little. It didn't stop her death glare at him though.

"It is only humans who think more than one lover is wrong. It's accepted and mostly applied within all other races," I supplied, in hope it would ease her troubles.

I didn't think it helped. Paige's brows dipped. She bit her bottom lip and shook her head. "I-I don't think…." She took a deep breath. "I don't know what to think."

"As for myself," Thorn started, "I have noticed you didn't claim the others until they used their powers or showed their other nature. I believe that will happen once I do too."

"Then don't. I mean—"

Thorn stiffened. His amber-colored eyes flashed with a red haze over them, and he opened his mouth slightly to show us all his teeth as they grew. I caught the change that swept over Paige. Her heart raced, her eyes dulled, her lids lowered a little, and she sucked in a deep breath.

She licked her lips before one word dropped from between them in a whispered growl, "*Mine.*"

"Yes, my queen," Thorn answered, his voice deeper, harsher. "Release her."

Alex dropped his arms, and she walked her way toward Thorn slowly, a small smile splayed on her luscious lips.

The door opened, and one of the women from the plane stepped inside. Her eyes slammed into Paige approaching Thorn. She hissed as her steps ate up the carpet moving toward Paige. I started for her, as did Alex and Nate, until a huge hound bounded into the room behind the woman and tackled her to the ground.

Ezra, in his canine form, stood over the woman's back and growled viciously into her ear. It wasn't a growl of a dog, and she knew it because she froze.

Saliva dribbled out of his mouth and splattered her in the face.

Paige, in the commotion, blinked out of her haze and stared down at Ezra. Then she smacked Thorn in the stomach. But I could tell it wasn't at full-strength.

"You did that on purpose," she sulked half-heartedly. The smart-ass grinned big and wide.

Though, I couldn't say I blamed him. I would have done the same. Luckily it had already been done without our knowledge, so there wouldn't be any way Paige could shut her claim on us down.

My mind ticked it over.

She claimed us.

We were hers.

If it had been any other, I might have hated it, but it wasn't.

It was the woman who'd caught my attention so many hours

ago. The woman I wanted to know. The one I'd felt a connection to even before the bond formed within her.

I knew I wasn't the only one pleased either. Alex and Nate didn't seem fazed by it. They kept an eye on her like she should be treasured as a rare prized jewel.

Even if Nate acted like an idiot, he wanted her, he liked her, and he was pleased by the events.

"Thorn, please," the woman begged.

Thorn slowly tore his gaze away from Paige and down to her. A tick started in his jaw. We needed her gone so we could talk about the mate bond more thoroughly.

There was also the matter of my feeding.

I glanced to Alex. He sensed my stare and met it. He nodded, and I dipped my head in appreciation. Though it felt like more, like a gift. It had me looking at him differently. At the man he was becoming.

CHAPTER ELEVEN

THORN

Iknew she was about to deny her claim on me; I wouldn't have it. I'd been dreaming of her for quite some time, and now that she was in front of me, I wouldn't lose her. Even after her power washed over me after mixing with mine, I worried she would be angry with what I had done. She had been a little annoyed. While I understood why, I also rejoiced in her claim, her scent, and her power surrounding me.

Like all the men in the room, others would sense the queen's claim on us.

My chest expanded from the thought of it, proud to walk about knowing she was a part of me and soon, hopefully very soon, I would have my own claim on her. I would be a part of her, and our powers together would thrive.

I didn't care she had others. It was a given she would have

more than one mate, though I'd assumed it would be of our own kind. Of course, Paige was different from the late queen.

She was special.

She would bring change.

"Thorn, please," Malvina begged. Honestly, I had forgotten she'd been in the room, too captivated by Paige's beauty. I didn't want to look away, but I dragged my gaze down to the floor to see Malvina sprawled on the floor with Ezra looming over her. I thinned my lips in distaste. She'd been a thorn in my side for quite some time.

"My queen, would you call Ezra off?"

My lips twitched as I watched Paige think about it. She sighed. "Ezra, come here."

With one last growl, Ezra climbed off and strode over to Paige, who crouched and cuddled the animal close. Now *that* made my gut heat in jealousy. I wanted to be the one she cradled.

I moved my gaze back to the problem at hand. "Stand," I ordered. Malvina got to her feet. Her gaze locked onto Paige and burned in fury. She had always thought I would come back to her bed. I hadn't because six months ago, our former queen had shared what the seer had visioned for me. I would be a part of the new queen's life, and she was the same woman I'd dreamed of.

Back then, Malvina had seen my status, as the highest-ranking guard with an ear directly to the queen, as a means to gain more power over our people for herself.

I'd seen it, ended it, and she'd never gotten over it. Even though she'd been with many others since then.

"What did you interrupt us for?"

Her eyes went to the floor, and she smiled coyly. "You

weren't in your room. I thought I would come find you and see if you're ready to head there."

Paige sucked in sharply, and a noise fell from between her lips. It sounded very much like a growl. I wanted to bask in her possessiveness. Some may have found her actions annoying or acted similar to how Nate had, but not I.

"Do not act like you come to my room every night. It's been *months*, Malvina, and it will never happen again."

Her upper lip rose. "Because of *her*."

"She is the new queen," I shouted. "You will bow to her."

She straightened. "I will not," she shrilled, and stormed from the room. I went to go after her, to make her bow if I had to. She would not get away with disrespecting the queen, but then a hand wrapped around my wrist. I glanced down to see Paige had a hold of me.

Her hand fell away, and then she ranted, "I want to punch her in the tit. No, I could rip both of them off and shove them down her throat." Paige huffed. "You'll need to get your ex under control, Thorn, before I do just that."

"I was about to have words with her."

She shook her head. "Not now. We have things to talk about, and actually, no you won't talk to her. I don't like the thought of you near her." She ran a hand over her face. Her brows dipped as worry appeared over her features. "You'll need to get someone else to speak with her."

I nodded. A smile crept onto my lips. "And wipe that smile off your mouth. You got me all claimy on purpose. I've not yet forgiven you."

I bowed. "I shall seek your forgiveness in some way, my queen." I breathed out the words of the last part and glanced up at her. I caught the shiver crossing her body.

She groaned and slapped both hands to her face. I straightened, stepped close, and pulled her into my arms. Before I could say anything, she did. "I'm a horrible, terrible person."

"You are not," I told her.

She nodded into my chest. "I am."

Over her head, Asher and Nate ushered Alex forward. It seemed they didn't know what to do when our queen was upset. Alex, though, moved in close, pulling Paige's back against his chest. His hands went to her waist.

"Why do you think you're terrible, Paige?" Alex asked softly.

"How am I not? I ruined everyone's life. My sister's, Eric's, my poor niece's and nephew's. You, Asher, and asshole." Nate's lips trembled in mirth. She shook her head again. "I'm not sure Thorn will see it as bad, but you all should. You're all here without wanting to really. I've got my stinking claim on you without knowing I did it and without getting consent in the first place." She lifted her head and moved away toward the door. "You should just leave." Her sorrow-filled gaze caught mine, and if my heart beat, it would have lurched. "If they leave, will the claim go away?"

Paige may not have noticed, but I did. Alex tensed. Nate's forehead ticked, and Asher's eyes flashed green for only a second, but I saw it. They didn't like the thought of the claim going away.

Would they show that to Paige? Make her understand they wanted to be there at her side?

"We have time to sort this out," Asher said. "For now, we should go back to your family and talk on other things, but first, I need to feed."

Paige nodded. She looked to Asher, then Alex, who was blushing, and waited.

Nate scoffed. "We'll meet you back in the room." He started for the door, grabbing Paige's upper arm.

"But… Asher might need more than just Alex," Paige said weakly. He wouldn't, the men in the room knew this. A mage's blood could sustain a vampire for longer than a human. Paige just didn't want to leave because she wanted to watch.

In a blink, Asher stood behind Alex. His mouth descended, fangs out, and latched onto Alex's neck. Alex let out a gasp and tilted his head more to the side, and then his eyes closed on a moan.

"Oh…," Paige muttered, and in the next second, the room was hit with the scent of her arousal.

My cock thickened in an instant. I held in my own groan and could tell Nate was doing the same with how hard he clenched his jaw.

Asher's eyes bled to green. He wrapped an arm around Alex's chest, bringing him back closer to his body. Alex panted out a breath. Another pulse of Paige's arousal shot into the room.

She'd be wet, so damn wet, and I wanted to slip my hand in her panties to find out.

"Fucking hell," Nate clipped. He took the couple of steps to Paige and turned her. She let out a squeal of surprise when he picked her up over his shoulder and stalked from the room with Ezra on his heel, who was making a sound which sounded a lot like a laugh.

I quickly followed, closing the door behind me.

In my years, I had been with men and women. I had a thought to stay and see if Asher's feeding led to anything more. We were all Paige's. Well, we would be, so I didn't see anything wrong in watching two of her men. We were all intoxicated on her lust. My cock throbbed, wanting release. But until I knew Paige would be for it and the other men didn't mind attention from the same sex, I would put a hold on everything.

Even if my dick hated me by the end of it.

Yet, I was sure the reward of having Paige would be worth it.

Nate shoved the door open to the sitting room we'd been in previously. Paige's sister and husband weren't around. Nate deposited Paige onto the couch and strode to the table with drinks on it. He poured himself a large glass of bourbon and sucked it down.

Paige stood, her hands on her hips. "Do you want to tell me why you took me from the room?" She glanced around, then added, "And where my family is?"

Nate growled low in his throat. He poured another drink and knocked it back. Ezra trotted over to the couch Paige had vacated and jumped up on it, lying flat with a groan. He settled in for the show.

I made my way over to Paige and curled an arm around her waist. I thought she would stiffen at my touch because it was new, but she didn't. She leaned against me.

It felt right. Perfect. My body hummed from the contact.

Too long had I been without it.

"I think, my dear, it would be best to let Nate have a moment, and I believe your sister and Eric are with the children."

She nodded, then tilted her head back to look up at me. "Why does he need a moment?"

I smiled. "We could… smell your arousal in the room, Paige. It was either remove you from what turned you on or start something you might not like."

Her cheeks heated. "Well, shit." Her tone implied she was thinking about what could have happened.

Nate picked up on it too. "Don't go down that line of thought." He drew in a deep breath, grumbled something, and poured another drink.

Yes, I could also smell a hint of what she'd felt in the other room now.

She nodded. "Right… so, ah… more talking."

My fingers traced her arm up and down. "Yes, more talking. Then I'll show you your room so you can shower before some rest."

Her brows dipped. "I slept…" She glanced out the window to the bright sun. "…yesterday. I shouldn't need to again for a while."

I shook my head. "You've changed, remember? You'll need more rest than you've had."

She shivered, and her eyes turned lazy. "I did like to sleep, so I don't mind that change."

"Good."

"Uh… if you keep going with the hand, things are about to get heated in this room," she told me on a whisper. Of course Nate heard. He shot us a glare, which Paige returned. Nate had met his match in our queen. She seemed perfect for him. For Asher. For Alex, and for myself.

Chuckling, I dropped my hands, but just for a moment. I didn't want to stop touching her. Instead, I rested them on her shoulders and massaged her. Her head dropped back, and she moaned long and loudly.

"Are you fucking kidding me?" Nate bit out when Paige's lust rose once more.

Even though I wanted to continue, I stopped my hands.

Paige opened her eyes and sighed. She stepped away from me and circled her arms around her waist. Right then I wanted to punch Nate in the face.

"Maybe I need to bang you all to ease the ache. The way you all make my body crazed isn't normal. It would settle down after a quick roll in the hay, wouldn't it?" She moved to have my eyes.

"Somewhat," I told her.

"Somewhat? What do you mean somewhat?"

"From what the former queen said regarding her bonded males, the connection created is strong. The desire and possessiveness you feel will lessen after the connection is made. However, it will still be present. I'm unsure just how much."

Paige pulled a hand up to her neck. Her beautiful eyes shone with guilt.

I stepped closer to her, wanting to remind her none of us were unhappy with the bond. But she backed up, shaking her head, her eyes to the floor. "Please," she begged. "Just stay there. Whenever one of you is close, I can't think straight."

"There is something you must know then, my Paige." I waited until she looked up. "None of your men have to accept the bond. If we so choose, we can dissolve it. It will be uncomfortable for a while, but with distance, it will weaken and then drop away to nothing."

Her eyes widened. "Even though I've managed to claim you all?"

"Yes."

She nodded. "Then, that's great. All of you just have to," she seemed to choke on the next word, "leave."

"I can't speak for the others, but I'm not willing to lose you, Paige Alice."

She tensed, blinked rapidly, and then threw her hands into the air. "I don't know why you would want this. You can have a normal… well, somewhat, existence. I mean, I'm a nobody."

"You're the queen. My queen. More than that, you were made for me and I for you."

She studied me. "You really believe that?"

"With everything I am."

Her bottom lip quivered. She turned away and sniffed. With her emotions high from my confession, I wanted to continue to tell her how long I had waited for her, how much I would cherish each day I had with her. Only, as I glanced to Nate and his clenched jaw, I didn't say any more. There would be a time when we were alone, but only if she could see a future with me by her side as well.

CHAPTER TWELVE

His words sang inside of me. They warmed me and sent a thrill in my belly. He truly thought I was made for him and he for me.

I wanted more than anything to believe his words. But the truth was, it scared me. I'd been picked on, put down, dumped, and told I wasn't enough, and all that was from *one* man.

I had four to deal with… *if* I did in the end.

Also, I still used my human brain. Hell, less than twenty-four hours ago, I was a supernatural community of one. I didn't yet fully understand that a connection like the one Thorn spoke of was allowed. One where we were all devoted to each other. It didn't seem fair I got four men, and they only had me. Yet, the thought of any of them with someone else burned my chest.

Everything that had happened, everything I'd been through

in such a short amount of time was piled too high. I worried I would tumble and break when more information got stacked on the already large amount.

A shiver raked over my skin—Asher and Alex were approaching. I spun to the door, and a few seconds later, it opened. Asher stepped in first. His previous pale complexion had a light dusting of color. He tipped his chin down at me and moved over to where Nate stood. Alex walked through next. I bit my bottom lip to stop my smile at his very heated cheeks. He closed the door, stood beside it, and put his hands behind his back, leaning against the wall.

"Everything okay?" I asked.

His eyes widened. Then he looked to the floor as he cleared his throat. "Yeah, yep. All good." He was so damn cute. Actually, cute wasn't enough since he was as hot as sin, but innocent as well, and so smart to do what he did with magic.

"Paige," Thorn called gently.

Oops. My heart had taken off in flight, and my vagina was appreciating the view of Alex a whole lot since I'd run my gaze down and he was supporting a massive erection. I had zero ideas how to rein in my reactions to them all.

Was his hard-on from me or from Asher while he drank his blood?

Oh hell… why was the thought of Alex getting turned on by Asher such a turn-on that my inner walls spasmed and my belly dipped in pleasure.

Growls sounded around the room. My body heated.

Thorn cleared his throat and clapped his hands together. "Maybe it's best we spoke of things now?"

I closed my eyes to try and clear my mind of the image of Asher and Alex in bed together. It didn't help, but I forced it to the back of my mind. I wouldn't, no, I couldn't let my body rule me. We needed to talk. We all needed answers, and then I would rest and maybe crack into pieces of guilt, horror, and sorrow.

Scrubbing a hand over my face, I nodded and headed back to the couch. "Yes, of course, we need to talk. First things first. Are you certain I'm the ghoul queen, and how did I become that way?"

Nate stayed by the table while Asher moved to sit across from me on another couch. Thorn took his place beside me, and Alex stayed by the door.

Thorn said, "Yes, I'm certain. The queen described you, and I can feel the queen's power running through you. Not only that, but your heart beats and your pupils turn a shade of red with a black ring around them. All signs the former queen had to show her power to others."

"Start from the beginning," Asher demanded.

Thorn leaned back and nodded. "Eight months ago, the queen of the ghouls announced to her bonded males and me that her seer had seen her death. She wouldn't explain how it would happen, but that it would be better for not only the ghouls but all other species. Even when we tried to gain the information to prevent her death, she refused to say. To save her people, and others, she was willing to die. The queen set out to find the one the seer saw would rule next. The one to bring us all together. You."

I sensed the color drip from my face. "How... why... I'm not...." I shook my head. "Why me?"

"You were foretold by the seer. You have a good heart, you're strong-willed, and you will fight for what you believe is right. To save us all."

"Save? What am I saving you all from?" I stood quickly, pacing the floor. "I'm twenty-five years old. A barista… and I've probably lost my job because I haven't shown up. I may have the strength of Superman, but I'm still scared of spiders. I don't understand how I'm supposed to save everyone. What happens if she got it wrong? What happens if I'm not really the one the seer saw in her vision?"

"You are," Thorn stated, his voice resolute. "I dreamed of you before the queen came to me and told me I would be a part of your uprising. Her trusted friend, who is a witch, placed a spell on me there and then. I was to be transferred to you when the time came. I left the community here to wait out until I could be by your side."

"Are you sure it was me in your dreams?" I asked, panic rising in my chest because it felt like the weight of the world was settling there.

"Yes. Completely sure."

"So what, the queen just up and changed me into a ghoul and then six months later she dies and all her powers transferred to me… how?" Too many things were running through my mind. I still couldn't believe I was the right person to be queen.

Queen.

Me.

Paige Alice.

It was fantastical to even think it. Then again, six months ago I was a human. I didn't know others existed. Now, I was thrown deep within everything.

"She disappeared the day she made you a ghoul. No one, not even her bonded mates knew where she'd gone. When she came back, she was weak. Weaker because she had made you."

"How did she make me?"

Thorn winced, and I knew I wouldn't like what he was about to say. "She cut out her own heart and replaced yours with hers."

I didn't like it.

At all.

With a shaky hand, I reached up and patted my chest. "I have her heart in me?" Thorn nodded. "Then how am I still myself and not a part of her?" It didn't feel like any of my body parts had changed. I closed my hand around my throat and squeezed to stop from gagging. I had someone else's heart inside me.

Ezra bumped his head into my side. Absently, I reached for him, and a sense of calm washed over me.

"Her heart became *yours*, Paige. You are no different."

"W-Where's mine?"

"Locked away safe."

Jesus Christ, my heart was in a jar somewhere.

"To answer your other question, the queen was betrayed by her sister Korissa. She wanted the throne, but she didn't know the queen had already chosen another to take her place. Korissa had picked the one night Marsala, the former queen, was distracted and grieving an old friend to slice her sister's head from her shoulders." I gripped my neck and looked to the floor. Thorn frowned and went on softly, "The queen's bonded mates caught her in the act. They killed Korissa… and then themselves."

My head snapped up. "What? Why?"

"They couldn't live without her and knew you would be reborn only moments after her eyes closed for the final time."

My gut twisted harshly.

They couldn't live without her.

Did that mean…? I shook my head. "We're not finishing this bond. I won't have you all tied to me to only end your lives." Ezra pushed into me more. I bit my bottom lip before it trembled. Already I didn't like the thought of them not being around if something happened to me. Already my body grew cold at the thought of anything harming them. Even if it was themselves.

Turning away, I walked to the window and looked out. I wrapped my arms around my waist. The castle bustled with people, all different kinds. I didn't know if I could be queen, but I had a feeling people were relying on me to be. For them, I would try.

However, I could put a stop to one thing. In a hard, emotionless tone, I said, "You need to leave. Asher, Nate, and Alex. Go while I've only claimed you all and the bond can still be stopped. I won't have you forced into a situation. I won't have you bound to me when… we don't know each other. You could be missing out on something else. Someone better. Thorn, I realize this is your place. I can't ask you to leave, but—"

"Don't," Thorn clipped. He came to my side and turned me with his hands on my shoulders, his grip unyielding, his eyes stony. "Do not reject us so easily."

"None of you know me. I won't fulfill the connection because you're all dropped into my mess."

"Do you not think we were chosen for you for a reason? Humans try to hunt for their one and only. They're lucky if they find that person. A lot aren't so lucky. Other races believe in finding their mate, believe in finding that one, *or more*, bonded partners for themselves. With us, we understand and accept we were born for you and you for us. It has been *seen*. It's Fate."

My eyes prickled. Tears wanted to show, but I refused them. I blinked and shook my head. "Fate can kiss my butt. I won't force anyone—"

"You won't be forcing us" came from Asher. Thorn moved aside as Asher stood. "I think we're going around in circles. We need to take this a day at a time."

"You don't have long before you have to go back for your job, right? Why not just leave now?" I suggested.

"We don't have a job to go back to," Asher announced.

The room pulsed, and then both Nate and Alex burst out with "What?"

"The council did not want us to leave. I barely made it away. It is why I had to feed again."

Nate threw out a hand. "I knew something was off. They fucking harmed you, didn't they?"

Asher nodded. "I imagine they suspect something is going on. I don't understand why they would refuse us the time off. When I told them we would be taking it no matter if they didn't give their approval, they beat me. I escaped, they hunted, I fought, and managed to flee. They'll be after us, so I'm afraid we're here for some time."

Fury bombarded my mind and clenched my stomach. My upper lip raised. "They beat you. *Hunted* you."

"Paige," Alex called.

Thorn's hand landed on my shoulders. He reassured me, "My queen, he's here. Safe."

"They beat him. Hunted him," I snarled, my gaze not believing he was whole and across the room.

Then, in a blink, Asher stood right in front of me. His hands cupped my cheeks. My skin tingled and my heart lurched. He pulled my gaze up to meet his. "I have fed. I'm whole."

"They'll pay," I told him.

He studied me, then nodded. "They will."

"You won't go back. None of you."

"We won't," Asher told me.

"But none of you can be mine," I added. I wanted them safe, even from me.

His lips twitched. "We shall see."

"Asher—"

Smiling, Asher pressed a finger against my lips and looked to Thorn. "When we spoke of the council back at the restaurant, about how we had been told why the ghouls were extinct, you didn't like it. Do you know more?"

Asher was lucky I wanted to know the answer to this, or I would have said something more about the matter of them not being mine.

Thorn nodded stiffly. "Centuries ago, and even before my time, our kind were close to extinction, but it was due to the council members alone even before the council was created. They feared our numbers. They feared our power. Most saw ghouls as the supreme rulers and because of those things the council members conjured up stories about our kind instigating wars over nothing, of killing innocent people, and other vile things. The queen fought hard to protect her people. But with the whispered words from the wrong people, it caused the council to be formed to assist. It was then the ghouls got pushed out completely. The queen faked her own death and then took the people she had left into hiding because she knew the council wouldn't stop until every ghoul was gone from the earth.

"Over time, other species joined her, especially those with power who were deemed as a threat to the council. Before long, our group grew to a new kingdom, the size of a small town. The queen's mission was for harmony, but as always happens, corruption brewed. Hence Marsala's death by her own sister."

"The council is evil," I stated clearly after scenting Thorn had told the truth about everything. "Something needs to be done."

Asher quickly glanced to Nate and Alex. "Master Delton, and the fae king died suspiciously. Gerrid and Keilor, two of the strongest alphas are missing, presumed dead."

I tensed. I didn't like what I was hearing.

Nate's lips thinned, and worry seeped into his eyes, but he nodded. "It seems the council is culling powerful people and blaming others for it."

"We need to look into this further and expose them," Alex said. His voice was strong and held disdain. Something I hadn't yet heard from him.

What I wanted was to go to the council's door, bust it open, kick their asses and kill them for ever starting this downward spiral for my people in the first place. When I glanced to all the men, I noticed they were already watching me.

"She's angry," Alex pointed out.

Nate snorted. "What gave it away? Her fisted hands, the steam coming from her nose, or the fact her eyes are glowing?" He looked to me. "Calm down. We can't do anything about them yet."

I hated anyone telling me to calm down. I ground my teeth together.

Thorn cleared his throat, gaining everyone's attention. "It's also good that none of you are leaving since Nate has his challenge with the alpha's son during the next full moon."

Anger evaporated as I sucked in a shocked breath. "What?" I gently moved around a smiling Asher to look at Nate. I knew Thorn was changing the subject, but I allowed it and went along as I wanted to know what this was about.

Nate groaned. "Fucking great. Throw me under the bus, why don't you."

"You can't," I snapped.

Nate glared. "I can and I will."

"I won't allow it," I told him coldly. My heart already beat heavily in my chest at the thought of him fighting someone.

Nate snorted. "You don't have a say in it. This is pack business."

I bristled at his harsh words. "But you're not a part of their pack. Why are they making you fight?"

His expression shut down to a blank void. Nate shifted his gaze to beside me. "I've been up a fucking long time. I need to sleep."

"Nate," I snapped. "We haven't finished talking."

"We have." He started for the door.

"Explain to me why you have to fight," I demanded.

"Thorn, either find me a fucking room to crash in or I'll do it myself," he said, ignoring me. When Thorn glanced down at me, he shrugged and went after Nate, who was already out the door.

I didn't like to be ignored, not when he would be risking his life, and I wasn't sure why. I followed him, but Alex blocked my path.

He gave me a thin-lipped smile. "It might be best to leave him for a bit. He's never in a good mood when tired."

"Is he ever in a good mood?"

His smile widened. "Yes. Just give it time."

It seemed I had a lot of time.

A man appeared behind Alex. I quickly pulled Alex to the side and bared my teeth. He bowed low and said, "I'm sorry to interrupt, my queen. Master Thorn sent me here to show you all to your rooms."

Straightening, I cleared my throat. "Ah, right, thank you...."

The man stood tall. "Gregory, your majesty."

"Yes, Gregory." Glancing over my shoulder, I caught Alex and Asher grinning, probably over my protectiveness, which I couldn't help. Rolling my eyes, I called, "Ezra." He bounded over, panting happily.

Gregory glanced down to Ezra and stiffened.

"He won't harm you," I told him.

Gregory's lips thinned, but he nodded and moved away from the door. He started down the hall, and I followed with Asher and Alex behind me.

The walk took a million years. At least it felt like it. I listened to Gregory as he explained the rooms or areas we walked by, trying to take it all in, but I knew I would get lost all the same. I also tried to listen in on Alex as he questioned Asher quietly about the council. My gut still fired with fury.

"Wait, my sister. She's with her husband and kids. Will they be near us?"

Gregory nodded. "Yes, my queen. She has been transferred already to a room near yours and your men."

"They're not my men," I said quickly.

The guys behind me quieted, and I regretted my reply. But then, why should I? It wasn't like they were hooked on me. It was the other way around.

"My apologies. I could scent them over you. I just presumed." He cleared his throat. "It's good that they are not since, besides Master Thorn, they are not of our kind."

I stopped.

The judgmental idiot noticed and gazed at me in question.

"Take. That. Back."

His head jerked back on his shoulders. His eyes widened. "I'm sorry?"

I stepped close, felt Ezra knocking my leg, then Asher and Alex getting close. I ignored them all and told him, "Since I am the queen, I will bond, claim, and sleep with whomever I want. No one in this place has the right to judge what goes on in people's love lives unless they become a danger. Do you hear me?" I tapped his chest and then held my finger there.

I didn't expect to see a smile bloom over his face. He tipped his head down. "Of course, my queen." He turned and started walking down the hall again, continuing on with his tour.

What just happened?

Alex leaned in, his lips close to my ear, and I shivered. "I believe he's happy with your reply."

"Why?"

"He must love someone not of his own kind."

"But… that's allowed no matter their species, right?"

"Not all species would agree, Paige," Asher informed me. "Maybe the former queen was one of them."

Well, that just sucked.

CHAPTER THIRTEEN

PAIGE

Gregory opened a door at the end of yet another hallway and dipped his head. "This shall be your room, my queen. The men each have a room going down the hall from yours on each side." He turned back from my door and pointed to another door outside my room. "I believe the wolf has already taken the second door on the right. Master Thorn is in the first door on the left."

"I'll take the first on her right. Alex, you're in the second on her left," Asher said.

"I'm going in for a shower, and then I'd like to see my sister."

"Her room is at the end of the hall. A family suite," Gregory informed me.

"Thank you." I smiled, just as Ezra strolled into my room

like he owned it. Gregory bowed low once more before walking back down the hall.

"Paige," Asher called. I turned just inside the room. "Do not worry about the council for now. You have a lot still to deal with here. They don't know where we are. You're safe. Your people are safe—"

"You're all safe," I interrupted, and then bit my lip for just blurting that out.

"We are. The council can wait for now. Let us worry about things in the present."

I didn't like it, but I understood why he was asking me to. There were matters here needing my attention rather than worrying about bastards who didn't know where we were. However, their time would come and soon, because I didn't like that people were living in fear outside of these walls because of the council.

"Okay," I whispered with a nod.

He smiled. "All right. Now, Alex will be taking a nap. After your shower, please don't wander the halls without someone assisting you. I'll be taking a shower too. I don't need sleep, so please knock on my door after."

I nodded. I wasn't stupid; I didn't know if my presence would be welcomed by all. Especially Thorn's conquests. My gut burned. I would take the help when offered. "Thanks, Asher." I glanced to Alex. "Have a good sleep."

He tipped his chin down and looked up at me through his lashes. "Call out to me if you need anything."

I shot him a wink before closing the door behind me. A smile crept onto my mouth as I leaned back against the door. Alex was a man I could easily fall for. Asher and Thorn were close behind him, and even though Nate drove me up the wall, I couldn't deny my attraction for him. I couldn't deny the pain I felt in my mind and stomach at the thought of something happening to him.

To any of them.

I quickly pushed that thought aside so it couldn't take hold and burn me. Instead, I glanced around the room. Though, calling it a room wasn't enough. Gregory said my sister had a family suite. This had to be one too. It was massive. A ginormous bed, bigger than any king-sized bed I'd seen, sat across the room near the windows. The gold bedspread looked soft and inviting. There were two doors on each side of the room. One probably led to a walk-in robe, the other to the en suite. The room also contained a seating area near an unlit fireplace where a TV sat high on the wall.

"This place is bigger than my apartment," I mentioned to Ezra. He grunted at me and made his way to the bed where he jumped up and lay down, closing his eyes. Rolling mine, I told him, "I get it, you're tired." I went over to the bed and quickly kissed him on the head. "Thank you for always having my back." He lifted enough to run his wet, warm tongue over the side of my face. "Lucky I'm going for a shower." He made a noise in the back of his throat that sounded like his laugh.

Ignoring him, I made my way to the right of the room, hoping the door I approached was the bathroom. It didn't really matter since Alex cleaned me up. But I still felt the need to wash away some of the worry with the hot water.

Opening the door, shock radiated over my body. The bathroom was something out of Beyoncé's house. There was a shower that could fit easily five people in with a nozzle down each end. Not a normal two-person sink, but four. Three toilets were in small separate cubicles. There was also the biggest

Jacuzzi tub I'd ever seen, a normal-sized claw-foot bathtub, and then, smack dab in the middle, were two flat, white couches. In between them was a bar.

Did they think I was going to throw a party in here?

I picked up my jaw and stepped fully in. The room was spotlessly clean, and I worried I would dirty it. Then again, bathrooms were made to be used, and there wasn't anything that would stop me from my shower.

Stripping out of my clothes, which I left on a couch, I walked to the shower and turned it on. Instant hot water soothed my shoulders; something that never happened in my old apartment. After I adjusted the temperature a little, I happened to glance back at the toilets and wondered why a castle for ghouls would need any. Only then I remembered all the other supernatural beings around the place. Of course they were needed. Then I thought why the hell was I thinking of it in the first place.

Shaking my head, I stepped under the warm spray and moaned. I tipped my head back and ran my fingers through my hair. Alex's magic was amazing, but nothing beat an actual shower after a revealing and long day.

I still couldn't believe the changes that had happened. Understanding and accepting my new life the first time after climbing out of a hole in the ground had taken me months. Yet there I was again, having to believe and trust more mind-blowing circumstances.

I was a queen.

I ruled people.

They looked up to me.

Me.

They would have expectations of my role, believing I was reborn to save their lives.

From what, I still didn't know, but if I had to guess, it would be the council. Regardless, I wasn't even sure I could be that person for them.

How the hell did someone simply become a queen overnight and be expected to rule?

I had no answers.

Had no idea how to wave that slow, weird way that queens were known to do. Did I have to talk to my people with a plum in my mouth? That wasn't me.

Yet, I found myself wanting to try.

For the ones who couldn't fight.

For the ones who need protecting.

I just wished I knew what I would be protecting them from. Again, the council popped straight into my mind. They sounded corrupted to the core.

Eventually I would find out more about them.

For now, I had things around here to sort out.

I also had four men to deal with. A vampire. A ghoul. A shifter. And a mage.

Four men who were so different to each other in their abilities and even some of their traits. Four stunningly gorgeous men who sent my mind and body into a wild spin.

Four men who I would have to keep my distance from, even when that thought felt like it cut my throat open.

For their sake, I would do it.

I had to do it.

Too much had changed in such a short amount of time, and I wasn't at the stage where any of this was normal for me in my mind.

Maybe with time…. Yeah, I wasn't even sure then.

Wanting to stay in the shower forever, I sighed, knowing I couldn't. It was tempting, though. But I wanted to see if my sister was awake. She always, okay, usually gave me good advice.

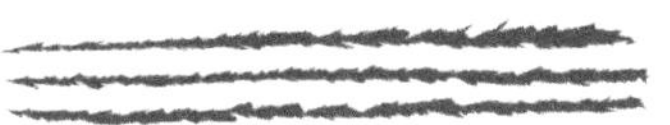

"DATE THEM," Yasmin said as she made the bed. They'd had the chance to get some sleep, since we'd arrive late in the night, or early hours really, and I'd been busy with the men.

Maybe she hadn't heard me properly. I tried again. "Did you hear what I said? I claimed four men. *Four*. Men I don't really know, but it seemed my ghoul side wants them for herself."

Yasmin nodded. "I heard you." She faced me. "They don't seem too upset with the claim you've made. And you claiming them makes so much more sense to me now. I thought they'd put a spell on you or something, but now I know it's all coming from you it's better."

Shock swept through me. "Better?"

She shrugged. "Yes. Better because I know they're not forcing themselves on you."

"But I'm forcing myself on them."

She shook her head. "It's not the same." I glared at her. "Okay, it is. But…" She took my hands into hers. "I'm only learning about this world. You've been in it for six months, which you should have told me. They've been in this world a lot longer. I've seen you when you're all crazy protective or getting horny, freaking out about the things that have happened. They haven't. They know what they're getting into. They haven't run from your claim. They look at you like they've known you forever, like you've been theirs forever. Like you belong to them. It's not one-sided. You've claimed them, but I can tell they're happy about it and would accept and complete the bond in a second."

"They don't know me. I don't know them. This is all too much."

"I know, but you'll get used to it, and I'm here to help." She smiled. "This is our life now, and we'll get used to it together."

I sniffed. "Have I told you how you're the best sister in the world?"

Her smile warmed. "You have." She hugged me close. "Don't get me wrong, it's all scary different, but exciting at the same time." She pulled back. "And at least I'm not the queen."

I narrowed my gaze, and she laughed and went back to finishing the bed.

"Have you told the kids anything?"

"We had to because they'll see a lot of strange things around here."

I gulped. I still hated how much my sister and her family's lives had changed because of me. "What did you say?"

She glanced over at me. "Get that look off your face." She walked up to me and shook my shoulders. "For the rest of my life, I will never regret coming here with you. I was speaking with Gregory. They have a school in the town that the kids can go to. It may hold shifters and children with magic, but it's still a school, and he'd said it's an amazing one. Not only that, he told me there's a job going in town, and I thought Eric will be good at helping you organize matters around here. Things are fine. They're good even because I get to keep my kickass sister in my life. I couldn't have lived without you in it, Paige." She hooked her arm in mine and led me toward the door. "Besides, the kids are excited to see the different people. They were wondering if Tinker Bell is real."

A laugh abruptly left me.

"I know. I told them I wasn't sure, but we could find out. They dragged Eric out of here to take in some sights even before having breakfast." I tensed. "Don't worry, your ghoul guy is with them."

My body relaxed, but I quickly said, "He's not my ghoul."

"Uh-huh."

We entered the living room as their door opened, hitting the wall behind it. We both froze for a second before Nate stormed in. "Your scent lessened. Did you think for a fucking second to have woken me before you left the area?"

"I had her," Asher said, and I jumped when he stepped forward from the shadows behind us. Ezra also made it known he was there by growling low.

Nate's jaw clenched. He glanced from Asher to Ezra, then back to Asher. He ran a hand over his face. "Fuck. Fine. I'm going back to bed. You good?" he asked Asher, not me.

"Yes."

Nate grunted and then stalked from the room.

Yasmin leaned into me and whispered, "And you think they're not into you."

Nate's reaction surprised me the most. He'd scented I wasn't close even in his sleep, woke and rushed after me. Like he was ready to protect me.

I'd thought he'd hated me.

Then again, he could still. After all, he was stuck here with me, and he seemed more than annoyed, pissed even, that I'd claimed him. However, he hadn't voiced it either.

Confusion dipped my brows.

I glanced to Asher. He was already watching me. Earlier, when I'd gone to his room knocking and asked if he wanted to come with me to see Yasmin, he had, without questioning it. He followed me down the hall, a couple of steps behind. I'd felt his eyes on me the whole way, and I'd enjoyed the lick of heat they produced over my body. I may have even put an extra swing to my hips.

I did like their attention.

I liked them.

"Tinker Bell doesn't exist. Fairies do though, but keep the children away from them because they're vicious creatures."

Yasmin's mouth gaped. My throat thickened. Did that mean he'd heard everything we'd talked about? Stupid, stupid me had thought a room separating us would be enough. I should have realized it wouldn't. Although, I had slightly forgotten he was around because talking with my sister consumed my mind.

Asher stepped closer to me. "Your sister is correct. We know what we're getting into."

My body stilled. I opened my mouth to say something but squeaked when he flashed forward so fast it was hard to track. He stopped right in front of me. Yasmin let out a gasp and took a step back.

Asher leaned in. "I cannot speak for the others, but I enjoy the idea of being yours. Of having your claim upon me." Slowly, he reached up and tucked a strand of hair behind my ear. "I understand everything that has happened is unnatural for you. I'm hoping with time you will finalize the claim. Until then, know I'll be waiting, at the pace you set."

My heart jackrabbited in my chest. He glanced down, as if

he could see my heart under the shirt I'd found on the bed when I'd finished my shower. His lips lifted in a smirk.

The room suddenly felt a lot smaller when he pulled his eyes up, and they were heated with desire.

"Oh my," Yasmin whispered.

"Mommy" was called by a six-year-old monster as Sophie ran into the room.

Asher stepped back, moving his gaze from mine to the doorway, but I couldn't drag my eyes from the man in front of me.

He wanted me.

He liked that I'd claimed him.

He was willing to take things at my pace.

What did I do with that information?

"Hello," I heard Sophie say. "I'm Sophie. Who are you?"

"Asher Evans."

"You're very pretty," Sophie commented, and that seemed to snap me out of my state since I stepped in front of Asher and faced Sophie.

Yasmin, who was beside her daughter, gave me a look. I shrugged. I couldn't help my reactions. They were irrational when it came to the four men.

Asher's chuckle swept over my head. Glad to see he found it funny how I was protecting him from a six-year-old's gaze. His hands landed on my shoulders, and I melted into his touch.

"Are you Auntie's boyfriend?" she asked as Ezra made it to her side and licked her face. She giggled and wrapped her arms around his neck. Yasmin just watched on. She seemed okay now with the thought of Ezra near her daughter.

"Who's Auntie's boyfriend?" Oscar asked as he stepped

through the door with Eric and Thorn following. Oscar's eyes narrowed on Asher behind me. "Who're you?"

"Oscar, this is Asher. A friend of your Aunt Paige's," Yasmin explained.

Oscar studied Asher for a moment. "Are you different too?"

"Yes," Asher stated simply.

"Are you like Mr. Thorn and Aunt Paige?"

"No. I'm a vampire."

I balked at the honesty. Yasmin and Eric didn't seem fazed by it at all; they both looked to their son for his reaction.

Oscar's eyes widened. "Cool."

"Mommy, we saw so many things out there. One boy even changed into a big pussy cat right in front of us. It was awesome," Sophie exclaimed with a cry of joy.

"That's…" She glanced at Eric. "…great?"

Thorn smiled. "I think the young boy was taken with Sophie and wanted to show off."

Yasmin's lips thinned. She clearly wasn't sure how to react.

"It was harmless, babe," Eric reassured her.

"So you drink blood," Oscar said, coming close our way.

The mention of blood had me thinking of Asher drinking from Alex. I tightened my legs together when my walls convulsed.

"Oh, look at your eyes," Sophie cried, and all of a sudden, I wanted to throw a bag over Asher's head and drag him from the room.

This was getting ridiculous.

Grinding my teeth together, I locked my emotions down and glanced over my shoulder to witness Asher's eyes bleeding back to his normal color. A groan slipped past my lips as his hands drifted down to my waist and gripped.

Would it be wrong to rub my butt on his crotch?

"Why do they change like that?" Oscar asked, and it was like a cold bucket of water being thrown over my lust.

There're kids present, Paige. Get your head out of the gutter.

It was all Asher's fault for practically telling me he wanted me and then touching me and showing his eyes off. Damn him.

"He was just showing you something he could do," Thorn said quickly.

"What else can you do?" asked Oscar.

With a breeze lifting my hair, Asher was no longer behind me, but standing on the other side of the room. Sophie laughed and clapped. Oscar's mouth dropped open.

Asher's smile caused my belly to roll in pleasure.

"This place is amazing!" Sophie yelled.

"It's pretty cool," Oscar said. He tried to wipe the big smile off his face to act the cool kid but failed. "Can you go out into the sunlight?"

"Yes." Asher smiled.

"Can you eat normal food as well?" Oscar questioned.

"Yes, and drink other things besides blood."

"Does your skin sparkle when you go outside?" We all turned to Yasmin who'd been the one to ask that question.

Asher chuckled. I looked back to watch, the sound making my heart happy.

"I think that's enough questions for now. How about the two youngest in the room go wash your hands before the food Thorn arranged arrives?" Eric said. Both kids ran off, heading toward the bathroom off their room. The place was amazing. Yasmin had shown me through before, and the suite was more like the size of a home.

Oscar paused at the doorway. "Will you still be here when we come out?" he asked Asher. I didn't even get a look in.

Asher glanced to me, and I couldn't think of anything else better than spending time with my family and him. I nodded.

"I'll be here," Asher replied. Oscar's grin widened before he nodded and disappeared to wash up.

CHAPTER FOURTEEN

ALEX

The room they supplied was extravagant. It was like a mini penthouse suite. All I wanted to do was rest. Except I had to do something first.

My dick had never been so hard for so long. Between my reaction to Paige and Asher feeding on me, I was already close to coming in my pants. All worries about the council, what my family would think, and the new life I'd been thrust into was at the back of my mind. At the forefront was the feel of Asher's teeth sinking into me, the way desire shot straight to my already hard cock. Already so damn hard because of the woman who had claimed me.

Me.

Alex Smith.

Top of his class mage, but a fuckup still in my parents' eyes because I hadn't married Emily Fortier to secure their ranking in the mage world.

Paige Alice wanted me, not because of status, but because I was meant to be hers.

She was meant to be mine, and I wasn't scared about it like I had been with Emily. This felt right.

But what would have happened if someone else had been on the team or it was another team altogether in the restaurant when Paige's powers rose? Would the result still be the same? Would she have claimed another or waited until our lives collided?

I didn't know, but time would tell when another used their magic or power in front of her. I'd see if she'd claim them. If it was only because of the power….

My dick shrank at the thought of it.

I'd always been a worrier. Overthought things. It was exactly what I was doing now. Should I just accept that fate had intervened, and I was meant to be claimed by Paige?

Time would tell, I supposed.

There was no denying the attraction I felt for her, though. She was beautiful, even in her smaller package. Saying that, her temper made up for her tiny size. While we barely knew each other, without a doubt she was perfect for me, and I couldn't wait to discover more about her.

God, I could still sense her arousal when Asher had bitten me. My dick, once again, hardened. Not only from thinking about Paige, but from the bite itself. I didn't know a vampire's bite would feel like that.

I would have come in my pants if Asher had fed while Paige watched or touched herself.

Walking into the bathroom, I palmed my rigid cock. I turned on the shower and stripped from my clothes, wondering why I wasn't fazed by offering Asher my blood. Drinking from the neck seemed intimate, almost personal. The knowledge threw me for a loop.

I was attracted to both men and women.

Asher and Nate, and even Thorn, were all good-looking guys. There, I'd finally admitted to myself I could appreciate their looks without anyone knowing.

Under the spray of water, I took my cock in hand and stroked slowly. I moaned, closing my eyes.

Would Paige have found it erotic if I pushed myself back on Asher? I'd felt his erection just touching my ass. Thinking about it then, I moved my hand over myself faster. Would Paige have liked to have seen Asher reach around and palm my dick? From the look in her eyes as he'd drank, it seemed like she would have enjoyed it. If not, she wouldn't have gotten turned on watching Asher clamp down on my neck.

"Goddamn," I grunted.

I wished I'd had the courage to have taken the moment further between us all. Even with Thorn in the room. He'd also seemed to look on with desire in his eyes.

As I stroked over my length, I pictured Paige and Thorn approaching. Asher already had his hand over my pants while he rubbed himself into my jean-clad ass. I thought of Paige dropping to her knees, undoing my pants and pulling me free while Thorn got to his knees and cupped Paige's breasts. Nate stood to the side with hooded eyes watching us all while he pleasured himself, then Paige would lick the tip of my dick, drawing a groan from my mouth like I was right then in the shower.

Thinking of Paige taking me into her mouth was enough for streams of cum to shoot out the tip as I moaned long and deep.

Never had I been so damn turned on before. If a simple fantasy drew such a reaction from me, I couldn't wait to see where this bond between us all would go.

The bathroom door suddenly opened, hitting the wall with the force behind the shove. Nate strode in wearing jeans only. Alertness rocked through me. I shut off the shower and climbed out, grabbing a towel and wrapping it around my waist.

"You gotta help me," he growled.

"What's wrong? Is it Paige? Is she all right?"

"No," he clipped, and then stormed back into the large space that doubled as a living room and bedroom. I grabbed another towel to dry the rest of me and followed.

"What's going on?" I asked, watching Nate pace at the end of the bed.

"I can't stop fucking thinking. Put a spell on me or do something to knock me out for a few hours sleep." He ran a hand roughly through his hair. "I keep thinking she won't be safe unless she's next to me. There ain't no way I'll ask her to go to sleep so I can get some shut-eye." He flung the blankets back on my bed and took off his jeans. I saw a flash of skin before he got in and covered himself. With my blanket.

I choked. "What are you doing?"

"I need to sleep. If you knock me out and if I feel someone's sleeping next to me, then I might actually get some rest."

He was seriously on edge. If he didn't get sleep, there was a chance Paige and Nate would butt heads. But… he was in my bed, and he wanted *me* to sleep beside him.

There was also the fact he was naked.

Naked.

"First of all, get on some damn pants."

He rolled his eyes, like being naked around me meant nothing to him. Then again, shifters never gave a second thought about being in the nude. "Smith, just get in the fucking bed. Knock me out."

Glaring, I conjured up two pairs of boxers and threw a pair at the cranky wolf. He grumbled but slipped them under the blanket and put them on. I pulled mine on and up under the towel, then dropped the towel to the floor. I made my way to the bed and moved the blanket up to climb in, only to pause. Even though I'd just come, the sight of Nate's erection caused my dick to jerk. I clenched my teeth and groaned inwardly.

I was getting turned on by everything and everyone.

"What?" Nate snapped. He glanced down. "Yeah, it won't go down."

"Didn't you...?" My face heated. There wasn't a chance in hell I would finish that sentence.

"Yes. Goddamn twice."

I sighed and dropped the blanket before scrubbing a hand over my face. This was so damn awkward. We'd been team-mates for five years and never had we talked about our dicks before. We worked, we got along, and we were like brothers to a point, but never had I thought, besides them being good-looking, about the what-ifs between us.

As far as I knew, neither of them swung that way.

I shouldn't have been thinking about that shit then either. Nate was there for my help. Sighing again, I took the blanket, slipped in, and rolled so Nate had my back.

"You gonna knock me out?"

"What happens if I do and you don't wake up from it? I don't have a bloody timer on my spell. Depends on the person. You could be asleep for half an hour or ten hours."

He cursed low, probably thinking about the times I had used my knock-out spell in combat. Those times were always to complete a quick mission and to get in and out. We never lingered, so I didn't have a clue how long it lasted. Maybe I should have tested it on someone.

"Want me to test it on you?" I offered.

He growled in the back of his throat. "No."

"Then you'll just have to go to sleep next to me." I closed my eyes and took a deep breath, trying to relax. But knowing the man, a guy I'd worked with for a damn long time, was awake behind me probably staring at the roof…. Nope, he shifted. I felt him sit up, slap the pillow, and fall back onto the bed. His legs moved restlessly. Up, down, up, down, over and back, I was ready to chop them off.

Rolling, I shifted close, put my leg over his, my arm over his chest where I grabbed his arm and tucked it close to his body while I rested my head near his shoulder. His body locked tight, but I ignored it, intent on getting some sleep.

"Sleep," I ordered.

"What the fuck are you doing?"

"If you move around the whole time you're in here, I won't get any sleep."

He didn't move, but he was still stiff in my arms. His breath skimmed my face; it smelled like bourbon.

A snort dropped from Nate's nose. "Never thought this'd happen."

I chuckled. "What? Us in bed or having Paige claiming us or being rogue from the council?"

"Fuck. All of it," Nate muttered, his body finally relaxing.

"I'd defy the council any day if in the end it means Paige is in my life," I told him. Without her, I doubted my life would have changed. I would have lived the days doing the same thing over and over. Following the council's missions. Working with men, but not really knowing them.

I never would have been charmed by Paige, opened my eyes to change, and offered my blood to Asher or my comfort to Nate. Not until she'd come crashing into our lives.

She was altering our world for the better, and it had started right away, even back at the restaurant. When she'd walked through my ward. Her being new to the world, to the differences our world presented, meant taking things slow. She was freaked over claiming us unknowingly and didn't understand how women of her status would and should have more life mates than one.

"She's gonna be a pain in the ass," Nate grumbled, his voice lower.

I couldn't help but laugh. "And you'll like it." I knew he would because he enjoyed going head-to-head too much with her. Not many would argue against Nate. Paige did, and he enjoyed it.

He scoffed. "Nah."

"Uh-huh."

He quieted, and just when I thought he'd drifted off, he whispered into the room, "Why isn't this weirder?"

It was my turn to tense. I opened my eyes and stared at his skin in front of me through hooded eyes. I knew what he meant —us lying next to each other. Hell, I was practically on top of him, and yet I didn't mind it.

"Maybe it's got something to do with Paige, the connection we had with her even before her claim."

"Hmm, maybe," he mumbled, and then in the next second, his breath evened out and his whole body sank deeper into the mattress. He was asleep.

I should have rolled away, but I didn't. Instead, I lifted my head slightly and glanced at Nate. In his slumber, he looked younger. There wasn't a permanent scowl on his face, though, which surprised me. I'd thought it'd still be there.

Then it felt strange I was staring at him.

Thinning my lips, I rolled over, giving him my back. Shock rippled through me and my stomach twisted in a good way when Nate moved with me. With an arm over my side and curling across my stomach, he pulled me back into the curve of his body.

My dick decided it was time to party and jerked behind my boxers.

I squeezed my eyes closed and thought of my family, which helped the erection to deflate, and finally, I got some sleep. The warmth from Nate's body lulled me into comfort.

CHAPTER FIFTEEN

ASHER

"Maybe we should let them sleep longer?" I suggested. At first I had been shocked to see Nate and Alex in bed together, but I had a feeling Nate would have been on edge and needed some type of comfort to get to sleep so he didn't worry about Paige. Not that she would know it or he would admit to it. On the surface, Nate was hard, but deep down, very deep, he was soft. He cared, and Paige had touched that caring side to him.

"Do you have a phone on you?" Paige asked with a wicked glint to her eyes.

My lips twitched. "Unfortunately I don't."

"Ezra, run and steal Yasmin's phone," Paige said, and Ezra bounded from the room. She nudged her hip with mine. "If I didn't have the meeting Thorn organized with the queen's advisers, I would let them sleep, but I have a feeling they'll want to be present."

She was right. Plus, they'd gotten enough sleep. Six hours had gone by that we'd spent with Paige and her family. The children were a treat to be around while they learned new things.

"You're correct," I answered.

I didn't trust anyone here with Paige besides her family, my men, and Thorn. She needed all the protection she could have when meeting with others who had been sworn to the former queen.

I heard Ezra approach before he ran into the room. I still found it unbelievable a hellhound, a creature from Hell itself, was linked to Paige. Not only that, but he acted like a tamed domestic dog. He was smarter than others we'd fought. He kept his power locked tight, which was how we hadn't sensed what he was to begin with. It made me wonder if he was superior to all other hellhounds. But also, how did he find his way to be with Paige? Something I would ask and soon.

When Paige held out her hand, Ezra dropped the slobbery phone into it. Paige wiped it on her pants, like it was nothing to her, then held it up in front of her. She giggled as she snapped a couple of pictures before moving to the side of the bed and taking some more.

Nate's eyes snapped open, landing on Paige. She waved the phone at him and grinned like a maniac. Nate growled in the back of his throat, causing Alex to open his eyes. He froze at the sight of Paige who stood in front of me. I saw him move slightly and then his eyes widened when he realized Nate was still behind him.

"Paige, give me the fucking phone," Nate clipped.

"Nope." She grinned. "It's too cute to delete." She let out a squeal and bolted behind me when Nate jumped from the bed for her.

"Asher, move," he demanded.

I smirked, crossing my arms over my chest and cocking an eyebrow.

Nate cursed. "Paige, I swear to fucking Christ, if you don't get rid of those photos, I'll… do something."

Paige laughed. "Sure, okay. I'll get rid of them."

We all heard the lie in her voice, could taste it in fact.

To try and control the situation, I shifted the conversation to why we were in the room in the first place. "We wouldn't have woken either of you, but there's a meeting in half an hour with the advisers of the former queen. Paige wanted us all there."

Nate straightened before nodding. "I'll get dressed," he bit out and then walked out of the room, slamming the door behind him.

Glancing back to Alex, I should have expected it, but his cheeks were burning. I could still taste his blood in my mouth. It had been intoxicating. Rich and filled with power. I wouldn't have to feed for a long time. However, I wanted another nip. I also wouldn't mind scenting his arousal and Paige's mixed together as it had been in the room earlier.

I had never thought of Alex any way besides working alongside him.

Until I'd tasted him.

Until I knew he'd been aroused by my bite.

Usually men enjoyed it, but not to the point of getting hard from it like Alex had. Unless they were interested in men. Did that mean Alex was?

I had been around so many years and enjoyed both men and women. I also liked the thought of young Alex being turned on by my bite.

Right then, his gaze swiftly raced over me and then Paige before moving to the floor. I smiled when his blush raced down his neck. What had he been thinking to cause such a delicious reaction?

He cleared his throat and sat up, pulling the blanket with him to cover his waist.

Christ, was he hard now?

"So, ah, I'll get dressed too," he said, then waited.

"Go on then," Paige teased; she was reading him along with me. She knew he was embarrassed and turned on. I drew in his scent, and the peppery aroma to his lust thickened.

Alex coughed. "Right." He nodded. "Um, if you'll just give me a moment."

Ezra let out a noise that sounded like a laugh. I glanced to him as he looked up, and the damn hellhound rolled his amused eyes before walking to Paige and nudging her legs.

Paige laughed. "All right, I've had my fun." She winked at Alex. "See you soon." She walked from the room with Ezra and then called back, "I'll be in my room. Meet me there."

Once she was gone, I turned back to Alex. He paled. "Nothing happened. We just slept beside each other. It might have looked different with Nate close, but it wasn't. He couldn't sleep because he was thinking about Paige. He was worried and wanted to go to her side, but he needed sleep so he wouldn't be so cranky. I'm not sure if it helped since Paige has taken photos."

My lips twitched. I didn't understand why he was trying to explain himself to me. Still, I found it amusing.

"I'm sure it won't happen again and, ah, the team will be as it always was…."

Ah, now it all made sense. He was concerned I would think the group dynamics would be harmed. I shook my head. "Alex, nothing has changed between the team. I'm not worried if things change between the team either. I understand what happened here, and you shouldn't feel you have to explain yourself to me. I'm not in charge any longer. We work together as one. After all, I'm sure we all want to make sure our mate is safe."

His eyes widened. "You've accepted this?"

I nodded. "I'm not a fool to fight it when I can feel the pull toward her. Paige is mine. Yours. All of ours. I've informed her I'm not going anywhere. I would like to finalize the bond, at her own pace."

"Should I tell her that as well?" he blurted. His action and words were endearing, and oh so sweet and innocent.

"That is up to you."

"I do want this bond."

Another smile graced my lips. I hadn't smiled so much in a long time. "I know."

"And you're good with sharing her?"

I would share Paige. I also hoped I would share something more than just a collaboration with the men. Only time would tell if that would happen. Maybe the bond with Paige wasn't the only one. I'd felt a connection toward Nate and Alex since I'd met them more than any others I'd worked with, which was why I'd chosen them to work on my team. I even felt one with Thorn, despite him pissing me off the first time he appeared. Though, I'd ignored it until we'd arrived here.

"I am."

He nodded, seeming lost in thought. Then he said, "So am I."

"I can see Nate agreeing eventually," I mentioned. "Thorn, of course, is all in."

Alex snorted. "Thorn is a given, and Nate's just being stubborn, but she'll wear him down."

I smiled. "I agree." I glanced over my shoulder, feeling the need to get back to Paige.

"Go, I'll be there in a second. In fact—" He clicked his fingers and was dressed in jeans and a shirt. "I'm ready now." He got out of bed.

Turning, I walked to the door, down to Paige's room, and entered without knocking, knowing Alex would follow because the destination was our queen.

We found her sitting on a chair, her gaze already on us. Her smile was radiant. If my heart beat, it would have stopped because I couldn't describe how beautiful her smile was. She pointed at the fire, which Ezra lay in front of, as if we didn't see it. "Look, they lit it."

I returned her smile because hers was contagious. "I can see."

She rested back in her chair. "Do we have to meet those advisers yet?"

"You are queen. I'm sure Thorn would push back a meeting for you," I told her, but then added, "Although, it is probably best to get this out of the way."

She groaned, and my cock jerked, my mind going to the sounds she would make once I was inside her. When I caught Alex adjusting himself, I knew he clearly had the same thought.

She nodded and stood. "You're right. Let's get this out of the way." Ezra grumbled as he climbed to his feet and accompanied Paige as she made her way toward us. Passing by, she ran a hand over my arm, then Alex's before walking out the door. We followed. We would always follow Paige. Even not knowing her for long, our connection was strong. And I already knew I never wanted a day without her in it.

As we went by Nate's door, it opened with a bang. He strode out with a scowl and stepped in beside Paige. She smiled up at him, and when his eyes narrowed down on her even more, she giggled.

"I will get those pictures."

She reached out and patted his arm. "Uh-huh."

Nate growled under his breath but said no more because Thorn appeared at the end of the hall. Paige's smile widened and she waved. Thorn returned the grin and waited for us.

"My queen," Thorn said with a smirk and a bow when Paige glowered at him. "Right this way." He turned and headed down another hall. We walked on silently. Thorn had informed Paige and me, which I would tell Alex and Nate, that our private rooms were soundproof. The rest weren't, so we would have to watch what we said.

As we moved further into the heart of the castle, the hall became busier with people. I could sense my own kind among them, as well as others. They all looked, and most bowed to Paige. It was the ones who didn't I took extra care to study—memorizing their faces and their scent.

Ezra pulled back his upper lip and snarled at a man who got too close to Paige. I stepped forward to get between our queen and him, but he simply dropped to his knees and pressed his forehead to the floor. "My queen." He breathed the words.

Paige's eyes widened. She glanced to me, Thorn, and then to the man on the floor. I heard a muttered, "She's out of her element. Some queen she'll be."

Paige tensed. She clenched her jaw and straightened before saying, "Rise, sir."

The man sprang up like a jack-in-the-box. His eyes never made it to Paige's, though; they stayed on the floor.

"Are you after something?" Paige asked.

"If you would be so kind as to allow my mate to see the doctor, she is close to giving birth, and I worry if she does it alone, there will be problems."

Paige's head tilted to the side. "What do you mean allow her to see a doctor? Can't she already?"

Someone scoffed. "Not when the doctor is ours." A witch stepped forward.

"Address the queen properly, Rylee," Thorn demanded.

When Rylee rolled her eyes, Nate's chest rumbled with a growl. The witch bowed her head half an inch and said, "My queen, we do not let our doctor work on animals."

Paige's hands fisted and she faced the woman completely. "Are you saying because his mate is a shifter, the witch won't help her through her birth?"

"Yes."

A door at the end of the hall opened and an old mage came through. "Queen, that is the way it has been for so long. They will have to seek the doctor from the wolf pack. We do not help them."

My upper lip rose. I wanted to rip the arrogant smirk off his face.

Anger burned bright in Paige's eyes. "Who are you?" she demanded. My lips dropped, and I fought a smile. She'd been worried about being queen, and yet even from the first moment I'd seen her to right then, I felt there was something important about her, and now I could tell she would be fine in her new role.

"Odin Servetus. The magic users' chairman and trusted adviser to the former queen."

The man beside Paige dropped to his knees. "The wolves won't help when we're not a part of the pack since we're horse shifters."

Paige's hand landed on the man's shoulder. He stiffened. "What's your name?"

"Michael Dill, my queen."

"I will find someone to help your mate, Michael."

Michael made a noise in the back of his throat. It sounded like a sob. "Thank you, my queen. Thank you. Thank you."

"It won't happen, you cannot—"

Paige's gaze snapped up at Odin. "Are you telling me what I can and can't do?" Her voice was hard and cold. My cock jerked once more.

Odin blanched and replied gently, "Of course not, my queen. I only advise."

People murmured around us. Paige ignored them all and said to Michael once more, "After we speak in here, I'll have Thorn come to you and let you know who will attend your mate."

Michael nodded, his hands clasped in front of him as if praying as he thanked her over and over.

Paige patted his shoulder once more and then strode forward. Ezra and Nate kept at her sides, while Thorn and I moved to her back with Alex behind us.

Odin moved aside, bowing his head as Paige walked by. As soon as all of us had entered the meeting room, the door closed.

Paige made her way to the seat at the end of the table. Once there, she stopped at the side of the chair and eyed the six others in the room—three women and three men, including Odin.

Thorn pulled out her chair and she sat. Pride filled me. I knew she'd be nervous, but she hid it well and looked regal. Nate stepped back to lean against the wall behind her with Alex. They both had their jobs and knew, without my telling them, to keep an eye on all the people in the room. I moved to them as well, but my objective was Paige. I would keep an eye on her emotions and guard her with my life, like Thorn and Ezra were. Ezra planted himself on Paige's right. Her hand landed on his head and she gently rubbed over his fur. Thorn stood tall on her left.

"Shall we get started," she called clearly.

CHAPTER SIXTEEN

Fury still consumed me. I wanted to shout and yell at everyone. Instead, I controlled it, even though it was hard. I needed to get to the bottom of the issue to fix it, because I *would* have a doctor or even a nurse visit Michael's mate by the end of the day.

Odin stood at the other end of the table, while the others took their seats slowly. Odin cleared his throat. "Queen Paige Alice, I have already introduced myself, but let me introduce you to everyone else." I nodded. He pointed to his right where a man, who looked Odin's age, in his forties if I had to guess, sat. Though, I knew they could be older than what they seemed. Even thousands of years old. "This is Barrett Caldas, mage."

Barrett didn't bow. He stared me down, causing Ezra to growl. It seemed, also like Odin, he was a cocky bastard. Next to him sat another man, but he appeared younger, not by much though. I hated how looks were deceiving.

"Beside him is Clyde Rick, head vampire." Clyde dipped his chin at me, but his eyes were to Asher behind me. I didn't like it. Odin pointed a hand to the left where three women sat. The first looked to be in her late sixties, the next in her forties, and the last seemed sixteen. Shock slid through me. Odin gestured to the first. "Alma Burnet, seer." Alma didn't bow or dip her head. No, she winked at me instead. I smiled in return. My shock over her age subsided slightly, but I still wondered if seers aged differently to witches and mages, who all seemed stuck in their forties, or did it mean Alma was as old as time? Odin shook his head and sighed. "Grace Hatty, witch." Grace stared at me coolly and then reluctantly dipped her chin down about an inch. "Lastly, Selma Bobbie, vampire." Selma glanced away from behind me at my men, causing my irritation to flare. Then she smiled sweetly and bowed her head while Odin took his seat at the end of the table. I didn't trust her, and it wasn't only because she'd been eyeing my men. There was an untrusting glint in her gaze.

Still, should I class them as my men?

Yes, I could, and I would. They were mine until they got smart and ran for the hills so I could protect them from this new change.

Until then, I would make sure people knew they belonged to me. Without a doubt, I was about to become a possessive bitch. Leaning forward, I rested my elbows to the table and clasped my hands in front of me. "It's a pleasure to meet you all," I said. Then I gestured to Thorn with a flick of my hand. "All of you would already know Thorn. At my back is Alex, Nate, and Asher. Also, beside me is Ezra." I patted his head. He leaned into it and panted. If Asher and the others didn't know Ezra was a hellhound until he changed, then these people wouldn't either, and I wasn't about to tell them. Not when they screwed their noses up at me when I'd introduced him. They thought he was beneath them all. He wasn't. They'd find it out eventually.

"I didn't realize Thorn would be... so close to you already," Odin commented. "He was, after all, just the former queen's high-ranking guard."

The shmuck looked down on my Thorn. What was strange was how I'd already thought they knew Thorn and the men were my bonded mates. I chanced a brief glance at Alma. Had she been the seer to inform the queen of everything? Alma's wicked smile and wink my way told enough. They had kept it between her and the queen, maybe even her mates and Thorn.

Reaching up, I took Thorn's hand in mine and brought it around to my lips where I kissed it. Looking up at him, I found him already gazing warmly down at me. A smirk played on his lips. I heard a cackle and knew it was coming from Alma. I had a feeling I would like the woman a lot.

Glancing back to Odin, I asked, "Did you know I would be showing so soon?"

Odin flicked a glance to Barrett and then Thorn. His jaw clenched. "No. As far as we knew, Thorn was on a mission to see what the council were up to these days. We were aware a new queen would arise, but when, we didn't know. Still, we were preparing for it." He glared down at Alma, who ignored him completely and kept smiling at me.

"Funny how the former queen's trusted advisers weren't informed," I mentioned.

"Are you saying Thorn is your mate?" Grace asked.

"Yes. Along with Alex, Nate, and Asher."

A fist pounded into the table. All eyes shot to Barrett. "This is an outrage," he bellowed. "They're different species. You can't have them as your mates."

Ezra got to his feet and snarled.

The room thickened with my rage. I sensed Alex, Asher, and Nate step closer to my back. I dropped Thorn's hand and stood, leaning into my hands on the table. "Are you telling me who I should have as mates?"

Odin stood too, his hands pressed down on the air in front of him. "No. He was just surprised, as we all are. He means no harm by it."

That I doubted.

"Ezra, go and get Eric for me. Only Eric," I told him without looking away from the people in front of me. Ezra huffed and went to the door with Nate following. He opened it for Ezra to slip out. Nate stayed standing by the door with his arms crossed over his chest, scowling around the room.

"Since I'm new here, I'd like to get some things that are concerning me out of the way. From what I've seen and heard, can someone tell me, even though we have mixed species within our community, it's still segregated?"

"Of course," Barrett snapped.

"Did the former queen allow mixed races to bond?"

Barrett's face scrunched up, even Grace and Odin looked disgusted by my question, but it was Clyde who answered with, "We've been around for many, many years, my queen. It is frowned upon being with someone from another race. The former queen was advised to keep peace in the community, it would be better to segregate the races."

"It is treason to be with another kind than your own," Barrett yelled.

Clyde turned to him slowly. "And yet, the former queen never once killed or sent away anyone when she found out what was happening behind closed doors."

"Because it never happened under her ruling."

Clyde laughed. "You are a fool to think it didn't. It happened, and Marsala knew of them all. She made sure to know of it to protect them from the likes of you and the people who follow your lead."

Barrett stood, his chair flying back. "How do you know this?"

Clyde smiled, flashing a bit of fang. "Because I was tasked to find out about them all and inform her." While Barrett shot daggers out of his eyes and breathed deeply, Clyde looked back to me. "She knew it wouldn't be for her to change things. It would be for the next queen to do so because you have already changed many things by taking a vampire, a shifter, a ghoul, and a mage as your mates."

All right, Clyde wasn't too bad of a guy. Especially if he went behind Barrett, Odin, and Grace's back about different species getting together. Selma I didn't trust as yet, since she sat quietly with a flirty smile on her face staring at Asher. Of course, it was my right to step in front of him more to block her view. She smiled when I glared down at her.

Clyde brought my attention back to him when he asked, "Are you willing to make the changes within the community?"

"I'm willing to do what's right for everyone."

He studied me, then nodded once.

There was a knock on the door. Nate drew in a breath and then opened it. Ezra strode in and came back to my side. He even snapped at Selma, who let out a frightened noise. I kept my smile from blooming. Some vampire she was. While I patted Ezra's head, I watched a wide-eyed Eric step through the entrance.

"Ah, hey."

"Eric, come down here please." I motioned to my end of the table. He did, looking at everyone suspiciously.

"What's going on?" he asked. Grace gasped. I wasn't sure if it was over Eric being human or how he didn't follow protocol by addressing me properly.

I didn't answer him. Instead, I addressed the rest of the room. "First order of business. As the new queen, I appoint new advisers at my side. Most I trust with my life, others will earn my trust in time. Nate, Alex, Asher, Thorn, Alma, Clyde, Michael, and Eric."

"What?" Odin screeched.

"You can't do this!" Barrett screamed.

"How dare you!" Grace spat.

It was only Selma who stayed silent with a bland look upon her face.

"I'll be organizing a meeting for tomorrow, a full-court announcement." I glanced to Thorn.

He bowed and said, "I'll make it happen, my queen."

"Thank you. For now, the four of you are excused."

"He's a human. He doesn't know our ways. This is blasphemy," Odin called.

"It doesn't matter what he is. I don't have to explain the reasons behind my choices. Now, please leave."

"It's not the end of this—" Barrett started, until Odin reached out and touched his back. Then he shut up and stormed from the room. Odin and Grace glared at us, then followed Barrett out.

Selma stood slowly. She looked to Clyde and rose a brow.

He stared back, but I couldn't read anything from his expression. She laughed, shrugged, and then swayed her hips as she started behind me. I didn't miss the way her eyes ran over Asher or the small touch she skimmed over his shoulders.

In seconds, I had her by the throat and slammed into the wall. "Never touch what is *mine*," I snarled in her face.

She smiled. "I was just testing how strongly you felt for your mate. I could have had some fun with him."

"Never," I bit out. "Try testing me again and you won't live another day."

Her hands came up. "Yes, my queen. My apologies."

I tightened my hold for a moment longer and then dropped it, stepping back. Selma straightened her tight dress and walked from the room. I wanted to rip her head from her shoulders because she was still smiling.

It wasn't until Asher moved in behind me and ran his hands from my shoulders, down my arms, and then to my waist that I relaxed.

"You have made some enemies today," Clyde commented.

Opening my eyes, I stared at him. "Will you be one of them?" Had I made the right choice? I didn't have a clue what a queen was supposed to do, but my demand was spontaneous, and as soon as the words left my mouth, it felt right. Of course second-guessing myself would be something I'd do because there was a lot of weight on my shoulders. Hell, it all freaked me out, but I tried my best to keep it from showing. It would be something a queen did, right? Hide her emotions, act noble, at least try to.

I wanted to grab Thorn's shirt, drag him close and yell, "Am I doing the right thing? Do I sit like this? Do I look like I'm pulling this off, acting all queenish?"

Before I could do it though, Clyde spoke. "No, my queen." His lips tipped up into a close-mouthed smile. I would have to wait and see if he spoke the truth, or ask Nate if he could smell it. Clyde continued, "I agree with the changes you've made and look forward to seeing what you will bring the people."

"Peace. Safety. Fun times," Alma voiced. We all looked to her as she clapped her hands together. I could only hope whatever she knew or had seen was right. "May I also suggest one other for your advisers?"

"Who?" I questioned. My interest kept my wayward thoughts at bay, which was good.

"Agatha Delmar. She is a fine young witch."

I glanced at Thorn. He nodded. "She is the one who placed the spell on me to have me at your side when your powers surfaced."

"What's this?" Clyde asked.

Alma waved his question away. "You'll know all soon enough." A knock sounded on the door. Nate huffed but opened it. A woman, actually she looked to be in her late teens, came through. I wondered how old she really was. Alma laughed. "Right on time, Aggie."

The girl blushed. Her eyes met the floor before she bowed at the waist. "My queen."

Asher gently applied pressure to my waist. Right, I was supposed to say something. "Rise, Agatha." She did, but still didn't look me in the eyes. "Would you like to be another adviser to me?" Just because Alma suggested her or had "seen" her, didn't mean I wouldn't give the girl a choice. There was no doubt that allegiance to me could be dangerous. She had to make the decision herself. "I can't promise being one of my advisers will be safe. This also goes for everyone in the room."

I took a moment to make eye contact with everyone. "Just because I said your name earlier doesn't mean you have to stay as an adviser. I didn't think before. I jumped ahead once more."

Thorn opened his mouth to say something, but I held up a hand. "Please, all of you think about it. I know my role won't be safe, and I don't want you risking your life just to help me."

Clyde stood and bowed. "Thank you for your concern, my queen."

I nodded. "All of you have until tomorrow. I will ask at the court meeting if you wish to stay as my adviser. I won't hold anything against you if you don't wish to."

"Good idea, my queen," Thorn stated. "If we announce who will remain as your advisers, it will show the people who they're able to seek for an ear with the queen."

"Should we worry about the old advisers?" Nate asked.

Clyde replied. "It would be best to keep an eye on them and who they speak with."

"Can we really speak freely and trust everyone in here?" Agatha asked, her gaze flicked to Clyde. He straightened and glared.

Alma waved her hand in the air. "It's fine, dear. Trust them all. You have my word."

It was good to hear her say that, especially when I wasn't fully convinced of Clyde myself. However, a little of that tension eased from me at Alma's words. And how did I know I could trust Alma? Because I could *feel* it, sense it. She was like a safe, warm grandmother who everyone wished they had.

"I... um...," Agatha started. When everyone looked at her, she blanched and shifted her gaze back to the floor. Then mumbled, "N-no one knew Marsala, I mean the former queen, and I were friends. I could, ah, be a secret adviser, find out things on the inside."

"You would be willing to do this?" I asked. She nodded straight away. Alma was also nodding.

"Grace is your coven mistress. You would go behind her back?" Clyde asked.

Her head lifted, and she glared at him. "I will never follow that woman's rules if it's the last thing I do."

Grace must have done something to piss Agatha off.

"Agatha, if she found out…."

"She won't. Not until she had to. Not until she knew… if, I mean, I would be under your protection, yes?"

"Of course," I said instantly.

She nodded. "Thorn has many men in the guard he trusts. Many men to protect us all. I know I'll be safe."

"Okay, Agatha, if this is what you choose to do." She seemed determined, and I had a feeling if I didn't agree and give my protection, she would do it anyway.

"Thank you, and please call me Aggie."

"Good, good," Alma called. "Aggie must go now before she's seen by too many."

Aggie bowed quickly and then slipped from the room.

"My queen, if you allow me, I'll seek out Michael and make the offer of adviser to him," Clyde offered.

"That would be good, thank you," I said. He bowed and left the room.

"It also reminds me, Michael needs a doctor for his mate. Would I be pushing it asking for the doctor the witches use?" I asked the rest of the room.

Nate stepped forward. "I have medical training."

"No," I blurted. Asher chuckled at my back. Alex and Thorn

were also smiling. Ezra even let out a huff. Alma smiled wide, while Eric looked confused. I ran a hand over my face. "Sorry, but, ah, for the woman's safety, it would be better if it was anyone but one of you."

Nate rolled his eyes but said no more. I didn't miss the twitch on his lips, though.

"Now that changes are in the works, I'll tell Divina she'll be allowed to see anyone she wants. She's a ghoul who was previously a doctor. She's happy to help anyone but has been restricted because of the fool advisers getting in the former-queen's ear, trying to run things like the council does for control over the community. Poor Marsala was tired of the bickering back and forth. She knew her time was limited. She wanted to spend it in harmony with her mates. So she gave them too much free rein, and it went to their heads. But things are changing already for the better." Alma clapped; it seemed she loved to clap. She got to her feet slowly. "It's been a pleasure to meet you, Queen Paige Alice. I look forward to the times to come. Stay strong and believe in yourself and your mates."

"Thank you, Alma."

She dipped her head and left the room. It fell silent after Nate closed the door. I then glanced at Eric and said, "I've changed my mind. I don't think you should be an adviser for me. I won't risk your life or Yasmin's."

"But—"

I shook my head. "I know I probably won't change these stubborn asses' minds." Chuckles surrounded me. "And I know you can be stubborn, but I also know you'll do anything for your family. Yasmin and the kids need to stay safe. You're already at risk for being my family. I won't add to it."

He sighed and ran a hand through his hair. "I understand. Still, you'll need to give me something to do."

"There's plenty of jobs around. I'll bring some that are open to you tomorrow morning," Thorn suggested.

"Thanks." Eric nodded. "I better get back before Yasmin gets worried."

"Ezra, can you escort him please?"

Ezra nudged my hand. He knew I was sending him to protect Eric, and I knew Ezra would do anything for me. After they left, I turned to the men and said, "Can we head back and talk in my room?" Already I was tired of being around others. I just wanted the men and me alone.

"Of course," Asher replied.

CHAPTER SEVENTEEN

NATE

My eyes were on Paige's ass the entire walk back to her room. It was a good distraction to keep me from hunting those prejudice pricks down and ripping them a new asshole. But fuck, Paige had handled the situation perfectly. It was a good thing I'd gone for the tighter boxers, else everyone would have seen the hard-on I had for her and her assertiveness.

Christ, I even got off on her taking that bitch Selma to the wall to stake her claim over Asher.

Why did I fight the bond?

At that moment, I didn't have a clue.

Being the last one through her door, I took the time to adjust my dick behind my jeans. Paige went straight for the couch near the fire. I closed the door behind me and turned back to see Asher and Thorn sitting on each side of her. Alex moved and took the seat opposite them. I grabbed the last one beside him. I'd honestly been surprised when my wolf or I didn't feel threatened by the other men in the room when it came to Paige. My wolf huffed, like I was an idiot and missing something. Maybe it was because we knew she'd need more than one mate. We'd already accepted them into our pack to protect what was ours.

She needed all the help she could get. She acted like the queen well enough in front of others, but I could also scent—and it worried me others would as well—how she was unsure of everything. We had to remember it was all new to her. It was like she took on the job easily, but it wouldn't have been for herself. She was scared still. She did it for the people. She had a damn heart of gold, and I knew I wasn't the only one who worried it'd get her hurt in the end. Alex, Asher, and Thorn showed their concern over her in their own looks or actions. Still, we'd have her back through it all and hope with time she'd fully accept her title as queen.

Paige broke the silence by asking, "Why would they live like this? It's so… old fashioned, judgmental, arrogant."

"People don't like change. No matter what race," Asher explained.

"They've been this way for a very long time. From what I've gathered, the former queen, Marsala, knew the battle would be too big for her," Thorn explained.

"And it's not for me?" Her brows dipped in worry.

Thorn reached for her hand. Their fingers twined together, and he rested them on his thigh. "She never wanted to believe her advisers would go against her, but Alma saw how Marsala wanted to change things. She also saw Marsala's death before the time was right. Before she could reach you. If that happened…." He shook his head. "Life for our society would have worsened."

"So she waited for me because they saw I would bring change and succeed? But in the process, how many will get hurt?"

"We can't worry about what will happen," I told her. "We just need to make sure to have each other's backs."

Her eyes looked glassy; it freaked me out.

"Or you all could leave and—"

"It's not happening," I clipped. I ground my teeth together. She was foolish if she thought we would leave her to deal with everything on her own.

"But—"

"No buts. We're here, we're staying whether you like it or not."

She glared up at me. It was better than the fearful look in her eyes. "If you keep interrupting me, I won't like you staying."

I snorted and rolled my eyes.

Asher's arm went behind her, his hand around her neck. She glanced at him. "This is our destiny. You were meant to become queen, and we were meant to be by your side. Whatever is to come, the good, the bad… we will deal with it all together."

Wasn't that what I said? Although, Asher said it more eloquently. His way had Paige smiling softly up at him, her leaning into him, and his arm circling around her waist. Thorn didn't care. He kept holding her hand while she rested into Asher. I was surprised jealousy didn't rear its ugly head inside me.

Then again, this was how it was supposed to be.

She was made for all of us.

My resolve lowered, wavered. I didn't think I was completely interested in being Paige's, but I couldn't stop thinking about her. Claiming her, sinking my teeth into her flesh while I fucked her hard.

Fucking hell, my dick strained against my jeans.

I wasn't ready to finalize the bond, though. I'd wait, fight for her, and spend time around her. Make sure this bond would be the best choice for both of us, as well as the rest, in the end. Asher, Thorn, and Alex were completely for it. I could tell, and I was sure she knew it as well. She wasn't sure about me, and that was fine. I liked what we had. I liked fucking with her to bring her attitude out. I also wanted to wait until after the challenge. If shit happened to me, she wouldn't be too hung up should I fail. That was what I hoped anyway.

"It's nearing midnight. How about you try and rest," Thorn suggested.

She shrugged and sighed. "I suppose. Plus there will probably be a shitstorm tomorrow at the meeting, so I better be on top of my game."

I could definitely use more rest and some damn food.

"Do you have guards for her door or are we taking turns?" I asked.

"I'll call my brothers-in-arms. I trust them completely to guard her rooms."

"Wait," Paige called, her eyes widening. "What am I supposed to wear tomorrow?"

Another snort left me. She gave me the finger, and my lips twitched. Yeah, she would be feisty in bed, and I looked forward to that day, but it wouldn't be soon, even if my dick hated me for it.

"It will be formal clothing for such a gathering, Paige," Thorn told her.

She bit her bottom lip before saying, "But I don't have anything with me."

Asher glided a finger across her jaw. Her eyes darkened as they swung to him. "You have Alex. He can magic anything you desire."

Her gaze flared and swung to Alex, who smiled shyly and nodded. "It would be a pleasure."

"Thank you," she cried. "Could you conjure up some pajamas?"

"Easy." His eyes didn't even change color, but his cheeks pinked, and then he clicked his fingers.

"Ah, fuck." I groaned and scrubbed a hand over my face. "Time to go," I stated and stood. I grabbed Alex's arm and pulled him up.

"I didn't mean to do that. I thought of it briefly, but I wanted something else. I didn't mean it," he rambled as I pulled him toward the door. "Do you want me to change it?" he asked when I opened the door.

"No," Asher growled.

Just before I pulled Alex out of the room, I caught Paige look up to Asher as his eyes bled to green. Over my shoulder, I called, "Thorn, get those guards here."

"Yes." I heard him shift, his fingers pressing digits into a phone, but then closed the door and dragged Alex down to his room.

"You seriously had to go with that?" I asked, opening his door and walking in. I dropped his arm and made my way to the bed where I sat on the edge. My dick throbbed for release.

He threw out his hands. "I didn't mean it. It was a quick

thought, and then I pictured something else, but my subconscious brought forward what I'd… ah.…"

"Desired," I said.

He nodded.

Christ, if I had that power, I would have done the same. Her smooth, milky skin under that red lace was seared into my mind. She looked stunning. Absolutely fuckable.

"Do you think…?"

"Yes." I nodded. "Their bond will be finalized tonight." If I had stayed, I'd be a part of it too. We weren't ready, though.

"That's good, right?"

"It is. They want it. Paige does too, even though she's scared of what it means." I glanced up from the floor to see Alex looking back to the door. "You'll get your chance. It'd be good for just the two of them though. All of us could overwhelm her."

"Yeah, you're right." He nodded again before meeting my eyes. "So you do want the bond?"

"Pretty sure. I'll see how things go."

Alex rolled his eyes. "You're going to wait until after the challenge in case anything happens. To try and save her some pain. But you know you're stronger than him, right?"

I hummed under my breath and shrugged. I wasn't so sure. I stood, needing to change the subject. "Anyway, can you click your fingers and get me some food?" I rubbed my gut.

Alex sighed. "Fine. I'm hungry as well." He made his way to a chair just as a tray of burgers and fries appeared on the coffee table in front of it.

"Perfect," I grumbled and dove for a burger. Three bites down and it disappeared. Another appeared, and I took that as well. Once I filled myself, I stood and stretched. "Gonna hit the shower and get some sleep." I headed for the bathroom.

Alex made a noise in the back of his throat. "In here? Again?"

"Yep," I replied without looking back.

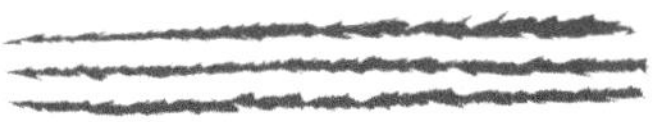

Paige

I HEARD my door close after Nate and Alex and sensed Thorn stand and move away. He clipped some words into the phone, but I didn't hear what he said as I couldn't look away from Asher. His green glowing eyes penetrated me. They also sent a shot of desire right to my breasts, causing my nipples to harden under the tiny red teddy Alex had put me in.

I would have laughed at Alex's choice and the shock that showed on his face when it happened, but wetness pooled between my legs, distracting me—as much as the vampire was right in front of me. Asher hissed out a breath. In the next second, I found myself on my back, bouncing on the bed, and Asher standing at the end of it. He shook his head, and the green haze receded. I got to my elbows and stared at him.

"Tell me to leave, Paige," he ordered darkly. When I didn't answer right away, his chest grumbled with a growl. His hand flashed out, and in the next moment, Asher gripped Thorn to his side by his shirt. "Tell *us* to leave, Paige," Asher demanded again.

I glanced from one man to the next, over and over. I couldn't seem to bring the words to my mouth.

I didn't want them to leave.

Was that crazy?

It was. It really was because I hardly knew them, yet I felt like I did. Felt like they were mine. *They are mine.* And they didn't seem to care I'd claimed them. In fact, both of them had voiced they wanted my claim and would be ready to take the next step to finalize the bond, at my pace. Right then, my pace was now.

They were my forever.

Meant to be with me, by my side, for the rest of our days.

Destiny.

Fate.

Made for each other.

Our lives had locked into each other's. Why would I deny two men who had voiced their desire to be fully mine? I couldn't.

"Paige," Asher warned. "My strength is lessening."

That was good.

Thorn pried Asher's hand from his shirt. Though, I was sure Asher had hold of Thorn in the first place to keep himself in one place because, as soon as his hand unlatched, his eyes darkened and he pulled his shirt from his body.

"I can scent you, love. Tell me to leave," he snarled.

Love.

I liked he called me that. I kept my mouth closed and smiled slowly. Thorn chuckled. "Sweetheart, would you like me to step out?" He would leave if I wished it, which said a lot about the man.

Asher went to grab Thorn again. Maybe he thought to throw Thorn my way and make a run for it. He was probably concerned I wouldn't want this. However, Thorn sidestepped.

Asher grumbled in the back of his throat, his fingers to his pants, and he undid the button.

I glanced to Thorn and could see the pronounced bulge behind his pants. Just like Asher's.

A pulse of lust swept through me. Asher's eyes flashed green and then back to his normal light blue, and his fangs peeked out. As Thorn's eyes hooded, he ran a hand over his face and shook out his body.

"Are you both sure—"

"Yes," Asher clipped.

"God, yes," Thorn replied on a groan. He grabbed his shirt at the back of his neck and tugged it free from his glorious body.

How did I get so lucky?

Oh wait, I remembered. I died, was reborn a ghoul, and the queen's power got transferred to me, and then met my mates. Funny thing was, I would do everything again if it left me in the position I was in.

With two of my mates in front of me, both seeming ready to seal the deal.

Sitting, and then getting to my knees, I said, "Come here, my mates." The possession, the endearment, the truth of my words settled in my chest. Feeling right.

I let out a squeak when Asher flashed to my left side, kneeling on the bed. His hands distracted me—one touched my back, the other my waist where he gripped my teddy. My body shuddered. I didn't know Thorn had climbed onto the bed to my right side until his lips were on my shoulder. I sighed contentedly. My head arched to the side and Thorn trailed his tongue up to my neck and kissed there.

Asher lifted a hand from my back to slide my strap down from my other shoulder where he too kissed. I gasped from the pleasure both of them sent right to my core. Having their attention, both of them at the same time, was nearly overwhelming but absolutely needed. Wanted.

If this was too soon, I didn't care. They were mine. I could feel it in my heart, my soul.

I reached out to them, to their erections straining behind their clothes. Both of my men let out a sound as soon as I touched them. Asher thrust his into my hand, while Thorn let me take my fill as I ran my hand up and down his long, thick length.

The next second, I was facing Thorn with Asher pressing against my back. I glanced over my shoulder and raised my brows. He shook his head. "I love your touch, but having more of it will make this night over for me."

Thorn chuckled. Asher glared at him, and when he looked back to me, he saw my thinning lips as I tried not to giggle. He growled, gripped my hair, and tugged my head back into his shoulder. A moan escaped me when his free hand slid to my waist and then up to cup my breast.

"Asher," I whispered.

"Ah, now who's losing it?"

I pouted. "Not fair."

"But you shall enjoy it." I heard a tear and felt a breeze hit my chest. I glanced down to see Asher had exposed my breasts. Thorn's lust-filled gaze caught my attention. "I think these beauties need attention, Thorn." Asher gripped one in each hand and gently caressed them.

"I think you're right, Asher."

While Asher ran his hands down over my stomach and slowly rocked his hardness into me, Thorn cupped both breasts and leaned in to suck the right nipple into his warm, wet mouth. I whimpered as he twirled my hard nipple around his tongue. "Thorn," I gasped and felt his smile against me.

When Asher's hand snuck inside my panties and held my mound, I moaned his name.

"Yes, my love?"

"Please."

"What do you need?"

His touch inside of me… but even more I needed his teeth biting into my flesh. The thought of it had me leaking more.

"Paige?" he clipped, sliding his fingers under my panties and over my lower lips.

Thorn bit down on my other nipple. I cried out and forced my breast into his face.

"My queen," Asher called low.

"Bite me, Asher," I ordered. He stilled at my back, his hand frozen in my panties.

"Love?"

"I need your fangs, Asher. Drink from me, please."

He sucked in a sharp breath. "Paige—"

I rocked my pussy over his hand and begged, "Please."

"Are you really going to leave our mate waiting?" Thorn asked, pressing a kiss on my breast before straightening. Mesmerized, I watched him undo his jeans. Asher must have been looking too because Thorn sent a wink over my shoulder. He stood from the bed and pushed his pants down his legs before standing and kicking them off. His dick sprang up and ready. Before I could take a good look at him, he climbed back on the bed. His grip moved to my waist. I snuck a hand down to take hold of him, but he clutched it, laughing. "Not yet, sweetheart."

Sweetheart.

I loved that as much as I loved it when Asher called me love.

I stilled as Asher tugged my long hair away from my neck. His tongue traced from my shoulder up to just below my ear where he gently nibbled before he whispered, "I would do anything for our queen, but especially our mate."

My body shuddered from his warm breath washing over my skin. When Thorn moved closer, my eyes lifted as he dipped his head and captured my lips with his. I moaned into his mouth when it opened, and our tongues tangled. He tasted and felt divine. Needing more contact, I ran my hands over his smooth skin.

Thorn fell back cursing. "Why did you push me?" he demanded from Asher. There was no answer; instead, Asher picked me up and set me, with my legs spread, over Thorn's waist.

Thorn's eyes widened, then lowered, and a grunt escaped him when Asher reached between us and shred my panties with his claws.

"Are you ready, my love?" he growled into my ear.

For what I wasn't sure, but I was ready for anything they would both deliver. "Yes," I whispered.

With his arm around my waist, Asher pulled me back flush against his chest, grinding his cock against me. "Take him while I feed," he ordered harshly, lust dripping from his rough voice.

Nodding, I lifted to my knees, reached down, and with Thorn's help, we placed him against my entrance.

"Fucking stunning," Thorn rumbled, running his hands up my thighs.

"She is, and she's ours," Asher stated darkly. His claws on my waist dug in, but not enough to hurt me. The noise from his chest, which vibrated against my back, was possessive. He raked his fangs over my neck and then struck. A gasp fell from my mouth, and a moan soon followed when Thorn thrust up inside me. I closed my eyes as bliss soaked into me. Asher pulled my blood into his mouth. He groaned as he took his fill as Thorn hissed low, then both paused. They stilled.

Something built inside me. It warmed my stomach, spread up to my chest, and aimed to where I was connected to Asher and lower where Thorn was planted inside me. My men grunted, their grips tightening, Asher's around my waist and Thorn's on my hips.

The warmth heated more, and they moaned. It seared into me, and I cried out, but as soon as it flamed to pain, it disappeared. Opening my eyes, I gasped. The room glowed with Thorn's and Asher's gazes; their other selves had made an appearance. I saw it and felt it with their claws scraping against my skin. Asher withdrew his fangs and licked my sensitive skin. I shuddered and felt Thorn twitch inside me. I bit my bottom lip and rocked down on him, drawing out his growl.

My back arched, a cry escaping my lips, and both men grunted. Lust, desire, need, want, and even love shone through me, consumed me, and I could tell those emotions weren't only my own.

I could *feel* them.

Feel their emotions.

Did that mean they could feel mine?

"Yes," Asher said against my shoulder before he kissed me there. "The connection has been completed. You're mine."

"And mine," Thorn clipped as his hands trailed up to cup my breasts. He lifted his hips into me, and I moaned. "Watch who takes you, my queen."

Asher's hands at my waist lifted me a little to my knees. It gave Thorn access to pump his hard, warm length in and out of me. "Open your eyes, sweetheart," he ordered. I hadn't even realized I'd closed them, having dropped my head back onto Asher's shoulder, lost in the sensation.

Opening my eyes, I dropped my head to meet Thorn's heated gaze. He thrust up again, and my mouth dropped open. His love washed over me. It had my heart beating double time, had me returning that love and comforting both of us. When I ground down onto him, my power sprang forward, and I felt my eyes change and sensed how he thought it was beautiful.

"You're mine," I snarled. Asher gently pushed at my back, and I lowered my chest to Thorn's and rode his cock. "*Mine*," I bit out again.

"Yes, my queen. I'm yours," Thorn stated with delight in his tone. His hand threaded through my hair. He tugged me closer and captured my mouth. A hand slid between us. Asher. He rubbed a finger over my slickness and then on my clit. I moaned against Thorn's mouth. Content they didn't shy away from touching me when I had someone else inside me, it made me think of them together, of them kissing, touching, and tasting one another.

Thinking it, my belly swirled. Thinking it added more wetness that coated Thorn's cock.

Both of them growled deeply.

Thorn's mouth tore from mine. He cursed and groaned. Gripping my hair tightly again, he asked, "What did you just think of to send that amount of arousal our way?"

Heat hit my cheeks, and I glanced away, but Thorn brought my gaze back down to his when he pinched my nipple.

"It must have been good," Asher said roughly behind me. His

hands ran over my back, my ass, where he slapped a cheek. "Tell us, love."

"You two. Together."

For a fraction of a second, they stilled, until Thorn rubbed up into me. "You don't mind if we do?"

I shook my head quickly. "It would turn me on. Seeing it and feeling the emotions when it happened… it would be a pleasure," I panted.

"One day soon, love. I would take any of your mates on in the bedroom if they allowed it," Asher said, his voice thicker. It had me moaning and rocking harder down on Thorn.

Thorn nodded. "I would enjoy anything from any of them."

Asher's finger sped up on my clit. My walls tightened around Thorn, causing him to hiss.

"Oh God," I cried out, losing myself to the sudden orgasm. Thorn growled deeply within his chest as he pulled me back down, claiming my mouth. I whimpered into it, still climaxing around him. He grunted, "Coming," and kissed me roughly as he throbbed and warmth filled my insides.

Thorn's hold relaxed. Asher must have seen it because next I was losing Thorn from within and was up on my knees. A scream tore from my throat when Asher embedded himself straight into me. Another climax overwhelmed me. Thorn held me while Asher fucked me hard and fast.

I loved every second of it.

Asher leaned over me, still drilling his hips, his cock pistoning in and out of me as he bit my shoulder. He growled, wrapping his arms tightly around my chest. I didn't think it possible, but another orgasm had me crying his name.

He hissed, withdrew his fangs and licked over the spot, still while I kept coming. He snarled, and I felt his longer length surge inside once more as he spilled his seed inside me.

A purring noise had me turning my head slightly to see Asher's eyes glowing. He pulled back his hips and slowly pushed back in.

"*Mine*," he grunted, his vampire riding his voice.

"Yes." I breathed the word.

His gaze shifted to Thorn under me. "*Ours*."

Thorn nodded. "Yes, our mate, and let's take care of her."

The purr in Asher's chest didn't subside as he pulled out. It continued as he lifted me from the bed into his arms. Thorn slowly climbed from the bed and went into the bathroom. Once out of sight, I heard flowing water.

Asher rubbed his cheek against mine, then pressed his nose in my neck and inhaled deeply.

When Thorn came back into the room, Asher growled low, and I linked an arm around his shoulders. Thorn stilled. "Ours remember."

Asher grunted and went back to purring. His vampire sent his pleasure, his happiness out to me. He loved me, loved that I was his mate, and I knew Thorn felt the same.

We'd completed the bond. I was theirs as much as they were mine, and I felt giddy from it. A laugh rumbled out of my vampire, while Thorn smiled brightly.

The fear over forcing them into the situation fell away. We all wanted to be here, be with one another, and be each other's forever.

After all, it was meant to be.

And I looked forward to finalizing the bond with my other mates.

CHAPTER EIGHTEEN

NATE

By the time I got out of the bathroom, which took me longer than normal since I had a hard-on to deal with, Alex sat on the bed with a book in hand dressed in nothing but boxers. *Alex*. He'd been Smith for so long, and yet here he was Alex. It felt right. Better even.

The room was only lit by the lamp beside him on the small table. Even without that I could see clearly in the dark thanks to my animal.

"Need boxers," I told him. Without looking, he clicked his fingers, and under my towel, I felt a new pair of boxers. I dropped the towel and glanced down. The boxers were tighter than usual and silk. I raised a brow at Alex, but his gaze was on the discarded towel on the floor. A tick started in his jaw while a grin popped up on my lips. I knew the guy was a clean freak, but I now understood it was worse. I gave him time to see how long it took for him to either deal with it or say something. I'd made it to the other side of the bed before the towel disappeared with another click of his fingers.

His attention returned to his book. "It's hanging in the bathroom."

A laugh escaped me as I climbed under the sheet. What was weird was that it felt normal. It wasn't strange, which didn't really make sense because it was Alex. A man I'd worked alongside for years. Out of the corner of my eye, I studied him while I settled back to lie flat with my arms behind my head. I didn't know what he was reading, but he was engrossed in it. His eyes flicked over the words quickly, and he turned page after page as I kept staring. I'd never noticed how fit he was or the fact he smiled to himself while reading. How his face lit up at certain spots in the book.

But why was I noticing now?

He was damn young compared to me and Asher. It showed a lot, but he still held his own. He was strong and fast with his magic. Not only that, but in body as well, which explained the six-pack I currently stared at.

Christ, why was I eyeing him up?

Was the connection to Paige the reason? If so, it would at least explain why my dick suddenly twitched as I ran my eyes over him. Though, it could have to do with the way he bit his bottom lip, the way his eyes widened and then hooded as he read on.

Then it hit me.

Something in the book had turned him on.

"What're you reading?" I asked to the quiet room.

Alex jumped; he even threw the book. "Nothing!" he shouted. He took a gulp of air. "Jesus, I thought you'd crashed, Nate. You been awake this whole time?"

"Yep."

He leaned out of bed, picked up his book and grumbled, "Go to sleep." He opened the book again, finding the page he was on and started reading again. Another wave of arousal hit my senses. My dick didn't care it was a guy it stood to attention for behind the boxers, ready for action. I sucked in a big breath, drawing in his scent more, and Alex's wide eyes snapped down to me. "What are you doing?"

I smirked. "Wanting to know what you're reading that's turning you on." I made a grab for the book, but he threw it across the room, then clicked his fingers, and it disappeared.

"I'm not... t-turned on."

I drew in another breath.

"Stop that," he demanded, scowling down at me with the color of fire over his cheeks. He slid down in the bed and turned off the light.

Rolling to my side, my eyes adjusted to the darkness and brought the room into clear focus. My wolf paced inside me. He wanted some action in any way he could. Fight or fuck.

"What were you reading, Alex?"

He sighed and rested an arm over his face. "A book," he mumbled.

"And it turned you on?" My tone was deeper, rougher.

He groaned in agitation. "Can you just drop it?"

"No."

"Fine. Yes, it turned me on, but I always seem to be aroused since Paige, ah, claimed me."

I snorted. "I know the feeling." I paused, letting him think the conversation was over. Then said, "What were you reading?"

He cursed under his breath. "Normal words."

"Normal words got you hard?"

He made a noise in the back of his throat. "I'm *not* hard. Just… I was… aroused. *Now,* can we drop it?"

I couldn't because my wolf and I liked teasing him, liked seeing him flustered and his cheeks tinted. Even more, we liked the thought of knowing Alex was hard. It shocked me for a second, but it also aroused us. With a quick movement, I reached out and gripped his erection. He cursed again, then yelled, "What the hell?"

"You're lying to me, Alex," I clipped. I didn't like he lied. I didn't like he hid it. What I did like was the weight of his erection in my hand. I ran my palm up and down. He gripped my wrist to stop me. I growled low, and he stilled.

"W-What are you doing?"

I wasn't sure. I'd never felt another guy's junk, but I was, and hell, it wasn't too bad. I enjoyed the way his voice hitched. I didn't want him to make me stop. The thought of stopping annoyed me and my wolf. So I didn't answer him; instead, I peeled his hand off my wrist and dragged it down to cover my hard dick. His breath picked up. Another shot of desire hit the room. I drew it in, and a rumble escaped from my mouth. I rocked into his hand while I ran mine up and down his length. His breath hitched again.

"Nate," he whispered. Yeah, he liked this. He wanted to touch me, and he wanted *my* touch. Fuck, that pleased me and my wolf.

"No," I bit out.

"You're touching me." His low, needy voice had me leaning in and nipping his shoulder.

"And you're touching me," I said roughly. He hadn't stopped touching me, even when I'd removed my hand. In fact, he was rubbing me up and down slowly. My wolf let out a rumble; he suddenly felt smug.

"But… we… should stop."

"No," I clipped harshly. His hand stopped for a moment, and I saw him look my way.

"Your eyes are glowing, Nate."

I knew they were. My wolf was close. He wanted more. He wanted to control. Not me, but *he* wanted *me* to control Alex. Hell, I even liked the idea of it. With a deep, rumbling growl, I gripped Alex and twisted him enough so I could rub my dick into his ass cheeks. The gasp that dropped from his lips jerked my dick hard. I pulled him back and ground my dick into him.

"Nate," he half warned, half breathed.

Another growl radiated out of my chest when he went to move away from me. He stilled.

"Just… wait. For a moment, let go," Alex said.

I didn't like it. My wolf really didn't want to, but I forced my hands to loosen. Alex managed to slip out of my grip. He flung the blanket back, and I thought he was getting out of bed. I made a grab for him when he quickly said, "Wait." It was only his heated eyes that had me stilling and waiting.

His eyes told me he wouldn't be stopping this.

He got to his knees beside me. A hiss escaped me when he clicked his fingers, and a tube of lube appeared on the bed. At the same time, our boxers disappeared. I could have come right there and then.

Mine. Ours. My wolf sounded in my mind and then threw me images of Paige, Alex, Asher and Thorn. *Ours.* He snarled with another picture of me and Paige together.

Fuck me. It all made sense now—why we'd been accepting of the other men.

The wolf saw everyone as Paige and mine.

He wanted to claim all of them as well. Like Paige did.

Ours.

Alex sat back on his calves, his erection jutting out. He was hard for me. Hard because I'd been touching him.

"Did I read this moment wrong?" he asked, and even in the dark I could see the hesitant look in his eyes as well as the blush coating his face and neck. He shook his head and went to move, but I grabbed his arm.

"You ever done this…?" I asked.

"With a guy? Once."

Fuck, why did I want to hunt that one guy down and rip his dick off to shove it down his throat? My wolf didn't like it either. Another growl erupted and kept rumbling from my chest as I got to my knees, slipping in behind him. "No more," I snarled.

"S-Sorry?"

I didn't say anything. Instead, I ran my hands down over his shoulders, his back. His skin under my touch, smooth and warm, appeased my wolf. I nipped at his shoulder. An image of me biting him touched my mind.

Claim, my wolf and I thought together.

With a hand to his shoulder, I pushed him forward. He went to his hands, his ass rising for me. My chest vibrated with a deep guttural sound. I ran a finger over his hole. On contact, his hips jerked forward. I pulled him back with a hand to his thigh.

He wouldn't take away from me what he was offering. "Mine," I bit out. The sound in my chest didn't stop. I grabbed the tube of lube. Even though my wolf wanted me embedded deep inside Alex, I knew I had to take my time.

"Yes," Alex whispered.

Yes? He knew he was mine?

My lips tugged up.

I lathered my fingers, his ring, and my dick in a lot of lube before throwing the bottle to the bed again. When I ran my fingers over his ring again, he whimpered. When I pressed one inside, he gasped. I joined another with the first, watching my fingers work his hole, stretching it. We didn't need protection. Neither of us could get any human diseases, which I was goddamn grateful for because my dick was already leaking at the thought of being inside him with nothing between us.

"Should... should I worry about your growls? Your dominance?"

Leaning down, I kissed his lower back. My chest wouldn't quit vibrating over the sound my content wolf made. He knew I was going to get what we wanted. He was happy.

Kissing his waist, I trailed my tongue up to his shoulder where I nipped again. "Probably."

When I pressed my fingers deeper, rubbing against what I was sure was his prostate, he threw his head back and moaned.

"Later," he muttered. Then after a few beats, he snapped, "Nate."

"You want me inside?"

He glared over his shoulder. "Yes."

My wolf howled inside me. As I forced his chest to the bed, I slipped my fingers free. He mewed in protest. I got to my knees and positioned myself behind him, gripping my leaking dick. I rubbed it up and down over him. He panted, and I saw him take a hand under him. His body moved slightly while he jerked his dick in his hand.

"Mine," I clipped, and reached for his arm. He let me pull it away from him. Stretching over his back, I pressed my cock at his hole. As soon as I inched in, I crouched and leaned into him more, holding his hands down on the bed.

I dragged my lips over his shoulder. Licking, tasting. With his head turned sideways, he opened his eyes, and I slammed deep inside. His mouth opened at the intrusion, his eyes darkening, and then he licked his lips.

Fuck me. He liked it.

Ours, my wolf chimed.

Slowly, I pulled out and then back in. Alex moaned. I grunted deeply.

Christ, he felt amazing. I buried myself as far as I could go and felt a tingle hit my spine.

"Nate?" Alex must have sensed something. He went to move but stilled when I growled menacingly.

He was ours.

My body grew. The half shift swept over me. My claws sprouted, along with my teeth. Alex gasped and rocked back onto me. My dick had grown, my pink tip would be out and deeper inside him.

"Mine," I snarled before moving back, gripping his hips and fucking him hard and fast. He took it all. He cried out, groaned, panted, and moaned for us.

"Nate," he called, and we knew he was close.

Still pounding into him, I grabbed his shoulder and dragged him up to his hands. With our increased height, we mounted him, jerking only our hips in and out while we lay over his back.

"Nate," he moaned again.

Our teeth latched onto his shoulder. We bit down, drawing blood. Immediately, he cried out and shuddered under us. Our bite deepened while his body kept shaking and coming. We growled around his skin. Our balls drew up, and finally, goddamn finally, our cum shot inside his ass as we moved in and out fast.

My wolf receded, sated. Carefully, I took my teeth out of Alex and licked the spot. I jerked inside him, the last of my cum squirting out. My claws, teeth, and body shrank down to my human form. Slowly, I withdrew. As if in a daze, Alex slumped forward, flat on his stomach. I moved to the side and brought him into me, curling my arms around him.

He yawned. "We'll talk about what happened in the morning."

I hummed under my breath, spent and tired. But damn happy since it seemed the bonding, not only with Paige, but with all of us, was underway.

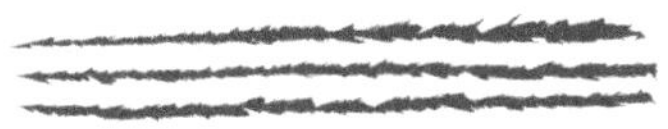

Alex

WHEN I WOKE, it was to the arm over my waist loosening and moving as Nate rolled to his back and then slid out of bed. I didn't open my eyes. Instead, my mind bombarded me with images of the night before. My body relished in the desire I'd experienced.

Never in my life would I have thought Nate and I would be in that situation.

Never.

Was I glad it happened? Yes. It felt right, good. That was if I didn't die of embarrassment first, and if I didn't, I would ask for it again. However, I knew I would never be good at dealing with the morning after with someone I'd just had sex with. Especially since it was something I hadn't ever experienced before. I either left or they did after the deed was done. So how did I act? Did we high-five? Tell each other good job? Go on like it never happened? I'd been with *one* other man and hadn't even stayed around after to worry about things like this. I'd also been with a couple of women, but those times weren't ones I stuck around for either. My studies, magic, and then work took up all of my time. I'd picked those people up at clubs and used them as a stress reliever, but I never looked for anything more.

I wondered if it was because I'd been destined for more.

For Paige.

For Paige and her men.

Heck, it wasn't that. I just wasn't the kind of guy who slept around. I enjoyed my own company. I didn't feel the need to seek out another being for pleasure when I could bring it on myself with my own hand… or fingers.

I heard the shower turn off. It was then I gasped and realized I should have used the time to get out of here. But then I remembered the room we were in was the one I'd been assigned. So instead, I sat up quickly and got out, standing beside it. I called up a spell to clean the sheets and make the bed.

Then I froze.

The bathroom door opened. Footsteps approached. Should I have turned and held out my hand for a shake? Worry churned my stomach. What would Paige think? Shit, she might not like what happened between us. We shouldn't have done it.

We had to hide it. No one could know.

Teeth nipping at my shoulder had me jolting on the spot. "Enough thinking," Nate ordered.

"I wasn't," I told him.

He snorted. "Sure. Explains why you're standing by the bed naked."

My eyes widened. I glanced down, and I *was* naked. With a click of my fingers, my body was clean, my hair was done, and a dark blue suit fitted my frame. Satisfied, I looked at Nate who… was… naked.

"I enjoy you looking, but we should get to Paige's," he said with a smirk because I *had* been running my gaze over him slowly.

Another click of my fingers and a black suit covered his amazing body. His brows dipped. "A monkey suit?"

I cleared my throat because he looked nearly as good in it as he was out of it. "Yes. We have to stand by Paige while she speaks with everyone. I don't think jeans will do it."

He sighed. "Fine." His jaw clenched.

"Ah… also, I don't think we should have done what we did last night. Paige might not like it, so we shouldn't, um, that's if you were thinking of doing it again… but we shouldn't do it again."

Oh shit.

Nate's lips thinned, his eyes narrowed, and his hands fisted at his sides. His nostrils flared. He stretched his neck, rolling his head around before lasering me with another glower. "It *should* have happened. It *will* happen again, and Paige *will* accept it," he clipped before storming to the door and opening it.

My power flared. I transported to the door and slammed it closed before he could step out. "Nate, listen to me. We—"

He crowded me, aligning his body with mine against the door. "What happened last night?"

The bite.

"Yes, about that—" I started.

"My wolf and I claimed you. We'll be claiming Asher, Thorn, *and* Paige. You're ours. What happened last night fucking rocked. I have a feeling it's because of Paige, because of her claim and power changing us all, but that doesn't matter because it happened. We deal, move on, and again, you're—" He leaned in more and rubbed his nose against mine just before he pressed his lips against my own. Shock blasted through me. With wide eyes, I took in his own big gaze, until I saw his green eyes darken and lower, his body relaxing against mine. As if the kiss was the final moment in the claim. It was done. I *was* his and for the life of me, I couldn't find the fight in me anymore. Nor did I want to. Not when he nipped at my bottom lip playfully and then deepened the kiss. I lost control and grabbed him to me, molding and melting with him. When we finally came up for air, he growled out deep and low. "*Mine.*"

My heart hammered in my chest, and my breathing left me panting. Too stunned and moved to say anything, Nate was able to move me aside and open the door again. He walked out while I gripped my chest.

He had claimed me completely.

Me.

A mage to his shifter.

His wolf wanted me.

Me. Asher. Thorn and Paige.

My dick was still stuck on the fact he wanted it to happen again before I rushed out of the room after him.

CHAPTER NINETEEN

I sat on the couch eating a bagel with cream cheese. I had about two hours before I had to leave for the meeting I called. My body ached in the best of ways. There was no way I could wipe the smile off my face. In fact, I was looking forward to another night of testing out the bed once more. Whether it was with Asher and Thorn again, or one of them on their own. Even if it was with Nate, if I didn't kill him, or Alex… or both of them together.

My hormones had amped up more after the previous night, and I couldn't stop thinking about it or staring at the men who'd made my body sing. Thorn sat opposite me reading something on his iPad, while Asher had just come from the bathroom and stood near the couch I was on, drying his hair.

"If you keep thinking about last night or looking at me like that, love, we won't make the meeting."

"Okay." I smiled, still eyeing him and allowing them to feel my desire.

He laughed.

"Finish your bagel, sweetheart," Thorn said. He was already smirking my way when I glanced to him. He enjoyed the way I'd moaned over the first bite of bagel. His rush of arousal hit me from where he sat. However, I couldn't help that I was starving; they'd used all my energy up.

I took another bite and chewed slowly. Thorn's eyes hooded. He licked his lips, and somehow, I felt that over my clit. I rubbed my legs together under my robe, and Thorn's mouth tipped up.

Before things got carried away, I said, "Can I ask you both a question?"

Asher nodded once, as Thorn replied, "Of course."

"How, ah, how did you both become what you are? I mean, if it's not something you want to talk about, I understand…. I just, um, wanted to know more about you both."

Asher moved over to the couch and sat on the armrest. He nodded at Thorn, who smiled. "My story isn't exciting or anything. I was turned by one of the former queen's bonded mates. I'd been out one night drinking at a bar after a long day of work at my family's farm."

"You're a country boy?" I grinned.

Thorn smirked. "I was, yes. I have my cowboy gear in the back of my wardrobe if you would like to see it?"

Yes please. I nodded and knew he felt my excitement when he chuckled. "One night soon, sweetheart. Back to the story. There were a couple of men there who were hassling a woman. I told them to stop. They did, after some fists were exchanged with faces. They left, and I thought that would be the end of it. However, it wasn't. They were waiting outside of the bar and then shot me." I gasped, worry clutching at my chest. "I'm all right, Paige, as you can see." I could, but knowing he'd been shot didn't sit well. "Justice, the mate to the former queen, found me. He killed the men before he dropped to his knees beside me. We both knew I would die, but he asked if I wanted to live but become something else. He saw what had happened and knew I was a good man, but by living, I would have to leave the life I had behind."

"Your family."

"Yes. My choice was either death or to live on as something else. I picked something else after I made sure I would be able to keep an eye on my family from a distance afterward."

"Do you regret your choice?" I asked, feeling kind of afraid of his answer because it meant he didn't like where his life now was.

He shook his head quickly. "It cut me deeply, knowing my family thought me dead, but… now I know what my purpose is. To be by your side. I would have picked it again and again because it led me to be here with you."

Relief washed through me. "D-Do you still see them?"

"Sometimes. At least my great nieces and nephews. My parents and brothers are long gone. They lived, loved, and were happy. It was all I wanted for them."

"How did you become a guard for the queen?"

"Training, and a lot of it. Justice took a liking to me. He taught me everything I know, and I worked my way up." I opened my mouth to ask another question when Thorn held up his hand. "We have so much time to get to know each other completely, but I'm afraid this morning we don't have enough to go into a lot of it. If you would like to hear Asher's story, then we should move on to it."

He was right. We had so much time, and knowing it warmed me within. "Okay." I smiled and looked to Asher. His pinched brows and thinned lips had me reaching out to take his hand. "You don't have to tell me now or ever if you—"

"I wish to. Only my change isn't as honorable as Thorn's."

"You have to know by now that no matter what your past entailed, I'll still be by your side. I'll still love you for the man you've shown me, and that man is caring, protective, and fierce when he needs to be."

His brows shot up. "You love me?"

Shock had me jerking my head back. I thought they would have sensed it. "Well, yes. Both of you. Can't you feel it?"

His eyes darkened. "I can, but hearing the words means something as well."

"Agreed," Thorn stated, his voice thick and rough. A wave of love swept through me from both of them. It caused a frantic beat to my heart.

Asher's thumb gently stroked my skin as he started talking. "I had been called to my family's house for a dinner. They were aristocrats in the town we lived in and wanted to make a good impression on someone. At first, I told them I wouldn't because I'd not long moved out to get away from them. Yet, as soon as my father told me he would cut off my money, I went because I was selfish and liked the way I lived. No one knew of the existence of *others* in the world."

He licked his lips. "We learned differently that night. The couple my father invited were new to town but flaunted their money around, so he wanted to be the first to invite them over because he wanted our family to be the talk of the town. We found out exactly who they were after dinner. First, they killed my sister, then my mother. Lisa had taken a liking to me. She wanted to keep me as her pet." A growl dropped from my lips. Asher squeezed my hand. "It's fine, love. They got what they deserved in the end. Lisa started the process. I didn't know I would become what they were and wake with a hunger like I'd never felt." Pain danced on his features and had him thinning his lips. I knew why a second later when he said, "They left my father alive to be my first kill. I didn't know at the time who I was feeding from. Until it was too late. However, I didn't grieve his death or my family for a long time after because the hunger had taken over. I killed over fifty people before it was sated. It was a week later when I finally came back to myself."

"Is that what it's like for all vampires when they're first changed?"

He shook his head sadly. "If they have a kind master, they're taken care of, taught how to feed, how long for so no death will occur. Lisa and David didn't care. They wanted me to go on a rampage. They didn't realize their mistake until I took their lives. Nearly killing myself in the process because with Lisa being my master, I didn't know our connection could harm her younger children. If it hadn't been for Cynthia, a vampire who happened to be in the area, I would have died along with them. She saved me and taught me the rules, how we were supposed to live."

My anger for Lisa and David quickly shifted. Jealousy burned in my gut, but I had no right. I should have been grateful for Cynthia's help, else I wouldn't have Asher by my side.

Asher reached out and tucked my hair behind my ear. "She

has been a long-time friend more than we were lovers. You have nothing to fear from her or my time. You are my world. Since the moment I laid my eyes on you."

Well… I couldn't say anything to that.

I nodded stiffly and rolled my shoulders back. "Okay," I clipped since my brain was still on the fact that they *had* been lovers. Asher chuckled. I looked at Thorn to find him smiling.

"Sweetheart, you'll now need to worry that we never cross any of your exes. I would kill them knowing they have touched you." His eyes tinted red before returning to normal.

Then I remembered. He'd said the possessiveness would grow once the bond was complete. I laughed. "Welcome to my world, guys."

Both growled low, causing me to laugh again.

Maybe it would be best to move on from the subject altogether for now or we'd all end up angry. Although there was one thing I needed to make clear for Asher. Glancing up at him, I pushed my love into him. "You do know none of it is your fault."

"The guilt over killing innocent people will always live inside me. It was why I chose to work for the council so long ago. To help other newborns, to erase the existence of cruel masters, and to protect anyone I could."

How couldn't he see he'd paid his dues by doing so much good? Smiling, I told him, "One day I'll have you seeing the amazing man I see in front of me, Asher. And when you do, I hope it'll ease the guilt you still hold."

"Anything you wish, love."

He was only placating me, I knew it, but I gave it to him. My glower made him chuckle. I knew I wouldn't get anywhere today with making him see my reason, so I chose to move on.

For now. "Do you think we can stop by Yasmin's and pick up Ezra on the way?" I missed my hellhound. He'd taken it upon himself to protect my family for me. It was sweet and very kind, but I did love having him at my side.

"Yes, of course," Thorn said.

"Speaking of him," Asher started, "how did it come about? Do you know why he was there when you woke?"

I shook my head. "I've never known how or why he came to me in the first place. How he even found me. But, for me, the reasons don't matter. I'll always be grateful and love him for it. He's mine and I'm his."

Asher and Thorn glanced at one another and shared a look I didn't understand. "What was that?" I asked.

"What, sweetheart?"

"You know what, that look."

"I'm not sure." Thorn smiled. "Are you hungry for more than a bagel?" he questioned, and it threw me because it had me wondering something.

"We'll get back to that look soon," I promised. "No, I'm not hungry for something *more* just yet. Soon though I'm sure. But I did just wonder where the 'food' came from."

"We have a certain group that visits the morgues close by. We also protect the area surrounding us from those looking to harm anyone in the society."

"Oh… well, there you go."

My door came open, and I saw Asher had already been looking that way before Nate strolled in and then Alex.

Alex, who was bright red in the face.

Alex, who somehow smelled different.

Alex, who looked everywhere but at anyone.

"Morning," I called.

Nate grunted, but there wasn't any heat behind it. Actually, I was sure that on his lips was a tiny smile. He moved differently, too. Instead of stomping, he was lighter on his feet as he made his way to the table with coffee and food on it. Which Thorn had delivered that morning. They both looked amazing and very edible in their suits. Like Thorn had after he'd gotten ready.

"Morning," Alex replied from where he stood near the door. He tugged at the neck of his shirt. I caught his throat moving when he swallowed thickly after Asher moved from the armrest and stepped close to him.

I glanced back to Nate, who stuffed his face with bacon. In his other hand, he held up a bagel with nothing on it, ready to shove it in his mouth. He flicked his eyes to Asher and Alex. "Leave him alone," he said around his mouthful.

When Asher's wide eyes shot to Nate's, I knew I was missing something.

"What's going on?" I even looked at Thorn when no one replied to see if he knew anything. His brows nearly met his hairline, and he looked from Nate to Alex and back again.

I put the rest of my bagel on the plate and stood with my hands on my hips. "What's going on?"

"Nothing," Alex blurted quickly and loudly. His blush spread to his ears and down his neck.

At the same time, Nate, in a rough tone, said, "Alex and I slept together last night."

"Nate," Alex yelled.

Eyeing Nate, I replied, "So? You did that the night before as well."

His brows rose, and he gave me a look that said he thought I was stupid. I glowered at him.

"I. Fucked. Him," he stated slowly.

My mouth dropped open, my heart raced, and my eyes flared.

Nate and Alex.

Last night.

Nate was inside Alex.

In bed.

A wave of heat sank into my gut and moved lower to press inside me. I exclaimed, "You mean I missed out on seeing it?" I slapped a hand over my mouth. I couldn't believe I just said that when *they* didn't know it would turn me on. They hadn't been in the room last night. Instead, they'd been together. Dear God, I wanted to see that.

I heard Alex choke on a cough. I glanced to him to see he was having a hard time getting his redness under control while he tried to breathe normally. I spun my head back to Nate when, to my utter shock, he laughed aloud.

Once he settled and after we'd all watched him, he went back to rolling his eyes at us and glowering before taking a gulp of his coffee. Then I witnessed in astonishment as he made another cup and walked it over to Alex, who was still red in the face but also shocked by the kind gesture from Nate. Alex took the mug with shaky hands and muttered, "Thanks."

Nate shrugged and went back to the food.

After a while, Nate looked at us all. "For fuck's sake, what?"

"So…," I started. I honestly didn't know what to say. I did want *all* the details of the previous night, but I was sure if we spoke about it, Alex would have a heart attack. I quickly added, "Nothing."

Thorn cleared his throat to grab everyone's attention, "I don't think that's all that—"

"Can we just focus on the day, talk about that later?" Nate interrupted. His gaze met mine. "Do you know what you're going to say?"

To try and save his mood from going down to asshole land, I went along with his change of subject. "I'm going to wing it."

Everyone stared at me.

"Wing it?" Thorn asked.

"Well, yes."

"You don't have anything planned?" Alex queried.

"Nope." I shook my head. I picked my bagel back up and took a big bite.

"And she's the queen," Nate mumbled, but we all heard. I shot him the finger. Immediately, he chuckled. Yep, he was in a good mood. It told me all Nate needed was a fine night in bed with someone…. My body tensed. Not just anyone, though. I wouldn't, no, *couldn't* allow it. I would kill a person if anyone other than one of my mates or me touched him. Just the thought of it burned my stomach.

"Love, what's on your mind?" Asher asked as he walked to my side. Both he and Thorn would have sensed my emotions shift.

I glanced around. All my men were watching me. "Not much." At my side, he wrapped an arm around my waist. I leaned into him, and it helped calm the fire inside me.

A knock sounded on the door. Since Alex was near it, he opened it, and in stepped a man in his thirties. He bowed at me, but his eyes were on our mage. I bristled.

"My queen, Gregory asked me to come and see if there was anything else you needed."

"No, I'm fine."

"Can I do anything for anyone in here?" he purred. His gaze

was right on Alex. I was about to tell him we were fine when something crashed Nate's way. I looked over and saw his cup on the floor, and he moved toward the male.

He shoved the man's chest hard.

"Nate," Alex admonished. I was too stunned to say anything.

"Look at him like that again, and I'll cut your eyes out and feed them to you. Now get the fuck out. We don't need anything."

The man paled. He bowed over and over and backed further out of the room. "Yes, sir. Sorry, sir." The fool looked over at Alex once more, and Nate dove for him, but Alex wrapped his arms around Nate, who struggled. Thorn got up and rushed to the door, slamming it closed after the man. He leaned against it.

"Calm the hell down," Alex ordered.

Nate stilled. He huffed and relaxed into Alex.

"What was that about?" I asked out of the corner of my mouth to Asher. I honestly found it quite arousing. Well, after the annoyance fell away since Nate took care of the problem.

"I think it's something we'll discuss after the conference today," Asher said.

Dang it. I didn't want to wait, but I had a feeling it could be a long talk. "Fine."

"Alex, could you do your magic on me and Asher?"

With a final look to Nate, who nodded, Alex smiled over at me and came my way. "It would be an honor."

CHAPTER TWENTY

Alex had dressed me in a simple long black dress and heels. My hair was in two braids, which I pulled over my shoulders. After Alex had done his work, I didn't want to leave the room with the way all the men had been staring at me. Even Alex and Nate. However, I knew if I started something, we would have been late or not gone at all. Which wouldn't look good since I'd organized this meeting.

We were surrounded by Thorn's buddy elite guards as we walked. Then Thorn was in front of me leading the way. Asher walked at my right side, with Nate on my left and Alex following close behind with Ezra beside him. Ezra had been in my sister's suite all night, and the way he sniffed all of us when we'd stopped in there, he knew exactly what had happened the previous night. He'd wheezed in his laughing way.

Yasmin and Eric wanted to attend, but I asked them to stay back for their safety. Eventually, Yasmin agreed when I brought the kids into it. Thorn had some of his men stay to guard them.

We stopped just outside the throne room. Thorn turned to me and asked softly, "Are you ready, my queen?"

I wasn't.

I didn't think I would ever be ready, but this was my new life, my responsibility, and one day it would fully sink in. I would completely accept my new role. For now, I was winging it and praying for the best. Although, with my mates at my side, it helped my confidence. Their unwavering support had *me* believing I could do this. Even when it scared me to a point where, if I still went to the bathroom, I would have shit myself quite a few times over.

I ran my hands down my dress, pushed all joking aside, and told myself once more that I was doing the right thing by accepting the knowledge of me being the ghoul queen.

For me, for my mates, and for our people who sought refuge against the council. I would be the best queen I could be.

Resting a hand against my hard-beating heart, I nodded. Thorn smiled before facing toward the double wooden doors. As soon as he did, two of his men in front opened the doors and stepped aside. At least ten others entered before we did.

I could hear the voices, the murmurs, the heartbeats. I could even scent the worry, the excitement, and the hate. It was an added bonus to becoming queen—at least that was what Thorn told me, and I trusted him completely. The power had been slowly manifesting.

The two mates I had finalized the bond with sent me calmness. It rolled into me, and I straightened, lifting my head high just as Thorn started into the room. With a slow pace, I followed, knowing my men would be with me every step of the way.

I blocked out what I could hear, what I could scent, and made my way down between pews. It took a while to reach the front since the room was so large, but eventually, I climbed the steps to the platform and stopped just in front of the throne.

Turning, I gazed out into the room. There were so many people in attendance, standing and watching me. Waiting. I didn't say anything until my men were in position. Asher and Thorn took a spot on each side of me, just a step back from the chair. Alex was next to Thorn, and Nate stopped on the other side of Asher. Ezra trotted to my side and faced the room, sitting on his hind legs beside the throne that was mine.

I was queen.

Queen to all of the people before me.

That was if they accepted the changes I was about to make.

With a clear, tremor-free voice, I called out, "My heart beats, my eyes shine with red and black, my strength is something to be feared." I brought forward my powers, even when previously I'd been apprehensive to use them, show them, but I knew now that transforming communicated to the people the power I had. It also showed everyone, especially my mates, I would accept them in any form they came. So I changed my eyes for all to see. I grew my claws, holding them out and away for people to witness, my teeth lengthened, and around them, I voiced distinctly, "My name is Paige Alice, and I am the new ghoul queen. Your queen."

"My queen" was shouted back, and most bowed their heads in respect. Some didn't, and I understood why. Half of them wouldn't trust me, some of them wouldn't respect me until I proved myself and my worth to them. I could only hope I did.

Then there were the ones who hated me even before knowing me. Without a doubt, I knew the former advisers had spread the word about how I would be changing things. Those were ones I didn't care about; except they were also the ones I would keep a better eye on.

Once people were back to standing and the silence filled the room again, I pushed down my power, turning back to my human-looking self, and then said, "Please, take a seat." They did, but I didn't. I wanted all to see me, hear me. "I am sorry for the loss of the beloved former Queen Marsala. I do hope I can live up to her standards, but also precede them with my own rules and regulations.

"I believe in change. Change for the better. From what I've seen so far, things haven't progressed from the older times. With my help, my love, my kindness, I wish things to change for a happier, healthier, and peaceful future. Before I incorporate these changes, I wish for you all to know my first decree, and that was to gain new advisers." I swung my arm out Thorn's way. "Thorn Jones, Alex Smith." Then with my other arm, I gestured to my other mates. "Asher Evans and Nate Felan." I faced the front before I could get distracted by my men. "I would also like to offer the position to Alma Burnet, Clyde Rick, and Michael Dill. Please come forth if you accept the position as my adviser." Some gasped when they'd heard Michael's name. Some muttered their disgust over the change. Many just watched.

Clyde was the first to the stage. He dropped to his knees in front of me and bowed his head. "My queen, it would be an honor."

Fear throbbed inside of me. I didn't know the protocol. Did I just ask him to rise? I had a feeling it wouldn't be enough. But then a whisper of knowledge came over me, and before my mind registered it, I had my hand out in front of me. I dug my nails into my palm and turned it over to show the blood blossoming. People started whispering. Asher and Thorn's fury washed over me. In response, I sent them tranquility, enough to relax them, for them to know this was what was meant to be done.

"Take me into you, so I know you trust me, so I know you will advise me with your best knowledge, and so I know you will care for my people as I would myself. Take me into you to earn my trust of you. It may not be easy, but it will be rewarded. You will have my ear. You will have my help. Take me into you, Clyde Rick, and become my trusted adviser. Swear your allegiance to me."

If he took my blood, I would know, to a point at least, I could trust him.

He lifted his head, revealing his fangs had dropped. He leaned forward, and I was happy to see he wasn't hesitant in his decision. When he licked the blood from my palm, a shudder ran over him. His hands fell to the floor, his head touched my feet, and again he said, "My queen."

"Rise and take a stand at my side," I ordered.

He flashed up and over to stand beside Alex. Again, I dug my nails into my palm as Michael stepped forward. I repeated what I'd said to Clyde. Michael also shuddered from accepting my blood. He took the side next to Nate. Alma, who had the help of Asher and Thorn, got to her knees. I repeated the bind while she held my hand. After she took my blood into her, she grunted, "That packs a punch." Asher and Thorn again assisted her, and she took the spot beside Clyde while Asher and Thorn moved back to my sides.

"What about the other men at your side who are your advisers?" someone called.

"They do not need to swear to me."

"Then how can we trust they have your ear?" another shouted.

It was time everyone knew anyway.

"Some already may have sensed or learned, but I will explain. Asher is a vampire, Nate is a shifter, Thorn a ghoul, and Alex a mage. I trust them all completely with my life, with my people, because they are my bonded mates."

More gasps, whispers, and talk started up around the large room. I gave everyone time to process.

"Has the bond been completed?" It was Odin who called out.

My eyes narrowed on him, and he smirked. I bit out, "That's none of your business."

"Your life is everyone's business. We have the right to know," Barrett yelled.

I clenched my jaw. They were starting shit and I didn't like it, but I would still allow it because I wanted to see where it would lead. "Thorn and Asher," I stated with pride. "Nate and Alex will be soon, *if* they are accepting of me."

"We are," they both said clearly. My heart pounded in my chest. Alex I knew wanted to be claimed fully. Nate I hadn't been sure of until then.

"That's sacrilege. Each race should stick to their own," Patrice, who had flirted with all my men, shouted. Silence fell over the room. She stepped from her spot in the second pew and moved forward. "The former queen would never allow such a thing. Shifters are lowly beings. They don't deserve the right to have your ear."

Ezra got to his feet and growled low at her.

"No one is above anyone here," I told her sharply. "I declare that in this community, people are welcome to share their time, their love with *whomever* they wish." I scowled down on her. "Even if they are from another race."

People started chattering once more, a lot sounded happy with my reveal. Some disgusted.

Her nose scrunched up. "You're a fool. Things have been in order, have been fine until you came along."

"In order? Tell me about this order when it leaves people in need of a doctor, without help or secretly loving someone they shouldn't. No one has the right to tell people who they can love. Everyone deserves assistance, no matter their race. As the new queen, I will make sure this will happen."

Patrice scoffed. Thorn stepped forward. "Have care, Patrice, on how you speak and act in front of the queen."

"Queen? What queen? For all we know, her beating heart and her eyes could just be a trick." She looked at me. "We haven't seen your strength, and if you're allowing such things to happen, I'm worried about your smarts also."

Gasps sounded around the room.

"Enough," I clipped, anger rolling through me.

She leaned in. "It won't be enough. I'm speaking for those who don't want this change. I'm speaking on behalf of those who think you're a joke." She stepped closer. "I challenge you for the right to become queen." She smirked. "I'll even take your mates off your hands. Throw away the ones who don't matter, but Asher I will keep, and I'm sure I could break the bond."

Rage stabbed and cut me open, leaving me raw and murderous. It was one thing to go at me, but my mates...

Never.

I didn't have to bring my power forward as it was already

there. I let it consume me. The changes washed over me quickly. I pointed a long, sharp claw her way. "I accept your challenge," I snarled.

Patrice hissed, her own claws and fangs popping out.

"Stupid move," I heard Nate say as I slowly approached my prey. "You'll be dead in seconds. I saw the queen rip the head off a demon possessing a body. This was even before she came into the queen's power," he said it in a bored tone.

Patrice's eyes flared with fear before she looked back to me and hissed out, "Lies."

Nate laughed. "You'll see then."

Ezra growled. He too slunk forward. "Ezra, no," I said. He stopped, glaring up at me but sat back on his rump.

Lifting my foot, I took off my right heel and then the left. Some laughed, even my mates. It meant I would be shorter, but it also meant I wouldn't be wobbling all over the place or risk spraining an ankle. Even if it would heal right away, I didn't want the distraction.

Walking down the stairs, I stopped at the bottom and offered Patrice a final chance. "Are you sure you want to do this?"

Her glance was brief, but I caught her looking to Odin. So he was the one behind it.

"Yes," she hissed. "What you want to change shouldn't be. We refuse to live like the scum you want us to be."

"Us? Who's us?"

She sneered. "You'll find out." She ran at me, her claws ready to strike across my neck. She wanted my head from my body. Only she didn't anticipate me racing toward her. I ducked and slid on my knees by her. I popped up behind her and wrapped an arm around her neck before throwing her to the side. She crashed loudly into the front pews. People managed to either jump or flash out of the way.

Patrice stood, let out a screech, and charged at me with her vampire speed. It was the same dumb move. If I hadn't had Ezra helping me learn to fight, I would have been useless to protect myself. But I wasn't. My hellhound taught me well.

I dodged her hands, threaded my hand into her hair, and threw her into the air. Some clumps of hair were left behind. I looked at them in disgust and dropped them to the floor as her body landed with a thud. She shook her head and got to her feet more slowly. I knew bones would be mending.

"Do you want to stop?" I asked, giving her yet another chance, which I probably shouldn't have.

"No," she croaked. Why? What was her point? She should know she couldn't beat me. She wouldn't have my position or my mates. Never my mates. So why continue?

Patrice screamed, stomping forward just as the doors banged open. A guard, bloody and bruised, entered.

Everyone froze.

"Felnick?" Thorn bellowed. His fear rocked into me. It had me gasping as dread filled deeply into my soul.

"They tried to take them," he said.

Thorn's gaze shot down to me. My body shook in fear. Yasmin. I looked to Patrice; she didn't wipe her smug smile from her lips quick enough.

"Did they get them?" Asher boomed. His anger revved up mine.

"No," Felnick replied before he staggered forward. Michael rushed to him and held him up.

Murmurs started.

Even though I knew they were safe and my body sagged a

little in relief knowing my family was still protected—and those soldiers would be rewarded for doing so—all I could see was red. Red because I was about to bathe in some blood.

In seconds, I had a hand wrapped around Patrice's neck and her back slammed into the floor. I kneeled onto her chest and heard a rib crack. "Who ordered it?" I snarled into her face.

"I-I don't k-know," she stammered.

"Who!" I screamed down at her.

Ezra howled. My gaze swung up to see him transform in front of everyone. People screamed and scattered.

"Stop," I yelled, and my voice, even over the noise, echoed around the room. People slowed and then eventually stopped. "Nate," I called since he was the closest. He came to my side and took my position over Patrice. "Do not let her move. If she does, break something each time."

He smiled. "Yes, my queen."

I approached Ezra slowly, my hands out, my heart beating chaotically. "Ezra, calm down, honey. It's okay. They're okay."

His red-tinted eyes locked onto me. I expected another howl or growl, but he whimpered instead. I looked around. Alex's eyes were purple—he was working something. Asher had Odin on his knees on the floor in front of him. Thorn stood below the stairs, keeping an eye on everything.

"Alex?" I called thickly.

"Magic. Someone is weaving a spell into the room."

"What does it do?" I demanded.

Ezra whimpered again. In his full hellhound form, he dropped to his side. The ground shook from it.

"No," I cried, rushing to him and dropping beside his head. I ran my hands over him, fingers gliding through his fur, my body shaking hard. "Ezra, fight it, please. Please." I looked up at Alex. "Help him."

His brows dipped. "I'm trying, my queen."

A new cool breeze swept my hair and dress around.

Ezra's wet, rough tongue licked at my arm. I looked down as tears clouded my vision. I blinked them away. I couldn't lose him. He was mine. Mine, dammit. No one took from me.

Yet they were.

It shattered my chest open.

"Ezra, please don't leave me." I sniffed and buried my head into his neck. Ezra's whine had me gripping him tighter. Had more tears pooling and falling.

"There!" Alex shouted. I pulled my head up to see him pointing. I searched and found Barrett huddled in a corner, his eyes closed, his lips moving in a silent spell.

"Asher," I yelled. Asher picked Odin up, threw him at Alex and then flashed to Barrett.

Ezra whimpered again. I glanced back down. He took a breath, his eyes widened, and then…. Nothing.

CHAPTER TWENTY-ONE

PAIGE

It had been two weeks since we buried my hellhound. Two weeks and I couldn't mend the gaping hole in my chest. It remained raw and open from the loss. From the thought of never seeing Ezra who had been there from the start. He'd been by my side, right from when I climbed out of the grave the former ghoul queen had buried me in. He'd taught me to hunt, to feed, to live, and to fight.

How was I supposed to go on without him?

He wasn't just any hellhound, he'd been mine. He was smart, cheeky, and fierce.

I wanted him back.

Back rolling his eyes or laughing at me. Back with his knowing looks every time I got aroused by my bonded mates.

Yasmin, my sister, sat on the couch beside me. She tucked a stray blonde strand behind my ear. "You don't have to do this," she told me.

But I did.

I wanted to go to the dungeons where Patrice, Odin, and Barrett were being held. Where they'd been suffering and starving. I wanted to go in there so I could question them myself.

I'd let myself have time after burying Ezra to mourn, and even though my heart remained broken, I wanted answers. They'd caused this hole inside me. They'd killed my hellhound. I wanted them to pay a hell of a lot more than they were. They'd taken someone I cared for away from me. There wasn't a chance I'd let that go unpunished.

"I do," I answered, my voice cold.

"Paige, please let your mates handle it," she pleaded.

I stood, shaking my head. "I'm the queen, Yasmin. If I want answers, I will do the work to get them. They took Ezra. They broke a piece of me. They will suffer by my hand, and it will show others what will happen if they try to take from me again."

After a moment, she stood, nodded, and took me in for a hug. "Okay," she whispered.

After I returned her embrace, I faced my mates at the door to my family's suite. I walked to them. Alex was the first to reach out and take my hand. They had been amazing since... since we lost Ezra. I hadn't as yet finalized the bond with Nate or Alex, like I already had with Asher and Thorn. But they never pushed me. They knew I wasn't in the right frame of mind. Instead, my sweet, amazing men held me when I cried, comforting me all the time. They even distracted me when I needed it. Nate did it by pissing me off. Alex when he showed me some magic. Thorn and Asher when they spoke of things happening around the castle. They'd even worked out with me daily on new fighting tactics. Nate had been the one to suggest it, saying I needed to gain some muscle on my puny body. We'd sparred right away after that comment, and I realized how good it felt. Not only did it take my mind off things, but my body also ached in a way that exhausted me. It was that night I slept for the first time.

My mates were perfect.

Especially when they were dealing with an overemotional woman.

But I wasn't sure I would ever get over losing Ezra. The loss had darkened me inside, and I held onto it, that blackness, because I refused to move on and forget him.

As Asher opened the door, he called back to Yasmin, "We'll have her back soon."

"Take care of her," she said.

"Always," Thorn replied before he stepped out the door first. Then I went, still holding Alex's hand. Asher and Nate walked out after me. Outside of the room, Thorn's men, my personal guards, surrounded us as we silently made our way down underneath the castle's floors and into the cold, damp dungeons.

Some of the guards stayed at the entrance while one opened the locked gated door and we walked in. He shut the door and stayed by it. We traveled to the end of the hall. I wanted to start with Patrice first. I had a feeling she would be weaker than Odin or Barrett. Along the way, I happened to glance into a cell and saw Malvina, the ghoul who'd disrespected me and had wanted Thorn for herself. I sent a questioning glance at Thorn who was looking at me, he said, "No one speaks to you that way, my queen."

I nodded. "Get one of the guards to see if she's learned her lesson. If he thinks she has, set her free but keep an eye on her." Afterall, I had a feeling her disrespect was rooted in her love for Thorn. I couldn't fault her for that. Although, if she didn't learn to back off and leave him alone, knowing we were bonded, then things would be hard for her.

He dipped his chin. "Yes, my queen."

As I stood by the door, I stared in through the silver bars to Patrice. No longer was she made up to perfection. Now she wore a tattered dress. Her messy hair hung limply around her dirt-caked face, and smudges of grime painted her body. But it was her glowing eyes that told me she was starving for blood. She hadn't had any in over two weeks. She was young for a vampire, which I'd learned meant she had to feed more regularly.

The door opened, and she flinched as I entered. Asher and Nate were at my back while Alex and Thorn stopped near the inside of the door, in case she got by the three of us first. I doubted it completely. There was no way I would allow it.

Stepping close to her, I looked down in disgust and unfiltered hate. "Who else was in on this?"

She laughed dryly. "No one."

"Patrice, one last chance. Who else was in on this?"

Her upper lip raised. "You're pathetic."

Bending, I gripped the knife I'd stored in my boot, lifted it, and sliced it across her neck. Her blood sprayed out, covering me. Her eyes widened, and she gagged on her own blood.

"Bag," I ordered. Someone dropped a blood bag into my waiting hand. I slapped it to her mouth, and she drank greedily. Her neck knitted back together. "Who else, Patrice?"

"Fuck you," she rasped.

In response, I threw the bagged blood on the dust-covered ground. She cried out, until I sliced her newly healed neck open again. That time, I waited. I let her suffer by carving her neck open over and over while it tried to heal.

"Bag," I clipped. Another was deposited in my hand. "Who else, Patrice?"

"Selma," she whispered.

Before she drank all the blood down, I took it from her and dropped it to the floor.

"No!" she cried.

I shook my head. "You shouldn't have been a part of it. You should have stayed well away from me. Instead, you took from me. You helped kill Ezra. For that, you will suffer." I turned and walked away, catching a guard's eyes. "Keep doing what I was. Until I say otherwise."

He bowed. Respect shone in his eyes. "Yes, my queen."

"And send someone after Selma. I want her down here."

"As you wish, my queen," another guard answered, and three of them peeled away from the wall outside Patrice's cell to do as I bid.

I would make a mockery of them, and make sure no one wanted to deal with my wrath again while I was at it.

As I moved toward Barrett's cell, worry seeped into my mind. Already I'd hardened myself to a point where a part of my innocence withered away. There were vile creatures out there, even within these walls, and it was up to me to deal with them. I had to be strong; I had to steal a fortress around my own emotions sometimes. What worried me the most about it, about this newer unbreakable side to me, was if my mates would despise seeing me like that and the queen I was becoming? Would they hate me? Would they find what I did disgusting? I could have had them handle this for me. They would have. They were used to fighting, killing, but I didn't want them to touch her. To have spoken with her. Did they understand why I had to deal with these vermin myself? I wanted to make them hurt, like I had the people I'd killed to feed, the ones with evil intent, and the ones Ezra had taught me to hunt.

Ezra. My chest speared with sorrow. I bit my bottom lip to stop the emotion taking hold.

Did my mates, the men who were made for me and me for them, understand I bloodied myself for Ezra? He had to be avenged, and I had to be the one to do it.

Would they think of me different because of these events?

"Never, love," Asher answered quietly. "You are beautiful and amazing. No matter what side you show us, we will always want you." Lately, he and Thorn kept their emotions locked away from me since I'd already been feeling so much, but they opened themselves wide. Hope, love, pride, even arousal crawled over and inside of me from them.

"Thank you." I let my gratitude show in my voice. I doubted there would be a day I wouldn't feel lucky to have my mates. Yes, even Nate.

Another guard opened the cell door. Stepping through, I looked down at Barrett on his cot in the corner of the room. He was in the same shape as Patrice, but being a mage, he hungered for food and water instead. He sat up quickly and curled into himself.

"Leave me alone!" he cried. I glanced at his ankle. It still held the device that took away his magic.

I shook my head. "I can't. I won't. Ezra was mine, and you killed him. Where do you think that leaves you?"

"Y-You can't kill me. I was protecting the people from that beast."

Lies. I could scent it. "No one knew what he was. As far as people knew, he was a dog. And *mine*," I said, low and harsh. "Why did you kill him?"

He shook his head.

When I stepped closer, he shouted, "What did you do to Patrice?"

"You'll find out if you don't talk, because I'll do the same to you." I gestured down my body. "You see her blood. Do you want yours to join hers?"

He quivered. His scent shifted. Sweat and fear. He opened his mouth and said quietly, "Since your family was safe, I tried to take matters into my own hands. The spell wouldn't work on your mates—"

"You tried?" I bellowed. My powers surged, my eyes glowed, my claws and teeth extended.

He whimpered and tried to scuttle back, but he was already in the corner. I enjoyed seeing and scenting his terror. He deserved it.

"They were safe. You were safe. I couldn't touch anyone but the mutt."

"Shit," I heard Alex curse behind me.

Facing Alex, I saw dread dipping his brows, darkening his eyes, slumping his shoulders. "What?" I asked.

He bowed his head, eyes to the floor. "It's my fault, my queen."

"Look at me," I ordered softly. He straightened. "What are you saying, Alex?"

I could tell he wanted to move his gaze away from me. Guilt flickered in his eyes, but his focus stayed on me when he said, "I layered a spell over us and you. I should have for Ezra, but I didn't think." His jaw clenched. "It's my fault he got to him."

"No," I stated, resolute. I pulled my power in and took the steps to be in front of Alex. I cupped his cheeks, staring into his agonized gaze. "It's not your fault. Never your fault. It's theirs. They wanted to hurt me, hurt all of my mates, but couldn't because *you* protected us."

"But I should have—"

"Don't take on that blame. *Please.* It's not your fault." Truth carried my words. I wouldn't blame Alex and didn't want him to blame himself either. I could only hope he heard the certainty in my voice. I would have shared it in my emotions with him, but we'd yet to finalize the bond. Something that would change and soon; I needed my mates. It would be safer for all of us to be connected completely. I wanted all them to know that even through my grief they're mine, something I hadn't shown them since we'd lost Ezra. They needed to know I would protect them, I would love them, and I would kill for them.

It was Barrett, Odin, Patrice, and Selma's fault. They were all guilty for the event.

"Okay," he said in an exhale.

Smiling, I nodded. "Okay." Leaning up, I brushed my lips against his. His heart galloped from the first touch of my lips.

"Hellhounds should be able to repel magic thrown at them. Why didn't that happen?" Thorn interrupted; I was sure it was more to himself than everyone. However, it had me turning back to Barrett.

He shook his head. "I don't know how it worked. I don't."

Maybe Ezra was different from any other hellhound. It was all I could think of.

Brushing the thought away, for now, I moved back toward Barrett and called over my shoulder, "Asher."

"Yes, my queen?"

"I need you to help me with something because I have a feeling he won't tell the truth, no matter what I do."

Asher stepped to my side as we stopped in front of Barrett. "Make him tell me if he's romantically involved with Odin."

Barrett let out a noise and buried his head into his knees, crying over and over, "No."

I was glad when Asher's eyes bled to green, and his fangs dropped. Thankfully, my libido didn't kick into hyperdrive—it certainly wasn't the time. The room chilled as his power thickened throughout.

Asher leaned forward a little. His voice was soft, almost lulling when he said, "Look at me."

Barrett shook his head repeatedly.

"Look at me," Asher's voice deepened.

Slowly, Barrett lifted his head and gazed into Asher's eyes. "Is Odin your lover?"

"Yes."

Asher sucked his power back in, and he returned to his human appearance as he moved back. Barrett blinked over and over, coming out of the trance Asher had put him in.

"I thought so," I said.

"What? You talk about changing things, and you're against me loving a man?"

I laughed humorlessly. "No. You have it wrong. I'm all about people loving whoever they want. But... you took someone *I* loved."

His eyes widened as understanding registered. He paled, and his heart beat erratically. "No." He gasped. "This is different. He was just a damn hellhound."

"Ezra was family!" I yelled, my hands balling into fists. Over my shoulder, I ordered, "Bring Odin in here."

"Please, no. Please don't do this. I love him."

"I love Ezra. If I'd begged, would you have dropped the spell? Would you have let me save him?"

His lips snapped closed.

Yeah, I didn't think so.

"Stop, unhand me," we heard shouted. "You can't do this to me. I have rights. I am an adviser."

I turned enough to see Odin being forced through the doorway by two guards. He looked in the same state as his lover. His ankles and hands were chained together. Only he still held a note of stubbornness, or arrogance and distaste. His face screwed up at the sight of me. "What's the meaning of this?"

With speed behind me, I swiftly moved behind Odin, gripped his head, and using my queen strength, I ripped it from his shoulders. More blood sprayed out, coating me. Barrett started screaming when Odin's body fell to the floor. I threw Odin's head over near Barrett.

"A life for a life," I called loudly. Barrett keened and rocked on his bed. I didn't sense any repulsion from Asher or Thorn. I even glanced to Alex and Nate, but to my shock, they showed understanding. Nate nodded.

"My queen," someone said.

Turning, I saw Felnick standing in the doorway. "Yes?" I asked.

"You have a call. It's important."

"Now?"

"Yes, my queen."

"Who is it?" Thorn asked.

"Lucifer."

What the fuckety-fuck?

CHAPTER TWENTY-TWO

PAIGE

We strode to the meeting room where I would take a call from Lucifer. "Are you sure it's the devil himself?" I asked again.

Felnick nodded. "Yes, my queen."

"As in *The* Prince of Darkness?" I queried and wondered if this was an actual dream. Then I glanced down at myself and saw the blood coating my hands, body, and probably face. It couldn't be a dream. *Dammit.*

"Yes, my queen," Felnick answered.

I glanced at Asher beside me. "What would he want with me?"

"I'm unsure, love."

Then to Thorn, I asked, "Was the former queen acquainted with him?"

Him.

The devil.

Lucifer.

I still couldn't wrap my head around the fact the devil was on the phone waiting for me. It was another moment where, if I still peed, I would be filling my leather pants about now.

"I had heard she'd spoken with him on a few occasions," Thorn said.

Laughter bubbled up, but I clamped my lips together to stop it from exploding. The former queen spoke with the devil on a few occasions.

The devil was real.

Hell was real… I guessed.

Of course it was all real, or else Lucifer wouldn't be waiting on the phone for me. But how did they get reception down there?

My mind and world had been blown wide open, and I wasn't sure I was ready for more things like this. Although, at least it would keep my mind off the gaping hole in my chest over losing Ezra for a while.

We entered my office—it had been the former queen's, but I'd taken it over just last week. Yasmin had been in and decorated it to what she thought I would like. She hadn't done too bad, except for the painting of, well, to me, it looked like two dogs going at it, but she swore it was some abstract art piece.

I made my way around the desk, and with a shaky hand, I picked up the phone and placed it against my ear. When I nodded at Felnick, he pressed the button.

Shit. How was I supposed to greet the Prince of Darkness?

A cool hand touched the back of my neck, and calmness

spread through me. I glanced at Asher with an appreciative smile. "Paige Alice speaking."

"Ah, Paige Alice, the new ghoul queen. It's a pleasure to hear your voice." His voice was smooth and soft, almost like a purr in my ear.

"I'm presuming this is… Lucifer?"

"You presume right, my dear." I could hear the humor in his voice.

"What can I do for you, Lucifer?" My lips twitched. Either this was some elaborate prank, or I was actually speaking with the devil.

"It's what I can do for you, my dear."

"And that would be?"

"It's not something to speak of over the phone. I shall be in your area in a couple of weeks. Please prepare some rooms for me and a few of my people."

I dipped my brows in confusion and pressed my lips together in annoyance. "You could have passed this message on to my guard Felnick. I was in the middle of something." I gasped at my own words. Did people talk to Satan like that? Would he smite me and send me to burn in Hell for the rest of my existence?

Lucifer snorted. "And what could have been so important that you would have missed *my* call?"

"Ripping someone's head off because he and his lover took someone from me." My voice darkened toward the end. "No one kills someone I love."

When laughter sounded on the other end, I wanted to slide my hand through the receiver and tear out his vocal cords. Instead, I hung the damn phone up with a slam.

My heart beat frantically, already worried, and that was even before my brain could register what I'd just done.

"You hung up on Lucifer," Alex croaked while pointing at the phone.

My hand shook as I ran it over my face, probably smearing blood everywhere. I shrugged off Asher's hand and placed both hands to the desk, leaning into it. What did I do? He could come here and kill us all, probably with a thought. Fear churned my stomach. Fear for everyone around me, not myself.

"My queen, would you like me to call him back and beg forgiveness?" Felnick offered. His whole body trembled.

"No," I said, yet I was unsure. After a moment's consideration, I voiced my thoughts. "I can't show weakness. He may be Lucifer, but he needs to know I won't be messed with." I glanced at my men. Alex seemed worried by the way he chewed on his bottom lip. Nate looked bored. It was Asher's and Thorn's smiles that eased the anguish in my belly.

I straightened and then jolted when my phone rang again. I waited a couple of beats before I answered it on speakerphone. "Paige Alice."

"Do you know no one has hung up on me before?" His voice was hard and cold. Eerily so.

"First time for everything," I blurted.

Lucifer hummed under his breath. "I think I like you, Paige Alice. Very much so."

The men, all except Felnick, grumbled or growled low. But my ears also picked up another snarl from the phone, then Lucifer cursed before he said, "I shall contact you before we arrive, Paige."

"How many should we expect?" I asked.

"Six."

"Very well."

"Until then," he replied with a smile in his voice, and then I got dial tone.

I ended the call and glanced around. Asher, Thorn, and Nate now all wore frowns. Felnick looked nervous by the way he shuffled from one foot to the other. Only Alex offered me a soft smile since the situation was over.

"I don't fucking like this," Nate announced gruffly.

"Me neither," Asher said.

"At least he sounded okay after Paige hung up on him," Alex offered. I gave him a grin. He was always quick to see the best in situations to ease my fears, even when worried. I loved him for it.

Nate shook his head. "It's Lucifer. He shouldn't have been okay with it."

Thorn nodded. "He's up to something."

"But what?" Asher put in. The room fell silent.

"Maybe I should call him back and tell him not to come," I thought aloud.

Felnick whimpered. I knew he was a hardass, since he was one who'd fought and killed to protect my family, yet it seemed when it came to the devil, he wanted to meld with the floor.

He shook his head again and again. "Not unless we want to die."

"He handled my hanging up on him well. I'm sure he'd be okay with me telling him he's not welcome."

"Question is, do we need to know what he wants to say?" Nate said.

I bit my bottom lip as I thought about it. Whatever he wanted to tell me couldn't be said over the phone. But if Lucifer came here, I was more worried about my men and people. Yet, if I did tell him no, it could mean we'd be worse off.

Groaning, I slapped the desk. "He'll have to come, and whatever he has to say or do, we'll need to be ready," I said.

Nate snorted. "There's no getting ready for Lucifer. He could kill with a blink of his eyes."

"I meant the castle." I hadn't, but it made me sound like I knew what I was saying. Ignoring Nate's obnoxious snort, I glanced at Felnick. "Speak with Gregory. Let him, and only him for now, know who will be coming and how many he's bringing with him."

He bowed, saying, "Yes, my queen." Then he rushed out the door, closing it behind him.

"Have any of you dealt with Lucifer before?"

"Never," Thorn said.

Alex shook his head.

Asher glanced at Nate, who sighed. "Neither of us have met him personally, but we've heard stories about him."

"Like what?" I asked, pulling out the chair at my desk and sitting in it. Alex took a chair opposite me. Nate leaned against the wall, crossing his arms over his chest. When Thorn sat on the corner of my desk, my eyes didn't stray from his butt… only it wasn't the time to admire or want to see it naked. Asher moved around my desk and sat in the chair beside Alex. His knowing look said I'd been caught checking out Thorn. Even Alex was blushing and smiling slightly. Nate rolled his eyes at me, but I caught his lips twitching. However, he thinned them and gave me a pointed look.

Right. It wasn't the time.

Just as my eyes strayed toward Thorn's rump, Nate sighed. I swung my gaze back to him as he started speaking. "We've heard tales of Lucifer never wanting to venture far from the underworld, yet he's willing to because he wants to meet you. We know he's a hard ruler, but like in all domains, people like to test things. He's ruthless, a womanizer, and you wouldn't want to be on his bad side."

Asher added, "He's feared by many. Even the council."

"Do you think he was the one who sent the demons after me in the first place?"

Thorn shook his head. "We can't be certain, but it's something we need to consider, especially with him coming here."

His cell phone rang. He quickly answered while I asked, "But wouldn't he have authority over all of them? So, it has to be him."

"There are millions of demons," Asher said, and I shuddered at the thought, "and being so many, there are ones who will do as they please. Lucifer is one man, after all. He can't keep an eye on everything. Demons are corrupt beings; they would do anything to gain power. So many seek more power to try and overthrow Lucifer."

"It would be good to believe Satan can be an ally," Alex murmured.

"There's nothing we can do about it now," Thorn said, ending the call he'd been on. "All we can do is wait. We have other matters to deal with for now."

I hated when he was right. "Selma. No one's found her yet?"

Thorn shook his head, his lips pressing into a thin line of worry. "That call was from my brethren. Unfortunately, she's disappeared."

"But can they tell if she's left the community altogether?" I asked.

His brows dipped, and I already knew it was more bad news. "They followed her trail. She's out of our area."

Dammit. I wanted a different answer.

Selma, a vampire who looked all of sixteen but was probably thousands of years old, had been on the Barrett-Odin bandwagon and, like them, hadn't wanted change to happen within the community. Somehow she'd escaped. Perhaps she'd been smart enough to know they would give her up, so she'd gone into hiding before I could get my hands on her. I had no doubt her involvement meant she played a big part in the attack on Ezra.

And all because they didn't want people to love who they wanted and, of course, they didn't approve that my mates were not of my own kind. They looked down on shifters especially, thought of them as lowly beings. It came as no surprise that they despised me making a shifter my adviser or how I intended to let different races work together.

They were old, I was new, and the change had to happen.

I wasn't the only one who thought my decision would be for the better.

Alma, the former queen's seer, and now mine, had seen how my bringing in these changes would better our community. I believed it also.

Of course, not a day went by that I didn't freak out about being thrust into the role of queen.

Even right then I felt like a fraud.

I would have given so much to be back in my small apartment with Ezra at my side. I'd work, see my family, hunt... all with Ezra.

But then I wouldn't have my men.

I wouldn't have bossy and scary Asher, my vampire. Angry

and annoying Nate, my shifter. Sweet and smart Alex, my mage. Cunning and fierce Thorn, my ghoul.

My life wouldn't have been complete without them in it.

Even when loss still stung me.

Love rolled over me, causing my fears and worries to recede inside me. I glanced up to Thorn as he stood from the desk and walked my way. When I scooted my chair back, he took my hand and dragged me up, wrapping his arms around my shoulders.

"Things will get easier," he promised.

Hands touched my waist, and a chest pressed into my back. Asher. "Eventually, you'll be too bored with nothing happening."

Resting my head on Thorn's shoulder, I shook it. "I doubt I could ever be bored." I couldn't ever be, not when I had my mates. They grounded me. I glanced at my glowering Nate and to my softly smiling Alex.

"She gets into too much trouble for things to be easy," Nate commented.

I shot him the middle finger.

CHAPTER TWENTY-THREE

THORN

It had been a few days since we'd found out Lucifer would be paying us a visit, and in that time, Paige's moods had been depleting. My gaze didn't stray from her as she sat reading on the couch with papers scattered around her. They were appeals from the people in the community. I'd told her we could all go through them, but she'd said she needed a distraction.

I understood she'd cared for her hellhound deeply, but I hadn't understood how strong their connection had been. Even though she had her emotions locked, there was still a tiny amount of heartache that seeped through. I hated to see her sad, but there wasn't a thing I could do. Maybe Asher and I had been right when we'd discussed Ezra being more than just a hellhound. The way he'd been with Paige was different from any other hellhound we'd previously encountered. Usually they were crazed beasts doing their master's bidding by destroying or killing. Ezra had expressions, had character, and I was pretty damn sure he'd had a soul.

He'd been different.

I glanced over Paige's head to see Asher at the desk going through his own work, but his attention was on Paige. He was worried about her as much as I was.

There was an abrupt knock on the door before it opened and Nate strode in, leaving the door ajar for two women—one a ghoul, the other human—and a shifter male to roll in trays of refreshments. Alex entered after them. Paige looked up as they bowed. "My queen."

She offered them a smile that didn't reach her eyes. She saved those for us when we were all alone, but it also seemed we were the only ones who got her to fully smile, as well as her family.

"Thank you," she said.

Asher stood and came around the desk. It was bad timing because he got close to one of the women and she smiled up at him with adoration while moving around the cart and happened to brush against him.

Power filled the room. I snapped my eyes to Paige as she jumped up, crouching on the couch. Her eyes changed, her claws grew, and a snarl dripped from between her lips. "Mine."

Her hands went to the back of the couch, and I could read her purpose—she was about to attack the woman. I flew out of my chair just as Nate raced at Paige. We circled her, holding her, yet with her power, she managed to take a few steps toward the screaming woman.

"Alex, get them out," Nate yelled. Alex's eyes bled to purple, and more power filled the room. A bubble popped up around the women and man, and slowly they floated out of the room. Asher flashed in front of Paige while Alex followed the floating people out.

"Clear their minds," Nate called.

"I know," Alex snapped.

Asher took the struggling Paige's face in his hands and forced her gaze to latch on to his glowing green vampire eyes.

"Paige, my love. Focus on me." His voice threaded softly through the room. He ignored her growls and leaned in to press his lips against the corner of her mouth but moved back quickly to avoid her sharp teeth.

"She needs to feed," I told them.

"She was about to eat," Nate said.

"No. She needs flesh. Fucking hell, I should have known earlier."

"Not your fault. Too much has been happening," Asher said.

"We need to clear her mind enough to get her into the kitchens," I ordered.

"Why can't we just call up for food?" Nate asked.

Asher shook his head. "It's the easy way out. She will hate what's happened, even feel weak and worthless for it. She needs to see how strong she can be. All she needs is a distraction to bring her back to us." With that said, he stuck his hand into her pants. Her growls paused. She hissed and then froze. Slowly her power eased, her claws retracting, as did her teeth. Lastly, her eyes swirled back to dark blue.

Nate snorted. He released his hold to cross his arms over his chest and seemed annoyed, but I noticed his eyes hadn't moved away from Asher's fingers teasing her under her clothes.

"Asher," she moaned.

"There you are, my love." He withdrew his fingers. She whimpered in protest before her face burned with the realization of her actions.

"I would have killed her," she whispered.

"Let's get you some food," I said and started to lead her to the door. When I glanced back, I caught Asher licking his fingers. Nate watched him, his eyes darker than usual.

"We'll catch up," Asher said. "I'm hungry myself, and Alex should be in soon."

The door opened and Alex stepped through. Paige wasn't fully with it, or she would have wanted to stay around to watch Asher feed. However, she kept my pace to the door, mumbling about being the worst queen ever.

Alex looked at us with concern. "I've got her," I reassured him. "Meet us in the kitchens."

He gave me a sad smile and nodded. As he started to shut the door after us, I heard, "You feed off me," Nate stated. "Not him today."

My lips tipped up. Nate was certainly more possessive of Alex since his wolf had claimed him—something Paige didn't know about yet. But Asher and I could read the signs clearly the day after it had happened.

I curled my arm tighter around Paige's waist as we made our way down the stairs. She grumbled under her breath some more.

"It's not your fault, Paige," I whispered into her ear.

She huffed. "I would have killed her, Thorn."

"We had you, sweetheart."

She nodded. Yet, since she'd opened her emotions probably unintentionally from her hunger, I could still feel her disgust and fear.

"We just need to make sure you feed more regularly." If anything, I felt guilty for not seeing it sooner. Our queen was starved, but she hadn't realized it.

"Just… hold me tighter. I wish the others had come as well."

"You don't trust I can handle you?" I teased, not letting my pride be wounded as I knew she was still scared.

"That's not it—"

I kissed her temple. "I know, sweetheart," I told her as we entered the deserted kitchens. The thing was, I knew she would hold herself together because of her people that lingered in the halls as we made our way to the kitchens. She hungered, but she forced it down, knowing her pains would settle shortly. "See, you made it. You're strong, Paige."

She laughed without humor. "If Asher hadn't stuck his hand in my pants, I would still be a growling psycho ready to kill things."

"Yet, you pulled it back in, walked out of there, made it downstairs and into the kitchens while people moved around, and kept your hunger from surfacing again. Sit here, sweetheart." I pulled out a chair at the counter and kissed her neck. "The hunger didn't win. You did. If she hadn't have gotten close to Asher, nothing would have happened."

She watched me as I headed to the walk-in meat refrigerator, that contained the freshest meals, beside the huge freezer and asked, "I thought my possessiveness would settle once the bond was completed."

I paused outside the door and glanced back. "I think it had something to do with being hungry and stressed, sweetheart."

"I'll need to be on top of it then since my new job is very stressful."

"That, and I'm sure your mates can help you stress less." I

winked and opened the door, but I didn't miss the smile, a real one, coming over Paige. I loved seeing her smile, especially when I felt her love shining through the devastation and worry. I grabbed some meat off the hook and took it back out to Paige, glad to see her still in a lighter mood. I hoped, with the help of some food, she might get some sleep.

As I cut off some human flesh and placed it in bowls, I asked, "How's Eric liking his job?"

She laughed, her eyes never straying from the bowl. "I never knew how much of a nerd he is. He's having the time of his life taking over the role of investment manager." She grinned warmly. "Thank you for helping him find it."

"My pleasure," I said, pushing the bowl and fork her way. On the first mouthful, she moaned in the back of her throat, and my cock thickened. To distract myself, I took my own forkful, only I should have looked away from Paige to be distracted because she was too seductive. Her eyes had fluttered closed. She licked her lips after each bite, and she moved around in her seat like she was riding a dick.

My cock throbbed. I'd wanted to be inside her since the last time. Even a couple of times a day, but after everything that had happened, I hadn't made a move in that area. She'd been grieving, and I would have been the biggest jerk if I'd started something.

Closing my eyes, I clenched my jaw and scolded myself. My poor mate was starving, and all I could do was think about sliding into her. How wet, soft, tight and inviting she would be.

"Thorn," Paige called softly. I opened my eyes to her. "Would it be wrong if you fucked me on the countertop where people made their meals?"

My fork clattered to the floor, and just as I made a move

around the bench, the door to the kitchen opened. Michael and his very pregnant wife, Leona, walked in, laughing about something. They froze and slammed their mouths closed when they spotted us.

All desire in the room fell away.

"It's all right. Come in," I offered with a smile and a wave.

Paige shoved the last of the meat into her mouth, making her look like a chipmunk with how big her cheeks were as she chewed wildly while the couple slowly made their way over to us.

Was she ashamed of what she was or just what she ate?

It was something I would ask when it was just the two of us. Then I'd reassure her it was natural and no one in our community cared. If they did, they wouldn't have followed the former queen in the first place.

I moved in beside Paige and wound an arm around her waist. She shivered at my touch, which caused me to smile.

Once they were close enough, they bowed, Michael helping his wife bend. "My queen," they said together. Paige shook her head and stepped up to them. She reached out and assisted Leona to stand. Only the woman was so shocked by it she gasped, her knees wobbled, and Michael had to pick her up in his arms.

Paige rushed over and grabbed a chair. "Here, sit her here."

Michael helped Leona into it, but all Leona could do was stare up at Paige in awe. Paige smiled down at her, asking, "How's everything going?"

Leona opened her mouth, then snapped it closed before she made a noise. Michael chuckled while I watched on with a grin. Finally, Michael came to his wife's rescue and said, "We must thank you again, Your Majesty, for the doctor and for allowing us to stay within the castle walls."

"It's not a problem. I like to have my advisers close, so thank you for moving in."

Leona cleared her throat, then whispered, "It's been many, many decades since shifters were seen as more than dirt under *others'* shoes. There's never enough thank-yous we could give for the things you've done."

Paige shrugged. "I can't understand how that happened, why shifters were seen as lesser beings to the rest of the supernatural community. But I'm glad I can be a part of helping others to see shifters are important as well. Even if it's within these walls."

"For now," I added.

Paige smiled over at me before glancing back down at Leona. Paige's hand fluttered out toward the horse shifter. "Is everything all right with the baby?"

Paige's features softened even more. I'd seen her with her niece and nephew, she loved children, and it had me wondering if there would ever be a time or a way she could eventually have her own. As far as I knew, even with her queen power, she'd be unable to get pregnant. The knowledge saddened me because she would be a great mother.

However, the former queen had only ever been with her own species, and ghouls were infertile, much like vampires. But our queen, our mate, had a shifter and a mage whose bodies were alive. Could it happen then? I enjoyed the thought of Paige pregnant too much. We were her family; we all would care for any child as our own, no matter its race. It was something I needed to find out.

"Yes, she's happy and healthy. Ready to see the world any

day now," Michael said proudly. Leona smiled up at him warmly while rubbing her belly. "We came down for a snack since it seems Little Miss is in need of chocolate cake."

Paige laughed lightly. "Chocolate cake sounds good to me."

"I'll see if I can find any," I told her.

"Thank you," she replied. Just as she was about to look my way, Leona took her hand. Paige's gaze snapped back down to her as Leona placed their hands over her belly. Paige melted. I'd never seen that look on her face or the one where it brightened blissfully as she giggled out, "She kicked."

Yes, I had to find out if our queen could have children. I knew it wasn't the time for it yet, but I prayed that things would eventually settle.

CHAPTER TWENTY-FOUR

"You feed off me. Not him today," Nate stated as the door to the office closed after Thorn took Paige out. I knew Thorn would be able to help Paige in the way she needed. There would also be guards following their every move, so I stayed back and arched my brow at Nate.

"Nate," Alex scolded. "I can help Asher out."

"No," he snarled. He strode right up to me, tilted his head to the side, and ordered, "Fucking eat." I glanced over at Alex, who looked irritated, his nostrils flaring, yet his eyes told me he found the protectiveness sweet.

I glanced back down to Nate's neck, the pulse ticking away under the skin. He'd never offered me his blood before. Was he only doing it now so I wouldn't get close to Alex? Had his wolf truly claimed Alex as a mate?

"We should talk about this."

He grabbed my arms, tugged me closer, and barked, "Another day. Just eat and hurry the fuck up before—"

My fangs dropped just before I embedded them into Nate's neck. On the first pull of his blood, as it touched my tongue, I moaned around the rich, earthy, yet tangy taste. Nate held me tighter, and his warm breath fanned over my shoulder and onto my skin where my shirt folded open. When his hands dropped to my hips, I placed a hand on the opposite side of Nate's neck and the other at his waist, dragging him close so he was flush against me. Nate's wolf woke, and he growled. His hands on my hips squeezed painfully. The wolf was uncertain about me taking his blood, and his damn mouth was close to my throat; he could easily rip it out. I needed to stop feeding, but I enjoyed his taste too much. Just like it had been hard for me to stop feeding from Alex for the first time.

Another growl rumbled out of him. I opened my eyes as they bled to green and saw Alex stepping up behind Nate.

"It's all right. You're all right," he cooed into Nate's shoulder, the same side as I drank from so our eyes held each other's. I felt Alex's hands on Nate's sides as they ran up and down gently, softly, reassuringly. "You're fine," he whispered and kissed Nate's shoulder.

Since I held Nate close, I felt the first stir of his cock thickening.

Christ.

My own dick responded. After another hard pull of his blood, where I savored his taste, I withdrew my fangs and straightened. Stepping back, I watched as Nate lifted his head. His nostrils flared. A moment later, he gripped Alex's hand at his side and dragged it around to his front, then down to run over his length behind his jeans.

Fuck.

I'd been with many men and women. Though, it had been many years since I'd desired for two men together. Until then. Witnessing Nate's dark gaze and Alex's heated one had me wanting to see them naked together. Where I may even join in on the fun. I hadn't been turned on in so long, except for the first night with Paige. She could draw my cock hard in an instant. It seemed watching my two brothers-in-arms touch each other could also have my cock rock-hard as well.

Never would I have thought I'd see this or feel it.

"Leave, Asher," Nate bit out.

"No," I clipped back quickly just as Alex undid the button to Nate's jeans and slowly lowered his zip.

Then the door burst open, and in it stood Gregory, blood dripping from his forehead. "Help, please."

Nate did his jeans up, and we all faced Gregory. "What happened?" I demanded.

He stumbled in. "Please, come with me. Help. Please."

Alex was the first to move toward him. "Tell us on the way," he said. Gregory nodded. He was out the door, running in seconds. Alex followed. I glanced at Nate, whose jaw was clenched before he took off after his claimed mate. I raced after them.

Nate and I caught up easily and heard, "The pack found us. He was going to leave for me, come here, but they won't let him. He got me away before they got him."

"Who?"

"My mate. My love. Jessup."

Nate stumbled. "Jessup? But he's the alpha of the wolf pack.

He has a mate. They have that fuckhead of a son. How is he your mate?"

Gregory shook his head. "The woman is the female alpha who joined with Jessup, but they aren't mates. Hers died. Jessup's brother. They came together to conceive, and that was it. He's mine. I'm his. No one knew until now. I messed up…. I shouldn't have gone there and pushed him; they don't accept it. They'll kill him."

When we'd first arrived, we'd had an altercation with the local wolf pack. Nate had accepted the challenge to fight Fenris, Jessup's son, to claim Paige. If he hadn't, Fenris was willing to fight anyone to prove he had the strength to stand at Paige's side and rule the people.

He was a bad seed, and Nate had even told me Fenris's own parents warned that if Fenris won, it wouldn't be good. So it wasn't hard to guess who would be behind the attack on the alpha when they found him with a man for a mate.

"You might have to move up the challenge," I told Nate.

"With fucking pleasure, but I'm not becoming their alpha," he replied as we ran by the kitchens. Paige stepped out. "Fuck," Nate cursed.

"What's going on?" she called, her eyes wide in alarm.

"Keep going. I'll be there shortly," I informed Nate. I wound back to Paige and Thorn. Four guards stood back from them. "Jessup, the wolf alpha, is in trouble. We're—"

"Let's go," Paige said and took off after Nate and the others.

"Christ," I clipped. "Stay close to her," I ordered the guards, and they followed Paige quickly. I looked at Thorn. "Nate may have to challenge Fenris early. If she's there for it…"

"It could be a shitstorm," he finished. We both rushed out the doors. The people who were still awake watched as we flew by them. "Is Alex there? He might be able to put her in a bubble like before," Thorn suggested.

I nodded. "It's an idea." And probably the best one, because if the challenge went ahead and Paige saw Nate in trouble, she could break all the laws of the challenge and probably break a few extra bones along the way. "Although, we may have to watch Alex too."

Understanding dawned on Thorn's face. "That's true. Let's see how it goes. I might call in more guards."

"Could be good."

Thorn and I stopped behind Paige in the woods just as she asked, "Gregory, what are you doing here?" She gasped when he faced her. "You're bleeding? Why are you bleeding? Who do I need to hurt? *No one* makes you bleed. You feed me, take care of us, make our beds."

Jesus. The things that came out of her mouth could have me bursting with laughter, but it wasn't the moment to do so.

"I'm fine, my queen, but it's Jessup who is not."

"How? Why? And how do you know?"

Gregory glanced from Alex to Nate and then me. I shook my head and said, "She doesn't know yet."

He bowed his head and met Paige's gaze. "I've only recently discovered Jessup is my mate. The pack as a whole doesn't know. But a few have discovered the truth, and a few don't approve. He wanted to keep me safe until he could change things…. N-Now they're making him pay for being with a man. He got me away, but he needs help."

Paige opened her mouth, but Nate spoke first. "Jessup isn't mated to the woman. They're the alpha couple, but she was mated to his brother. They only came together to have a kid."

Paige nodded, then clapped her hands and said, "Right, let's go save Jessup and kick some bigotry ass while we're at it." She started forward until Alex grabbed her arm gently.

She glanced at him, and he told her, "I'm sorry, Paige. I do enjoy seeing you kick ass"—a few of the guards chuckled—"but Nate will have to take point on this mission. It's a wolf pack we're dealing with, and Nate being, well, a wolf, he'll be better at sorting it."

She nodded and curled her arms around Alex's waist. Of course, he blushed, gazing down at her like she was the treasured prize she was. "You're right." She stepped back and took his hand. "I'll hold myself back."

Nate snorted. "I'll believe it when I see it."

She glared over at him. "You say shit like that and I won't." She glanced at her guards. "Sorry, I'm not acting very queen-like."

They bowed, and one said, "You be whomever you wish when you want, and we will follow you, my queen."

Tenderness bloomed inside of her and shone out. I knew Thorn would be feeling the same. "Thank you." She smiled.

"Please, my queen, may we move forward?" Gregory asked. Fear had his body twitching.

"Of course. Lead the way, Nate."

Nate grunted and took point. I followed behind him to his left and Thorn to his right. Gregory stepped up behind us, then Paige and Alex, swinging their joined hands. After them, the guards joined the line. Only one had his eyes on my mate's ass. When I let out a hiss, all eyes shot to me, and when the guard saw I was directing my glowing eyes on him, he blanched. There was his one chance. If I caught him ogling her again, I would make him pay in pain. He nodded as if reading my thoughts. Good.

Turning back around, we rushed through another couple of miles before we stepped into a clearing that held at least thirty cabins scattered here and there. I hadn't understood why the wolf shifters kept to themselves in this area when all the other shifters lived in the village behind the castle. That was until Thorn had explained that the former queen allowed the wolves their own area because of their large group, as long as they swore their allegiance to her.

Passing a few cabins, we entered the open space where we found Jessup strung up by his arms to a pole in the middle.

Gregory cried out. He made a run for Jessup, but Paige grabbed him and held him close. "Not yet," she said. "It's all right," she added, patting his back.

Upon Gregory's cry, Jessup slowly pulled his head up. There wasn't a part of his face that didn't look cracked, bruised, or bloodied.

He was alpha, the strongest of them all... how had this happened?

My answer came when five shifters, in their human form, stepped out from between the cabins. The one at the front was Fenris.

"You dare come onto pack land without an invite?" Fenris snarled, his upper lip raised.

Nate stepped forward. "We had concerns for the alpha. We came to help. No invitation needed."

"I'm alpha now." His gaze flicked to Paige, and he licked his lips. "And soon to be king by your side. We'll rule well together."

Paige opened her mouth to respond, but I caught Alex tightening his hold on her waist and she snapped her mouth closed. Instead, she just glared Fenris's way.

"Do not fucking look at her," Nate growled.

Fenris tensed. "Do not fucking come on my lands and talk to me that way. I'm alpha here. I'll deal with you in the challenge."

"How did you become alpha?" Nate nodded to Jessup, who's head had dropped back down, but his eyes stayed half open and on the ground while he listened. "Jessup isn't dead, or did he step down?" Nate questioned.

Fenris spat to the side. "He's filth. He's no alpha."

"So he stepped down?"

Fenris's jaw clenched.

"They were going to kill him in the morning" came a voice. The alpha female stepped out.

"Mom, get the fuck inside," Fenris clipped.

"Don't you 'Mom' me, boy. You disgrace our ways. You do this to your father—"

"He's no father of mine," he roared.

She shook her head. "You disappoint me. Disappoint the pack. There was no fair fight. You all took Jessup to the ground when you caught him and beat him senseless, then strung him up to make anyone too scared to go against you and your ways." Her eyes moved to Paige. "Times are changing."

"Not in this pack," Fenris yelled. "Fine, you want a fair fight? Release him and I'll rip his throat out."

She laughed humorlessly. "You would fight a man in his condition? Pathetic."

"Have care, Mother," he warned. Other shifters, some in their wolf form, some human, emerged from inside the cabins.

"Or what? You'll fight me? You'll beat me? Because you want power, you want to be alpha and have the pack fear you instead of leading it with love, happiness, and an iron fist? When has Jessup steered the pack wrong? He hasn't been challenged in decades."

"He steers us wrong by fucking that piece of shit over there," he screamed. "He's not pack. He's not wolf. Not even a fucking shifter."

The alpha woman shook her head. Fenris glared at the obvious disappointment in her eyes. "Times are changing. We need to keep up with them."

"We don't and we won't." Fenris threw out a hand toward Jessup. "Take him down. We fight for the alpha position."

Nate took another step forward. "On behalf of Jessup Falk, I'll fight for his right as alpha. I'll also be completing the challenge, set for the full moon in a couple of days, tonight."

"No!" Paige cried out just as Fenris smiled wickedly.

"Accepted." Fenris laughed.

CHAPTER TWENTY-FIVE

*P*anic gripped my chest. I started forward but was grabbed quickly. I fought their hold, not even knowing who held me. All I could see was Nate stepping closer into the circle as he removed his T-shirt. "Nate, no, you can't do this," I told him, my throat thick with tension.

"Paige, stop. He has to," Thorn said into my ear.

"No, he doesn't." I shook my head again and again. "No, I won't allow it."

Fenris let out a belly laugh. "Hear that, mutt? She won't allow it. You gonna stop to please your pussy?"

"Shut the fuck up. We doing this or not?"

"Not," I yelled. They ignored me.

Nate nodded, and I wanted to reach out to him to smack him upside the head or pick him up and run for the hills to protect him. I knew I couldn't, and I hated it. Wolves were proud creatures who lived by their own set of rules. If I interfered, it could mean bad things for not only us, but Jessup, Gregory, and Jessup's pack. I had to think about others rather than just me and my feelings. Still, knowing Nate was about to fight and could possibly be hurt, killed me inside. I gripped Thorn's arms around my waist and whimpered.

"He'll be fine," he whispered.

"He's strong," Alex said quietly from our side. Even though he was trying to reassure me, Alex looked like he'd swallowed something foul. He disliked what was about to happen as much as I did. I took his hand in mine again and brought it up to hold it against my chest.

"Skin or fur? I'll let you pick since I'll kill you in either form." Fenris grinned evilly.

"Skin," Nate replied. "But if the shift comes over either of us, there won't be any repercussions."

"Agreed," Fenris answered, then charged Nate, who braced.

Fenris hit Nate in the face so hard Nate's head whipped to the side. I slapped a hand over my mouth to keep the scream building at bay, not wanting to distract him. Alex's hand in mine squeezed harder, while Thorn held me tighter. Out of the corner of my eye, I saw Asher step up to Alex and place his hand on his shoulder. To my surprise, Nate grinned, only it wasn't a nice one. Fenris's cocky smile disappeared when Nate slowly turned his head back to face him.

Fenris went to hit him again, but Nate grabbed Fenris's fist in one hand and used the other to punch him in the gut. Fenris stumbled back, barely catching himself from falling, and snarled at Nate. Fenris bounced from one foot to another, his hand cocked in front of him like some type of boxer. Using his fingers, he called Nate forward, only Nate didn't move. He stood there and crossed his arms over his chest.

"Fight," Fenris roared.

Nate raised a brow.

"Fight me," Fenris yelled.

Nate relaxed his arms at his sides and took a step forward. Fenris charged again, jabbing his fist to the left, but Nate gracefully moved back. Fenris jabbed to the right, and Nate twirled out of the way.

I wanted to race in there, grab Nate's shoulders, and shake the shit out of him. He needed to end this fight before my nerves ate at my beating organ.

Fenris swept out his leg, kicking Nate in the thigh before bouncing back. He spun back in, grabbed Nate on the back of the neck, and kneed him in the stomach before moving out of reach. Another smile splayed across Fenris's face. He was sure of himself now that he'd gotten a couple of shots in.

"Nate, stop dragging this out," Asher called.

Fenris's smile vanished. He straightened, glancing from Asher to Nate. It was then Nate snapped out his leg, kicking Fenris in the chest, sending him flying backward and landing with a thud on the ground. Growling low, he rolled onto all fours and, still in human form, charged Nate.

Nate braced again, and as soon as Fenris was close, Nate jumped, flipping in the air and landing on Fenris's back. His knees dug into Fenris's spine, his arm locking around Fenris's neck, squeezing. Fenris dropped to the ground, skidding along the dirt, scraping his skin, which would heal easily.

"Do you yield?" Nate offered, his voice rough and thick.

"No," Fenris rasped. He rolled, flipping Nate off, and jumped to his feet as Nate did. With a nod, two other shifters stepped up behind Nate and grabbed his arms.

"Foul play," I yelled. Dropping Alex's hand, I forced Thorn's arms off me and started toward them, ready to help.

In seconds, the coward Fenris punched, kicked, and then extended his claws, slashing at Nate's chest and stomach.

"Paige," Alex clipped in a vicious tone, one I hadn't heard from him, so it had me looking back. "I have this," he told me. His jaw clenched, his eyes glowed purple, and his hands and mouth moved. My clit pulsed, but I told it to get lost. I glanced back to Nate in time to see the shifters holding him stiffen.

Their arms fell away. Fenris cursed them but realized something was happening when their eyes widened. They let out a howl of pain right before we all heard their spines snapping in two and they tumbled to the ground.

Holy shit.

Nate lifted his head as his chest rose and fell rapidly. He was bloody and sore, but the smart-ass prick winked at me before shifting his gaze to Alex. I turned, and I'd never seen Alex look so scary before. His pulsating power had his hair sticking up everywhere, swaying in the invisible breeze only around him. His body was tense, his hands fisted at his sides, and his eyes were glowing brighter. He nodded once at Nate. I didn't catch what Nate did, but it had Alex relaxing, his power subsiding.

A harsh snarl had me facing Nate again. He'd shifted to his wolf form. His jeans shredded, falling to the floor. Fenris followed and changed into his wolf. Where Nate was a dark brown, Fenris was a light amber color.

They circled each other, growling. Fenris jumped forward, nipping at Nate, but Nate was too fast and bounced back, only to jump forward and snap his jaw at Fenris's side. Fenris let out a scared noise and tumbled back, popping back up onto his paws. They circled each other again, snarling.

Other wolves around the circle scraped with claws into the dirt, growling, wanting to join the fight, but stayed back.

I caught the alpha female stepping up to Jessup's side, and with the help of Gregory, who somehow made his way over, they helped him down from the pole. Were they readying him to escape if something happened?

Fenris bound forward, snapping his teeth at Nate's side. Nate shuffled quickly to the left, curling his head into Fenris and latching onto his ear, ripping it from his body. Fenris howled, leaving his neck unprotected. Nate clamped his massive jaw onto it and bit down. Fenris growled and whimpered, and when he rolled to the side, Nate held on, using his large paws to hold Fenris to the ground while he tore into Fenris's neck, ripping fur, skin, and muscles out.

As Fenris took his last breath, a howl started up around us.

The noise cut off when Nate moved off Fenris's dead body. He shifted back to his human body, crouching. When he straightened, naked, he used the back of his arm to wipe at his mouth. Not caring about his nudity, he turned around, gazing at each shifter.

"Anyone else want to challenge me?"

Not a sound was made.

I heard Alex click his fingers, and the blood on Nate disappeared. There were still scrapes and bruises, which would heal, but he looked better. Nate was also dressed in jeans once more. It seemed Alex was as jealous as I was, noticing the female shifters eyeing Nate. I liked I wasn't the only one worrying or being possessive of the men. I'd gladly have Alex's help, and I enjoyed, a lot, knowing there was something going on with the both of them. It made me hope all of my bonded mates would have the same type of connection with each other. I also had to admit, it turned me on and had me thinking I would very much like to see them together.

I caught Nate smirk at Alex before he looked toward Jessup, who stood with the assistance of the female alpha and Gregory.

"The pack is still yours," he said.

Jessup nodded. "The Falk pack appreciates the assistance. We'd also like to extend an offer to you to join our pack and become our beta."

My heart faltered.

Would he accept?

Did he miss being in a pack surrounded by his own kind?

Hands on my shoulders had me jolting. Alex's scent and heat touched me next as he molded his front to my back. Together, we stood there waiting for Nate's reply. Both anxious.

Nate glanced back to us, his eyes moved to Asher and even Thorn, then back to Alex and me. He faced Jessup again. "Thank you for the generous offer, but I already have my own pack."

My body relaxed into Alex, and I felt his muscles loosen as he slid his arms around my chest. He kissed the side of my head.

Jessup smiled. "I can see that."

"Why don't you all come in for a coffee?" the alpha female asked.

Coffee? Right now? What I wanted was to take my mates back to the castle, yell at Nate a little, and then have them surround me in bed, so I knew they were okay. I wanted them, all of them, to rest with me. I hadn't had them all in the same bed by myself. Usually it had been just Asher and Thorn together or by themselves. But I needed Alex and Nate to join us that night.

"It would be so they could talk privately about things," Alex said into my ear.

Nate glanced to me. I nodded.

"Lead the way," Nate told her. We slowly followed Jessup and her up to the biggest cabin.

"Please wait on the porch," I said to the guards.

They bowed, and one replied, "Yes, my queen."

When I walked in, with Alex at my side, the others were already seated around a living room, except for the alpha female. I could hear clattering in the kitchen. I pecked Alex on the cheek and made my way in there to help her.

"Can I help?" I asked in the doorway.

She glanced over her shoulder, her brows rising. "I didn't think the queen would lower herself to—"

"You don't know this queen. I still pick up my own laundry."

She turned back around, but I didn't miss her smile. "Amelie," she offered.

I walked over and helped with some mugs of coffee, since I knew how my guys took their drinks. "Hi, Amelie, I'm Paige."

"It would have been good to meet you properly under different circumstances."

"I agree, and I'm sorry for… your loss." After all, Fenris was her son.

She frowned. "I can't say it was a loss."

Well, okay then. "Should we get these into the room?"

"Yes. They'll be waiting on us."

She was right. As we entered, the room was quiet. I squeezed through the gap between the couches that were in a L-shape looking toward the wall where a large TV was fixed above a fireplace. I put the tray down on the coffee table and then handed out the drinks to my men before taking my own and sitting between Asher and Nate. Thorn and Alex stood behind the couch we were on while Jessup, Gregory, and Amelie were opposite us on their own couch.

The cabin felt warm and homey, especially with the knitted blankets flung over the back of each couch.

"Do you have someone else who can step up as beta?" Nate asked. His leg bounced up and down. He seemed on edge, but I had a feeling it had to do with the overflowing adrenaline from the fight.

"Yes, there are a few candidates." Jessup glanced at Amelie. When she nodded, he looked back to Nate. "The former queen allowed us onto her property because she trusted us to keep an eye on the outer regions. It gave our pack something to do, a purpose. There are many packs that would step into the role quickly if they knew about this community. We want to make sure the Falk pack is imbedded at the queen's side if the community grows."

Meaning, they wanted to stay in the position they were in and didn't want me to allow other packs to take their role if more were to flock to our area.

Why wasn't he asking me, though? Why wasn't he looking at me? Was it some wolf thing?

"You said our queen had to prove herself in the role before you followed her. Has she? Would you be faithful to her and her own?" Asher asked. "We won't risk our mate for anything."

Amelie stood. "With the changes she's already made and assisting us because one of her own asked for help, it has proven Paige Alice is more queen than the one before. She is humble, smart, fierce, and a woman who would fight for not only hers but others to make sure everyone is treated the same. We would follow, stand by, protect, and risk our own lives to make sure she is safe." She bowed. Jessup, with Gregory's help, stood and bowed as well.

"Thank you," I said, my voice soft. My cheeks heated. They saw me in a light I would never see myself in. I appreciated their kind words. "I would love to have the Falk pack at my side." Amelia and Jessup straightened, both smiling until I added, "However, I have a question."

They froze. "Yes?" Jessup said.

"Will Gregory be safe here? Will the pack care you're mated to a ghoul who's a man?"

Gregory's eyes filled with tears. "Thank you for caring, my queen."

"I will always care about my people." I smiled warmly.

Jessup took Gregory's hand. I looked to him as he said, "I'll make sure Gregory is safe here. Fenris was the leader of the few who hated same-sex matings and other races mixing."

"With him gone, we'll have things back in order," Amelie said.

Jessup nodded. "We will."

"My queen," Gregory called. "I would still like to work in the castle, if you'll allow it?"

"Of course, Gregory. I'd be lost without you." I smiled. While his grin was back, it was wobbly and soft.

Nate suddenly stood. "Now that's settled, we're going," he stated roughly.

Jessup and Amelie shared a look, one full of knowing. Jessup chuckled. "Of course, I'm surprised you handled it this long."

"Handled what?" I asked, also standing.

"Nothing," Nate clipped.

"Nate." I glared. "I thought you'd be in a better mood since winning out there, but it doesn't seem like it." It was then I punched him in the stomach.

"What the fuck?" he yelled.

"That's for scaring me, you asshole."

"Are they always like this?" I heard Jessup ask.

"Yes," Alex, Thorn, and Asher replied together.

"I had it handled," Nate seethed through clenched teeth in my face.

"I know that now," I yelled, "but I freaked out at the time. Do you know how hard it was to stand back and watch?"

"Yes," he hissed. "It's about as hard as it is watching you risk your life."

I jerked my head back. All right, he had a point. "Hmm, well, okay. But tell me what you need to handle now."

Nate scrubbed a hand over his face while others laughed around us. Nate sighed. His hands landed on my arms, and I was pushed back into Asher. He then walked around the couch, got near Alex, bent and flung Alex over his shoulder and slapped his ass. Alex cried out in surprise.

"Bring her," Nate clipped.

"What's going on?" I demanded.

"Wolves like to fuck after a fight," Amelie stated with humor in her voice.

My mouth dropped open. Nate glowered over at me. "You wanted to watch, right?"

I was sure the biggest smile I'd ever had covered my mouth. I jumped at Asher. Thankfully he caught me in bridal style. "Let's go!"

CHAPTER TWENTY-SIX

NATE

Alex didn't complain as I raced through the woods back to the castle with him over my shoulder. Asher, with Paige in his arms, who giggled like a maniac, and Thorn, kept to my pace. Alex gripped my waist and held on. He didn't say anything until we got close to the opened area.

"You need to put me down."

"What the fuck for?" I demanded. I didn't want him away from me; he was the only one I'd claimed, the only one I knew who was willing to let me fuck them the way I wanted—rough and hard—so I wasn't letting him from my reach.

He smacked my ass. "People will see. It's bad enough the guards and wolves did. We can't have the people know… know about, ah… you know." I just knew he'd be blushing beet red.

Was he worried about himself or me?

"If you don't—"

"No, I don't care, but we should put up a pretense—"

"Alex," Paige called. With his hands digging into my butt, Alex lifted himself enough to capture her gaze. "Fuck them," she announced, and shit, I wanted to laugh.

"But—"

She shook her head. "I'm queen. I rule here, not them, and until that changes, I, as well as all of you, can do what we like when it comes to our relationships. Don't hide your feelings for anyone. Please. If they don't like it, they can leave."

"Okay," Alex replied in a whisper. It was fucking sweet he'd been worried, but I didn't give a shit what anyone thought, and neither did my wolf. If we wanted to take our mates in the middle of a field, we would.

We ran out into the clearing. It was late, and only a few people were scattered around the area. They watched us until we disappeared through the castle gates. Some frowned, a lot smiled, and there was even a chuckle or two when they realized, from Paige waving, that there wasn't anything wrong.

Before we knew it, I had the door to Paige's room open and was stepping through, allowing Alex to drop to his feet. He started to step back until I hauled him back close to me with a growl in the back of my throat.

His eyes widened as he looked up at me. I heard the door close, but I didn't move my gaze from Alex, who licked his lips. As I watched his tongue, another rumble fell from between my lips.

Paige wanted to watch—something I fucking loved the thought of. Especially since the room was already mixed with her sweet scent of arousal from just seeing Alex and me close.

Leaning in, I pressed my mouth against Alex's. I heard Paige gasp, and as I opened Alex's mouth by nipping at his bottom lip, another hit of arousal scented the room. Alex's hands tightened on my hips. Our heads tilted this way and that. I couldn't get enough of kissing him. It still surprised the fuck out of me. Kissing a guy, a team member, but hell, he was my mate. He knew what he was getting into with me, and he'd accepted it.

I slid my hand from the back of his neck down to cup his ass cheek and squeezed. He let out a whimper and tore his mouth from mine, panting. His hooded gaze lifted to mine and then moved over to the others in the room. I looked there too.

My heart gave a lurch.

Thorn stood behind Paige. His hand was down in her pants and her legs shook. She gripped his arm as if it were the only thing that held her up. Asher, without a shirt, sat on the bed. His hand ran up and down his length behind his slacks.

Alex stopped breathing for a moment seeing it, until I grabbed him and turned him like Thorn had Paige. His heart thudded hard in his chest when I slowly glided my hand into his jeans. He moaned when I threaded my hand round his erection and leisurely dragged it up and down him.

"Take her to the bed," I ordered.

Thorn smirked. He withdrew his hand, and I knew Alex, like me, was watching. When Thorn licked his fingers clean, Alex's cock throbbed in my hand while mine jerked in my jeans. Asher stood, his slacks dropped to the floor, and he stepped out of them, kicking them away.

Naked.

Asher was fucking naked in front of us. He stepped out of the way so Thorn could help Paige onto the bed. She lay at the head of the bed, watching us all with lust burning in her eyes. She bit her bottom lip when Asher kneeled on the bed, helping her get rid of her top, and Thorn removed her pants, gliding them down her legs at an unrushed pace.

Jesus Christ.

Thorn moved back to get rid of his own clothes, and Alex and I got a full view of Paige bare on the bed.

Claim her. Fuck her. Mark her. My wolf rumbled over and over in my head.

Alex sucked in a sharp breath, and I realized I held him a little tight. I released my grip, removed my hand and then helped him take off his shirt. His arms lifted automatically, and I threw the fabric to the floor. Paige, up on her elbows, watched me as I slid my hands over Alex's smooth skin, savoring his hard muscles.

I popped the button to his jeans, and—Alex clicked his fingers. His and my jeans disappeared. Our cocks shot up. I chuckled, as did Asher and Thorn at Alex's eagerness. Over his shoulder, I caught his face heating. I bit my mark on his skin and thrust my hips into his ass cheeks. "Don't get embarrassed in here," I told him.

"I agree," Paige said. I glanced over. A growl dropped from my lips when I saw she had her fingers playing with her clit. "It's hot, how excited you get," she said, her voice low and thick with desire.

Alex nodded. He took my hand and pulled it down to his dick. Smiling, I grabbed his erection and jerked him up and down. I curled my other arm around his chest and nipped at his shoulder before licking there. My mark was still on him. It would stay there forever, and I fucking loved seeing it.

With my body, I gently pushed him over to the bed, still jacking him with each step we took.

"Please," Paige whispered. She was drenched below, and

seeing it, scenting it, the wolf and I wanted to lick her juices clean.

"P-Please what?" Alex asked.

Only she didn't answer because Asher slid onto the bed, pressing beside her and taking her nipple into his mouth. Thorn sat at the end of the mattress and ran his hand up and down her calves. Her legs spread under his touch. Her scent was intoxicating.

Overwhelmed, I pushed Alex's upper body forward. Before his hands landed on the bed, he clicked his fingers, and a tube of lube landed on the bed near us. Thorn picked it up and went to pass it, but he got too close to Alex, and my wolf and I didn't like it. A low snarl sounded out of me. He paused, his eyes widening.

Alex pushed his ass back onto me, grabbed the lube and lifted it over his shoulder. I snatched it out of his hand and opened it, rubbing it over my length and then Alex's hole. Immediately, he backed into my touch.

"It's all right. He didn't touch me," Alex said softly, probably because I couldn't stop the rattle of my growl in my chest. Alex cleared his throat.

"Why...?" Paige trailed off when I turned Alex enough for her to see I had my fingers inside Alex, stretching him. Alex's head dropped. I could hear his ragged breathing easily and the little mew sound Paige made.

Asher kissed her shoulder. "Because his wolf is as possessive as the man is, and he doesn't like his mate being touched by others."

Paige's head tilted. She may not have realized it, but she leaned closer our way, her gaze riveted on where I toyed with Alex. "But... he didn't mind me touching him."

Asher cupped her breast, tweaking her nipple with his fingers, and her breath hitched. "That's because he knows you'll be his sooner or later. Thorn and I are more dominant—" I snorted, then gnashed my teeth at him. Asher smirked. "He doesn't trust us completely to not take away what's his. That is, until he's claimed us."

Shock radiated over my wolf and I. It had me removing my fingers. Alex let out a complaint and glared over at Asher.

Thorn smiled, and I caught Asher's brow rising. "That is what will happen, right? Your wolf sees us all as his?" I nodded once, waiting for his reaction. Asher's eyes bled to green, his fangs dropping. "We'll have to see who gets topped, wolf. I don't give in easily."

My upper lip rose, and my claws flashed out. The half change came over me. My body grew, my hair lengthened, and my teeth sharpened. The wolf and I were one in body. "I'll take you on and make you mine, vampire."

Asher snarled. "We will see."

Alex groaned, but in annoyance. "Can we have a pissing contest later? We've got better things to—" He cried out when we entered him, our pink tip sliding further into him, in our half form. He was right. We had better things to do. We'd take Asher and force him to heel later. We'd do the same to Thorn if he wanted to fight for dominance as well.

Paige's heart took off in flight. She rubbed her legs together but then spread them when Thorn was back to rubbing his hand up her leg. She licked her lips and then bit the bottom one as we pulled back out of a panting Alex, then thrust back in again. We gripped his hips hard and pounded into our first mate, who accepted us with ease, even when he was damn tight.

Thorn sat with one leg on the bed, the other hanging off the bed with his foot planted on the floor. Paige let out a squeal when Thorn pulled her down the bed a little by her calves. He dipped down and licked her wetness, eating her like she was his favorite ice cream. She squirmed under him. Her mouth dropped open in a silent moan. Alex pushed back on me hard—he liked watching Thorn devour Paige's pussy.

She reached out under Alex, and when he uttered, "Fucking hell." We knew she was jerking him off. Blindly, she sought out Asher with her other hand and wrapped it around his large length, tracing her grip up and down.

It was lucky we knew she was going to be ours. We knew she wouldn't fight when it came time to claim. So we let her have attention from her other mates. Alex leaned in and took her left nipple into his mouth, while Asher took her right. She gasped and bared down on Thorn's mouth. All while we fucked Alex from behind.

The sight… Christ, it was amazing. We wanted to howl in pleasure.

Thorn pulled back and shoved at Asher, moving him enough so Thorn could pick Paige up. He shifted her around our way. Alex swore again when he looked down at her pussy.

"Get him on the bed," Thorn ordered.

We embedded our dick in Alex, causing him to groan, and with our hand on his hips, we ushered him forward, so he moved closer to the bed. We pushed him lower as Paige wiggled down the bed more.

"Will you let me finish the bond, Alex?" Paige asked huskily.

"Yes," he hissed.

We threaded our hand between Paige and Alex. Gripping his dick, we held it against her entrance. Pulling our cock out of him, we pushed in and forced him to slide right inside of Paige.

Both screamed at the same time. When Alex stilled, we panicked and went to grab him.

Thorn snatched our arms and shook his head. "Let the bond connect."

We ground our teeth together. We didn't like to see either of them so still. Alex grunted. At the sound, we shook off Thorn's hold and went for Alex again—something smashed into us, and we were ripped away from Alex, landing on the floor with a thud. We heard Asher say, "Relax, it's okay. They're okay. They'll fight it out. Just keep going."

Sounds of flesh slapping against flesh filled the room. Alex groaned and Paige gasped. We knew they were good, they were together, fulfilling the bond. We wanted to see but were beyond pissed at being held back. With a roar, we rolled the weight off us, our hands wrapping around Thorn's neck as we squeezed. His grin was fucking evil right before his fist landed on our cheek. Our head snapped to the side. We let out a low, deep growl.

"Yes. God, yes, Alex," Paige cried. We paused, raised our head, and looked over to see Alex drilling into Paige, and yet she still yelled, "Harder."

He did, and then next, Paige screamed his name. We scented her cum just before Alex cursed, then grunted, "I'm coming."

Thorn pushed us to the side. He went to stand, but we grabbed him around the waist and pulled him under us. Alex moved onto the bed; he was okay. He picked Paige up and seated her between his legs. He kissed her neck, and she smiled lazily. Wrapping his arms around Paige's waist, they both looked down at us on the floor.

We'd been distracted enough to have Thorn buck us off him. He had time to grab the edge of the bed before we hauled his body back toward me. We flipped him over, and his fist connected with our fucking face again. We wrapped our hand around his wrist and slapped it to the floor. We snatched his other arm and brought both up above his head.

Leaning down, we snarled in his face. It pissed us off even more when he laughed. We spotted the lube on the floor near us. We'd give the fucker something to laugh about.

Yes. Fuck, claim. Make him ours.

Thorn's eyes widened when we took both his wrists in one hand and then clasped the bottle. He tried to shove us off, but we quickly flicked the lid open and used our knees to spread his legs, squirting the substance on him. Thorn's eyes glowed red, and he struggled against our hold. We heard a bone snap in his wrist, yet we didn't let go.

"It's fine, Paige. They both like it," Asher whispered.

Thorn lifted his head, snapping his sharp teeth at us. We gnashed ours back before we rested our chest against his. Using our knees, spreading his apart more, we pushed a hand under his ass, lifting enough to slam our cock inside him.

"Ours," we clipped roughly as he stilled. We pulled out and thrust in. Our mate clenched around us and let out a deep, grunting moan.

We smiled wickedly. He liked it. He wanted it, and we'd give it to him.

We withdrew again and rolled forward inside his heat. Thorn's eyes closed, his mouth parting. We could see his sharp teeth. Then a noise caught our attention. We looked up and spotted the vampire behind our soon-to-be female mate fucking her while she watched us and sucked on our mate's cock.

Our chest vibrated with a noise. Conflicted, we wanted to

continue watching them, but the beast under us got a hand free and raked his claws down our chest. Roaring, we grabbed his arm and pulled it away to bend and latch our mouth onto his shoulder.

"Ours," I told him around his skin.

"Yes," he moaned.

With our teeth sinking into his flesh, Thorn cried out as we fucked him faster. We kept our teeth in him so the mark would stay, so people would see he was ours. His legs rose over our hips, holding on while we pounded into him.

We shifted our eyes in time to see our mate holding Paige's head and crying out through his release into her mouth. The vampire kept an eye on us even as he took his pleasure, even as he gripped the female tighter to him. She licked our mate one last time and then reached back to grip the vampire's neck, holding on as he drilled his dick into her wet pussy.

"Asher," she yelled as her orgasm scented the room again just before the vampire bared his teeth and pulled out of her to spread his ejaculating seed onto the female's skin.

"Nate," our mate under us whispered. "Faster."

We growled around his skin. Wanting to please our mate, we fucked him with everything we had. His hands landed on our ass, holding us, gripping us.

"Fuck, coming," he bit out.

He tightened around us more, drawing out our end, and we came inside him. Spent, relaxed, and damn happy, the wolf receded, my body shrank, and I slipped from Thorn. He let out a noise but rubbed his hands up and down my back. I released my teeth from his skin and licked at the bite. Pulling back, I peered down at it, and I felt a bark of pleasure from my wolf at the sight of our mark still there after his skin healed.

I moved my gaze down to capture Thorn's; he was back to his normal self. He didn't seem fazed by me claiming him; he just stared back, his eyes light with humor. Then he lifted his head and pressed his lips against mine. Shock hit me, but then I deepened the kiss, sliding my hand to the back of his head.

"I can't wait to see the wolf take on the vampire," Paige commented from the bed.

Breaking the kiss, I pecked at Thorn's lips once more before looking up. First, I checked on Alex, to make sure he was okay and fine with the new connection the wolf and I had made. Alex smiled down at me as he ran his fingers through Paige's hair.

Then I looked to Asher, who seemed amused, if the smirk was anything to go by. "Yes," he said. "It shall be entertaining. Hard to tell who will win, though."

I let out a huff, ignoring his taunt because the wolf and I were confident we'd best him. I stood, holding out my hand to Thorn. He took it, and I pulled him to his feet. I ran a hand over the side of his face. Content to have him as a mate, yet I still wanted more that night.

I was tired of fighting it.

My wolf agreed with me on my next thought.

Yes, he roared.

This was our destiny. This was our pack.

The vampire I would get to eventually, but for now, it was time to complete the bond.

I needed Paige.

I had to claim her.

Her whole being spoke to me in ways I'd never had. She drove me fucking insane, but I couldn't see my life now without her. Without any of them. I glanced at Paige. "I'm going for a shower. Are you too tired to finalize the bond with me?"

She gulped. Heat hit her cheeks, and before worry could steal my breath, she shook her head and said, "I'm not tired. I would like that."

"Good," I grunted.

With that organized, I walked toward the joined bathroom with a smile on my face and my dick already growing at the thought of being inside her.

CHAPTER TWENTY-SEVEN

"Should I shower as well?" I asked nervously after Nate disappeared into the en suite. The door opened again, and Nate stuck his head out.

His voice was rough and deep when he said, "No. Just clean your skin and the bed." The door slammed closed, and I glanced up at Alex.

His cheeks burned as he stammered, "Uh... he's, um, I mean... he's, as in, Nate is okay with my..." His brows rose. "... cum inside you, but he wants Asher's essence off you and the bed," he finished in a rush.

It was my turn to blush. Then I scolded myself for it because I shouldn't be embarrassed by what we'd done. Asher, and now Alex, were my mates, so we could do what we wanted with each other.

Asher laughed. "It seems, until the wolf can claim me—if he can and not the other way around—then we need to make sure I'm not scented around you while he claims you."

Oh.

I glanced to Thorn's neck to see the teeth marks there.

Thorn smiled. "It's okay, sweetheart. It didn't hurt." He actually stood straighter and seemed proud to have the mark. I still couldn't believe what I'd seen or how turned on I'd been watching Nate take Alex and then dominate Thorn. The way their bodies moved, the way they touched each other, fucked each other... dear God, if it was a TV show, I wouldn't get anything done. Instead, I would watch it every day and all day long. Just thinking of the way Nate's hips pistoned in and out of Alex and Thorn had me rubbing my thighs together. To top it all, bonding with Alex was more than I'd imagined. The way he held me down, the way he pinched my nipples and clit, the way he fucked me like I wanted was mind-blowing. I could feel him in me, feel the desire swirling inside him, the desire that had his dick growing right before my eyes.

I glanced up at him as he said, "It's you who has me hardening. I can sense how turned on you are. What were you thinking?"

I smiled sheepishly. "About us together and about Nate with you and Thorn."

Alex ran his thumb over my bottom lip. "You really don't mind Nate's claim? About us... fucking?" I'd never heard him swear; it was cute and yet sexy at the same time.

"I don't mind at all. I love getting pleasure but also seeing you all have it as well. If it's the five of us together or you with Nate alone and I hear about it, then I'm happy."

In the next second, I was on my back with Alex over me.

"You really are amazing and meant to be ours, Paige Alice. I'm honored to be known as your bonded mate."

I cupped his cheeks, then ran my hands up through his hair before meeting his gaze again. "I'm glad, because I love you all the same."

His eyes closed. He sucked in a deep breath, and I felt his love pour into me. I gasped, arched up into him, and wrapped my arms around his neck, dragging him down to me to kiss him senseless. He rocked his erection into my hip. A throat cleared, but I was too lost in the sensation, in the scent of Alex and his hard, smooth, wonderful skin while I glided my hands down his back.

"We should clean before the wolf—"

A hard, urgent knock sounded on the door. Alex and I froze. In the next blink, Alex clicked his fingers, and all of us were dressed and the bed was made with clean sheets.

"Enter," Asher barked.

The door swung open. A pale Felnick entered. "There's a problem, my queen."

I groaned, rubbing a hand over my face. "Another one? Is it Lucifer on the phone?"

"No. Our brothers-in-arms, who were sent out into the world, have found Selma. She's locked herself in a room with a few humans, threatening to kill them, and won't come out until she speaks with the queen in person."

"She's here?" Thorn questioned.

Felnick shook his head. "She's in New York."

The door to the en suite flew open, and Nate, only in a towel, stomped in. He pointed at me and snapped, "Don't even fucking think about going."

Bristling, my anger surfaced. I stood quickly with my hands

on my hips, only realizing I was dressed in a snowsuit. It had me blinking down at it and then glancing over at Alex. His jaw unclenched enough to bite out, "No one has the right to see your skin after...." After I'd been thoroughly fucked, he left off, and I appreciated that he had. My face heated, while I heard Thorn and Asher chuckle, as Nate snorted.

It was sweet he was being protective.

"But a snowsuit?" I pressed.

"Yes." He nodded, and I had a feeling he wouldn't change my outfit even if I wanted him to.

Sighing, something I hadn't done in a while, I faced Nate again. "If you weren't so hot and muscular, and tall, and good-looking with your warm skin—"

Someone cleared their throat loudly.

Damn Nate for distracting me with his body. My eyes narrowed even more at his smug smile. "If you weren't meant to be my bonded mate, I would so kick your ass right now for ordering me."

He rolled his eyes. "I'm here to protect you. I'll easily tie you to the bed if I have to."

That had me picturing it. Tied to the bed while he got all growly and bossy and assholey.... Wait, that couldn't mean I liked his hard-edge moods, right?

Fuck. I thought it did.

Still, I wouldn't let him get away with it.

"Ah, my queen," Felnick called.

"Yes?" I asked, facing him.

"What should we do about the issue?"

Right. Selma. Honestly, it wasn't a decision I could make on the fly. There was so much to consider. I glanced at my men, then asked, "What do you all think?"

"It's a trap," Nate declared.

"Something is amiss with the request," Asher said.

"Why would she leave the sanctuary to then ask to see you or she'll kill humans? She could have just spoken with you here," Alex pointed out.

"Like Nate said, it has to be a trap," Thorn added.

Thinning my lips, I nodded. Staring at the floor, I said quietly, "But I can't risk lives just because I'm worried it's a trap."

"Yes, you can," Nate boomed. "You're queen. Your life is worth more than anyone's. You're the change for the future. The people need you above anyone here."

I shook my head. "I'm not above anyone's life. Everyone is important."

"My queen, if I may?" Felnick asked, his head bowed.

"Yes?"

"It is honorable you would even think to risk yourself for others. The way you already protect your people, allowing them to live their lives fully and by taking the harshness that darkens some doorsteps is beyond what some queens would do. You do not see your life more important than any others, so it's our job to do it for you. Already, I can foretell that if something happened to you, everything would fall into the pits of Hell. People like Odin, Barrett, or the members of the council would take over, would rule cruelly. If you would allow us to care for your life, like you would others, to protect the good you will do in this world, then it is a task we'll take on happily."

If I didn't think my men would harm Felnick, I would have thrown my arms around him and hugged him tightly. The way he saw me shocked me, but how could I risk my life after that speech?

"She's leaking," Nate clipped. "You fucking made her leak." He stomped toward Felnick. Thorn wrapped his arms around Nate's chest and held him tightly, while Felnick backed into the wall. It had me wondering again about how Felnick could be fierce and protective against anyone but Lucifer, during the phone call, and my bonded. Then again, my men were badasses, and I was sure Lucifer could make anyone piss themselves, and I didn't even know the man, devil, whatever.

Arms circled my waist. Alex stood at my back before he leaned in to kiss my neck. Asher stepped close and took my hand in his, running his thumb over my skin; both had me sniffing and closing my eyes to compose myself before Nate killed Felnick.

"Look, she's fine. Her bonded calmed her," Thorn told Nate.

I opened my eyes as Nate glanced our way. He took me in from head to toe first before he glanced to Alex and Asher. Then his upper lip raised at my vampire until Asher stepped back a little, away from Alex. Rolling my eyes, I stated, "And you said I was crazy when it came to claiming and being possessive."

He growled low. My clit twinged as if that growl had been just for her.

If only we hadn't been interrupted with this new situation, because by now, I would have finished the bond with my annoying and arrogant wolf. Still, it was something to look forward to.

Sorrow stabbed at my chest.

Ezra.

I'd forgotten all about his loss, so guilt twisted my heart painfully.

"Paige," Alex whispered. "It's okay—"

"Leave us for a moment, Felnick," Thorn ordered. "We'll have an answer on what to do soon."

He bowed and backed out of the room, closing the door behind him.

"I should feel guilty for forgetting him, right?" My eyes misted again when I looked up at Asher.

"Fucking hell. She's leaking again." I ignored Nate's mutter and the need to slap him because Alex wrapped me up tighter, right before there was a bright light and a feeling of weightlessness. Next, I was sitting on the bed between Alex's spread legs. He gently pulled my back against his chest. With a click of his fingers, I was redressed in shorts and a T-shirt.

My other men approached. Thorn sat on my left, Asher on the right, while Nate stood at the end of the bed with his arms crossed over his chest, glaring down at us. Yet I could still see the concern in his eyes. He hated when I was upset, and knowing he felt something showed me more about the mate he would be. Already I knew he was protective to a point he would tie me up. He could be sweet, happy, and amazing like he'd been whenever he was around Alex.

Thorn reached his hand out to Nate, whose jaw clenched when he gazed down at it, then stopped. I caught a faint smile before Nate took Thorn's hand. They shared a look, one that was full of heat and tenderness. One I wanted to witness all the time between every single one of my bonded.

"Paige?" Alex whispered as his hand sifted through my hair.

"I'm sorry. For a moment I forgot about Ezra. The sorrow slammed into me, and then the guilt over forgetting took over."

"You don't have to feel guilty, love," Asher said, taking my hand in both of his. "You're not forgetting him. You never will. There'll be times in your day when you're distracted, where you'll smile, laugh, and even feel the best pleasure of your life." His brows rose, and I couldn't help but laugh even when tears dropped onto my cheeks. "But the loss of Ezra will always be inside you, and when you feel other things, it only means you've pushed it back enough to live in the moment. It means you're living, love."

My bottom lip trembled, yet I nodded. "I know you're right…. It's just… when I remember, it hurts."

"And it will for a very long time," Thorn said.

"But we'll be at your side to help you through that pain," Alex mumbled against my temple.

Nate grunted. When I looked up at him, he nodded.

"Fate really did the best job in her life when she put us all together," I told them, smiling softly.

"I agree," Alex said. The rest grinned over at me, though Nate's was more of a smug smirk.

"Now, what are we going to do about the Selma situation?" Alex asked.

"I have a feeling if I say I want to go see what she has to say, you'll all lock me in a tower."

"Damn right," Nate growled.

Shaking my head at him, I glanced at Thorn. "Do you think your brotherhood could get in there without the humans being harmed?"

"Vampires are faster, sweetheart. I'm afraid there will be some casualties."

That was what I feared as well.

"I could go," Alex announced, and coldness washed through me.

"No," I cried. Turning, I placed my hands on his cheeks and

said again, "No. If none of you will let me risk myself, then I won't let any of you do the same."

His hands landed over mine, and he smiled. "I have skills that some may not even know of. I'm strong, Paige. I was top of my class. Why do you think Asher selected me right out of school? I can do this easily."

"I'll go with him," Thorn said, and I swung my gaze to his. Tears already pooled in my eyes. I blinked them away and let them fall onto my skin.

"I've already lost Ezra. I can't lose either of you."

Alex's hand traced up and down my back while I kept them both in sight. "You won't. Have faith in us."

"Why can't the brotherhood just go in?"

"There's a high chance there'll be fewer casualties with Alex there," Nate stated. "He's good at what he does." Alex preened at Nate's words, his chest puffing out, and a wide grin overtook his mouth.

Fear still held me back from agreeing. It felt like my throat had closed off, suffocating the words they wanted to hear because I didn't want them to go.

But then… I had to believe in them, in their skills. Before we'd even met, they were soldiers. They did this type of thing every day. Even though I wanted to lock them up in their own tower, I knew I couldn't suffocate their abilities.

I had to trust them to come back to me.

Clearing my throat, I opened my mouth, choked, and then cleared my throat again. Finally, I nodded. "Okay," I whispered. "I trust you both to come back to me in one piece, or else I'll find a way to bring you back and make your lives a living hell."

Tears erupted in my eyes once more, panic seizing my body. Then Alex dragged me back into his arms, hugging me close.

He kissed my head. It wasn't enough, so I tilted my head and captured his lips with my own.

"Promise me you'll stay safe," I said against them.

"I promise." He nodded.

Looking to Thorn, I reached my hand out to him. He crawled onto the bed and moved my way before hovering over me as I lay back onto Alex's chest. "Promise me you'll keep safe."

"I vow to you I will do everything in my power to come back."

With my hand to the back of his neck, I drew him down and kissed him just as fiercely as I had Alex. My heart raced behind my ribs. I hated the thought of them leaving the community, the safe sanctuary we had here.

My hands trembled as I loosened my grip on Thorn. He moved back and stood beside the bed, smiling warmly down at me. Alex lifted me, and I was in Asher's arms. They wound around me as Asher sat me on his lap, and then Alex got off the bed to stand beside Thorn.

"I'll walk them out," Nate said, his voice hard and rough. He disliked this as much as I did.

However, I nodded. "I want to be updated every half hour until you're both back here with us."

"We will," Alex said. "No trap will keep us from coming home."

"You'd better be right," I told him.

They made their way to the door, opened it, and walked out. Nate gave us a look before he closed it after them.

"Did I do the right thing by letting them go?"

"Yes," Asher whispered.

"Then why does it feel like I didn't?" My face stung with the number of tears that bombarded my eyes. I bit my bottom lip to stop the tremble.

"Because you love them, and it will never be easy to watch them walk into battle, but you're strong enough to know you're doing the right thing to save all the lives you can." His hand threaded into my hair, and he tipped my head back with a gentle tug. "It doesn't mean you have to stay strong behind closed doors when I'm here to catch you."

With that, I buried my face into his chest and cried.

CHAPTER TWENTY-EIGHT

ALEX

With the bond between Paige and I complete, I finally felt like my feet were firmly set on the ground. I hadn't realized I'd been floating around the world missing something until the moment Nate claimed me and one foot got placed down. But then, when Paige's power bonded us together, my other foot solidly got pushed to the ground.

My life, my purpose, finally made sense. I was theirs and they were mine. I also felt like I belonged to Thorn and Asher. Even with my own family, I hadn't sensed being wanted, needed, or loved… until now. Until my new family.

All because of Paige.

I couldn't thank Fate enough for choosing me to be a part of something so important, giving me people I would cherish for the rest of my long existence.

Smiling, I glanced to Nate and Thorn as we stood in the war room with Felnick and twenty other brothers-in-arms. Thorn had just informed them that he and I would be involved in the capture of Selma. Nate had stated how Paige wouldn't be joining us before anyone else could question it; there wasn't a chance we'd let Paige out into the world. There was too much at risk. We still didn't know why the demons had been after her in the first place or who sent them. Or were they working on their own accord?

Before we entered the war room, I'd voiced my other concerns—ones Nate and Asher would have to keep an eye on. Grace, the coven mistress who had been against Paige's changes for the community, hadn't as yet done anything to move against Paige, and even though we'd made sure to keep up to date with Agatha, a witch who was keeping tabs on her coven mistress for us, there was still a risk something could happen to Paige because of that woman.

Nate, in his grumpy way, told me he wasn't that stupid. Of course he'd keep an eye on things.

"Thorn and I will transport to the hotel she's holed up in and scout the area before entering."

"Is it advisable for the queen's bonded males to go into battle?" one of the guards from the brotherhood said.

Thorn snapped his gaze the guard's way. "Just because we're mated to the queen doesn't mean we'd sit on our asses and let everything go to shit when we have the strength and the power to help."

The guard bowed. "Of course, sire."

"Now I understand why Paige is against being bowed at and called queen. I'll never get used to being called sire," Thorn grumbled. He moved to the wall of weapons and strapped on some knives and guns. My magic was my weapon. Hands touched my thigh. Startled, I swung my gaze down to see Nate fitting me with a thigh holster.

My pulse raced. I wanted to smile, to gush even, but that would piss him off. "What are you doing?"

"Shut up. Just fucking humor me like you did when Asher ordered you to carry one weapon. Know you're strong in magic, Alex, but for my own sanity,"—he shoved a gun into the holster—"you're taking this."

I ran my hand over his shoulder. "All right." I couldn't help but grin since he'd never worried like this about me before, but now we were mated, he was a wreck. I didn't wipe the grin away quick enough. When Nate looked up at me, he growled low and kept doing so when he slowly stood in front of me.

The room quieted, sensing the rising pissed-off wolf.

His hand gripped the back of my neck, and he slammed his mouth onto me in a hard, punishing but delicious kiss. He broke it when he sensed Thorn close because in a blink, Thorn crashed into us, and Nate was kissing him too.

When Nate broke the kiss, his eyes were dark, his wolf there, and he ordered in a dark voice, "Have each other's back. Come home. Pack first."

"Pack first," I told him.

"We'll come back," Thorn reassured him. He stared at us both before snarling, turning, and walking out of the room.

"He... the wolf... I've never—"

"Never what?" Thorn snapped.

The guard blanched. "Never seen a wolf take more than one mate," he blurted.

"Congratulations, sire," Felnick offered.

Thorn smiled. "Thank you, brother." I didn't know much

about Thorn, and I needed that to change. What I did know was that he was a respected, good man. One Nate's wolf claimed without question. And that told me a lot more than anything else. Nate didn't take people into his pack easily. But it seemed knowing Thorn was Paige's also made the choice simple. We were now in each other's lives forever.

It was definitely time to get to know him.

WITH A HOLD ON THORN, I transported us into a corner of the lobby in the hotel Selma had selected to stay. There were already members of Thorn's brotherhood in the surveillance room and dotted throughout the hotel waiting for us. I drew in the power that escaped on the transport and then blocked Thorn and our essence. We didn't want to give away we'd arrived to anyone who was working with Selma.

"You said you didn't know much about the vampire, but do you think she would sink low enough to work with demons to trap Paige?" I asked as we walked toward the surveillance room, only to come to an abrupt halt. Snapping my hand out, I took hold of Thorn's arm.

He spun back to me. "What?"

"Magic and—" Doors crashed open. "—demons," I called over the noise of all different types and sizes of demons rushing into the room snarling, growling. "Ready?"

"Always," Thorn yelled. His eyes changed to red, while mine shifted to purple as I called my powers forward. Thorn grabbed the guns from his hips and fired at the fast-approaching demons. A lot fell to the floor, but not enough. I swept my hand out, picking up at least ten of them, flinging them into the wall. Bones breaking echoed around the room. My lips moved over a spell, and knives shot out of my palms, aiming at the closest demons.

Thorn's gun fired over and over until he ran out and threw them to the floor, grabbing two others. I shot off another spell, telling him, "They shouldn't run out of bullets."

His grin over his shoulder was wild and wicked since his teeth had sharpened from his ghoul side. "Thanks." He went back to shooting everything he spotted while I blinded the monsters with a sunshine spell. They screeched and screamed, covering their eyes, giving Thorn more time to shoot a lot of them. When that spell faded, I had another ready. The floor liquefied, and demons sank into it, crying out in surprise. They clawed at the ground once it solidified.

I moved my eyes to the door when another wave of demons crawled, ran, and flew in. They were stronger ones. When a ball of fire flew my way, I swiped it to the side and shot off my own. It hit him, only he smiled as the flames ran over his body.

Fuck.

Since fire didn't work, I formed a spell for ice and engaged it. The demon's eyes widened. He dodged right, but I already had another two erupting from my palms. One hit him. He howled in pain and sank to his knees, frosting over.

A hit to my back had me stumbling forward. My back burned. I crafted a spell to heal whatever had me in agony. Pain still laced through me as I turned to see Grace standing there smiling.

"Now," she yelled, and two other witches stepped up to her sides.

Anger had my feet lifting off the floor, had me spreading my hands, had wild wind whipping around me. My lips moved, but no sound came from them as I locked onto their own spell and broke it apart inch by inch. I managed to glance at Thorn, checking he was okay. His eyes were wide watching me. He wasn't focused and demons approached.

"Behind you," I said, my voice hard.

He spun in time to decapitate the two heads off the demon, then sliced another down the middle. He must have lost his guns at some point to be using the swords he'd had strapped to his back.

The witches staggered a step forward, bringing a smile to my face. "You won't best me," I told them.

Grace's brow dipped in concentration. She changed up her spell, and I quickly countered it with my own alteration, using my hands in the air, drawing patterns and swirls.

Grace let out an agitated scream.

"Where is Selma?" I demanded.

Grace swiped at her forehead and laughed. "Not here." She smiled. "She was never here," she said, her voice different.

"That's Selma's voice," Thorn called. He leaped to the other side of me and attacked the demons there, his blade effortlessly cutting through an acid ball shot his way.

"Do you know where Selma is?" I asked.

"She had other orders," a new voice said. A man stepped out of a darkened corner. He licked his lips, his eyes glowing red. "You have delicious power." He looked at Grace. "I want them both."

"The mage is strong—"

"You promised to make it happen," the demon roared.

Grace frowned and nodded.

The demon smiled and gazed up at me. "I'll be seeing and

playing with you both soon." His eyes shifted to the others in the room. "Those who drag them down into Hell will be rewarded." Then he vanished.

Grace cried out. A fog floated up around her, and she laughed maniacally.

Jesus, she was gaining more power.

"You don't have to do this," I told Grace.

"I feel amazing." She smiled, then pulled the witch to her left close and sliced her throat open. Grace's lips moved. She grabbed the other screaming witch and stabbed her in the heart.

Blood magic was the darkest. Fear pierced my chest. I could maybe counter it, but I didn't have the time, and I had to keep our promise to Paige and Nate.

"Thorn, to me," I yelled, landing back on the floor. Thorn wrapped his arms around me. I went to transport us out, but nothing happened. The floor beneath us vanished as Grace opened a portal straight to Hell. I gripped Thorn to me and floated above it. Demons surrounded us. I pushed them back magically, but more ran in. There was a pop—my protective bubble fell away. Three demons jumped at us before I could get us high enough. They locked their arms around our legs, and then there was a clap and we were being dragged into the portal.

Into Hell.

Blackness surrounded us as we kept falling. Thorn released his hold and pushed off me to wrap himself around a demon and sliced over and over with his claws at his chest. The demon screamed in pain and fury before exploding. He went for the next, all while we still fell, and I took on the last.

As our backs hit the solid ground with a grunt, the demons

were dead. The blackness around us evaporated into nothing. The first thing that hit me was the heat; the next I noticed was the dirt-covered ground since a few jagged rocks pushed into my back and butt.

Groaning, I rolled to the side to find Thorn slowly sitting up.

I did the same, wincing from the pain in my back, chest, and ass. Glancing around, I took in the street we'd landed in.

Wait… Hell had streets?

My eyes widened; shock radiated throughout me. It seemed Hell had more than just streets. Hell looked a lot like Vegas. In the distance, there were lights flashing, music played, and I sensed the magic surrounding the city.

All in Hell.

Thorn and I were in the desert part of Vegas Hell. The heat beat down on me. I hated blistering warm days. I shielded my eyes and looked up into the sunny sky. Was all of this magic? An illusion? It couldn't be because I could only sense the magic coming from the city area.

Glancing back to Thorn, I said, "Paige is going to kill us."

He snorted out a laugh and stood, his hands going to his waist while he stretched. "Christ, you're right. So we'd better find a way back to her quickly."

Standing, I brushed at my clothes. "I have a feeling we'll find the only way back in that place." I pointed to the city. He looked behind him and cursed.

"Are we really going into a city full of demons?" he asked.

"We'll have to."

He cursed again. "For Paige," he said.

I nodded. "For Paige. Hey, maybe Lucifer will be in there

somewhere and take us with him since he wants to see Paige soon anyway."

Thorn slapped me on the back as I stopped beside him. "Your optimism is outstanding." I shrugged. He added, "Great fighting back there."

I knew my cheeks were warmer than just from the sun; I didn't do well with compliments. "I didn't do much."

He scoffed and slung his arm around my shoulders, as if he'd done it a million times before. We started walking before he said, "Not much... yeah, we'll go with that."

"Your fighting skills are... ah, amazing." Which they were.

He glanced down at me and smiled. "Thanks." He released his arm from around me. "You ready to jog?"

I hated jogging. "Sure." I nodded as my lips thinned. For some reason, Thorn found it amusing and started laughing.

CHAPTER TWENTY-NINE

THORN

*A*lex glanced at me again, after we'd been running for a little while, and after I'd kept him from tripping about five times. His good mood and optimism seemed long gone since he was scowling around the area. Finally, he got up the courage to ask, "Why are you smiling? We had our asses handed to us. Grace, with an extra boost of blood magic, is probably on the way back to the community to harm Paige. Selma is still God knows where. Your men weren't even there. We're stuck in Hell, running into a city where there will be millions of demons who would take great pleasure in killing us."

"We're alive. We fought well together. Paige will be protected with Asher and Nate. Plus, there're all the people she's charmed, even in the short amount of time she's been there. Selma will reappear, and we'll take care of her then." My smile faded. "My men did their duty. They knew, like I did, what would be involved. Battles can be lost. It saddens me deeply this was one of them, and when we get home, I'll grieve with the rest of my men for their losses. Now isn't the time."

"I'm sorry," he blurted, and I knew he meant it. I could hear it and see it in his frown and furrowed brows.

Alex hadn't meant it. He'd spoken without thinking, and I reacted. Their loss sat in my gut, churning painfully, but I had to push it aside. I had to think positive because it all counted to help us get home. So I offered him a smile—it was weak, but there—and he returned one just as weak.

I went on answering his concerns. "We may be in Hell, but Lucifer does want to meet Paige, and hopefully he wants an ally in her, so maybe he'll keep us safe. We may have to fight again, but I'm confident in our skills."

He harrumphed, unsure of my words, but I believed them. Alex was a powerful mage, one who kicked ass against three witches and demons easily, without even breaking into a sweat. I was glad he was on our side. If it wasn't for the blood magic he seemed fearful of, then we would have walked out of that place.

"Who do you think that other demon was?" he asked, helping me push away the mournful thoughts of losing my men by changing the subject. I valued him for it. Alex was slightly puffing and sweating from jogging. We were miles away from the city, though, and I wondered if he'd make it. I would mention to Nate to up Alex's physical activities. He caught me looking at him since I hadn't answered him; he glared, but his cheeks were pink. "If I wasn't sure they'd sense me using my magic, I'd transport us or float all the way there."

Yep, he needed to not rely on his powers, something he might be realizing since he was suffering from exercise.

Although, it had me wondering how his body was so fit when he didn't seem to like to work out.

For now, I'd let it slide. I had a feeling he'd listen to Nate and Asher more than me, until we got to know one another better.

"To answer your question, I think the demon is one who's trying to rise up in ranks here. However, he seemed weak on earth, which was why either he or Grace sought each other out to help one another. Grace probably promised him helpful minions, and in return, he gave her all the power he had to open the portal to Hell. He'd be here rejuvenating his strength somewhere, expecting us to be dragged into his lair. Then Grace would have felt drained opening the portal, which was why she had to use blood magic, in the end, to make sure the portal stayed open long enough to get us here. If we hadn't killed the demons on the way down, they would have delivered us to their master for the reward they were promised. If somehow they managed to get us to him, then right about now, he'd probably be stripping us of our power."

Alex stumbled over some loose rocks again. I caught his arm and found him staring at me in shock. "That sounded really accurate."

I grinned. "I've been in the brotherhood for a very long time. I've learnt how people think and strategize a lot of outcomes before they can even happen. Usually I'm spot on, which was how I became the commander of them all and had an ear to the former queen."

He nodded. "That makes sense."

Asher had spoken to me before about Alex, how he'd been the best in school and sought after from the council for many teams, but Asher had been the first captain to approach him personally. He'd picked their team right after. He'd told me how he was young in mage years, but still had a lot to learn, not in work, but within himself. He wasn't confident of his worth. He was shy around people who interested him, yet he'd grown in the month since Paige had come into our lives.

He interested me like Asher and Nate had.

Our family couldn't have been more perfectly put together than if I'd tried to do so myself.

I was pleased to have him in my life. Pleased and happy to have the family I now had, and I would do anything to protect them all.

"Can I ask you something?"

"Sure, anything," he answered.

That made me smile, yet I wasn't sure he'd like my line of questions, and it annoyed me to even think of upsetting him. Still, it was something all of us should know about him. "Blood magic, you seemed disgusted by it."

He glanced off to the side and sighed. His eyes returned to in front of him, which was probably good; he wasn't the steadiest on his feet while running. "I've studied it, had a cousin lost to it, but shockingly, I've never had to fight against it."

"You're strong, Alex," I told him.

He shrugged. "My cousin killed his whole family because of it. I've never wanted anything to do with blood magic, but with the life we now have… I'll have to make sure I know everything there is to counter any type of blood magic." He almost looked green from the thought.

"Do you believe you can counter it?"

"I'm not sure, which is what scares me most."

"I'll help you find out somehow."

He shot me a quick look of surprise before tripping, and I had to grab him again. "You will?"

I smiled. "Of course. We're family now. We help each other out."

"Thank you," he mumbled, his cheeks tinting once again.

"Anything at any time, Alex, I'm there."

He bit on his bottom lip, but I saw his grin. "Are you happy with…?"

"Everything that's happened?" He nodded. "Yes. Hell yes. Paige is amazing, perfect really. I wasn't sure we'd all get along; it worried me. I didn't even think any of you liked me. Especially Nate, but how he's claimed me, changed that."

"Nate's prickly. He always has been, and I think he always will be, but that's just him. He's changed a bit since, um, claiming us."

I laughed. "I can tell. He's almost sweet, in a possessive way toward you. I look forward to knowing you all more."

"Same with you, I mean, getting to know you."

I bumped his shoulder. Once again, he tripped, but my arm went out around his waist, steadying him. I gave it a squeeze before letting go as we kept up our steady pace. "The future looks bright, even with everything still to deal with."

He nodded, smiling again. "It does."

My ears picked up on a sound. I grabbed Alex's arm and pulled him to a stop. He looked at me, and I held my finger up to my lips. Even over his heavy breaths, I heard it again—a howl.

I spun back the way we'd come. "Fuck."

"What?" Alex snapped.

"Hellhounds and demons running this way." I glanced down at him. "They've got our scent."

"They're hunting us," he concluded.

I nodded. We both started running again.

"Should we risk me using my magic?"

"Let's save it for our last resort."

"Thorn...."

I glanced at him from over my shoulder; they were gaining on us quickly. "Yeah?"

"I'm not fast, and I won't be able to keep going for much longer," he admitted. Shame shone in his eyes before he looked ahead of us. We were about a mile out. I wasn't sure we'd make it without being caught and either ripped apart—because there were a lot of those fuckers—or taken to someone who could be stronger than the both of us.

"Sorry," I said.

"What for?" He gasped when I picked him up and flung him over my shoulder. He held on as I changed to ghoul and sped over the terrain—triple the speed of what we'd been running.

"This... is... humiliating," Alex panted. He grabbed the top of my jeans, holding on and trying to steady his bouncing.

"It's not. Keep an eye on them. If they get close, it'll be you saving our asses."

"You... have... a nice one... to save."

It was my turn to almost trip. I righted us and laughed. "Are you seriously checking me out while we're running for our lives?"

"No," he fired back quickly, bringing out another laugh from me. Him admitting that he liked how I looked was something to explore another time—when we weren't running to save ourselves.

After a while, I asked, "How we doing?"

"They're closing in, but we're still far enough away."

"Okay," I clipped. It was good having Alex watching them because all I had to do was concentrate on getting us to the city.

Fuck. As we drew close, I caught the bustling city and also the sentries who stood surrounding the place.

There were too many. We couldn't take them all on.

They spotted us. A roar erupted through the thick, warm air. Stopping, I placed Alex on his feet.

"What?" he said, then looked to where I was. I heard his gulp as they raced toward us.

We were surrounded.

"Time to use my magic?" Alex asked.

A snort dropped from my lips unexpectedly. "Yeah. Can you get us in there?"

"I can. We'll just have to see if we'll be detected afterward."

They grew closer.

"Let's do it."

Alex's power rose. His eyes changed to purple, the shade glowing, the air chilling, and yet he waited.

"What are you doing?" I asked anxiously. They were nearly upon us.

"Hold on to me," he said, his voice thicker, deeper.

I wrapped my arms around his waist just as a blast shot out of him and slid over the desert. I witnessed the surrounding army fall to the ground just before light shone around us, and that same feeling of being transported took over me.

I opened my eyes to see we now stood in a small, darkened room. The light under the door shone enough for me to make out we were in a broom closet. "Are you okay?" I asked when Alex stumbled forward after I released him.

"Just weakened a little. Give me a moment. I'll be okay."

"What did you do to them?"

"Put them to sleep. I'm not sure how long they'll stay like that."

My hands slid from his arms up to his shoulders. He lifted his head and blinked up at me. "Alex, there were thousands out there."

He nodded. "I know. I could kill them, but it could have knocked me out. A sleeping spell was easier."

The power he held inside of him was amazing.

I tugged him toward me and kissed him hard. He moaned under my lips, and I found his tongue to play with my own. Pulling back, I said, "You saved us."

He stared up at me in a bit of a daze. "Don't say that yet. I'm not sure where I've landed us. I just made sure it was a room no one was in." Smiling, I kissed him again. He gently pushed on my chest and muttered, "If you keep doing that, my weakness will continue."

I laughed, and he covered my mouth. Grabbing his hand, I pulled it down to whisper, "I'll go out and scope the area—"

"No. Just give me a moment and we'll go together."

"All right." I pulled him against me again and twisted enough to sit us in the cramped area with him between my legs. He didn't even fight it. He rested back against me and breathed deeply. He sounded asleep, but I knew better. He'd still be alert; he was just trying to gain some energy back.

"Couple more minutes," he mumbled.

"Sure," I whispered.

Laughter and then music started outside the room.

Christ, where the fuck were we and would we have to fight our way out? We needed to find out where Lucifer was. He'd be our best chance to get out of there. Hopefully.

Right then, I wasn't too sure of anything, and I didn't like the thought of Alex having to use his reserves of power. It could harm him more than help.

Usually, I wouldn't let worry seep into my veins, but fuck, with Alex there it did. He was family. He was ours, and I didn't want him to risk himself more. Absently, I massaged the back of his neck since his head was turned into my shoulder.

"We could wait until their party stops," I suggested. "They could be drinking and pass out by the end of it."

"No. They'll sense us soon. I'm blocking our scents and power from them, but I won't be able—"

"Fuck, you shouldn't be doing it. You're trying to get energy back, not waste it."

He chuckled low. "It's not a waste, and it's easy to do." Groaning, he started to move away until I pulled him back. "We have to make a move now. My magic is already building."

"Alex."

He turned in my arms and smiled. "Trust me."

I searched his eyes. Already they looked livelier. "I do."

"Good." He pecked my lips, blushed for doing so, and then quickly stood. "We'll go out there. I'll block our powers, and hopefully they'll think we're new demons or something so we can get out." He wouldn't meet my gaze now. I'd deal with that later, make sure he knew I wanted his lips on mine any time, or else I wouldn't have kissed him before.

"Sounds like a plan."

He nodded, opened the door, and stepped out. I followed quickly. My body buzzed, and I saw we were in some type of living room before I caught his "Motherfuck—" He froze as all eyes were on us. Out of the corner of his mouth, he said, "Seems they blocked my block and knew exactly what we are."

Of fucking course the demons didn't allow anyone to goddamn hide.

They stood from the couches, from the stools at the bench,

from the table where they'd sat playing poker. They all stood smiling like they'd just won the lottery.

Only we were their winnings.

The front door in front of us burst open. I stood in a fighting stance while Alex called his power up. The sunlight blinded us for a moment, and I blinked rapidly.

A long, loud noise sounded throughout the room. The demons, to my utter fucking shock, sank to their knees.

Alex gasped. I swung my gaze back to the doorway, and my mouth dropped open. I couldn't believe it.

CHAPTER THIRTY

PAIGE

I didn't know how long went by, but eventually, Asher sent a message to Nate telling him he'd taken me down to my sister's suite to get my mind off things. They'd probably only just woken up, but it was a good idea. The kids were always a good distraction.

Especially when Alex and Thorn's emotions inside me were lost. I felt the loss even more since I'd just made the connection and bonded with Alex, but Asher told me they would have blocked the connection for my sake.

I knocked on the door, and it sprang open by a smiling Sophie. She wrapped her arms around me and hugged me close. Lifting her head, she dug her chin into my hip. "Hiya, Aunty Paige."

I ran my hands over her head. "Hiya, Sophie. Is your mom awake?"

"I think so. I didn't call out this morning. I snuck out my room and heard her yell at Daddy about doing something harder."

Oh shit.

Asher choked, holding back a laugh.

"Ah, yeah, okay. I'm sure she'll be out soon."

Asher choked again, and I elbowed him. Curling my arm around Sophie's shoulders, I ushered her back into the living room. "You know you shouldn't answer the door on your own."

"But there's men who watch to keep us safe. Mommy told me."

"I know, honey, but your mom and dad would still like you to never answer the door without them around."

She sighed. "Okay." She skipped over to Asher, her arms already raised. He scooped her up and swung her around, drawing out a giggle. "Hiya, Uncle Asher."

He stilled, just blinking down at her.

"What's wrong with him?" she asked.

I laughed. "Nothing, honey. He's just happy that you're calling him Uncle Asher."

"Oh." She grinned. "Mommy said I could when I asked. And I get to call Nate my uncle Nate, and Thorn my uncle Thorn, and Alex my uncle Alex. Even though Alex does supercool magic and I wanted to marry him, Mommy said I couldn't because he was your boyfriend, Aunty Paige. Then I asked how come you get to date, like, four boys, but she said she'd tell me when I'm older or that I had to ask you... so...?"

I didn't know what to say. What I did think, though, was that I was going to kill my sister for leaving it up to me.

Maybe it would be best for the simple answer. "Because I love them all, and they were made just for me."

"That's amazing!" she cried, and then squished Asher's cheeks together. "Isn't that amazing!" He nodded, smiling, also trying to hold in his laughter again. Sophie didn't. She giggled and announced, "I want to be just like Aunty Paige and love lots of boys."

Oh fuck.

"How about we make a start on breakfast for everyone?" I suggested quickly.

"Yes," she cried. "I'm starving."

Oscar was the next to rise, just as I had the bacon and eggs cooking while Asher talked, and Sophie got the cutlery and cups out. My nephew walked in looking like a little monster himself with his shuffling feet, messy hair, and tired eyes. He made his way straight to Asher and leaned into Asher's side. I looked on, my heart melting as Asher put his arm around Oscar and said, "Morning, buddy." Oscar grunted back in reply.

Asher would have made an amazing father. The only time I saw his expression that soft was when he was with me and the rest of the men. Outside our rooms, he was cold and hard. It was beautiful to see the difference he held, the gentleness to him, for the people important to him. I wished I could give my men children.

Sadness washed through me. I couldn't regret what I'd become or where my life was at because I had my men, but I would have loved to have extended our own little family with their kids.

Asher's gaze lifted, his gates opened, and he flooded me with contentment and happiness. I smiled warmly at him and went back to cooking. No, I could never regret where my life was because I had four beautiful, amazing men. If only Ezra were around…. I shook my head from that thought before it took me under.

"Aunty," Oscar mumbled.

"Yes, little man?"

"Can I have pancakes?"

"You can have anything. As soon as I'm done here, I'll make you some."

"Thanks. Uncle Asher, do you want pancakes?"

I glanced over my shoulder to see Asher's eyes shine, his chest expanding. I could feel how honored he was the kids were calling him uncle.

"Morning," my sister announced, walking in with a satisfied smile and fresh from the shower, dressed in jeans and a woolen sweater.

"Morning, Mommy," Sophie cried and ran at Yasmin to hug her. "I got up myself this morning, and then Aunty Paige was here. Did Daddy end up doing it harder?"

I laughed and Asher chuckled when Yasmin choked on her own saliva. "W-What?"

"I got up without calling out like you asked, and I heard you yell at Daddy about doing it harder."

"Ah, right…." Yasmin looked at us for help. We were too busy enjoying her embarrassment.

"It's all right, Soph," Eric said as he walked in. "I took care of it."

"Goodie," she yelled, and then went back to grabbing juice out of the refrigerator.

"Eric," Yasmin whispered in a harsh tone.

"She doesn't know any better."

"But others do." She gestured her head toward us.

Eric just smiled and called "Morning," before he planted a quick kiss on Yasmin's cheek and walked our way.

I froze when a frantic knock sounded on the door. Asher was up out of his seat and at the door in seconds, opening it. He stepped back, and Aggie, the witch who was spying on her coven mistress, moved in. Her eyes wide with worry.

"Eric, take this," I said, handing him the spatula. "Ollie wants pancakes."

"So does Asher," Oscar said quickly.

"I'll let your mom know if we can make it back in time."

He grumbled, "Fine." I gave him a quick kiss on the cheek, then Sophie and finally Yasmin. Only when I went to pull away from my sister, she took my hand. Our eyes met and she studied me.

"I'm okay," I told her.

"Promise?"

I nodded. "I will be. Alex and Thorn went on a mission. I'm just… jittery without them."

She gave me a soft smile. "They'll be okay."

"My queen, please," Aggie called.

My heart lurched. Whatever she had to say was important.

Yasmin squeezed my hand. "Go. Be safe."

"I will." With a quick fierce hug, we parted, and I rushed to the door. Asher slipped out first, then me and Aggie. Felnick already stood there with six other guards waiting for an order.

"Down to the office. Felnick, call in more guards because you're in with us. I want four guards to stay here with my family," I told him.

"Yes, my queen." He dropped behind to organize the men while we kept going until we reached my office.

Once inside with the door closed, I went behind the desk and faced Aggie, demanding, "What's wrong?"

"Grace didn't come back last night," Aggie said, ringing her hands together in front of her while Asher slowly moved around to my back. Aggie went on, "She told us she had to head into the city to get more herbs. Something she'd done in the past, but she never came back. I overheard two of her close friends say they hoped her plan goes well. I don't have a good feeling."

The door banged open, and Felnick entered with Alma in his arms.

"Alma," I cried and rushed around the desk, only to have her grin over at me.

"Put me down, handsome. Maybe next time we can do a different kind of riding?" Alma winked up at him while he blushed and set her on her feet.

"What's going on?" I asked, stopping at her side and taking her arm to lead her over to the chair.

She patted my hand with her free one. "Don't fret. I'm fine. Just exhausted from all the darn stairs in here. May I suggest getting elevators?"

"Noted." Asher grinned.

"Good."

"Miss Alma, you said it was urgent to get here, which was why you asked me to carry you," Felnick said.

"Oh yes." She smiled. "I've seen it. The council will soon know of our existence. War is coming. How you choose to approach it will decide on the outcome."

"Can't you just tell us what way to approach it?" I asked.

"No, dear. The powers that be won't let me."

"Can you tell us when at least?" Asher questioned.

"Nope."

"But it must be soon since you've told us now," I said, more to myself than anyone.

Alma smiled up at me as I leaned my butt against the desk in front of her.

"Soon could mean anything. Days, weeks, or even a month," Felnick added. I glanced to him and caught him looking away from Aggie quickly. She didn't see his hungry gaze as her eyes were on the floor.

Until she lifted them and said, "I could go there. Pretend—"

"No." I shook my head. "What you're already doing for us is a risk. I won't have you attempting a bigger one."

"But—"

"No" was clipped. At first, I thought it was Asher. I turned to him, but he shook his head. I glanced to Felnick, who stood with his fists clenched, his jaw locked, and glaring at Aggie like he would kidnap her to protect her.

"I can do whatever I wish, Felnick."

"Oooh, this is good." Alma clapped.

"You cannot when you are so willing to risk your own life all the time."

Aggie's hands dropped to her hips, and her chin lifted in defiance. "Who are you to tell me?"

Felnick's teeth ground together before he bit out, "You'll find out exactly when you're older."

Aggie snorted. "That makes no sense. I'm old enough to know now."

Oh, this was awkward because she totally wasn't getting his point. He wanted her in a naked way. He wanted her in a way he had a say in her future and decisions.

"Fine. You want to know who I am to tell you why I won't allow you to risk your life?"

"Yes."

"Right now? Here in front of everyone?"

Her head jerked back. Confusion washed over her features, dipping her brows and pinching her lips. She opened her mouth, closed it and then opened it again to stutter, "Y-Yes, um, at least, I think so." She glanced at me. "Do I?"

"Yes, you do," Alma said.

Aggie nodded down at her. "Okay." She looked back at Felnick. "Then yes, I want to know."

"I'll be the man in your future, Aggie. I'll be the one in your bed, claiming you as mine, and you'll be the woman who will want to stay there and not risk her life because you'll see a future with me."

Wow, that was awesome.

Aggie's cheeks shot to a deep red. "Uh… no."

Felnick blanched. "No?"

Alma scoffed. "Oh, don't you pretend you don't like him. You've been crushing on him since you were a youngin' I heard."

"Alma!" Aggie yelled.

Felnick was now looking smug. "We'll talk more about this later then."

"I…. What…?" She shook her head. "No, we won't." She glared.

"We'll see." He faced me. "My queen, your guards will be ready for when the time comes for war. I'll even ask around to see if there are others willing to join the fight."

Alma gurgled. We all looked to her; she shook her head.

My brows drew down. "No to others joining?" I asked. She

winked. "But war is coming here, we'll need all the people there are if what I hear about the ruthless council is right."

Alma shook her head but said nothing. Obviously, she couldn't speak on the matter.

"Alma," Asher called. She gazed up at him. "Is the war coming here?"

She winked. That was a yes.

"We're missing something," I stated. Alma touched her nose.

"The council will come for us?" Aggie asked.

Alma winked.

"If they come here, will we win?" Asher asked quietly. She shook her head.

"Which is why we don't need more guards," I said quietly. "They'll win no matter." Alma winked, then gurgled, but I was lost in the fear. It was like an invisible fist surrounded my heart and squeezed it tightly. I couldn't lose anyone. The people, *my* people, we had to get them out. Oh God, my family. The kids. All the children.

The door opened and Nate strolled in. "Alma, do we have a chance if we take the fight to them?" He'd been listening at the door.

When Alma lifted her hand and shook it side to side, I knew it meant it was a possibility. It still meant risking my men, my guards. It meant there would be a war with only a slight chance we'd win. But if we didn't take it there, go to them, we didn't have a chance at all.

"I don't fucking like this," Nate announced.

Everyone nodded, looking dejected.

"At least there's a better chance for us if we go there, or we'll risk losing our lives and the people under our care," Felnick said. We could all hear the tension in his voice, the worry.

I dropped to my knees and grabbed Alma's hands. "Can we run? Can the mages and witches move our community someplace else?"

She shook her head. "The fight is inevitable."

"Meaning even if we move, it'll still happen in the future," Nate said.

Asher's hands landed on my shoulders. Softly, he said, "You knew this would come, love."

I bit my bottom lip and nodded. I straightened and turned into him, gripping his T-shirt. "I just didn't know it would be so soon. It kills me knowing you will all walk into danger with me."

"If we don't, the council could ruin so many more lives. They've killed innocents, probably kidnapped some more. They need to be stopped, and we're the best chance to do it." Nate told me things I already knew; it didn't mean the mind-numbing fear would ease.

Asher tucked my hair behind my ear. "Take that fear and switch it to anger when the time comes."

I wished I could walk into the battle on my own. However, I wasn't stupid. For the people, I would have a better chance of protecting their future with my men and whoever would be willing to go with us at my side.

"I will," I told him, because I knew I would.

CHAPTER THIRTY-ONE

ASHER

She was amazing. I could feel her terror, but I knew without a doubt she would do what she had to for the future. To make sure the people she protected were safe from the clutches of the council. We all knew there would come a time we'd have to do something about the council members and had hoped it wouldn't be for a while, but fate had stepped up our timeline.

Looking to Nate, I saw the resolve in his eyes. When the time did come, we would do everything to make sure our mate would live on for a happier time within the supernatural world.

"For now, and until Alex and Thorn are back, maybe we should get back on the subject of Grace," I suggested.

"Ah, yes, Grace," Alma murmured.

An explosion erupted outside.

I flashed to the window and peered out, sensing Nate at my side. We both took in the chaos. People were scattered below, running away from the huge hole in the gate.

"I knew there was something else I forgot to tell you," Alma said.

"What?" Paige demanded.

Alma sighed. I glanced back to see her studying her nails. "It seems Grace has taken to the dark side, Obi-Wan. She's come to kill you using blood magic." Another explosion rocked the castle. "Better get out there before she takes her anger out on innocent bystanders."

Nate tugged his shirt from his body, and Paige yelled harshly, "Look away, Aggie."

"I've got it," Felnick said, crossing the room quickly to cover Aggie's eyes.

Nate snorted and removed his pants. "Open the door for me, Paige, and stay here."

The queen called for her power. Her eyes changed, her claws extending along with her teeth. "You are not leaving me behind. Neither of you are," she snarled, looking from Nate to me, and when I nodded, she then glanced back to Nate.

He cursed yet didn't fight with her any longer. The shift came over him. His body morphed, bones popped, and in seconds, he landed on all fours as his huge wolf form.

"Felnick, stay here with them," Paige ordered, her hand on the door handle.

"But—"

"Felnick. Alma and Aggie are important to me. Actually, take them to my family's suite and guard all of them."

Felnick tipped his chin down. "Yes, my queen."

She swung the door open, and Nate bounded out before Paige ran into the hall. I quickly followed, the air surrounding me fluttering papers from the desk around the room. I caught Alma's laugh. Together, we raced down the busy hall of people scattering for safety. However, some stopped to watch in awe to see the queen herself running into the threat.

It wasn't that long ago her fear had control. Looking at her now, I would have thought nothing could scare her. Her people, our people, should be proud of the type of queen Paige was.

Along the trek, twenty or so guards joined our line of defense, but already I could hear the fighting had started outside. I locked my emotions away from my mate. She glanced at me and nodded, then did the same. We couldn't be distracted.

Just as we reached the front door that led into the market area, we heard, "Come out, little queen. It's time to test your strength."

Guards pushed the doors open. We stepped out together. Grace had brought demons along with her. It was those the guards had been fighting while Grace stood just inside the gate and stared on smiling.

Any time someone approached her, they sank to their knees and cried out in pain. She'd protected herself with a spell.

"Ah, there she is. Welcome to the party, little queen." The fighting around us stopped. Everyone, even the demons, watched as Paige walked on slowly, taking in everything.

"I'm just happy you're calling me queen at all, Grace. It means you do see me as one."

Grace's upper lip rose. "You may be queen for now, but I'll rip your powers from your body when I take your heart."

The wolf gnashed his teeth and snarled at Grace even as

demons roared and stamped their hooves or feet into the ground.

Paige threw her head back and laughed.

I saw the way Grace's features blanked, her confidence lessened all for a second before a scowl marred her face. "I wouldn't laugh, little queen. My army and I have you outnumbered."

"Take out the main player and the army will fall," I said.

Grace's gaze flicked to me. "You don't stand a chance, vampire."

I shrugged. "We shall see."

She cackled and looked back to Paige. Grace's confidence had her pulling her shoulders back, had a smirk lifting her lips, and an evil glint shining in her eyes. "Tell me something, little queen. Where are your two other men?"

Paige's steps faltered until she stopped completely. "What are you saying, Grace?"

"I heard they went on a mission. I heard they were ambushed. I heard they were taken out." Her smirk grew into a smile.

"What did you do?" Paige demanded, her voice deeper, darker. Her ghoul side would be after vengeance. Fury leaked through her block, but before she could act, we needed answers first. When I took her hand in mine, she gripped me hard, but I knew she'd understand I was just trying to help her. Like the wolf was by stepping in front of her and pressing his body against her legs.

"They're dead."

"You lie," Paige bellowed. She managed a step forward even with the wolf and me holding her.

Grace leaned forward a little. "I don't."

"Do you forget bonded mates can feel when the other has passed?" I question.

Grace's lips thinned. Then she threw her hands out as if to say it didn't matter. "I'm unsure if she'd feel it when they're in Hell."

Fuck.

Even I wasn't sure of the consequences, and when Paige glanced at me, she saw it on my face. Her jaw clenched, her body tensing.

In a low, hard voice, she asked, "And *you* were a part of their ambush?"

Grace, sensing her mistake, took a step back but then stopped.

"Is this how you got more power? Why you switched to using blood magic? You aided the demons?" a voice called from behind us.

"Aggie, Jesus Christ, get the fuck back," Felnick hissed. He'd left Paige's family suite, had disregarded Paige's orders. Even though he did it for the woman he saw as his, he would pay for not listening.

"Ah, sweet Aggie. Come here, dear."

"So you can drain my powers? Where's Montana? Where's Renee?"

Grace didn't answer, and as Aggie stepped up to my side with Felnick at her back, I caught the tears in her eyes. "Even though they followed you blindly, they didn't deserve death just so you can darken your soul."

"Felnick?" Paige snapped low.

"They're safe. The guards are with them. Michael is there with some shifters. Alma sent me after Aggie." When Paige nodded, Felnick relaxed a little, until Aggie took another step forward.

"Now isn't the time to step up, Aggie. I will bury you." Grace stretched her arms out, lifting her hands, and then black smoke swirled. "I will suck the life right out of you, child."

"I'd like to see you try," Aggie clipped.

"Aggie," Felnick snapped. He wrapped his arms around her to pull her back. She stood on his foot, elbowed him in the ribs, and shot off a beam of white light toward Grace.

"Attack," Grace yelled.

Mayhem broke out. The demons attacked anyone they were close to. It was time to let my vampire loose. Especially when my dead heart nearly jumped in my throat when Paige bounded over her wolf and charged the demons who'd surrounded a bear shifter.

Jesus, she would be the death of me.

PAIGE

AS I CHARGED THE DEMONS, who were all around a lone bear shifter, fury washed through me. I jumped Nate and raced the bear's way. Out of the corner of my eye, I caught Asher's vampire side bursting out of him. A wave of arousal had my nipples hardening, my clit throbbing, and my body humming.

Now isn't the damn time, body.

In their normal state, my mates turned me into a puddle of desire, but when I saw their monster, it was as if my monster readied my body to take my men. Even in the middle of a fight apparently.

Shaking my head, I pushed off the ground with my feet and landed onto the back of one demon. My arms flung over his enormous hunched shoulders, and I easily slid my claws into his chest. He howled, bucked, and tried to grab me. I locked my legs around his waist and shredded his heart inside his body. The demon dropped to the ground on his knees. I pushed off him, taking his head with me.

I glanced up to see Asher. His green eyes were trained on me, the other demons around the injured bear shifter were on the dirt. All headless. Black blood dripped from Asher's claws.

He was ferocious and amazing to look at.

"Take him inside for help," I told Asher.

He snarled at me. "No. Protect *Mine*." He wanted to stay at my side.

"Please, Asher."

A demon got close to him. Asher's hand snapped out in a blurred movement, and the demon was missing his head.

"No," he demanded.

"It's all right, my queen," Clyde said, appearing out of nowhere. "I'll take care of the shifter. Keep Asher at your side."

"Witches," someone yelled.

"Aggie?" I called, glancing at her, and found her floating in the sky with a bubble surrounding her body as she tried to fight every spell Grace threw at her. Sweat covered her face, worrying me. She could run out of steam before taking Grace down. We had to help.

"They're with her," Aggie said through clenched teeth. Felnick stood below Aggie, moving this way and that with his sword raised high and slicing anything that got too close.

"Fuck," I bit out.

A whimper caught my attention. Nate. I searched around me, knowing he wouldn't be far, and he wasn't. Only what I saw had a haze of anger washing over me. A witch stood over him. Her lips moved, spelling him in some way. Yet he still tried to attack; he crawled toward her on his belly.

"Asher," I called.

"Yes?"

"It's time to feed," I told him.

"The witches," he hissed. Then he curled his arm around my waist. Wind whipped me in the face as he flashed us close to Nate. Asher's hands went to my waist right before he threw me at the bitch attacking Nate.

Shock crossed her features as I crashed into her. She landed on her back on the ground. I rolled to break my fall, and then on all fours, I crawled back to her. Her hands glowed, but all I wanted was her death. Nothing else worried me. She'd hurt what was mine. She would pay.

As I pushed her shoulders in the ground, I ignored the burning sensation at my waist and dropped my mouth to her neck where I bit. My razor-sharp teeth easily slid into her soft skin. I tore out a chunk, spat it to the side, and then went in for more. She screamed, wiggled, and fought, but it wouldn't be enough.

More screams of terror sounded around me before they were cut off and I felt the thump of something hitting the ground. Asher was at work.

Nate was at my side, growling. Even though I ate at her neck, she still managed another loud yell, and then I saw Nate get a hold of one of her arms in his mouth. The pain at my waist disappeared as I heard her take her last breath.

Lifting off her, I pushed my claws into her chest, cutting through her ribs and grabbing her heart, crushing it into nothing.

Nate whimpered at my side as he shoved his nose against my waist. I sat back and lifted my top. Two handprints were burned into my skin, near down to the bone.

Nate licked at my face as I ran my hands through his hair. "I'll be fine. It's already healing."

"You will not best me," Grace bellowed.

Asher stopped at my side and slowly helped me up, and we watched Grace take a step closer to Aggie before she threw a black ball of something at her. It surrounded Aggie's bubble.

"Shit," I whispered, seeing the bubble slowly being eaten away.

Aggie cried out in frustration. Her hands shot out—white light built in each palm. Her eyes slid to mine, and then in my mind, I heard her voice. *"Her defenses will be down for only a second. You'll need to get to her and kill her."*

Clenching my jaw, I nodded.

Taking Asher's hand in mine, I whispered, "Get ready."

"I heard." Aggie must have told all of us.

Around us, the guards still fought the dwindling demons and what was left of the witches. I saw Clyde drinking from one witch, and the bear shifter was up and back to fighting, even when I'd thought he'd be out of action for a while.

A howl swept over the area. Nate lifted his head and joined in.

The wolves were on the way, and close. As I looked toward the gate, I saw the first few race through, attacking where they could. Helping.

Quickly, I moved my gaze back to Aggie just as the last of Grace's spell consumed Aggie's bubble.

"No!" Felnick bellowed as the blackness reached out for Aggie, latching onto her foot.

Her eyes slid to us then back again.

This was it.

CHAPTER THIRTY-TWO

PAIGE

My heart gave a fearful hard thump, but I had to steel it. I had to push it back. For the people. For Aggie and for us.

The blackness slid up Aggie's body, but it was as if she ignored it; however, I could see how hard she gritted her teeth. Aggie's whole body went into the push of her power as she flung her hands forward and shot two orbs of white light at Grace.

It surrounded Grace's own invisible bubble. Grace gasped as her barrier started to get devoured.

Asher's arm shot around my waist. He flashed us forward as a gap appeared in the bubble. I felt his hesitancy in what he knew he had to do. "Do it," I clipped. He did. Asher threw me through the gap. I rolled, pushed up, and jammed my fist into

Grace's stomach. Blood sprayed. I gripped the flesh and organs inside her.

She let out a noise, glanced down, and gripped my wrist. Grace looked up and then smiled. But before she could get cocky, Nate was inside the bubble. He jumped onto her back and latched his powerful jaw around the back of her neck.

Fire from her hands burned my skin. I clamped my lips closed so I didn't scream. The scent near had me gagging. Nate whimpered. His whole body shook like he was being shocked over and over. He dropped to the ground.

Slowly, I glanced up. "You'll pay for that."

"I don't think—"

A screech of pain had me turning my head to see a lifeless Aggie fall out of the sky. Felnick managed to catch her and lay her gently to the ground. His hands slid over her, and when he looked up with pain-filled eyes, I knew she wasn't alive.

I wanted to cry, to let the anguish consume me, but I couldn't.

Grace, in the distraction, managed to push my hand out of her. She laughed maniacally as her body healed quicker than any creature before.

"Poor, poor Aggie. She was no match for blood magic. Just like you won't be."

My wrist still burned, but I straightened and then smiled. "That's the problem. I'm never alone."

Asher's hands wrapped around her chest, his claws digging in between her breasts. A bout of jealousy had my upper lip raising and growling. My vampire smirked until blackness—the same stuff that killed Aggie—burst from Grace's hands.

Asher laughed. He leaned down and said, "Blood magic does nothing to me, fool. I'm made of darkness and blood."

He stabbed his claws inside her and peeled her chest and ribs open with ease. Grace's hands dropped, her eyes blinking sluggishly, her body slowly dying. The only thing that kept her heart beating, which I could clearly see, was the dark magic.

I stepped up to her.

"I am queen. I am the *ghoul* queen. I was meant to rule over all races. I was meant to change the ways. I revel in the knowledge you'll die knowing you failed. To me, to Aggie, to the shifters, and my people because you are weak and contaminated."

I thrust my hand into her open chest and pulled out her heart. I lifted it to my mouth as the life in her eyes faded and bit into it as it beat for the last time.

The remaining demons vanished into the air, the last witch standing, who fought on Grace's side, turned her glowing hand on herself, and her body fell to the ground. A guard bent to check her vitals. He smiled over at me. She'd killed herself so she didn't have to face our wrath.

I looked back at Asher. He let her body drop to the floor while his green glowing eyes devoured me. He'd never be fazed by what I did, how I was. In fact, if the bulge in his pants was anything to go by, he enjoyed seeing my monster as much as I did his.

Something nudged my thigh. I threw the heart to the ground and looked down. Nate sat there and rubbed his head into my thigh. I crouched and wrapped my arms around his neck, taking his scent into my dead lungs. He licked my face, even though his dark eyes told me he was pissed about something.

Standing, I gripped his fur and took a step toward Asher,

using the back of my arm to wipe away the blood around my mouth. I needed my men. Both of them.

"My queen."

Pausing, I turned my head to see Felnick there.

The fog from my men lifted and I remembered.

Oh God, Aggie.

"Aggie," I whispered, ready to run to her side. Until Felnick's hand shot up.

"My queen." He bowed his head. "I couldn't save her. I failed her."

Over his shoulder, I saw Clyde picking up Aggie in his arms.

"What's going on?"

"He was willing to save her."

"He changed her?"

"Yes." Sadness overtook his eyes. "I didn't have a choice."

"It doesn't mean she won't be yours," Asher said, his vampire side no longer around.

"She'll have a bond with her master—"

"If it's meant to be, no bond with the master can change it."

"Felnick," Clyde called. "Come with us. She'll need you too."

Felnick's eyes widened, surprised. He'd honestly thought he'd lost any chance he had with Aggie. Felnick had been scared Clyde wouldn't want him around his new addition into his clan.

"My queen," Felnick said, though he didn't look back at me.

"Go. Be with her," I told him.

He took off, stopping at Clyde's side to take her hand in his. Clyde said something. Felnick looked up in shock, his lips thinning, but then tipped up before he nodded.

"What was that about?" I asked.

"Clyde has offered for Felnick to stay in his place and for her to feed upon him first."

I dipped my brows in confusion. "Isn't Felnick a ghoul? Does he have the blood to fill her?"

"Do you bleed, love?"

I glanced down to my arm to my tee where blood stained it from my wounds. "Yes, but I have a beating heart."

"That is true, but there will be enough blood in Felnick to supply Aggie with what she needs before he will have to feed to replenish the blood drained from his body."

Oh, I got it now. The blood from our kills stayed in our body, which was why my people bled without a beating heart.

Honestly, I still had a lot more learning to do.

Since arriving, each day seemed to have spun by in a blur of activity. The only moments that took their time was when I was with my men. Even still, they weren't long enough. I couldn't wait for the day where I had nothing to do but lounge around. If it ever came.

"Will Aggie be all right? Does… I mean, she'll still be a witch, right?"

Asher nodded. "She will, love. She'll be a hybrid. Half witch, half vampire."

"Are there many hybrids?" Seemed strange since there'd been many rules about cross mating and such.

"No. She'll be the first here. At least that I've sensed so far."

That made more sense.

"My queen" was voiced from our side. I turned to see a man who was even bigger built than Nate.

"Yes?"

He dropped to his knees and bowed, his forehead nearly touching the dirt. "Thank you for your assistance in saving me."

He had to be the bear shifter.

"You're welcome…"

"Leon Walton, my queen."

"Please stand," I asked. He did and towered over me, though that seemed normal around here. "Are you a part of Thorn's brotherhood?"

A pang of loss cracked my chest.

No. I ground my teeth together. They weren't lost. They were alive, and I would get them back.

"No, my queen. I'm a mere shifter. We don't belong with the brotherhood."

I scoffed; I couldn't help it. It seemed Thorn had to fold within the old laws as well. I knew he wouldn't have been discriminating on purpose; he would have followed the orders of the old advisers or queen.

Upon my scoff, Leon's gaze snapped up from the ground to meet mine. Asher and Nate rumbled out a growl. I fisted my hand in Nate's fur and took Asher's hand.

"It's all right." I lifted my chin and addressed Leon, "You were willing to fight for the people without even being a part of the brotherhood. Your courage is amazing. If you would, I'd like to invite you and four others you trust completely to safeguard my own family. But you will also be working together with another four brotherhood guards, if you accept."

He closed his eyes and dropped his chin. "What you bestow upon me is the biggest honor. Members of my sleuth would protect your family with our lives."

Dropping Asher's hand, I reached out for Leon's, only Asher, with his glowing eyes and descended fangs, grabbed my hand back and pulled it to his side. His grip unwavering as he hissed at Leon.

Leon tipped his head to the side, his lips twitching. "She is your mate, vampire."

"We're a little out of sorts after everything," I told Leon.

"Of course."

"How many are in your sleuth?"

"I have eight brothers, a sister and her mate, and they have four children."

Wow, okay, that was a lot of siblings.

"My queen," Gregory said, stopping at our side.

"Gregory." I smiled. "What are you doing here?"

"Jessup," he said simply.

"Yes, please thank him and his pack for his assistance."

"It was the least we could do," Jessup called, walking up to our huddle.

"How are you healed already?"

I was surprised when Jessup and Gregory blushed. Nate at my side snorted. Even in wolf form he still managed to do that.

"Ah…." Jessup rubbed the back of his neck. His naked neck. On his naked body. "I shifted, and a mate can, ah, help the healing process after."

"You're naked," I pointed out in case he didn't already know.

He chuckled. "Comes with the territory of being a shifter. We don't care about nudity."

I glanced down at Nate. I jabbed my finger on my chest and then down at him. "We care about it. You don't go around naked in front of anyone."

He huffed, not liking being told what to do.

"How are you not naked?" I asked Leon, noting he wore jeans and a flannel shirt.

He grinned. "My sleuth and I leave clothes all over the place. Seems my sister doesn't want to see us naked, and her mate doesn't want anyone looking at her naked either."

"I think I'll like them. That's what you should do…. Not

saying that naked isn't fine. Anyone who wants to go around naked can. Being naked for some is natural—"

"Love, how about you stop saying naked?"

"Good idea." I nodded. "Jessup, thank you and your pack for helping. Gregory, could I please ask a favor?"

"Of course, my queen."

"Are you able to set up some rooms for Leon?"

"Oh no, my queen," Leon said. "Please and thank you for the kind offer, but we live in the village, and we'd like to stay there. Our cubs go to the school there. We'd need to stay close. Since there are eight brothers of mine, we can rotate shifts to attend your family. Four on four off and so on, if you wouldn't mind." He dipped his head.

"Leon, that's fine, but as long as I'm not taking you away from any jobs you have in the village. I didn't even think of it before."

"Our jobs will be replaced by another easily. Nothing to worry about. It is honestly an honor to work for the queen."

I bit my bottom lip, feeling guilty for taking them away from the village, from their sleuth.

"Please, my queen. We would be looked upon as well-respected individuals if you allow us to still have the jobs to guard your family."

"As long as everyone in your, um, sleuth is okay with it."

His smile took up half his face. "They will be, but if you'll excuse me, I'll go and speak with them now."

I nodded. "All right, thank you."

"No, my queen, thank you again. My brothers would have been here, but they were far away fishing. They should return soon, and then I'll have your answer, which I'm sure will be a yes."

"Okay, Leon. If I'm not available, please let Gregory or Eric know, and they'll inform me."

He bowed, turned, and raced off.

"Your kindness has made that man's day, and no doubt his family's. Shifters have never been sought after from a queen, until now." Jessup smiled.

I glanced down at Nate. My fingers sifted through his fur on his shoulder. "Shifters were never a lesser being. We're all equal."

"But it is those who see it that makes a tremendous queen, such as yourself," Jessup said.

I shrugged. Asher chuckled. "Our mate doesn't do well with compliments."

I glared up at him. "No, I don't. Can we start cleaning up around here. I could use a shower. If only Alex was…." Misery twisted my stomach. I gripped Nate tighter to me and told Asher, "They're alive."

"I'm sure they are, love."

"They are." They had to be.

He nodded. "You would know, my love."

"I would, and I know they're alive. They'll come back. They'll… they're in Hell, Asher. Hell." I spun to Gregory. "I need to call Lucifer. Get me on the phone to Lucifer. Now."

His gaze dimmed. "I'm sorry, my queen, we have no way of contacting him."

"But he called me."

"I heard he had, but he wouldn't make it traceable. The former queen never had a number to contact him. If the devil wants to see you, *he* shows, *he* calls, never the other way around."

Frustration had me throwing my head back and yelling. How was this fair?

"They're in Hell, Asher. Can they survive Hell?"

"They would do anything to come back to you, my love. Anything."

Nate whimpered at my side and pressed himself into me. My insides were a swirling pool of fear, worry, and misery.

"Take the queen inside. We'll take care of this mess," Jessup offered.

"No!" I shouted, then took a deep breath. "I need to keep busy. I need something to do."

Asher nodded, and Nate started to move off. "Nate," I called and he turned. "I-I'd like you here with me." I couldn't let them out of my sight. Not now.

He barked, only I didn't talk wolf.

"I believe he's going to get dressed so no one here sees him naked," Jessup offered.

"Right, well, that's good." I nodded and then shot Nate a thumbs-up. I was sure I saw him roll his eyes at the gesture before leaving.

My gaze drifted down to Grace. I wished she wasn't dead already. Just thinking of what Thorn and Alex were going through in Hell made me want to kill her again and again.

They had to be alive.

No, they were. Deep inside me, I would have felt their loss, and even when their links to me were blocked, I would still know.

I would.

CHAPTER THIRTY-THREE

I stood back and eyed my work. I screwed my nose up. What had I been thinking painting Alex's room in purple? I tried to get the same color to match his eyes, but now it just looked like a squished eggplant. However, I wasn't the best painter. Thorn's room could contest to that when I'd messed up his walls, and maybe I got some on his floor and bed, in a deep red.

"We have to do something," Nate mock whispered to Asher behind me.

Asher hummed. I didn't know if he was agreeing or disagreeing.

Okay, maybe I might have lost my mind a little. The wolf pack wouldn't have me back until I fixed their plumbing. Something I'd tried to help with since I'd been human not that long ago, compared to them at least. But now their water only ran cold water. Thankfully, Leon's brother had experience in plumbing, but he was still working on the other problem I'd made.

People around the castle stepped out of my way these days since I'd stopped everyone I passed and asked them if I could help with anything. With a few mistakes with sewing, cooking, gardening, and home renovations, they learned to dodge me, so they wouldn't feel guilty and have to accept my help. At least they'd gotten over the queen asking to assist people. And that was only because my rant about how queens were able to do whatever they wanted in a time of need and support, or anytime for that matter, had been spread when the first person questioned why the queen would sink so low as to do mundane things.

It had been two weeks since Grace had come in ready for a battle and informed me that Alex and Nate were in Hell.

Two weeks.

Two long-ass, frustrating weeks.

Every minute that passed, I made sure I kept busy, else I'd be a mess in the corner of a room, holding a dolly and asking for my mommy.

Nate growled in the back of his throat. "You know they're alive or else we would both know it. Our souls would have lost a part of itself."

I knew they were. *We* knew they were since Nate had claimed them both and had made his own connection to them. We just never ventured to the part where we were unsure. Would we feel the broken bond even from Hell?

I quickly pushed that thought away and went over to the paint tin. "I know," I muttered.

"Paige, you need to rest. You've only had a few hours sleep in two weeks, and you need to feed," Asher said. "Your people are concerned about you."

"You also look like shit," Nate added.

Straightening, I swung my eyes his way and lasered him with a glare.

His brows raised. "You do." He walked to the door and opened it. I saw Gregory standing there. "Make her a meal, normal food and flesh. Bring it up but leave it outside the door. Have a guard watch it."

Gregory smiled, and he dipped his head before walking off. Nate closed the door and turned, crossing his arms over his chest. "You need a shower, rest, and food before this fucking meeting tomorrow, and I'm going to make sure you get all three."

I snorted, rolled my eyes, and picked my brush up to walk back to the wall. He was right. I knew he was. I should have wanted to look my best for the ceremony in front of all to swear Aggie, Leon, and his brothers into my close fold; however, I just couldn't bring myself out of this depressed state of worry to care enough. I was also concerned that if I slept, I would dream. Even though I hadn't had that dream I used to have since I'd been there, I had no doubt my mind would twist and show me Alex and Thorn dead. I couldn't handle it.

I was beyond pissed they weren't back and beyond angry I had no way of contacting Lucifer. No matter how hard I'd tried. I swore to Christ, when Lucifer got his ass into gear and showed up, since apparently a couple of weeks didn't mean two weeks in his books, if he appeared without knowing my men were in his world, I would carve him open and feast upon his insides with pleasure. He had to know something.

"Right, that's fucking it," Nate clipped as I started brushing the wall with more paint. I ignored his words. He'd been threatening to beat my head against the wall for the last week. I knew he was all talk. "Vampire, are you ready?"

"I've been ready for some time, wolf," Asher answered, his voice low and thick. Slowly, I turned, and the paintbrush dropped from my hand. Both of my men were getting undressed.

"W-What's going on?"

They didn't say anything, just removed their pants like they already had with their tops and shoes. Nate's body shimmered and shifted; his half form shot forward. His tail swished back and forth. I wanted to rush over to him and play with it. My clit pulsed and my nipples hardened. Nate drew in the scent around him, and he shot me a cocky smile.

"Already turned on, angel?"

I gave him the finger. He chuckled around his sharp teeth. My gaze went to Asher as he hissed. His body had grown a little. His claws lengthened, his eyes glowed, his fangs dropped, and he licked his lips, watching Nate like he was a delicious meal. Asher's long, dark hair blew from the open window behind him. Usually he kept it tied back in a braid, but tonight this wasn't the case, and it made him look like an incredibly hot monster.

Both had my body shaking with need.

In a blink, Asher was beside Nate, picking him up and throwing him into the wall. The room shook. I expected some guards to rush in, but the door stayed closed. Nate jumped to his feet and rushed at Asher. He leaped, wrapped his arms around Asher's neck, and swung his body over Asher's back with his arms still locked around his neck. I expected Asher to be flung over Nate's shoulder, but Asher flipped himself over and wrapped his arms around Nate's waist. I would have been worried for both of them, if it wasn't for the erections they both sported—turned on from the fighting.

Nate bucked, but Asher didn't move; in fact, as Nate growled, Asher hissed into his neck before latching his teeth onto Nate's shoulder. Nate let out a roar before stilling for a moment, and the roar turned into a rumble of his chest. Asher's hand glided down and wrapped around Nate's hard-on, stroking him up and down.

My knees wobbled. I sank to the floor on my knees and kept my gaze on the two beautiful monsters.

Asher licked at Nate's neck before saying, "Do you hear, wolf, our mate—well, she's not yours yet, but listen to her heart pattering in her chest. Smell her desire. She likes a show, but are you ready for *me* to claim *you*?"

"Never," Nate clipped. He unleashed his claws, dropped his hands, and stabbed them into Asher's thighs. Asher snarled. His eyes swirled from green to black, something I hadn't seen before, and back again. If I had to guess, I would say it happened because his vampire was pissed.

I knew I'd been right when Asher's hold dropped from Nate for a second, only to come back and rake his nails up Nate's stomach and chest, leaving blood-welling red marks. I nearly missed Nate shuddering against Asher. Then he picked Nate up and threw him across the room. Before Nate could even get up, Asher flashed to his side. A low growl was Nate's only warning before Nate was picked up and thrown against another wall. Only Nate landed on his feet in a crouch this time and stood as Asher reached for him again. Nate's arms went around Asher's waist, and he slammed them to the floor. His hands snapped out to hold Asher to the floorboards. They snarled, hissed, nipped, and growled at each other.

"Open your legs, vampire. Let me have you." Nate's voice was rough and deep. His tail… well, it wagged in excitement while he ground their cocks together, causing Asher to still for a second, but when Nate's feet slipped between Asher's and started to spread Asher's legs apart, the vampire smiled up at him. Only, it wasn't a pleasant one.

I gasped when their bodies floated up to a standing position. Asher leaned closer to Nate, their arms still held together above their bodies. "Not happening, wolf. *I* claim *you*."

Nate snapped his teeth in Asher's face. Asher laughed darkly. He managed to free one hand and dropped it around Nate, where his cute, fluffy tail swayed side to side. Somehow, I'd spread my legs without thinking about it and was rubbing my fingers over my jean-clad pussy as I watched Asher circle his hand around the base of Nate's tail. It stopped moving.

Nate's warning growl echoed around the room, and then it was Asher's turn to fly into a wall. Before he did so, Asher spun in the air and landed on his feet. He pushed the hair out of his face and grinned.

I blinked when Asher disappeared from sight. Nate's growl grew louder as he spun this way and that.

"Wipe that smile off your face, angel," Nate snarled at me.

I didn't realize I'd been smiling, but I couldn't wipe it away if I tried. I liked what I could see. I also enjoyed Nate calling me angel a lot.

A breeze swept over me. A whisper touched my ear. "Take your clothes off, love." Another breeze and Asher was gone. I heard a slap, and Nate cursed, snarling at the air as he rubbed his butt cheek.

Covering my mouth, I laughed silently but stood and quickly undressed. Nate's nostrils flared, and his dark gaze swung to me. His growl turned rougher. His eyes stayed locked on me as I made my way to Alex's bed.

Asher winked at me from where he leaned against the wall behind Nate. My vampire was playing a game of distraction to get what he wanted, and it was working because Nate never wavered from looking at me.

This was fun.

A thrill shot to my pussy, wetting me more than I already was. Nate breathed it in and took a step forward. He shook his head and glanced around the room. Asher was already on the move, flashing so unbelievably fast that we couldn't keep an eye on him. Nate snarled, reaching out, trying to grasp the invisible.

Feeling playful myself, I also wanted to gain the one bond I hadn't. Nate would be mine… and in turn, if Asher claimed Nate, then it wasn't my fault. Not when both of them turned me into a lusty mess.

I climbed onto the bed. Nate, hearing the squeaks of the mattress, whipped his eyes my way. Smiling, I lay on my back. He was close to the end of the bed, so when I dragged my legs up to place my feet on the bed and then spread them, he had a straight line to my drenched pussy.

He sucked in a harsh breath and took a step my way, only to stop, shake his head violently, and then glance around the room, searching for his prey.

I needed to play dirty to get his attention focused only on me.

I lifted up on one elbow and slowly glided my hand over my breasts and moaned. His dark gaze shot right back to me, and he let out a louder rumble.

"I know what you're doing, angel. It won't work."

I shook my head. "I don't know what you're talking about."

His upper lip raised, and he snarled, knowing I was lying. Yet, he didn't take his eyes off me. Instead, his gaze drank me in. It roamed over my skin, heating my body more. I moved my hand down over my belly, where it quivered under my own light touch. I then dipped my fingers into my curls and watched Nate take another step toward me, his hands fisting at his sides. His erection leaked at the tip, and I wanted to lick it away.

At the first touch with just one finger to my sensitive and throbbing clit, I threw my head back and moaned again.

Next, my hand was thrown away from my pussy, and there was a beast of a man between my legs, taking in his first taste of me. His tongue swiped over my folds, then from the bottom of my slit to the top where he circled his tongue around my nub. I cried out, lying flat on my back and gripping the sheets.

"Oh God," I yelled, and felt Nate's lips and mouth stiffen on me. A warm sensation started in my chest and weaved low to where Nate was connected to me. Nate stilled for a moment, then growled, which vibrated over me, causing me to twitch. It was then I remembered Thorn's words. Any sexual fluids would complete the bond; it just happened to be while Nate was between my legs. His hands and claws dug into my thighs, holding me tighter while the bond heated to the painful flame and then disappeared. Nate groaned. A burst of crazed desire shot into me. Desire, respect, annoyance, and even love... I knew it was all from Nate because I felt the same for him and made sure he could feel my own emotions.

He groaned again before giving me one last swipe of his tongue and climbed up to hover over me.

"The bond's complete," he stated.

Smiling, I nodded and cupped his cheeks. "Yes." I ran a finger over his plump, wet bottom lip. "Now kiss me, my mate."

He nipped at my finger. "You're annoying."

"So are you."

"You're a pain in my ass."

I laughed, feeling so much lighter. "So are you."

"I… care about you."

My heart thumped hard. "I know." I lifted up and pressed my mouth to his. Against his lips, I whispered, "And I care about you."

He grunted. "Good." His arms wrapped around me. He captured my mouth in a demanding, hot, hard kiss while he slid his hard cock inside me. He ate my whimper into his own mouth, and if he didn't feel so good, I would have smacked that cocky smirk off his face.

Only his mouth then lifted off me, his head turned, and a snarl ripped out of him. Looking over his shoulder, I saw Asher with his hand wrapped around Nate's tail, stroking it up and down.

Nate had been claimed.

A giggle escaped me. Nate gave me a dirty look, but then pulled out from within me and thrust in deep. "Yes," I cried and saw him smile, until his growl came back, and he glanced over his shoulder again.

I couldn't see where Asher's other hand was. When I saw Nate's eyes widen, he pumped himself in and out of me and bit on his bottom lip, all while his chest rumbled with the same growl.

"Yes, wolf, fuck our mate," Asher bit out.

Nate did. His hips moved faster, but then he stilled. His growl changed up a bit, one of warning.

"I told you, wolf. You're mine," Asher said, and then I felt a powerful thrust. Nate threw his head back and roared. Asher's hand dug into Nate's hips, and then we were all moving together. I clamped my legs up around both men to feel Asher move in and out of Nate while Nate entered me again and again.

Nate's head dipped. His mouth latched on my nipple and sucked. It drew the orgasm straight up and out of me. My walls clamped around Nate's cock, and he groaned. Asher hissed behind him, their hips still moving back and forth, and then Asher bit into Nate's shoulder and both of them shuddered above me, moaning.

Nate panted into my neck. "We're doing that again, but it'll last longer, and I'll have you, vampire."

Asher chuckled. I could already see both of my men were back to their other selves. "I'd like to see you try again, wolf."

I loved their teasing, their friendship, and even their love for each other. They may not admit it to one another, but I could feel it from both of them, and it wasn't just aimed at me.

CHAPTER THIRTY-FOUR

My body had recharged with a good round of lovemaking, a shower, food, and sleep. I'd never get over the separation anxiety I felt for Alex and Thorn, but I had to pull myself together and make sure I was still there for the mates I had around me. And for my people and my family too—a family who had banned me from their suite because they were sick of seeing me… sick of my moods, sick of my interfering in their own lives.

Okay, I probably went too far when I told Eric he needed to knock my sister up because she wanted another child. And that if he didn't do it, I was sure she'd find someone around the place who would easily take her to bed and impregnate her.

Yes, it wasn't my best moment. Especially since Yasmin had

confided in me quietly how Eric said he didn't want any more children, but she did.

Thankfully, when I went there that morning, dropped to my knees and begged for forgiveness for being over-the-top stupid, Eric sighed, nodded, and let me in. Asher was off seeing to something, so I had Nate following me into their home close behind. In fact, since the bond completed, he hadn't left my side, and I lost count of the times he buried his nose in my neck to draw in my scent.

I didn't mind at all; in fact, I thought it cute.

Just after I'd entered my sister's quarters, I was attacked. It had only been a couple of days, but when the kids wrapped their little arms around me for a hug, it felt like I'd been missing them for years.

Yasmin stood in the doorway to the kitchen with her arms crossed and a glare fixed on her face. I offered an apologetic smile. She turned and walked back into the kitchen.

"Is Mommy cranky with you?" Sophie asked in a whisper before she ran and jumped into Nate's arms. He spun her, causing her to giggle.

"She sure looks it," Oscar said.

I ruffled his hair and told him, "It's fine. I'll go talk to her." I glanced at Nate. "Wait here, please." He grunted and then was too busy defending himself when Oscar charged him and leaped onto his back. Nate fell, pretending with them. There hadn't been many moments I'd seen him with my niece and nephew, but when I did, I loved watching their interaction. Actually, I loved all of my men and how easily they melted around the kids.

I quickly pushed that thought aside, or it would lead me

down a path I wasn't ready to travel. One that was probably filled with longing and hope.

When I entered the kitchen, Yasmin stood leaning against the counter. I smiled again, but she didn't return it.

"Sisters before misters. You always said that," she told me.

"I have." I nodded.

"What you told Eric was hard, cruel, and could have damaged our marriage."

"I know, and I'm so sorry. I've been crazy since Alex and Thorn haven't returned to me."

Her eyes softened a little. "I understand, but you're never to interfere in my marriage again."

"I won't. I promise."

"Okay," she said.

"Okay as in you'll forgive me or just okay?"

"I'll forgive you. Just this once."

I ran at her and hugged her tightly. "I am so very sorry."

She curled her arms around me. "I know you are. I also know you have a lot on your plate. The battle didn't go unnoticed, and then with the news of Alex and Thorn, plus with the visit from Lucifer, which I still can't believe, a lot is going on."

I nodded. "There's so much to deal with." I pulled back, my smile sad. "You know I was always the procrastinator on many things in life, but now it seems everything is just flying at me so fast it's hard to deal with. It's hard to get my head around, but I have to, and not only for myself but for the people depending on me."

She tucked my hair behind my ears and then rested her hands on my shoulders. "You're not alone in dealing with everything, Paige. You must remember you have your mates, you have us, the guards, the wolf pack now. You have so many who are willing to help you in any way. Even to help you get through your emotions. Just lean on us all a little more. It's okay to feel worry and fear for those you care about."

Nodding, I stepped back. Her hands dropped, and I started pacing. "Everything is still so new. I'm not sure how I'm supposed to act, what I'm supposed to tell people. I feel like a failure for showing my emotions. I need to show strength."

"The queen can show her people it's okay to care. It's okay to lose it when something bad happens. It makes you human… well, not human, but more approachable, more like the people who look up to you."

She was right. I tried to push my emotions down and do things that kept me busy to hide showing my emotions. I didn't need to hide them. Everyone felt, and even though I was the queen, I could still be me.

Stopping, I faced Yasmin. "You're right."

"Thank you, but another word of advice. What the queen shouldn't be doing is trying to fix plumbing, nearly burning down the kitchen, and decorating. Leave that up to the rest, the ones who know what they're doing."

A laugh escaped me. "I will."

"I'm glad. One last thing."

"Yes?" I said hesitantly.

"What the hell are you wearing?"

I glanced down at myself and laughed. "Alex's shirt and Thorn's pants."

"They are way too big for you. You look like a child."

I smiled. "I know, but they're comforting. There is something I could use your help with."

"What's that?"

"I have that ceremony this afternoon, can you help me pick the right dress for it?"

She snorted. "I think it's best I do."

"I love you, Yasmin."

"And I love you."

My sister was the best in the world.

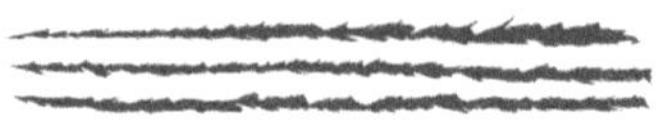

Nate

"WILL YOU FUCKING QUIT DOING THAT?" I snapped, but not too harshly. I couldn't have made it harsh even if I wanted to because, even though I was pissed and concerned for Alex and Thorn, I was still happy, and that shit made me feel guilty because I didn't have my other mates here to share the happiness I got from Paige and Asher.

Christ, I was a ball full of fucked-upness.

"No, I don't believe I will, wolf," Asher said at my back as he nipped on my neck and continued purring. His vampire fucking purred. He was too damn satisfied after we'd fought again, and he'd managed to win. Though, I was sure my wolf was happy to give up if we got to feel the way he made us the night before. I hid my grin in the pillow. We knew we had to move, but we were being lazy. I was on my stomach with Asher practically covering my body with his weight. I liked it. Never thought I'd say that shit, but I did.

Paige walked out from the bathroom with a towel wrapped around her. She'd only left the bed moments ago after sucking me until I came down her throat while I enjoyed eating her pussy as Asher fucked me. "Are you both still agreeing with Yasmin with her choice of that?" She pointed down at the dress over the lounge chair. I didn't even look at the fabric. I couldn't stop looking at her gorgeous body, knowing she was mine.

Ours.

Christ, I was one lucky wolf.

"It's perfect, love," Asher said, running his claws up and down my back, drawing out goose bumps.

"For the millionth time, she picked well," I told her, then winked. She grinned, her eyes warm as she looked at us. Even the night before and moments ago, I never once sensed jealousy, and she'd kept our links open. In fact, I knew for certain she enjoyed a fucking lot watching Asher and me together. It'd be the same when I took Alex and Thorn as well.

All of us were made for each other. Shit. Being with a guy had never been in my thoughts until Paige came into our lives and blew our minds wide open. Though, I thought perhaps I was the only one who hadn't been with a guy previously. It was safe to say I'd been missing out.

Paige was our heart and soul. She was everything.

We had the perfect pack.

Even though my wolf and I hadn't claimed Asher in the way we had Alex and Thorn, we still saw him as ours, and the possessiveness was still the same over him that it was for them. Found that out only a couple of hours ago when a bitch of a vampire checked him out as we'd walked down the hall. I'd known where her thoughts had gone, and they were picturing him naked. It was lucky Asher was fast or she wouldn't have any eyes to look at him again.

Of course, the fucker thought it was funny, until someone

brushed up against me in the kitchens, and Asher had her body flying through the room. It was lucky Paige had already changed things, and people seemed happier about said changes around the place because they found our actions cute. At least that was what Gregory told us on the walk back to Paige's room.

"Are you two getting ready any time soon?"

"Or you could come back to bed with us, angel," I said.

She pointed a finger at me and wiggled it side to side. "Don't tempt me, Nate. But, can I just say I love this… seeing you both like this. Happy." Her smile dimmed.

"Don't, love. Don't feel guilty for feeling happy in the moment because Alex and Thorn aren't with us. They will be eventually. They aren't lost to us forever. I'm sure of it. I'm also sure they'll want to hear about everything they've missed. Like the vampire beating the wolf."

I growled in the back of my throat, even though my wolf wasn't present since he was sleeping contently. "Be smug, vampire. It won't last."

Paige giggled. When I shot her a glare, she covered her mouth to try and hide it. I couldn't keep the glare when she was so fucking adorable. Also, when I felt fucking happy.

Goddamn, I wished Alex and Thorn were here.

"Come here, angel."

She shook her head. "I can't. You'll distract me, and we have to get to the ceremony soon."

I held out my hand while Asher went back to kissing and purring over me. "Come on, just for a little while."

Her lips thinned as she thought it over. Then she moved toward the bed and sat on the edge. I curled my arm around her waist and dragged her down, lifting enough to lay half over her. "This is better," I said.

She smiled. "I never would have thought that the big bad wolf was a cuddler."

"I never have been, but you're a bad influence on me."

She ran her hand through my hair. "I'm glad."

I hummed under my breath and rested my head against her shoulder. Asher's hand left my back, and I knew when Paige's hand disappeared from my hair that he'd taken it in his hand. I heard his kiss to her skin.

He leaned over me more so he could see Paige. "Back to what you were saying, love. I can only speak for myself, but I have never been this happy in my existence. What we have is beyond what I could have imagined in finding my perfect clan. You all complete me, and I look forward to the future we'll have."

I grunted. "Not long ago, I was thinking the same. Only I would have said pack, and I wouldn't have been that corny to say you complete me, but I'd think it."

Asher's fangs raked over my skin, his growl playful. "As soon as Alex and Thorn are home, we will tell them the same."

She licked her lips, which was distracting. "It hasn't been the same without them, and yet…."

"It has because we've all been together."

"Yes," she admitted guiltily.

"I know it's impossible not to feel guilty because I feel it as well, but we just have to remember that they're not lost to us. They will come back, and we'll all feel whole again," I told her. "It's not bad to be happy, to enjoy us, and for me to enjoy you both, and the same for Asher."

She nodded. "I know. I'll feel better when they are home."

"And they will be soon," a new voice drifted over us. Paige let out a scream. Asher's weight shifted as he flashed up and in front of us while I lay over Paige more, protecting her. Alma stood just inside the door. She rolled her eyes and waved her hand. "Oh, stop hissing at me, vampire. I come in peace."

"Maybe, crazy lady, come at a time when we're not fucking naked and in bed," I suggested angrily.

"How did you get in here?" Asher demanded.

She lifted a key in her hand.

"How did you get that?" I clipped.

Paige let out a muffled noise.

Fuck! I pulled back so I wasn't covering her face.

"Alma, what are you doing in here, and stop looking at my men like they're candy!" she demanded. "Asher, get some clothes on," she snapped.

Alma cackled, her hand covering her stomach while she kept laughing.

"Alma," Paige bit out. Annoyance swept through me, which came from Paige, and I knew she'd been feeling my rage. She ran her hands up and down my back.

"Right, yes, as I was saying, you all better get dressed."

"You didn't say that at all," I growled.

"Doesn't matter. Lucifer is on his way. I'm sure you'll want to greet him in the throne room."

Paige went to sit up, but the towel had slipped down and her breasts were on display. Even though the crazy woman was old enough to be her grandmother, she wasn't seeing Paige's tits.

"Thank you, Alma. We'll prepare," Asher said.

In other words, get the fuck out.

Alma snorted, obviously reading the brush-off. "Toodaloo." She waved and left.

"Wait," Paige yelled, but the old woman didn't return. Paige looked up at me. "What do you think she meant before?" Her eyes widened, and my heart stalled.

Both of us realized at the same time. While Asher chuckled at us, I bolted off the bed and ran to the bathroom, only to rush back and help Paige out of bed. I kissed her swiftly but hard and then said, "They're coming back." I reached out, sensed Asher close, and grabbed him, dragging him into our huddle.

She laughed cheerfully and shook us both. "They're coming home."

"They are, love. Let us prepare for them, and for Lucifer."

Shit. Forgot about that fucker.

CHAPTER THIRTY-FIVE

Dressed in the long black gown my sister picked out, I paced the staged area of the throne room. In a rush, we sent word to my people that the ceremony would be delayed due to Alma foreseeing the arrival of Lucifer, finally. Of course, mentioning his name put people in a nervous tizzy. No doubt the castle would be spick-and-span in an hour or so.

I probably should have been scared knowing the devil was on his way, but nothing could override the glee I felt knowing Alma had seen that Alex and Thorn were coming home too. They must have got a hold of Lucifer in Hell somehow, and he was bringing them back to me.

I glanced at the doors again and saw Felnick shake his head. He was on the lookout for them. He also had guards lining the walls in case something bad happened.

Again, no fear bombarded me even thinking that.

It was probably stupid, but I trusted Alma would have warned us in some cryptic way if Lucifer was coming here to harm us.

"My queen, are you sure you won't wear the crown?" Gregory asked for the fifth time.

Rolling my eyes, I looked down at him where he stood below the steps of the stage. "No. No and no. I'm not a crown-wearing kind of woman."

"But… it will show Lucifer—"

"Nothing. I promise I'll wear it when it's necessary, like… I don't know, public meetings with royalty."

"Lucifer is royalty," he said, his voice high and anxious.

That was true. Damn.

I looked to the crown on a cushion in his hands. It gleamed with diamonds, rubies, sapphires, and other types of jewels. The thing was over the top and in the face.

"Fine," I grumbled.

Gregory beamed. He raced up the steps, but Nate moved to my side, grabbed the crown from the cushion, and set it on top of my head with a smirk. Unfortunately, it wasn't the time to junk punch him.

"Fucking hell, this shit is heavy." If I wasn't a ghoul, the weight of the crown could possibly break my neck.

"I've always found crown-wearing annoying myself," a new voice said into the room.

We froze for a second, and then Asher had Gregory out of sight before he flashed back to stand in front of me. Nate was at my side, his arm out, curling around my stomach, holding me back. Guards rushed toward us, but in a blink, they froze.

"No need for that."

I peeked around Asher to see a tall, dark-skinned man wearing a navy blue suit with a white shirt under it opened at the neck, dipping down his smooth mocha skin. It fit him to perfection. His piercing blue eyes crinkled at the corners, humor evident. His lips curved up in the corners. His black hair was shaved low, and for a second, I felt like I wanted to run my hand over it.

I shook my head. Grabbing Nate's arm, I moved it from my body. He was hesitant until I looked at him and smiled with a nod. He grumbled under his breath but dropped his arm. I stepped around Asher and moved in front of him instead.

"Lucifer, I presume." He was nothing like I'd imagined. Maybe what didn't help was how I'd watched the show *Lucifer* on Netflix.

"And you would be correct, my dear." His voice was made for sin. Smooth, rich, and something I could listen to all the time. Damn him.

"How did you get in here?" I asked, trying to seem unfazed. He stood there alone. I wanted to demand where my men were, where his people were, why had he shown without announcing himself? But I realized he would be all about games, and it would come down to how well I played them.

He chuckled. "I have my ways." His eyes went behind me to Asher, then slowly slid to Nate. I wanted to punch him in the face for staring at them too long.

When they moved further to the side, and I heard a whimper, I called, "Thank you, Gregory, that will be all." I heard a door slam, and then a grinning Lucifer was back looking at me. "Why wasn't he frozen? And if you wouldn't mind—" I swung my hand out toward my guards. "I promise they won't attack."

"So that man wasn't a mate?"

"Gregory?" I laughed. Lucifer nodded once. "No. My guards?"

The room erupted in the noise of my guards rushing forward. "Stop," I yelled. They did. "Please, go back to your positions."

Lucifer, with a smile, watched as my guards went back to the walls around us. He met my gaze and said, "You'll promise my people will be safe?"

"I promise, as long as none of your people harm mine in any way, yours will be safe."

He chuckled. "Very good, Paige. Perfect wording." His hand flung out and people appeared around him. Three women and six men—all dressed immaculately, except for a guy at Lucifer's side. He was dressed in jeans and some band T-shirt. His messy black hair held a tinge of blue to it. His eyes, which looked like a black abyss, held mine, and I couldn't seem to look away.

"Paige Alice, I would like you to meet...." I heard him sigh. "Is she listening to me?"

I licked my suddenly dry lips when the corner of rocker guy's lips lifted. He stood in a casual posture, his hands down at the sides of his slim waist. I just knew he would be perfect, like my men were, under his clothes, and I wanted to know what his caramel skin tasted like.

"My queen," Asher called.

Slowly, I drew my eyes from rocker guy and looked up at Asher. He dipped his chin down toward Lucifer.

Oh shit. Had he spoken?

I faced the devil again. He looked annoyed with his arms crossed over his chest. "Are you listening now?"

I nodded, but then a deep chuckle touched my ears. It came from Lucifer's side, and I slid my eyes to rocker guy. Our gazes caught and locked. He winked, and a thrill trembled throughout my body. My nipples hardened.

The rocker guy's body jerked forward. I realized Lucifer smacked him in the back of the head. My power burst forward, my heart beating louder, harder. My eyes glowed, my claws shot out, and through my long, sharp teeth, I snarled, "Don't." I glared down at the man I wanted to hurt for doing such a thing.

"Don't?" Lucifer whispered.

The room shook. More power threaded through the air, swaying clothing and hair around. Before my eyes, Lucifer changed. His eyes bled black. No white showed at all. He grew taller, larger. His shirt and jacket disappeared as wings sprouted from his back. His own claws held a silver-tipped edge. He didn't just have one set of teeth, but two, all long, pointy, and no doubt sharp.

"Did you tell me don't?" he demanded, his voice hard, cold, and vibrating around the room. Some of my guards shook from where they stood. His people watched on, either bored or with a smile. While Asher went all vampire and Nate half shifted, Lucifer's suit tore as his body expanded.

"Yes," I hissed. "I fucking told you don't. You don't harm anyone under *my* roof."

"*He* is one of mine. I can do to him what I wish."

I took a step forward. Both my men moved with me. Nate growled in the back of his throat, and Asher's own chest rumbled.

"Not here. This is *my* domain. You do not rule here. *I do.* I will do everything I can to protect people I see being hurt for no reason. Fucking touch him again and you'll see how that goes for you."

In the back of my mind, I knew this was crazy. I knew I

should be cowering from the force of Lucifer's power licking and burning my skin, but I couldn't stop. I couldn't back down. I wasn't weak, and I would do anything to protect the guy beside him. Why? I didn't know, but the need to drag him to my side and curl around him, shielding him with my own body from any harm was strong. I was sure I would kill anyone who laid a finger on him.

This is stupid, Paige. He's the fucking devil. I tried to talk myself down. It could have worked if Lucifer hadn't started reaching for the man beside him because then all I saw was red.

I ran and sprang at Lucifer, ready to take him to the ground and rip his head off while I plunged my hand into his chest and dragged out his heart.

But I froze.

In midair.

My body was literally frozen in midair.

I could still hear, still see and move my eyes, but my body wouldn't move. By the sound of Asher's hisses and Nate's snarls, both of them were in the same predicament. I glanced at the guards and saw them frozen.

I'd fucked up big-time.

We were screwed.

Lucifer was going to rip us all apart and feast on our own bodies. He'd hunt my people down and kill them... all because of me.

Even when I thought I was doing the right thing, when my instincts were running my mind and body—and were usually right—I'd been wrong.

I wanted to cry, to scream and beg for my men, for my people. I wanted to ask to spare everyone and take my life only.

Before me, as Lucifer stepped close, his body morphed back

into his human guise. Only his wings didn't disappear; he used them to float up to get in my face.

He studied me, then flew around to face his people. "She is ferociously beautiful, is she not?" No one commented. He spun back to me. "I think I might take this time, while you're not going for my throat, to introduce you to my people. Do you agree?" He cupped his hand behind his ear. "Oh, wait, that's right; you can't speak right now. Not to worry, my dear, I'll go on." His feet landed back on the ground, and he stood before the woman. "These are my concubines. Corazon, Aretha, and Virginia." For the first time, I actually took them in. Corazon looked like a young version of Salma Hayek, Aretha looked a twin to Halle Berry, and Virginia, well, she looked like Charlize Theron. Of course he would have women in his bed who were stunning. Virginia was the only one who smiled and waved at me. Lucifer kissed her neck while his other two glared at Charlize. He moved over to the men. "At the back, we have my loyal guards. Ozuna, Rami, Xi, Jair, and Glenn." I would have laughed at Glenn's normal name, if I wasn't damn frozen. For now, it was a good thing I couldn't move because I was sure I'd have kept laughing since his guards resembled Dwayne Johnson, Vin Diesel, Jason Statham, Bruce Willis, and Glenn looked like Chris Hemsworth when he starred in *Avengers*. I didn't know if they truly looked like that or if that was the form they'd picked. "Lastly, my son, Azrael."

As soon as I looked to his son, I was captured and lost in his dark, yet kind, gaze.

"For fuck's sake," Lucifer cried. I forced my eyes back to him. "So, you see, queenie, I can do what I wish to my own son since he's of my flesh and blood." He walked close to Azrael, who stood still and just stared up at me with a small smile on his face, while I wanted to yell at him to run.

Lucifer stopped behind his son. His hands rested on his shoulders in what seemed like a nice way, but I didn't trust it. I tried to yell, scream, and curse, but I couldn't.

"Do you like what you see here, queenie?" Lucifer asked, cupping his hand under Azrael's chin. Lucifer smiled. "I think you do. You're very distracted by him."

I tried again to move my mouth, my hands, my legs, but nothing.

"What about if I do this?" One claw popped out and he scraped it down Azrael's cheek. Blood welled and dripped down to his shoulder, his T-shirt.

My chest burned from my attempts to break free.

"No? You don't mind?" He laughed. "Then I guess I'll do this." He sliced across Azrael's neck, not cutting, but scratching, only I really didn't like to see it. To witness Azrael flinch. A savage howl started in my belly, swept up my chest and out my mouth. Only it was muffled.

Lucifer clapped and laughed. "Oh, she didn't like that at all." He grinned. "Hmm, let's see what else I can do to my own son." Lucifer walked around Azrael's body. All of his claws were out now, and he used them to slice at his son's shoulder, his arm, his chest, cutting through the material easily.

An untamed part of me ignited in my stomach. It went up in a blaze and burned bright throughout me. In the next second, my snarl was loud, free, just like my body, and I finished the jump to the ground, landing in a crouch.

Asher and Nate made noises behind me, but I couldn't look at them. I kept my eyes on the devil. My power still rolled over me. I pulled my upper lip up and snarled at him again. He was too close to what was mine.

Mine? I blinked at the word, confused.

Lucifer's hand reached out toward Azrael. Not wanting him harmed any more, I leaped. Arms stretched out, feet kicking off the floor, I grabbed Lucifer by the neck, hand circling, my own claws dug into his skin. We fell. Lucifer landed with a thud with me on top of him.

"Stop," he yelled. I didn't, but then I saw his hand out and knew he was talking to his guards. Then his hands were at my waist and he pushed, and I flew over his head, dropping to my back. I rolled, jumped up, and faced him again. He was already on his feet, spreading his legs, bracing. I moved in and jabbed my fist at his face. He dodged. I kicked at his legs, but he jumped them. His hand pushed at my chest, and I went crashing back into the pews. I got to my feet and charged, fist ready for his face, but I faked and then ducked, circling my arms around his waist. I took him to the ground, straddling his waist. I punched my claws into his chest. He cried out and grabbed my wrists.

Clapping started.

It had me pausing before I could reach his heart. I glanced up and saw Lucifer standing near his guards, still clapping. I looked back down and found nothing under me.

Lucifer beamed at me. "I do believe you are perfect."

CHAPTER THIRTY-SIX

PAIGE

Blinking, I stood and drew my power in as I backed up a little to stand in front of Azrael. "What is this?" I demanded at Lucifer.

"A test." Lucifer smirked.

I jerked my head back, confused. "A test?" When Lucifer stepped forward, I took one back, nearly tripping on my stupid dress. At least it hadn't been a hinderance when I fought.

I felt Azrael's heat. I wanted to face him, soak in it while I kissed and tasted him.

Why him?

What made him bring out my possessiveness like my men....

No, he couldn't be.

No. I had my men. I didn't need another one.

But why did I feel a connection toward him?

"Yes, a test, and you passed with flying colors, Paige Alice." Lucifer winked.

"A test for what?" I demanded.

"Not many can break my power, but you did. I'm impressed." He nodded with a big smile.

"That doesn't answer my questions, and can you please allow my men and guards to move?"

He shook his head. "Not just yet. I do believe they'll need to calm down first." He moved forward again.

I clenched my jaw, and Lucifer smirked. "Now, now, queenie. Don't get your panties in a twist. They'll be free as soon as I sense they have their rage under control."

There wasn't anything I could do, so I nodded. "While we wait, will you tell me what the—" A moan escaped me when a warm hand touched the back of my neck under my long hair. Spinning, the hand followed around to the front of my neck. I looked up into Azrael's dark eyes, startled by how familiar they seemed, and yet I couldn't place from where or why.

Azrael graced me with a smile, and I then realized his skin looked scratch-free. I reached out and touched his smooth cheeks, neck, and then he let me lift his T-shirt so I could make sure he'd healed... or had it all been a trick to begin with?

His hand covered mine over his chest. I glanced up. "No marks," I said.

He shook his head and lifted my hand back up to his cheek, flattening it there. His eyes closed, and he leaned into my touch as my heart hammered in my chest. I would have given anything to have kissed him right then. In fact, I started to lift up on my toes, since he was another tall man in my life, to take his mouth with mine. His eyes opened before he chuckled and shook his head. Humor danced in his eyes, along with desire. I hadn't read him wrong. He liked me, but why was he denying me a taste?

"This is sickly cute," Lucifer said dryly. I'd forgotten where I was and who was in there. I twisted back and moved into Azrael. My hands went behind me, to the thighs. Ready to protect him if I had to. Even when he chuckled at my back, his warm breath blowing into my hair. I wanted to smack him for laughing, but Lucifer spoke again. "But it can wait. We have other matters to speak of."

"What matters?" I asked.

"We shall adjourn to somewhere more comfortable with refreshments before we get started," he told me, and I didn't like being told what to do under my own roof.

Learn what fight to fight, Paige.

Sighing, I nodded, then thought of something. "We will, but first my men, guards, and then you'll need to tell me where Alex and Thorn are."

He eyed me impassively, which didn't last because then he laughed. "Demanding little thing." He looked to his son behind me and raised a brow. I didn't see what Azrael did, but it made Lucifer laugh again. "Fair enough, I would too."

He swept his hand out. My guards knew to stop as soon as they were free, so I wasn't worried about them. Nate's roar rolled over the room, as did Asher's snarl. The wind blew and Asher's vampire form stood in front of me. Nate shifted fully on his jump. He skidded and stopped in front of Asher, both wouldn't, or couldn't, stop the rumble from the chest in displeasure.

"Fine men you have, queenie, but it's unnecessary," Lucifer said.

I leaned around Asher to address him when two figures

appeared between our group and theirs. My heart lurched, my body shook, and my belly swirled in delight. I shoved Asher out of the way. Somehow, I knew he let me move him or it would have been impossible, and then I dove at Thorn and Alex. Our arms wrapped around each other and a sob caught in my throat. Tilting my face up, I caught Thorn's lips first in an emotion-filled, hard kiss, then moved to Alex's mouth to do the same. My body settled and my heart soothed. I had my men back and in my arms.

"We're okay, sweetheart," Thorn mumbled against my neck.

"We're here now, dove," Alex murmured against my lips.

I pulled back enough to hit them both in the stomachs. They grunted. I heard laughter, but I grabbed them both close to me again and cried into their shoulders, overwhelmed with happiness at having them with me again. Their hands rubbed up and down my back while they soothed me with reassuring words.

"I love you both so much," I told them.

"Love you, Paige," Alex whispered into my hair.

Both their grips on me tightened. "I'll always love you, sweetheart," Thorn said softly.

"Neither of you will leave me again," I demanded.

Alex smiled and Thorn said, "We can only hope we won't ever need to." I knew they couldn't promise it, yet I wanted them to because it scared me to think it would happen again.

Sniffling, I buried my head back into them. I didn't want to let them go. I could have stayed there, in their arms, forever.

They were back.

They were with me. Home.

Elation had my head spinning.

My men were in my arms.

More warmth hit my back—Asher and Nate. They curled around us, and I felt whole again.

Whole, yet... rocker guy.

He should have been a part of this—a part of our family, our pack.

But I couldn't touch on that, not just yet, not when I'd just got Thorn and Alex back. If it wasn't for having to deal with Lucifer, I would have taken my men to the bedroom. Asher, Nate, and I would show them how much they'd been missed.

However, even with Lucifer and his people there, I lifted my head. Alex was the first to capture my mouth with his again. I moaned around his insistent tongue making his way into my mouth, knowing he needed this as much as I did. He finished with a quick peck, and I turned to Thorn. He was ready, his mouth on mine in seconds. His hand on my waist tightened its hold as we deepened the kiss. Both of us taking each other's whimper into our mouths.

Regrettably, I pulled back, then leaned back in to kiss his chest. I smiled a little shakily up at them. "It's good to have you both home."

"It's good to be home," Thorn replied.

"We're sorry for the fear you must have felt," Alex added.

I took a hand of each of theirs into mine and nodded. "I know."

"We took care of her," Nate said at my back. He thrust into my lower back. He thrust his *hardness* into me. My eyes widened, and I spun around.

"Nate, what have I said about being naked in front of people?" Rough laughter started, but I ignored it.

Nate grinned. "Alex?"

A click of fingers and then Nate was dressed in jeans and a

T-shirt. I caught Alex brush Nate's hand as he stepped closer. "We knew you would both take care of her," he said.

Nate grunted. Then Thorn was there curving an arm around Nate's shoulders. I didn't miss the pressure he applied to Nate's arms. "We had trust in you both."

"As did we," Asher stated. "Though, someone had her moments." He smirked.

As I turned to Asher, ready to rant, his hand covered my mouth and he faced me back to Lucifer. Shit. Right. "Thank you, Lucifer, for bringing my bonded back to me."

"It was lucky my son found them," Lucifer commented with a grin.

My eyes shot to Azrael. He dipped his chin down, smiling.

"Thank you," I said again to the right man.

Thorn made a noise in the back of his throat. "Had no one—"

"We must adjourn," Lucifer called loudly. "We could use some refreshments and comfortable seats."

I drew my brows down. It certainly seemed like the devil was keeping Thorn from saying something, but what? I kept my gaze on Thorn. He shook his head, giving me a thin-lipped smile.

"My queen," Gregory said, appearing from somewhere. "I have set up the library for the meeting. It is most private for such types of things." Meaning he would have gotten anyone in that area, since it was close to Thorn's room, away for their own safety. This man was amazing.

"Thank you, Gregory." I faced Lucifer. "Shall we?"

"I believe so, my dear."

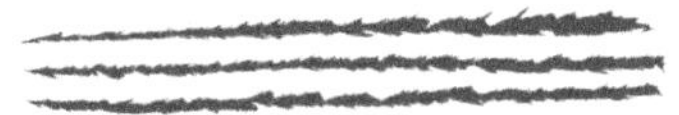

LUCIFER SAT across from me with his three concubines on the long leather couch while I sat leaning into the corner of a chaise lounge. Thorn stood on my right and Asher sat on my left. Nate had shifted back to his wolf form to sit on the floor at my feet, and Alex stood behind me with a hand on my shoulder. I was glad he did as I needed the comfort that he was back. Thorn may have sensed it as well because he reached down, resting his fingers lightly on my other shoulder.

Lucifer's guards, all but one, stood behind him. It was Glenn who was with Gregory helping with refreshments. Azrael stood over near the windows smiling. He seemed to always smile, and I wondered why. What made him so happy?

No one said anything as Gregory and Glenn puttered around. A wet nose touched my hand. I looked from Azrael to Nate, who jerked his chin toward Lucifer.

Fuck.

Had I been so lost staring at Azrael that I hadn't even noticed Lucifer's attention boring into me? Was he waiting for me to speak?

"Have some restraint, queenie," Lucifer said, his lips twitching.

I could feel my cheeks heating. He was right. I should have some since my own bonded mates were in the room and they were witnessing me lust over a demon—if he was even that. I didn't know. A man who was Satan's son. How could I have been so thoughtless? Did it show Alex and Thorn I didn't care they were back?

Nate snapped his teeth at Lucifer, sensing my turmoil.

Alex's hand pressed down. "My queen—"

I shook my head and then tilted it back to have his eyes. "Not my queen, never my queen from any of you. You're my bonded mates. We're one. A family." I reached out for Nate. "A pack and clan." I took Asher's hand. "I'll hurt anyone who tries to say it's disrespectful you call me by my name and not queen around them."

Alex's eyes softened, and he nodded. I glanced at Thorn, who smirked. "As you wish, sweetheart."

A female groaned. "How many more gag moments will we have to endure?"

I snapped my head to Aretha who'd spoken.

Leaning forward, I rested my elbows on my knees. "Whose house is this?" I didn't let her answer and went on in a darker tone. "Whose mates have just been brought back to her after two weeks of fear that I'd lost them forever? I will do what I want, whenever I want, and you can keep your mouth shut."

She spluttered, "You can't talk to me like this."

"Under my roof, I can. If I were in your domain, I would bite my tongue and think you were nothing but a bitch." I glanced at Lucifer, raising my brow to see if he was going to fight me on my decision.

"She's right, Aretha. This is her domain. She is alpha here. You're stupid to think you could act like that and your outburst didn't embarrass me." He glanced over his shoulder to Xi. "Take her back. Keep her locked in her room until I can deal with her."

"No, Lucifer, darling, please. I'll keep my mouth shut."

"No," he clipped.

Maybe I should have felt bad for getting her into trouble with the devil, but I didn't. She screamed as Xi approached, and when she sneered at me, I could see in her eyes what she'd planned before she even acted it out. She launched at me, her hands out ready to wrap around my neck. I wasn't sure why she thought she could attack me with all my men surrounding me, but she tried.

Yet, it wasn't one of my men who stopped her. Azrael, with speed that matched Asher's, flashed forward. His arm wound around her waist in midair, she jerked to a stop and then was thrown backward into the windows. They shattered, and she flew out them. No one seemed too bothered about it. Honestly, I wasn't sure how my own eyes could have followed the fast actions of Azrael, but they had…. Maybe it was another power of being queen manifesting.

"Xi," Lucifer ordered.

Xi disappeared from where he'd stood, but in the next blink, he was back with Aretha, struggling like a wild woman in his arms. But Xi stood holding her through her struggles, emotionless.

"Master?" he asked.

"Just take her back."

They disappeared.

"It is common for her to have outbursts at home. I didn't think she'd be foolish enough to do it here."

I nodded. I wasn't sure if I should apologize for speaking to her the way I did. After all, she was a concubine for Satan, but something held me back from saying anything. As I'd stated, this was my domain. I'd accepted the position. Claimed it. I would do what I wanted, when I wanted without comment from another. I'd never liked to be questioned even when I was a human, but now even more so.

With the tilt to Lucifer's lips, I knew I'd made the right choice by biting my tongue and not saying anything.

"Would you mind if we moved onto the matter of why you requested a meeting?"

"This is lovely," Virginia commented after a sip of tea.

I glanced from Lucifer to her. "Thank you."

I went to move my gaze back to Lucifer, but a grinning Virginia added, "You have a wonderful home."

Even though she seemed sweet, nicer than Aretha and Corazon, my attention was caught in a suspicious way. Why was Lucifer allowing her to interrupt as such? "Thank you again. I haven't been here long or even seen the village yet, but I do believe you're correct. It's beautiful."

"You haven't been here long and yet… I feel you've changed so much." She winked. "Impressive." She snuggled into Lucifer. "Don't you think, Luca?"

"I do, my lovely."

Virginia rested her head against Lucifer's shoulder as if they were on a date and watching a movie together. Something was going on. Something was about to happen, and I wasn't sure if it would be good or bad. Yet, I readied for it, and sensed my men around me do the same.

Her gaze moved to Thorn. "How well do you know a woman named Alma?"

I leaned forward. "What of Alma?" I demanded.

Virginia beamed up at Lucifer. "She's protective, isn't she?"

He chuckled. "That she is."

"What about Alma? She'll not go with you. She'll not work for you. She belongs here. We're her family."

To my utter shock, Virginia's eyes welled. "I have never met anyone walk into a leadership role and shine in their new position such as you have. Your love and kindness are beyond what I'd have imagined. It would be an honor to be claimed, as you would say, into your family." The air shimmered around her, and then I was looking at Alma cuddled up to Lucifer. "Thank you, dear."

CHAPTER THIRTY-SEVEN

ASHER

Paige flung herself back into the couch. She wasn't the only one shocked. When Alma's body shifted back to Virginia's young one, she smiled once again.

"What's the meaning of this?" Thorn demanded harshly. Nate stood on all fours and pressed himself against Paige's legs. Alex's eyes change to purple. His magic swept out, and I could see the clear wall erected in front of us, keeping Lucifer and his people on the other side.

"Relax." Virginia grinned. "Paige is safe with us. She always will be."

"Who are you?" I clipped.

Lucifer's hard eyes locked onto mine, even my vampire side wanted to look away. Somehow, I managed not to, and I was sure it had to do with the woman in my life. Her power mixed with Alex's and Nate's when I'd fed on them, strengthening mine. My clan offered me more than respect and love. It gave me more power. It rolled through me and locked my body and then my eyes on the biggest threat in the room.

"Now, now, boys. We all know you're both tough. Cut it out." Virginia laughed. We both looked at her at the same time, so no one lost in the stare down, and I was happy with that.

"Again, could you inform us who exactly you are because right now it seems we have all been tricked into thinking you were the seer who had been with the former queen for a very long time. We find it unjust to have been lied to this whole time."

Lucifer nodded once at me, at my choice of words since they just bordered on respectful.

Virginia straightened, yet she still leaned into Lucifer. "Of course, I can understand why you're all confused." She took a breath. "The night before sweet Marsala gave her heart to our young Paige here, she requested an audience with my Luca. Since we'd been out on a date discussing a certain something, I went along with him. She'd asked us for a favor. After some thought, we complied, but of course, we had demands of our own. One was for me to come and stay in my twin sister Alma's stead to make sure…. It doesn't matter just yet. It is me who you met, not Alma, who is away on a holiday with her beau."

"Is it because of Alma being your sister why you've kept the secret of this community's existence?" I asked.

"Correct." Virginia smiled. "At first it was for my sister's sake to keep the secret of Marsala and her community from others. Now there have been other reasons we'll get into shortly." She moved her gaze to Thorn. "Yes?"

"It's been you all along?" Thorn asked.

"It has." She nodded.

"But how have you been seeing things?"

"Alma and I have the same power."

"And you've been helping us, why?" Paige asked.

Virginia shrugged. "I liked it here. I loved the people, but I saw Marsala had lost her authority among her people. The people who couldn't help themselves needed someone who would do it for them. As soon as I saw Paige arrive, and by the way she took control, I knew things were going to be amazing."

Paige waved her hand in front of her. "Wait, let me get this straight. Was it you or Alma who 'saw' it should be me to take Marsala's spot as queen?"

"Oh, that was Alma. It was me who knew Aggie would be a darling to have on board. Alma told me all about her, and as soon as I met Aggie myself, I loved her like a daughter I didn't have."

"You have two daughters, lovely," Lucifer added in.

"Bah, they're bitches. Aggie's not. It was also me who knew Clyde could be trustworthy. It was me in that room with you for the first time and since."

"Why?" Alex asked. Nate woofed; he too wanted to know why Lucifer's concubine stayed within the walls taking on a persona of her twin sister.

"There is another question I have," I said. It may not be a good time to interrupt the knowledge of getting to know why all this happened, but this question had me suspicious of the woman.

"Yes?" Virginia asked.

"How is it Alma is so much older than you appear now, if you are twins?"

Paige clicked her fingers and pointed my way. She sent me a wink as if to say "Good one, Asher."

"That's simple. It's because I've been living in Hell."

"You don't age down there?"

"No." A sad smile crept onto her lips. "I offered Alma some time down there with me, but... well, she doesn't like my Luca very much, and she has always believed aging is the way of God."

"I know this is getting off topic again," Paige started, looking away from the man who stood near our couch. I could sense something going on between the two of them. It felt very similar to the connection I'd shared with Nate, Alex, and Thorn the first time around Paige. Did that mean he was meant to be her bonded mate as well? There was also something very familiar about him. He'd already proven himself when he protected Paige from Lucifer's concubine. I just wished I knew all there was about him right then so I could encourage the connection Paige had with him. If it meant more protection for our Paige, then I would welcome whomever in, as long as Paige agreed to it as well. I was sure I wouldn't be the only bonded male of Paige's who thought like that too.

I shook my thoughts away as Paige continued. "But how did you have a life with Lucifer and your twin believe in God's ways?" Yes, we could all presume God was real, or how else would Lucifer be sitting on the couch?

Virginia giggled. "Simple really. I fell in love and would do anything to keep that love. It doesn't mean I don't believe in God's law-abiding ways." Lucifer snarled low, and Virginia patted his thigh. "I do, to some extent, but Lucifer has my heart over everything. I'm sure you can understand that?"

Paige glanced at all of us, leaving Azrael for last, albeit briefly, before she looked back to Virginia and nodded.

"Good." Virginia returned her smile.

"I'm surprised you allowed your concubine to stay here, Lucifer," Thorn said. That was true. I'd heard he was possessive to a point he'd killed people for looking at his women.

He smirked. "I have found it is easier to let my lovely have what she wants over fighting her."

Corazon snorted, picking at her nails. "She gets everything she wants."

"Corazon," Lucifer warned.

The woman rolled her eyes but said nothing. I was guessing she didn't want to be sent back.

"Why...?" Paige started as a blush coated her cheeks.

"Why does he have concubines when he has me?" Virginia asked, smiling.

"Yes." Our mate nodded.

"Well, they're used for a power source. I can't always be used, or it would drain me."

"How are they used as a power source?" Thorn questioned.

Virginia glanced up at Lucifer. He nodded. "Lucifer is an angel, but what many don't know is he also has another side to him."

"Vampire," I said softly. I knew a part of him felt like kin, but I'd brushed it off, thinking our darker sides had originated from Hell.

Virginia looked up at me and nodded. I could feel Lucifer's gaze on me, but I ignored it. No wonder we'd had a struggle of dominance. It was our vampire sides working against each other. Usually, I would have seen he was more dominant, but mine had become stronger since Paige and my clan had connected. Although, I wasn't stupid enough to believe I would win a fight with the devil. His abilities went beyond all of ours, which had me wondering yet again why they were here trying to get in Paige's good graces.

They wanted something from her, but what?

Did it also mean we'd have an alliance with Lucifer?

For Paige's sake and safety, it was something to take into consideration before making the final decision.

I ran my hand down Paige's thigh. She shivered. I left my palm flat just above her knee. Meeting Lucifer's eyes, I stated, "I would like to know the other reasons you are here. Why Virginia wanted to involve herself within these walls."

After a beat, he answered, "The demons who attacked Paige, to begin with, weren't sent from me. The first one, Valino, who encountered Paige, sensed her changes within. He sent a mental message to his brethren before he was killed."

The one in the restaurant. We hadn't thought he was strong enough to contact his brethren in Hell, unless they'd already been on earth of course.

"Does that mean they work alone?" Alex asked. "They were after Paige because they knew she would be queen and wanted to use her to gain their own kingdom?"

"There is always that possibility. I have many demons who are loyal to me, too fearful of what I would do. But there are always creatures in any domain that are trying to gain strength to overthrow me and anyone with power and authority." Those were things we'd already known, but then he added, "However, I fear the demons that are Valino's brethren are working alongside someone."

"Then they were the ones who ambushed us and were working with Grace," Alex said.

Paige's heart skipped a beat. Nate snarled and I tensed. None of us liked hearing his words. They were our clan, our family, and they were tricked. We could have lost them all together and it didn't sit well at all.

"Ambushed you?" Paige demanded in a low, vicious tone.

Alex pushed calm out to all of us. It was new. I could feel Alex, and not just through his link with Paige. It meant we were all connected on a new level. Nate's snarl dropped off into an unsettled growl in the back of his throat, and I relaxed a little, feeling his calm.

"Remember, dove, we're fine."

The sound of her teeth grinding together reached me. She nodded once.

"What happened?" she clipped.

They told us the story of what they'd been through, and in return, we filled them in on the battle with Grace.

"I wished we'd kept her alive so I could kill her again," Paige stated.

"I'd also like to get my hands on her," Thorn said, his jaw tight. "In fact, I could do with a snack."

Lucifer chuckled at that.

I interrupted with "Do you know who the demon working with Grace was?"

Lucifer nodded. "From what Alex described, he is Rebellious. He'd been a guard, but when I'd caught him," his jaw clenched, "flirting with Virginia, I handled him. I thought he was dead. Obviously, I was wrong. I have no doubt he would be working with the same people who are trying to capture Paige."

"Why are they after her?" Alex asked.

"With Paige comes power and her people. There's been a

rumor that if a demon was to eat the ghoul queen's heart, her power and followers will be theirs."

"Is it true?" I demanded.

Lucifer shrugged. "No one knows because no demon has killed a ghoul queen."

"And no one ever will," I stated coldly and was surprised when Lucifer, the devil himself, nodded.

"How dangerous is Rebellious?" Thorn asked.

Lucifer shrugged. "Depends on who he works alongside. On his own, any one of you could take him down. If he's able to gain more power, he could be a problem."

Fuck, we needed to know who he worked with. I had a feeling it was the council.

"Do you know of the council?" Alex asked.

Lucifer snorted. "Of course." His teeth ground together. "They're a group of people who think they're too powerful to be touched."

Virginia's hand landed on his. "My latest premonition involved the council, Luca."

His body locked. "What of them?"

"They've been informed of Paige's existence and whereabouts."

"And?" he clipped.

Virginia opened her mouth, made a gargle noise, and then frowned.

I spoke for her. "From what we gathered, if they are to come here for her, the chance of our survival is slim. If we pay them a visit, things look better." I paused for a moment and added something that had been on my mind. "However, I have been thinking, when we do go there, we will need people of the supernatural community to know of their... wrongdoings.

We'll need proof to take them down without anything coming back on us."

Lucifer's lips tipped in the corners in a small smile. "I would agree with that assessment. Without proof and people seeing the evidence, things will go south for you all if you just show and murder the lot of them. You'll need others to see Paige and the good she's doing for her people, that aren't just her own kind."

Paige's hand shot out. "Wait. Hold on. Are you saying there's a chance, if we manage to take all of them down in the right way, nothing comes back to bite us in the butt? People will see me as their new... I don't know, council member?"

"Correct." He nodded.

Paige's panic hit us all. Quickly, I curled my arm around her and dragged her close.

"I won't do it." She shook her head. "Already I have enough on my plate here, and I struggle each day to make sure I'm doing it right."

"Already you're succeeding in ruling like all queens should be," Virginia said.

Lucifer nodded. "You rule like I do now. I respect it."

Paige gulped. We all heard it. I thinned my lips to keep from laughing. I didn't think she'd take that as a compliment having been compared to the devil.

Lucifer laughed. "I'll rephrase that, my dear. You rule like I do since Virginia came into my life. Before I had her, I killed anyone who pissed me off for the littlest thing. Now, she grounds me. We kill when necessary. We protect our people. We give orders when needed, and change things to match the times. Before Virginia, I didn't have respect from my people.

They lived in fear. After her, they follow me for a different reason… because they want to."

"But… you're the devil," Paige said.

If it had offended, I was ready to flash her away, but it didn't. Instead, he smiled.

"I'll never be a saint. There were too many sins on my soul, and really it would be boring to live my existence as a good Samaritan like my dickhead brother Michael. But it doesn't mean I can't alter my world, or my thoughts for the people I love." He winked. "But back to what I was saying. If killing the council is the path you'll have to follow, you'll need to give the people something, or *someone* new."

"What about you?" Paige asked, hopeful.

Lucifer snorted, then chuckled. "No."

Virginia shook her head. "His life belongs in Hell. It's where he's needed."

Paige sagged against me. "My love, it's not something to worry about now," I told her.

"I agree," Thorn said. "Things aren't set in stone. We still need to find proof to take down the council, and this is before they even think about coming here."

"We should send a notice of our visit. So they know we're coming, and then they won't have to come here." Alex glanced at Virginia. "Would that work? Would they stay away and wait for us to come to them?"

Virginia winked.

"Gregory?" Paige called.

"I'll have it done by the end of the day, my queen."

"Thank you. Please state we'll be there within two months." She glanced to Virginia, who nodded, and then Paige smiled over at Gregory, who bowed. Paige's nerves were all over the place. She still feared a lot of things, but I could still feel her interest in Azrael, and also her arousal and happiness that she had her clan all together. What I also sensed was confusion.

"Sweetheart," Thorn called.

She tipped her head up to him. "Yes?"

"What has you confused?" He'd been reading her too, and no doubt, Alex and Nate had done the same.

She nodded, glanced back to Lucifer, and asked, "Why are you both helping us?"

When Virginia smiled up at Lucifer, he nodded. She looked back at Paige and said, "It's simple. We believe you're the best candidate to offer our support to for the future. All we're after is a peaceful existence." She paused a beat. "However, there is one more thing."

Paige's heart skipped a beat. "What's that?"

"We needed to make sure you would be the perfect mate for our son."

CHAPTER THIRTY-EIGHT

PAIGE

"I'm sorry, what?" I mean, I knew there was a connection with Azrael, but I didn't realize Virginia was his mother. And my mate? I had four already. *Four.* What was strange was how I couldn't sense any unease from Thorn or Alex. They showed me nothing through the link, even though it was open. However, Asher was wary, and Nate pressed closer and growled low in concern.

"You. Are. Our. Son's. Mate," Lucifer said slowly and with sign language.

I wanted to punch him. Even more, I wanted to look at Azrael, but suddenly, I felt shy. Was this some type of arranged marriage? Were they for real? This was why they were supporting me, so they could get rid of their son? Were they mean parents? Of course they were mean, well, Satan was, because he'd cut his own son up… although there wasn't a mark on Azrael in the end.

"It's very amusing watching her as she thinks," Lucifer commented.

"True, so many emotions cross over her features. Right now, she's back to confusion."

"What was the screwed-up face one?" Lucifer asked.

"She was probably worried about everyone's sanity," Virginia answered.

Running a hand down my face, I suddenly stood and started pacing in front of my couch. Only that got me closer to Azrael. My eyes widened. I looked away, so I didn't get lost in his eyes, and backed up, tripping over Asher's feet. Quickly, I jumped up, ignoring my face heating.

I pointed to a chuckling Lucifer. "You… he… this isn't…. I mean, you can't just offer up your son to me." I threw out my hand Azrael's way. "He looks like a nice guy, and he… ah, helped with your concubine trying to hurt me. Still… I have four bonded males already."

"Are you saying you don't feel the connection between you both?" Lucifer asked, now frowning.

I didn't want to admit it in front of my men. Yet, it was ridiculous to deny it since I attacked the devil himself trying to protect Azrael.

Biting my bottom lip, I nodded.

"So you do feel it?" Lucifer questioned again. I was sure it was to annoy me.

Glaring at him, I said, "Nodding does mean yes."

"Let me tell you a story then," he replied, ignoring my snark. In fact, he'd been very lenient with me. Was it because Azrael was their son and them thinking he was my mate?

I dipped my brows in confusion. "Story time now?"

"There's always time for story time. However, this is important right now." I nodded. He relaxed further into the couch while I took my seat back and didn't look at their son. "It started on a cold, dreary night—"

"Are you serious right now?" I demanded. His jaw clenched in reaction. "Is this an actual real story or something made up?"

"It's real. I'm just setting the mood."

I rolled my eyes. Who'd have thought the devil was a narrator? I thinned my lips and bit down on them when he started again with "It was a cold, dreary night in New York City. I had been out looking for a certain someone when Marsala appeared out of nowhere."

I really wished he would just get to the damn point. But if I interrupted again, there was a chance he'd once more start from the beginning, and I couldn't have that happen.

"Marsala and I had known each other for a long time. I wouldn't say we were friends; however, she was a person I could rely on to deal with my wayward demons in her area. She needed a favor. A protector and teacher for her replacement."

I stilled.

Ezra? Sorrow grabbed at my chest. I quickly blocked my mates from my emotions. I erected a wall between us so I couldn't feel theirs either as I wanted to feel that pain. I deserved that pain.

"After some thought, I offered her someone since he was to be punished for disobeying us. You know who I'm talking about?" Lucifer asked.

I nodded. If I opened my mouth, I would have sobbed. Tears brimmed my eyes. Should I have cared it was in front of Lucifer? Probably. It showed weakness, but I'd already been gushy and loving in front of him, so I didn't care what he thought.

Then I wondered if they blamed me for Ezra's death. Had he been their faithful hellhound and I'd got him killed?

"He died under your care," Lucifer stated.

I nodded.

"You cared for him?"

I nodded.

"You still care for him?"

Another nod. I also wanted to shout at him to shut up, or I would burst into tears. Thorn took my hand, kissing the back of it. Asher's hand touched the base of my neck. Nate whimpered and rested his head on my knees. Alex's hand went to my shoulder, where he applied pressure.

All of them offering me their support.

I loved my men.

Loved them.

But whatever was to come, it was me who would deal with it.

"It was unfortunate to lose him. It—"

My lips unlocked, and I said darkly, "It wasn't unfortunate. It killed a part of me, and I'll forever feel his loss. He was my friend, my teacher, my companion, and if it wasn't for my men, my family, I would have found a way to end my life because it wouldn't have been worth living without him. I loved him. I still love him, and I always will. You can punish me for his loss because I would do the same since he was so special."

Sniffling, Virginia wiped at her eyes. "You really are perfect. The way you love is strong and with everything you have. Your body, heart, and soul. It's beautiful."

I ground my teeth together, not understanding what was going on.

"Azrael," Lucifer called.

Great, we were back to arguing over setting us up.

I opened my mouth to say something but snapped it closed. I really wasn't in the mood to speak, especially after talking of Ezra since thinking of him saddened me. All I wished for was to go to my room with my men and fall into bed with them, knowing they were all safe.

However, out of the corner of my eye, Azrael stepped closer. Asher stiffened, and Nate growled. I turned my head his way to tell Azrael we'd speak of it another day, if they were staying, when his body wavered, almost shimmering.

I snapped my lips closed. Heat washed through the room. It burned hotter for a moment, forcing me to close my eyes. Something was happening. Something to Azrael. Panic clutched my gut.

Then the heat stopped.

Asher muttered, "What the fuck?"

Nate whimpered. I glanced down to him to see him jump forward, then back. I shifted my gaze to where he was looking.

My jaw dropped. My eyes widened at where Azrael had been standing a moment ago. But....

It couldn't be.

I was seeing things.

I had to have been.

My throat closed, my eyes welled, and my heart pumped erratically in my chest.

Anger had me standing, had me shaking my head, fisting my hands at my sides. "How could you do this to me? It's not him.

It's not. This is beyond cruel." Nate went to all fours and snarled.

Hands grabbed my shoulders. "Sweetheart," Thorn said, his voice thick with emotion. "Look at him. Really look at him."

I shook my head again and again. "No. I won't. Leave!" I yelled.

"Dove," Alex tried, coming to my side. His fingers glided through Nate's hair since he was just in front of me. "Just look. It is him."

"No," I sobbed.

Alex's free hand touched my jaw. He gently tilted my head his way to have my gaze. "Trust me?"

Sniffling, I nodded.

"Then look. Please." He threaded his fingers in mine and held on tightly.

I rubbed at my chest, trying to still my erratic heart. I was scared out of my mind it was a stupid, cruel prank. Slowly, I faced the hellhound that had been Azrael.

Azrael sat on his hind legs, letting me have my inspection. I ran my wet eyes over his silky, messy black fur and large stocky body. A spine full of jutting bones, razor-sharp teeth with two long fangs hanging out of his mouth. His jaw opened, his tongue rolled out, and he panted. I moved my gaze up to his red glowing eyes.

He looked exactly like Ezra, but it could still be a trick.

The hellhound stood and walked my way, moving as Ezra had. He stopped just in front of me, and through the red haze, I watched his eyes roll before his tongue came out and licked the side of my neck and cheek. His warm breath washed over me…. He even scented how Ezra had—of fire, earth, and honey.

Opening my eyes, I met its gaze. "Ezra?"

A rumble came from within his chest, and he dipped his head.

I made a noise in the back of my throat; a sob wanted to tear free, but I didn't allow it.

Thorn stepped up beside us. I glanced at him. He smirked softly. "He came to us in Hell. It was lucky he'd sensed Alex's power because we'd been stuck in a house full of demons. He saved us, took us back to his home, where he transformed into Azrael. We would have come home sooner, but we had to wait for Lucifer to return to his kingdom. Since Alex couldn't teleport out of Hell without his permission, Alex's power wouldn't work. Also, time in Hell moves a lot slower than here. It's only been a week for us."

Nodding, because all of it made sense and there wasn't anything they could have done differently, I reached out and ran a hand through his fur. He leaned into my touch. "How?"

It was Lucifer who spoke quietly. "When Marsala said she was in need of a guard for the new queen, it happened to be when Azrael was in trouble for disobeying us. We thought it would be good for his punishment."

"Also a learning curve," Virginia added. "He was spelled to stay in his hellhound form for added punishment. We didn't know you would form a connection. When he was… killed here on Earth, he was sent back to us in Hell. He told us what happened and since then has wanted to be back at your side."

Lucifer nodded. "However, he had to heal since he is part human, like his mother. The mage's power was able to work on him. If he was a full hellhound, it wouldn't have. Then, before I could get us here, I had things to attend to in Hell, which couldn't be put off."

Virginia giggled. "Our Azrael wasn't happy waiting. He tried everything he could to get back, but he doesn't have the power to open portals."

I bit my trembling bottom lip and drew my gaze back to Azrael. "I thought you were lost to me." Tears welled. Azrael whined and licked my neck and cheek again. My Ezra had never been one to think of personal space or what was gross.

"You wanted to come back to me?"

He nodded, his lips pulling back into a smile. Or a hellhound version of one.

Then a thought popped into my head. Everything that had happened. Everything that I'd done around him. My eyes widened. "You watched me get dressed, and in the shower, and… " Heat hit my cheeks. Some nights he'd been in the room, and I'd touched myself, thinking he'd been asleep. Had he really?

He let out a huffing noise… the same sound Ezra made when I'd assumed he was laughing.

"Ezra—Azrael," I scolded.

His body shimmered and next in front of me stood the man.

"I prefer Ezra," he told me with a warm smile.

Fresh tears welled and fell. I wanted to reach out to him, to drag him into my arms and never let go. But this wasn't the Ezra I knew. This was a man I didn't know. How was I supposed to act? What was I supposed to do?

Everything in me told me to hold him, to— Why was that bitch looking at him?

Corazon's gaze slowly ran up and down Ezra. I wanted to punch her in the face so it dinted and she couldn't see out her eyes.

"Dove," I heard Alex say.

She licked her lips as if she remembered she'd had a taste of him. I ground my teeth together before lifting my upper lip at her. Only she didn't notice the threat. She didn't notice her life was dangling in front of her. She rubbed her thighs together, her gaze on Ezra's ass.

A growl erupted from my chest.

"Sweetheart," Thorn said, his hand touching my arm.

Laughter sounded in the room, but I ignored it, as did Corazon since she was lost in eye-fucking Ezra. She moved forward on the couch as if she would come at him.

"Grab her," Asher cried as I flew at the woman reaching for Ezra. Arms curled my waist and drew me back into a hard body.

His scent calmed me a little.

"What's wrong, Paige?" Ezra asked.

"This is delightful," Lucifer said.

"That bitch was eye-fucking you and about to make a grab for your ass. She looks at you like she's had a taste and wants more. No one goddamn touches you."

The room fell silent, except for the rumbling coming from the chest of the man who was holding me. Ezra—I couldn't see him as Azrael since I'd accepted him as being Ezra—turned me in his arms. I tried to keep my gaze on the bitch who looked like she wanted to crawl under the couch, but a hand cupped my cheek, and my head was pried away from her direction to meet with Ezra's warm gaze. Using his free hand, he took mine and brought it up to his chest where I felt the rumbling on his skin. It sounded content.

"She's never had me. She never will because I am yours, if you want me?"

Someone sniffled. However, I couldn't look away from the man in front of me. He was stunning. He was strong. He was a part of Hell, born son of Lucifer. He could be scary and fierce. He was also Ezra, my hellhound who'd I missed with every beat of my heart.

He *was* mine.

I couldn't deny it, and I would never try.

"I will always want you," I told him.

CHAPTER THIRTY-NINE

THORN

*E*zra clutched Paige to him and then kissed her like she was his much-needed breath. I couldn't say it hurt seeing it, because it didn't. When Alex and I had been in Hell, we'd spoken of the connection we'd felt with Ezra. The man who refused to go by Azrael because he'd been Paige's Ezra, and that was all he wanted to be. The only ones who refused to call him that were his parents.

Paige jumped, and Ezra caught her with his hands on her sweet ass, holding her tightly to him as they still kissed.

I quickly addressed the room while holding an agitated Nate back. "I think it is time to rest in our rooms."

A beaming Virginia bounced up and clapped her hands, so much like Alma would have done. "Yes, I agree. Let the kids have privacy, Luca."

Lucifer nodded, and, in a blink, he stood by his woman with an arm around her waist. We hadn't seen much of them in Hell, which I was grateful for. I wasn't sure I liked Lucifer, but he was giving his son what he wanted and loved most in his life—Paige. For that, I was grateful. The times we'd seen Virginia in Hell, she'd never once hinted at being Alma. They liked their secrets, which meant we would have to keep a close eye on them. Even when they were being accommodating in helping us with their advice. I had a feeling that had a lot to do with who their son would be bound to, though.

A moan filled the room from Paige when she ground her crotch against Ezra. He returned it with his own groan, the content rumble in his chest never stopping.

"Out," Lucifer commanded.

I made sure Paige's men were the last to head to the door. Nate still wasn't too pleased to leave. I had to grab a tighter hold of his fur and tug him with me. He licked my hand, pleased I was home, at least that was what I guessed. Immediately after, he went back to growling and fighting my every step. It seemed Nate had claimed Paige and wasn't happy about leaving her with someone his wolf hadn't claimed.

God, I'd missed this, his antics. Actually, I'd missed them all. Alex and I had spoken about home much and how we couldn't wait to be here.

"Wait," a rough, thick voice called.

We turned back to see Ezra helping Paige stand on her shaky feet.

"What is it?" Asher asked. He stood beside me with his hand clasped around Alex's arm. It had been nice knowing Paige had missed us and how much she had, but she hadn't been the only one it seemed.

We were truly a family.

One that had extended to contain Ezra.

Alex and I both knew as soon as Paige found out the truth, she wouldn't let him go. I had been skeptical about Asher and Nate taking it well, but Alex reassured me—for Paige's sake and to see her happy—they would be fine.

"Stay," Ezra said. "You're all Paige's and she's yours. I won't jeopardize anything you already have."

Paige cupped his cheeks, turning his head back to her. Her smile was soft when she pecked his lips. "You're amazing."

He shrugged. "It helps I already know them all and have felt the connection you have. Though, I'm not sure Nate is too pleased I'm back."

"Nate, shift back." I grunted when he tried to lunge forward again. The bastard was strong; thankfully I nearly matched it.

My hands fell away when his body started to shake. He grew taller and wider. His tail stayed in place when he stopped the shift in his half form.

"Thorn, Asher, you'll have to hold me back until he's claimed her," he growled between sharp, long teeth.

"I've got him," Asher said. He lifted his chin toward Paige. His voice lowered, "Spend time with her."

I shook my head. "But Ezra needs—"

"She needs all three of you."

"Are you sure you can handle him on your own?" Already I wanted to get over to where Ezra guided Paige over to the couch. Even if I liked the feel of Nate against me, where he had my dick hardening, I still felt the pull to go to Paige.

Asher smiled, full fang. "Yes."

Nodding, I dropped my arms. Nate made for Ezra, but Asher was there, throwing him across the room. Asher followed and ignore Nate's snarling and wrapped his arms around Nate from behind, taking him to the floor.

"Settle, pup, and yield for me," Asher demanded.

"Fuck you, vampire." Though, when Asher's legs knocked Nate's apart, Nate's struggles lessened a little. I grinned, understanding dawning on me. Asher had claimed the wolf. I wished I'd been there to see it.

A moan had me looking toward the couch. Ezra watched Alex's hand up Paige's dress. He'd have his fingers inside her, and I wanted to see. Stalking over to them, I stopped and stood before them, crossing my arms over my chest.

"Alex, our mate is dressed in far too many clothes," I said, and caught Alex's grin against Paige's lips. Ezra looked on with desire burning within his eyes and a small smile on his lips.

Alex clicked his fingers. Suddenly, Paige sat on the couch in nothing. Ezra, Alex, and I had only boxers on, all of them tented with our erections. I glanced over to the corner to see Asher was also only in his underwear while he still rolled around on the floor with half-shifted Nate.

A war started up inside me. I wanted to watch everything that was going on, but I couldn't, and when Paige cried out, I moved my gaze quickly back to see her arching as Alex's finger sank deeply into her while Ezra sucked, bit, and licked at her nipple.

Leaning in, I took hold of Paige's thighs and spread her legs apart, hooking one leg over Alex's and then Ezra's. Standing back, I nodded at my good work because now I could see perfectly between her legs. I could see how drenched she was.

Paige whimpered against Alex's mouth before she drew her lips away, turned her head, and kissed Ezra. Alex slipped his finger free and Paige complained, but then his hand glided up her body, took Ezra's hand and moved it down to between her legs.

On his first touch, Ezra's hips jutted forward into Paige's side. Immediately, Paige dropped her hand and slipped it under his boxers to grip him. He groaned harshly into her mouth.

Alex stood from the couch. He grabbed my wrist and roughly pulled me his way. He shifted quickly and pushed me down onto the couch beside Paige.

"Ezra," she whispered. "Please," she begged.

"What?" he bit out, desire riding his demanding voice.

Reaching around her, I took Ezra's chin in hand and forced his burning red gaze, meaning his hellhound side was close, to mine. "She wants you inside her."

His smile was wicked. He nipped at my hand before moving to his knees on the floor.

I glanced down as something dropped to my lap and found a tube of lube. I ripped my gaze up to a cheekily grinning Alex. He rose a brow. Did he seriously think I would knock this option back? I'd been staring at his ass for the last week, wanting to feel it around my cock.

With jerky motions, I lifted my ass, shoved my boxers down, and lathered the lube over my leaking length. Paige had me looking at her when I heard a giggle.

"Yes, sweetheart?"

"I just love to see you all wanting each other." She lifted her chin toward the other men. I caught Asher pushing himself into Nate, who was grinding his teeth together in pleasure. He was refusing to let Asher know he liked being fucked.

My gaze swept back when Alex climbed onto my lap. With a quick glance to Ezra, I was pleased to see he wasn't repulsed by our actions. In fact, he got distracted by Asher fucking Nate. I had a feeling he wanted to take on the wolf as well.

Only, as soon as Paige touched him, Ezra's attention was right back on her. He took her hand, and she gently tugged him closer, between her legs.

"You're mine?" she asked.

"Always."

"It means a connection with all of us," she told him.

He nodded. "Gladly."

"Then you'll accept being my bonded male."

His eyes heated even more. "With pleasure."

"Remove your boxers, mate, and be one with me."

His body shuddered at her words. He pushed down his boxers as Alex cupped the side of my neck, and I lifted my gaze to his. I slid my hands to his waist and then glided them up over his skin to his shoulders, where I could force him down to finish the kiss we'd started in Hell.

He lifted enough to grind his ass down on my cock.

Christ, yes.

A grunted groan had us breaking the kiss, but it didn't stop Alex from rocking over me or me pulling him free from his boxers and jerking him up and down. Before I glanced at Ezra and Paige, I caught Alex biting down on his bottom lip.

Ezra had his head buried in Paige's shoulder. Her eyes were closed, and she panted through the intensity we'd all experienced when finalizing the bond. It also meant Ezra had his cock inside Paige, something I wish I'd seen, but I had my hands full, which I didn't mind at all. They needed their first time private... well, somewhat private.

Alex shifted up, reached through his legs, and gripped my

dick. Slowly, he sat with the tip of my cock slipping inside him for the first time.

"Fuck," I clipped.

Alex moaned as he surrounded me with himself. His head dropped back. Leisurely, I reached up and ran my hand from his neck and down. I loved his skin, so much smoother than the rest of us.

Ezra breathed deeply. He picked up his head and stared at Paige in awe. She smiled warmly back at him, wrapping her legs around his waist as he slowly pushed in and out of her.

"You're incredible," he told her, leaning in to nip at her lips. "Unbelievable."

"So are you, my mate, my Ezra, my hellhound."

Nate's cry of release was soon joined with Asher's, but I couldn't look that way. Not when I'd moved my gaze back to Alex, and he'd forced the rest of me inside him with a gasp. His heated eyes met my own. He kissed my chest, my neck. It wasn't enough, not when he started to rock up and down on me. I wrapped an arm around him and gripped his hair to drag his mouth up to mine. We drank each other's moans down. His movements switched to a faster pace.

Purring started over in the corner; Asher's vampire was content.

"Quit it," Nate grumbled.

"No," Asher clipped, never stopping the noise. Alex and I chuckled against each other's mouth, only to stop and glance to Ezra and Paige when Paige cried out.

My hand shot out to grip Ezra's as it lay against the top of her breast. Ezra lifted his head from her shoulder he'd been kissing to glare at me.

"Stop, it's okay," Paige called, and when she smiled, I really knew it was okay. Then, when Paige opened her emotions to all of us, pure ecstasy reached me. I grunted and released my hold on Ezra's arm to grab Alex to me. My balls drew up, and Alex started fucking himself hard, up and down, squeezing my cock each time.

Fuck, he was tight.

"Christ, you feel good," I said against his lips.

"Paige," Ezra yelled. Alex and I looked over, still while he moved over me. Ezra bit out another groaned, "Fuck."

"Yes, hell yes, Ezra," she cried, holding him tightly to her. Her eyes slammed closed as her pleasure peaked, and we all made a noise when we felt her ride over into her orgasm. Ezra growled low, pumping faster; then he made a sound deep within his chest, coming inside our mate before he slowed and slid in and out unhurried.

A small hand snaked between Alex and me. Alex pulled back enough where we could both look down and see Paige's hand stroking Alex's hard cock.

"God, yes," Alex murmured.

I lifted my hand to his face, my thumb to his lips. He drew it into his mouth and sucked on it. I turned my head to claim Paige's mouth. Alex whimpered through his release as it squirted out and onto my chest and stomach. His ass tightened even more, drawing out my own cum into him.

Alex slumped against me, breathing hard. Paige and I broke apart, and my eyes landed on a grinning Ezra, where he rested his head against Paige's chest. I moved my gaze to the top of her breast and caught his handprint burned into her skin. He'd marked her as his, and it didn't bother me because I knew, like all of us did, he was a part of our family.

"I could use a shower, food, and sleep," Nate said from

across the room. After I helped Alex off my lap, he clicked his fingers and I felt my skin clean. I wasn't the only one he'd cleaned up either.

"I wouldn't mind feeding," Asher stated, his eyes trained on a blushing Alex from where he and Nate sat leaning against the wall. They'd been watching us and were already hard again.

Remembering Nate being inside me, I couldn't help but want it again since it had been so long.

Nate's eyes also shone with lust.

"We'll go to my room," Paige said, and then she cried out when Ezra swept her up into his arms.

He started for the door, but Paige wouldn't like the thought of all of us naked. I called out, "Alex, clothes please." I heard his click and felt silk against my skin. I started laughing when my body, as well as everyone else's, was covered from chest to feet in silk pajamas.

Happiness had my chest swelling. We were all possessive and protective of one another.

We were perfect together.

CHAPTER FORTY

PAIGE

As soon as we'd entered my room, Alex had replaced the men's pajamas with boxers, and I was in a short purple see-through teddy. I went straight for the bed and sat on the edge of it. I lifted my gaze from the nightie, smiling. It quickly drifted from my lips, and I bit my bottom one to keep my moan contained, already aroused again. And I wasn't the only one. Watching Asher drink from Alex was erotic in itself, but seeing Alex between Asher's spread legs on the couch and with his hand in Alex's boxers amped up my desire to a new height. I didn't know how I could possibly want more after what we'd just done, but I did, and I knew my males wouldn't deny me.

As I watched Asher and Alex, I didn't even need to ask for attention. Ezra, my newly bonded male, dropped to his knees in front of me, and I shifted my gaze down when he pushed my legs apart.

"I've been wanting a taste for a fucking long time," he said huskily.

Smiling, I reached out and ran a hand through his wild hair. "Who am I to deny you then."

He grinned. Thankfully Alex hadn't put anything but the teddy on my body, so when my legs were wide, Ezra could see how ready I was for him. He groaned and ducked in. On the first swipe of his tongue, I planted my hands on the bed and lifted my pussy to him.

When he sucked on my clit, I cried out, slamming my eyes closed, only to quickly open them and look down at his heated gaze. His tongue swirled around, and then he licked down, flicking his tongue over my entrance.

"Ezra," I whimpered.

"You taste better than I imagined, and I did a lot of that." He kissed my thigh and pushed two fingers inside me. I clamped down around them, causing him to hiss out a breath.

A moan sounded over at the couch. I lifted my hooded gaze and saw Asher had pulled down the front of Alex's boxers. His hand ran up and down Alex's length at a fast pace. Their eyes were on me and Ezra between my legs.

A growl to my left had me searching for my other two males. Nate had Thorn on the floor, on all fours with Nate behind Thorn, fucking him slowly. Their eyes were also on Ezra and me.

Nate grabbed Thorn's shoulder. He pulled him back to wrap his arms around Thorn's chest. Nate kissed Thorn's shoulder as he pumped into Thorn harder, drawing out a ragged groan from my ghoul. God, I loved seeing them together.

I glanced back to Asher and Alex. Alex's arms were holding Asher tightly. His hips ground up and down. I knew he was rubbing his ass against Asher, who licked and nibbled at Alex's neck.

Ezra surged up, his fingers still sliding in and out of me, but when he claimed my mouth, his finger disappeared. I heard a rip and pulled back to look around at my exposed front.

"Fucking stunning, isn't she?"

It pleased me our new member of the family didn't mind what was going on around us. How my other men shared their desires with each other. In fact, as Ezra glanced over to Nate and Thorn, I could sense his lust at their show.

"Christ, yes," Nate said roughly.

Alex and Thorn hummed their approval, and Asher called, "She is, and she's all ours."

I felt Ezra's smile against my breast before he latched his lips around my nipple. Yes, he liked being a part of our family, loved our connection. He was just as special as the rest of them. Something I had always known when he'd been only my hellhound, but more so now that he proved he was my mate and within our fold.

Ezra cupped my other breast and massaged it. I felt his hand between us before the tip of his dick pressed against my entrance.

His mouth went away from my nipple with a pop. He blew cool air over it. "You'll have me inside again?"

"I'll always have you inside me."

He surged forward and embedded deep. I cried out and gripped his shoulders. He buried his head into my neck and rocked in and out of me. I savored his touch, his feel, and already I couldn't wait for the next time with Ezra, even with Asher, Thorn, Nate, and Alex.

"Fuck," Nate clipped. "So goddamn tight," he added just as I caught, even without touching himself, Thorn's cum squirt out the tip and onto the floor. Nate's hand snaked down and tugged on Thorn's cock, drawing more out of him as he bit Thorn's shoulder and grunted through his own release into Thorn.

Seeing it had my walls clamping tighter around Ezra. He groaned, his thrusts more urgent, knowing I was close. My lower belly swirled, and I tipped my head to the other side in time to watch Asher's fangs slide into Alex's neck again. His bite harsh, his eyes green, he was lost in his release against Alex's back. Alex then arched, his cum shooting out and coating his lean stomach and Asher's hand.

"Ezra," I yelled as my orgasm crashed into me. I held Ezra tighter against me and heard his sharp intake of breath before he released inside me.

A woman sure could get used to this.

After we all showered in the actual shower that time, to which I thanked God for my large bathroom, I crawled back into bed. The men moved around the room, some drinking, some eating, while Thorn and Alex spoke of their time in Hell. I listened intently and kept pushing the fear down. They were home. They were safe, I reminded myself.

It was strange yet comforting to see Ezra mold into the family as if he'd always been there. Since his presence was the same, I guessed it made it easy to adjust to him, and in a way, he had been always there, only not in his human form. When he spoke, my other men listened. I could already see the respect they held for him.

Eventually, Alex drifted over to the bed. I opened my arms,

and he pulled the sheet back enough to climb in. Rather than lying beside me, he hovered over me until I spread my legs; only then did he rest on me gently. I wrapped my arms around him, and then with one hand, I ran my fingers through his hair. He sighed into my chest.

"Am I too heavy?" he asked groggily. He must have been exhausted since they'd refused to sleep much in Hell. It wasn't that they were scared; they just didn't trust the demons, and I couldn't blame them, even when they had Ezra's protection.

"You're perfect where you are," I told him, and then it didn't take him long before he drifted off. My other men then retired with us. Nate and Ezra close to my sides, while Asher lay behind Nate and Thorn behind Ezra. I'd been blessed with such amazing men in my life. I loved them fully, and I was beyond elated they shared love between each other as well.

Nothing was perfect. I wasn't foolish enough to think what we had would always be sunshine and roses, but I'd enjoy each and every day as they came because my men would be by my side.

"We still have so much to deal with," I said softly into the room. My body tensed just thinking about it all.

"I have been thinking on the matter," Asher said.

"And?" Nate clipped.

"I believe the best way to gain people's attention is, as Lucifer said, to have proof. It is time our queen makes herself known. Not with just the council, but with others."

"What will it gain?" Thorn asked.

"Attention," Ezra added. "If people see what kind of queen Paige is, how respected she is, who she has at her side, others may be willing to listen to Paige and her ways. It will be an asset before things go head-to-head with the council."

"Agreed," Asher said. "I think we need to use the month before seeing the council to our advantage."

Nate grunted. "You're talking about traveling to see other communities, aren't you?"

"Yes. The ones we've heard of. The lost alphas, the fae king, the vampire master, all their people?"

"It could be a good idea," Nate said. "We can speak of our thoughts regarding the council's part in their deaths or disappearances and see where it goes."

"Not everyone will trust," I told them, my stomach swirling with unease. "It wasn't simple here, and it's not like everything here has been smoothed out with our people. I can still see problems popping up. So how will it be for the other kings or queens who know nothing about me, who have thought the ghouls extinct? Can we really ask them to trust us when the community and my people have been hidden for so long?"

"All we can do is try," Asher said softly.

"It won't be easy," I replied. I felt sick to the gut. I hated the idea, but they made good points. We needed more people with us to go against the council. And if we could get their support, we had a better chance at defeating them.

"No, it won't," Thorn said. "But Asher and Ezra are right. To have others at our back, for people to see the poison within the council, it's best we at least try. If the people we go to, see what we have and witness how the missing or dead rulers have been respected, their replacements—and their people—will do anything to have their missing comrades back and seek vengeance of those kings who died."

"What happens if their replacements are in with the council already?" I questioned.

Thorn's lips thinned. "I'm sure between all of us we will be able to detect such things. Three of your bonded worked with the council for many years. Together, we'll work out who is or isn't to be trusted."

I didn't like the thought of traveling and going into unfamiliar communities, but I believed in my men and their abilities. They would know the rules. They would guide me. All I could do was pray it would lead us to success. I forced myself to relax a little, even when fear for them touched my heart. "What will we use the other month for?" I asked, trying to distract myself.

"Training," Ezra said. "We'll need to make sure we're as strong as we can be."

That was a good idea. We all needed to be at our best for this horrid situation.

"Especially since we'll be going into others' territory," Nate grumbled.

Nerves still fluttered in my stomach. "What about here? Who will take care of the kingdom when we're gone?" I wouldn't leave my people unguarded.

"I'll speak with my parents and see if they will come back while we're gone," Ezra said, and the room quieted.

"They'd do that?" Thorn asked, sounding as surprised as I felt. We were talking about the devil. Though, from what he'd already shown, he wasn't anything like I'd expected. Then again, Ezra was their son, and I was sure that had a lot to do with it.

Ezra chuckled. "My mother has managed to mellow my father in the years they've been together. One thing I am certain of, they would do anything for me... within reason."

"If they're not able to, there is always Felnick and the shifters," Thorn said. They were options, and I knew, if asked, they would do everything within their power to safeguard our land. It still scared me, though, even the thought of asking them because they had their own lives, their own families to take care of.

"Again, there's so much to do," I told them, letting unease seep into them.

Ezra's fingers tickled up my arm before resting his hand flat on my shoulder. "There is, but we'll do it all together." Tipping my head back, he leaned in, knowing what I wanted, and pressed his lips against mine. A little of the panic subsided.

"Agreed," Nate grumbled from my other side. I turned my head his way. He lifted his gaze from Alex, whose head still rested on my naked chest as he softly snored. Nate's lips grazed against mine. More of the fear dashed away.

"We'll protect one another," Asher said from behind Nate. His hand slid over Nate's shoulder, reaching out for me. I removed my hand from Alex's hair and took it.

My men were my world. With them, it had me believing I *could* take on anything.

"We will," I told him. Because I would do anything to keep them all alive.

"Family is always first," Thorn muttered lazily. He got up to his elbow behind Ezra and smiled down at me. "For now, though, sweetheart, let's get some rest."

Laughing, I nodded since my worry was under control. "Rest with all my males sounds like heaven."

Thorn pressed a kiss to the tips of his finger and then moved them to my lips, where I kissed.

Yes, whatever was to come, I would do anything, fight anyone, kill everyone I had to, making sure I would come home with the men I loved. With the family I'd claimed.

CHAPTER FORTY-ONE

PAIGE

"Again," Nate bellowed down at me.

I groaned and rolled to my stomach. Slowly, I clambered to my feet and bared my teeth at him. "You yell at me one more time, I'm going to take your balls from your body."

He snorted, but before he could open his mouth, Thorn said, "I rather like his balls. Maybe take some toes instead, sweetheart."

I shot Thorn the finger, and he chuckled. Until Alex used his power and put him in a bubble. When Thorn started floating up to the roof, his eyes widened. He stumbled around like a fish out of water, cursing up a storm. He pounded at the outer layer, but we all knew nothing would penetrate it. We'd all tried.

My anger disappeared, and I started laughing. But then my feet were knocked out from under me, and I landed with a thump on my back on the floor. Asher stood over me with his hands on his hips.

"Being distracted could get you killed."

"I know," I clipped.

"It could also get someone you love killed," Nate called. I twisted my head to see him standing behind Ezra with his hand around his throat. I knew he wouldn't harm Ezra but seeing it had me screaming at myself under my breath. They'd been teaching me how to protect myself for the last two weeks, and we'd now moved on to trying to show me how to work within a team. To make sure I not only had myself covered but those who would fight alongside me. I thought I'd made progress, but it was obvious I still had a lot of work to do. My body chilled in worry. I fisted my hands and pressed them against my churning stomach. I wouldn't be ready in time.

We were leaving in two weeks.

Two weeks.

It wasn't enough time.

A sense of failure and worry spread through my veins instead of blood. I didn't want to be the weak link. I had to get better.

Slapping the floor as I stood, I ignored Asher's hand he'd held out to help me.

"Love—" he started, but I shook my head.

I ran a hand over my sweaty face. "Don't give me sweet, encouraging words. I don't want them right now."

He nodded. "All right." He dodged left. I slid right and gripped his arm to take him to the ground, but he was too fast. He easily slipped out of my hold and wound his arm around my throat, pressing his front to my back. I grabbed his hand and bent, flipping him over my body. He landed in a crouch, stood, and turned. His movements were a mere blur with every punch and kick as he drove me backward. I deflected each one.

Out of the corner of my eye, I saw Nate approaching Alex, who still held Thorn in a bubble. I ducked under Asher's punch, unsheathed my blade at my ankle, and threw it across the room; it landed just before Nate's toes.

His gaze hit me, but Alex had also noticed Nate now.

Asher tripped me. I fell on my back, rolled, and jumped up.

He stopped and smiled at me. "Better."

It was a good thing I didn't breathe, or I would have been out of breath. Still, my heart was beating so hard in my chest I was surprised it didn't fall out.

It was wonderful to hear his praise, but it wasn't enough yet. Soon we would be walking into the fae territory, and even though we'd asked for permission and it had been given, I didn't like not knowing what would happen. Actually, all of the meetings we'd set up had been agreed upon since they were all willing to meet with the new ghoul queen. Of course they would want to know if I would be a threat to them and theirs. They'd learn I wouldn't be, unless something happened to someone I claimed as mine.

I'd read up on fae between training, yet the information was limited. And those who had been around the fae told me never to trust them. They were conniving, tricky creatures. They could fly, glamour, and talk their way into your home and bed. I'd heard they were the most stunning creatures in existence, and yes, I'd seen pictures in the books I'd studied. Yet, all I could think was that I saw more beauty in my bonded mates.

I wasn't holding out hope in their help. The fae kept to themselves a lot. For all I knew, the new king, who was the son of the former one, wouldn't care what was going on outside of his kingdom. I had asked why we were even going to see them, but Asher assured me they would be an advantage to have on our side. The council were the ones behind the former king's death. Alex was certain the facts my men already had to show the fae, as well as what they could tell us about that night, would be enough for them to not trust the council and hopefully stand with us. Or if not, then to stay out of the fight when it was time for us to go to them.

Only time would tell.

After the fae kingdom, we were moving on to the two missing alphas. The first was from a lion pride consisting of at least five hundred members. The other was a tiger in charge of his streak. Nate had informed me one night while studying that tigers usually didn't group together—they tended to be solitary creatures—but the alpha that had gone missing had been looked up to by many of his kind, which was how he became their leader.

Their groups had also given us permission to enter their territory. However, I had a feeling it could have something to do with wanting to take a good look at the ghoul queen they'd never heard of. Even the fae would want the same, to discover my power and determine if I would be a threat or not.

We had to be careful with how we did things, though, or it could bring us more trouble than just the council.

Lastly, and it was thanks to the woman who'd saved my Asher, we were allowed entry into the deceased master's clan lands to visit the vampires since she'd now taken over as their master. I wasn't looking forward to seeing Cynthia. The interaction Asher had with her concerned me as I could likely kill her if she tried anything. However, Asher told me everything would be fine and Cynthia would listen to what we had to say.

It was also likely she'd help us—another thing Asher was sure of. His confidence in her had me wanting to punch her in the face in a fit of jealousy, which was something my men found amusing when they felt and saw how pissed I became every time Asher spoke of her.

Still, I pushed all of that down to worry about when the time came and, instead, got into a fighting stance. I curled my fingers at Asher and said, "Come at me."

He smirked and then disappeared.

Only that time I brought my powers forward. It helped me see his movement better. Just as he stopped behind me, I twisted, grabbed, and dropped him to his back on the floor. Though, I was sure he allowed it because when I straddled his waist, his hands slowly slid up my thighs. The movement paused, and he rolled me to my back, got to his feet, and crouched in front of me. Nate's growl was pointed at the door, so was Ezra's in his shifted form, and as Thorn's feet touched the floor, he withdrew his sword. Alex, with his delicious power, aimed his glowing-white hands at the door.

It was then I heard it—the heavy footfalls of maybe three people. Quickly, I stood just as the doors to the gym burst open and in them stood a puffing Leon and two of his brothers.

"What's wrong?" I demanded, taking a step forward, until Asher's arm swung out to hold me back.

"Yasmin." My sister's name from his lips had my heart taking off in flight and angst twisting my stomach. He went on. "She was outside with Sophie and two of our brothers. They...." He shook his head.

Jake, Leon's younger brother, continued with "We didn't know the real Sophie was actually inside, since the fake scented the same as the real one. We were all fooled."

Fear grabbed at me. "Then who was Yasmin walking with? Is my sister okay? What happened?"

"We don't know who the imposter was, but the fake Sophie attacked them."

"Where's Yasmin?" I yelled.

Leon's frown said enough, even before he admitted, "We don't know. We have every shifter out searching for her."

I shoved Asher's hand from me and raced from the room. My men followed, as did Leon and his brothers. The guards who'd been outside the gym joined us as well.

"Does Eric know?" Thorn asked.

Leon shook his head. "We kept it quiet. Until…."

"Until we knew more," Jake finished.

"We're sorry we failed you, my queen." Leon's lips thinned. He hated himself, but I couldn't allow it when they would have done everything they could have.

"Your brothers who were with Yasmin?" I asked.

Sorrow crossed his features before he steeled his expression into a blank one. "One didn't make it. The other is with a healer."

We made it outside. Jake pointed at the entryway that led out toward the town behind my castle. I kept moving. "Whoever has done this will pay in flesh and blood," I told him, even knowing it wasn't going to be enough.

Yasmin.

She could be next.

She could die.

I shook my head. I couldn't let that thought settle.

"Thank you, my queen," he said softly.

"Asher?" I called.

He veered left. "Blood, off into the woods."

"That's where our kin were found."

"How do you know Yasmin and Sophie were out here with your brothers in the first place?" I asked, pulling to a stop behind Asher. He lifted his nose and sniffed the area.

"We keep each other informed of all movements. Plus, we questioned a shop owner who they passed. She saw Yasmin and who she thought was young Sophie walk from the castle together with our brothers not far behind. She said she overheard Sophie saying she wanted to show her mom something."

A trick. Yasmin would follow Sophie anywhere, just like most of us. Only we would have sensed the power used to alter the appearance of whoever was behind this. Though perhaps not since two bear shifters, who had good senses, hadn't. I clenched my jaw and glanced around. Two pools of blood marred the leaves, dirt, and grass. Leon's brothers. My heart ached for them.

Nate and Ezra, who had both shifted at some point, took a few bounds forward and growled. They glanced back, then forward, and took off running. We quickly followed. I hadn't even considered how people would react seeing Ezra back as we'd run through the township and even the castle. He hadn't shifted around anyone but us, and in training only. All they knew

was that he was a part of Lucifer's entourage. Lucifer had since left with Virginia and their people, but were coming back when we traveled. It was something to worry about later.

My throat closed as we entered a clearing and I saw Yasmin being held with a knife to her neck by a woman I didn't know.

The woman smiled. "Finally, it took them plenty of time to let you know."

"Who are you and what do you want?" Asher asked.

Nate and Ezra pawed at the ground, snarling from where they stood just in front of me.

"If anyone moves, I will slice her open."

"Answer my mate's questions."

"My queen," a guard called. I glanced to the side as he stepped forward. "Her name is Tenaya. She is Grace's daughter."

Fuck.

Fuckety fuck.

Yasmin stared at me with tears in her eyes. Her lips trembled as she smiled sadly at me. She knew this could be it for her. I shook my head slightly, telling her there was still hope. I had my men, the guards. We could kill this bitch without harming my sister.

Dread filled me to the brim. Even with the strength, the magic around me, they were still a distance away. If Tenaya saw Alex disappear, she would kill Yasmin with a quick swipe.

Please, please do not take my sister away from me, from her family. Please.

Another guard moved close. "She is also the one in battle who took her own life."

Tenaya laughed. "Yes, it was so easy to fool you all with all the blood around. So easy to cover the beating of my heart with a spell."

"What do you want?" I pressed. There had to be something she wanted or... no, no, no. It couldn't just be for revenge. I hadn't even remembered her besides when she pretended to take her own life. I'd been so far away, I didn't recognize her. Now closer, I saw the resemblance to Grace.

Her smile was pure evil. "I see the panic in your eyes. You know why we're here."

"Please don't kill her."

"Then you shouldn't have killed my mother."

"She murdered people for power, sent my mates to Hell, conspired with demons," I called. "Yasmin is an innocent human being."

Her grip tightened on my sister, and Yasmin whimpered. I fisted my hands. I wanted to tear into the woman. Rip, bite, and kill.

Instead, I locked my body down. Tears welled in my eyes. "Please, please don't kill her. She has a husband, children."

Tenaya smiled again. "Oh, I know."

"Why?" I asked on a whisper.

"Because you took my mother," she answered simply.

My eyes connected to Yasmin's. She mouthed, "I love you. Take care of them."

My body shuddered in anguish. "I'll do anything."

"I'm not stupid. We make a bargain, and you'll all kill me in the end—do not move," she yelled. The guards stopped. "All I want is to see your pain, and I have." Quickly, she removed the knife from Yasmin's neck. We all rushed forward. A scream tore out of me when she plunged the knife into Yasmin's chest. Into her heart.

I stumbled. Asher grabbed me. Alex appeared out of nowhere and caught Yasmin as her body sagged. Tenaya stepped back, still grinning, only her eyes widened when Ezra leaped. His mouth surrounded her neck and face. I heard a snap just as Nate joined Ezra, and they shredded her to pieces.

Dropping to my knees beside Alex cradling Yasmin, I reached out and gripped her hand in both of mine. Her hand was loose, no strength evident. A sob caught in my throat. Yasmin gazed up at me as her breath stuttered. Blood spurted from her mouth.

"You t-take care of them," she wheezed.

"No, you'll be here to do it." I shook my head again and again.

"I love you so much…. Not your fault."

I dug my top teeth into my bottom lip. "I love you, but this isn't goodbye. It can't be." Her lips pulled up before she went lax against Alex. "Yasmin," I yelled. "Please, please, Yasmin."

Hands dropped to my shoulders. "She's passed out, love. Just passed out."

I lifted my gaze and looked at Alex and Thorn. When Nate pressed himself between them, I met his gaze. Finally, I glanced at Asher. "Get Eric," I ordered.

"Sweetheart, are you sure—"

"Get Eric, now!" I bellowed. Asher disappeared, and the warm breeze blew over us.

I wouldn't—couldn't lose my sister… but if Eric didn't agree, then I would have to say goodbye, and that thought had me trembling in fear.

Ezra, still in his hellhound form, moved to my side. I ignored the blood around his mouth and curled an arm over his neck, pulling him close. Thorn went to his knee on my other side, Nate trotted around to my back and pressed in, while Alex laid his hand over mine still clutching Yasmin's.

I wasn't sure their support and comfort would be enough for what was to come, but I appreciated it all the same. They would be the only reason I got through this.

CHAPTER FORTY-TWO

EZRA

Her pain slipped through her walls and had me shifting back to my human form beside her, needing to comfort and protect her. Her arm stayed around me, and I wrapped mine around her waist. When I shifted, thankfully my clothes stayed on; my father had told me it was something to do with the magic within me. I was just glad as Paige hated if anyone saw any of her mates naked. Just like we would be if another saw her bare.

My heart ached for Paige, but also Yasmin. To see her so still with a dagger sticking out of her chest, it was so fucking terrifying. She was a good sister to my mate, a great mother, and from what I'd seen, wife. She didn't deserve this.

If she died…. I couldn't even consider it, as it would mean Paige would lose a part of herself—like she had when I'd died in my hellhound form, from what I'd been told. I hated… fuck no, despised that I'd put her through that anguish. If I could have gotten back to her, I would have in a heartbeat.

Paige trembled against me. Tears ran down her cheeks, but she ground her teeth together in the hope of holding them back.

The air around us blew harder as Asher stopped at our side. He carefully took Eric off his shoulder and set him on his feet.

"What's going on?" Eric demanded.

With a clenched jaw, Asher placed his hands on Eric's shoulders and turned him our way. He paled, and a mournful cry fell from his lips as he dropped to the ground and crawled to Paige's other side.

"Yasmin," he choked. His hands fluttered out before pulling back again.

"It's okay to touch her," Alex reassured. "I have her body frozen in place so… nothing moves." He gulped, unsure if he said the right thing, but a reassuring and wobbly small smile from Paige had Alex relaxing a little. One of Eric's hands brushed his wife's hair away from her forehead while he used the other to gently press two fingers against her neck. Over her weak pulse. The pulse that we could all hear slowing even more.

"Eric," Paige started, her voice shaking, "you have to listen to me."

"Yasmin," he whispered, leaning into her, putting his face next to her. "Baby, you can't leave me. You can't leave the kids."

"Eric," Paige tried again.

"Honey, we need you." He laughed humorlessly. "I can't survive without you." He made a pained noise in the back of his throat, then shook his head. "We can get through this. We can."

He straightened to his knees as his tears dropped freely. "Tell me she can get through this. Then fucking tell me who did this so I can kill them."

For some insane reason, I wanted to yell, "She has a fucking knife sticking out of her heart, how do you think she'll get through this?" Yet I clamped my lips closed because I knew, along with all of Paige's men, that our mate would have a plan, and by the way she looked up at Asher, I knew exactly what it was.

With Asher's slight nod, Paige moved her gaze back to Eric. "There is only one way."

Eric nodded. "Becoming something more?"

"Yes," Paige whispered.

"What?" he demanded. "A shifter? A Ghoul? A vampire?" He laughed humorlessly. "I've been living here and it's still crazy." He looked back down to Yasmin, his bottom lip trembling. "But I would do anything to have her with me."

"You know everything will change?" Thorn questioned.

"I know."

"Your children—"

He shook his head. "Will want their mom in their life. No matter what she is."

"Yasmin?" Paige whispered.

His watery gaze fell on hers. He reached out and took Paige's hand that rested gently against Yasmin's shoulder. "Will never regret the choice we make for her because she'll want more days with her children."

Paige glanced down at her sister and took a shuddering breath. "She wouldn't want to die," Paige said, more to herself than anyone.

"No, she wouldn't," Eric stated. He sniffed, wiped at his face, and straightened even more. "So, what shall she become?"

"Eric, has she ever said anything to you about what she would prefer?" Asher asked.

Eric nodded. "Yes."

"A vampire," Paige uttered.

Eric looked at her. "How did you...?" He shook his head. "Never mind. You two know everything about each other, even if you haven't spoken of it. Yes, a vampire."

Jealousy hit me, only it wasn't mine. It was Paige's, yet it was quickly replaced by guilt.

"It doesn't have to be me, love," Asher said softly.

She shook her head. "It does. You're the only one I trust to do this, to help her through this, to guide her properly. I... just... I hate to say it, but I won't be able to be around when you do it."

Understanding dawned through me. She'd already thought of Asher siring Yasmin. She wasn't comfortable, but like the amazing woman she was, she'd put herself, her needs aside for others she cared for.

Tightening my hold around Paige, I said, "Alex, take Yasmin to your room with Asher and Eric. Nate, go to the children and reassure them things are fine. Paige, you'll be with me and Thorn."

Paige nodded. She looked at Eric. "She'll be okay."

"She will be. We can't lose her."

"No, we can't."

"I will do everything in my power to make sure your sister lives, my love," Asher reassured, bending to kiss the top of Paige's head. She tilted back, waiting. Asher pressed his lips against hers.

"I know you will. I love you." She was so free with showing her feelings, it was beautiful. The night I watched her dig her way free from the ground was when I knew she would be my mate. I'd cursed everything I could that I wasn't allowed to show her my true form. I'd been spelled to stay as my hellhound for at least a year as punishment for disobeying my parents. Yet it had also been a blessing as I'd been by her side from the beginning, to teach her, get to know her, and love her deeply.

"As I love you."

Not only could I feel her anguish, her guilt, her love, but I could see it in her tense body, her drawn brows, and in her eyes. I curled her in tighter against me and kissed her temple. Asher's hand landed on my shoulder and gave it a squeeze.

"Take care of our mate," he said.

"With my life," I answered.

"Always," Thorn added.

In a blink, Alex disappeared with Yasmin and Eric. The breeze picked up, and Asher swept away to meet them. Paige drew in a shuddering breath, even when she didn't have to breathe. Nate, still in his wolf form, stood and licked Paige's face.

She nodded. "I know she'll be fine. She's in good hands." Her lips thinned before she whispered again, "She'll be fine."

Nate's body contorted with the change. It was smooth and fast, but painful. Still, the man didn't show that it affected him. His expression stayed neutral. Then he was kneeling beside Paige, pulling her into him.

"You're naked," Paige muttered.

Thorn and I snorted. Fear bombarded her, yet she still managed to care that someone would see her mate naked.

Nate let out a huff. "No one is around. How about you stop

panicking and worrying, which gets you nowhere, and go to the training area to kick Ezra and Thorn's asses?"

I winced. It was harsh, but Nate worked Paige in a way that got her annoyed or pissed enough to be distracted. It was what she needed.

"You're a dick," she mumbled with a sniff.

"Yes."

"At least you're my dick."

He kissed her neck. "That I am."

"Fight or fuck?" Nate asked her. My dick jerked behind my jeans.

Her eyes narrowed on what was left of the witch. "Fight."

I stood and held out my hand. "Then we'll battle." It would be good for all of us. The witch had died too soon, too easily, and I needed to get rid of some of the burning adrenaline inside me. I bounced on the balls of my feet as Paige took my hand, and I pulled her up. Thorn got close while Nate also stood.

"I'll go to the kids," Nate said. He leaned down, pressed his lips to Paige's swiftly, then up to Thorn's. He hesitated when his gaze met mine. I puckered my lips and made kissy faces at him. It was good to see Paige smile, even if it disappeared a second later and her eyes drifted off toward the castle.

While I was distracted by Paige, Nate moved in front of me. With one hand he pinched my cheeks so my lips stayed puck-ered and kissed me hard and fast. My wide gaze caught his shining wolf one. "You're the only one not claimed. That'll change."

I mumbled through my squeezed cheeks until he released them. "Beast to beast, I'd like to see who wins."

His eyes flashed. His teeth lengthened and a snout appeared.

"I'll bend you to my will, hellhound," he growled roughly, his wolf riding his voice.

I rolled my eyes. He snapped his teeth in my face before he called forth the rest of his shift, his body twisting and snapping. Nate landed on all fours in his wolf form and strutted to Paige, pushing his head under her hand. Her eyes shot down to him, and she smiled softly, curling her fingers into his hair. Nate bumped his body into hers before he took off on a run, straight back to the castle, not only to reassure the kids—Paige's niece and nephew—but to be there for them.

Thorn stepped up behind Paige, and just as his hands landed on her waist, a form appeared out of nowhere. It was lucky Thorn and I had fast reflexes, or Alex would have been dead. Thorn stopped short from throwing a dagger at him, and I pulled back on my punch at the last second.

"What's wrong?" Paige demanded, fear evident in her high-pitched tone. She grabbed for Alex, taking his arm. "Shouldn't you be with Yasmin?"

"My powers still hold her suspended." He reassured her and looked at us. "I'm taking Paige to my room, both of you meet us there," Alex stated. He curled his free arm around Paige's waist, and with a bright flash of white light, they disappeared.

Thorn and I shared a look before racing toward Alex's room.

We arrived and turned a corner to find Paige in the face of a woman I'd never seen before. I chanced a glance at Thorn, and he said softly, "Sakura, vampire."

Guards stood behind the other woman and glared down at her, while Asher and Alex stood at Paige's back. Eric must have been in the bedroom with his wife.

"Please, please, majesty, allow me to be the one," the woman begged, her eyes down to the floor.

"For the last time, I don't know you, and you expect me to trust you? I've never seen you around. How can I trust you have good intentions?"

"What are you asking of our queen, Sakura?" Thorn questioned.

Only it was Asher who spoke. "She wants to be the one to change Yasmin. I heard her approaching and warned Alex. We both came out here before she could barge in. The guards showed soon after she arrived."

"Why do you want this?" I questioned harshly, wanting an answer she'd yet to give Paige. Yasmin was family as far as I was concerned. We had to be cautious of everyone who tried to be a part of our close-knit connection. I didn't know this vampire, and it seemed neither did Asher or Alex. I glanced at Thorn.

He caught my gaze and said to all, "Sakura is a part of our elite force. She has been one who guards your sister and her family on and off." Thorn looked to Alex's bedroom. "Is Eric able to hear?"

Alex shook his head. "No, the room is soundproof."

"We can't leave my sister suspended much longer without risk." Paige then mumbled to herself, "There's always risk." She lifted her eyes to Asher. "We need to finish this. Can you please—"

"No, he can't. You don't understand the connection," Sakura cried, then snapped her lips together. She went to grab Paige. I snatched her suspended hand and spun her, so I had her back to my chest and locked my arms around her tightly.

"Never touch the queen," I snarled.

Sakura shook in my arms. She stank of fear and determination. "Please, please, let me speak."

Paige's brows dipped as she glared down at my hands. "Ezra." I dropped my arms but stayed where I was. Paige nodded and then said to the vampire, "I know I don't know the connection between a fledgling and their master, but Asher does, and he hasn't advised against it. I trust him and his knowledge that it wouldn't be bad by siring my sister."

Sakura shook her head. "Your bonded male would make an excellent sire; I have no doubt. I know their connection would never come between a bonded pair or group. Bonds are stronger than anything, even a master's hold," she said softly, then dipped her head, eyes back to the floor. "However, Yasmin and I have grown... close. I believe she would prefer if it was I who changed her."

Paige's eyes grew wide. "Close? Ah... as in... you mean you're a friend of my sister's?"

"Yes."

"Oh, right," Paige said, laughing a little. I could sense from her how she'd jumped to another conclusion and then thought she'd been silly for it.

"And something else," Sakura confessed even quieter.

"Leave us," Asher ordered roughly. The guards filed down the hallway.

Paige's anger twisted through me; she had her hands fisted at her sides. "Do you mean you've come between Yasmin and Eric?" I now understood her anger. When I'd first been with Paige and stuck in my hellhound form, she often spoke about how special Yasmin and Eric's relationship was. She would hate anything or anyone that had come between her sister's marriage. Our Paige wished many times to have had a connection like theirs with a man.

Now she had it with us all. It honored me to be a part of it, to have her love and be free to give it back.

"No," Sakura said quickly. "It… no, it wasn't like that. It… I do not wish to explain when you should hear this from someone in your family."

Paige turned her head to capture Alex's gaze. "Get Eric out here." She then stared back at Sakura, who still looked to the floor as Alex disappeared into the room.

Paige's anger still simmered. I moved from behind Sakura, knowing Thorn would grab her if she tried anything—though I couldn't imagine her attacking—and moved to Paige's back. I ran my hands from her shoulders, down her back, and stopped at her waist. She leaned into me, sighing, letting the anger lessen enough that it didn't cloud her mind.

My body hummed in contentment and amazement every time I touched her and she accepted it without a thought. I was really hers, connected for eternity. It made me fucking ecstatic, like a child learning something new and thrilling for the first time.

The door opened to Eric demanding, "What's going on? Why are we not helping my wife?" He saw Sakura. His eyes widened in surprise then welled. "Sakura," he whispered.

The vampire sniffed and dashed for Eric; their arms wrapped around each other in a tight embrace. In a second, I had Paige turned away from them as she screamed and tried to move in my arms to get to them.

"You cheating, motherfucking, stinking asshole. I will *kill you*. Kill you, bring you back, and kill you again," she roared.

"Paige," Eric yelled as he pushed Sakura behind him. Over

my shoulder, I caught him stepping closer to Paige until Alex grabbed him by the shoulder, shaking his head.

Eric sighed. "Paige, I would never cheat on my wife, on your sister. She's the love of my life. You know this."

"Take a moment, *mi corazón*," I whispered into her ear, then kissed her neck. "Let's listen to them, and then if we don't like it, I'll help to gut him like a pig."

She drew in an unnecessary breath, shook out her hands, and then straightened. When she nodded, I dropped my hands and moved to her side as she turned to face Eric.

"Explain," she ordered.

He swiped a hand over his face. "Okay, all right. It's not what you think. Well, it is—" Paige made a grab for him. Asher and I held her back when Eric yelled, *"But,* there's a but...." Paige settled. "Jesus, you should know to trust me, Paige."

"I'll trust you when I know why you were hanging off a woman I don't even know like she is… is… something to you."

"To us. To me and your sister. She's something to us."

Paige's head jerked back. She shrugged off our hold and threw a hand out. "Explain that."

Eric threw his own hands up in the air. "Explain you, explain this place, the people, the connection you have with five men. I don't know how anything works, but since spending time with Sakura, Yasmin and I have both… I don't know, grown to like her… a lot."

"You *and* Yasmin?"

"Yes! I wouldn't cheat on my wife."

"Sakura?"

She nodded and lifted her head, her eyes meeting Paige's. "I believe they are my bonded."

Eric's head whipped around. "Wait, what?"

"Say what?" Paige said.

Eric stepped up to Sakura and took her hands. Paige grumbled behind her thinned lips. Eric ignored her. "Do you mean like Paige has with her men?"

"Yes," Sakura said softly, glancing away from Eric. "I didn't want to say anything. Your marriage is important to me. I care for you both enough to let this go since the bond hasn't been completed." She blushed. How was this woman a guard?

"She has only light duties with other members of the force," Thorn explained as if reading my thoughts. I nodded. Knowing Thorn, he would have employed Sakura if she had asked or if her family had pushed her into the duty. The ghoul was hard when he had to be, but soft under it all.

"She wants to be the one to change Yasmin," Paige said.

"You do?" Eric asked.

"Yes, but… even if either of you do not want me as a bonded, then I would still like a chance to sire Yasmin, so then when I do leave, I will know within myself that she is well or in need of help."

"You would do that for them? Leave if they don't want you?" Thorn asked.

She didn't look away from Eric's gaze. "I would do anything for both of them."

We all heard Eric swallow thickly. Paige didn't look away from Eric's thumb caressing Sakura's hand.

"Yasmin would want you to sire her," he told her.

"Eric," Paige warned.

He faced Paige. "She would." It was his turn to blush. "You, ah, look, this is awkward as hell, but we've been spending time with Sakura. We know there's something we feel about her that we can't and won't deny. There's a connection. We haven't said anything because it's still new."

Paige studied him—his firm posture, his determined eyes. Still she asked, "Are you sure Yasmin would want this?"

"Yes." His voice held strong. "Sakura should sire Yasmin."

I could feel the war within her. She wasn't sure what to believe since she knew nothing about Sakura. Shock and fear, as well as sadness, rolled around inside her. Thorn and I both reached out to her at the same time. We brought her back against us, and just our touch seemed to help.

"Okay," Paige said quietly. "Save my sister, please."

Sakura's bottom lip trembled, and she bowed her head. "It would be my honor, my queen."

Alex opened the door to the bedroom again. Eric quickly hugged Paige, plus Thorn and me since we were so close. "Thank you." He kissed her cheek, and I growled out a warning. Eric smiled and then went to Sakura, curling his arm around her waist and leading her into the room.

"You've done the right thing, love," Asher said. "I'll keep an eye on everything with Alex."

She smiled softly. "Thank you." She blew Asher and Alex a kiss, to which Alex returned and Asher dipped his head, and they followed Eric in, shutting the door after them.

Leaning down, I kissed Paige's neck. She trembled. "You haven't practiced fighting against my hellhound side in a long time, mi corazón. How about we see how you fair?"

"Sounds like a good distraction. Also, what does mi corazón mean?"

I smiled softly. "It means 'my heart,' which is what you have always been, in Spanish. Would you prefer it in French? *Mon cœur*, or Russian—"

"No," she whispered quickly, almost shyly. I could hear her heart picking up its pace. She liked my name for her, and I loved that she did. "I like it in Spanish, how you said it first."

"That's how it'll be then," I told her. "Now, should we go?" I asked, starting down the hall with her hand in mine and Thorn at her other side. "I'd also like to see how well the ghoul can do."

Thorn laughed. "I'd beat your ass, furry head."

Biting my bottom lip, I smiled and hummed under my breath.

"I could," Thorn stated.

Glancing down at Paige, I rolled my eyes. She started giggling, then smiled her thanks for entertaining her.

"You'll be on the floor in a second, hound."

"Yes, you're right. Only it'll be with my cock buried in you while I dominate your ghoul." Paige's scent shifted; her arousal sang to me. I loved how turned on she got from watching her men in bed together. I had yet to see what they were like. If they were as good as our mate, then I knew I'd be more than satisfied in bed.

Thorn tripped. "Jesus, you sound like Nate. You've been hanging out with him too much, and you're wrong. It'll be you under me while I allow you to taste our mate's pussy."

Paige moaned. "Now all of *that* is a welcome distraction of what's really going on. I'll race you." She grinned, and then her power filled the area before she sped off down the hall.

Of course we followed.

CHAPTER FORTY-THREE

THORN

*E*zra was brilliant at distracting Paige. He was a worthy mate for our queen. He'd managed to bring a smile to our lips and ease the ache in our chests over Yasmin. Though guilt stabbed at me for smiling when Paige's sister's life was on the line. Maybe it had something to do with how positive I was that she would pull through and be all right.

Paige had just entered the room, and I was closing in. I dove and curled my arms around her waist, taking her to the ground but twisting in the air so I would land on my back with Paige sprawled over me. I heard Paige's cry of surprise, Ezra's laugh, and then a snarl.

In a second, I was up with Paige pushed behind me as a flash of something barreled into Ezra, taking him to the floor.

Paige's power burst out of her. She transformed before my

eyes as she moved to the figure over Ezra, gripped it in a roar, picked the figure up, and threw it across the room. I stood there gaping like a newbie fool as she glanced down at Ezra, saw blood on his neck, and lost it. She screamed as she advanced on the blur of motion, as if she could track it easily. Paige raced back toward Ezra, reached out, and the blur stopped enough for her to take hold and throw the form across the room again.

"Stop this, Aggie, or I will kill you," Paige demanded harshly around her mouth full of teeth. Her eyes glowed brighter than I'd seen them. Her body also seemed altered, taller, wider.

Wait, Aggie?

Paige growled as she tracked Aggie's movements. I could only see a faint trace of her as she zigged and zagged all over the place.

Paige leaped, spun, and crashed Aggie's back into the wall, pinning Aggie to the stone by a hand around her throat. Aggie's green vampire eyes shot daggers at Paige before she looked back to Ezra. Still, Aggie snapped her teeth as she kicked and scratched at Paige, trying to tear free to get back to Ezra. Paige took hold of one of Aggie's hands, but the other was still free and marking Paige.

Finally, my mind woke up, and I wanted to kill myself for being so slow, so slack, allowing the queen, but most of all, my mate, to deal with such a threat.

I moved, taking Aggie's other arm and slamming it against the wall. I moved close and yelled, "Aggie, stop."

She didn't. Her gaze didn't move from Ezra. He slowly got to his feet with his hand on his neck. He would heal, but the wound seemed to be taking its damn time.

"Aggie, enough," boomed from across the room, at the other entrance into the fighting area. "Do not move," the familiar voice added. Aggie froze, her arms and legs dropping. She hung against our hold while she kept staring at Ezra like he was her favorite dessert.

"Paige, I'm fine," Ezra tried, but we both knew Paige wouldn't calm, not with Aggie being a threat to her bonded male. She wouldn't stop until it was safe for Ezra, even if Ezra could take care of himself.

Clyde was at our side instantly. He bowed. "I apologize, my queen. She was unguarded for a moment. We thought she was getting stronger at denying her hunger."

"Why isn't she looking away from Ezra?" Paige demanded darkly, pulling Aggie away from the wall by her neck and thrusting her back against it. "I don't want to hurt you, Aggie. Just look away and get out of here."

She didn't remove her stare or move.

Paige's anger intensified. It burned through me and fed my own.

"She bit him, Clyde," Paige snapped.

"What and who is he, my queen? If I know, then I'll understand why his scent called to her. Why she won't look away after one taste. He came with the devil, said to be Lucifer's own son, and goes by Azrael, and yet you call him Ezra. Like you did your hellhound, but he perished."

Tension filled Paige, and I didn't like it. Clyde was a trusted adviser. He'd sworn his allegiance to her. We could trust him, not only because of that, but because I'd seen him with Aggie, who he'd sired, and also Felnick—a fellow guard who was devoted to Aggie before she was sired by Clyde. He'd treated both of them like they were his treasures. He'd proven himself in many ways in my eyes.

"That's because he is all you've just said," I told him. I felt

Paige's eyes on me. We'd slipped up; we knew we would, but at least it was only around Clyde. In public, we were supposed to call Ezra by Azrael. "How did you find out he was Lucifer's son? That wasn't knowledge the queen or Lucifer wanted people to know since the devil knows he's not well-liked, and it could bring more danger to not only Ezra but also to our community. As far as we knew, the people only think of him as Azrael, a replaceable lackey to Lucifer." The devil himself helped spread the knowledge that he wouldn't care if anything happened to Azrael. He was only leaving him behind as punishment and to keep an eye on Paige.

"A concubine of Lucifer's slept with a vampire of mine while they were here. When he told me, I made him swear to tell no other, and as far as I know, he hasn't."

"Then why did you question the queen about it when you already knew?"

"I didn't know Azrael and Ezra were one and the same. I also wanted to see if I had the trust back that I give freely."

"You do, to some extent. My men will always come first," Paige said.

"I can understand that. You hold in your hand someone I will put before anyone else. Even others I have sired."

It was lucky Aggie thought highly of and looked up to Paige. It was unfortunate considering the situation we were in, though.

"Does what he is explain why she won't be distracted from Ezra?" I asked.

"Unfortunately, no." He turned to Ezra and bowed in respect. I had to guess it was because he knew Ezra was related to Lucifer. "If you will, could you please remove yourself so my fledgling may calm down, and then we should be able to find out."

"I won't leave—"

"Ezra… fuck, I mean, Azrael, please. I can't hurt her, and I don't want you harmed either. Please."

His jaw clenched, but I knew he would do anything Paige asked. Just like any of us would.

"I'll send some guards and wait back in your room," he answered grudgingly, then stormed from the room.

I waited for Aggie to start up again, but she just watched him go, staying motionless like her master had ordered. Yet I could see the pain in her eyes, in the way she swallowed again and again.

"Aggie," Clyde called. "Look at me."

Slowly, she pulled her gaze away from the door Ezra had exited from and met Clyde's gaze. "Please release her."

"Clyde," I called, unsure.

"She won't move. Release her."

"I won't risk her going for Azrael," Paige said.

"She won't. I swear it, my queen."

Paige grumbled under her breath as she dropped her hands and took a step back. I removed my own hold and moved to Paige's side.

Aggie stumbled forward. Clyde flashed in and caught her. She let out a sob. "I couldn't stop myself. I couldn't."

"It's all right, darling. It's all right," Clyde reassured, running his hand over her hair.

She lifted her head and looked to Paige. Red-tinged tears stained her cheeks. "I'm so sorry, my queen. So sorry. I didn't want to. I didn't mean to, but the hunger took over. It felt like I had just woken new when I caught his scent. It was the most delicious scent I have ever experienced."

"It's okay…. I mean, it's not. I nearly killed you, Aggie. I never want to do that. You're my friend, and I'm sure if I did, Felnick and Clyde would come after me."

Clyde's jaw clenched. I didn't like seeing it because it meant Paige was right. He would come after her no matter her being queen. I could understand the bond between master and fledgling, but this was something more.

"Are you both bonded?"

Aggie's blush said enough.

"What about Felnick?" Paige asked.

"He is with us as well," Clyde replied.

Paige laughed. "It seems we're setting a trend with more than a couple in a bonded match."

Curling an arm around her waist, I tugged her close and kissed her temple. "I wish we could take credit for it; however, there are many bonded groups with more than two people. Yet we are the first here with a mixed-species group."

"Well, at least we have that." She smiled up at me before looking back at Aggie. "I think it's best if you stay in your quarters until we leave and take Azrael since it seems it's only the newly born who are affected by his scent." She glanced at Clyde, who nodded. "It means we'll have to watch Yasmin closely as well or move her to someplace else with guards."

"What's this about Yasmin?" Aggie asked.

Paige blinked quickly, her body tensing. I moved her in front of me to wrap both arms around her and told them what happened.

Aggie reached out a hand, and Paige took it. Then Aggie

said, "I'm sorry this is happening and then I added to your stress."

Paige shook her head. "You couldn't help it."

I nodded. "Exactly. We'll need to find out why he's so enticing to the newly turned, especially since we're going into vampire territory soon."

Paige looked up to me and said, "We'll need to speak with Azrael and his father." She glanced back to Aggie and Clyde.

"We won't say anything of who he is. We promise," Clyde announced.

Paige nodded. "Thank you."

"However," Clyde said, "if you're not careful with his name around everyone, rumors will be spread, and it's bound to come out."

He was right.

So far, we'd been lucky and only kept him around us. We hadn't even announced he was one of Paige's bonded mates. The whole situation was damn awkward.

Paige must have come to the same conclusion because next she said, "You're right. I'll speak with Lucifer and Ezra about it."

"He's your bonded as well, right?" Aggie asked nervously. "Or else you wouldn't have acted like that if he wasn't."

I caught Paige's smile. "Yes."

"People are already speaking of you two. Putting together their own thoughts. You had to know it would be this way with you in the spotlight."

Paige sighed, something she still did often, even when she didn't have to breathe. "Yes. We were stupid to think questions wouldn't be asked or we wouldn't be watched too closely since all we do is research and train. I'd hoped, since we were leaving soon, that we could blame the trip on how close we got."

"Don't worry. We'll think of something," I told her.

"The truth is always best," Aggie said.

Paige studied her, then nodded. "It's because of Lucifer's concern for his son that we've said nothing."

"Come on," I said, tightening my hold on her for a moment. "We'll go and get this sorted."

"I'm sorry again, my queen," Aggie said softly.

"*Paige*, Aggie," she emphasized. "We're friends, even after this."

Aggie's bottom lip trembled. "Thank you."

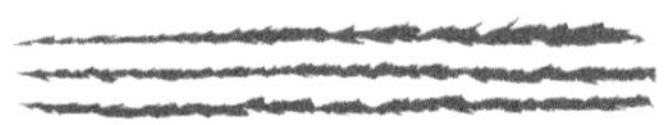

I OPENED Paige's bedroom door and shifted back so Paige could enter. I nodded to the men outside before stepping through and closing the door behind me. Paige already had Ezra in her arms fussing over him.

"Are you okay? Does it hurt? Do you need anything?"

Laughing, Ezra grabbed her hands, stopping her from inspecting his neck. "I'm fine. As you can see and feel, it's healed."

She pushed her forehead into his chest and mumbled, "I was so scared." She gripped his tee and lifted her gaze to his. "She had you on the ground, tearing into your neck. I was so damn terrified. I could have lost you again."

His expression softened. "You won't lose me, mi corazón. Spells no longer work on me with the protection from Alex. I would have removed Aggie, but I didn't want to hurt her."

Paige groaned in frustration. "Next time remove her, even if it harms her. She'll heal just like you had to. You come first, Ezra. You."

He tucked her long blonde hair behind her ear. "Okay, Paige."

I molded myself to her back and saw her glare up at him. "You're just saying that to make me happy and stop harping."

He smirked. "Who, me? I would never."

"I could kick you right now," she told him.

I grinned at him while he chuckled. "You would never," he said before dipping his head and kissing her lips. Like always, as soon as one of us touched her lips, she was lost in the moment. My body tingled as I watched them hold each other close and deepen the kiss. Christ, it was so damn pleasurable to witness them together. Paige's arousal swamped the room and swirled with Ezra's and mine.

I wanted to get lost in the sensation, to take it further. Unfortunately, we had things to do.

"Sweetheart, Ezra," I said gently, kissing the side of Paige's neck and reaching out to touch Ezra's. They pulled apart, both panting. I gave them a thin-lipped smile. "Sorry. You can finish this soon, but for now, we have to figure out why Aggie was drawn to you."

"You're right," Paige said with a touch of annoyance, though understanding lit her words.

A hand landed on my waist. I glanced down to see Ezra's smooth skin touching me. Looking back up, I took in his smile. "We'll get to the bottom of this, and then you'll bottom for me."

A sharp bark of laughter dropped from my mouth. Christ, he was cocky.

"You wish, little doggy." I shoved his shoulder. "Now call

your father and see if he knows why a fledgling would be enticed by your scent from miles away."

Ezra winked, then glanced down at Paige. "He's hot when he's bossy."

Paige laughed. "That he is."

If my heart worked, it would be pumping blood to my cheeks. I knew Ezra was a smart-ass, even when he was in his hellhound form when I'd first met him, but to have the man in front of me, this was different. I liked it. Not that I'd let the man know.

It was amazing how the Fates found the perfect mates for Paige. Not only for her but for all of us. We got along, we each brought something different to the group, and we were all on the same page when it came to sexual needs. Male and female.

Perfect.

I rolled my eyes and pulled my phone from my back pocket. "Enough you two." I handed the cell phone to Ezra. "I presume you know how to get in touch with him."

"I do." He nodded with a smile and pressed some numbers before putting it on speaker for all of us to hear.

"Ghoul, how did you get this number?" Lucifer answered.

"How did you know it was my phone?"

The devil laughed. "I know all."

"Meaning Mom would have found everyone's phone number and given it to him," Ezra explained.

Lucifer huffed. "You spoil my fun, son. How are things? Do you need me to come kill, maim, slice, or burn anyone?"

"No, we—"

"Is Paige treating you well? She's cute, but that temper of hers—"

"Hello, Lucifer," Paige called.

"Ah, sweet Paige. It's good to hear your voice, my dear." His voice was light. In the few days he'd stuck around, we'd discovered Lucifer had a big sense of humor. He taunted and teased Paige a lot because he knew he could get a rise out of her.

"I'm sure it is," Paige replied deadpan, then coughed out, "Asshole."

Lucifer chuckled. He also enjoyed how Paige didn't care Lucifer was, well, the devil. She said anything she wanted, and he'd respected that.

"We have a situation, wiseass," she added.

"Tell me," he said coolly. Paige explained what happened and about how we felt regarding our people knowing exactly that Azrael was Ezra and also Lucifer's son.

"Fuck," he barked. After a long, drawn-out groan, he said, "We didn't think you had any of their blood in you."

"Who's blood, Dad?" Ezra asked, his voice low and annoyed.

A member of our family calling Satan "Dad" was something I wasn't sure I'd ever get used to.

"Your mother's grandmother was of a mixed breed. She was a seer, a witch, and also... a unicorn shifter."

My eyes widened as shock swept through me. I met Ezra's equally surprised gaze.

Paige asked, "What am I missing?"

"I'm guessing the men are looking at each other in shock?" Lucifer commented.

"Yes."

"It's because, my dear, unicorns—whether purebred or mixed race—have been extinct for centuries. Their blood called to newly turned vampires. It was like a drug for them. They fed and fed until the victim died, and then the vampire usually died soon after as well from ingesting too much unicorn blood."

"Why?"

"Unicorns are as humans have made them out to be, magical. They're made of light and all that is good. Too much of their blood, for ones as dark as vampires, kills them."

Paige's gaze shot to us. "Aggie—"

"I believe she did not take enough to harm her. However, have her master feed her his blood, and since it was a small amount, it should counteract the diluted amount of unicorn blood Azrael has."

"Why wouldn't Ezra's blood call to older vampires since their senses grow with age?"

"For about two weeks, a fledgling's senses are stronger than even the oldest master vampire. Until they have themselves under control and their senses settle, they will be a risk for our son."

Paige glared down at the phone, slightly offended Lucifer felt he needed to warn us. "We'll keep him away from any new vampire."

"Or if we happen upon any, we will protect him with our life," I said.

Ezra's gaze warmed on both of us. "I can also make sure I protect myself more."

"Yes, you will," Paige said.

"I know you're in good hands, son. Which is why I'm not there dragging you back to Hell. Now, as for the other matter, I believe it would be for the best if the truth came out also. I have trust in your family, son. I know they will protect you, and you will do everything you can to make sure they're safe too. However, it would still be wise to have extra protection. I'll be sending Xi to you."

"Dad—"

"No, he is skilled in all areas. As I said, it's not because I think any of you are incapable, but it would ease mine and your mother's heart if you allow us this. Not only for you, son, but for your mates."

There, right then, when Lucifer mentioned Ezra's mates, I knew the devil had won the argument.

"Fine," Ezra bit out.

"Thank you, son. Speak soon and stay safe, or else there'll be hell to pay," he said on a laugh and then hung up. Ezra passed me the phone back, and I put it in my pocket before I hid my smile behind a cough and turned my back to them for a moment. Lucky I had, else I would have attacked the man appearing out of nowhere.

Xi, who Paige described as looking like the male actor Jason Statham—not that I knew who he was—stood with his hands clasped behind his back.

"Xi," I said.

He tipped his chin as Paige turned, and then he said, "Queen, ghoul, and young master."

"Thank you for coming to assist us, Xi," Paige said, her lips twitching at Xi's robotic tone and serious expression. "And please call us by our names. Paige, Thorn, and Ezra." Paige winced. "I mean—"

"Ezra," Ezra said with a smile and a wink. "Always Ezra."

"As you require." He tipped his chin down again. "If you do not mind, I would like to wander the area to make sure things are safe."

"That's fine," Paige said. "Thank you."

His brows dipped before he bowed and walked out of the room.

Paige spun to Ezra. "Is he always like this?"

"As far as I know. I was never around him much. But I know his family has been working with ours for many decades. He's the best fighter Dad has. Xi would never betray him, and he would do everything in his power to follow through with Dad's orders because Dad saved Xi's and Xi's father's life."

"That's, well, sweet," Paige said.

It was, but knowing Lucifer, there would be a reason why he saved them. Maybe it had something to do with gaining a loyal guard in Xi.

"I suppose," Ezra replied. He ran a hand through his hair, causing it to stick up everywhere. I wanted to reach over and feel how soft it was myself. However, we still had a lot to do.

"Sweetheart, I'm going to Alex's room to let them know we'll need to transfer Yasmin to another wing of the castle and let them know everything that's happened."

"Thank you. I'll speak with Gregory about sending notice out regarding Ezra."

"You don't want to hold court for it?"

She pulled her bottom lip in and bit down on it. A sense of unease shot from her. I wanted to hit myself in the head. Of course she wouldn't want to hold court regarding Ezra, because the last time Ezra had been in that room, he'd died.

"Forget I said anything, sweetheart," I said softly, taking her hand and leaning down to kiss her temple. "Contact Gregory, and I'll be back soon. I'll also come back with news of Yasmin."

"That would be great, thank you." She smiled.

"I also thought we could test something out." I wasn't sure if my idea was a good one, but it could be okay with all of us around.

"What's that?" Ezra asked.

"Having Asher feed from you to see if a master goes crazed as Agg—"

"No!" Paige cried. "I won't risk Ezra's life, and how would you feel if something happened to Ezra? Asher also wouldn't be able to live with himself."

"I think it's worth trying," Ezra said. Paige's gaze swung to him. "We'll be going into vampire territory. I won't risk any of you fighting for me."

"What about their newborns?" Paige demanded.

"We have to confirm with Asher, but I heard they keep them far away from court matters. They won't be within the area because they won't want to start a war over a youngling," Thorn said.

"All we can do is ask Asher," Ezra said. He hugged Paige to his chest, and she wrapped her arms around him. "You'll all be there. With Thorn and Nate's strength and Alex's power, things will stay in control."

"If Asher doesn't agree, then we keep Ezra away from the vampire territory," I suggested.

"Fine," Paige mumbled into Ezra's chest. Ezra smiled over her head at me. I was glad he was on board with my idea, and I would make sure nothing happened to cause anyone heartache.

CHAPTER FORTY-FOUR

ALEX

*N*ever in my years had I seen a person be changed over to a vampire. I didn't realize just how hungry they woke. Yasmin, not herself, clung to her husband, feeding on him greedily while Sakura sat behind Yasmin, trying to control the intake.

Sakura lifted her gaze to Asher and me standing at the end of the bed. "She needs more blood." She'd already been through the bagged stuff we'd brought in. We didn't think she'd need Eric, but she had, and yet she still craved more.

"Because she lost so much to begin with," Asher pointed out quietly, answering the unasked question flittering through my mind.

"I could—"

"No," Asher snarled. His quick transformation startled me.

His hand snatched out and drew me to stand in front of his body, holding me tightly. "No one has yours."

It wasn't really the time to pop a boner, and yet there it was at his possessive tone. I patted his hand on my stomach. "Okay, big guy. No one feeds from me."

"But me," he bit out around his fangs.

Another pat to his hand, and I said reassuringly, "Yes, that's right. Only you."

Sakura stared at me as if I had grown another head. Maybe it had something to do with the powerful grumpy vampire at my back I was coddling.

"Guards," I called. The door opened, and two stepped through. I felt bad I didn't know all of Thorn's brethren, but there were many. "Are either of you able to donate blood?" They eyed Asher and paled. I quickly reassured him. "Not him. Yasmin, on the bed."

"I have a mate," one said, stepping back.

"I'm able to."

"Make sure he's replaced outside," I told the other before he left. "What's your name?" I asked.

"Tim. I'm a...." He glanced around.

"A shifter?" I guessed from his smell.

"Yes. A cat."

"A tiger?" I blurted, but then thought it rude, so heat hit my own cheeks.

"No, just a cat." He lifted his chin, indicating he wasn't ashamed.

I nodded. "Asher, can you help switch out Eric?" The man in his wife's arms just moaned loudly. Another blush hit my face because I knew that moan. I'd used that moan when Asher had fed on me and I'd come in my pants a couple of days ago.

Tim walked to the bed with a straight face and stiff posture. "Wrist or neck?" he asked.

"Neck," Asher said roughly. "It's better blood for a newborn." Asher nipped at my neck, causing me to shiver and remember his bite flaming my body, before walking around me as his features morphed back to his human form.

Asher nodded down at Sakura, who pried Yasmin's teeth from Eric. Yasmin snarled and writhed on the bed. She went to grab for Eric, but Asher moved him quickly over to the couch while Sakura wrapped her legs around Yasmin's arms, and Tim climbed over her, placing his neck in front of Yasmin's face.

"Ready?" Sakura asked.

"Yes," Tim said.

She released Yasmin's head, and Yasmin sank her teeth into Tim's neck. Tim hissed out a breath and a growl but stayed still.

"She's relaxing, not taking in as much," Sakura said. "She'll sleep soon."

I nodded to her and then looked over to Asher to see him helping Eric sit and giving him a bottle of orange juice. A sudden pang of jealousy swept through me. It was ridiculous I felt jealous over Asher taking care of Eric.

Except... he was mine.

I shook my head and clenched my teeth before stalking across the room where I grabbed the glass out of Asher's hand and held it up for Eric instead. I was the only one the men in our group could take care of. Well, except for each other. I didn't want them to show their sweet, caring sides for anyone but Paige and me. Asher's amused gaze locked on my glare.

Yeah, it's okay for him to go all possessive, but I can't feel the same way? Instead, he probably finds me cute and funny. God, I wanted to preen under his gaze. I liked he thought of me that way.

That was messed up. We seriously drove each other crazy, yet we all liked that about one another.

The perfect match.

Eric pushed my hand away. He nodded. "Thanks."

"You'll need to rest," Asher told him.

"I will. She'll…."

"Yasmin will be fine," I said.

We all looked over. Sakura was smiling fondly at Eric. "She's nearly done, and then she'll sleep. Once she wakes, she'll be more herself. Hungry still, but she'll manage it a little more, and we'll have donors ready."

"I can give her more."

Sakura shook her head. "You've given enough. You need to replenish for her. She will want to… um, that is—"

"Once she is in control, she will want to fuck and drink from you many times to regain the connection she had with you," Asher supplied blandly.

Eric coughed, nodded, gave a thumbs-up, and then muttered, "Right, yeah, okay."

The door suddenly opened, and Thorn stepped through. My heart gave a stumble. It happened every time I hadn't seen one of the others in a while, and then when I did, it was as if my heart wanted to reach out to them and climb inside. I'd mentioned that to Paige during a moment of quiet time a couple of days ago, and she'd said she felt the same. We both smiled over it.

I didn't mind if the others didn't feel it. I liked having something shared with Paige. I knew I was… more in touch with my feminine nature than the others. I didn't care. I liked it because not only did it bond me with the guys in a different way, but it matched me to Paige in more ways than they had. Well, that was what I thought, and I was sticking to it.

Thorn's cocky smile had me rolling my eyes. With them, I enjoyed playing annoyed about how they all knew how my heart acted. They always gave me a look or a smirk or smiled over it, like they did with Paige. Obviously, I wasn't annoyed in the slightest. I simply loved their reaction to it. However, I think they enjoyed it when I acted annoyed.

It was all confusing and yet easy.

Thorn glanced away to the bed, just as Yasmin's eyes fluttered closed and she slumped against Sakura. "Do you have a room far away from this area?"

"Yes," she answered.

"Good. Tim, if you'll excuse us, please."

"Of course, brother." Tim stood from the bed. There wasn't even a wavering to his footing, so I knew Yasmin hadn't taken much from him. He walked from the room quickly.

Once the door shut, Thorn announced, "There's been an issue. It'll explain why Yasmin will have to be far away from here until we leave for our travels."

"What's happened?" Asher demanded.

My mind swirled as Thorn explained everything. It hadn't felt like we'd been in the room long, and so much had occurred. Now Ezra and Thorn wanted to test out Ezra's blood with Asher. It had my gut clenching in fear. If anything happened to either of them, nothing would be the same.

Sakura stood with Yasmin in her arms. "I'll take her to my room. She would hate it if she tried to attack a mate of her sister."

Eric also stood. He swayed a little but stayed on his feet. "I'll help you."

"Actually, Eric, we need you to take over from Nate with your children for a while. We'll need him with us in case…. Just in case."

Eric scrubbed a hand over his face. "Of course. Shit, the kids. They'll need me." He glanced at his wife in Sakura's arms, looking torn with his dipped brows and thinned lips.

"Go. They need you also. I'll send for you when she wakes and after she's fed again. You know she would want you protected as well."

He nodded and made his way over to them. "I know. All right, as soon as she's okay to see me, please have someone come for me."

"I promise," she whispered, looking up at him. He leaned down and kissed Yasmin on the lips quickly, then glanced up and pressed his lips against Sakura's cheek. She closed her eyes. I could tell she was cherishing the touch. I knew I got the same blissed expression on my face every time one of mine touched me.

Eric faced us. "Good luck."

I clenched my jaw. We may just need more than luck. Strength, power, and love would hopefully help us, or I could be jumping to conclusions, and Asher wouldn't be tempted to tear out Ezra's neck because of his unicorn blood. I started praying to anyone who would listen that would be the case.

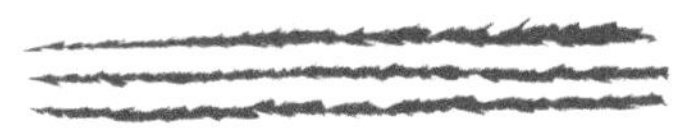

"How is she?" Paige asked as soon as we'd entered.

Unconsciously, I made my way to her and took her hand as Asher pulled her gently back into his body. "She's good," I told her with a smile. "Sakura's moving her to another area, and Eric will be with her later."

The door opened and Nate stepped in. There went my heart. I caught Paige's smile and shared one with her.

Nate slammed the door, faced the room with his hands on his hips, and roughly announced, "We are not fucking doing this."

"Nate—" Thorn tried, taking a step toward him, but Nate's hand shot up.

"No," he clipped. "This is a risk we don't need to take. We'll keep Ezra away from any vampire. Simple as that."

"I assume Eric told you everything?" Asher asked.

"Yes," he hissed.

"How are the kids?" Paige asked. I'd dropped her hand after Nate's first words, ready to go to him, and now she was wringing them in front of her, worried about her niece and nephew.

Nate's eyes softened a little. "They're confused. They know something's going on, but not what. They're smart, though. They know to trust us, trust the people around them. They were happy with Eric home. He composed himself well around them."

She nodded. "Good, great. I'll get down to them, um, soon."

"You agree to this as well?" Nate asked.

Paige shrugged. "I see their point, but of course I'm scared senseless like you are about them both."

"I'm not scared," Nate bit out. He was, but he'd never admit it, else he wouldn't have been fighting us on it.

Ezra moved around us and started Nate's way. Nate glared at him. "I'll have you all here to help. That's even if something happens in the first place. I have a feeling it won't, though, because mature vampires don't go crazy like the newborns do when scenting me."

"You said it there: we don't know if Asher will be able to contain himself."

Ezra reached out and clasped Nate's jaw. I saw he applied pressure. "This, in a controlled environment, is the best way to go. You know it. Deep down you do."

Nate's jaw clenched, and his nostrils flared. "Fuck," he snapped. "Do it then."

My heart jumped into my throat when Asher stood at Ezra's back. His head dipped into Ezra's neck, and I heard his deep inhale. I took a step closer while Thorn and Paige moved in to surround them. I could work from afar; I didn't want to get in their way in case they had to use their strength to stop him.

"Does he smell different?" Paige asked, her voice tight, her emotions locked down.

"No. Just the same as always," Asher said.

My dick decided it was time to party when Asher licked up Ezra's neck. Ezra hissed out a breath, then gasped when Asher bit into him. Asher groaned, drawing in Ezra's blood. Ezra shuddered, gripping Nate harder.

"Ezra?" Paige said.

"I'm fine. G-Good in fact." He moaned. "Shit, someone touch me."

"Not yet," Thorn replied.

"Asher?" Nate clipped.

Asher's eyes opened, the glow to his eyes brighter than they had been. He stared at Nate but didn't stop drinking.

"Asher," I snapped.

"Someone touch me. Fuck, no one told me this could feel so good," Ezra whined.

"Asher," Thorn growled out.

"Please," Ezra moaned. He dragged Nate's hand down. "Yes, there, just up and down."

"Asher," Paige whispered.

Asher's hand snapped out. He grabbed Paige around the waist and drew her close. He licked at Ezra's neck and then turned his face to slant his mouth over hers. She sagged into him, wrapping her arms around his neck. Paige moved enough for me to see Asher's hand over Nate's as they stroked Ezra's cock under his jeans.

Mine throbbed at the sight. When Ezra rested his head back on Asher's shoulder, his eyes closed, and his lips parted a little as he just took in the pleasure of them touching him. I could barely contain my need. I hadn't realized the height difference. Ezra was just a little taller than me really, while Asher, Nate, and Thorn were all taller. Thinking of Thorn, I looked to him to find his gaze already on me. Slowly, he took the few steps to me. Reaching out, he trailed his fingers down my arm as he circled around me and pressed his front to my back.

"I like seeing you watch them. Witnessing your dick grow hard behind these pants." When he said pants, his gliding hands slid low over my hips and butt, and one hand stopped over my bulge, giving it a squeeze.

Paige broke the kiss, staring up at Asher. He smiled. "His blood is rich, smooth, and delicious, but it doesn't make me want to devour him." Nate snorted. "Well, except in a sexual way."

Paige smiled. She relaxed into Asher more, the panic falling from her body as her desire surged to full speed. My own fear had diminished with Asher's control. He wouldn't have been able to stop if Ezra's blood had called to his vampire.

It meant newborns were the only risk we had when it came to Ezra.

Thorn nipped at my neck, then sucked on my skin, causing me to shiver in delight. I tilted my head to the side for him to have better access, and he didn't disappoint. His tongue trailed up and down it before laying kiss after kiss.

A moan had me opening my eyes and looking across the room. Nate had Paige up in his arms, her legs around his waist while he took her mouth in a brutal, hard kiss, which she returned.

"Alex," Nate barked as he broke the kiss, and I knew what was annoying him. With a click of my fingers, clothes disappeared. All of us were suddenly naked. Nate pressed Paige's back against the wall as he slowly pushed his stiff cock inside of her. I loved how hungry for him she looked. How she bit her bottom lip and her hands threaded into his hair right before she pulled him down for another bruising kiss, like she wanted him inside her at all points she could, pussy and mouth, while their hearts and souls bonded.

She was beautiful. I could stare at her all day long and never feel like it was enough.

A hissed-out breath had my eyes gliding over to Asher and Ezra. However, before I could take in what they were doing, Thorn's hand wrapped around my erection and stroked over and over. My eyes closed. I dropped my head back to his shoulder and ground my ass into Thorn's own hardness.

"I wanted to do this when we were stuck in Hell. I saw you in the shower running your hands over your body, and I wanted to be the one touching you. I wanted to take my time, kiss, bite, and lick every inch. I've been inside you once, Alex. I'm going to need to again."

"Yes" was all I could say.

"Go lay on the bed," he ordered darkly.

To get what I wanted, I did as I was told and lay back. Thorn stood at the end of the bed, running his fisted hand up and down his length as his hooded eyes slid over me slowly.

"Fuck me, you asshole," I heard, causing both Thorn and me to glance over to Ezra and Asher. Ezra had been doing what I did to Thorn, backing his ass up against Asher while Asher drank once more from Ezra. Only after Ezra shouted that, Asher licked his puncture marks closed, picked Ezra up and roughly dropped him onto the bed on his knees.

Asher's eyes glowed. His clawed hands gripped Ezra's hips and jerked him back, rubbing his cock against Ezra, who growled in the back of his throat.

"You want me to fuck you, Ezra?"

"What do you think?"

Asher's hand slapped down on Ezra's butt cheek. "Do you want me to fuck you, Ezra?"

Ezra's gaze lifted from the bed and met mine, his eyes were pure black. Slowly, he turned his head to look over his shoulder and snarled, "Careful, vampire."

"Then answer me, hellhound."

"Yes," Ezra hissed. "Fuck me."

Me, being the helpful person I was, clicked my fingers, and tubes of lube landed on the bed. One near Asher and the other between my own legs as I watched Thorn climb on the bed. His strong, muscular form and smooth skin were meant to be admired, and I was. Like all of them, he was built to fight and to fuck. I squirmed on the bed, knowing I was about to be the one fucked by such a stunning man.

Paige's cry of pleasure sounded around the room just before

Nate's low groan, him no doubt coming inside of Paige's sweet warmth. I could hear their kissing, as well as Ezra's growl being cut off by a satisfied, low moan, and I knew Asher was finally pushing into the needy man. But I couldn't look away from Thorn as he ran lube over his erection while gazing down at me like I was his dessert and he was about to devour it.

"Need prep?" Thorn asked, his voice thick and rough.

"No," I whispered. Movement to the side caught my attention. Nate sat in a chair with Paige on his lap, both still wonderfully naked as they watched the show in front of them. My face burned with heat, usually shy about what I said or did or how I looked, but being with Paige and these men, I soon stopped worrying about such things. Though it didn't stop me blushing. Nothing would.

A hand to my cheek pulled my eyes back up to Thorn hovering over me. His thumb ran across my bottom lip. I nipped at it, and his eyes flashed. He sank his thumb into my mouth, and I swirled my tongue around it and spread my legs wider, lifting my hips a little to accommodate Thorn's size as he pressed his tip to my hole and slowly pushed in. Thorn glided his thumb in and out of my mouth, and that thrilling sensation, along with how he filled me, had my gut clenching in delight.

"Christ," Thorn cursed. "You're fucking tight, beautiful, and sweet." He turned his head slightly. "Isn't he, Paige?"

I tilted my head enough to see her but still keep Thorn's thumb in my mouth. She lay back on Nate with her legs spread and Nate's hands between them massaging her clit.

"Yes, so, so beautiful. All my men are."

"I agree," Ezra said on a moan, bringing my gaze from Paige to him. Somehow, he was close, his face inches from mine. Thorn's thumb dropped away from my mouth, and both his hands gripped my thighs as he drilled in and out of me, causing my breath to catch, and then I lost it altogether when Ezra dipped his head and bit at my chest. Lower, he swirled his tongue around my nipple, and I lifted my gaze, drawing in a breath to see Asher behind him, thrusting hard and fast, rocking Ezra's mouth, lips, and tongue across my skin as it trailed up to my neck. My body tingled, and my balls drew up; they all had me on edge.

"How's he feel?" I asked Asher.

"Like home, like you all do, but more, like mine. Like Paige's."

"Yes!" Paige cried. I faced her, seeing her gripping the arms of the chair and grinding her hips down and around on Nate as she climaxed over Nate's fingers inside her. "God, I love you all," she muttered, relaxing back.

"More, vampire," Ezra demanded. Asher leaned over Ezra and sank his teeth into Ezra's shoulder. Ezra roared. His cum shot out and landed on the bed and me. Ezra saw it. A pleased smile came over him, and he bent his head to take my mouth with his. The kiss surprised me. I soon got carried away with it, and the way Thorn's cock kept touching my prostate each time he pushed himself in.

"Fuck," Thorn yelled. "Fuck." The feel of his cum squirting inside me pushed me over the edge. It was sudden and explosive. I whimpered into Ezra's mouth and felt my release land on my stomach.

Coming back to myself, I panted out my breaths and tried to control my fast-beating heart. I found myself up the bed further with Paige curled into my side and Thorn behind her up on his elbow looking down at us.

"Good?" he asked me with a knowing smirk.

"Yes."

"Does he always do this?" Ezra asked from my other side where he lay on his stomach. He was referring to the purring vampire at his back who was currently taking care of Ezra by running a washcloth over his back and butt.

Nate grunted and held out a glass of orange juice to Ezra. "Yes. Yes, he fucking does, and it's annoying as shit."

I called bull on that. Nate's soft eyes on Asher said another story.

"I will never, never stop loving seeing you all together, loving one another and enjoying each other. Having you all feel what you do about each other, and not just me, makes me feel… it's so hard to describe. It's just amazing," Paige said softly.

"I agree, sweetheart," Thorn said, kissing her hair.

Ezra nodded. "Even though I'm new to this, I'm damn grateful to be a part of our group."

"Our family," Paige said.

"Clan," Asher clipped between purrs.

"Pack," Nate bit out.

Thorn laughed with Paige and me before saying, "I think family is the best way to describe it without getting into an argument."

"Whatever we all are," I started, "we're perfect, and we'll get through anything to keep us all together."

Paige kissed my cheek. "Yes, we will."

CHAPTER FORTY-FIVE

PAIGE

"You didn't say anything to me," I said gently to Yasmin. We sat on a couch in Sakura's private room. It had been a week since she'd been changed. A long week without seeing her. She hadn't wanted to see me that day either, but we were leaving in a couple of hours, and I couldn't leave without saying goodbye. She looked even better than she had as a human. She no longer had bags under her eyes or eczema spots on her skin; in fact, her skin seemed clear and her hair shiny. She looked perfect, except for the fact she kept swallowing over and over. I hated I was causing her pain.

"Can we argue about this another day?"

I glanced away, tears threatening. "We're leaving. We have to go now to get things done before we meet with the council."

"I should have known. Sorry."

"Don't apologize. Ever. I'm the one who should. I got you in this—"

Her hand flashed out and gripped mine tightly. "Don't you apologize. It is not your fault a crazy witch's daughter wanted revenge. I should have been smarter, and honestly, Eric and I knew staying human wouldn't be an option in the end. Us changing was bound to h-h-happen, um…."

"Should we get Sakura in here?" I asked since she was eyeing my neck like it was a morning coffee she needed to drink.

"Yes."

The door opened, and Sakura stalked in. She was probably listening on the other side. She went straight to my sister, sat beside her, and held her wrist up. Yasmin bit into it and moaned. Her eyes closed as she took a deep pull of Sakura's blood. I watched as Yasmin leaned into Sakura and the vampire looked at my sister like she was something special while running her free hand down Yasmin's hair. I'd seen them together, with Eric, before he'd left to be with the kids and before I asked Sakura to give us a moment. They'd been… infatuated with one another.

I didn't see any jealousy as Eric lightly kissed Sakura on the lips just after he had Yasmin. Or from Eric when Sakura cradled Yasmin in her arms and kissed her neck just as I entered. Of course, they both froze when they saw me.

It truly was like they'd bonded as I had with my men.

Yasmin licked Sakura's wrist before pulling it down to her lap where she held Sakura's hand.

"I never told you about Sakura and I getting close because you've had so much to deal with on your own."

My heart ached. "I'm still here to listen to you."

She smiled softly. "I know, and I'll still always rant to you, but this was new. At first, I thought I was gaining a friend. Okay, it might have been a friend both Eric and I felt comfortable with hugging and kissing in greeting. But I realized only recently, before the... before what happened, that I felt more for Sakura. I wanted more than what we'd started. It was just *that* morning I spoke with Eric about it, and he also said he sensed something with Sakura as well."

"And now?"

Yasmin smiled. "Now, I have Eric and I have Sakura... if she'll have both of us."

Sakura grinned shyly. "You both know I will. My life would be dull without either of you."

"The kids?" I asked.

"They'll eventually know because, well, we don't like being apart for long. Also, the children are old enough to know things around here are different than a normal human's ways. Should I feel bad about that? For wanting this to work with Sakura and bring it in front of my children?" She shrugged. "I don't know."

"It's not bad to want happiness. I can already see Sakura brings that for both you and Eric. I'm sure the children will see it and understand. They're smart. They take after their father."

"Hey," Yasmin yelled, and we laughed.

"If things are meant to be, they'll work out," I told her. My stomach twisted. "I'm going to miss you. I'll have Alex pop me back when I can."

"I know you will, and I'll miss you like crazy as well. I wish I could hug you, but I don't trust myself yet, and I'm sure your guard could rip my head off with just a thought."

I glanced back at Xi. He stood statue-still with his arms down, hands clasped in front of him. I snorted. "It could be a possibility." Xi even freaked me out. He was a silent ninja, popping up when I least expected him. Once was while I was in the bath with Ezra. Apparently, he'd called, and when we didn't answer, since we'd been under the water kissing, we came up for air and there he was standing over us. My scream brought the rest of the men into the bathroom. They got a good laugh out of it. I was grateful when Xi left after my men's coaxing, leaving Ezra and me to get back to what we'd been doing.

The announcement went out to my people regarding who Ezra was exactly, what he was to me, and that if anyone wanted to speak of it, to contact myself or Lucifer. I was certain the mention of Lucifer helped keep the haters away. However, I wasn't stupid enough to not believe there could be ones lurking, wanting to best Lucifer or myself. And by doing it, they would harm Ezra, which was why Ezra was never alone. We knew he was strong, he was powerful, and he could protect himself and others against an army, but it was still fresh in my heart and mind how we'd lost him. I was sure it was the same with my other men because two of them went with him everywhere, along with ten other guards. I had my own guard in Xi. I'd been surprised when Xi didn't stick like glue to Ezra. His answer when I asked was "You hold his heart. You are their center. If you die, they will want to. It is you who I protect, child." I could have done without the child part, but he made sense, and I didn't argue with him because I knew he was right—the men would follow me to the grave if I died, and I didn't want that to ever happen.

Pressure suddenly hit my chest. I was about to leave the safety of the castle and walk my men into dangerous situations. Then there was my sister dealing with being a vampire and not being able to see her children in so long. There wasn't only that.

I worried about my people, about what could happen in our absence. Virginia had come back to help watch over things and Lucifer promised to pop in and out, of course, wanting to see Virginia, which was reassuring if anyone acted up for Felnick, Clyde, and Aggie.

Although, leaving really didn't sit well inside me.

"I love you," I told Yasmin.

"I love you too. Always."

I shifted my gaze to Sakura. "Thank you for taking care of Yasmin."

She dipped her chin. "You're welcome, my queen."

"Stay safe while I'm away."

Yasmin smiled. "I will."

"I shall make sure your family will be safe, with my life."

I couldn't ask for anything more. I knew Sakura would keep her word. It would be like me promising to take care of my mates with my life.

After leaving their suite, I slowly made my way back to the other side of the castle. Only I took the long way around, out through the market. Most people greeted me with a bow, smile, or a call, which I returned each and every one. Even with the man stuck to my back.

"Can you step back a little?" I asked Xi through gritted teeth. He was doing his job a bit above and beyond, especially since I also had about ten other guards at my back.

"No, I cannot."

I grumbled under my breath, before I was distracted when I saw Michael, Leona, and their little bundle of joy, Zoey, their little horse shifter. I hadn't had a chance to make it to the birth since it was the day Lucifer had shown up and Ezra had come back into my life. However, as soon as I'd heard about Leona giving birth, I was at their room instantly.

"Michael, Leona," I called with a wave.

Both of them smiled brightly upon seeing me. When I was close, they bowed their heads. Thankfully they didn't go into a full bow like they used to. Leona even tried it when I'd come to her room and she'd been breastfeeding. I tried to make them promise not to bow, but they refused, saying it wasn't right. So I got them to compromise to this.

"My queen, do you need anything?" Leona asked, gesturing to the stall they were in front of. It was one with an array of clothing of different types and styles.

"No, thank you. I think Gregory has stuffed my suitcases full to the brim already. Plus, I have Alex, and he can just conjure anything I wish."

"That must be wonderful." Leona smiled.

Michael wrapped his arm around Leona's waist. "You're not thinking of adding a mage to our Equidae, are you?"

Leona blushed and then giggled. They were so darn cute together. Leona shook her head. "You're enough to handle."

Michael grinned. "Good." His gaze shifted to me. "My queen, we'd like to thank you again for gifting us with the stroller for Zoey."

I waved it off and bent over the stroller, cooing at the cuteness who slept soundly inside. "How can we not spoil such sweetness?"

"That's true." Michael beamed. He was a very proud father, and Leona was an amazing, doting mother.

"Please, while we're gone, make sure to keep in the castle grounds," I said, lifting my gaze from Zoey and then straightening.

Michael nodded. "We will, my queen."

"Thank you. I better be going to see if I need to do anything else before we leave."

They dipped their heads. "Safe travels, my queen. I hope everything works out." Leona smiled.

"As do I, Leona." Or else my men and people were doomed to live a life of pain and hate.

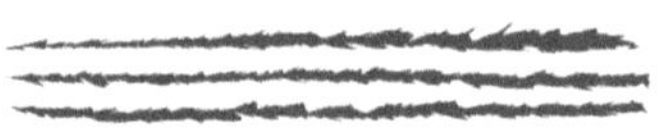

"ARE WE THERE YET?" I asked for the billionth time and got the same reaction from Nate, a scowl and a growl as he looked back at me in the rearview mirror. It had me smiling at least. But seriously, I'd been sitting for four hours in a... what Asher called Nissan Nv 3500 4x4, that had been converted to a six-seater so I could have all my men in one vehicle. Nate and Thorn sat up front. I was in the middle seat with Alex and Ezra, and Asher was spread out on the back one sleeping since he hadn't gotten much in the last few days.

I hadn't been the only one worried about leaving the castle. He worked with me on making sure everything would be settled before we left. Another 4x4 was in front of us that held Xi and some guards, and another was behind us with more guards. I was bored out of my mind.

"Try and sleep," Nate clipped.

"I'm not tired."

"I could think of something to do," Ezra said with a cheeky grin, and then I was up out of my seat and on his lap.

"Set her down and put her seat belt back on," Nate snapped.

"But, Dad," Ezra whined. I laughed behind my hand.

"Now, boy."

"Will you spank me if I don't?"

"I'll do more than spank you if you don't listen," Nate growled out.

"Um… yay," I offered, causing Ezra and Alex to chuckle.

"Ezra," Nate warned.

Ezra sighed. "He's no fun." Still, he kissed my shoulder before putting me back on the seat between him and Alex. Alex reached around me and put my seat belt back on.

"Where is this portal we have to take to the land of fae?" Jesus, that sounded like something someone would say in a book or movie. Not in real life. Then again, my life had been a fantasy since I ended up with five different and so very amazing men.

"It's about another hour away. In Texas."

I screwed up my nose, and Ezra flicked it, smiling. I grabbed his hand and held it on my lap, then took Alex's. "The fae picked Texas to have a portal in? I didn't expect that."

"They have many around the world," Thorn explained. "But the Texan one is closest for us to get to."

"Let me guess, the council has one close to them also, which is how they got someone in and out to kill the former king?"

"It had been activated that same day, yes," Alex said. "But they had a cover for why it was used, of course."

"Of course," I mumbled.

Alex squeezed my hand. "Don't worry. We'll stop their corrupting ways."

"I have faith in you all. I just hate how hard it's going to be."

"Shit," Nate cursed.

I sat straighter and gripped the back of their seats as I searched out the front window. "What? What is it?"

"The car in front of us is braking. There shouldn't be any slowing or stopping until we reach closer to town. This is a straight path."

"Meaning?"

"Something's happening," Thorn said.

"Asher?" Nate called.

"I'm awake."

I jumped at his voice behind us but kept looking out the front window. Waiting, watching to see if anything was about to happen. Nate suddenly braked hard as the car in front of us did, and things from the woods moved out on the road surrounding the vehicles. I had to think "things" because I didn't know what they were since they were all clothed in black from top to bottom. Mesh covered their eyes, making it hard to see if there were normal eyes peeking out.

"Asher?" Nate called.

"Open the top and let me out first."

"No," I cried, undoing my seat belt and turning on the seat.

Asher leaned forward and cradled my face, saying, "You are to follow what we ask to keep everyone safe."

"Then you shouldn't throw yourself into danger. The men can handle this."

"We fight with the men. We fight our battles together. It's the way of a good ruler. We don't hide, love."

Shit, I knew he was right, but it still scared me. Reluctantly, I nodded and flopped back to my butt, leaning into Ezra.

"Send the queen out and you can all keep your lives," someone called from outside the vehicles.

"I'm going out as well," Alex said.

"No," Nate, Thorn, and Asher clipped together.

Ezra snickered. They all glowered at him. His hands shot up.

"Hey, don't look at me. I'm sticking by Paige's side like a good boy. Like I was told. I just think it's cute you all get domineering with Alex."

"It's ridiculous," Alex complained. "I have the power to end them all in seconds, yet you all want me to hang back and be the last line of defense with Ezra."

"We've spoken about this," Nate snarled. It was the first I'd heard of it.

"Yes, and I hated it then as well," Alex snapped. "You all treat me like I'm a little boy. I'm not. I'm damn powerful and you all know it."

"Can we talk about this later?" Thorn said. "They're looking ready to attack."

It was true. Some had drawn their bow and arrows, others had swords, and some even had guns. All of them were pointed toward our vehicle.

Nate pressed his finger to let the bulletproof, custom-made sunroof open. I watched him take in a deep breath. "Demons, they reek of sulfur."

"Then I need to be the one to—fucking hell," Ezra finished. I looked to where he was to see Xi standing on the roof of the vehicle in front of us.

"It is you who will live if you leave now. My name is Xi Huang. I am second in command to our lord Lucifer. In the vehicle with the queen you want is Azrael, son to Lucifer—"

"Fuck, should he have announced that?" Thorn asked.

"If you wish to live, then leave." Xi shrugged. "Or don't, and suffer the wrath of my blade and hands."

"We want the queen—"

"So be it," Xi snarled. He threw out his hands, and I heard

screams. Demons fell to the ground, convulsing on the dirt path with blades sticking out of their throats.

Asher flashed out of the sunroof, his body too fast to track for most, yet I could see the outline of his hazy form as he raced around the one hundred men—or demons—surrounding us. They didn't know what hit them. All they could do was fall to the ground after their heads had been severed.

I twitched in the seat, gripping the seats in front of me, watching and wanting to get out there myself to help.

"There'll be other chances to fight," Ezra said in my ear.

"I know what Asher means now. We fight together. It shouldn't be only them out there." A few guards had joined the battle. I winced when one fell to the ground with a huge hole in his abdomen.

"We would be as well if I didn't know they could handle it," Nate said, his voice calm yet cold.

"How is that handling it?" I demanded and pointed to the fallen comrade. Only he wasn't there any longer. He was up again, fighting. "What is he?"

"A ghoul," Thorn said, pride held in his tone.

The car rocked. Something had been thrown into it. I climbed over Alex, who was already looking out the window.

However, as soon as Nate growled out, "Paige," I was pulled back against Ezra's chest, and then I saw a demon stand on the outside. He, it, whatever it was, didn't face our way. He was looking at the person who threw him.

Asher, in all his glory, stood on an embankment, his glowing green eyes glaring down at the demon. His fangs and claws were on full display, and I wasn't the only one impressed or turned on by him. I could scent it off all my men. Our response had me smiling.

In the next second, the demon disappeared and Asher stood in its place, holding a head up before he threw it to the ground.

Beside me, Alex's eyes shone purple. He lifted his flat hand up in front of him, and when he closed it, the demon at Asher's back squished into a ball of goop.

Asher spun around then looked at Alex through the window. "Keep doing that from where you are," he said.

"I'm better out there," Alex said through clenched teeth.

"No," Asher clipped.

More demons around Asher turned into goop thanks to Alex, while they continued to argue. "Just because you've fucked me doesn't mean you can coddle me."

"I can and I will," Asher bit out.

"Oooh, wrong thing to say, man," Ezra sang.

Alex flew up through the sunroof and stood up there, firing sparks of yellow bolts at demons, who melted on the spot.

"Is it wrong I want to give them both head right now?" I asked as I watched Asher tear through more demons while glaring up at Alex.

Ezra and Thorn laughed while Nate snorted. "Not the time, angel."

"Damn," I muttered. "Actually, I'd like to see them both suck each other off—"

A hand covered my mouth as a nose brushed into my hair. "Mi corazón, now isn't the time to speak of it and get us all hard and wanting."

"Fine," I mumbled behind his hand. I pulled it away and sat up. A roar had me twisting back to stare out the front windshield. What I saw I couldn't comprehend, and fear twisted what felt like an invisible knife in my chest. "What is that?"

"A chimera," Thorn said.

I didn't have a clue what that was, but it scared me enough my body shook. "We need to get everyone back in the fucking cars now," I yelled.

Ezra tried to curl his arms around me. "Relax, Paige. It's fine."

"No! Asher, Alex, back in here now!"

"Paige," Nate barked, suddenly in my face. "Relax. That's Xi."

Blinking slowly, I opened my mouth and then closed it.

The beast ate, tore, and bit anything in its path. It looked to have all areas covered around it because it had more than one head. I could see the main head looked like a lion while the one on its back looked like a goat or sheep, but the tail wasn't to be outdone. It ended in a snake's head. It wrapped around a demon and sank its fangs into the body, easily piercing the protective gear they all wore.

I was in awe. My hammering heart settled a little knowing it was Xi and he was on our side, because there was no way in hell I would want to go against him.

"Catch Alex," Nate warned.

Somehow, Ezra gently pushed me out of the way just before Alex fell back through the sunroof, hitting his head on the edge.

"Alex?" I cried when I saw he was unconscious.

"He'll be okay. Beside the egg on his head, which he'll fix," Nate said. "He's just used a lot of juice in a short amount of time."

I nodded. I understood that was a lot of power, yet I still looked him over just in case.

Asher flashed inside the car, into the back seat. His angry gaze didn't sway from Alex while he ground his teeth together. I had a feeling it would be Alex who got a spanking. Nate started the car and slowly drove forward.

Seeing Alex unharmed, I sat back in the seat with his legs on my lap. "We know it's the council sending these hitmen after me, but how did they know where we would be?"

"It could either be someone has ratted us out, or they guessed our plans and had mercenaries lay in wait just in case," Thorn said.

"I hope it's the latter one," said a tired voice. I swung my gaze to Alex.

I grabbed his hand in mine, so he knew I was there. Ezra squeezed Alex tighter to him and then laid a quick kiss to his head. When his eyes fluttered open and landed on me, I scolded lightly, "You scared me. Again."

He gave me a smile. "Sorry."

"Sorry is not good enough," Asher snarled.

Alex groaned. "Don't start—"

Asher gripped the back of the seat, leaned over, and got in Alex's face. His hard expression sent a shiver of fear through me. "You know what dark spells do to you. They drain you faster than any defensive spell. You put yourself in harm's way. Why?"

Alex's nostrils flared in agitation. "There were too many. I could help, so I helped."

Asher growled in his face. "You knew the formation we would stick to. You knew when you had to step in if something like this happened. You changed it. Why?"

"Because I have the power to help. I just proved it to you."

"You proved you went too far. You passed out. What could have happened if there were some left and you were already on the ground taking a nap? We follow rules for a reason, Alex. You've never gone against my orders before. Why *now*?"

Alex's eyes flashed purple and back again. "Because you

could have died." He gripped Asher's shirt in a fist. "They were coming at your back. I had to protect you. I protect the people I love at all costs."

Asher crushed his mouth to Alex's, and my pussy spasmed. Nate caught my gaze and gave me a knowing smirk. I shot him the finger.

Asher pulled back and ordered, "You will do as you're told. You will yield to me in the field. I know what I'm doing. Trust me, even when we're sleeping together, that I will do *anything* for our clan to keep *everyone* safe to live a long fucking life together."

Alex paled. "I panicked."

"You did."

"I'll listen next time."

"Good." Asher studied his face. "I love you also."

Alex blushed, then nodded. "Okay."

Asher sat back in the seat and crossed his arms over his chest. "We'll need to make sure we're on alert at every stop we make. They may have easily guessed our plan because they know Nate, Alex, and me. Also, if the shoe was on the other foot, they would do the same as we are, gaining trust from people who could stand against them."

"Should we call for more backup?" Thorn asked.

"No. We handled this fine, and we can't go into anyone's territory—that even means the council—with a large number of soldiers or it will look like we've come to battle and not talk. However, I think we may have to adjust when we get to the council since Nate, Alex, and I are already wanted by them."

Alex, from where he still leaned against Ezra, who was giving him a shoulder rub, said, "We know the layout of the council building. I could plant members of our team, or even extras from the castle, within the building dressed as an elite enforcer to try and keep suspicion down and to let us have more people on the inside."

"It's a sound idea," Nate said.

"Yes," Asher agreed. "Let's see first if we can't gain more people to aid our mission from the ones we see."

Nate grunted. "Agreed." He pulled the car up alongside the other. "We're here."

Shit. My stomach bottomed out. Already on this trip we'd been through one battle. Would walking through this portal bring another?

I didn't know, but we had to find out, and I hated that we did.

CHAPTER FORTY-SIX

*W*e stood in front of a formation of rocks that looked like something out of the old television show *Stargate*. Except the center of it was full of rock, not an empty entryway into nothingness.

"Where's the control panel to get the thing started?" I asked, and everyone looked at me. I shrugged. "You know, you dial in a certain sequence of shapes…." I glanced up at the edges. There weren't any shapes or patterns. "Huh, okay, so is there a magic button to press?"

Thorn pulled out his phone and pressed a few buttons before putting it to his ear while smiling at me. "Yes, Thorn Jones, bonded mate to Paige Alice, ghoul queen, waiting for acceptance into the fae realm." He paused before looking up at something, so I also did. All I saw were more rocks. "Yes. Thank you." He hung up and pocketed it. The men moved, all surrounding me. I had Asher, Xi, and Thorn in front. Alex and Ezra were at my sides and Nate at my back. The other men were scattered from Alex's sides and behind Nate.

Next, there was a flash of bright white light, and Thorn was the first to step into the bubbling glare. I made a noise in the back of my throat and went to grab him. Xi turned and said, "He is fine, Queen." Then he stepped through, as did Asher.

"I'm not sure about this," I told my remaining men.

"Stop being a chicken." Nate laughed, pushing against my back, but I didn't move.

"I hate you, asshole," I snapped. Nate laughed again and applied more pressure.

"Come on, mi corazón. We'll do it together with Alex." They both took a hand and forced me forward.

"What happens if we get lost in the swirling portal and end up being spit out somewhere else?"

Some of the men behind me laughed but were kind enough to cover it with a cough.

Alex smiled. "I'm not sure what portal you've stepped through in the past, but these types are just one step through, and you're there. They can't take you someplace else."

"Right." I nodded. "I knew that. I was just testing you."

"More like delaying while you get yourself together," Nate said, humor evident in his tone. I dropped the guys' hands and whirled on him to give him a piece of my mind, but I was picked up. I buried my head in Nate's chest, wrapped my arms and legs around him, and closed my eyes as I felt him walk forward.

"Open your eyes, angel," Nate said into my hair as he forced my legs down to touch the ground. I unwrapped my arms, opened my eyes, and hit him in the chest.

"Next time I'll kick you in the balls. I would have walked through on my own when I was ready."

He snorted. "We didn't have all day."

A throat cleared. I turned, and my mouth dropped open. I quickly snapped it closed and got myself together by straightening and replacing the glare I'd shared with Nate to a neutral expression.

"King Nelydriel. Elf and ruler of all fae," the equally tall man at the king's side announced. I suddenly felt underdressed. I also should have asked if I needed to bow to a king, or because I was queen, I didn't have to. I didn't know what I was meant to do, but my gut and heart said not to bow, so I listened.

Instead, I took a step forward and said, "Paige Alice, ghoul queen and bonded mate to Asher, Thorn, Nate, Alex, and Ezra."

One of King Nelydriel's dark brows rose; it was totally different from his long white hair, not blond, but pure white. The top half was pinned back, showing off his pointy ears. Heat hit my cheeks because I pictured myself touching his ears while kissing his face.

Oh, fuck no. No! I cut that vision off and clenched my teeth, double-checking my mental shields were up. This couldn't be happening now. He wasn't even using his power for my ghoul side to place a mark on him.

I licked my suddenly dry lips and ignored the way his turquoise eyes shined down along my body as he took all of my short self in. I couldn't help but return the gesture and ran my eyes down his firm, fit body, over his expensive, long-at-the-back and down-to-his-thighs gown-type top, and... oh crap. Were those stockings? I thinned my lips, so I didn't laugh.

However, when I got to his cute boots, a sound escaped from me and I quickly brought my gaze back up to his narrowed eyes.

Look bored, Paige. Look bored, and do not get lost in those fucking eyes.

"Paige," Alex whispered. "Something doesn't feel right."

"I thought you would be taller," the king mentioned and sounded snobby while doing it.

"And I thought you would have wings, be three inches tall, and nice."

Someone, from his fifty or so men on his side, barked out a laugh, then quickly shut it off before I could see who it had been. The king's lips twitched while most of his men stiffened and the shorter man with a rounded potbelly beside him gasped. "How dare you compare the great sire to the common folk fairies."

I screwed my nose up. Just fucking great. There was prejudice and probably bigotry there as well.

"Get over it," I told him, and he seemed to choke on his saliva. He stepped forward, but I suddenly had Asher, Thorn, and Xi in front of me. "It's all right, guys," I told them, reaching out to part Thorn and Asher. Thankfully they didn't fight me on it.

"Paige," Alex called. I glanced at him. "Something isn't right."

"What?" I whispered. Unease filled me.

He scrunched up his forehead in confusion. "I don't know."

"Rallis, enough" was clipped. I looked back in time to see that at his king's words, Rallis moved back to his boss's side. The king held out his hand to me. "Welcome to Airrile, Paige Alice. May I show you around before we sit to speak?"

Paige Alice. I sure noticed it wasn't Queen Alice. I took

another quick look at Alex, who shrugged. Shit, until he knew what was troubling him, I couldn't be rude and run for the portal.

I glanced at the king's hand and fought the pull to touch him. Though, I noticed it wasn't as strong as what I'd felt with my men, which was good. But then my eyes flicked over his shoulder to a man with long black hair and the pull suddenly intensified. Strange. This didn't make sense. Why did one man's appearance call to me, and yet, it felt as if the other man was the one who held some type of connection to me?

What the hell was going on? Had I finally lost it? Was it this place? Were we even on Earth?

Scolding myself and the runaway thoughts, I forced my eyes back to the king and then placed my hands behind my back and nodded. "Thank you, that would be nice." I fixed a mock smile on my face. I didn't like this guy's attitude since he pretty much ignored my men and looked down on us. I was sure my body was on a high from walking through the portal or something because the king was a stuck-up douche. Unless it was the portal that did something to me. I needed to get this over with and then speak with my men privately about it.

His lips twitched again, and I wanted to punch him in the face because it looked cute on him. So what? His looks were nice, but it didn't mean anything. All I had to do was focus on the stockings and boots because they looked damn ridiculous, and the attraction I felt to his looks would fade.

The king dropped his hand and dipped his chin. "Right this way." He turned and started forward. His people parted for the king, only I wasn't sure if they looked up to him or feared him. As I passed the man with black hair, I shivered and felt like sniffing him, licking him, and even peeing on him. What the fuck?

I pushed it all down, stabbed my fingernails into my palms, and looked out in front of me. That was when I noticed the rest of the area and sucked in a sharp breath.

The warm sun shone down on rolling hills of green pastures and woodlands. A breeze swept over my skin, and I took in the birds singing their songs in the trees near us. The path we were on led us down to a town about the size of New Orleans. The buildings were like something out of a Santa's village that I'd seen in movies, old and beautiful.

I pressed my hands against my stomach while it fluttered even more.

I'd thought my castle and surrounding lands were amazing, but this was picturesque.

"Stunning, isn't it?" the king asked.

I shrugged, blanking my features, and said, "It's okay." He fought a smile, and I heard someone make a sound in the back of their throat, either a scoff, a snort, or a laugh, I wasn't sure, though. What I did know was that it wasn't one of my men. Ignoring it, we walked down the path in silence for a little while, until I asked, "Do you have a name?"

"I do" was all he said. I ground my teeth together.

"You may refer to him only as King Nelydriel," the suck-up said from the king's other side. He spoke in a tone that told me he thought I was so below his master's princess boots I wasn't worth the time of day.

I stopped walking. It took them a few beats to notice. However, the black-haired elf did, and then the others turned to face me. I fisted my hands at my sides, so I didn't punch the king's little minion in the balls. "I think you need to bring your head back out of the king's ass to breathe the fresh air and see with your own eyes that whatever you think about you, about your king, and about your world, doesn't make him or any of you better than my people or me. We all bleed in the same way, and if you keep up the hoity-toity crap, I'll have my hellhound bite your head off." Ezra gave off a growl in the back of his throat. It was too bad it sang to my ears and he looked too handsome for me to think it was threatening in any way. Although it wasn't a show for me and it had the minion taking a step back, which was good.

The king's brow rose again, and I wanted to rip it right off.

"My queen, maybe we should leave," Thorn suggested.

"I think you're right." I turned and started off, fighting the sudden ache in my chest. I caught Alex relaxing before he saw me looking and nodded. He was happy we were going.

"You're leaving?" the king called.

"You've got a view of my butt, which means I'm walking away, so yes, we're leaving."

"No queen should speak or act as you do," the minion called. "It's crass."

I whirled back around. "What's crass is the way you and your king have acted since we've shown up. I would have spoken and acted with respect and manners if I'd been shown it in the first place." I spun back around and started stomping away.

"You came here wanting us to join you against the council. Now you're walking away from that chance?"

I froze because the voice was one I hadn't heard before. It was soft yet deep. I wanted badly to turn around, but I didn't. I dug my nails into my palms once more, and said, "What makes you think that's what we came for since you would be aware that my mate spoke to the king of evidence we have to share regarding his father's death?"

He cleared his throat. "Even though we're in a different dimension, Paige Alice, we still have ears everywhere. We heard they had found out about the new ghoul queen. About how they were coming to your territory to, no doubt, cut you all down. However, you had put them off by stating how you were coming to see them. It was either a stupid or smart move. I haven't figured it out yet."

"Smart. It means my people stay safe." Finally, I turned, my gaze settling on the man with the long black hair standing with his arms crossed over his chest. His battle attire, like all of the guards, looked like it had been made out of hardened gray scales. "Shall we speak in private, *King*, or would you prefer this public show still?" I asked, crossing my own arms over my chest.

Asher hissed. Nate and Ezra growled, readying themselves with arms out for a shift. Thorn and Xi pulled swords free, and Alex called his powers forward as the air around us shimmered. All of them moved to surround me.

I stayed still while the space around us morphed into an empty room the size of my throne room back home. I didn't let the shock register on my face, but I was surprised as hell since I had felt the sun's warmth and the soft breeze from outside, yet none of it had been real.

That wasn't the only thing that changed. The appearance of the man we'd thought had been the king altered into the man with black hair, which meant…. I glanced at the actual king and watched as his black hair disappeared, replaced by the fake king's long white hair and clothes. They had pretended to be one another in appearances.

The guards at his back had their weapons out and trained our way, while his minion smirked, and the fake king grinned like he found this all hilarious. The rightful king dipped his chin down and announced, "My name is Cedrick Nelydriel. I am the true king of Airrile."

My body hummed and my heart raced, but if my mates heard it, they could take it for the shock of what happened. Lastly, as something inside me clicked, making things feel right, my pussy throbbed.

Fuck no. I would fight this mark, this connection. I didn't need another mate, and besides, he had his own lands and people to take care of. I fisted my hands, planted my feet firmly on the floor, and locked myself down.

Nate and Ezra looked at me. I shook my head and showed my determination of not wanting this. Asher reached back and took my hand in his, running his thumb over my skin in reassurance.

I knew they would tell me the Fates had picked this man for me, that he was meant to be in our lives for a reason, but I wouldn't have it. I had my men. I loved my men. There wasn't room for anyone else. Fuck this bond. Fuck my body and heart.

No!

"What is the meaning of these parlor tricks?" Thorn demanded.

"We have had our own problems with the council. People coming under different pretenses, but all were seeking to end my life." He waved a hand to the man now with long black hair. "My brother, Kiered, thought it would be safer if he acted in my place to see if you would also be a threat."

Nate snorted. "You let your brother take the fall if something happened."

Cedrick's jaw ticked. "I didn't *let*." He glared. "I wasn't given the choice. Apparently being the king means my life comes before anyone else's. Something I hate and would change if I didn't have everyone going against me. I also wouldn't allow him to go it alone, which is why I am here pretending to be him as a guard so I can fight my own battles."

"Ha," I let out and pointed at Cedrick. "Sounds familiar. You guys would have me in bubble wrap tied to a bed if I didn't fight for my right."

"I'm sure tied to a bed has some benefits," Kiered said with another grin and a wink.

"Kiered," his brother bit off as my men made some type of noise or growl at the man.

Kiered raised his hands. "Hey, I'm not saying *I* want to tie her to a bed. Relax." I caught his quick glance at Xi. Interesting.

"This is the man you had in your stead?" Thorn questioned.

Cedrick's brows dipped, and he shook his head. "His skills at fighting are beyond most."

"Aww, bro. I love you too," Kiered teased, and I liked him a lot more now that he wasn't pretending to be the toffy king. But did it mean that was how Cedrick was all the time? If that was the case, I was sure my mind, body, and the Fates wouldn't be that cruel and want him to still be in my life. Not that I would allow it.

Kiered stepped forward. "Now, are we able to move this into a room that's more comfortable?"

"I have the meeting room set up, your highness," Rallis said with a bow and a glare my way. I still wanted to stick my finger up at him.

"Please lead the way, Rallis," Cedrick replied, then glanced at me. "After you."

I ground my teeth. I didn't want to walk in front of him. Then again, I also didn't want to have him in front of me either because I knew I wouldn't be able to help myself—I would check him out... unless I had my men do something arousing, then my attention would easily sway to them. The only problem with that was how easily I could get lost in what they were doing and forget everything else around me.

Like now, when my mind wants to run with a thought of them in bed together.

Focus, Paige. Focus goddamn it.

As I straightened my red silk shirt out, Asher, Thorn, and Xi parted. I took the first step forward, then another. My body shivered because I could swear his eyes were on me.

"Holy shit, you're checking out her ass," Kiered whispered. However, he must have forgotten about our advanced hearing. I heard a slap, and then Kiered cursed and some of the men chuckled. I glanced to my men and saw even they held a smirk or a grin over it. I wanted to stamp my foot and tell them to be offended; he was looking at my butt in the first place. I stopped myself from shaking it and let the annoyance go. I was the only one overreacting.

We followed Rallis down a long hallway. Male and female elves scattered out of the way. Honestly, we must have looked a frightful sight. Xi and Asher had blood all over them; I hadn't even thought to get Alex to fix their appearance, not after he had been depleted. Though, I knew he was back in full force, or else he wouldn't have called for his powers in the room earlier.

Leaning into him, I asked, "Was it the glamour that had you on edge?"

He nodded. "I could feel magic, but I didn't know where

because it didn't make sense it was coming from everywhere." He glanced at me. "I'll know what to look for now."

I took his hand and squeezed it. Smiling up at him, I told him, "I know you will."

As we went by some windows, I looked out and found the scene they had set in the room was exactly like what I saw out in the real world. It was still beautiful. It had me wanting to go out there and actually see it for real.

A woman walked out of a room in front of us. She sneered, and then her gaze went behind us, which changed her expression into a coy smile and sweet, soft eyes.

No doubt one of the elves behind us was her beau.

We passed by, still following Rallis, when I heard, "My lord, how are you this day?"

My head twisted. I squeezed Alex's hand tightly. I wanted to turn around and smash her face into the door for even speaking to him, but I fought it, and it hurt. My body burned. Ezra and Nate moved closer. They reached out and touched me, a hand to my lower back and one sliding into my other hand. The skin-on-skin contact with my bonded helped cool me.

"Very well, Elizitenth," the king replied.

"May I help with something?" she called.

"Not right now, thank you."

The king was brushing her off calmed me even more. I shook my body out and kept my gaze ahead. We turned a corner, and a group of women scuttled to the side. All of them blushed and giggled, looking at my men and then at the ones or a certain one behind me.

Would slicing their throats open with my claws be too bad, really?

Now I had Asher reaching back, as well as Thorn, to touch

me in more ways. One at the hip the other on my arm. I was sure I looked like a fool, but I didn't care, else I would go on a killing spree.

"Is everything all right?" Cedrick asked. He was closer now; goose bumps broke over my skin. My dead skin. How was that even possible?

"Fine," I ground out.

We turned another corner and then down the hall we paused at the double wooden doors while Rallis opened them to another room about the size of the first one we'd been in. Only this one had four large tables, two bars, and a row of long tables off to one wall where food would have probably been set in long meetings.

Rallis moved aside. We entered and went straight for the largest table smack dab in the middle of the room. My men and I spread out on the left side. I sat in the middle. Xi stood at my back with Nate, while Thorn and Asher sat to my right, then Ezra and Alex sat on my left.

Opposite me, Cedrick sat. He was right there in front of me. Right there with his long, perfect hair, his stupid, amazing eyes, and cute, lickable ears.

I could be strong. I could be.

CHAPTER FORTY-SEVEN

PAIGE

Someone cleared their throat. I jolted a little in my seat and glared over at the man who'd made me lose my train of thought. Cedrick glanced at Asher. At least I hadn't been the only one lost in the stare.

"Shall we start?" Asher asked.

"Of course." Cedrick nodded.

"We came with proof of the council's involvement in the death of your father."

Cedrick's hand shot up. "We already know it was the council."

"How?" Nate demanded.

Cedrick pulled his gaze up to Nate. "It's a thing called interrogation. The people we captured eventually talked."

"So you know it's the council's usual MO?" Alex asked.

"What do you mean, their usual?"

Alex's power filled the room. I gripped the arms on the seat, so I didn't maul him. I didn't even look at him because I knew I would be a goner. At least twenty files dropped with a bang onto the table. He leaned over them and spread some out.

His fingers drummed on the table. "These are files on higher-up members of society who have died suspiciously, been murdered, or disappeared without a trace. They were members of different types of races. Ones who their own people thought highly of. Including the former ghoul queen, your father, and the currently missing alphas of the tiger and lion clans. However, I haven't even mentioned the mage, witch, mermaid, troll, or sphinx. The list goes on, but you get my drift. The one thing they all have in common are the groups the council sent out to investigate."

Motherfuckers. God, I hated the council.

"What does this have to do with us?" Rallis asked from where he stood behind the king. Actually, the only two who sat were the brothers. His other men lined the wall.

"Nothing, if you choose," I said, leaning into the table and resting my elbows on there to clasp my hands in front of me. "It'll keep being nothing if no one stands up to the council. Murders, kidnappings, disappearances will continue happening by their hands if there is nothing or no one to challenge them."

"Why are you the one to challenge them?" Cedrick asked.

I looked to his shoulder. "Because they threatened my people and my land by stating they were coming there. We're not stupid enough to believe they would have come in peace. They would have slaughtered innocent people, and I won't stand for it. I'm going to the council to set my own challenge so one day there will be peace. There will be days filled with minimal occurrences. Days I can look forward to spending with my men and my people, without the threat of them hanging over our heads."

"Will you allow us to take time to think about it?" Kiered asked.

I glanced to Asher as he said, "We leave in two days to travel to speak with the shifters. After that, we're going to a vampire clan whose master was murdered."

"You're hoping they'll step in as backup?" Cedrick asked.

I nodded, staring at his chin. "Yes, and that's all we can do. Hope. If any of you chose not to attend the meeting with the council as… let's say witnesses, then it's fine. We won't hold it against anyone."

Cedrick nodded. "Two days."

"Do you have somewhere in your town we could stay?" Thorn asked.

"It would be an honor to have you as guests here in our palace."

Shit. I didn't think being under the same roof would be good, but at least I had my men to distract me.

Wait… he said castle, right? I wanted to see the outside because I didn't remember one in the scene he'd set in the room earlier. I knew it was him because when he'd used his magic, he'd set off my mark for him. Why else would I want to hump his leg like a madwoman and kill every woman he'd been with or looked at him.

Speaking of… crap, was I really going to have to do this?

Yes, I was. Damn it.

"Thank you," I said, dipping my chin in respect. "There is something you might have to warn your people of though."

"What?" he demanded.

I cleared my throat and shifted in the seat, suddenly uncomfortable. Nate snorted behind me, obviously guessing what I was about to say. I ignored that and Ezra's snicker.

"Look, ah, there's no simple way to say it. I'm a little possessive of my men."

"A little." Ezra laughed.

Alex covered his mouth, and I knew he was smiling wide behind it. At least Thorn and Asher only had a small smirk.

"Okay, I'm very possessive of my men. I don't like it when women or men flirt with them."

"What do you mean by *very* possessive?"

"She's near killed over it. If we hadn't been there, she would have," Asher explained mildly. "We are also possessive of her. Please pass it along as well." Asher lifted his gaze to behind the king and narrowed his eyes. "You've been undressing her since we arrived. If you do not cease, I'll have your blood join with the rest over my clothes."

Cedrick spun around on his seat. "Out," he clipped low to one of his guards, who quickly bowed and left. My stupid body tingled at Cedrick's tone. Kiered chuckled but cut it off when his brother glared at him. Cedrick looked back to two men and ordered, "Let it be known, because if someone doesn't listen, they'll suffer the consequences. Not Paige and her mates."

"You would allow them to come into our lands and spout foolish rules like this?" Rallis questioned snottily. I just knew he needed his balls rearranged on his body.

When his king looked to him, Rallis gulped, paled, and stepped back. "Forgive me for speaking out, my lord."

I didn't trust him. Admittedly, I didn't know him, but there was something about him that set off alarm bells throughout me. He was so far up the king's good-looking ass it wasn't funny. Yet, he still seemed scared by him. No matter, I'd be keeping an eye on him. I may even have a chat with Cedrick's brother to see if he'd be willing to speak of Rallis and either confirm my mistrust or defend him.

"It's been happening a lot lately, Rallis," Kiered commented while looking at his fingernails. "Is there a reason why?"

"N-No, sir. I just worry for the king is all."

Kiered hummed under his breath. "Anyway, I think we should all freshen up before dinner."

Oh fuck. Did they expect me to eat? What? Normal food? I mean, Alex could bring in a meal for me, which was how the ghouls in the group, including myself, were going to be feeding, but I wouldn't be comfortable eating in front of them.

Ezra's hand slid to my leg. He smiled over at the king. "We'd love dinner, but I'm afraid some of us are on liquid diets."

Kiered chuckled. "But of course. We'll make sure to have something for everyone."

Unease twisted my stomach. I stared down at the table, trying to think of a way to get out of it but couldn't come up with anything.

"Unless you would prefer to retire to your rooms?" Cedrick mentioned. Since I hadn't expected his offer, I lifted my gaze to find him already staring at me. My damn cheeks heated. "I presume something happened on the way here, so you must all be tired."

"We were attacked. So a rest would be good, thank you," I told him.

He nodded. "Kiered will show you to your rooms." He glanced to his brother. "Take them all to the fourth floor."

"Where—"

"Fourth floor," he bit out.

"Of course." He dipped his head then clicked his fingers, and a man stepped close. He spoke in a different language quietly, one I didn't understand, but the guard nodded and raced out of the room.

"Should we be worried about that or what's on the fourth floor?" Thorn asked casually. I was glad he mentioned something because it seemed suspicious.

"Nothing to fear. I'm just removing some others on that floor so you can have it to yourselves."

Kiered looked away when I shifted my gaze to him. What was this about? I wouldn't jeopardize my men if there was a problem.

"Who was on that floor?" I demanded.

"Not of your concern," Cedrick clipped.

"Love," Asher called. "It's fine. I could do with some rest though." Meaning he understood what was said and knew we had nothing to worry about.

"Okay." I nodded, trusting him completely.

"Will you need a room separately?" Cedrick asked suddenly as I stood from my seat.

Nate snorted. "We're fine in the one room."

"Let's just hope the bed's big enough for all of us," Alex murmured, being cheeky for some reason.

"Also, that it's sturdy," Ezra added with a smug smile after.

"Guys," I scolded, not understanding why they were speaking of it in front of the others.

Something snapped. I looked over to see Cedrick dusting something off his hands.

"Right this way," Kiered called from the doorway. His grin was the biggest I'd seen it. I noticed my men were also smirking or smiling over something.

I would get to the bottom of it when we were in the room.

Out in the hall, Kiered started for the stairs. He glanced back and asked, "You're mated to all six of them?"

"Six?"

"Xi isn't a part of the bonded group," Thorn put in.

"Oh, I thought he was." Kiered's gaze slowly ran over Xi in appreciation. Maybe they weren't bigots here. To my utter shock, Xi blushed and looked everywhere but at the man.

"No, he's my guard," I told him. "He was sent from the devil himself because he's the best there is."

"Really," Kiered drew out slowly. Xi's face heated even more, and I caught him miss a step, but he grabbed the railing, righting himself quickly. Interesting, very interesting. I grinned, thinking Xi deserved a little happiness, and I could tell he wasn't disgusted by the thought of Kiered.

"He will need a room to himself right next door to us."

"I'll make it happen," Kiered said. He winked at me.

Ezra groaned. "You guys need to install elevators in this place."

Kiered laughed. "It's in the pipework; however, since we aren't in need of them, it keeps getting pushed back."

"Why aren't you in need of them?" I asked.

Kiered turned on the step at level three. He levitated a foot off the floor and floated up ahead easily, then landed. "See, easier for us."

"That's pretty cool. I forgot you could all do that." We moved to the next set of stairs and started walking up them. "What was also amazing was the glamour in the room earlier. I can see it was a true picture of what's out there." I pointed to a window.

Kiered nodded. "Since the first assassination attempt, we had to move the portal into a secured room in the castle because a couple of times the assassin tried to kill the king on the spot and they'd thought to escape into the woods when they'd realized they were outnumbered. Thankfully, they were hunted and caught."

"How many attempts have there been?" Xi asked.

"About five."

Xi cursed just as we reached the fourth floor.

"You say you keep the glamour up until you know you can trust the person. How did you trust us so quickly?" Nate asked.

Good question.

"Yes, ah, well, we didn't until Cedrick revealed himself to you all."

"Are you saying he knew to trust us?"

Kiered shrugged and led us down the hall. "The guards can start picking a room as we walk down. But you'll be in the second to last room, Paige Alice."

"Just Paige," I told him.

He smiled. "Just Paige."

"Why did your brother trust us, Kiered?" Thorn asked again.

"You'll have to ask him. I'm not sure."

I had a feeling that was a lie. I caught my men looking at each other. Damn it, they were all thinking it had to do with me.

"Although, you telling Rallis to pull his head out of the king's ass was a good indication. No one has spoken so freely before. It's nice."

"Our queen has a habit of speaking freely. Just another reason we love her," Alex said, and I grinned at him, wrapping my arm around his waist. He curled his around my shoulders.

Xi sorted the guards into rooms as we continued down the hall. When we were the last, Kiered called Xi's name, stopping in front of a gold brass door. Honestly, I wasn't a fan of the décor inside. It was over-the-top lavish. It all said "we have money… let me show you." I'd never seen so many paintings in my life.

"This will be your room," Kiered announced and pushed open the door.

"I would like to see the queen's room first, please."

Ezra clutched his chest and gasped. "He said please."

Xi scowled at him. There was lightness in Xi's eyes as he looked at Ezra, which I was sure many would never have been able to spot. My mate loved to give Xi a hell of a time, but it was all in fun. Xi knew it too. It also seemed he was very patient.

"That's really nice of you, but I promise the room won't have any booby traps." Kiered smiled. Xi blinked at him and clasped his hands behind his back. Kiered looked around at us. "Ahh, okay. This way." He chuckled to himself as he mock-whispered to me, "Is he always so serious?"

I nodded. "Always."

Kiered smiled widely before moving off to the next room. I had a feeling he took that as a challenge, and he was going to see if he could break Xi out of his robotic emotions. The only time I'd seen him smile was fighting those demons earlier.

Kiered opened the next door and swung it all the way in before stepping back and sweeping out his hand. "After you, sweet Xi."

Ezra snorted, and I covered my smile with my hand when I

noticed a blush on Xi's cheeks as he stepped through ignoring us. I waited in the hall until he came back out and dipped his head. "You may enter."

"Thanks, Xi." I smiled.

"However," he started and turned to Kiered, "I would like to know whose room is on the other side." He pointed to the last door in that hallway.

Kiered coughed and ran a hand at the back of his neck. Were the tips of his ears tinting red? "The king's."

Ezra laughed. "Makes me wonder why he would want us on his floor."

"Yes, I wonder why," Nate said sarcastically.

Well, it had better not have anything to do with me, because I didn't want that. Why would he do that? Did he sense some-thing? Oh shit. Did I share my lust into him? Did he think he was mine now? I wouldn't have him. I wouldn't.

I had my five. Five was more than enough.

Roughly, I heard Xi say something, but I didn't take it in because I was freaking out in my mind. I didn't want my men to think they weren't enough for me. They were. They would always be. Why were the fucking Fates doing this to me?

Wait… the bond hadn't been completed. I could get away from him, from here, and never see him again. Then things would go back to how they were.

Besides, I didn't like white hair. I liked blond, black, brown… not white. I snorted to myself. The way he dressed wasn't a turn-on. Not that I was looking for things to turn me on about him, because I wasn't, and I refused to think about his eyes, ears, and body.

"How's she doing?" someone asked.

"She'll be fine," someone else replied.

Guilt stabbed at me. How greedy could one ghoul be? I had five amazing, perfect mates. They were the absolute best, all challenging me in different ways. All accepting me for who I was. I didn't need another.

And that was final.

I would refuse to complete the bond.

I would dodge Cedrick at all costs.

Blinking, I focused in front of me to see I was sitting on a large bed in an extravagant bedroom. I'd thought mine was big. This was twice its size, with a little kitchenette of its own. Asher stood with Thorn leaning against the wall talking quietly. Alex and Nate lounged on the bed behind me, and Ezra sat between my legs on the floor. Reaching out, I ran my hand through his hair. He turned quickly, getting to his knees.

"Hey," he said.

"Hi, sorry to space out there for a moment."

He took my hands in his and pressed his cheek against them. "It's okay. We understand you've sensed the connection with the king."

I sighed and glanced to my other men. Nate and Alex moved forward on the bed to sit on each side of me. "I've felt the connection, yes. However, I'm refusing to accept it."

"Why, love?" Asher asked, straightening from the wall to come over with Thorn. Both stopped in front of us.

"Because I have five amazing mates already. I don't need or want another." Before he or anyone else could say anything, I shot my hand up. "Please don't say anything. I know you all think this is out of our hands because the Fates picked this choice for me, but the fact is there's a choice to complete the bond, which means it's an out for this connection. I'm taking that out."

"Would Cedrick have a say?" Thorn asked.

"No, yes, well… I don't know." I lifted one hand out from under Ezra's head and ran my fingers through his hair. "You guys didn't know about the connection until Thorn said something. I mean, you felt a little of something, but that was it. If he asks, we'll ignore it, play it off as we don't know what he's talking about. Then we'll leave and I won't have to see him again."

I disregarded my heart since it felt like it was weeping in my chest or ready to explode at the thought of leaving without Cedrick.

"If he decides to join us on our quest?" Alex asked softly.

My stomach fluttered. "I doubt he would. He's king. He'll have too many other things to take care of here. It looks three times the size of our place. If anything, I think he could send some men, but that's it."

Asher hummed under his breath. I glowered up at him and snapped, "What?"

"Nothing, love."

"Asher." I shook my head. "Actually, I don't want to know. Can we do something else for a moment and then talk business after?"

Asher smiled, showing a bit of fang. "I'm rather parched. Nate, would you—"

"Yes," Nate clipped before Asher could finish.

"Perfect," I said. "Entertain me, my mates."

"Always, my queen," Asher said. As soon as Nate was in front of him, he spun Nate around to have his back to his front. Nate squirmed, bringing on his half form. He snarled as Asher scraped his fangs on his neck. Nate reached behind him, grabbed a handful of clothes, and pulled, flipping Asher over his head.

The fight was on and it brought a smile to my face.

"Alex, they're in too many clothes. Thorn, Ezra, come up on the bed with us." I laughed when Ezra jumped up quickly and bounced flat on the bed.

This was what happiness was made of.

CHAPTER FORTY-EIGHT

CEDRICK

The women of my land were the most beautiful of all kinds. They had been cherished by many; stories were told of how exquisite they were. Of course, I had indulged in many different women in my time and found them pleasurable. They were tall, legs going on forever. They were soft and thin, with long silky hair and eyes that shone.

Yet, they dulled in comparison to Paige Alice.

Paige Alice, the ghoul queen.

The way my body reacted to her was something I'd never felt. No woman had hardened my cock in seconds after seeing her for the first time. Hell, I had wanted to pull her from her mate's body after she'd come through the portal in his arms and cradle her to me. That was even before seeing her stunning features. She was small. The top of her head only came to my chest. She had curves I wanted to caress, and when her scent drifted over to me, I wanted nothing more than to smell it for the rest of my life.

Had she placed some type of spell on me?

I hadn't heard she was a sorceress.

Shaking my head, I stalked to my windows in my room and looked out. Clenching my jaw because of my stupidity, I exhaled. No, she hadn't put me under a spell, and I knew it. She was meant for me because she was my intended. My bride.

A knock sounded on the door, and it opened before I called out. I knew who it would be. *"Yes, Kiered?"* I asked through our minds. It was a gift all elves had, to be able to speak with each other as long as the person receiving it was open to allow it.

"She's not who I expected."

He could say that again. Aloud, I replied, "Who did you expect?"

"A cold, dead thing that dragged around her body slowly and moaned for brains."

I glared over my shoulder and faced the window again, so he didn't see my smile. "I think you have zombies and ghouls mixed up. However, you're correct. No one could predict what type of woman she would be without seeing it for themselves."

"What type of woman is she, brother?"

"A take-charge, caring, funny, sexy woman."

"Is she... your bride?"

"Yes."

"Is this why you got rid of your women on this floor, to have her close?"

Turning, I sighed and leaned against the windowsill. I ground my teeth together and admitted, *"I can already tell no woman will do but her. However, I won't be taking her as my bride."*

His brows shot up near in his hairline. "Whyever not?"

"We're polar opposites."

He laughed. "I see no difference. You would do anything for your people, like she does hers. You're both rulers, have a lot hanging over your heads."

"She has *five* men already. Five, Kiered." I shook my head. "I would never leave my people either. It hasn't been long since I became king, and we both know father ran things down when he was ruling. I'm to make a difference."

"You already have, brother. All look up to you in respect and not fear. Father was a sadist; we both know that. He didn't touch us because we were his kin, but it didn't stop him from showing us his real side. I know it kills you that we couldn't save everyone when he was… in a mood. It hurts me also, but you must trust the palace is better off without him. However, we need to show others that coming into our lands and killing one of our own won't go unpunished." He walked closer and then sat beside me against the window. "You know the council has reigned long enough over everyone with their vicious ways. They're like Father in many ways. Are you willing to have them continue on the path of destruction, which could come into our lands again and again?"

"I agree. You know I do. The council will get what's coming to them, and they'll deserve it. Which is why I will assist Paige in their takedown by sending as many men as we can spare with her."

"Our men are legends in their own right. Still…" He knocked his foot against mine. "She'll need your help and protection."

"She has *many* to protect her, and I'm sure the shifters she's to see will be willing to assist to get any information they can on their alphas."

"Are you jealous of her mates?"

I scoffed. "No." A part of me might have been because they got to have who they wanted, and from the looks I saw exchanged, I could tell they shared their bodies as well. It didn't disgust me. In fact, if I was honest, they were all attractive men. All different in their own ways. I could tell the connection they all shared was one of love. They didn't fulfill the bond because it was convenient or because they presumed they would gain more power from the connection. They honestly loved each other.

Not all bonds worked out like that. No one knew how or why the Fates picked as they did. Sometimes it worked, other times it didn't, but I always thought when it didn't work, it was because of the people involved. They didn't put enough into it. One was greedier than the other and expected more out of it.

I shook my head. No matter what it came down to... none of it was for me.

"You are." Kiered laughed. "This is funny coming from a man who sleeps with many women and men in one night, all in the same bed." He sobered when he saw I wasn't finding it amusing. He didn't yet understand why I couldn't have Paige Alice as my bride.

"It never comes down to attraction or sex with a bride connection. Before we can commit, we have to take everything into account. Everything, Kiered. If I leave to be with her, who will rule Airrile?" He opened his mouth to answer, but I shot in quickly with "You can't take this on, Kiered. You're skilled in fighting, yes, but in power, I am the only one who will be able to keep our darker brothers on this side. Father's elder powers only passed onto me, brother. I wish we had been equal, but we are not, and it is left up to me to keep peace within our realm."

"The other elders could assist; they've sat back long enough."

"They never assisted with Father because they all thought along the same path as he. Rule with pain, with fear. I won't subject the people to them."

Kiered clenched his jaw and glared at the floor. "She is your bride, brother. Your one and only. Now you've seen her, met her, you will no longer love or be with another because they could never satisfy you in—"

"I know what it means, Kiered," I clipped as I straightened and started pacing the room. "It is a sacrifice I make for our land, our people."

"You're stronger than I could ever be, brother."

Maybe I was. Though I was worried what kind of man would I be when I didn't have my bride to complete me.

"She could move here—"

"She has her own people to take care of."

"They could also come here."

I laughed without humor. "Can you imagine what our people would think of us allowing outsiders to live within our realm forever? Vampires, witches, ghouls, shifters?" I huffed. "Maybe after I've been king for a decade or two, I can make such a change. For now, I'm still gaining the trust of the people, and I won't jeopardize it to satisfy myself."

"Are you sure—"

"Whatever it is you're about to say, yes, I'm sure." I walked toward the bathroom. "Now, can you please see to a meal for them and send it to their room?"

"I think the vampire feeds from a few in the bonded group."

My dick throbbed at the thought of seeing it while he drank

from Paige. "Right, then send the rest something." I opened the door and turned back to add, "Shifters eat a lot. I presume hellhounds have the same appetite."

"Did you know he was a hellhound?"

I smirked. "Not until she told Rallis her hellhound would eat him."

Kiered chuckled. "I was sure he shit his undergarments. I can see she eyes Rallis with caution."

I grunted. "She's smart. When you go back with the meal, be sure to have a quiet word to them about him."

He nodded. "I will. Last question. Have you tried to mind speak with her?"

Since she was of another race, but still my bride, I would have been able to mind speak with her still. However, I wasn't willing to try. In doing so, would be another step to completing the link. "No, I haven't and won't."

He offered a sad smile. "Enjoy your cool shower." He winked, then blanched. "That sounded wrong." He went to the door, opened it, and shot out of the room.

Smiling, I enjoyed the new Kiered. Actually, he wasn't new; he was more himself, more out in the open than he had ever been when Father had been around. My brother was loud, liked to tease, was conceited in a funny way, and now didn't care what others thought of him. He preferred men, but had hidden that part of him as Father hadn't approved. If he hadn't pretended to like women, he would have been forced to fuck them in front of people, like our cousin had.

I despised the man.

Hated him with everything I was.

Yet, I hadn't been strong enough to put a stop to him. If only I'd had the elders' power rushing through me back then. I would have slayed him on the spot for his foulness. In reality, it was a good thing he was assassinated in the end.

Thinking of him always soured my mood. Yet, there was another reason turmoil spread through my veins and deadened my heart.

Finding a bride was the most amazing feeling in the realm. It had been; she took my breath away, had my body singing in tune with hers… and I wanted more than anything to claim her.

Denying a bond…. I could already feel the ache from not being near her. I would hurt for a long time, until distance helped dull the pain. However, it would never go.

I just hoped it wouldn't be the same for her.

I prayed she hadn't felt this bond within her and no pain could touch her from this since it would be my decision to not complete it. I could speak to her about it, explain the reasons why. Let her know it had nothing to do with her, but my commitments as king. I had a feeling she would understand, but a small part of me feared she wouldn't and I would see the anguish within her that I had caused. So really, I was being selfish by not saying anything.

Two days.

Only two days I had to pretend she didn't mean the world to me.

I could do it.

I had to.

A SCREAM of rage had me transporting myself from the shower to the destination where I felt the anger. I stood in the middle of Paige's room with swords in each hand and gasped at the chaos around me. Her men fought hand to hand against steel and arrow. Paige, dressed in what looked like a little nightie, had a man bent in half on the floor. His feet actually touched his face. It was then I caught another man sneaking closer to Paige, coming up behind her as she demanded answers from the man under her.

In seconds, I stood at her back and brought both swords straight down the middle of the man. Each half fell different ways.

I glanced down to Paige to see her looking up at me with wide eyes. A blush coated her gorgeous face. Her unbound hair wound around her shoulders as if caressing her.

"Alex," she called. "Clothes."

I heard a click and then something pressed against my skin. I looked down to see a black shirt and trousers covered my body. Nakedness didn't bother me, yet it seemed to Paige.

I searched for Alex, who was throwing some type of ball of light toward someone, and nodded when he looked over. He grinned and it caught my breath. Yes, I could see why Paige would be taken with him.

Another opponent moved behind Alex, but before I could say anything, the vampire was there ripping the head off with his bare hands. He then snarled something low at Alex before kissing him hard and flashing off.

I turned back in time to split three more threats in half with ease.

"How does he fucking move with grace like that?" I heard Paige ask. Then heard a grunt before she said, "I'm not talking to you, asshole. Now tell me, who sent you?" A beat later, she cursed, then called, "Thorn!" I didn't have time to look because more advanced. Only then I was taken to the ground and covered by the tiny woman who had her hands over my face.

Suddenly, the room fell silent.

She lifted her head, but not her hands off my face until I dragged them down to my chest. I stared up at her while she looked around the room. "Alex?"

"I'm fine. Not drained at all."

"What have we said about overdoing it?" was barked from Thorn, I thought.

"Relax, they're unconscious, not dead. A simple spell," Alex replied.

"And the spell seconds before that? The fire?" That sounded like the shifter, Nate.

No one got to answer because there was a knock. We all looked over to see Kiered standing there in the opened door with a quivering parlor maid. She shook so much that things on her tray rattled, while Kiered gazed around the room in shock.

"What did I miss?" he asked.

"That is what I would like to know," I snapped.

"Sweetheart, you can hop off the king now," Thorn called.

Paige's gaze snapped down to me, and it was then I realized my hands were on her hips. I gave them a squeeze, feeling that I touched no clothing, but skin. Her nightie must have ridden up. She bit her bottom lip. I wanted to take my cock out, bury it inside her, and watch as she threw her head back on a moan and rode me like my dick was made for her. Which it was. I wanted to run my hands up until they cupped her breasts; then I would bring my mouth up to taste her skin, at her neck first before sliding lower to her erect nipples.

Wait... they were, in fact, currently erect and ready for tasting. Her body reacted to me already.

She shifted back lightly, but I gripped her, so she didn't move lower over my body to find out how hard I was for her.

"Criosd, tha thu mar sin bòidheach," I said, hoping she didn't understand my language, since I had just told her she was beautiful. If she did, I would find another language she didn't understand since I knew over one hundred.

She frowned. "What does that mean?"

Thankfully, I didn't have to answer since Ezra was there lifting her off me with a smirk playing on his lips. He winked down at me, then twirled Paige in his arms and bent her back to kiss her neck. "Now we can get back to what we were doing."

Her eyes closed. She gripped the man tightly even as he straightened them upright and she smiled up at him like he was the one to create chocolate. Until she blinked and glanced around at the destruction in their room.

"Uh, soon. Right now I want answers." She turned to me as I climbed to my feet. I would have repositioned my hardened dick if she wasn't already looking at me. "Do you know what they are? Are they yours? Did you try to kill us?"

I couldn't help but roll my eyes. "If I wanted you all dead, you already would be."

"Brother, maybe we can adjourn to your room while we have this place cleaned up and the prisoners taken to the dungeon?"

"Fine," I clipped and then stalked from the room. It hurt to think she would suspect I would be involved, which counted for my short, sharp response. However, even after I regretted it, it also could be good to push her away.

"Please excuse my brother. He's under a lot of strain at the moment." I heard Kiered say as I entered the hall from her room.

Someone snorted, another chuckled, before an amused voice said, "I'm sure he is."

My step faltered. Did they know? Did they suspect I was hers and wasn't accepting this bond? My gut clenched, twisted, and then dropped. Would they understand if they did know?

It wasn't Paige. I would never reject *her*.

Throwing my door open, I stormed through. I didn't realize the parlor maid had followed until I'd turned back to the door.

"My lord, shall I lay their refreshments in here?"

"Please." I nodded and waved my hand toward the table. "Place them there."

She curtsied and did as I asked. As she took the plates off the tray, the others entered, and I noticed Paige was now dressed in human clothes of jeans and a top. The others also had more clothing on. Kiered kicked the door closed and moved to the table to deposit his own tray. However, the door shot open and hit the wall.

"Merde," the French word dropped from my mouth before I could stop it.

After everyone looked at me, they slowly moved their gaze to the door.

"Thera, now isn't a good time," I told my ex-fiancée, but of course she didn't listen. She gazed around the room as she stepped through the door. Thera and I had been promised to one another when my father was around. She was manipulative, cold, and a bitch. She also didn't understand why I called off the wedding as soon as I heard word my father had died. She still refused to move from the palace, telling me I would come to my senses in the end because it was a politically good move. It was utter shit. I never trusted her father, another elder, so I would rather die than have any part of that man have more say in what went on in the kingdom. Meaning, his daughter would be his own little pawn.

As far as I knew, she had been off visiting her parents. What she was doing back I didn't have a clue, nor why she was staring at the people venomously.

"Darling, you should have told me we had guests. I would have made sure I was home from the start."

Movement had me shifting my gaze to the side to see Paige's men surround her. Asher even had his arms around her upper arms as he held her to him. What was going on?

Thera stepped closer to me. Kiered stopped her with a hand on her arm. "Thera, such a pleasure to see you. Why are you back?"

"Do I need a reason to return home to my husband? I think not."

Paige made a noise in the back of her throat as she screwed her nose up and narrowed her gaze.

I pulled my eyes from her and said, "Thera, you know the arranged wedding was canceled as soon as my father died." I crossed my arms over my chest. "You will never be my wife, as I've said multiple times. So, explain to me why you come barging into my room without notice."

She laughed. "Oh, darling, you never complained before." She smiled, shrugged off Kiered's hold, and went to come at me.

"Enough," Paige snapped.

Thera froze and eyed Paige since Ezra and Nate moved aside. Asher still held his mate. Thera took a step toward them. Ezra and Nate both growled in the back of their throats. Smartly, Thera stopped. Her nose turned up. "Who are you to speak to me as such?"

Before Paige could say anything, I said coldly, "She is a guest of your king. It is you who is in the wrong by coming in here thinking you have the right, when in fact you don't."

Thera ignored my words and asked again, "Who are you?"

"Thera, you will leave instantly," I ordered.

"I am Paige Alice, ghoul queen. Who is it you think you are? As far as I can see, you are not wanted or needed in this room and never will be."

Thera gasped dramatically and turned to me. "Will you allow this?"

I had wanted to keep things peaceful, but enough was enough.

"Yes," I told her.

She sneered. "Father was right. You're a weak king." I felt a tap on my mind. She wanted access. She was trying to force it.

"Don't, Thera," Kiered warned, sensing what she was trying to do.

"What's she doing?" Paige demanded.

"Trying to pry open my mind to speak with me. It won't happen, Thera."

She screamed and stamped her foot like a spoiled child. Unfortunately, she turned to Paige, drew a dagger from her sleeve, and threw it at her. Paige cried out when Nate, who moved in front of her, stumbled backward.

Even though he'd caught himself and Thera's aim wasn't good since the blade ended up in his arm, Paige saw red.

Before our eyes, she changed. Her eyes shone red with a black ring around the pupil, and her nails extended into claws. She let out a vicious snarl, and even though Asher still held her, she managed to get out of his hold and race to Thera.

Paige grabbed her by her hair and threw her across the room.

"Love," Asher called.

"Sweetheart," Thorn said.

"Let her go," Ezra mumbled.

None of them assisted her.

Thera got up off the floor with more daggers in her hands. She looked as if nothing had happened to her. Hair, clothes, and appearance all perfect. Whereas Paige looked feral, and I liked it. No, I loved it because she was herself. Her wild, wonderful self, protecting her mate.

"I'll kill you," Thera bit out.

"You can try." Paige smiled.

The room thickened with Thera's power. I stepped closer to Paige, but Alex was there with his hand on my arm, shaking his head. "I have it," he told me on a whisper. "She's safe, magically, and she'll fight her own battles physically."

I eyed him, lost in his glowing purple eyes. His magic swept over me and caused me to shiver. I nodded down at him, since I seemed to be the tallest out of the men. Alex was also the short-est, just above Paige.

Why I compared myself to the men I didn't know. It wasn't like it mattered since I wouldn't be a part of their group.

"As long as she isn't outnumbered," Asher stated.

Nate snorted. "She'd even try to keep us out of it then and take it all on."

Thorn nodded. "She's stubborn."

"In a cute way, especially when she gets angry with us," Ezra added.

Why were they telling me all this?

Thera threw a dagger. Paige dodged it beautifully as she made her way toward the woman. Thera threw the next dagger, and Paige easily moved out of the way. She was on Thera, a hand wrapped around her neck. She picked Thera up off the floor and held her high.

Elves were strong, but it seemed ghouls were stronger, or at least the queen was.

Thera struggled, choking and gripping Paige's arms.

"Why do you want to harm me? I have done nothing to you."

"H-He s-said I-I h-had to," she got out slowly.

Paige dropped her. Thera landed in a heap. She sat up slowly, rubbing her neck. "What are you doing?" Thera whispered.

"Who said you had to harm me?"

"My father."

"Why?"

"Because the council ordered it—and I will follow through," she yelled, lifting herself up and stabbing Paige in the chest.

We all cried out, until we heard Paige laugh. She leaned into the knife, cupped Thera's face and smiled down at her. "The only way to kill a ghoul is to slice off our heads." Thera paled and then her eyes widened when Paige went on with "You should have learned more about us and how I now have the right to kill you instantly." Paige whipped Thera's head quickly to the side, snapping her neck.

Thera dropped to the floor. Dead.

Paige straightened, glanced down at the knife sticking out of her, and asked, "Does someone want to help pull it out?"

CHAPTER FORTY-NINE

PAIGE

The room had been cleared of maids and the dead body. When it finally happened, I wanted to smack all my men in the face and kick them in the shin. Usually I only got that feeling with Nate, and maybe sometimes Ezra. Not with all of them. Even Cedrick was being foolish.

"I think Alex should put her to sleep before we remove it," Thorn suggested again.

Cedrick nodded as he stared down at my chest. "I would agree," he murmured.

"Sounds good to me. Then it won't hurt her," Ezra added.

"Just pull the thing out quickly," Nate said. He bent and poked at where the knife was still inside me. I flinched, which caused Alex to smack him in the back of the head.

"That hurt her."

The most annoying one came from the most sensible one. Asher tapped his chin and said, "Maybe if we distract her with an orgasm—"

"Are you all serious right now?" I took the hilt of the dagger, and while they all called out for me to stop, I pulled it free with a small cry of pain. I dropped the dagger to the floor and glared at them all. "That's the last time I ask for help. Next time I have something hanging out of me, I'll deal with it myself."

"Why did that sound dirty and yet not?" Ezra asked.

I punched him in the stomach. He wheezed as I then stepped around them to go to the couch.

"Sweetheart, come on now. We didn't want to hurt you," Thorn said. I ignored him and winced a little when I sat. Already I could feel the skin knitting back together. Thorn took the seat beside me, and just as Nate was about to sit on the other side, Alex appeared out of nowhere, scaring Nate enough he cried out in surprise.

Then a scowl took over his features before he kicked at Alex's foot. "You're fucking lucky you're pretty or I'd move you."

"I know." Alex smiled.

Leaning back, I looked up, and up again, at Cedrick. My heart fluttered, remembering his naked body appearing in the room. I knew his body would be perfection, but his silky white skin, his hard muscles, his tall form, and his long, thick dick would be seared into my mind forever.

Even then I wanted to see it again. I wanted to cherish each and every inch of the man with cute pointy ears. God, those ears drove me crazy. I could stare at them, at all of him, for hours. Like all of my men.

Regret filled me, and my healed chest twisted from it.

However, I couldn't bring myself to tell him he was mine. He was made for me. He had responsibilities, and I couldn't come between him and his people.

"You know, don't you?" Cedrick asked. My body jolted, and I realized I'd been staring at him standing in front of me. It shocked me when he knelt, resting his clasped hands on his thighs. The others quieted around us and stopped trying to reason with me about why they didn't want to hurt me. I understood it, but maybe we had to stop coddling each other when it came to helping one another. Even if it hurt.

"Know what?" I asked softly and caught Kiered's pained look behind his brother.

Oh crap… was this about my mark on him?

"You're my bride," he announced as his icy eyes held mine. They told me more than his blank look. In them I could see hurt, respect, and resolve.

"Sorry, what?" No one said anything about being a bride. What did he mean? Was he expecting me to leave my lands, my people, to become a doting wife?

"Love," Asher called, then his hands were on my shoulders, his calmness rolling over me. "For elves, they call their mates brides. That is what Cedrick means."

Oh.

"Ah… okay, um, it sounds very *Bride of Chucky*, but to answer your question, I didn't know I was your bride. As far as I knew, I had marked you to be my bonded mate."

His eyes widened; then he caught himself and blanked his features.

"You've marked me?"

Alex took my hand as I blushed like a little girl who had her first crush and he was talking to her. "Yes."

Nate, from where he'd planted himself on the floor between Alex's legs, said, "We guessed it happened when we first showed. You were using your power to glamour that room?" Cedrick nodded. "Paige marks her mates when they first use their powers in front of her. Though, it seems you also marked her to be your bride."

"What do you mean?" Asher asked.

"Alex noticed it before we got interrupted. He pointed it out to me only recently and I saw it when you changed."

"What are you talking about?" I demanded.

"On the back of your shoulder is a mark, one that looks a lot like an autumn leaf."

Cedrick, with wide eyes, looked over his shoulder to his brother, who shrugged. He turned back and asked, "May I see it?"

I nodded and leaned forward for Thorn and Alex to grip my tee and lift it. Cedrick walked around the back of the couch and stopped beside Asher. Both of them leaned in. One of them traced a finger over my skin, causing me to shiver.

"I have never heard of a bride receiving a mark," Cedrick admitted. He sounded in awe. "It is beautiful."

It was *his* finger lightly grazing the mark, causing my body to react even more. My nipples hardened, my pussy pulsed, and I bit my bottom lip to stop myself from moaning. I wanted to turn around and claim his lips.

We'd marked each other.

Even though I had five mates where the marking happened nearly instantly, it still shocked me how a part of ourselves knew we were it for each other.

"Does this mean the bond is complete?" I asked, wondering if it was different for fae. When I felt Cedrick straighten, his finger dropping away, I pulled my shoulder forward enough to glance down.

A dainty sugar maple leaf, colored in browns, greens, and ambers, sat just at the back of my right shoulder. I thinned my lips, so I didn't smile. It reminded me of when Ezra had first left his mark on my chest. His handprint. I glanced to where he stood leaning against the wall closest to the couch. He smirked down at me, as if knowing my thoughts.

I wanted Nate and Asher to fuck me and bite me again. To leave their marks deeper so they stayed permanently on me. I wanted Alex and Thorn to brand me in some way as well. We may have emotionally marked one another, but I wanted theirs to show on my body, so I could walk around proudly showing who I belonged to.

Smiling to myself, I decided I would voice what I wanted eventually because I knew they would give me it. I also knew it would be something they would love. It was just unfortunate it would have to be later.

All happiness faded and my chest ached. My smile dropped and I blinked down at my lap.

My men sensed my mood shift, and all reached out to touch me in some way. Ezra even came over to sit on the floor between Thorn's legs to be close and curled a reassuring hand around my calf.

"It doesn't have to be this way," Ezra murmured.

"What doesn't?" Cedrick asked. Obviously, his hearing was as good as the rest of ours.

I licked my dry lips. "How this won't work." It hurt to say the words; it felt like even my throat wanted to close off on the words and take them back.

"I know," he said before I could say more. I lifted my gaze

to his as he walked around the couch and sat in the chair Kiered pulled up. Anguish filled his gaze, and I knew mine replicated his. It pained me even more. He smiled sadly; one corner of his mouth tilted a little. "You have your people to take care of and I have mine. Neither of us could change it. Our father wasn't the kindest ruler. I'm only just gaining the trust of my people. If I were to leave and have another elder rule—someone who went along with our father's ideas—it wouldn't be good for the people, but also for everyone outside of this realm."

"My brother's power keeps the dark fae in line and secured behind their own binding," Kiered said. "To lose him now would risk those wards, and if they were free, they would do anything they wanted to ensure chaos."

I never understood what a fae king had to deal with. In retrospect, it seemed a lot more than I ever could.

"I… um… my staying wouldn't help the matter, would it?" It wasn't like I could stay, but I still wanted to ask. However, I already knew the answer when he closed his eyes as if he'd been cut.

"No," he whispered, opening his eyes again. I wanted to crawl into his lap and comfort him, and myself. It tormented me more knowing we both knew we were each other's mates and understood we couldn't complete the bond.

We would have been better to have lived in the dark a little longer. I'd thought I could walk away if he didn't understand what we were to each other. I wasn't sure I could now.

But I had to.

Why would the Fates do this?

Why would they hurt us like this?

Walking away would no doubt break something inside of

me and Cedrick. Already, even without the connection, I could see how he suffered inside like I was.

My bottom lip trembled. I bit down on it, but Cedrick saw, and he made a pained noise in the back of his throat. He started to reach for me but stopped himself, clenching his jaw.

"The room should be cleared by now," Kiered said, seeing his brother's conflict. "Shall we rest for the night and speak of matters on the morrow?"

"No," Cedrick started, his voice sounding hard. He straightened his back. To me it looked like the king was present, gone my destined mate who I couldn't have and who couldn't have me back. "We need to speak of other matters."

It pained me to say so, but he was right. So many other things were happening. "He's right." I nodded once. "We do, and first on the agenda would be if you knew who attacked us in the room. Second would be if we need to worry about Thera's father."

He leaned forward, elbows to his knees. It wasn't a posture I would expect from him. To me, Cedrick looked regal, and I would have thought he would also act that way always. Although, maybe he was treating us to his relaxed self and the way he was behind closed doors.

He clasped his hands together and stared down at them. "We have a traitor in our palace," he announced, then looked up to meet my gaze. I would have gotten lost in his gaze, but that was news no one who ruled would want to happen.

"Rallis?" I said.

Kiered snorted. Cedrick gave me a small smile. "You've been around him not long and you already suspect something?"

"He just seems that type of guy. No one can be that far up someone's ass without a reason. He either has a crush on you and you're lovers, or he wants to live up your butt so much so you don't suspect him of anything."

Cedrick's smile grew, while Kiered laughed loudly. "We're not lovers, and I don't believe he has a crush on me. We also think he's behind some things that have happened."

"What things?" Thorn asked.

I leaned back into Alex more and waited to hear the answer. I saw Cedrick notice my movement and was glad to see no jealousy in his expression or body.

"Little things. Mixed messages, undelivered messages. Tasks unfulfilled because he didn't agree with them. Thankfully, all have been mild where I haven't had to punish him. But lately it has been happening more frequently."

"Why haven't you confronted him?" Nate asked.

"We've been having someone follow him, hoping he will make a mistake and take us to whomever is pulling his strings."

"You don't believe he could be behind something bigger?" Ezra asked. He smirked, already knowing the answer.

"I can see you don't believe it even after questioning it. No, someone is leading him into annoying me or making me look a fool to my people."

"Maybe the two are connected," I mumbled more to myself in thought.

"What do you mean, love?" Asher asked.

I lifted my gaze and met Cedrick's. "Or maybe all of them are connected. As in Rallis, Thera and her father, then those men who were sent to attack us. They could all be following someone on the council. They're threatened by us. Trying to end the threat before it arrives, before we get into their territory. Which is also why we were set upon on the way here."

Cedrick slowly straightened. His eyes widened a little like it all clicked into place. "You're right. I hadn't seen it before because I thought nothing of the marriage arranged with Thera." I frowned. I couldn't believe he'd been set to marry that goddamn beautiful skank.

Well, she was dead now, and I smiled at the thought of it being me to kill her.

"Dove, that smile seems a little crazy. Bring it down a notch," Alex suggested. Nate snorted, Ezra chuckled, while Thorn and Asher smiled when I checked on them. Making sure my crazy wasn't scaring them, I guessed I was good since they all stayed where they were.

I looked back to Cedrick. His small smile said he'd guessed my train of thought and didn't mind.

At least, I hoped.

"As I said, I thought nothing of it because my father and hers were close friends."

"Isn't Therolidi, Thera's father, friends with someone on the council?" Kiered asked suddenly.

Cedrick stood and started pacing. "How could I have been so stupid? Yes, he is, but why would he plot to assassinate our father? It never meant he would be in power. The throne would always go to me."

"But he had Thera to try and steer you in ways he wanted," Ezra said.

"Yes, he did. But I wouldn't lead blindly. I hardly listened to her...." He froze. "Unless she was queen and I suddenly died, then everything would be in her control."

"How does Rallis play into this?" Asher asked.

Kiered laughed. "He's always been more in love with Thera than my brother."

"He's been helping them."

"Who did Thera's father, Therolidi, have involvement with on the council?" Nate asked.

"Jessica, at least I think that was the name I remembered mentioned."

Already I'd felt Alex, Nate, and Asher tense.

"She was in charge of our group when we worked for the council in their elite enforcers."

"You all worked for the council?" Cedrick asked.

Ezra rose his hand. "Not me. I was Paige's protector and teacher when she was first changed into a ghoul."

Thorn cleared his throat. "I was from the former ghoul queen's guards, sent out to meet with Paige after the queen's powers transferred to Paige."

"How is it that none of you won't go running back to the council with all this information about Paige? For all I know, one of you could be helping—"

"Don't," I clipped, cutting off Cedrick. "Before you say something you'll regret, don't say anything more against Alex, Asher, and Nate. They are bound to me. I know what they're feeling, I know they're true, and they want to take down the council with me."

"There is also the fact we became wanted men by the council as soon as we refused to do as they'd asked," Asher stated prickly. "I would never go against my mate. Never. Even if it meant ending my own life in the process."

"Asher," I whispered, reaching up to take his hand on my shoulder. "None of that talk. No one will be ending lives, because you all know I would follow you just to kick your ass."

Asher gazed down at me, his eyes softening. "I know, love."

"Dad would also kick your ass for upsetting us," Ezra said.

"Dad?" Kiered questioned.

"Who said Asher would end up in Hell?" I demanded. My men were good men. No one got to go to Hell if I had any say in it. They deserved to walk through the pearly white gates and high-five God.

"Love, I have done many things in life that I shouldn't have. I won't be seeing upstairs in my death."

"There's nothing wrong with Hell," Ezra huffed.

I patted him absently. "You have only sinned to protect those around you, I'm sure," I told Asher.

"Love, I'll be sure to go wherever you go. Nothing nor no one will keep me back."

I hummed my approval. "Good." Then I thought. "You only said that to shut me up."

"Never, love." Asher bent and kissed my forehead with his upturned lips. The guy was playing me, but I'd let it slide until it came down to the matter where I would fight tooth and nail to get Asher where he belonged. In Heaven.

"You know she won't drop it. She'll fight with God if she has to." Thorn smiled.

Asher chuckled, as did most of my mates, before saying, "Yes, I know."

"Let's get back to why you all think Hell is such a bad place. I never suffered." Ezra glared.

I leaned down and cupped his cheeks. "No one is dismissing Hell, honey. I love you. I love that's where you come from. I just want what's best out there for my mates, and I thought Hell might not have been it. However, as long as we're all together, I don't care where we end up." I kissed his nose. "Besides, it won't be for a long time, and I'm sure if it's soon and we do end up in Hell, your dad will send us back because we'll have driven him insane."

He grinned. "You're right."

A throat cleared. I gave Ezra a quick kiss and then sat back, looking to the elves.

Actually, right then, I wanted to take a "holy shit" moment. I was in front of elves. Elves. Real-life pointy-eared, tall, sword-wielding, arrow-fighting elves.

Yes, I knew there were other supernatural creatures. I was one. But it just hit me all of a sudden. I walked through a portal into another realm, a realm full of more different species. Dark and light ones. I'd even read there were trolls, leprechauns, and merpeople there.

If I had more time, I would explore, because it did seem this place went on forever. Their kingdom wasn't the only city nestled in Airrile, but from what I'd read, I knew it was the biggest.

I'd thought the human world had enough things that went bump in the night, but here was larger, and Cedrick had to deal with it all.

I was in awe of the elf.

I could never ask him to leave such a place for me.

Just like I knew he wouldn't ask me.

There I went, back to the sour feeling inside me because our choice to accept the bond and one another was taken out of our hands.

Then why was Cedrick chosen for me?

It didn't make sense.

"Are you saying Ezra is related to Lucifer? As in the devil? Satan?" Kiered asked. Cedrick and he stared down at us, paler than they had been.

"Yes." I grinned. "But don't worry, he won't interfere in anything unless he has to."

That didn't seem to reassure them.

"He's mellowed in age," Ezra added. "Thanks to my mom."

"That's true." I nodded.

"The devil. You know him?"

I waved a hand around. "It's a long story of sorts, and right now I know three of my mates who need to eat."

Nate grunted, and his stomach growled like it was a beast itself.

"Then come. We'll take the food back into your room and leave you to rest. I have a few people I need to speak with. They'll join the others in the dungeons, and I'll contact you when it's time for questioning."

I stood from the couch. "Sounds like a plan, and thank you for not arguing with me about going into the dungeons."

He glanced down at me as we walked out of his room side by side. His body heat warmed me all over, along with his eyes. "I don't agree, but I'm learning from watching that you would do it no matter what I say."

Laughter behind us, along with rattling of trays, sounded. I glared over my shoulder and then looked back up at Cedrick. "At least you're learning."

"One day I would like to hear the story about Lucifer though."

Butterflies took off in flight in my stomach. He'd said one day. I shouldn't have, but I did have hope.

CHAPTER FIFTY

I floated in the darkened sky, looking below to the dirt mound surrounded by woods. I watched and waited for something to happen, as if I expected a situation. And when I saw the dirt shift, little rocks and soil tumbling to the side, I knew what I was waiting for.

I knew it as well as the next breath I needed.

Dirty hands popped through the earth. They clawed out from the ground, digging their way free.

Fear clenched my stomach, despite knowing I shouldn't be scared.

The scene was surreal.

A head broke free next and tipped back. A growl shuddered through the area. Wild red eyes took in everything. It was a woman. Her light-colored hair was either blonde or white, but filthy from the muck. She pushed at the dirt and then leaped from the hole she'd been buried in. As she landed in a crouch, her eyes frantically darted this way and that. Her head tipped again, her nostrils flaring. She scented her surroundings.

Another growl rumbled from her, tore from her, the sound almost animalistic.

The dress covering her small frame was in tatters.

My stomach tightened when I saw her clutch at her own gut as she slowly stood, as if I could feel the hunger eating away at her.

The wind brushed through the area, her hair and dress swaying in the breeze. Suddenly, she spun right and crouched again. A low, humming rumble echoed out of her mud-caked mouth and into the woods.

Again, fear bombarded me.

The woman looked crazed. Her body tensed when we heard a branch break close by. Her upper lip pulled back in a snarl, a warning, and I felt mine doing the same.

Into the small clearing stepped a....

….

Wait….

What was happening?

I blinked rapidly and shook my head. This wasn't right. This was a dream… a dream I hadn't had in a long time.

What in the fuck was happening?

My body jolted as if shaken by something, and I landed on my hands and knees on the dirt ground. I lifted my head and drew in the scents around me. It didn't smell like the outdoors. Familiar scents rushed into me, but I couldn't remember what they were.

Suddenly, I was knocked to the floor. I rolled and then sat

up, flicking my hair out of my face. I glanced down and saw I wore the same nightie I had when I'd first crawled out of the ground. When I'd become a ghoul.

That was right... I was a ghoul.

I had strength. I could hear things from afar and yet... I couldn't hear anything at all.

Nothing was making a sound; it was as if I was deaf. There wasn't a sound of birds, people, or the wind rustling.

Nothing.

Fucking hell, where was I and what was going on?

I remembered... shit, what did I remember? That I was a ghoul, I dug myself out, but then nothing. Why?

I drew in another whiff. My chest ached like I had something jammed in there. I grabbed it and looked down. There wasn't anything there, or perhaps I couldn't *see* what the problem was. I screamed and dropped to my back, gripping my head at the severe stabbing pressure on my temples.

"Stop, stop, stop," I yelled.

Then it did.

Slowly, I opened my eyes and sat up. I was smart enough to know what I saw in front of me wasn't real. I wasn't actually in the woods at night. I was... after another intake of air, I sensed I was in a room. The air was clear, but stuffy.

Disoriented, I lay back on the ground. Coldness touched my back. It wasn't from dirt though, maybe concrete or metal.

Another breath in.

God, there were those scents that had me longing.

Were they people or food?

They didn't smell like food.

Pine, blood, a sweet spice like cinnamon, and—

"Roll" came from a deep, panicked voice through my mind.

Only I was too shocked hearing a voice in my head I didn't listen to its warning and something invisible smashed into my face. My nose cracked, blood gushing from it while I covered my face and yelled from the pain.

Jesus Christ, did a Mack truck hit me?

I sucked in a sharp breath as my nose healed. I lowered my hands and opened my eyes; they felt puffy, so I knew they'd swelled from the hit, whatever it had been.

How was I supposed to fight something invisible?

But that voice… it warned me. It also seemed like I'd heard it before; a part of me was telling me I had. Still, it felt new, but one I wanted to listen to. How was that possible?

Whatever was going on was fucked up.

Fear clutched my beating heart and twisted.

Something about my heart triggered my mind, but when I tried to grab that thought, it fled.

Heart, heart, heart, I chanted over and over.

Beating.

My eyes widened.

Shut the damn front door. My heart hadn't been beating when I'd crawled out of the ground. Why was it now? Did it mean I was human?

I pounded the ground with my fists in frustration.

"Move," sounded inside my mind, and that time I didn't hesitate. I was on my feet and running a couple of steps forward, spinning this way and that.

"What else?" I yelled into the still night sky. I gripped my head and whimpered as something clicked inside it, then disappeared. My heart raced at an onslaught of completeness. I felt as if a part of myself that had been missing was found. It didn't make sense, yet nothing had since I woke back in my dream.

"Paige, I'm sorry. I didn't want to complete this mind link, but I had to. You're safe now. It's time to wake up."

"Who are you?"

"What do you mean?" he demanded in a rough, sharp tone, one I sensed alarm in.

"I don't know you."

"Paige, I'm Cedrick Nelydriel, elf king to the realm Airrile."

"Sorry, buddy, it's not ringing any bells."

"What about Asher, Nate, Thorn, Alex, and Ezra?"

I had a little tingling of something, but it slipped away. *"No. Nothing. What's going on? Where am I?"*

"What surrounds you?"

"The woods where I had been buried after... wait, I don't know if I should be telling you this."

Silence, and I didn't like *not* hearing his voice. Panic twisted my insides. *"Cedrick?"* I called, twisting around in the darkened area. *"Cedrick?"* I yelled.

"I'm here, Paige."

The voice sounded so close. The sudden warmth at my back had me tensing. Slowly, I looked over my shoulder and then cried out, turning and stumbling away.

His hand grabbed mine before I fell to the ground. "Paige, relax. Please, I'm here to help you."

His touch and his voice helped me settle. It even spread nerves through my belly. He helped me stand and then slid his hand down my arm, causing me to shiver, to my hand where he held it. I lifted my gaze from our hands to see he was still staring down at them.

"Who are you?" I whispered.

He caught my eyes, and I sucked in some air at how beautiful he was. He smiled. "I already told you. Cedrick Nelydriel, I'm the—"

"Yes, yes. Elf king of such and such." I shook my head. "Who are you to me?"

His smile upped a notch. It had me wanting to lean into him. His head tilted to the side a little as he studied me.

"God, your hair is absolutely stunning, and those ears, I want to kiss them, touch them—"

He choked.

"Fuck. I said that aloud, didn't I?"

He shook his head, and it didn't go unnoticed how the tips of his ears and cheeks were pink. He licked his lips as if they were dry, and said, "No, you said that in your mind. Only, I'm able to hear it now."

Wait, what? "I'm sorry—what?"

Since we still held each other's hands, he used his other to reach up and tuck my hair behind my ear. His finger glided down from my temple to my cheek and chin; then he cupped the side of my neck.

"How opposed would he be if I kept his hands always on me?"

His eyes widened.

"Shit." I closed my eyes and dropped my head, so I didn't look at him. "Can we stop it?"

"We can learn to stop projecting."

"You're not projecting. It's only me."

His grin grew even more. "For that I'm grateful or else you would have punched me a few times."

I laughed and glanced up at him. "Really?" It shouldn't have, but it had me feeling better.

"Yes."

"Okay. Good." I nodded. He chuckled. "Now, can you tell me who you are to me?"

"Your mate."

"My mate? As in the Australian term, like, on ya cobber, I mean, on ya, mate? Buddy? Pal?"

He threw his head back and laughed. "No. Nothing like that, though I'm not even sure what you first said. What I mean is that you're my intended wife." My eyes sprang wide. He quickly added, "A couple who were fated to be with one another forever." I jerked my head back. He groaned. "I'm not explaining it right. We're bonded mates… at least mostly bonded. We're one step closer with the mind link we now have. Meaning we're touched in some way, but there is only one way for us to complete the bond, and that would be for us to… you see, we would have to… I mean that we're to…."

I searched his face, his was once again blushing, and then a part of my mind produced an image of us naked on the ground. "If we were to sleep with each other, we would completely be bonded?"

"Yes."

"And you want to do this here and now?"

He choked again. "No, no. Christ, woman, you say whatever you think, don't you?"

I smiled. "Yes. So then you come into this place—"

"Your mind."

"What?"

"You're stuck in your mind, Paige. You won't understand it right now, but someone in my realm locked you in your mind and tried to have you forget your other bonded men."

I stepped back in shock, my hands covering my belly. "I have more?" I yelled.

He gave a laugh until I glared. He sobered and then nodded. "Yes. Asher, Thorn, Alex, Nate, and Ezra."

I leaned toward him and whispered, "Am I a slut?"

His lips thinned, and he shook his head. "No," he said darkly.

"Huh, he doesn't like me saying that about myself."

He stepped closer. "No, I don't. You're loved, cherished, and important to all of us. We've all lived a long life, Paige. Having you as our bonded mate completes us. We feel full, at peace, happy, and even loved. Not all have more than one partner. But when it comes to someone special like yourself, it's as it's meant to be. Fate put us all together for a reason. Whatever it is, I'm delighted to be a part of it. Your other men are... they're great men, and together, we're whole. A family."

I didn't know what to think or understand completely how I felt because there were so many emotions rolling around inside me. My mind spun, and my hands shook. Honestly, how he described the connection we shared sounded amazing, wonderful even. Hell, I wanted it, I did, and I knew my... mates would all be different like myself because no human could understand something like this.

"There's no jealousy among anyone?"

He blushed *again*. "No."

I narrowed my gaze. "You're leaving something out."

"It doesn't matter. You'll remember everything as soon as you're out of here."

I placed my hands on my hips. "Cedrick."

He ground his teeth together. "As far as I know, they share one another as well."

"Oh... well, that's... something I wouldn't mind seeing."

Cedrick groaned, rubbing a hand over his face.

"Wait, you said as far as you knew. Why wouldn't you know

if you're mine also?" I paused at that, not liking he wasn't involved. *"God, it all sounds so weird. I have five, no six, husbands... men. Six. The sex must be outstanding."*

He snorted, coughed to cover a surprised laugh, and then shook his head. He ran a hand over the back of his neck as he sighed. "I'm new. We only met yesterday."

"And I wanted to be with you then?" I threw up my hands in the air. "Jesus, I must be—"

"Do not say anything bad about yourself," he warned, his hands clenched at his sides. "In our worlds, it's different. The Fates have a play in our lives, in our mates. Desire, need, and hope fill us once we find each other and a small connection is made. However, not all races know that what you have in front of you is an intended mate. People often mistake it for lust. Though, some do, like I did with you. From what I'd heard, you didn't know about me until I'd used my power and your ghoul side reacted to it."

"So it, *this*, the connection, means a lot."

"It means everything, which is why it pains me that we can't be together—"

"Why?" I demanded.

"You will know all of this when we're out."

Biting my bottom lip, I nodded. Even though I wanted to know as the thought of him not wanting me swirled through my brain, but his words said the contrary. He thought highly of a mate, so there had to be a good reason why we couldn't be together.

"All right. How do we get out?"

"A kiss," he stated.

A giggle escaped. Then I cackled so much I had tears running down my cheeks. I slapped my hand to my leg as I bent over still laughing. I gasped, "A kiss." I shook my head. "How very princess-y."

"Pardon?" Cedrick asked, his face stoic.

I straightened, finally calm enough. "You know… a kiss from a prince always rescues the princess. I just never knew it would be from my own mind." I snorted out another laugh. "Why a kiss? How will that help me?"

"I'll have to drag your mind from this point in time that you're stuck in. There's a chance it will hurt. A kiss from a mate is distracting and could help with any pain you may face."

"Oh," I said quietly. I hated pain. I even considered not having a child since giving birth scared the hell out of me. I mean, I loved my niece and nephew…. Something tickled a part of my mind again. Something about my family. I lifted my gaze. "Is my family okay?"

He seemed confused, the pinch to his brows told me so, before he said, "Sorry?"

"My family… you know what, never mind. You're sure I'll remember everything once you drag me out?"

"Yes." He nodded once.

"Good. Let's do this." Only it was then I thought of something. "Hang on, if our minds are in here, where are our bodies? Will we be waking into danger?"

Cedrick shook his head. "The men and I disposed of the danger. It's safe to leave, and our bodies should be in the old medical wing. Where we found you."

If I was safe, it meant I had time for another question, right? "What happened to me?"

He took my hand, and I eagerly held onto his. His jaw clenched suddenly. He seemed angry.

Did I want to know why?

Yes, I had to. I didn't hide.

"You may not understand everything right now, but I'll try. You and the other men were attacked. We thought it was to kill you all under the council orders. However, it seemed they were sent to drug you instead. It took some time, but you all fell asleep, and that was when they came in to get you."

The council wanted me dead? Me and my men? Why? What had we done? And what damn council?

"You're right. I don't understand a lot. So maybe it's best we do get out of here."

"Of course. Wrap your arms around my neck." I did, and he lifted me so we were eye to eye. "I'm sorry if this causes you pain."

I didn't answer right away; I got lost in his angelic features. How could one elf be so good-looking? I wanted to know everything about him, and I couldn't wait to remember my other men. Excitement had my stomach in knots.

I gave Cedrick a small smile. "I'm sure you'll be able to take my mind off it."

"It will be my honor to try, my beautiful Paige." Slowly, so the tingle in my groin intensified, he leaned in while staring into my eyes. His were warm and full of desire, and I knew mine burned for him. I couldn't wait to taste him.

He brushed his lips against mine teasingly. Feeling impatient, I growled under my breath and felt his lips pull up as he pressed them against the corner of my mouth.

"I do not like that this will be our first kiss," Cedrick admitted against my cheek.

"We'll have to make up for it then."

He let out a breath, maybe a little laugh. He nipped at my neck. "I will do my best."

I panted the words, "I have a feeling I'll like your best."

He lifted his head, and before he could say more, I pressed my lips against his. He froze for a second, probably worried about the pain, until I tightened my hold around his neck and hooked my legs around his waist. His hands slapped down on my bottom and he squeezed.

"Yes, dear God, yes."

"Cedrick will do, beautiful. I'm no God."

I pulled back quickly, swearing again. "No reading my mind, mister."

"I can't help it. You're projecting. Not that I mind at all." He smirked. "Shall we try again?"

"Yes," I answered a little too quickly.

That time he didn't smile; instead, he dipped in and claimed my lips like he owned them. The kiss was hot, heavy, and so delicious. I moaned into his mouth, opening up to his tongue that glided along my bottom lip. Hell, he tasted of cherries, chocolates, and whiskey. How was that possible?

All I knew was that I wanted more. I wanted all of him.

Until... I whimpered into his mouth. It felt as if my brain was being pulled and pushed from my head without an actual opening. My head throbbed as if someone was stabbing me over and over. I wanted to scream, to cry out, but I also didn't want to lose the connection I had with Cedrick. He kept me grounded. He kept me whole. If I let go of him, I would lose myself.

"Nearly done."

I couldn't reply because the pain intensified. I was sure my brain was on fire, sizzling away under my skull. A scream got through my block. I knew it by the way Cedrick twitched.

"I'm okay." I tried to reassure him, but even in my head I sounded weak.

The pain grew again. Like a knife being drilled into my eyes and slowly the blade was being dragged up over my forehead and skull, right to the back.

I couldn't stop it. I had to let it out.

Pulling back from the kiss, I gripped my head and screamed. I dropped back, but nothing around me registered beyond the pain.

Then it was as if a switch was turned off and the pain stopped.

I panted out unnecessary breaths. My heart was erratic in my chest. I picked up panicked voices but couldn't open my eyes.

"Paige, love. We're here. You're okay." *Asher.*

"You're out, beautiful. You're free." *Cedrick.*

"We're right here, sweetheart. We're not leaving you." *Thorn.*

"Do you feel my hand, dove? Can you feel it?" *Alex.*

"Let her relax. Let her get herself together. Paige, it's fine. Relax, angel." *Nate.*

"Yes, rest if you need to, mi corazón." *Ezra.*

My men were there. *My* men. My bonded mates.

Nate, Asher, Alex, Thorn, Ezra, and even Cedrick.

I remembered them.

God, how could I have forgotten them?

My chest constricted painfully. If I'd been stuck in my mind forever, I wouldn't have had them. I wouldn't have remembered them and wouldn't have known what I was missing out on. Or how much love I would have lost. It hurt knowing that could have happened. Although right then, it quickly switched to anger.

I cleared my healing throat. I must have screamed so much I'd hurt it. "W-Who did this?"

"Thera's father. Do you remember her? Do you remember us?" Thorn asked. He glanced to Cedrick. "We were told you didn't know who we were."

I nodded as another pang of hurt and anger twisted inside me. "I hadn't. All of you were wiped away from my mind," I whispered and then smiled. "I remember you all now though." Opening my eyes, tears filled them. I saw all of them hovered over me in different ways so they could fit as I lay on what felt like a cold metal table. I looked from one to another and then over again. My bottom lip trembled. "He took you all away from me." A sob caught, and Nate was the first to pull me into his arms and off the table. He took a couple of steps and sat us on a couch. I curled into his lap, wrapping my arms around his waist while wondering why a couch was placed in a room that looked like something out of a doctor's office, only a nightmare kind.

The room was all white and silver, but a lot of the silver on the desk, table, chairs, and cabinets had corroded with rust. I shivered from the sight and from the thought of being in there unconscious, prone on the filthy metal table.

I scented Alex at my back, rubbing a hand up and down it. Ezra was to my side, pressing into me and kissing my shoulder. Without looking, I knew Thorn, Asher, and Cedrick would be standing around us, watching, listening, and guarding.

After composing myself, I looked up and met Cedrick's gaze first. "Did he do this because of what I'd done to Thera?"

That I could understand. He took away what meant the most to me, like I had done with him by taking his daughter.

Cedrick shook his head. "Let's get somewhere comfortable and we'll explain what happened."

Nate grunted. He must have agreed because he stood with me in his arms and walked us from the room. I rested my head on his shoulder and then felt a hand on my shoulder and one on my leg. Alex and Ezra. Both needed comfort from touch as much as Nate and I did. I was sure my other men did as well, but they would be willing to wait and let Nate, Alex, and Ezra get their fill first. It reminded me again of how perfectly we worked together.

CHAPTER FIFTY-ONE

NATE

Having her in my arms wasn't enough. My wolf and I wanted to be buried inside her, marking her with our scent all over again. The fear of waking without her in our room would live with me for a fucking long time, and it'd take a while until I could let her out of my sight. Even if it was with one of our men. My skin crawled at the thought of leaving her alone and having something happen to her.

As we walked down the hall, my mind took me back to the last few hours.

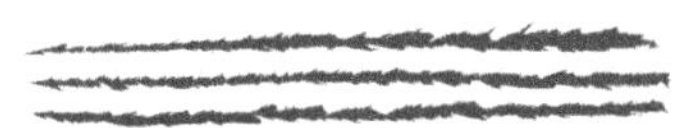

My head was knocked to the side. "Wake up" was yelled, so close to my face that the warm breath washed over my skin. Groaning, I clutched my head and sat slowly.

"Kiered?" someone asked, and I opened my eyes to see Cedrick kneeling in front of me, but he was looking over at his brother who knelt over Ezra. Asher and Thorn were helping Alex sit from his spot on the bed, while I was on the floor.

"What the fuck, man?" I asked, my throat dry and scratchy. I rubbed at my cheek; it still hurt like a bitch from his hit.

"Where is she?" Cedrick demanded.

My mind felt foggy as if it was stuffed in Jell-O. "What are you talking about?"

"Where is Paige?"

My mind spun, locked on his words, and my heart beat hard in my chest as I quickly stood in search for her. Only I stumbled a little, blinking rapidly as I sucked in a deep inhale. Her scent was in the room, but fainter than it should have been. I closed my eyes and paid more attention to my hearing. The people around me quieted as if sensing what I was doing. I could hear scuffling in the floorboards, mites or some type of bugs. Muffled sounds came from down the hall, but nothing right outside or too close.

I couldn't scent or hear her close by.

I breathed deeply through my nose and clenched my hands.

"Nate," Asher said softly. "We'll find her."

I shook my head roughly and lifted my upper lip off my teeth in a silent snarl.

"Nate, hold your shit in until we have all the damn information," Thorn demanded.

My skin rippled over my body. My teeth lengthened, as did

my claws. Fur sprouted over my face. It grew longer on my body.

"Jesus, is he bigger than usual?" someone muttered.

I lifted my head back and howled into the room.

"Nate," Alex called. His scent grew close until he was right in front of me. Then Asher was there, Thorn, and Ezra. They surrounded me. They belonged to me, but our bonded female, our Paige, wasn't there.

Someone had taken her.

Someone would pay.

"Calm down. Think, talk, then hunt," Ezra said. He gripped my face in his hands and shook my head slightly. "Think, talk, then hunt," he repeated.

"Kill," we growled out harshly.

"Yes," Ezra bit out in his own growl, his eyes glowing.

I pulled the wolf back, even when he fought me for control. I dragged him back down inside me and held him tight. *Soon*, I promised him.

"We need answers now," I stated.

"And we'll find them." Asher nodded. We all looked to Cedrick.

"This is what I know. All of you came back in here to rest, and I went to speak with Therolidi regarding his daughter, but he wasn't at his home. I ran into Rallis though. He's in the dungeon with the other guards, who were rousing. We came here to get you all and found you passed out."

"How were we knocked out?" Ezra questioned. Yeah, he was kind of new, but he'd been a part of this from the start, even as his hellhound, so it was easy to be comfortable with him. Cedrick, even though I knew Paige and he were connected, they weren't bonded fully yet, so I wasn't ready to trust everything he said. Although, he looked as stricken as the rest of us with the loss of Paige.

He ran a hand through his hair and looked around the room, like he was searching for something. "It doesn't make sense."

"What?" I demanded harshly, my wolf riding my tone.

Ezra and Alex faced Cedrick, but they both reached back to lay a hand on me. Alex at my outer thigh and Ezra curled his hand around my wrist. Their contact, along with Asher's on my neck and Thorn's on my shoulder, helped ground me more.

Fuck me, but I loved my pack.

However, the most important part was missing.

We had to get her back.

A sad whimper escaped me, feeling her loss hit me once more. Our mates' fingers rubbed at my skin, calming me. We hadn't even claimed one, the hound, but he was still ours. I knew it and the wolf did also. The time would come, but it wouldn't be until Paige was back in our arms.

"How did this happen? None of you would just fall into slumber and risk your mate."

"No, we wouldn't," Asher agreed. "Especially since a lot of us need very little sleep to begin with."

"Then it happened to us without us knowing," Alex said more to himself as he stared at the floor in thought. He lifted his gaze and turned to see all of us in the room. "The food?"

I shook my head. "Not everyone ate."

"The fight," Kiered said softly. We all looked to him behind Cedrick. He stepped closer. "Look on yourself to see if you can find a mark of some type."

"Fucking hell, the fight was a setup—not to kill Paige or us, but to put us to sleep to get to her," I said while searching my body.

"There," Thorn said. His hands went to my lower back. I kept still as everyone crowded around me. Fingers ran over my skin. "It looks like a goddamn freckle, but it's not." I felt a fast, sharp prick of pain and then turned as Thorn held up what did look like a freckle.

"Motherfucker. How did they get that on me without me knowing?"

"Distraction," Asher said as he picked something off his arm near his elbow. "They used the fight to see if they could take her on their own, or if that failed, they drugged us. We wouldn't have felt it because we were getting knocked around at the time."

"Jesus Christ," I yelled. "We need to find her." I pulled Ezra around since he hadn't found his and dragged his tee from his body. I found it on his hip and pulled it free.

"Who deals with this type of magic? A magic I hadn't sensed before," Alex asked, glancing down at his in his hand.

Cedrick stepped closer to him. I grabbed Alex and Ezra and pulled them behind me, holding out my own for him to look at. I ignored Ezra's snort and Alex's grumble. Cedrick didn't say anything about my mistrust of him and held his hand above mine where the device was.

He shook his head. "Any one of my people who has the power to control earth magic. I can sense the herbs, dirt, and leaves within it myself. Used with the correct wording, which they obviously had, it all becomes a powerful sleeping spell."

"Can you do it, Alex?" Asher asked.

I caught Alex roll his eyes before looking over his shoulder to Asher. "Yes, of course."

"Do what?" Kiered asked.

"Trace where the spell was cast," Alex said as his power filled the room. His eyes closed but not before I saw them change to purple. His lips moved with his own spell. The window suddenly opened with a bang, causing a few of us to jump, and I wouldn't admit I was one. A breeze blew in and swirled around Alex.

He then smiled.

"I have a picture in my mind. A medical ward, but it looks run-down. It's dark, but a man with shoulder-length, dark brown hair and eyes cast the spell from there. It's within the walls of this castle."

"Merde," Cedrick whispered. He spun to his brother. "Right under my nose." His jaw clenched. The floor beneath us shook as his eyes glowed brighter. "Right under my nose." He looked to Alex with intense anger in his eyes. I wanted to step in front of Alex again, but I didn't. Mainly because Alex placed his hand on my arm in a warning not to. "Can you teleport?"

"Yes."

"Using that picture in your mind?"

"Yes, and with two people."

Cedrick nodded. "I'll take the wolf and hellhound."

My wolf liked being called instead of my actual fucking name; it annoyed me though.

"Let's go," Alex said, and then he disappeared with Asher and Thorn. Cedrick glided quickly to my side and swept Ezra up in one arm on the way to me. As soon as his arm wound around my waist, everything disappeared around me. My head spun for a second, and then my feet jarred when I landed on new flooring, we arrived shortly after Alex, Thorn, and Asher.

"Therolidi, step away from her," Cedrick demanded in a low, cold, and hard tone.

I lifted my gaze and growled. My wolf was already prowling

close to the surface. Especially when I saw Paige unconscious on a metal table and a man standing over her with a knife to her neck.

"Where is Thera?" Therolidi asked in a mild tone and with a smirk I wanted to wipe off his face. He glanced to Ezra and me as we both growled. "Calm, beasts. I've already told the mage not to use any magic, and the vampire, if he so much as moves a hair, I'll cut her head off."

I sensed Alex, Asher, and Thorn close, but I didn't dare look toward them and take my eyes off the threat.

"Move the fuck away from her, and we'll think about letting you live," I snarled.

The motherfucker laughed. "I have a knife to her throat. None of you can tell me what to do."

"Why do you want her?"

He scoffed. "I don't. The council does, and I want her out of the way."

I felt Cedrick tense behind me. "You knew she was my bride."

"The whole kingdom knows, you foolish boy. Everyone feels the pull you have for each other."

"So you wanted her gone for your daughter to step back in?" Thorn guessed.

"My daughter would have eventually won his heart, but she wouldn't with this thing in the picture." He sneered down at Paige like she was dog shit under his foot.

My body stiffened when I felt a wave of something come off Cedrick. Christ, it warmed me. I rolled my head and then lunged when Therolidi punched Paige in the face.

"Do not move," he roared. Everyone froze. I knew the others had moved too. I could see more of them from the corner of my eyes. Asher's gaze caught mine, then moved behind me to Cedrick. I dropped my gaze to his fingers. He shifted them slightly.

Be ready, they told me.

"What does the council want her for?"

Therolidi laughed. "What does the council always want? Money, but more importantly, power. They believe they can get that from her."

Fucking stupid mongrels.

They'd never learn. As soon as we got Paige out of this and walked into their comfortable world, or what they thought was comfortable, they would soon learn they weren't safe behind their compound doors.

"Now, where's my daughter?"

"Dead," Cedrick announced, then yelled. "Now!"

Paige's body suddenly rolled. If it hadn't been for Asher flashing forward to grab her, she would have crashed to the ground. I dove over the table with Ezra at my side, but Therolidi, by Alex's magic, was lifted into the air and slammed into the roof with such force bones broke. The ground shook. Thorn shoved the table toward Asher. He placed Paige back on it and held onto her and the table as the floor, fucking *concrete* floor, split open. Ezra tackled me and we rolled out of the way.

Therolidi's scream of horror had both of us glancing up to see his arms being torn by an invisible force from his body.

"No one touches our mate," Alex clipped, his usual sweet, soft voice gone. The powerful mage stood in his place as his lips moved once more and blood poured from Therolidi's thighs while the bottom of his legs dropped to the ground.

"What a damn sight," Ezra whispered, and I could hear the awe in his voice. Shit, pride came out of me in waves. Our Alex was not to be reckoned with. Only now wasn't the time to get a fucking hard-on over it. I snorted when I caught Ezra adjust himself.

"Alex, bury him and let him suffocate," Cedrick demanded. His hands and legs were spread wide, and I realized he'd been the one to open the floor in the room. Alex nodded. He lowered a whimpering, crying elf into the ground, and as he begged for his life, Cedrick closed the hole over him. He sealed it and set the room back to as it had been, as if nothing had happened in the first place.

"We could have questioned him some more," Thorn announced in the quiet room.

"And have him hurt her more?" Cedrick asked.

"No, I just meant after we'd captured him."

"I wasn't in the mood to have a conversation," Alex said, clenching his jaw.

I strode over to him and brought him into my arms. "She's safe now," I told him. He sighed, relaxed a little, and leaned into me. *She's safe now*, I reminded myself and my wolf. Though we weren't happy just yet, not until she was awake and yelling at us or giving us the finger for something. Still, I had the need to reassure Alex. I didn't like to see him so serious when his nature was never like that.

Ezra approached and pressed into Alex's back, nipping at his neck. "That was totally badass."

Alex let out a surprised laugh. "Don't," he said a second later.

"Well, it was."

Alex lifted his head and turned enough to kiss Ezra's cheek. "Thank you, both of you. I'm better now."

"Good," I grunted. I still rubbed my hand up and down his

back as I looked to the others. "Now, why the fuck hasn't she woken yet and how did her body roll off the damn table?"

"I believe Therolidi has locked her in her mind to be able to transport her."

"Locked her in her mind?" Thorn questioned. "But she has strong mental shields. She blocks us all the time when she doesn't want us knowing what she's feeling."

"Our powers over the mind are stronger, especially when that someone is asleep and doesn't realize their mind is being messed with."

"Fuck," I barked. "Fix her," I ordered, and then added, "It still doesn't explain how she moved."

"Cedrick made a mind link with her," Kiered announced.

"And that's supposed to explain it how?" I asked.

"I reached in and spoke with her. If you wait one moment, I will do it again." He closed his eyes. I didn't like when his brows pinched or his lips thinned. He opened his eyes. "She's been locked on a loop on the night she woke from the grave she dug her way out of. She doesn't know any of you or even me."

"What the fuck?" I yelled, then curled Alex into me more when I felt him tense. Ezra moved closer into Alex's side as well.

"Can you help her?" Asher asked.

"I should be able to, but it may cause her pain."

I winced at the thought of Paige in any pain.

"If I know Paige correctly, she'll want help to remember everything," I said.

Cedrick nodded.

"But what do you mean you've made a mind link with Paige?" Ezra asked.

"Our minds will always be able to reach one another's, and

we're able to speak telepathically," he said. "She's calling for me. I must go. I don't want her to worry more than she is."

"You're keeping out something." I glared.

Cedrick sighed. "It is one step closer to having our bond formed. I shouldn't have made it since we are unable to be with one another, but I had to."

"That's how she rolled out of the way," Alex said.

Cedrick nodded.

Well, crap. I couldn't dislike the guy for protecting her.

"Kiered, pull over that table," Cedrick ordered. His brother did, and Cedrick climbed on top of it. He lay back. "I will do everything in my power to bring her back with little to no pain."

Thorn rested a hand on his arm. "Thank you." Asher nodded, as did Alex, while Ezra gave him a wink.

I sucked it up, since I was grateful for his help and now the wolf and I knew he'd protected her. I rubbed at the back of my neck and said, "Yeah, thanks. You'd make a good mate for her." And he would, even if I hated admitting it. But the extra protection for her would be good. Plus, he was okay-looking, I supposed.

"Thank you. All of you," he said with a smile and then closed his eyes.

"Wait," Paige called out. She forcefully twisted in my arms so hard I had to place her on her feet. Only I didn't release her altogether; my hands went to her waist. She pointed to another room. "What's in there?" she asked Cedrick.

He glanced to his brother and then back again. "Another room."

Paige shook her head. She took a step closer and rested her hand to the door. "It… I don't know, doesn't feel right, but I feel a need to go in here."

Cedrick's eyes glowed brightly. The ground moved a little, and then he was right next to Paige, touching the door. "Yes, I feel it now that you've pointed it out. I wouldn't have if you didn't say anything."

I didn't have a fucking clue what they were talking about because I couldn't sense shit. All I knew was that I wanted to get out of this freaky hallway from the medical wing of doom.

Kiered joined in. "Someone blocked this room from anyone being able to hear or feel anything from within it."

Cedrick snarled, "More of Therolidi's tricks."

"You elf lot sure do love mind games and illusions."

Cedrick straightened and waved his hand in front of him. The door and walls wavered revealing, *oh fucking wow*, another door. Only this one was more rotten than the rest down in this dingy, stinky-as-hell place.

Kiered reached for the handle, but then his body shook violently.

"Brother," Cedrick cried.

Paige grabbed Cedrick's arm when Alex yelled, "Don't touch him." Alex stepped forward. His eyes glowed, his lips moved, and Kiered suddenly stilled and his hand dropped away. Alex floated him down to the floor. Cedrick dropped to his brother's side.

"Merde, that hurt," Kiered muttered.

"You're all right?"

"Yes, brother. I should have been more careful, but it

wouldn't release me. It's lucky you have a strong mage in your bonded group."

"It is," Cedrick said. He turned and took Alex's hand, causing Alex to blush tomato red, and lay his forehead against it before kissing his skin. "Thank you."

"Ah, yeah, um, no problem," Alex mumbled.

An unease filled me. He hadn't claimed Alex and was touching him.

I wanted to rip his hand off and my wolf agreed. But a part of me, for once, held back since I knew he was meant to be in our group, but mainly because he'd helped Paige when we couldn't. Logically, we knew we needed him. It still didn't stop me from reaching out, taking Alex's wrist, and pulling his hand from Cedrick's grasp.

Kiered chuckled. "The possessive wolf comes out."

Cedrick smiled and helped his brother up from the floor.

Paige giggled. She stepped close and patted my chest. "He's just a playful puppy really."

I growled low and nipped at her. She moved back, laughing.

"Yeah, playful." Ezra snorted.

"Can we get back to the damn door issue?" I asked. Alex twisted his wrist in my hand and slid it up to hold my hand instead.

"It's unlocked now," Alex said.

"Thank you once more." Cedrick nodded. I didn't know if he realized himself, but his eyes slid over Alex in appreciation. I stopped from taking his eyeballs and let him look since he wasn't touching. Besides, Alex was easy on the eyes. Fuck it, all of them were.

Goddamn good-looking mates.

I had to reason with the wolf that we wouldn't kill everyone who looked at them like they wanted to fuck them, despite us hating it.

Cedrick, proving he was an okay guy again, trusted Alex's words and reached for the handle. He twisted and pushed, and it opened wide.

A pained noise ripped from within him and Kiered.

"Mother," Cedrick whispered.

Holy fuck.

The woman, chained to a chair with tubes running all up her arms that were hooked up to some type of machine, didn't lift her head. I wasn't even sure she was alive. Her body looked sunken in. No fat remained on any inch of her. Fuck, she looked like a skeleton.

Cedrick and Kiered raced into the room, one on each side of their mother. They reached out, pulled their hands back, and then reached out again. Kiered rested a hand to her bony shoulder while Cedrick slowly lifted their mother's head. She showed no response.

Paige moved in. I wanted to grab her and drag her back out because I didn't like the fucking feel of the room. As soon as the door had opened, my skin crawled.

"Paige," I called.

Of course the infuriating woman ignored me. Hadn't she been through enough? If this was another fucking trick, I would kill people.

I stepped in after her and felt Alex behind me. I glanced over my shoulder to see Asher, Ezra, and Thorn had also followed. We looked around the room for any type of trap or threat. When I couldn't see or sense anything, I focused back on Paige.

She had her fingers against the woman's neck. "She's alive, but her pulse is very weak."

"Fuck, Cedrick. Fuck," Kiered whispered.

"Are you sure this isn't a trick?" Asher asked.

Cedrick nodded.

"You've never mentioned her before," Thorn said. "Are you sure this is her?"

Tears pooled in his eyes and his brother's. Cedrick clenched his jaw. "Yes, it's her. God, it's her."

Asher and Thorn shared a look. I knew that look. It was one that said we weren't sure to trust this. However, the brothers were adamant that it was their mother. Kiered kept whispering into her ear that they were there and she was safe.

"Do you know what this is?" I asked.

Cedrick shook his head. "Kiered, go and get Yeno, Grandith, and Juri. They'll be able to help her."

Kiered nodded once and disappeared from the room instantly.

"Who are they?" Paige asked.

"They never confirmed it, but they were her intended."

"But your father…."

Cedrick shook his head, gazing sadly down at his mother. "Mother's parents, the former king and queen, believed it best, like my father had, to set up an arranged marriage for business purposes. Yeno, Grandith, and Juri were mother's guards."

Paige went around the chair and curled her arm around Cedrick's waist. She looked up at him, and he stared down. When Cedrick nodded, I knew they'd been having a conversation within their minds.

Why did a sudden pang of sadness for the guy hit me?

Hell, my wolf even whimpered a little.

Maybe it was because Cedrick had been through a fucking lot.

It brought up memories of my own fucked-up life before I worked with the elite force. I'd been with a drunk dad who'd changed my mother into a werewolf without her consent, and then she lived through her days stuck in half form. Not that it stopped my motherfucking father from screwing her to conceive me. She ended her life when I was five, leaving me stuck with him until I killed him.

A hand to my back had my body jolting. Growling, I spun to Paige, who stood there with a pinch to her brows. Worried for me. Christ, I didn't lock down my emotions enough.

"I'm fine," I clipped, crossing my arms over my chest.

"Okay," she whispered. She got to her tippy-toes, and even then, I had to bend a little so she could place a peck on my lips. "I don't believe you, but I'll get it out of you later."

I scoffed. She rolled her eyes and went back to Cedrick. Shit, even his eyes looked darker in concern for me. Made me feel like a dick for getting lost in my head while he was dealing with finding his mom like this. I nodded once at him, letting him know I was fine. Thankfully he turned back to his mother where Alex stood on the other side using his magic to put her in a trance while he gently removed all the shit she was hooked up with. The needles and bounds.

When the last strap was free, along with yet another needle, the woman let out a gasp. She started to droop forward, but Cedrick caught her and supported her back against the chair.

"Mother? Mother, it's Cedrick."

She moaned and shook her head.

"Mother?"

Four forms appeared behind the chair. One was Kiered, so the others must have been the men Cedrick wanted there. As soon as they appeared, they cried out and surrounded the woman, all of them speaking at once, saying different things.

All of them were also crying.

"Paige," I called. She looked over at me, her own eyes filled with tears. "Maybe we should step out?" I knew if I was them, I would want my privacy.

She nodded. Turning, I started for the door and knew the others would follow. I itched for answers, but they would wait. What I longed for most was to have my pack surrounding me.

In the hall, and once the door was closed, I ordered, "Here, please." Paige was the first in my arms. She pressed in, and I heard her letting go, crying. Alex and Ezra were on each side of her, wrapping us up at my front while Asher and Thorn curled around my back.

This was what I needed. To feel them all, to know they were safe.

I was sure I wasn't the only one needing it.

CHAPTER FIFTY-TWO

The door to the new room Cedrick supplied burst open, and a very pissed off Xi entered. "Did no one think to wake me from my slumber?"

Oh shit.

"He must have been drugged earlier than us for him to sleep through the fight," Asher mused. The room filled with more tension.

"Whoever did it saw him as more of a threat than us," Ezra said, sounding annoyed. "That pisses me off. I'm damned threatening."

Since he was close from where I paced, I patted his arm. "Yes, you are."

He glared at me, so I leaned in and kissed him quickly. As I pulled back, my hellhound was back to smiling.

"What is this fight? And who drugged me?" Xi demanded, pulling swords from his back. I was sure I hadn't seen the hilts there before. Were they magical?

Ezra rolled his eyes. "Relax, Grandpa, the fight is done, and the drugs have worn off. Hmm, maybe I need some of those drugs when he gets on my nerves."

"Ezra," Xi growled.

Ezra batted his eyelashes. "Yes, Xi?"

Laughing, I slapped Ezra's stomach. "Stop goading him or I'll let him eat you."

"I could eat you," he said low with a wink.

I gasped. "Oh my God, you didn't just say that."

He threw up his hands. "I can't help it. Things like that just come out with you."

It was lucky I found him cute and silly.

"Stop around anyone but us or there won't be any action at all," I warned. He used a finger and a thumb to zip his lips with an invisible zipper. Nate snorted. I whirled around. "What does *that* snort mean?"

He smirked. "Like you could hold off from having sex."

"I can and I will if that's what you want," I said with a glare and my hands on my hips. Okay, I probably couldn't when they drove me into a frenzy of desire all the time. Even just standing there eating a cookie, I wanted to jump his bones because he was damn hot. Bastard.

"Nate, shut it," Thorn scolded. Ha, at least he knew I would try to keep myself from sex and he didn't want those few days I would last to happen.

"May we please get back to what the fuck happened?" Xi roared. I'd never heard him say so much. It told me he was at the end of his leash in patience.

"Sorry, Xi," I started, and then replayed what had occurred in the last few hours or so.

At the end, Xi embedded his swords into the floor, crossed his arms, and said, "I do not like this place. It gives me the heebie-jeebies. Too many tricks and illusions. We need to leave at once."

Ezra gaped at him. "Did you just say heebie-jeebies?" He looked to Alex and asked, "Did he just say heebie-jeebies?" A smiling Alex nodded.

Xi ignored him and crossed his arms over his chest. "What is this new mess with the mother of your new mate?"

"Well, he's not my full mate just yet," I said. He stared me down blankly. "Anyway, we're not sure. They're seeing to her in another room and we're all praying she lives for their sake."

"She does seem loved," Alex said.

I nodded. "Yes, she does." It had me wondering for the millionth time what had happened. "I guess we'll get answers eventually."

"I still say we should leave," Xi said.

"I know you do, Xi, but I can't until I know everything will be okay," I told him. I wouldn't just up and leave because Xi was worried without saying anything to Cedrick. I had a feeling that even if I tried, my whole self would revolt in some way.

"At least we don't need to question the survivors," Alex said. "We know everything. They were Therolidi's minions sent to kill or drug us, and we know Therolidi wanted to hand Paige over to the council, our old boss in fact, since they were chummy. What's left for us to know?" He shrugged.

"Then we kill them," I suggested.

Nate snorted, then smirked. Asher and Alex had a small smile, while Ezra was all-out grinning. It was Thorn who approached me and said, "Yes, our little bloodthirsty mate. We'll kill them." He grinned and spun me to hug me from behind. He laid a kiss on my shoulder. "I do love how your mind works."

Hell, I wanted to preen at his compliment, but I wasn't sure if that would look psycho since I had just mentioned murder. So I simply tilted my head to the side and puckered my lips. Chuckling, Thorn bent and pressed his mouth against mine.

Xi growled in the back of his throat, bringing my attention back to him. "Since I missed the fight, I think I have the right to kill them."

Damn. If I said no, I was sure he would get his panties in a twist. Even though I was in the mood to take some anger out on the mongrels, I would find another way to relieve some tension.

"Okay, Xi, and see if you find out anything new that we haven't told you."

He bowed, picked up his swords, and stormed from the room.

"It was a good choice, love. Xi lives by honor, and he would have struggled not being here for you."

I nodded at Asher. "I guessed as much. Plus, I didn't want a pouting Xi around."

Ezra laughed. "I second that."

"However, now I have all this energy and I don't know how I should get rid of it. I also have a need for some entertainment." I glanced over my shoulder to Thorn. "Would we have time?"

His eyes darkened as he scraped his bottom lip with his top teeth. "I'm sure we would."

I scented my other men before their heat hit me as I turned in Thorn's arms to face him.

I caught Nate as he pulled his tee over his head. "Alex, please fix the door and make the room soundproof. Plus, get everyone damn naked to save time."

Alex's power swept through the room, causing me to shiver and then moan as my clit pulsed. Then, I was gloriously naked, surrounded by my men. One was missing, but it was by our choice, and it wasn't as if I liked that choice either. I would have loved him there with us.

Something buzzed against my clit, and my body shuddered. I looked down, but no one touched me.

I glanced up and found a grinning Alex. "You were thinking. I had to distract you."

Smiling, I curled a hand around the back of his neck and pulled him closer. "Distract me again, please."

"My pleasure," he murmured against my lips, and then my clit buzzed again and again. I cried out, dropped my head back, and knew it was Nate's chest I leaned against. I made sure to keep my hand around Alex's neck when my body was lifted. Thorn picked me up easily. I wrapped my legs around his waist as he slid inside of my wet, throbbing pussy.

"Fuck, I can feel that, Alex."

Alex chuckled. "Fun isn't it, but I'll stop for now. We don't want to tire her out before we've had our fill of our mate."

"Good thinking." Ezra grinned. He squeezed in to kiss his mark on my chest, and then he claimed my mouth in a hot and heavy kiss. Pulling back, he winked and moved from my shoulder to behind Alex.

Thorn's hand on my hips tightened. He grunted, lost for words as he worked himself in and out of me, with Nate's help as he supported me from behind. Knowing my men had my weight as Asher moved in to lean down and take a nipple into his mouth, I reached down and palmed his erection. He hissed out a breath before biting down on my nipple.

"God, yes," I cried, feeling his fangs penetrate my skin. He'd only taken a sip before he licked over the puncture wounds and kissed down my body to tongue my clit even while Thorn still fucked me. Thorn slowed though, letting Asher drink me in, dipping his tongue in to take more wetness from Thorn and me.

A gasp had me prying my eyes open and smiling when I saw Alex had turned enough for Ezra to be on his knees in front of him. His head bobbed up and down on Alex's hard cock. A wave of desire from the sight had me clamping down on Thorn.

A growl rumbled up from Nate at my back. "Get the fuck off him," he snarled. Ezra didn't listen; he taunted my wolf with a wink. Alex tried to step back to calm Nate, but Ezra grabbed the back of his thighs and sucked him all the way in and swallowed around Alex. It, of course, caused Alex to curse and get lost in the sensation.

Oh shit, Nate hadn't claimed Ezra or the other way around. He wouldn't enjoy seeing them together until that happened. His emotions were all over the place when they slipped out and into the room. He was pumped full of pleasure, but angry at the same time.

Suddenly, I was lifted off Thorn. "You can have her back in a second," Nate said just as he turned me, picked me up and buried himself inside me. He was thicker than Thorn, so I threw my head back and cried out from how full I felt.

He lifted me up and down slowly on him and nuzzled his mouth into my neck, kissing, licking, and marking me. "Had to be inside of you… fuck," Nate clipped as I clamped down around him, a surprise orgasm taking over me. I moaned and bit into his neck, trying to mark him myself. He growled low, a different sound to any other. It was the wolf telling me he liked what I was doing.

"Jesus, fuck, you always feel good."

"Hmm, so do you," I said.

"Now I got you to come, I've got to take care of something," he said into my neck.

"What?"

"Ezra."

My heart skipped a beat. I would have clapped if I'd let him go. "Um, yay," I mumbled instead. He chuckled before he slowly slid out of me and helped me stand. My legs felt like jelly, but in the best way. I glanced back to Asher and Thorn; my pulse raced. They were lip locked in a tight embrace. Their hands ran over each other's bodies while they ground their cocks against one another's.

"May I have your attention for a moment, dove?" Alex stepped up beside me.

"You can have it any time you want," I told him, taking his hand he held out to me.

He grinned, a blush coating his cheeks. God, I loved him. I loved them all so darn much. He licked his lips nervously; it was always cute to see. "Will you join me on the bed?"

I nodded. "Always." He led me around to the side where the rest of the room would be visible. He knew, while we made love, I would still want to see the other pleasure my men gave each other—especially if there was a fight about to happen.

Nate and Ezra stood apart eyeing one another. Nate glared while Ezra looked smug.

I gasped when I was pushed forward, my top half bent over, and I rested my elbows to the bed, glancing over my shoulder to see Alex with darkened eyes as they ran over my body slowly. The blush was long gone, even when he ordered, "Spread your legs more."

My nipples hardened, and my pussy throbbed. I did as I was told, because in the bedroom, I did like to be told what to do.

Alex ran his hand up and down his length while he used his other hand to reach out and run a couple of fingers through my wetness. He drew his finger up to his nose and inhaled before sucking them into his mouth.

"I love your scent, love your taste, love all of you," he whispered, and I noticed Thorn and Asher were watching him also while they jerked each other off.

"I love everything about you, Alex."

"Asher, take Thorn to the bed next to us. I want you to bury yourself inside of him while I do our Paige. It'll leave more room for Nate and Ezra to play."

A cool breeze blew over my skin as Asher flashed to our side, and then Thorn was in the same position I was, bent over the bed, his ass on view for Asher. Only Asher had a hand at the back of Alex's neck while he took his mouth in a heated kiss.

"Sweetheart," Thorn uttered. I glanced back and found him close. His lips touched mine gently once, twice, and a third time before we deepened the kiss. Wanting more, needing to touch him more, I wrapped my arm around him and scooted closer.

I could never, not ever, get enough of my men.

Alex's hands at my hips distracted me. I pulled back, panting even when I didn't need to. Thorn smiled smugly at me, knowing he was the cause because of the kiss. Only he let out a hiss and glanced over his shoulder. I looked also since I could feel the tip of Alex's cock at my needy entrance. Asher was also lined up with Thorn, and they slowly pushed inside of us. I gripped Thorn's hand, my belly already tightening with an oncoming orgasm from just the feel of Alex entering me and seeing Asher pushing into Thorn.

"Fuck us," Thorn demanded roughly.

Asher laughed low. "Are you sure you can handle it?"

"Hell yes," Thorn replied. "Paige?" he asked.

I glanced over to Alex. "Please, Alex, fuck me hard."

He sucked in a sharp breath, tightened his hold on my hips, and leaned over me a little before he did indeed fuck me hard. I got lost in the sensation, the in and out, the slapping of skin, the sounds we all made.

"Christ, I'm coming," Thorn yelled.

"Yes, come," Asher said, wrapping his arms around Thorn's shoulders and forcing him to stand up a bit. I got to see Thorn's cum shoot out over the bed, hear his cry of ecstasy. All of it had me moaning as my own release overcame me. Alex grunted. He swelled inside me, and I milked all of the cum out of him.

"Thorn," Asher clipped and then groaned as his own seed spilled into Thorn.

My mind spun as the room around me wavered. The next thing I knew, I was sitting on a clean bed between Alex's legs next to Thorn, who lay with his head resting on Asher's thigh as Asher ran his hand over Thorn's hair, purring. I wiggled back, resting into Alex more. His arms slid around my waist, holding me close. He kissed my neck and shoulder. I smiled contently, relaxed and sated wonderfully, ready for the show about to start. As were Asher, Alex, and Thorn.

"Well, wolf, that's got me all randy. Are you ready to submit?" Ezra asked. The tip of his cock shone with precum. If it had been me watching us, then I would feel the same. Ready for my own release.

"We'll soon find out who comes out on top." Nate smirked. Then right before our eyes, his body altered, changed, and morphed into his wolf.

"He has grown," Asher commented. I nodded. It was all I could do because I was in awe whenever Nate shifted. I'd been told it hurt each transformation, but he made it look so smooth and painless. Nate barked, got down on his front legs, and growled.

I glanced to Ezra. His smile was a little wild. He clapped his hands once and then spread them wide. "Beast form, I love it." His body flew into his hellhound form. One second it was Ezra the man, and then the next his hellhound stood on all fours and let loose a deep growl, responding to Nate's.

"Oh shit, this'll be good," I said eagerly, rubbing my hands together. "The spell to block out sound is still in place?"

"Of course," Alex said. I felt his smile against my shoulder.

Nate was nearly as large as Ezra's hellhound. He had grown. How it was possible, I didn't know, but it was something to think about later. The wolf and hellhound stared each other down with their glowing eyes as they circled one another. Constant rumbles dropped from their mouths.

Ezra jumped forward then back, trying to goad Nate into action. But I knew Nate wouldn't take the bait. Ezra would have to be the one to attack. They circled some more. Ezra snarled and then lost his cool and dove at Nate, nipping at his flank, but leaving himself wide open also. Nate went to go for the top of Ezra's neck, but no doubt realized he couldn't because of the bones jutting out from his spine, so he ducked lower and bit at his neck before knocking into Ezra and taking him to the ground.

They snarled and snapped at each other as they rolled

around on the floor. Neither was going to come out unscathed from this fight of dominance. I had a feeling Nate would win and hoped Ezra would just give in so they didn't hurt one another too bad.

Nate managed to get to his feet, grab Ezra by the throat, and throw him to the side. Ezra went skidding over the floor and crashed into a table, which fell on top of him. A rush of concern filled me. My blood sped through my body.

"It's fine, love," Asher said, taking my free hand since the other was already clutching Alex's. He kissed the back of my hand and then placed them down on his thigh. "They know what they're doing. Nate didn't even break his skin when he threw him, and Ezra is stronger than you think."

I nodded and relaxed again into Alex, knowing if anything did happen, my other men would fix it. Ezra stood. Wood dropped away from his body as he shook. He licked his lips, eyeing Nate and growling.

Nate took a step forward and snarled. Ezra answered it. Nate swiped at the floor, his nails easily carving into the wood. Ezra jumped at him, Nate dodged, but Ezra was there latching his jaw around the back of Nate's neck. Nate snarled. Ezra growled and shook Nate back and forth.

Nate rumbled out some more noise, but Ezra wasn't letting go and I was sure Nate knew it.

"Should we do something?" I whispered.

The men around me chuckled. Alex kissed my neck and whispered, "Look lower on them, dove."

I scanned over them and down. I spotted Nate's erection first—large, hard, with the pink tip out and leaking. He was enjoying it, and it was obvious Ezra was as well. While holding Nate in a grip around the neck, he moved over Nate more and mounted him. It was then I saw his own long, thick cock. Longer still than Nate's since his pink tip extended out further in his hellhound form.

My heart thumped so fast in my chest I was sure it would jump out of my body.

Nate snarled, glancing over his shoulder. Ezra growled back —it almost sounded smug. Ezra adjusted again. His dick was right near Nate's ass. Slowly, Ezra pushed inside. Nate stilled, dropping his head. Ezra let go of Nate's neck and licked at him. Nate lowered himself a little so Ezra got a better grip with his feet on the ground. Ezra then pumped in and out with his length. Ezra licked at Nate again. Nate grumbled but tipped his head to the side to receive the lick on the face. Still, Ezra fucked Nate hard and fast.

"Does it bother you, love?" Asher asked.

In answer, I took his hand and gently pulled it down where I spread my legs and let him feel how unbothered I was by it. Watching them, even in their shifted forms, fight and enjoy each other, love each other, got me aroused. I was close to climax already.

"Christ, you're drenched," Asher said roughly. He didn't pull his hand away, which I was grateful for. Instead, he inserted two fingers inside me, and I ground back against Alex's hardness. His arousal was proudly on display. He hissed out a breath and cupped both my breasts, rolling them around in his hands, teasing each nipple while pushing himself up against me.

"Yes," I moaned, gripping Asher's wrist while his fingers drove in and out in the same rhythm Ezra was to Nate.

Thorn twisted around in Asher's lap and took a hard Asher into his mouth, causing Asher to groan and grip the back of

Thorn's head. Through hooded eyes, I caught Thorn get to his knees and run his own palm over himself.

As I rode Asher's fingers, panting drew my attention to Nate and Ezra. Nate had given up on stopping Ezra licking his face and just accepted it as Ezra pumped Nate. Nate suddenly tensed. He let out a grumble and then a sound in the back of his throat as his cum shot out his tip and landed on the floor. Asher cried out, holding Thorn down on him and came down his throat. Wetness touched my back as Alex hissed out a breath of "Yes!"

I locked Asher's hand between my thighs. As Asher fucked me with his fingers, Alex used his magic to buzz against my clit, sending me over the edge with a cry. Thorn groaned. I opened my eyes to see him pumping his hand faster over himself as he leaned up near Asher and then he shot his load onto Asher's groin.

Ezra howled as he thrust into Nate a few more times before stilling and gently slipping himself out of Nate. They both dropped to the floor in a heap around each other. Nate slowly shifted back, bones crunching and popping. When he lay there as a man, Ezra gave him one last lick before shifting back also.

"Next time, I might let you take me," Ezra teased.

Nate grunted and gave him the finger. Though, he didn't seem upset over what happened at all.

God, I loved my men.

CHAPTER FIFTY-THREE

While Nate, Ezra, and Asher rested, Alex insisted he was fine and suggested I make a call to my family. Of course I took him up on it. Seeing Yasmin glowing as she sat with Eric and Sakura standing behind them like she was their guard, helped ease more tension I didn't realize I'd been carrying. Then again, of course I was worried about my family, but they reassured me everything was fine back home.

A few hours later, I was sitting in a living room off the bedroom we'd been supplied when the door opened and Xi walked in. At least he didn't break the door.

"How did it go, Xi?" I asked as Thorn handed me a bowl of meat he'd had Alex transport him home for. It was then Asher had ordered Alex to have a rest. "Thank you." I smiled up at Thorn, which he returned.

"They are all dead," Xi announced plainly, almost as if he was bored.

"Uh, thank you," I offered. Though, I wasn't sure thanking someone for killing people was good.

He hummed under his breath and said no more.

"Xi, did you find out any new information?"

His jaw clenched. "No."

Ah, he was pissed off. Killing them for nothing had bored him. I would hate to think what he did for fun in Hell.

"Xi, have something to eat and sit down," Ezra said from where he sat between my legs. "I'm sure we'll speak with Cedrick soon, and he'll let us know what's going on."

"Then we can leave?" Xi questioned. I was sure the heebie-jeebies wasn't the only thing Xi wanted to get away from. There was something going on with him.

"We've been here one night, Xi. We were planning to spend two nights here anyway," Asher said. He stood by the wall reading some type of papers, and Nate stood with him with his own handful of papers. They looked important, but I knew if I needed to know anything about something, they would tell me, or I'd kick their ass if I found something out too late.

"It's been two nights. It's past midnight."

I waved my hand around, not bothering to answer. If he didn't understand I wouldn't leave without seeing and knowing Cedrick was okay, then he'd figure it out, or he'd just have to learn to be patient.

Before I could even blink, Xi had a sword drawn. His arm extended to the right, the tip of the blade touching Cedrick's neck.

"Xi," I cried as I leaped over Ezra in a panicked frenzy. However, Xi was already withdrawing his sword.

"Be careful where you pop in without notice," Xi warned, then walked over to the opposite wall to Asher and Nate to lean against it. He took a rag out of what I guessed was his back pocket and started cleaning a sword.

Was Lucifer actually punishing me? Did he really think I was too moody for his son so he sent Xi to drive me insane? I believed it could work in the end.

"Are you okay?" I asked, reaching out to place my hand on Cedrick's arm. A shiver raked over my body. His scent hit me, and I wanted to lick him, kiss him, and mark him. It felt as if I hadn't seen him in years.

He looked down at me with warmth in his eyes. "I am now, my lady." He glanced to Xi. "I apologize for appearing out of nowhere. I'll know not to do it again."

Xi didn't look at him but nodded once and kept cleaning his sword.

"How's your mom?" I asked, bringing his attention back down to me. Heat hit my cheeks because his eyes were so intense I could almost drown in them.

Was I this bad with my other men before we'd completed the bond?

It wasn't that long ago, yet it seemed eons ago because so much had happened.

He smiled. "Better. A lot better. She's been seen by a healer we trust and is already on the mend."

I grinned. "That's great." Only my gut bottomed out. It was cruel of me to think it, but knowing she was okay so soon and that Cedrick would be all right, meant we could leave.

Leave one of my mates.

Leave one of my men.

Even when we hadn't finalized the bond, the thought of

leaving him behind gutted me from breastbone down to my lower stomach. It had me pressing a hand against my stomach from the ache inside me.

"Are you able to tell us what that was down there?" Asher asked.

"Never felt creeped out as much as I did walking into that room," Nate commented. He walked to the table to grab an apple. He turned, leaned against the table, and took a bite. He was always eating, well, if he could. He told me it was because shifting took a lot out of him.

"I would like to explain what we've found out. Are you all comfortable here or would you like to speak in the meeting room?"

"Here's okay, if it's all right with you?" I asked, suddenly feeling unsure of what to say, how to stand, or if I was dressed nicely enough. Hell, it felt like I was in high school and the most popular jock was speaking to me. I swore if I giggled at anything he said, I would slap myself.

Humping his leg was out of the question, right?

God, that thought seemed familiar. I was sure I'd thought it before for one or all of my other mates.

Slowly, I removed my hand and put distance between us before I jumped his bones. I went back over to the couch and sat. Ezra moved back to lean against my legs. Thorn sat on my right and Asher to my left.

"I'll go get Alex," Nate said.

"Thanks," I said, glancing everywhere but at Cedrick.

Nate grunted and disappeared into the next room.

The door to the living room opened and Kiered entered, smiling. I caught Xi straighten from the wall, but other than that, he didn't look the man's way or stop from cleaning his blade. Mentally, I rubbed my hands together. I had a feeling Kiered was why Xi wanted to up and run away fast. He was interested in him, or Kiered liked Xi and made it known to the man, and it freaked him out. Then again, it could be mutual feelings and that could also concern Xi, worried it would get between his mission to protect us. It may just need my interfering, but first I would find out how they both felt.

"Hi, everyone. Did I miss the discussion?"

"No," I told him with my own smile. "We're just waiting for Alex."

"Good." He nodded, and then moved over to the wall beside Xi. From across the room, I could see Xi tense. He shifted to the side, away from Kiered, but Kiered removed that space between them.

I got a "holy shit" moment when I saw Xi's lips twitch. I'd never seen him smile except a scary one when he was fighting.

That confirmed it.

He liked Kiered.

Thorn placed his arm around my shoulders and brought me close. "Sweetheart, don't get involved."

I gave Thorn wide eyes and pointed at my chest. "Who, me?"

He chuckled and kissed my temple. "Yes, you."

"I don't know what you're talking about." I rolled my eyes and smiled.

The door to the bedroom opened and a fresh-looking Alex walked in with Nate following. Alex moved over to sit on the floor with Ezra, between Thorn's legs, and Nate sat on the arm of the couch on Asher's side.

Cedrick took a chair opposite us. I hated the distance between us. As far as I was concerned, he should have been sitting with all of us.

He relaxed back and gave me a small smile, as if he knew what I was thinking…. Crap, he probably did. Still, I wouldn't take it back.

"Five years ago, my brother and I were out visiting close towns when the palace was attacked. When we arrived home, our father told us our mother, Queen Castilina, died in battle." His jaw clenched as he glanced to Kiered and then back to the coffee table in front of him. "We believed the story because our father was marvelous at lying. He mourned for months; tears would shine in his eyes whenever he spoke of her. He, with his army, went out in search of the survivors of the dark elves who were said to attack us and killed them all."

"It would be easy to believe," I said, hoping he'd be able to forgive himself.

He shook his head. "I shouldn't have. He'd always been a deceitful bastard. I should have made sure myself. I should have done something."

"You weren't the only one tricked, brother. There was nothing any of us could do." Kiered stepped over and laid a hand on Cedrick's shoulder as he faced us. "We never thought Father would hurt Mother. She even believed it herself. He was enchanted by her beauty and power. He'd thought the world of her, even though he knew she didn't love him. He saw her as his treasure because she brought him status. He became king after all, so he easily could turn a blind eye on the love she held for her guards. Her true grooms… mates."

Cedrick nodded. "That is why, since she thought she was safe, she sent her mates to guard us on our travels. It was the biggest mistake we all made. Our mother for believing in our father, for sending her mates away. For us and her mates listening to her pleas in the first place and giving in when she said she would die if anything happened to her children, to us." A tick started in his temple. "She didn't realize we would become nothing without her in our lives. Her mates were mere shells without their soul with them. They only stayed alive because they promised to care for us."

"The one good thing the council has done is get rid of your father," Asher said, his voice hard and rough.

Cedrick nodded. "Agreed."

"So what actually happened to her?" Ezra asked as he tilted his head to the side and rested his cheek on my knee. I reached out and ran a hand through his hair while I watched Cedrick struggle through this new development. I wished I could take away his heartache somehow.

Cedrick paled more than his fair skin already was. Kiered did too as he removed his hand from Cedrick's shoulder and sat on the armrest beside him. Like he knew when they spoke of it, he wouldn't be able to stand anymore.

"The machine you saw her hooked up to syphons her power and eventually her life source."

My pulse raced. "They were taking her life slowly."

"Yes," he snarled. "Slowly and painfully for five fucking years."

"What did they do with what they syphoned?"

The tick in Cedrick's temple intensified. He sneered, his upper lip raised as he bit out, "Our father wanted it for himself." He shook his head. "He injected himself every day. In the beginning, the power he gained was beyond any our kind should have."

"How did he get killed if he was so powerful?" Thorn asked. I glanced around at my men. All of them looked sickened by the news, as well as angered.

"Because Therolidi, his most trusted friend, killed him on behalf of the council. It was also Therolidi who told me the council had planned his death. The people we caught and questioned could have been from Therolidi since they confirmed his story of the council doing it."

"He tried double-crossing the council. Hoping you would go after them and not find him out," Alex commented.

"I can only guess that was his plan. But I know for certain it was Therolidi who killed our father because Mother heard it all. He murdered him right in front of her, then planted his body elsewhere."

"The council knew what your father was doing and got Therolidi to murder him, but didn't stop Therolidi from doing the same, draining your mother of power and life force. It doesn't make sense," Nate commented.

"Maybe Therolidi was more manageable than their father," Ezra suggested.

"It could also mean the council are doing the same, syphoning power and life source from others, and they supplied Therolidi with a taste to be able to kill your father in the first place," Asher said.

"You're correct. While our mother rested, I took two of mother's guards into the dungeons and we spoke with Rallis, who is now dead."

Ezra laughed. "*Spoke*, you make torture sound so casual."

Cedrick shrugged. "Rallis overheard our father speaking of it with Therolidi, how he stumbled upon it happening within the council's walls when he went to see them six years ago. Of course, when the council found out what our father was doing, they had to put a stop to it instantly. They didn't want their secrets going further. Therolidi and his friend on the council worked together to kill and then cover up Father's death. He would have told them of his plan for me, how he wanted to be in control."

"They would have let him go and continue as your father was doing because, like Ezra said, he was more manageable than your father. He must be sleeping with Jessica. A lot of men think with their cocks, and this would be a perfect example. He seemed stupid enough to think he'd get away with everything. Even trying to take us out for the bitch," Nate said with a scowl.

This was maddening, sickening. I wanted to scream in anger and throw up in fear and anguish knowing what the council were doing with people. But also because of what Cedrick's mother had been through.

"The more I hear about the council, the more I want to face them and kill them. This can't keep happening," I said. Ezra let out a sound, and I quickly released his hair. I hadn't even realized I'd gripped it so tightly. "Sorry," I muttered.

He turned his head and smiled big, then winked. "We can try rough play another time, mi corazón."

My face heated. An unexpected laugh fell from my lips before I could stop it, but I quickly cut if off. It wasn't the time for fun and games, though Ezra always did help settle a darker atmosphere into a lighter one.

"Anyway," I started and playfully shoved at his head, causing him to chuckle, "this must be why the council is taking other powerful members of the communities."

"I agree, love," Asher said. "At least we know they'll have advanced strength and power."

Worry creased my brows and churned my stomach. "Will we have enough power to fight them?"

"From what our mother has said, the weaker the subject, the

weaker the dose. It depends on who they have and how long they've had them for."

"Since we don't know, we have to consider the worst. However, I believe we'll be strong enough to take them on. Are you still willing to give us some men to fight with us?" Thorn asked.

Cedrick nodded. He glanced up at Kiered, who smiled and nodded. Cedrick looked back to us and met my gaze. "There's one other matter with having Mother back at the palace."

"What?" I asked.

"I am no longer king."

My heart spiked. My mind spun. Could that mean…? I didn't want to jump to any conclusions; I didn't want to get my hopes up.

"W-What does that mean for you?"

"With the power I received from Father after his death, I was able to transfer it to Mother since it was rightfully hers anyway."

"Did it hurt? How was that possible?" Alex wondered. He was always after answers over many things. Ezra ruffled his hair, and Alex blushed. "Sorry, I didn't mean to pry."

"I do not mind." Cedrick smiled. "It didn't hurt as much as what Paige experienced when I pulled her from her mind. Mother and I had to reestablish the mind link a mother has with her children when they're born, and I transferred it that way. It had been suffocated with how she was locked away, cut off from the world, from us all, spelled so we couldn't trace her energy. I would have passed by that room if it hadn't been for you, Paige. It could have been too late. But with the new power boost from myself, it helped rejuvenate her quicker than anything else could have."

"I wasn't even sure how I knew, really. I just didn't want to leave before seeing in that room," I told him with a shrug, playing it off like it was nothing because he was eyeing me like it was everything. I wanted to crawl into his lap and see what he would do with me just from the way he was looking at me.

"It was everything," he said softly.

"It was," Kiered added. "Mother would love to meet with you soon if you would visit with her before leaving?"

Smiling up at him, I nodded. "I would love to meet her."

"I'll take you to her as soon as we're done speaking here," Cedrick said, bringing my attention back to him. I nodded, and he smiled in return.

"Will your mother be able to handle being queen so soon after? Is she strong enough to keep your darker brethren in check?" Asher asked.

"She is," Kiered said. "With the power transfer from Cedrick, she would be able to take on an attack if needed. Especially since she is also reestablishing the bonds with her mates as we speak."

My face ignited. Yet I tasted regret because Cedrick and I couldn't do the same… at least, I didn't think we could. But he wasn't king anymore. Did it mean he didn't have responsibilities, or would he still have them alongside his mother?

"It means, my beautiful, that I am able to stay by your side no matter where you are."

My eyes widened. I scooted forward on the couch and felt Ezra look back at me with uncertainty. *"Are you serious?"*

His smile was the biggest I'd seen from him. *"Yes. Very serious."*

"You're mine? As in my mate, my husband. You'll be with me everywhere? At my castle? At my home?"

"Correct, and you're mine also."

My body flamed, my nipples hardened, my heart raced, and my clit throbbed. I wanted him, and now, so nothing could come between us again.

"I have a feeling we need to leave the room," Kiered said, his voice light with humor. "He's just told her he's able to become her mate fully with Mother ruling the court."

"Leaving would be a good idea," Asher answered. "I'll take the wolf out."

I couldn't seem to look away from Cedrick. I was lost in the thought of making him completely mine.

But… did he understand—

"Yes, beautiful." He said through the link. *"I'm very well aware I shall have to share you with five other men. I am glad you have them in your life. They help you in many ways. I've even seen it in the short amount of time with you all. However, this may seem selfish or stupid, but I have only deep need for you, my mate, my wife. I only desire for you. There may come a time when I seek pleasure from our men, but until then, I only wish to be with you. Would this be possible?"*

"Yes." And I knew I wasn't lying. I knew my men, my family well. They would accept his wishes, for his sake and for mine, so I could claim him as mine.

His smile turned sly. *"It does not mean I wouldn't want to watch you with them. It excites me even thinking of it, seeing the pleasure upon your face. I do not feel jealous with them touching you or having you. I know they are yours and you are theirs."*

My body hummed. Nate drew in the scent and snarled. A breeze swept my hair over my face and then the door opened and closed. Nate's snarls lessened.

"Is he okay?" Cedrick asked.

I stood as the rest of my men did. Thorn chuckled, as did

Ezra, and I caught Alex smiling before he said, "He'll be fine once you're brought into the family."

Cedrick tilted his head to the side slightly in confusion.

Alex blushed, so it was Thorn who added, "Once the bond has been finished between you two, he'll accept you as part of Paige's family. Until then, his fur is a little ruffled and he doesn't like others playing with what's his."

Cedrick nodded. "I have spoken with Paige, but I need you all to understand that, for now, I'll only have her in the bedroom. It doesn't mean I won't like watching you all together, but for now, Paige will be my focus."

Thorn grinned. "We can understand that. Maybe just watch. You don't touch any of us in front of Nate either. His wolf has claimed us all... well, almost." His eyes flashed to Ezra who looked decidedly smug, then to Asher, who smirked.

Cedrick's eyes widened.

"Unless you have the strength to dominate him and then claim him, his wolf won't like you getting too close to us guys," Ezra added.

A throat cleared. "I believe a mind link with them all could help the matter," Xi said.

Ezra clicked his fingers and pointed at Xi. "Good thinking, old man. Cedrick would then scent like us with a mind link."

"Could we all speak of this after?" I asked, then slapped a hand over my mouth. I was suddenly impatient for alone time, but I sounded rude getting what I wanted.

My men laughed. Thorn kissed my cheek. "We'll leave you to it." He started for the door and slapped Cedrick on the shoulder in passing. "Welcome to the family."

Alex kissed me on the neck and then blushed as he whispered, "Have fun." He nodded and smiled to Cedrick as he walked by him.

Ezra nipped at my bottom lip before giving me a quick peck. "I'd say enjoy yourself, but I know you will." He winked. He slapped Cedrick on the arm as he went by. He glanced back to Kiered and Xi. "Are you two going to stand there and watch? Kind of kinky there, Xi."

Xi went beet red, mumbled something about killing Ezra, and stormed from the room.

Kiered grinned and said, "Don't worry, I'll make sure your hellhound still lives." He raced after Xi, slamming the door behind himself.

I looked up at Cedrick and gulped. His eyes were darker than usual and intense again. His jaw clenched as his hands fisted.

"I have never even asked you. Would you want to be my wife?"

Was he serious?

We were made for each other.

He was mine. I could feel the rightfulness all through me.

Yet, it was charming he was asking. "It depends. Would you be happy with a ghoul as a wife? Just so you understand, I eat, um…." I glanced away, steeled myself, and looked back, jutting my chin out and up. I had to stop being self-conscious and worrying about what people thought of me eating flesh. I was a ghoul, and I was a proud one. "I eat dead people, Cedrick. If it's something you can't handle, then I know this couldn't work for us."

"I accept you for you, Paige. Being a ghoul and all. No matter what you eat."

My heart skipped a beat. "Really?" I whispered.

"Yes, beautiful."

I smiled big. "Then yes, Cedrick. I want to be your wife," I told him, and then made a run and leaped into his arms. Thankfully he caught me as he laughed. He spun me around and then pressed me close against him, wrapping his arms around my waist while I locked mine around his neck and then my legs around his waist. We both grinned at each other, which slowly disappeared as Cedrick dipped his head and for the second time —only this wasn't in my mind—he kissed me.

I moaned into his mouth over the first taste of him, and he drank the sound down. His hands slid down and cupped my ass, holding me tightly against his hardness. And God, he was big.

I pulled back enough to say, "I'm going to need you inside me, right about now."

He chuckled. "Then I shall make it happen." He placed me back on my feet and pulled his top over his head. My knees felt weak at the sight of his perfectly smooth, pale skin. I licked my lips, my mouth suddenly dry. He watched me as I looked upon him when he undid the tie to his pants. I quickly whipped off my tee and threw it to the floor, then got rid of my jeans, kicking them off to the side so I stood in front of him in panties and a bra. At least they were nice ones; they always were when Alex dressed me. This time they were black and lacy.

His pants fell to the floor and pooled around his feet. He wore no underwear, and I was grateful to see how hard he already was for me.

"You do this to me, beautiful," he told me as he stroked his hand up and down his long length.

"You've driven me crazy since arriving, so it's fair." I smiled and reached behind me to unhook my bra. Leisurely, I dragged the straps down my arms and then dropped it to the floor. Cedrick's eyes stayed glued to my chest. He swallowed hard as his hand moved faster over himself.

"The panties," he bit out as he kicked his pants off his feet. I pushed my panties down to my thighs and wiggled my hips so they slid down my legs and then stepped out of them.

"So beautiful. I've never seen anyone as exquisite as you."

I couldn't stop the snort. "Your women are the most stunning I've seen."

He shook his head and narrowed his gaze on me. "They are nothing compared to you. Let me prove how much I cherish your body, mind, and soul."

"Yes, please."

"Shall we enter the bedroom?"

"No, it's so far away, and I need you now."

He flashed his teeth in a bright smile. "It's the next room."

I nodded. "Too far away."

He took the step to pick me up in his arms. "I love how eager you are for me, beautiful."

I wrapped my legs around his waist and let out a mew when my pussy pressed against his cock.

He hissed. "Already soaked. I can feel it."

"I'm ready for you, honey." I kissed his neck. He groaned and, using his hands on my ass, pulled me against him as he walked us to the couch. I slid up and down on him with each movement, driving us crazy with desire.

He turned and sat. One of his hands slid between us so he could run two fingers over my wet folds.

"For me," he clipped.

Biting my bottom lip, I nodded. "All for you."

When he inserted two fingers inside me, I dropped my head

back and cried out. Only he gripped the back of my hair and pulled my head back up so our eyes caught. "You'll be my wife. We'll be connected forever."

"I can't wait."

His eyes brightened with a glow in them. *"Me either."* He freed his fingers from within me and brought them up to his lips. He pressed them against his mouth and then gently tugged my body forward using my hair. I knew what he wanted, so when my mouth touched his fingers on his lips, I opened and swirled my tongue over his wet fingers. His eyes glowed more as his own mouth opened and his tongue joined mine and we both tasted myself on them.

"Up," he ordered with a smack to my ass cheek. I lifted to my knees and moved closer, and while we licked his fingers, I slowly sank down onto his cock. My pussy opened up to him, but with his length and girth, he filled me snugly.

He groaned and I gasped as the bonded connection took place. He removed his fingers from between our mouths and kissed me like it was the last kiss he'd give me. Even while the fire built inside me and took over, I didn't release him.

His emotions opened up to me, his desire, his pleasure, his happiness, and even love. I knew he was feeling my own when his arms wrapped around my waist tightly and his voice swept into my mind with *"It's more than I could have fathomed. I feel you everywhere, and still I want more."*

"I know what you mean." God, did I. Having him in my mind while he was planted deep and his emotions swirled, overwhelmed me in the best way. I wasn't sure my heart would ever settle down.

Slowly, I pushed up from his cock and then sank back down. Our hands dug into one another at the sensation.

"So tight, so wet, perfect," he murmured into my mind, kissing down my neck.

"You were made for me."

"And you me."

I nodded, closing my eyes, getting lost in the feel of him. Of Cedrick. My mate, my bonded, my husband.

When he dipped his head down, I took the chance and licked over the tip of his ear. He stilled, and next I was in the air before my back hit the couch. He made a sound in the back of his throat before he thrust back all the way inside me. His hips pistoned in and out roughly, savagely, and wonderfully. I gripped his shoulders and took it all with pleasure.

I also made a note to myself that touching his ears drove him insane.

Smiling, I nipped at his neck. He groaned and tipped his head to the side. He gripped my breast and brought a nipple to his mouth. His warm breath tickled over it. When I glided my tongue over the shell of his ear, he bit down on my nipple. I cried out and tightened my legs around his hips as he fucked me faster than even before.

"More," he demanded, and I gave it easily. I licked and nibbled on the tip of his ear. "Merde," he yelled.

My lower belly clenched and twisted in the best way. I was so close. "Harder, honey," I whispered against his ear before licking and sucking on the arch of it. He grunted and ground down onto me as he thrust harder.

"I can't hold on," he said, and it was those words, knowing he was as lost as I was, that drove me over the edge. He spoke in a language I'd never heard when my orgasm hit and my walls tightened around him even more. I gripped him to me, and he brought his mouth back to mine for a sweet but rough kiss. He pulled back and stared into my eyes. When they tightened in the corners and his mouth opened a little, I knew he was there. He swelled inside me, and his hot seed filled me as he groaned long and deep, dropping his forehead into my neck. I couldn't resist. I licked and sucked at his ear. His body shuddered over me, and he swelled even more before squirting the last of his cum into me.

His body relaxed against mine. He spoke again in a different language in between kisses over my skin.

"Thank you for accepting me." I received through my mind. I hadn't even thought he was feeling insecure over my acceptance of him being different from myself, but it was what I picked up from him at that moment.

I cupped his cheek. He lifted his gaze to mine, and I pressed a gentle kiss to his lips. *"Thank you for wanting me as your wife. I will forever hold you in my heart, soul, and mind."*

CHAPTER FIFTY-FOUR

PAIGE

Butterflies flew in circles in my belly. My nerves were high. I glanced down at my simple dark blue dress, the only casual but nice one I'd packed, and then up to Cedrick. "Are you sure I look presentable enough?"

He smiled down at me and placed an arm around my waist. "Yes, I'm sure Mother would approve even if you wore a sack."

I slapped his stomach. "No she wouldn't."

"If I'm happy, which I am, she would."

Still, his words didn't settle my nerves. She was his mother after all.

A knock sounded on the door to the living room we stood in. "Come in," Cedrick called. The door opened and my mates walked in. All smiled, except Nate. Alex even had a blush going.

Asher dipped his head toward Cedrick and said, "Welcome to the clan."

"Thank you. I would shake your hand, but I believe a certain wolf, who is currently glaring at me, would take my head off."

Nate grunted.

Asher smirked. "He is a bit possessive. Much like our Paige, but you'll find that out."

I snorted. "You're all the same. Unless you know he's a bonded mate, then you're ready to throw me at him."

The men chuckled, except Nate. I rolled my eyes at him and his glare narrowed more.

"Only because we know he'll add to the family," Ezra said. "Otherwise we would burn the bastard alive." He shrugged, went over to the couch, and sat. His eyes darkened as he drew in a deep breath. He licked his lips. "Hmm, smells divine over here."

"Ezra," I warned. He grinned wide and winked.

"Did the others speak of what we discussed before they left?" Cedrick asked Asher.

"They did. I think the mind link is good to try. It would bring us together and be an advantage in battle."

Cedrick nodded. "Then if you all would allow me access to your minds, I would like to try. Since we are connected through Paige already, it shouldn't be that hard."

"I don't fucking like people poking around in my head," Nate clipped.

"I promise the link will only allow us to speak through our minds and connect us in a way that family is supposed to be. You can block me anytime you wish."

Nate huffed, crossed his arms over his chest, and leaned against the wall.

"That's him agreeing," Alex offered.

Cedrick smiled at him and nodded. Nate growled in the back of his throat, and I saw Cedrick quickly look away from Alex.

"Please, close your eyes."

My men did. As soon as they had, Cedrick smiled at me and took a step back. His eyes glowed before he closed them. His body lifted off the ground, and he hovered in the air an inch or two off the floor. He spread his arms wide. I saw my men sway a little. I was glad at least some of them were sitting—Ezra and Alex. Nate stumbled to the left and then straightened, his jaw clenched, and he opened his eyes. They widened.

Together we watched Cedrick float back to the floor. The rest slowly opened their eyes; Alex even blinked rapidly a few times.

I dropped the shield in my mind.

"This is freaky. I can sense all of you in my head." Alex was the first I heard.

Nate gripped his head. *"I don't fucking like this. It feels weird having you all in my head."*

"You will get used to it," Cedrick promised.

"It could come in handy." Ezra then sent a picture that had my body quivering. It was of all of them touching, tasting and pleasuring me in some way. My men laughed, some even groaned. Cedrick was one of them.

"Not fair, Ezra." I glared over at him, and he just grinned back.

"Asher is right, though. It will be handy in battle." Thorn smiled.

Asher nodded. *"If we can communicate wherever we are, then we'll know if anyone needs help."* He looked to Cedrick. *"Thank you, Cedrick."*

Cedrick bowed his head. *"Thank you for trusting me, even those who were reluctant."* He looked to Nate with a small smile, one I wouldn't mind licking off his lips.

"Like his ears, I want to lick and suck on them or play with them."

Cedrick went bright red as I heard snickering from Ezra.

"You all heard that?"

"Yes, sweetheart," Thorn said.

"Oops."

"His ears are cute," Alex thought at us and then realized what he'd done and burned just as brightly as Cedrick had.

Cedrick coughed out a breath and shifted on his feet. He cleared his throat and said, "Shall we all go and see my mother? We leave tomorrow, correct?" My poor mate was in need of a change of subject.

Asher nodded. "Yes. However, before we leave the room, there is something we need to test first." He glanced to Nate, then Alex. "If you would, Alex."

"Me?" Alex blurted, his voice high. When no one said anything, Alex sighed. "Fine." I wasn't sure what was going on until Alex moved over to Cedrick. I glanced to Nate. His stance was tense. Alex rubbed his hands together and stuttered out, "D-Do you, ah, I-I mean, I know you don't like guys that way, but um, so we know if, um, we need to see... that is…. Blast." He ran a hand over his hot face and then let out a squeal when Cedrick hooked an arm around Alex's waist and brought him flush against Cedrick's front.

"Is this enough to tell?"

"Um…" was all Alex said as he stared flustered up at Cedrick.

I hid my smile behind my hand as I watched them. Cedrick dipped his chin and said, "It is not that I do not like men. I do.

However, Paige is my world at the moment and then eventually, when we get to know one another, I would like to explore more with you and the rest of the men."

"O-Okay?" Alex blinked slowly. "I mean, I think it's okay." He turned his eyes to me. "Is it?"

Removing my hand, I smiled wider and nodded.

"That's good," Cedrick said. He glanced over Alex's head to Nate. We all searched him out, finding him still against the wall. I didn't see any jealousy. He looked somewhat relaxed, so the mind link seemed to have helped his wolf settle.

"Let's go," he barked and opened the door before exiting.

"Is he always like this?" Cedrick asked as he released Alex from his arm. Alex stumbled back a little, but Thorn was there to steady him.

"Nate's a grumpy pain in my ass," I told him, taking his hand as we walked toward the door. "But I wouldn't have him any other way. I love the douche."

I heard Nate grunt; it was light, so I knew he liked what I'd said.

"He grows on you, like a fungus," Ezra teased and then tripped when he moved out of the room. Laughing, he shoved at Nate who'd been the one to mess his steps up. "See what I mean."

Cedrick, who was smiling, nodded. We walked down the hall, and as we did, the people moved out of our way, bowing in respect. Only one woman stepped in front of us. She bowed so low we got a view of her ample breasts just about ready to spill out of her dress.

"My lord, it is good to see you." She straightened and smiled coyly while twisting a strand of her hair around a finger. I wanted Alex to light her hair on fire.

"Elizitenth, we're very busy at the moment. We'll speak later," Cedrick told her. We waited for her to move. She didn't. Would throwing her out of the way look bad?

Her eyes moved down to our joined hands. She raised her gaze and said, "When am I able to move back into my room beside yours, my lord? I have missed you."

"Oh fuck," Ezra muttered.

He fucked her.

She was in a room right next to Cedrick's? Wait a goddamn moment. We were put in a room next to his.

My powers rushed through me. My teeth, claws, and body grew. I dropped Cedrick's hand and spun to face him. "You put me in her room?" I snarled.

"She's in my room?" the harpy shrilled.

I snaked a hand out, grabbed her around the neck and smiled with all my teeth showing when I heard her choking. Slowly, I turned my head to her. "Shut. The fuck. Up." I shook her and looked back to Cedrick.

"I see what you mean by possessive," he commented over my head. Was that a smile on his face? I would knock it off as soon as the wiggly bitch died.

"Love, let go of her," Asher said coolly. "She isn't worth it. This is mild since you have both completed the bond. If it occurred after, the woman would be dead by now."

Cedrick's eyes flashed. He looked down at me and cupped my cheeks. His thumb traced over my lips, ignoring the sharp teeth. He didn't look repulsed by me, how I looked, or by my actions. All I could see in his eyes was warmth.

"My beautiful Paige, she means nothing to me. She never has and never will. You are my everything from this day and until my last breath."

I dropped her and called back my powers. "You have a way with words, Cedrick." I curled my arms up around his neck and pulled him down so I could kiss him. I needed to show her he was mine.

The woman staggered to her feet, rubbing her neck and breathing hard. "D-Does she know how many women you had on that floor? One woman was never enough—" She broke off on a scream when I lunged for her.

Arms circled my waist and I was lifted off the floor and flung over a shoulder. "Let me go. She deserves to die. They all do." I kicked, punched, and yelled at whomever was carrying me. All I could focus on was the whore being shoved aside by Nate. "Punch her, Nate. I give you permission." The asshole just laughed and made his way down the hall.

A door opened as we went through. The last thing she saw was my middle finger before the door closed again.

"Put me down," I demanded. I was placed on my feet, and I glared up at Cedrick with my hands on my hips. Then I kicked him in the shin. "You put me in her room! You had many women please you!" I kicked him again.

"This was all before you captured my heart and soul, my beautiful." His hands landed on my shoulders, and he rubbed up and down my arms. "There will never be another woman in my life and bed but you."

I snorted and punched him in the stomach. "How can I satisfy you when you've had multiple women on your floor there to just jump into your bed? There's only me, Cedrick. You tied your knot to little old me, and now you're stuck. I bet you're regretting it, asshole." I threw out my hands in frustration. "Well, tough shit, you're stuck with me forever."

He grinned down at me. "I wouldn't want it any other way,

Paige Alice. You're more than enough for me. In fact, I now understand why you need so many mates."

I gasped, suddenly wanting to mess with him more since it annoyed the hell out of me he'd known I was his mate and he put me in a room where his former plaything slept. "Are you saying I'm too much?"

"No!" he cried, then groaned. "Does anyone want to help me?"

My acting skills weren't the best, but I thought I would try for the moment since I wasn't ready to forgive him for being inconsiderate. "You'll all regret taking me as a mate one day. I'm an over-the-top psycho." Before anyone could see, I pinched my arm so hard it brought tears to my eyes. Then I thought I should really stop messing with him since he'd come into a relationship where I already had five partners. It wasn't fair. I had to find a new way to torture him. Though, killing all the women in their sleep could make me happy too.

"Fucking fix her. She's leaking again," Nate growled.

"She doesn't have her period anymore. She talked for hours about how grateful she was about it after she figured it out. So it can't be that," Ezra said. Now I just wanted to punch him for that comment.

A slow clap caught my attention. "She could win an Oscar for that performance," a cool, rich voice said. Spinning around, I spotted Cedrick's mother and two of her mates sitting on a couch. One of them was smiling up at me and clapping. He winked.

"What do you mean?" Cedrick demanded as he stepped up beside me.

I slapped him in the stomach. A few laughed, but I ignored them and said, "You brought me to your mom after my little reaction out there?" I glared up at him and then released the glare to gaze back to his mother. Cedrick resembled his mother a lot, only he was more masculine, of course. He even had her white-colored hair.

I bowed. I couldn't help it. She looked more queen than I would ever be. Elegant. And all she was doing was sitting on a couch. Hands landed on my waist and pulled me back up.

"I'm sorry you saw that, Your Majesty."

"Please, call me Castilina, child." She smiled. "You also have nothing to worry about. I understand your reaction, and I'm grateful to know you care for my son deeply enough to want to hurt others before you." She took her mates' hands. "I have had my moments also."

One of her men laughed. "We lost count of the people she threatened over us."

I grinned. "It's good to know I'm not the only one."

She giggled. "You're not, and my son is the same I predict. Except with your already bonded grooms."

I nodded, thinking of the guard when we'd first arrived.

"Six altogether, how lucky are you."

My chest expanded with happiness. "Very."

"May we get back to where your tears went, beautiful?" Cedrick questioned.

The one who'd clapped laughed. "She pinched herself to bring them on. She was playing you, son."

"Son. Why does he call you that?"

"He is my mother's mate. Kiered and I have spent time with all of them more than the father we had. They treated us with kindness and patience, teaching us so much. We see them all as our fathers and long ago asked them to treat us like we were their own."

I gazed up at him, taking his hand in mine and squeezing it.

"That is the sweetest thing ever. I forgive you for putting me in her room. For now."

Cedrick laughed. He lifted my hand and kissed the back of it. "Thank you… I think." I grinned before he faced his mother again as he said, "Mother, may I formally introduce you to my wife, Paige Alice. Ghoul queen." He glanced around and added, "I would also like you to meet our bonded males, Asher Evans, Thorn Jones, Alex Smith, Ezra Morningstar, and Nate Felan. Everyone, this is Castilina, my mother."

Castilina smiled warmly. "It's a pleasure to meet you all. This is Juri." He was the clapping one. "And this is Grandith. My other mate, Yeno, is off getting more food for me, even though I'm stuffed to the brim."

"They never do listen," I teased my own men.

She laughed. "No, they don't."

Cedrick sighed. "We are standing here."

Castilina brightened. "How about you all leave us for some girl time?"

"Not happening," Yuri clipped. He glanced up at me. "No offense to you, but after everything that has happened to our mate, she will have two mates with her at all times."

Nate grunted and I caught Thorn, Asher, and Alex nodding.

"We know that feeling well," Ezra said. I couldn't say I blamed their protectiveness. I would have been the same if one of my mates disappeared for hours having God knows what done to them.

The queen frowned. "Yes, I am sorry for what Therolidi did to you."

I waved a hand in front of me. "It was nothing compared to what was done to you. I'm so very sorry." Tears filled my eyes. Now seeing her, speaking with her, even when it was a short moment, it pained me to know Castilina had been treated the way she was.

Her own eyes filled with tears. When her hand came out, I went and dropped to my knees, taking her hand in both of mine.

"We will heal from the physical and mental wounds inflicted upon us. It is why I think we've been blessed with so many mates." She gave me a wobbly smile, which I returned.

"Your people usually don't have so many mates?"

She shook her head. "No, usually we only have one. But I wouldn't want it any other way. My men complete me in different ways."

Nodding, I grinned and said, "I know exactly what you mean." I was surprised with how comfortable I felt with Castilina. Her people must have loved her as queen before they thought she perished. However, since she was coming back from death, would it be received well or had her former husband turned people against her? If he had, could she handle the situation on her own? She could still need Cedrick's support. "You understand I have to leave here tomorrow, and Cedrick has said he will come?" She nodded. I gripped her hands tighter. "I can't have him come if I know your people will be disgruntled over your appearance and cause you trouble. You need all the support you can get if that happens."

More tears filled her eyes, and she looked up over my head. "You have been blessed with a magnificent wife, son."

"I have, Mother."

She gazed back at me. "Even though you know it will pain you to have a bonded away from you for a long period of time, you are willing to sacrifice that to help me?"

"Of course," I said instantly. I would never want Cedrick to regret coming with me, nor worry about his family every day.

She leaned forward and cupped my cheek. "You honor me, child. I assure you, my people will rejoice at my return. I shall not use his name, but he ran this kingdom down. I did what I could to stop him. My people saw this. They know I will rule strictly but fairly. Cedrick would lose himself if he is not at your side in this battle you take." She smiled. "You are a brave woman, Paige Alice. What you're about to deal with is beyond what anyone else has taken upon themselves, and you do it for your people, yes, your family also, but you show your people the strong female you are, and they will respect you always."

As I dipped my head, feeling my cheeks heat, her hand dropped away. A throat cleared, and I sensed the queen look up. "Our mate doesn't do well with compliments. As far as she's concerned, she would rather run into battle than have people say nice things about her," Asher said.

Castilina laughed. "I can see that, and again it shows me what an admirable woman you are, Paige. Now rise, child, and stand by my son please."

I did as asked. Cedrick curled his arm around my waist again. Castilina looked at us with fondness.

Sudden power surged into the room. Panic filled me until Alex called, "It's okay." Then I relaxed.

The queen's eyes glowed, much like Cedrick's had. It then extended to around her body, and she floated up to her feet with ease. Her hand shot out, and she moved it in all different directions. "I bless this union. I bless the union Paige Alice has with all of her bonded mates. I bless your travels and pray you all stay safe through your hardship."

In a blink, she was back to her normal glow. Still looking

wonderful, no older than thirty, and yet she would have to be older because Cedrick seemed in his late twenties.

"I wish you all the best of luck, and I do hope you will visit when you can."

"Of course we will," I reassured her. There wasn't a chance I'd keep her son away from her.

"Thank you." She smiled, then laughed lightly. "I'll leave my tears for the actual farewell tomorrow, which will embarrass Cedrick."

"Don't worry, I'll cry with you, and then the men will really freak out."

She snorted, then covered her mouth in surprise. "I do like you, Paige."

"Thank you. I like you too, Castilina."

A knock sounded on the door right before it came open without anyone saying anything. Kiered walked in with a bright smile upon his face. Behind him, he dragged Xi in by the arm. Xi didn't look angry, maybe nervous with his frantic eyes searching the room.

"Mother, I have wonderful news," Kiered announced. "I would like you to meet my mate, Xi Huang."

My mouth dropped open and a shocked noise fell out, which had Xi glaring my way.

Castilina clapped her hands and said, "This is a blessed day. Juri, go and collect Yeno. He needs to be here. Xi Huang, welcome to the family. It will be a pleasure to get to know our son's mate." Juri disappeared in a blink of an eye.

Xi bowed low. "Thank you for accepting me; however, it was not needed because I am not his mate."

"Say what?" I said through the link.

"Xi's being stubborn," Ezra stated.

"He's being protective," Asher said.

"I agree. He knows what we walk into, and he doesn't want Kiered to care for him or worry," Alex shared.

"But then how did they find out they were mates if Xi's not accepting it?" I put in.

"What happens when two people come together sexually?" Thorn asked.

Nate snorted. *"Bam, they find out they're bonding as mates."*

"Xi had sex?" Shock had me coughing.

My men laughed around me.

"What do you mean, Xi Huang? You do not want this bond with my son?" Castilina sounded confused and a little hurt for her son's sake.

Kiered stepped forward. "Don't worry about what he says, Mother. He wants this bond and he cares for me as I care for him." He glanced back at a scowling Xi with a warm smile and soft eyes.

Juri reappeared with Castilina's third mate. "What's this I hear of more blessed news?" he asked. He came forward to clasp Kiered's arm and then shook his hand. "Congratulations, son." He glanced to Xi. "Is this fine warrior your mate?"

"He is, Yeno."

"I am not," Xi stated.

Yeno's brows dipped. "What's going on?"

"Kiered, my dear, you cannot have a mate who isn't willing to accept you. It always turns bad for the both of you," Castilina said gently.

Kiered sighed. "He does accept me. He's just being stubborn and trying to protect me."

"Why?" Grandith demanded, now standing beside Castilina with his arms crossed while glaring at Xi.

"Because of what he is," Kiered answered.

The queen straightened. "What are you, child?"

Xi's eyes flashed with pain. He closed them quickly and then reopened them, hardened. "I am no child, and that is another reason I cannot be with Kiered. I am over fifty thousand years old. I am a chimera, and my other half could kill Kiered instantly."

"Are you saying your other half won't accept Kiered as yours?"

Xi's jaw clenched. "He accepts him. However, it doesn't make it safe."

Nate stepped closer. "I know my beast isn't the same, but I always used to worry for my mate, if I accidently shifted in a moment of weakness and they were near, but I know my beast would do anything for our mates. He wouldn't harm one hair on their heads, unless they were being stubborn." He shot me a look, and I rolled my eyes. "Even if we were injured, we would recognize our mates and keep them safe. Have faith in your beast because they are a part of you also."

Ezra shifted closer. "I agree. Hellhounds don't have the best temper, and I know I'm only half one, but I know my beast side would never harm a mate. You can have happiness in your life, Xi. I know my father would want this for you."

"My beast is different than others. We have three minds inside of one. I cannot be certain something won't happen."

"Do you not trust my son?" Castilina asked softly.

"I…." Xi's hands fisted. He looked to the floor, but then nodded.

"Then if you do, trust that my son can take care of himself. That my son will accept you as you are, all of your beasts as well. My son will not only charm you and make you happy for the rest of your days, but he'll also have your beasts wrapped around his finger so that none of them would do him any harm because, as it's been said, you are a part of those beasts also, and you will love him with everything you have in time. Just as they will. Do not be afraid of something that could be so wonderful. I wish I hadn't listened to my parents so many years ago by putting status before love. Then again, I wouldn't have my sons, so it is as it was meant to be. Just how you two were meant for your lives to cross and find each other."

"Your mother is amazing," I sent to Cedrick.

He smiled down at me. *"She is. It's why the people love her. She leads with her heart."*

I could tell Xi was dumbfounded. He didn't know what to say or do, but he kept his eyes on the floor as no doubt thoughts ran around in his mind.

"Should we leave?" Alex asked, always the kindest out of all of us.

But I wasn't that kind. *"Heck no, this is drama I want to see. I never thought Xi could have another facial expression besides his stoic one."*

My men shifted and either looked the other way, coughed, or covered their mouths to hide their amusement.

Xi finally lifted his head and searched Kiered's face for something, but I wasn't sure he found it. Instead, he asked, "Are you certain this is what you want? I am old. I am a chimera. I am—"

"Grumpy?" Ezra offered. "Like a robot most of the time? A killer?"

Xi ground his teeth together. "I would have said colder than most people. Emotions don't come easy for me."

Kiered gave him a small smile as he stepped closer to Xi.

"Where did Xi get his name from? He looks American, but his name is from elsewhere," I asked Ezra.

"Dad said he was adopted when his real parents left him in an alley."

My heart lurched. Xi did deserve this happiness.

Kiered reached out and ran a hand down Xi's arm to his hand where he threaded their fingers together. "I will always accept you in any way or form. You're mine."

Xi's eyes shifted black and then back. He looked to Castilina and bowed. "Will you excuse us, Queen Castilina?"

She smiled wide and nodded. "Of course, and as I said before, Xi Huang, welcome to the family."

He bowed again. "You honor me." He straightened, picked Kiered up over his shoulder, and stalked from the room.

Happiness had me giddy, and I hugged Cedrick to me tightly —pleased for his brother and for Xi. "This day has been a wonderful one."

Castilina walked over and rested her hand on my arm. "Will you stay for a drink to celebrate?"

Leaning my head against Cedrick's chest, I nodded. "I would love to."

This was a future I wanted, one I would fight for. I refused to allow the council to tear this away from me.

CHAPTER FIFTY-FIVE

ASHER

The following morning, we said our goodbyes to Castilina and her mates after they had a royal announcement of her reappearance. It was like she'd said; her people greeted her back with open arms, and I didn't have any fears about taking Cedrick from the fae. Kiered was also coming with us since he and Xi didn't want to be far from one another. But Kiered would transport back to Airrile the night before our meeting with the council to lead members of their force to the destination if they were needed.

Paige sat in the back of the vehicle reading over pages regarding the shifters. We were meeting the tiger and lion packs at the same time. Both betas were willing to greet us together. I had a feeling it was because they didn't trust anyone and hoped meeting together would help their outcome for survival. They would soon discover we weren't there to fight, but to help and give them answers, then ask if they would stand with us against the ones who needed to be taken down.

"I thought packs of different species wouldn't be seen with one another," Paige commented.

Nate grunted. "Usually no, but Asher thinks they're worried we're there to harm them. They probably thought making an alliance was the lesser of two evils and would give them enough strength to fight against us."

"Will they attack before listening?" Cedrick questioned from where he sat next to Paige. I was in the front driving, Thorn sat next to me, and in the middle seat were the rest of our clan. Nate, Alex, and then Ezra. I wasn't sure if Alex noticed he was in the middle for a reason. The other two would have done it that way to protect him. If Paige hadn't have had Cedrick next to her, I would have asked her to sit in the middle of all of us. Even on Alex's lap. However, Cedrick was fast, and he could easily move her with a thought if a threat came at us.

I wasn't sure why the men of my clan and I treated Alex as the weakest since it was the opposite. He was the strongest, yet his young features and sweet, shy manners had us fawning over him. I'd also noticed Thorn, Nate, and myself starting to do it with Ezra. Which was ridiculous because he was a hellhound for God's sake. But we couldn't help it. Our reactions were instinctive.

At least we all knew that Paige came first, above all of us, and we never took offense to it. We loved one another equally. I knew it and could feel it.

"I don't believe they will. We've told them we have some answers to their alphas' disappearances. They'll want to know first."

"Then we'll need to make sure they don't set a trap," Ezra said.

"We will. Even if they did, Cedrick and I could get us all out of there," Alex mentioned without looking away from the book he was reading.

"I won't run," Paige countered. I looked at her through the rearview mirror and caught Alex twisting in his seat to see her.

"I'm not talking about running. Just stepping away until they're not so restless."

She reached out and ran a hand down the side of his face, smiling. "I know you wouldn't run. I shouldn't have said it like that. But I think… and I'm only basing this off Nate being so prickly"—Nate huffed, and though he didn't turn, I still saw his grin—"they're scared, worried, and want to protect their people. They'll be angry and most likely act harshly. We need to keep our cool. Show them we mean no harm and have no secrets right from the start. I think what would help is if Nate and Ezra walked in there in their shifted forms."

"They could take that as a threat also."

"I have a feeling they won't. They'll have others with them, right?" She looked to me, and I nodded. "Then I'm sure they'll have some of their own people in shifted form as well. I also say we leave Xi outside the building."

"I agree," Thorn said. "If we need him, Alex or Cedrick could get him in seconds."

"I'll agree with anything as long as I'm near Paige," Cedrick said.

She snuggled into him. I waited for the jealousy, but it never came. Like with all the men in the vehicle, Paige was all of ours, and sharing her was a part of it. Besides, I enjoyed all the different parts to her she shared with each of us individually. As of now, she was still schoolgirl shy with Cedrick. She was attentive to Alex, cheeky with Ezra, snappy in a fun way with Nate, sweet with Thorn, and wild with me.

I couldn't love another woman as much as I loved Paige Alice, and I would never stop being grateful for the treasure Fate dropped into my lap with her and also with our men.

"We're here," I announced as I pulled the car into an abandoned parking lot of an old factory. Already I could feel eyes on us and knew they would be listening to everything we said. Cedrick's gift to us all came in handy. *"We're surrounded. Keep this link open, and if you need to say anything, say it in here unless we want them to hear."*

Nate grunted. *"Well shit, I guess this mind thing is good."*

"That's a thank-you from Nate," Alex told Cedrick, who smiled.

"You're welcome then."

Nate grunted once more before opening his door. I also got out, as did Thorn, who stretched and acted relaxed.

Nate tipped his head back and scented the air. Ezra did the same on the other side of the car as Alex helped Paige out of the back. Cedrick followed after her and placed his hands on her shoulders. He still looked like a king even though he wasn't now. His knee-length black shirt looked similar to what his guards wore, as if it was made out of dragon scales, but silky enough it seemed comfortable. His black pants underneath looked like cow hide, and his boots came up to the top of his calves. The rest of us wore our own combat gear, except for Paige who wore dark jeans and a long-sleeved black cotton shirt. Though she had one too many buttons undone for my liking. I had been itching to reach out and do it up for her.

"Xi," I called, needing to distract myself or I would follow through with that thought.

"Yes?"

"You and the rest of the men will wait out here. I'll send Alex out if we're in need of anything."

"I do not like that plan."

"It's not up for discussion, Xi," Paige called, her tone hard and unyielding. Xi noticed too because his body tensed, but he nodded once, even when he didn't like it.

"Kiered, wait here too," Cedrick said. Kiered saluted his brother with a smile.

"It will mean we have someone I'm able to communicate with tele- pathically outside," Cedrick explained telepathically.

"Very good, Cedrick," I sent him.

"Nate, Ezra," Paige said aloud, and both men removed their clothes. It was Paige's turn to stiffen.

"Couldn't you have both shifted with clothes on? Ezra, you don't even need to get naked for it. Nate, you have spare clothes in the car."

Ezra's chuckle sounded through my mind. *"But, mi corazón, there is no fun in that."*

Nate snorted but said nothing.

"I'll show you fun." Paige shot a mental image of her flogging Ezra and Nate while they lay in a bed together.

"Angel, that shit will just get me hard, and now's not the damn time." Nate growled as he shifted into his wolf form.

"Mi corazón, now you're just teasing." Ezra leaped forward, and in one swift move, he was in his hellhound form, raising his head to the sky and snarling.

"Does the mind link work in their other forms?" I asked into the link, suddenly nervous it was a bad idea. *"Ezra? Nate?"*

"It feels weird, but I'm here," Ezra answered.

"Same. It's like I'm foggy, but I still know what's going on. I still have thoughts and can help suggest to him, but he's in charge," Nate explained.

Relief had me pushing my shoulders back. *"Paige enters first with Ezra and Nate on each side. Alex is directly behind her with Cedrick and Thorn on each side. Alex, you be point to get her out if needed. I'll be at the back. Do we have it clear?"*

"Yes, boss," Alex chimed in.

Nate let out a bark, and Ezra growled. I didn't need their verbal acceptance through my mind.

"I'm ready." Cedrick nodded.

"In position," Thorn said as he stepped beside Alex who was already behind Paige.

"Have I told you lately I love how you take charge? It really turns me on." Paige sent to me.

I palmed my face and heard Alex and Cedrick stifle a groan. Thorn let drop a quick chuckle while Ezra just laughed in our minds and Nate scoffed.

"My love, any talk about being turned on or sex will not help us."

She looked over her shoulder and gave me wide eyes. *"I can't help it."*

I gave her a small smile and nodded. "Let's move," I voiced, and Paige started forward, her hands threaded through Nate's and Ezra's fur as they walked.

"Eyes everywhere," Alex said.

"I can feel movement through the ground to the left," Cedrick told us.

"Thorn, keep a look out."

"Got it."

"Right ahead," Ezra warned. A Native American man, clad in only jeans, stepped into the afternoon light from a darkened

doorway. I waited for some type of reaction from Paige to see if a sudden attraction hit, but there was nothing. Her features didn't even change from the cool expression she showed. However, I did feel her concern of gaining more mates wash away, for now. She'd confided in me the previous night about her fears of traveling and the possibility of meeting more bonded mates. She didn't want any more. She loved who she had and was concerned that if more were added to the mix, she would have less time for the ones she had.

Of course, I tried to tell her that if the Fates chose her to have more, it would be for a reason that we weren't able to see yet and how it would be added protection for her. When she glared at me, I laughed and told her we would deal with it if it happened and that no matter how many men she received, we all knew she loved each of us all the same. Even if her time with us was sparse.

"Paige Alice, I presume," his deep voice called.

"You would be correct, and you are?"

"Detroit Heming, beta to the lion shifters." His eyes slid over all of us but went back to Ezra. "A hellhound. We weren't informed you had one. He'll have to stay out here."

Paige smiled. "I'm sorry. I go nowhere without my mates."

Detroit's eyes flared for a second. "He's your mate?"

"Didn't I just say that?" I asked through the link.

"Humor him, my love."

"Yes."

There was scuffling going on behind him and behind the broken windows that surrounded the parking area. More people moved closer for a better look.

"Are we having this meeting out here or in there?" Paige asked.

I shifted my gaze all around. I didn't like the number of shifters close to the openings of the building. Nate lifted his head and snarled. Ezra then did the same.

Nate growled into our minds. *"The wolf is on edge. It feels like a trap."*

"My hellhound agrees."

"Do we get Paige out of here?" Cedrick asked.

"Not yet," Paige instructed.

Paige dropped her hands from Nate's and Ezra's fur and took a small step forward. She spread her arms out and asked, "What's the delay? We come in peace. We have our guards standing back near the cars. They're not infiltrating your area. We don't want to fight. We want to talk, and that's it."

He studied her. I didn't like the way his eyes ran over her and stopped on her damn breasts. I knew I should have done up that button.

"You keep looking at our mate like that, we will have a problem," I clipped.

He pulled his gaze up and over to me.

"Asher," Paige warned through the link.

"No, my love. They have to know the consequences, so they do not ogle you like they want a taste."

"It's disrespectful, dove," Alex added. *"You're queen. Remember that."*

"Detroit, let them in" was bit out from inside. The tone was male. It sounded amused and irritated at the same time.

Detroit sighed, turned, and walked back into the building. The darkness swallowed him up. Paige went to go after him until I called out, "My queen, please allow me to enter first."

She stopped, glanced to me, and showed her worry for me, but nodded anyway. She made me proud. I dipped my chin, then lifted it and started forward. I brushed my fingers over her arm as I passed.

"Be careful," she sent me.

"No one will take me from you, love," I promised, because I would do anything to make sure we all got a taste of peace after everything we had already endured.

Stepping through, I sensed movement to my right and left in the doorway. Spinning, I knocked one out and had the other pinned to the wall in seconds. "Tell me why I shouldn't take his life."

"Asher," Paige called.

"Hold," I demanded. Picking the man up by the neck, I faced the room holding the choking man in the air. Since I knew he was a shifter, I dug my claws into his flesh around his neck, ready to rip his throat out if needed.

A man stepped into the light that shined down from the window above. "They weren't supposed to be there. Detroit?"

Detroit huffed. "It was a test. We needed to see how fast you were."

"I will not bring our queen, and *mate,* in here if there are more tests around each corner. Believe I am fast. Believe Alex is a powerful mage. That Ezra and Nate together, even separate, are vicious. That Thorn is strong, and that Cedrick is tricky. But not only that, you all need to believe we fight for everyone, not only our own people, alongside a woman, a queen, who is all that I mentioned we are, but more. She will bring about a good change to all of our communities. She is fierce but fair and so very much loved. Meaning, we will do anything to keep her safe."

"God, I love you."

"And I you, my love."

"Let him go. You can all enter in peace" came a woman's voice from a distance.

"Raquel," the unknown man clipped.

"No, Waylon. I want to hear what they have to say. Besides, they have news about our alpha, and yours, Detroit. They've proved they don't want to fight, else we would have had our asses handed to us. Let them in, you stubborn pricks."

I dropped the man to the ground as lights flicked on all around me just as the man and Detroit drew back into the room more.

I could sense them, but they all stepped out of their hidden areas and about fifty shifters moved further into the building. However, more still walked or waited throughout the rest of the building. The final number was unclear, but if they did plan anything, I knew we would be able to stop them.

"Paige," I called. Ezra entered first, growling low in warning, then Paige stepped through with Nate at her side. Ezra waited for them, and together, the three of them followed me the same way the others had gone. I ignored the footfalls and shuffles around us from the shifters moving back into hiding and kept walking through what looked like a reception area. I entered a room through double doors, and it seemed to be a large conference setting. A big round table was set right in the middle. At the opposite end from the entrance was a woman, my guess was Raquel who spoke before. Detroit, Waylon, and the woman were the only ones sitting. About ten more shifters in their animal form stood at their backs, then behind them, another ten men and women stood guard.

"Please, come in and take a seat. My name is Raquel, and I'm the beta for the tigers. Waylon is our enforcer."

"It's nice to meet you. I wish it was under different circumstances," Paige said as she sat in the chair right across from Raquel. Alex and Thorn moved the chairs out of the way so Ezra and Nate could sit on the floor next to her. I knew they were glaring down the other end at Detroit. Alex, Thorn, Cedrick, and I stood at our mate's back.

"So do I. The alpha of our pack is my mate."

Paige's pain rolled through us. She slid her hand forward on the table. "I am so sorry for your heartache and worry. We do hope to bring him back… bring them both back."

"As long as they're alive," Raquel added.

Paige smiled sadly at her and nodded. "Yes."

"So you know who has them?" Detroit demanded. His fist pounded into the table. "Who's to say this isn't some trick of your own and you have my brother yourself?"

Paige sat back in her seat more and shook her head. "You're a fool to think I would do something like this." The lions behind him roared and hissed. Ezra and Nate stood and snarled back at them. Paige laid a hand on each of their heads. "It's okay, guys." They settled and sat back down as soon as the noise stopped at the other end. "Do you know anything about me?" Paige asked.

"We only know you're the new ghoul queen to a race we thought were extinct."

Paige nodded. "The former queen had to take our people into hiding. Over time, we also gained people of other races. They sought out our community for refuge away from the council."

"Why? As far as we know, the council has been just," Raquel said.

"So many thought that as well. Alex, Nate, and I did too, when we worked for the council as their elite enforcers," I told them.

Their shock showed from their widening eyes and how their pulses raced.

"The council is corrupt, and they are the ones who are behind your alphas' disappearances," Alex stated.

Shouts and conversations started up down the other end. Raquel's hand rose. The sound stopped immediately. "You'll need to give us more information for us to believe this story."

Alex clicked his fingers. A file dropped into his hand. He walked it down the other end and then slid it over the table to Raquel since she seemed the more sensible one. She opened it and sucked in a breath. She quickly passed some papers to Detroit. He took one look and paled.

What they were seeing were pictures Alex had found in Councilman Gerald's computer. They were of the elite enforcers he was in charge of kidnapping both alphas after they'd beaten them senseless.

"Where did you get these?" Raquel asked, her voice thick with emotions.

"I managed to hack into a council member's computer before I was detected and found these. The people you see taking your alphas are members of the elite force."

"Why did you look into them in the first place?" Detroit questioned. I wasn't sure he bought the photos or if he still thought this was all a trick from us.

"When I came into my queen powers, I was attacked by demons. Someone sent them after me. It was lucky I had my men at my back, or I would have been taken. We found out the council was behind it."

"For what reason?" Detroit asked.

"For power," Cedrick answered. "I'm unsure if the news has been heard here as yet. In the realms of Airrile, we lost our mother five years ago. After my father was murdered, I became king." They looked upon Cedrick in a new light, with a lot more wariness. "It was only yesterday we found my mother alive. My father had made us believe she was killed when the palace was attacked. However, instead he'd locked her away to drain her of power and life force, to which he took within himself, making him stronger."

Gasps and shouts of outrage echoed around the room.

"This is what the council is doing," Paige announced. Everyone quieted once more. "Cedrick's father got the idea when he stumbled upon it in the basement at the council compound six years ago. Alex, Nate, and Asher have worked out that the cases, which seemed suspicious, could have happened for this reason."

"You think our alphas are being drained of their power and life force?" Raquel uttered, without taking her eyes from the images in front of her.

"Yes," I answered, and since they had been missing for a year, I wasn't sure about the chances of finding them alive. Yet, Castilina was down in that room for five years. However, only one person had been draining her. If all the council members were in on this, that was ten people.

We wouldn't know anything until we were in there.

"What are you asking from us?"

"To be witnesses and offer backup if needed when we go to the council."

Detroit stood. "Why would you go there?"

"Because I know my people, my family, won't be safe until something is done about them. I'm going to be the something," Paige answered.

Raquel finally lifted her head. Tears glistened in her eyes.

"You have the tigers at your back. Let us know when and how you'll need us, and we'll be there."

"Raquel," Waylon pressed.

She shook her head. "No, Waylon. This is Zion we're talking about. Our alpha, my mate." She stood and turned to her people. "Who will stand with me and back Paige Alice?"

Roars erupted around in the room, but also outside of it.

Raquel turned to Detroit. "What of the lions? Will you join?"

Detroit's jaw ticked. He glanced back at his people on his side, and I caught a woman nod. Who she was, I didn't know, but she did scent like Detroit.

He faced us. "We will be there also. Send us in, and we'll get everyone in their basement out."

Paige stood. She dipped her head a little and straightened. "Thank you."

"No, Paige," Raquel said. "It is us who should thank you. We've been doing everything to find out what happened that night, but came up empty-handed. You've given us hope, even if it's a small amount." She bowed. Her people followed suit, and then she turned and walked out of the back of the room.

Detroit nodded. "We've been in limbo not knowing. Now we have a plan of action; it gives us something to fight for."

"Something right?" Paige pressed with a small smile.

Detroit laughed, but it didn't last. "Yeah, I suppose. Call us when the time comes."

"We will," I told him, and then he, along with his people, left the building. I held up my hand until I knew there wasn't another being about, then lowered it.

"That went better than I thought it would," Thorn said.

"It did." I nodded.

"We will be able to count on them. They want revenge, but

also to find out exactly where their alphas are," Cedrick commented.

"I agree. I would also like to thank you all for listening to my instructions and trusting I had everything under control," I told them with a small smile.

"It was hard, but like old times." Alex grinned.

"It's also a turn-on, like Paige said." We all looked to Ezra. Paige and Alex laughed, while Cedrick and I smiled.

Paige clapped her hands. "Now it's time for the vampires. For Asher's former lover and now friend who I hope I don't kill."

"Love" was all I said.

"Yeah, yeah, I know she's nothing to you now and all that jazz. But if she looks at you like you're her dinner, I'll be snapping the fangs right out of her mouth."

Fuck.

CHAPTER FIFTY-SIX

PAIGE

We drove to the airport and got on one of two private jets belonging to the former queen. Actually, they were my private jets. God, that still shocked me. Even though with all we had been through, I was sure it would take me another year or two to get used to the fact I was a queen.

On the two-hour flight, we took the time to rest, eat, and used it for alone time. Xi wasn't pleased again he couldn't get on the same plane as I was, but Kiered calmed him enough to climb onto the other one with the rest of the guards. I was looking forward to some quiet time with only my mates on board. The plane had already been stocked with the necessities, knowing in advance from Thorn what we would need. The only food we didn't have was for Asher, but that was supplied from any one of us.

I had a need to be his dinner that night.

Ezra, Alex, and Nate were all arguing over who would feed him while Cedrick sat back smiling. Thorn's laughter indicated he also found it amusing. He couldn't feed Asher since he didn't have enough blood running through him like I had with my heart working for me. Still, it didn't stop Asher from marking him with his teeth and getting a tiny nip from Thorn when he wanted. It was something Thorn enjoyed.

"Asher," I called and held out my hand.

His eyes bled green. He stood and glided over to me. In seconds I was out of my seat with him sitting in it, and I was positioned on his lap.

Asher swept my hair over my shoulder, and I shivered. The others quieted and went back to their seats. They were fine with me feeding Asher. I could tell from the way all of them watched us with either a smile or heated looks.

"You know you have nothing to worry about, love."

"I know, but I can't help worrying. She was a big part of your life, Asher."

"She was, but now you are and will always be."

I hummed under my breath. "Maybe if you keep telling me that while we're there, I won't have to hurt her."

His chuckle shook my body. "You are vicious, and I love it."

Turning to have his eyes, I smiled. "I'm glad you do." I pressed my lips to his. It was only meant to be a quick kiss, but when kissing any of my mates, it was so easy to get lost in the feeling. Which was what we did. Asher's hand threaded into my hair, and he dropped the other to my hip and up under my shirt where he gently traced the skin there, causing me to grip him closer to me.

His lips trailed over my cheek. He nipped at my ear, and I tilted my head to the side to give him better access. When he slid his tongue down over my neck, I bit my bottom lip and whimpered. He sucked on my skin before I felt him graze his fangs across it, and then he struck. It was fast and painless, but oh so very pleasurable. I grabbed hold of his arms and ground down on his lap with his first pull of my blood into his mouth. He groaned around me, and it vibrated right down to my clit. I moaned, tipped my head back, and rubbed my hands up and down his arms.

My heart was already beating hard in my chest, but on his next pull, it went haywire and my skin felt alive. "Asher," I moaned.

Another pull, I orgasmed in my jeans without a touch to my pussy. My body quivered and shook. I panted out a breath, and licked my lips just as he swiped his tongue over my neck.

"Delicious as always, love."

"Hmm" was all I could say, which made him chuckle.

"Is watching Asher feed from our mate always that intense?" I heard Cedrick ask.

Ezra laughed. "It's more sometimes, especially when we're all in a room naked together. Asher has a way of sending very pleasant vibes to the ones he's feeding on."

Cedrick made a noise in the back of his throat, and I had a feeling he was now thinking of wanting to see how it felt for himself.

"Alex, I'll need fresh clothes and a clean body," Ezra admitted, and I couldn't stop the giggle. I opened my eyes to see him staring down at the wet patch on his pants.

"I have to admit I am in need of the same," Cedrick said, and I swung my gaze to see, but his shirt covered the front of him.

"Same," Nate grunted.

"Let's just say all of us then." Alex smiled.

"Yes," Thorn said.

"Of course," Asher replied. "Our queen makes me crazed enough to act like a teen and jizz my pants."

Another giggle burst out of me, and I looked around at all my mates smiling over at me. We needed more moments like these. Happy and carefree.

OF COURSE THE vampire's lair was an old mansion in New Orleans. Like that wasn't cliché. We'd just pulled through the huge-ass gate and stopped out front of a gothic-looking place. I climbed out after Asher and Thorn and stood out in front while thanking Fate for once that we hadn't been attacked on the way there from the airport. My nerves weren't the best in that moment after keeping an eye out the whole way there for trouble, and I knew they wouldn't settle until we got this out of the way. With Asher far away from Cynthia as soon as possible.

"We're getting the stare down from the sentries placed about," Ezra sent through the link. The mind connection had been the best asset to our family since it made communication so much easier. Yet I hoped Cedrick knew we wanted him within our fold because we cared for him, not for what he offered us.

It was something I needed to make sure he understood.

Asher nodded. *"I see them. Don't worry. Cynthia will have the place under control."*

I screwed my nose up and looked to the cobblestone ground. *"Of course, Cynthia will have the place under control. She's wonderful. She's perfect. She's dead."* Glancing up, I realized everyone was looking at me. *"Huh, I didn't block that, did I?"*

Nate, Ezra, Cedrick, Alex, and Thorn grinned, all at different watts, but still they were grinning. Asher frowned. Oh shit. Was he upset I mocked his precious Cynthia?

"You do understand I'm dead also, love?"

"What?"

"I'm of the undead. Do you have something against it?"

I placed my hands on my hips and turned to him more. *"Sorry, what?"*

"Dove, you said and I quote 'She's wonderful. She's perfect. She's dead.' Asher is concerned you have a dislike to dead beings." His lips twitched because he knew that was an idiotic thing to say. So silly. I laughed, and then laughed some more.

"Asher, you fool. I'm dead. Well, I was. I still think I am. Thorn's also dead. No, I don't have anything against dead beings. In fact, I love a few of them. I meant that she would be dead. That I would kill her fully."

Before he could say anything, our attention went to the steel doors as they slid open with a creak. A woman, who looked very similar to the younger version of Catherine Zeta-Jones, appeared. Asher had had sex with her.

I wanted to throw my hands up in the air as my insecurities took hold and told me Asher had settled for little plain old me.

"Merde," I uttered under my breath, taking on Cedrick's French swear word.

Some of my men coughed. Asher reached for my hand and took it, sending me serenity and love. I felt like dropping his hold, but I was being petty. All of my men had a past, and I had to remember it. I didn't have to like it, but I had to remember all of them were older than I was. So I would suck it up…. Well, until she pissed me off.

Like she currently was as she gazed down at Asher adoringly.

Clenching my jaw, I gripped Asher's hand tightly. Heat hit my back. Nate's scent swept over me, and then Alex's as he stepped up to my other side and took my free hand.

I touched their minds and said, "Are you guys just trying to stop me from killing someone for looking too beautiful for her own good?"

"Who, us?" Alex smiled as he stared forward, giving nothing away as we had our private conversation.

"I don't care if you kill all the exes." Nate's hands dropped to my waist.

"Really not the greatest thing to say." I could feel Ezra's humor.

"She is nothing compared to you," Cedrick said. He moved to Asher's other side and I was grateful because I hoped his steely look would get her to back off. I didn't like the smile on her as she descended the many stairs.

"I agree," Thorn added.

"As do I. Please do not kill anyone on my behalf, my love, because no matter what you do or how you act, I will love you."

Thinning my lips, I hated how he just blew my anger right out of the water.

"Asher, my darling, it is so good to see you." Cynthia made her way directly to Asher, ignoring everyone else in the process. I wasn't having it. Not only was it disrespectful to not acknowledge me as queen, but she had chosen to try and push my buttons already by making it clear she thought nothing of me, even as his bonded mate.

Unless she didn't know. A smile crossed my lips. I was more

than ready to inform her. Ezra swore through the mind link when he looked at me. *"She's smiling."*

"Shit, that's not good," Nate commented.

"Not in this situation at least," Thorn said.

"Beautiful, now isn't the time to lock us from your thoughts." I sensed Cedrick look around Asher to me, but I kept my eyes on the bitch in front of us.

I wanted to roll my eyes. They were overreacting. Maybe.

Just as she started to reach for Asher, who tensed, I dropped my mates' hands and stepped in front of Asher. My smile grew. "Hello, I'm Paige Alice, ghoul queen, and bonded mate to Asher, Thorn, Nate, Cedrick, Ezra, and Alex. I don't believe we've met, and I'm sorry, I haven't heard who you are."

"Ha, she just peed all over you, Asher," Ezra teased.

"She also peed on you, Ezra, but, my love, you did it beautifully. She was disrespectful." I could sense Asher's unease. He didn't understand why Cynthia would act that way. Maybe she wasn't the upstanding vampire he thought she was after all.

Cynthia glanced over my head to Asher. "Oh, yes, my apologies, Queen. Welcome to the Barrick Clan's residence. My name is Cynthia Mirrer." She waited for some type of reaction from me, but when she didn't get it, she once again glanced to Asher. "Though, I find it strange you've never heard of me."

I tilted my head to the side in an act of confusion. "Really, why's that?" I straightened. "I'm new to all this, sorry, but your name doesn't ring any bells."

Her jaw tightened before she was back to smiling. "Why, I helped Asher through a troubled time in his past. We became close. I thought he would have mentioned it, being your mate and all."

Oh, bitch.

"We've been very busy in such a short amount of time, Cindy. I'm sorry you haven't come up."

Nate snorted, Ezra chuckled, but my other mates hid their amusement well.

"It's Cynthia."

"Yes." I nodded. "Shall we get down to business?"

A tick started in her perfect forehead. "Of course, but do you mind if I greet Asher since we were so close?"

"Greet him all you like." I waved a hand around. She went to step around me, smiling once more, but I grabbed her wrist. "Just don't touch him. I'm very possessive of my men."

She looked down at me and must have heard the seriousness in my cold tone or seen something in my expression because she then nodded. "Yes, Queen Alice."

I nodded and released her arm. I didn't move. I stayed looking up at the ugly place when I heard, "Asher, it is lovely to see you after so long."

"A pleasure, Cynthia. However, if you disrespect my queen, my bonded mate, as you did once more, it won't be a pleasure next time."

She made a noise in the back of her throat. "I didn't think you would want to bond to something so—"

"Watch what you say here, Cynthia," Asher snarled. "Why are you acting as such? I spoke highly of you, and this is how you pick to show yourself to my clan?"

She laughed without humor. "Your clan. Of mixed race?"

"My clan. My family, my pack, my everything. I never knew you to be prejudiced, Cynthia. What's going on with you?"

"Something's happening. The guards are moving," Nate said into the link. He pulled me close and then gently pushed me toward Alex, who slid an arm around my waist.

A rattle startled me. I glanced back and saw the gates were closing.

"Kiered just told me Xi is concerned also." Cedrick added into our minds.

For some reason, I wanted people on the other side of that gate before it closed us all in fully.

"Cedrick, can Kiered take Xi to the other side of the gate?"

"Yes, but why?"

"I don't know. I just feel like we need to."

"That's all I need to know."

"No," we heard Xi clip.

I shifted my gaze to them standing near the rear vehicle. Xi started toward me but Kiered grabbed his wrist and they disappeared for a second to reappear outside of the property, just as the gates finished shutting.

"I am sorry, Asher."

"Cynthia, what have you done?" Asher's gaze moved all around the area. Into the link he ordered, *"Gather around Paige, now!"*

My men quickly surrounded me. Thorn held his swords out and up, ready. Nate half shifted while Alex called his powers forward, only to groan and clutch his head. He swayed and I reached out for him, crying his name as terror seized my heart and cooled my body. My hands shook as I ran them over him, searching for a wound but finding nothing. Dread twisted my insides painfully.

Ezra helped me steady him. "Alex, what is it?" he questioned with panic in his voice. Our others surrounded Ezra and me with Alex. Each trying to pay attention to what was around them and off what would be concerning them the most. Alex.

"Tell me what's happening?" Asher demanded into our minds

as he stopped next to us and threw Cynthia to the ground. She rolled over and stared up at me with a tired look.

"What's wrong with Alex?" Nate's panicked tone rolled through everyone.

"Alex? Dammit, Alex, answer us," Thorn called.

"I have Kiered seeking help. We need to find out why Alex is as he is," Cedrick said.

"Alex, please, tell us what's wrong," I begged aloud, cupping his cheeks under his hands and holding his head.

Alex's weight took Ezra and me to our knees with him. His pain-filled gaze met mine. "Father" was all he said before crying out and gripping his head once more.

"What does he mean?" I yelled at Ezra.

"I don't know. I don't fucking know." I had never seen the pure fear in Ezra's features before, and I knew my own would show the same. Wide eyes, pinched brow, lips shaped in a frown or thinned.

"He means me" came a voice. Nate and Thorn parted enough for me to see a man standing on the top of the stairs near the front doors.

"What is this?" Asher snarled. He picked Cynthia up by the throat and threw her so she sailed up the stairs to land next to the man.

The man, who I presumed was Alex's father, glanced down at Cynthia in distaste before smirking back at us.

Alex moaned. He lifted his head and sucked in a shuddering breath. He licked his dry lips and whispered, "Help me up." Ezra and I did, only we didn't dare release him to stand on his own since his body shook like it had just run a marathon. "I should have known you would be a part of this."

"You were always the slow one in the family."

"What did you do to him?" I demanded, glaring up at the short, stout man in front of us. Alex looked nothing like his father, and I could never see my Alex having that sneer of hatred on his face. How did my Alex turn out so pure, so sweet when he had a father as such? One willing to hurt his child for the council's sake.

"And you must be the pathetic ghoul queen." He looked me over, causing Ezra, Nate, and even Asher to growl under their breath. "I'd heard my son had taken up with you. Tell me something, bitch, how are you better than the one he'd been intended to? One with pure magic running through her veins? One made from a fine magical family?"

"Simple, my pussy is made of magic."

A startled laugh dropped from Alex and Ezra. Nate, of course, snorted, while my other men smiled.

The douche's face turned a dark shade of red. "You disgusting piece of rubbish."

"Watch what you say," Alex warned, his tone harsh and deadly.

"His name, Alex?" Thorn asked.

"Anthony Smith."

Anthony's gaze locked onto Alex. "You dishonor our family for this?" He waved a hand my way.

"Yes. I would do it over and over again because I never understood how I could have been born into such a cold, uncaring family. Paige has shown me love, as any mate would."

"Mate?" he yelled. Spittle flew from his mouth. "Mate?"

"Yes, mate."

"Tell me it hasn't been completed," he ordered.

Alex straightened even more, seeming to gain energy back.

"It has." Alex smiled. "I am also mated to Nate. He and his wolf chose me to be one of his."

Anthony paled just before he spit to the side. "You'll never be accepted back into the family. You are dead to us."

Alex laughed, but cut it off with a snarky smile. "I have my family. I do not need any of you."

"Alex, what did he do to you before?" I asked through the link, needing to know so I could prepare if it happened again.

"Since I am of his blood, he used it against me and blasted my mind with a magical stunning spell. Families are able to cross through our barriers easier than any other."

"Can he do it again?" Asher asked.

"He's already trying. I'm managing to block him now that I'm prepared for it."

"I shall help, Alex. My mind skills are above most," Cedrick said. I reached back and squeezed his hand.

Alex looked over his shoulder to Cedrick and smiled. Tension eased from his face and body, so I knew Cedrick already helped him block his father out, no matter the family connection they had for each other. Like Alex said, we were his family now, and I would make sure none of Alex's former family wanted anything from Alex again.

Obviously, they never deserved him in their lives.

"You can't protect your mind from me forever, Alex," Anthony warned.

"I can, Father, because I have help from people who actually care about my well-being."

Anthony scoffed. "Is this about your cousin? Your tantrum took you into their arms because you couldn't handle a little heat?"

Alex's magic resurfaced; his eyes glowed brighter than they

ever had. He took a step forward. Ezra's and my hands fell away from him. "A little heat? You allowed my cousin to test his spells on me while I was magically bound."

Anthony waved a hand around. "He had promise. We had to test his skills."

"If any of it killed me, would you have cared?"

"We would have missed your powers." He licked his lips as if he could imagine tasting something delicious.

It dawned on me then. "You'd offered him up to the council."

Anthony's gaze slid to me. "I didn't have to offer. The boy wanted to work for them to get away from us."

I couldn't say I blamed Alex. I would have as well if my family were mental cases.

"The council wanted to see if his powers would increase under them."

"So they had more to drain from him, you mean," Nate growled.

Anthony smiled. "Yes."

"Did they promise you his powers?" Cedrick asked.

He smiled, and it wasn't pleasant. "No, they were going to the magical members on the council."

"Then what were you getting from knowing about it and keeping your mouth shut?" Thorn questioned.

"Money and status."

"Jesus fuck, does everyone care about money and status?" I demanded loudly, frustration taking over my mouth for a moment.

"Unfortunately, most do, love," Asher answered.

Cynthia scoffed. "All you cared about was money and status back in the day. You act like you don't now, but look at you, a mate to a queen. My, you have grown."

"I learned money and status wasn't everything the moment I met Paige. In the short span of our time, she has shown me there is so much more to life. As have the men in my clan. Even if Paige hadn't been fated to be queen, I would still be with her no matter if we lived on the street because she opened my eyes to a love so consuming it's everything."

A pained expression washed over Cynthia's face, and her eyes darkened.

"She loves you."

Asher's gaze was full of surprise when it swung to me. *"No."*

I nodded and offered him a small, sad smile. "I'm sorry," I gave her. It was her turn to look at me in shock.

"What are you talking about?" I felt "fool" was left off the end of her sentence.

"Paige," Asher called.

I shook my head and stepped up beside Alex. "Asher spoke highly of you. I didn't like it, of course, because I'm a possessive woman, but he thought of you as a close friend. I'm sorry he didn't love you as you do him. I'm sorry your feelings are crushed as he stands with me. I'm sorry for your pain as you look at him, knowing you have lost him. I would never want that for another person. Especially not someone who cares for one of my mates as much as you do." I paused, letting my words sink in and watching as a few tears overflowed from her eyes. "But I can't say I'm sorry for meeting him, because my life wouldn't be the same without him in it. He helps me in so many ways. I love him with every breath, with every heartbeat, with every look, touch, and taste." I glanced to Anthony. "I love all my mates the same and will do anything in my power to make sure their future, *our* future, is one filled with harmony." I glanced back to Cynthia to find her looking at Asher longingly.

"I thought we would eventually be together. I was giving you time to love me as I love you. Maybe I shouldn't have done that. I should have told you how I felt many, many years ago because then we would have been together, and you wouldn't have found her. But I listened to your dreams of being something by working for the elite enforcers. You wanted to do good for the people. I respected you for it. I understood why, and then I let you walk out without saying anything. Since then, I thought you would see what I could have been for you. I kept waiting. I shouldn't have, and I should have stopped you from walking away from me. I should have held on to you and never let go." She looked to me and studied me for a couple of beats before looking back to Asher. "Now it's too late." She closed her eyes for a moment from whatever she saw on Asher. When she opened them, more tears dropped. She took a large gulp of air and then composed herself. "I wasn't the only sister who fell though."

"Shut up," Anthony yelled. He went to grab her, but she easily sidestepped him.

"What do you mean?" I asked.

"My sister hunts you all, not only for your powers and life source, but because she also loves a man who can never be hers."

"Shut your fucking mouth, vampire," Anthony bit out.

"Who?" Nate clipped.

"Jessica. Sister by blood, but not sire." She laughed without humor. "I asked her to take care of you since she just started out on the council when you arrived there."

"Jessica is your sister?" Asher asked.

"Yes."

"But you're nothing alike," Alex said.

"We had different mothers." She dodged Anthony's hand again. "There's something you should know—" She cried out as blood bloomed on her chest.

"Father, no!" Alex screamed. "He's shredding her heart."

Only it was too late. Whatever spell Anthony used had already taken hold, and he smiled gleefully as blood soaked more and more of her gown. I watched as Cynthia met Asher's gaze one last time and she mouthed, "I'm sorry."

"Forgiven," Asher called solemnly, just as she dropped to the ground. Completely dead.

CHAPTER FIFTY-SEVEN

The area around us was silent for a moment, and then chaos reigned down upon us all. The vampire sentries appeared from nowhere, flashing into existence after their master was killed. They went for Anthony but were bounced off an invisible wall. Still, they kept trying and trying.

More mages appeared behind Anthony. Alex cursed. "My family have come to help him."

I chanced a glance away from the battle to Asher. He stared down at Cynthia's body. My heart ached for him. I pushed the thought away of Asher regretting his chosen path when he could have had one with Cynthia and concentrated for a moment on more so wanting to wrap him up in my arms and tell him he would be okay, but we didn't have time. "Cedrick, why can't Kiered and Xi get back in?"

"There's something blocking them. It's as if the house and grounds are wrapped in a protective bubble," he replied.

Alex added, "It will be linked only to those under Anthony's coven. I was cut from being a member a long time ago."

"Shit." I'd seen that before when I'd first met Alex and the others, and I'd walked right through Alex's.… I had walked right through their protective bubble.

Could I walk people back with me?

We would have to join the fight soon, and we may need all the help we could get. I sent the plan to my men.

"I'll go and try to counter their spell to get the others through," Alex said into our minds. I grabbed him and kissed him quickly.

"Stay safe and remember you are stronger than any of them. You're amazing, Alex Smith." He nodded with a smile, and a light blush coated his cheeks. There was my mate. I looked to the others around me. *"Ezra, Thorn, and Cedrick, please help him. Cedrick, find out if you can trick them with an illusion. Ezra, see if you can frighten them. Nate, you're with me."* I took Nate's hand in mine and turned toward the gates.

"You also need to stay safe, sweetheart," Thorn called.

"I will," I said back through the mind link.

"What will you have of me?" Asher asked. His voice sounded low and full of hurt.

"Place Cynthia's body somewhere safe. She'll need a proper farewell after all this."

I stumbled when Asher blasted me with his love. I let mine wash over him more slowly as Nate straightened me and we finished the mad dash toward where Xi looked like he was about to have a heart attack as he banged on the invisible wall right in front of the outside of the entrance.

The gaps in the gates were wide enough for a small woman,

like me, to slip through. But then how would I get them back over to this side? That was *if* I could get them back through. Then there was also the risk, if I did go out there and couldn't get Xi back through, he would probably keep me out there for safety.

Stopping at the gate, I said, "If I can get through and drag you back through the magic shield, are you able to break the gate wide enough for you both?"

"Yes," Xi hissed, his eyes pure black. Oh, he was angry and wanted to hurt people. Kiered stood back waiting, rolling his eyes at his mate. He was calm and collected; really they were perfect for one another.

"Promise me you won't keep me out there even if I can't get you through?"

He snarled at me, his upper lip tipped as he kept growling. Nate got closer and growled in his own way, which had Xi stopping and nodding. I wish I could speak beast; I was sure they just had a conversation.

"All right." I nodded. When I started to move closer, hands gripped my waist and I was suddenly turned in large, extra-hairy arms. Nate looked down at me in his half form. Concern bled in his eyes. Reaching up, I cupped his cheek. "I'll be fine. You just keep an eye out, okay?"

He nodded, stuck his nose into my neck, and drew in my scent. "I'll be a bigger dick if you get hurt from doing this."

Laughter bubbled out of me. I kissed his cheek and stepped back. "Then I better make sure not one hair on my head gets damaged."

He grunted.

Turning back around, I moved closer to the gates. Slowly, I put my hands up and pressed them forward, expecting to feel something stop me before I touched the metal on the gates, but there was nothing there. I pushed a hand past the poles on the gates and found that same tingle I got when I walked through Alex's shield. Quickly, I turned my body enough to slip through the tight gap between two poles. My whole body hummed from the shield.

As soon as I was through, Xi grabbed me and pulled me all the way out. Nate snarled at his roughness, but I ignored it because I knew he was worried. I was his mission. If he kept me alive, the others would do anything to stay alive, and that included Lucifer's son.

Xi's hands trailed over my body, searching for any injuries and causing Nate to growl threateningly at the man.

"Do I need to leave the two of you alone?" Kiered sniffed.

"Ew, no. He's like a father figure to me with how protective he is."

I regretted saying anything because Xi suddenly stood and his chest puffed out. His eyes, even though they were still black, seemed to soften as he took me in.

Kiered groaned. "You've touched on his fatherly instincts."

It was my turn to groan. "Now I'll never get rid of him."

Kiered moved, stepping in front of Xi. Xi's gaze moved down to his mate, his lips starting to tip up right before Kiered kissed him. "You good now? Your girl is safe, your mate is safe, can you come back to me?"

"Yes." He nodded, though his eyes didn't switch back. His beasts were close to the surface.

Kiered patted his cheek gently. "That'll do." He faced me. "Now, how are we going to get back in there and kick some mage ass?"

"Get me through the shield and I will get us in," Xi ordered.

Nodding, I faced toward Nate, who was looking at the destruction near the house. Bodies littered the ground. My pulse raced, my insides cooled, and I prayed none of them were my mates, but I didn't want to risk checking in on them in case I was a distraction.

A hand touched to my back, and Kiered whispered into my ear, "They'll be okay. They're tough, strong, and would do anything to make sure they stay safe for you."

Smiling, I held up my hands in front of me. "Take hold of me. A hip or arm. But make sure you're touching skin. Then pray this works." Kiered placed his hand on my upper arm while Xi's cupped the back of my neck. Stepping forward, my hands were the first thing to hum. "Okay?"

"Yep," Kiered said, but his voice was rough. His hand on me tightened and I felt it shake. I glanced over my shoulder to find him clenching his jaw and his body quivering a little. It was the same with Xi. I dropped my hands.

"It's shocking the both of you?"

"Just a little," Kiered said. When I turned to him, my eyes widened in surprise. His hair looked like it had been blow-waved by a hairdresser who didn't know what they were doing. I couldn't tell with Xi since his head was shaved, but his face was tight, lips thin, and brow pinched. His hands were fisted down at his sides.

"Don't lie to me," I pleaded. "Look, I'll go through, help them, and then we'll get you both in there."

"No," Xi barked. He looked to his mate. "Stay out here."

Kiered glared, his hands slapping down on his hips. "Like hell. We're doing this together." His eyes blazed into mine. "Just be quick with it and we'll be fine."

"Xi has to break the gates. How long is that going to take while you're both being zapped?"

Xi sighed. "It won't take long. Let's do this so I can beat someone senseless."

"But—" When they both stared me down, I knew I didn't have a chance in stopping them, and now I wished I hadn't even come out to get them. Only the image of all the bodies pushed back into my mind and having Xi, hell, both of them in there would be an advantage. Sighing, I nodded once. "Fine."

Turning around again, they placed a hand on me once more. This time I didn't prepare with my hands out. I stepped right in and reached back, wrapping an arm around each man to try and help. Their bodies still convulsed, but Xi managed to grip the bars, and with a roar that shook the ground, he didn't just bend them to fit through, he broke them apart and threw the poles to the ground. Kiered stumbled forward, away from the shield, and gasped for breath. Xi, even with his body still shaking, took one step away, crouched on all fours and shifted with another roar of fury.

I took the chance to look around and noticed the mages were no longer behind their own barrier but fighting either hand to hand or magic to vampire strengths and gifts with others. They were separated at least. It could mean we had a better chance of taking them out one by one.

Xi's shifted form aimed all of his heads toward his mate. He took a step to Kiered, who didn't look scared at all. I was even fearful of what Xi in this form could do. Kiered stood his ground as the heads leaned in and sniffed him. The snake swept out it's tongue and licked him. I took a breath when their attention moved to the fighting. It let out another roar, and I caught people stop what they were doing to look our way. What I should have been doing was paying attention to Xi still, because I then felt hot breath on the back of my neck.

I froze.

Nate grumbled out a warning, and I hoped he didn't do anything else.

I got a sniff, and then he bounded forward, his eyes set on a mage off to the left. Shaking my body out, I called my own powers forward and felt the change instantly.

"He's amazing, isn't he?" Kiered sighed with awe as he watched his mate dodge a spell right before he opened his mouth and bit the mage in half. I was sure I could still hear the mage's cry of agony as Xi chewed.

I shuddered but pushed it all to the back of my mind when I caught Anthony advancing on Alex, who had his back to him while he fought another foe.

I lifted my head and let out an ear-piercing scream, then raced right for him.

Nate, in wolf form, landed at my side as we ran with all our strength. My attention never strayed from Anthony. A need to kill him flared inside me. Nate snarled and dropped behind me. A snap of bones followed, then someone cried out in pain. Still, I stayed on track.

Just as I was closing in, Anthony turned and threw a spell out at me. My body lit with fire burning over it, only it didn't hurt, nor sting like I expected it would. I lifted my gaze to a stunned Anthony.

"How?" he breathed. His gaze shifted to his side, and Alex had turned. His lavender eyes glowed more vibrant.

"Did you not think I would protect my mate?"

"But she, you…." He shook his head. "A protection spell? I should have cut through that."

"Because you used black magic?" Alex laughed, but it wasn't his normal light one. It was sinister. His hand rose, and the fire surrounding my body evaporated, leaving me naked. With a click of his fingers, I was dressed in fighting leathers. "You underestimated me and mine, Father. Look around. It has cost you your precious coven."

"I still have people," Anthony yelled, and he was right. Ten or so mages still battled against my mates and Cynthia's vampires.

"It won't last. *Look*, look into the future you have given your coven." Cedrick appeared behind Anthony and placed his hands on the man's head. Anthony screamed over and over. He dropped to his knees even as Cedrick never took away his hands. My mate was showing him his future, even if it was an illusion.

"Paige." My name was bellowed. I twisted and dove to the ground before rolling and popping back up into a crouch. A woman stood not far away with her hands out at her sides. Her lips moved, and I knew she was conjuring another spell. Instantly, I rushed right for her. A flash of red shot out of each of her hands. That time I managed to dodge the balls of light before I jumped into the air and landed on her. In the fall, I gripped her head and twisted swiftly to the right. Her neck snapped before her back even hit the ground. Someone screamed, and then I was tackled to the ground with another woman on top of me. She slapped at my face, pulled my hair, and yelled at me. I punched up. The force behind it had my hand sailing right through her stomach. Her eyes widened above me, and blood spurted from her mouth before she collapsed dead to the side. I pushed her all the way off and lifted my gaze.

Silence.

There was utter silence for one peaceful moment.

Did it mean the fighting was done or more was to come?

I stood and looked around; my mates and our people were doing the same. We all noticed the others watching me. I straightened and said loudly, "It didn't have to come to this. All we want is to live in our world in peace." I shook my head and waved a hand toward Anthony who blankly stared up at the sky at Cedrick's feet. "Did Anthony speak for you all? Did he bring death into your lives because he worked with a corrupt council who kill and steal innocent people in their greed to be stronger and more powerful than the rest? Why can't we all live together without fearing others? Why can't we all get along and not worry if someone has an extra boost in strength or power than the others? I want a world where even those who are stronger will help those who aren't. They will stand with anyone no matter who or what they are. I'm here because the council threatened my people, my family, and I'm in need of people to stand with us to stop the killings and kidnappings."

"Who will govern us all if the council isn't around to do it?" someone called.

"I will help find the right people to do the job. Until then, I will step in along with my mates. My mates who are from different factions in this community. But I want you all to know, I'm not after anything by doing this. I want harmony between us all. I want to live with my family in happiness and not worry or fear." I threw my hands out, waving them around. "Is this how you want to go on? Fighting? For what? Money, power? It isn't everything in the world."

"Mages, witches, will you stand down today?" Alex called. "You have heard my mate. All we want is to find peace, and in doing so we know it isn't under people who are cruel, who kill over meaningless things."

"Who says we'll allow them to stand down?" a red-haired male vampire stepped forward. "They came into our territory to fight, to bring war by killing Cynthia, our master. They deserve to die."

"We only followed our leader here when he sent us an SOS call. For all we know, it was you vampires who started this."

"Anthony killed Cynthia," Asher snarled. "I know she wasn't an innocent body in this matter. She conspired with the mage to trap us here because they want our mate, our queen, to drain her powers and life source to extend and grow their own. This is how the council have been working for years. Cynthia made a mistake. We all knew she regretted it in the end, but it never had to come to murdering her. There is no point fighting one another when all the blame falls onto the council. They also killed your former master. We have proof to show you. Then, through Anthony, they killed Cynthia. The mage also offered up his own son, his own flesh and blood, to be drained like he was nothing. It's people like this we allow to govern us. Will you let it continue? Or are you willing to stand with us and fight who is really at fault, not each other?"

Murmurs started up around us all. We watched and waited to see what the outcome would be. I just prayed it wouldn't end in more bloodshed.

A woman moved into my view. She dipped her head just a tiny bit. "If the vampires are willing to let this go, we will leave peacefully. I will put it to the other covens and see if we will offer our own help against the council. We also offer the vampires Anthony Smith for the misunderstanding today."

She was giving up their coven leader to be tortured and

killed. I respected that choice because Anthony deserved it. However, would Alex be able to live with letting it happen? I glanced to him and found him already looking at me. He gave me a small, sad smile but nodded.

Even if the choice came back to bite him in the butt, I would be there to help him get through it.

Nodding, I turned back to the woman and said, "That's all we can ask for. Please give one of my mates your details and we'll speak. But know we see the council in a week's time."

"Alex has my details."

"I do, Mother."

Mother? That was Alex's mother? She offered up her own husband without a care or tear over him? My gut burned in anger. But it wasn't because of that. No, it was the way she looked to her son, a man who was honorable, sweet, and amazing, without warmth or love. Instead, she turned and started to walk away.

"Wait," I called.

She faced me once more.

"I need you to understand it's fine if none of you stand with us. If no mage or witch comes to our aid or wishes to witness the proof the council will give when we see them. However, I will warn you to stay away, *far away* from me and what's mine. Especially Alex. If anyone causes any trouble for any of us, I will hunt you down and kill you myself."

She smirked. "And you say you want peace, yet there you are threatening us."

"I have a right to threaten the mother of my mate since it was your husband to cause all this in the first place. It was *your* husband who stood with the council in draining people, and it was *your* husband who treated my mate like he was nothing because *he* has a heart. So yes, I think I have a right to threaten you because I stand by what I say. I protect people from bullies, from people who think they're better than others."

She studied me before glaring, turning, and walking toward the gates. We all sensed the shield drop before the rest of the mages and witches followed Alex's mother out.

"Vampires, what say you?" Asher called.

The red-haired one moved closer to me until a certain wolf stomped to my side and growled. The vampire smirked but dipped his head. "I am Finnegan McGregor, now master to the clan, and I speak on behalf of my people. We stand with you, Paige Alice. You seek what we are after. From the recording today, we will contact other clans we trust and show them what has occurred, as well as the proof you have over the council murdering our former master."

I wasn't sure I liked that the whole thing had been filmed, but it could be good for us in the end. We didn't act out of turn. It showed exactly what we were about. "Thank you, Finnegan. We appreciate it. Alex will leave the files with you. However, be sure you trust the other clans completely and also that you destroy the footage after you have shown them."

"I will, Queen of ghouls." He bowed once more before ordering a man to take Anthony inside and then moving over to Alex.

"Can we leave now?" I asked, suddenly drained from everything that happened. Though I was still pissed at Alex's family. Killing Anthony over and over would be good. Maybe someone knew a necromancer and we could make that happen.

"I vote for leaving," Nate answered first, from his wolf form. *"They keep looking at Paige like they want to fuck or suck on her for hours after witnessing the way she fought."*

"I second that vote," Ezra agreed. He was now back in his human form.

"Paige isn't the only one being admired," Thorn fumed. I glanced over to see him watching a couple of vampire women approaching Asher.

Actually, it was happening everywhere. Some stood close to Thorn—not that he noticed—and others eyed Cedrick. One even reached out as if to touch his hair. I waggled my finger at him when he saw me looking.

"Can I pat your wolf?" a guy asked and then licked his lips.

I was about to tell him where he could go—straight to hell—when there was a commotion in the house. Five people appeared in the doorway. They looked crazed with their wild, frantic, glowing green eyes searching for something. They lifted their heads and drew in a deep breath.

My stomach bottomed out.

"Alex!" I yelled. *"Get Ezra out of here now,"* I ordered.

Alex disappeared from where he stood, appeared behind Ezra, and then both of them vanished out of sight.

The fledglings flashed down the stairs and sniffed the air again. A disgruntled man and woman appeared at the top of the stairs. "They broke out. Just broke out because they could smell something."

"Maybe it was all the blood," I suggested. I would have crossed my fingers for them to believe me, but I didn't want to make it obvious.

Though Finnegan knew I was full of shit since I'd yelled to Alex and then his sudden action to get Ezra out. Worry seeped into my veins. Would he question it?

I relaxed a little when he said, "Yes, must have been." He

moved over to them. "Children, feel the new bond. Do you sense it?"

They hesitated, and I worried we hadn't gotten Ezra away fast enough or that the smell of his blood still lingered.

"I can't scent his blood anywhere. It must have been on him," Asher told me, as if he knew my worries already, which he probably did.

A guy, who looked no older than sixteen, finally answered Finnegan, "Yes, master."

"Good, please go back into the safe rooms. It's nearly time for your feeding." They shuffled away without another word, and I relaxed even more.

If it would come down to it, I'd think of something to say to Finnegan to explain about getting Ezra out of there. I hoped he was smart enough to leave it alone though.

"Xi, pull the guards out and have them head back to the hotel we're staying at," Asher ordered. Xi grunted but got to work with Kiered at his side. "Finnegan, we'll be in touch. However, I would like to attend the send-off for Cynthia, if you'll allow me?"

I ground my teeth together in jealousy, and then I wanted to punch myself in the face, maybe even stab myself, because feeling jealousy was so wrong. Asher lost someone he cared about. I wanted him to be able to do what he wanted and needed to, for himself and her. For closure.

"Of course, Asher. You are always welcome here. We'll have a burial for Cynthia in a few hours."

"Thank you." He nodded and walked the rest of the way to me. "We're staying close to rest for a few days as I thought this would take longer. That's where Alex would have taken Ezra."

I took his hand and we made our way to the car. "Rest

sounds good, but I would like to pop home tomorrow, even if it's just for a few hours."

"I would love to see it," Cedrick said from my other side.

"And I would love to show you."

"We'll make it happen, sweetheart." Thorn smiled from where he walked beside Cedrick. Nate was on Thorn's other side, and he bumped his head into Thorn until Thorn threaded his fingers into his fur. "You big baby," Thorn teased. Nate growled low in a playful warning.

Another meeting slash battle down, where the outcome was promising. Now all we had was one more to go.

The worst one.

Or, if everything fell into place, it could be the easiest.

Please let it be the easiest.

CHAPTER FIFTY-EIGHT

PAIGE

"I still can't believe Lucifer contacted Ezra *after* the fight to inform him that if Ezra was in his hellhound form, the fledglings wouldn't have gone crazy," I complained as we walked through my castle.

Cedrick chuckled. "I think he'll be sure to find out all information straightaway from now on, especially after your phone call to yell at him." He shook his head, smiling. "Only you would scold the devil."

I harrumphed. "He deserved it."

His smile grew. "Yes, beautiful, he did."

At least, I thought he had. Okay, maybe I had gone too far when I threatened his balls a few too many times. I rolled my eyes. "Anyway, this is my sister's suite." I pointed to the door. "Well, the kids should be here probably, with the bear shifters or their father, Eric. Yasmin is still dealing with being changed over to a vampire."

Cedrick's hands landed on my shoulders. "Relax, beautiful. From what I've seen so far, I love everything about your home. I look forward to living here once this is over."

"Really?" I asked, turning in his arms and smiling widely, as I —quite possibly looking crazy—peered up at him.

He grinned back. "Really."

Tipping my head back, I puckered my lips. He chuckled and leaned down to claim my mouth. I curled my arms around his waist, but then slid them around his neck when he picked me up off the floor to deepen the kiss.

The door behind us opened. "Aunty Paige" was screamed by a little monster. Cedrick quickly placed me on my feet in time for Sophie to crash into the back of my legs with a tight hug. She buried her head into my hip. "You're back. I've missed you so, so, so much." She pulled back to stare up at me, but then her gaze drifted to the side. "Whoa, you're tall."

Cedrick laughed. "I am, and you must be Miss Sophie. It's a pleasure to meet you. I'm Cedrick."

"You were kissing my aunty. Does that mean you're her mate as well?"

"It does."

"Cool," she drew out. "Can I call you Uncle Cedrick?"

"I would love that." He reached out to ruffle her hair, which had her smile brightening even more.

"Do you change into anything like Uncles Nate and Ezra? Or are you really fast like Uncle Asher? Or maybe you're like my aunty or Uncle Thorn?"

"I'm different again, sweet one. I'm an elf."

She gasped and pushed me aside to get closer to Cedrick.

Rolling my eyes, I crossed my arms and waited to see what she was about to say. "Are you like an elf on the shelf? Are you magical like Uncle Alex?"

I giggled but covered it with my hand. Cedrick looked confused as he looked up at me. "What is an elf on a shelf?"

Shaking my head, I smiled. "I'll explain later. Sophie, Cedrick isn't like one of those, but he is a bit magical like Alex."

"That's so awesome."

"Sophie, you're supposed to wait by the door, not move out it," Oliver, my nephew, said as he appeared in the doorway. "Aunty Paige." He smiled and was about to step out to give me a hug when he saw Cedrick. "Who're you?"

"Prince Cedrick Nelydriel, from the fae land Airrile." Cedrick bowed. "I have heard all about you, Oliver."

"Yeah?"

"Yes, your aunt talks about you a lot."

"He's Aunty's boyfriend like Asher, and Nate, and Ezra, and Alex, and Thorn." Dear lord, did she have to list them all. "Isn't that the bestest?" she cried, and grabbed Oliver's arm waving it around. "He said I can call him Uncle and that he's an elf, but not like an elf on the shelf," Sophie informed her brother.

Oliver nodded. "That's cool."

Sophie smiled. "That's what I said." She sobered and then looked back up at Cedrick. "Wait, you said you're a prince? Like a real-life prince? Do you have a crown?"

"I am, and yes I do."

Sophie screamed, jumping up and down. It was then Leon and Jake, the bear shifters who helped guard my family, appeared with guns drawn. "What?" Leon yelled before he noticed Cedrick and me. "My queen, you're back." He bowed, as did Jake, both putting away their weapons.

"Only for a little while, guys. It's good to see you both."

"You as well, my queen." Jake smiled and Leon nodded, also grinning. Then they both looked at Cedrick.

"This is Cedrick Nelydriel, Prince of Airrile, my new bonded mate."

"Welcome, Prince Cedrick. I'm sure you'll love it here as we do now. We have such an amazing queen," Leon said with a bow, and I blushed right away.

"I'm sure I will. She is wonderful."

"Can we go now?" Oliver asked.

"Of course we can." Jake tapped Oliver on the arm with his fist. "This little guy is keen to watch the guards fight, and Miss Muppet would like to wander the stalls. She heard there may be cotton candy."

My brows dipped. "The guards are fighting?"

"In competition, yes." Leon nodded.

"What for?"

"To be on the force to protect the queen and her wonderful family."

My body jolted in shock. "People want to beat each other up so they can work for me?"

Jake laughed, and Leon grinned, showing all his teeth before saying, "Of course, it's an honor. But don't worry, it's not fighting to the death, else we wouldn't be allowed to take the children to see. Yasmin said so." He glanced down at the children. "We must be on our way. Our best wishes for the times ahead, my queen."

"Thank you, Leon and Jake. Kids, give me big hugs." I opened my arms, and they walked right into them. I wrapped them tightly and kissed the tops of their heads. "Be good, and remember, who loves you the most?"

"Ezra," Sophie shouted.

"Nate." Oliver grinned.

"No!" I cried. "I'm going to have to talk to those two. Now, who is it?"

"You," they said at the same time.

"That's right. Have fun."

Sophie turned to Cedrick. "Can I give you a hug?"

"I would love one." He bent so she could wrap her arms around his neck. She let out a squeal when he picked her up.

"It really is high up here," she commented when he straightened. Laughter rang around us all.

Leon clapped his hands and held them out for Sophie. "Come, missy, let's get you hyped up on candy so we can hand you back to your parents."

"Yay," she cheered.

They started off down the hall, but before they were out of earshot, Leon said, "Children, you know we both adore you, but we have to talk about the rules again. What's number five?"

They groaned, but recited, "Don't open the door to anyone. Only an adult can open the door."

"Yes, so what happened?"

"I'm sorry," Sophie said. "I heard Aunty's voice and got excited."

"That's okay. We all make mistakes. Just please try and remember it from now on."

"We will." Oliver nodded.

Cedrick's hand touched my waist. "They are good men."

Smiling, I leaned into him and nodded. "They are."

"You are a wonderful queen, Paige. I can see it in your people and how much they love you."

I shrugged. "They hardly know me."

"Yet, they look at you as if you've saved them. I know with time, when they do know all there is to know, they will adore you more." He turned me toward him and looked down at me. "I'm happy to be by your side, with the other men, while it happens."

Reaching up, I traced the backs of my fingers over his smooth, pale skin on his cheek. "I'm so glad you've come into our lives."

"As am I." He pressed his lips against mine.

"All right, you two, keep it behind closed doors. Unless I can join in," Ezra teased as he and Alex walked up to us. Alex and Ezra popped back with us for the few hours, while Nate, Asher, and Thorn stayed back to go over things with Xi and the other guards.

"Did you see Sophie and Oliver? We just did," Alex said. I loved how my men all warmed to my niece and nephew as if they were their own.

"That reminds me." I looked to Ezra with a mock glare. "Are you telling them to say they love you the most when I ask them?"

"I would never…. Okay, maybe." He grinned cheekily.

I playfully slapped him on the stomach. "Come on, let's go and see Yasmin so we can get back to the others." I didn't like being away from them for long; it made my skin crawl with unease.

Since the door was still wide open, we walked in. I wasn't even sure if she, or even Eric, would be there or at Sakura's. I chanced it anyway. I started for the kitchen when I heard voices coming from the bedroom area.

"Hello?" I called.

I was sure I heard someone answer, which was why I made

my way to the bedrooms. It was why I opened their door without thinking and then screamed. I covered my face with both hands and chanted, "Oh my God, oh my God."

"What's wrong?" Alex asked. I felt him move me aside and enter the room, only to yip and brush by me when he quickly exited.

"Huh, I didn't think about that move," Ezra said.

"Is now a good time to meet them?" the smart-ass Cedrick asked with humor in his tone.

"Shut the door. Shut the door!" my sister yelled.

Blindly, I reached out, grabbed the knob—not Eric's that had been dangling—and pulled the door closed with a loud bang.

Turning, I stalked back out into the living room and paced. "That was something I could have gone without seeing." I groaned and placed a hand on my stomach. "I feel sick."

"You do realize other people have sex, right?" Ezra asked with a chuckle. "It's not just you."

"Shut up," I scolded.

I stopped by Alex and rubbed his back since he was sitting on the couch with his head buried in his hands. "You could have told me they were… that all three of them… that they were…."

"Fucking, doing the tango, bumping uglies—"

"Ezra," I warned.

Ezra threw his hands up. "Our poor boy can't even say it. I was just helping him along." If only he would wipe that smirk off his face, then I may have believed him. Then again, I probably wouldn't.

"Paige, it will be fine. Don't worry," Cedrick tried.

"Fine? You saw more of my sister than I would want you to. As well as Eric and Sakura." I scrubbed a hand over my face.

I froze when I heard the door being opened and then foot-falls coming our way. Was it too late to make a run for it? Save me and my mates from this embarrassing moment?

My sister came around the corner with a bathrobe on. Her hands went to her hips as she glared at me. I scowled right back.

"Don't you know about knocking?"

"I called out. I thought I heard a reply, so I came to see. Maybe you shouldn't be doing that during the day."

Ezra choked on a laugh, but when I shot him a deadly look, he stopped. I lasered Cedrick with one as well since he was smiling like a maniac.

"Like you can talk. If you're not doing your queenly duties, you're doing your men all the damn time."

"So what? I'm allowed to."

"And I'm not?" she yelled.

"Ladies, I think we all need to calm down," Eric said as he turned the corner into the living room wearing only jeans. Sakura followed him, but at least she was dressed properly in pants and a shirt.

"Calm down?" I demanded.

"Paige," Cedrick murmured into my ear as he stepped close and put his hands on my hips. "It was an accident. Let's forget about it and move on, beautiful. I would like to meet your family."

"Oh my," Yasmin breathed. "Is he yours?"

I grinned over at my sister. "He is."

"Yasmin," Sakura clipped. As soon as my sister looked to Sakura under Eric's arm, she warmed, her eyes softened, and her body relaxed while she took in the couple she loved. It was wonderful to see. Sakura smiled shyly, her cheeks heating. "That's better."

Alex suddenly stood and blurted, "I'm sorry for seeing parts of your body I shouldn't have."

Everyone looked at his burning cheeks and laughed.

"Alex," I called and held my hand out. He walked right to me, placing his hand on mine. I tugged him close and kissed his cheek. "You're the best."

"For now," Ezra added with a wink.

"Yasmin," I called after she'd walked to Eric's other side and curled into him, taking Sakura's hand and resting it against Eric's stomach. "Eric and Sakura, I would like you to meet my mate Cedrick Nelydriel, fae prince to the land of Airrile."

"It is a pleasure to meet all of Paige's family."

"Um, sorry about what you saw, but, ah, welcome to the family," Yasmin offered.

Cedrick chuckled. "Thank you."

AN HOUR HAD GONE BY QUICKLY as we sat around and caught up on things. I now knew Yasmin had controlled her hunger in such a short amount of time. Though, I thought it had to do with her wanting to get back to her children. The people treated my family with kindness, and Yasmin even admitted they made her feel like a pop star. Lenora, Michael's wife, had stopped by to spend time with Yasmin, which was good to hear. I knew they would get along.

"How are things with the guards, Sakura?"

She opened her mouth to reply, but the door opened

abruptly, and Alma entered. Actually, it was Virginia in her twin sister's form. I could tell when she cried, "My son." She rushed over to Ezra, raining him with lots of kisses.

"Fucking hell," Ezra complained, but I could see the soft smile he had.

"It's so good to see you." She beamed, cupping his face in her hands.

"Mom, it looks weird you being in Alma's form and so vibrant. Can you change back?" Ezra asked, pulling her hands away from his face.

"Of course." Her body shimmered, and then there stood Virginia, a woman who looked too young to have a son Ezra's age. She faced me and smiled. "I thought it good to present myself as Alma in front of your people. I didn't think they would like to deal with me as Lucifer's woman."

She would be correct.

"Good thinking, Virginia."

She wiggled her fingers at me. "Come, come, let me take a look at my daughter-in-law." I moved over to her with a smile. She was crazy—in a charming way. She gripped my wrists and studied me. "Hmm." She nodded to herself. "Very nice."

"What are you talking about?" Ezra asked.

She ignored her son and turned to Cedrick. "You must be the new mate. You are a mighty fine fae." She curled her arm around my waist and nudged my hip with hers. "You must be pleased."

"I am."

"I can see why. Would you spin for me? I do like a nice ass."

"Mom!" Ezra yelled. "If Dad heard you say that...." He shook his head.

She scoffed. "He knows I like to look, but I would never touch when I have such an outstanding man in my bed."

Ezra groaned. "I don't need to know anything about your bed."

Virginia laughed. She hugged me tighter to her side, and then her face went blank.

"Give her a moment," Ezra said with a roll of his eyes.

Virginia sucked in a deep breath and blinked rapidly. She turned me, put her hands on my shoulders, and smiled brightly. The only thing that concerned me were the tears in her eyes. "Oh my hell. This is—" She coughed on what she was about to say. Though she didn't seem too concerned about what she saw in her vision. Did I dare believe it was good news?

"This is what?" I asked. She opened her mouth and choked on her words. I thinned my lips, wishing she could say something more. "I hate that you can't say anything."

She nodded but wouldn't stop smiling. She then raced toward Cedrick and hugged him tightly. The shock on his face brought a grin to my lips. She pushed him back, patted his arm, and then moved to Alex for a hug. Alex let out a sound when she squished him to her. Finally, she was back to her son and hugging him.

"I must run and tell Lucifer."

"Is it about the council? Our meeting?" Alex asked.

Virginia opened her mouth, made a sound, and closed it. Her brows pinched in agitation. So it could be about the council.

"What is any of this about?" Cedrick questioned.

"Cedrick, I'd like you to meet my mother, Virginia Morningstar. Seer."

Cedrick's eyes widened. "You see the future?"

"Yes, it can be a blessing and a curse."

"I believe it would be."

Yasmin cleared her throat; to be honest, I'd forgotten they were in the room. "Can you at least hint at something?" Worry tightened her voice. She glanced to me and then back to Virginia, who shrugged.

"You know what?" I started. "Let's just not worry about it now. Besides, it doesn't seem too bad if you're smiling."

Virginia shrugged and then announced, "I must go, and you all should as well."

"Why?" I questioned, fear taking hold inside of me. "Is it the others? Are they okay?"

Virginia pointed at Alex. We all jumped when his phone rang. Slowly, he pulled it out of his pocket. "Nate? Right, yes. We're coming back now." He hung up. "They have news from the council. We're needed back there."

I glanced to Virginia, but she was already gone.

"I don't like this," I admitted.

"Me either," Yasmin whispered.

CHAPTER FIFTY-NINE

*I*f I could go back and hit myself for wanting to go home, I would because saying goodbye to my family was hard. Cedrick wrapped me in his arms, while Alex held Ezra close as we transported back into the motel room we'd left from. Alex also carried a container of food for Thorn and me. Apparently, Nate had ordered him to grab some before on the phone.

I had a feeling it was so Thorn and I would be at our full strength, which was possible after feeding.

My stomach was in a nervous flutter of knots though. I wasn't even sure I could eat. At least not until I knew what was going on.

Dizziness swept through me when we reappeared. Asher, Thorn, and Nate stared at us from across a table. I stepped from

Cedrick's hold, as did Ezra from Alex's, and we looked back, waiting for them to tell us what was happening.

"The council have contacted us."

"How?" Alex asked.

"Somehow they knew where we were. A bellhop dropped it off."

Lifting my arms, I ran my hands through my hair from the stress taking shape in my mind. "I don't like it. They know where we are. They knew we were going to Cedrick's. The only place they didn't show was when we saw the shifters."

"As it's been said, we believe they're doing what they suspect we would do. They've realized we aren't stupid and want people at our back if it comes to war."

"It'll come to war," Nate grumbled.

It would, we all knew it. None of us liked it, but it was certain. They wouldn't give up what they were doing and suddenly turn over a new leaf in life where killing and kidnapping were bad.

We would have to fight them.

My heart thumped harder in my chest. It all felt daunting. My hands shook from the fear I had for my mates.

"What did it say?" I whispered.

"They're moving up the date of the meeting," Thorn said, his hands clenched at his sides.

"When?" Cedrick asked, his voice cold.

"We have a couple of hours to get there," Asher bit out.

"They can't do this," I yelled, and then picked up the chair in front of me and threw it across the room. Arms circled me and brought me into a chest. Cedrick. More warmth surrounded me. I could smell Ezra, Alex, and Nate.

"Unfortunately, they can do it, sweetheart," Thorn said gently from close by.

"And if we do not abide by it, it won't look good for us," Asher added.

Fuck.

Fuckety fuck.

Nate's nose pressed into my neck. "You smell different."

I shrugged, not sure what he meant or how I smelled different than any other time. I was too concerned about what would happen soon.

"It's probably because she's been away for a while," Thorn said, and Nate hummed under his breath before sticking his nose back into my neck and sniffing.

Having them close helped my anxiety, but I still felt the turmoil floating in me. Nate kissed my neck. "They're trying to get us unprepared and without our backup. But they won't. We don't need days for it to fall into place. Kiered and Xi left as soon as we heard to speak with the vampires. Kiered will also take Xi to the shifters. We're not trusting communicating through devices just in case. They'll come. They'll assist us."

"Did my brother speak with our mother?" Cedrick asked.

"He did," Thorn answered. "She's sending your people near the council compound. We'll speak to them when we get closer."

"Love, you need to eat." Asher smiled softly. "We have an hour here, but then we need to move to make it there in time to speak with the people before going into the trap."

I snorted. "Yeah, a trap. Maybe I could go alone and—"

"No," Asher clipped.

"Like fuck," Nate bit out.

"Not a chance," Thorn told me.

"As if," Ezra said.

"We'll be by your side always, and if you try to leave, I'll have Alex place you in your own bubble, one we can move around where we want," Cedrick warned.

"I'll do it, too, if you try anything to risk yourself for any of us."

My bottom lip trembled. "You all suck, but I've never felt loved and cherished as much as I do from all of you. Bastards."

They chuckled.

Sighing, I nodded. "All right, I'll eat, and then we'll all go kick some ass."

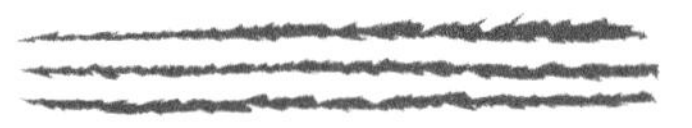

WE ALL STOOD a couple of blocks away speaking with the large number of people who showed. The lion and tiger shifters were there. Cedrick's guards had just arrived, so he was off speaking with them. Asher was by the vampires having words.

By now, they would all know what they had to do. The vampires were taking the right, and the shifters were infiltrating from below. Alex had given them the tunnel system that led right into the dungeons. The fae would be taking the left, and some of our guards would enter through the back, if possible, while my mates and I would walk right through the front door.

As I stared off down the road, my mind drifted over my time with my men. I couldn't have predicted where my life would go. No one would have thought I would become a queen. A ghoul queen at that. But I wouldn't change any of it because it took me right to my bonded mates.

I thought Fate may have screwed me over, but I was wrong. My life was better with my mates in it. All of them.

No regret lingered inside me over having my family brought into this mess. It was meant to be. The children loved it. My sister and Eric did as well, even after everything that had happened.

All I had to do was fight for our freedom from the council so we could live peacefully without them breathing down our necks or threatening any of us. We'd be safe, our people would be safe, and the other races would be safe.

All we had to do was win.

I glanced down, fiddling with the gown Alex had dressed me in. It was large and puffy at the bottom while the top squeezed me so tight I was sure my boobs were going to burst out. Maybe Alex picked it for that reason, since the council was a formal event and I had to dress over the top for it. Not only that, but I was a queen and was supposed to look the part. I allowed it, after a few complaints and sour looks, once he promised that when, not *if*, it came down to fighting, Alex would change my outfit instantly so I could move more freely.

"We'll be okay" came from my side. Thorn smiled down at me before he took my hand in his. "Do you believe it?"

"It's scary."

"I know."

"I want to believe it, but the council has done so much damage without the people knowing. They're capable of so much."

"So are we. You've killed with your bare hands. They hide behind their minions and use them as their weapons. We can take them."

Since he said that, I realized it was true. They did use the elite force a lot, and I already knew Nate, Alex, and Asher were confident in fighting them since they had been the top of their classes.

Confidence. That was what I needed.

Hell, I had it in my men. I just needed to have it for myself.

I nodded. "You're right. We can take them."

Thorn leaned in and kissed my temple. "There's our mate."

"We're moving out," Nate called.

I swallowed; my throat felt thick. As we moved to our vehicle, I wanted to tell my mates how much they meant to me. I wanted to tell them to be careful, to fight hard, and kill anyone they thought would be a threat. But the words didn't seem enough. Instead, I dropped my shields and let them feel everything I wanted to say.

They circled me, touching me in some way. I could feel and scent them all. My hellhound, my vampire, my mage, my shifter, my ghoul, and my fae.

Before I could let my emotions take hold and break me down in panic and fear, I straightened and nodded. "Let's get this done."

Xi and Kiered had already left in their own vehicle. They would be having their own private moment before shit hit the fan.

We rode in silence, this time in a limousine, because appearances mattered. Too soon we pulled up in the front, and out the window I took in the daunting skyscraper building. The front looked like an old church, but at the back, it branched up into something modern and ugly.

The driver opened the back door, and Thorn was the first to climb out, then Asher, and Cedrick. It was Cedrick's hand just in the door that waited for my hand.

Closing my eyes, I took one moment to myself and prayed for the last time.

Please, whoever is listening, no matter what happens, protect my mates.

Opening my eyes, I smiled at my remaining mates and then took Cedrick's hand. He helped me slide out in this monstrosity of a dress. I stood and moved aside for Nate, Ezra, and Alex. I could see Xi and Kiered standing up near the door waiting for us.

People milled around, looking our way. Some were vampires, witches, mages, shifters, and other things I hadn't yet sensed before to recognize what they were. There were a lot of humans as well.

It seemed the people had been informed of our rescheduled visit.

Asher took my hand on my other side while Thorn and Nate stayed in front of us. Ezra and Alex were at our backs, and together, we made our way up to their doors.

Into the link, I complained, *"Alex, I see a lot of suits, even for the women. I could have worn pants. I feel overdressed."*

"Trust me, they'll think you're a little flaky from what you wear and then, bang, when stuff goes down, you'll be in your fighting uniform."

"So it was a ruse. You should have told me that, Alex."

I didn't need to look—his voice told me he was smiling. *"But it was fun to watch you freak out over it. Plus, you do look fantastic in it."*

"Especially your breasts," Ezra added.

My face heated. *"You monsters."*

"Well, I am, not sure about magic boy."

Nate and Thorn moved aside a little when we got to the

door. The two guards there bowed when they saw me and then opened the doors for us.

"Is that usual?" I asked in their minds.

"No. They're usually stationed inside the doors and at the bottom of the stairs, but not at the door to open it."

"I feel special."

"You are special, beautiful." Cedrick winked down at me.

"Thank you." We entered, and the guards followed us in, along with Xi and Kiered.

"Please sign in at the desk, Paige Alice," one guard asked.

"She will," Nate answered for me. I sent the guard a smile and a nod of thanks. His head jerked back a little, as if surprised by it, and he looked to the other guard who also seemed shocked. What had the council said about me? That I truly was a monster made from darkness?

At the desk, a young woman stepped around it and bowed. "Queen Alice, it's a pleasure to have you here at the council headquarters. My name is Kimberly, and I'll be your guide today." She waved out her arm. "If you would please sign in." Thorn stepped up to the desk and went to pick up the pen. "Oh no, it has to be the queen."

"Why?" Nate clipped.

Kimberly cringed. "The one invited must be the one to sign in."

"That rule changes here and today," Thorn said.

"Please!" Kimberly cried.

"It's a fucking trap," Thorn stated through the link.

"Alex, can you sense anything?" Asher asked.

He closed his eyes so they didn't shine. *"A binding spell, I think. Hard to tell from back here."*

"Someone wants to bind Paige to themselves to have control over her."

"Alex, are you able to diffuse it or protect me from it?" I asked.

"Yes, already doing so. I'm not leaving anyone out this time."

Ezra's love for Alex washed through the link. *"Not your fault, and it turned out better with me in my human form."*

"Thorn," I called aloud. "It's no trouble. I wouldn't want Kimberly to get into trouble from straying from protocol."

Kimberly bowed over and over as I stepped up to the desk. "Thank you," she also kept muttering.

"Shit," Nate bit out. Kimberly whimpered, but quickly stopped moving her body and mouth.

I forced a laugh. "Now, Nate, don't be so grumpy." I smiled at Kimberly. "Don't worry about him. He's all bark with no bite." I wanted her at ease around me. I wasn't who the council made me out to be. I needed as many people to see that as I could.

Her smile back was hesitant and wobbly. Her fear was obvious.

Picking up the pen, I felt a slight tingle, but other than that, nothing. I quickly signed my name and put it back down. I lifted my gaze to her and smiled again. Her eyes widened a fraction before she caught herself and turned. "Right this way, please."

It seemed she wasn't our only guide. The guards from the front door walked at each side of Kimberly. As we walked, we kept getting stared at, so I made sure to smile and wave as I went. It annoyed me most of them were as shocked as the guards had been. But some of them looked at me like I was the shit they'd just walked on.

Kimberly led us to what looked like a waiting room and

said, "If you'll just wait here a moment, I'll make sure they're ready for you."

I nodded. "Of course, thank you."

She blinked slowly, nodded, and then walked through the double doors in front of us.

"Queen Alice," Kiered called, stepping close. "I just got this delivered to me as we waited outside. A gift from our mother. Yeno dropped it off." He lifted his hand, opened his palm, and inside it sat a broach in the shape of a leaf. It looked very similar to the tattoo on my shoulder.

Through the link he told us, *"It's a camera. Mother wants to show everyone what will happen behind those closed doors. She'll be broadcasting it on... I think Kiered said Youtubiler."*

Ezra coughed through his sudden laugh. *"YouTube, man."*

The guards eyed him, but one stepped forward. "I will have to check it."

"They'll look for anything magical. They don't want to be bugged," Asher said into our minds.

"Cedrick, will it pass?"

"Kiered believes so. It's very new, as in it only got designed this morning, which is why the delivery was late."

I took it from his palm and offered it out to the guard. It was then I realized he'd been blocking us from sensing him as his power erupted when he closed both hands around the broach. His eyes glowed purple, like Alex's, but they weren't as pretty or vibrant. Since I didn't need to hold my breath, I thinned my lips, watching to see if we were found out.

He dropped his top hand and nodded before passing it back to me. "It's fine."

I took the broach, and Nate helped me pin it to my shoulder strap. We continued to wait and wait. I knew the council members were screwing with us. They were probably watching from behind those closed doors.

I stayed in the one spot and made sure to keep the smile on my face.

"I'm so fucking bored," Ezra complained.

"You're not the only one," Nate said.

"How long do you think they'll make us wait?" I asked.

"It's hard to say, my love," Asher replied.

"Sweetheart, I forgot to ask, how was the visit home?"

Thorns voice startled me because he'd been so silent. "It was great. I wish you all could have made it."

"We'll be home soon," Nate said.

"I'm looking forward to it," Cedrick added. "The time there wasn't enough for my first time, but I got to see how our mate's people love her." He smiled down at me. "She was surprised when she found out how the guards are competing against one another to win a spot in the enforcers unit."

"It's because she leads with her heart. The changes she's already made have been taken wonderfully," Asher said. "Who knew so many were living the old ways?"

"What do you mean?" the other guard asked. Not the mage.

Smiling, I asked, "What's your name?"

"William, and that's Kyle."

"Well, William, I'm new to all this, so when I was told I was queen and then presented with a castle and the people in it to take care of, it was a lot to take in, and I worried I would be too different to rule." He nodded. "However, what I saw when I first arrived was a lot of bigotry and hate among different races. My first order of business was to ensure people, no matter who they were, could love and be with who they wanted. Without hate involved. Anyone who didn't like it was offered a chance to leave because I would never want anyone to be where they didn't feel comfortable or at home in." I smiled as I watched them both take in what I'd said. William seemed to like what I said, but Kyle frowned. I shrugged. "It may have something to do with how human I still felt, but I also knew, since I have six bonded mates of different factions, that I would fight to have them at my side. Just because we are different from one another shouldn't mean we couldn't love. Do you agree?"

"William," Kyle clipped. William glanced to him and Kyle shook his head.

William rolled his eyes but then said, "It's not for me to say."

"Then do you believe that people in a position of power have the right to do what they want? Even if it means killing those weaker or kidnapping them for other purposes?"

Kyle snorted. "Who's doing those things? Point them out and the council will take care of it. They take care of everything."

I shrugged again and kept on smiling. I was sure my face would ache so damn much from all the pretending. My heart ached for him, for all the ones who were blind to what the council really were. Evil.

"So you can't say." Kyle smirked.

Ezra and Nate growled under their breath. I shook my head. "It's okay, guys. He can say whatever he wants. The truth will be told eventually."

Kyle's smirk dropped.

Moving my gaze to the doors, I said, "I only wish for peace. I don't like fighting, competing, or bullies. All I want is to live with my mates, surrounded by my people who are happy, healthy, and safe." I looked back to Kyle. "Is it too much to ask for?"

He said nothing but held my stare.

"Whose coven are you connected to?" Alex asked.

"Morrison's," Kyle answered with a glare for Alex.

Alex's lips thinned before he said into our minds, *"They're worse than my father's coven."*

"That explains the hostilities," Cedrick said.

"I see that look. But I've heard about you, Alex Smith. You were an enforcer for the council like Nate and Asher. A mixed team, a weak team. You all ran when the mission went wrong and people got killed. You all ran to be with the woman who caused over twenty deaths."

"What are you talking about?" Nate demanded, his tone harsh.

"That's what we all got told," William said.

Kyle shot him a glare. "It's what we got told and what we believe."

Were the council listening to this? Were they waiting to see how we would react?

Well, it was time to get the show started.

I took a step forward. "It may be what you heard, but I don't see everyone believing it, and good on them for being smart. Do you want to hear my side of it?"

"No," Kyle snapped.

"Yes," William answered.

I smiled warmly at William. "Then I'll explain for those who wish to know, like yourself. Then you can judge for yourself. That night—"

The doors opened and Kimberly stepped out. "The council is ready for you."

Of course they were.

CHAPTER SIXTY

PAIGE

We entered in our little group, but with Xi and Kiered walking beside Alex, and Ezra at the back. The room was something like out of Harry Potter. It was circular and you stepped down at least twenty or so stairs into the middle where the council sat on a podium, leaving room in front of them on the empty floor. I wanted to snort at the thought of them wanting to be higher than whoever they spoke to on the floor. If they wanted to look down on me, that was fine. I would take it. I didn't care, because soon they would be stopped.

We slowly descended the stairs and stopped in the middle of the floor. Thorn and Nate moved aside a little, so they all had a view of me, and I had one of them.

They ranged in people. Older, younger, and middle-aged. Four were women, six were men.

I'd seen Gregory before on footage. He was the one who'd organized the kidnapping of the alphas. It was easy to guess who Jessica was. She eyed Asher like he was her salvation, even after everything they'd been through. Bet she regretted not giving him the time off now. My men could have been back working with the council if they'd done as Asher had asked. They forced my men's hands by rejecting their request and then trying to apprehend Asher so he wouldn't go anywhere since they knew, via demons, that the ghoul queen's powers had resurfaced in the area they had been on a mission in.

"Paige Alice, I would say welcome to the council compound, but unfortunately it's under terrible circumstance. Asher Evans, Nate Felan, Alex Smith, and you are suspects in twenty murders of humans," one of the middle-aged men said from where he sat in the center of the group.

I tilted my head a little and studied him. I sensed he was a shifter, but I could be wrong. "Forgive me, you seem to know who I am, but I do not know you." I knew all their names. I'd read the written files Alex had on them. I knew how each one was involved in something disgusting and why the council needed a clean slate of members, but I hadn't put faces to their names.

His jaw clenched. He didn't like I didn't know him. I had to hold back my smile from growing. He cleared his throat. "My name is Chryston Hem, alpha to the bears." Right, no wonder Leon and his people fled from this alpha. I'd read he liked to spend time with the young women of his sleuth. He was a rapist. I blanked my features. "Beside me is vampire master Samuel

Person." He drank from people without ensnaring their minds. He liked his victims to scream. "Down his side there is Aaron Jilt, mage. Stephen Kinston, troll. Jessica Frank, vampire. Fiona Gemming, Valkyrie. Along my side we have Quinton Heil, wendigo. Gregory Kelton, vampire. Desirae Hunt, witch. Sapphire Wills, fae." Aaron liked to play with young boys. Stephen raided businesses for money and supplies. Jessica… well, I just didn't like that bitch since she was my men's former boss. Fiona liked to eat people, literally, but not like I did. She did it while they were still alive. Quinton often joined Fiona and made a game out of it where they hunted the people down. Gregory sold women. Desirae and Sapphire collected men. Men who were weaker and didn't have the power or strength to stand up for themselves. They used them however they wanted. Pimped them out to others, and then killed them after years of torture because they grew bored with them. They were also in a relationship together. I wasn't sure how Alex gained all the information he had, but it was valuable, and it fueled my anger toward them. I had to remind myself that they deserved everything that would come to them.

However, Alex hadn't noted Sapphire was fae; he'd found witch on her file.

"Cedrick, do you know her?" I asked into his mind.

"She was sister to Lenora. Thought dead. Her name is different, used to be Leanna."

"Now you know our names and what we are. Can we move on?" Chryston asked with a smirk.

I waved a hand around. "Of course."

"Before we move on, Chryston. I'd like to know the mates we haven't heard of," Desirae purred as she eyed Ezra and licked her lips.

Rage surfaced inside me. I wanted to slap the bitch, rip her apart, and then spit on her.

"Ezra, *my* hellhound. Cedrick, *my* fae, and Thorn, *my* ghoul." I didn't give them their last names. I'd hoped they didn't know about the connection Ezra had to Lucifer.

"Hellhound. I thought them mindless, killing beasts," Stephen commented.

"I'm sure he's a beast in bed." Sapphire smiled and then giggled with Desirae.

Keep it together, Paige. Keep it together. They will get what's coming to them.

"All my men pleasure me in bed, but I wasn't sure you all needed to know that."

"We didn't." Chryston glared down at the sluts. "Back to the matter at hand. Will the guilty party step forward?"

"Guilty? We are not guilty of anything. You say we killed twenty humans, but where is this proof?" I demanded.

"Kimberly, bring in the only survivor," Samuel ordered.

Kimberly scuttled out a door to the side of their podium. She rushed back in, her face pale. "He's dead."

"What?" Chryston snarled. "How?"

"K-Killed himself," Kimberly stammered.

All eyes turned on us. "You've done this—"

I laughed and shook my head. "How? You've had people watch all of us since we arrived. I didn't even know you had a witness."

"Because there wasn't one, since it never happened," Alex said loudly.

"Lies," Fiona hissed.

"I would like to tell you my side of the story of what happened that night. If I may," I asked. They all looked at each other, and I was sure they communicated mentally like I could with Cedrick. I wondered if it was a gift from Sapphire.

"Very well. Speak."

I fisted my hands at my sides. I felt like barking like a dog, but didn't. Instead, I told them, and whoever was watching through the broach, in detail everything that happened the night I became ghoul queen.

"Why would demons come after you?" Gregory questioned.

This was where I could throw them under the bus with the proof we had. However, I wasn't sure it was the time.

"It doesn't matter," Jessica said. "Asher, Nate, and Alex are under arrest for treason. No one leaves the elite enforcers without permission. No one." She clapped her hands; the door to the left of the podium opened, and enforcers streamed into the room surrounding us.

"Come peacefully and no one will get hurt."

"No!" I cried. "You cannot take them."

"Love," Asher called, his hands on my shoulders. "We'll go. It's okay."

I looked to the floor, pretending to be lost in thought, but used the link to speak with with Asher instead. *What are you doing?*

Nate, Alex, and I will secure the room outside. You need to give them everything we know on them.

Throw them under the bus, Alex clipped.

But what happens if they do something to any of you?

Angel, have more faith in us. We can take these guys on with a hand tied behind our backs, Nate said.

You had all better come back into the room in one piece.

We will, dove. Nothing will keep us away from you.

Finally, I nodded and straightened. Asher dropped his hands

and he, with Nate and Alex, were escorted from the room with half of the enforcers while the other half stayed put.

"Kiered and I believe they will attack soon. The guards who stayed behind seem to be ones who don't like our group."

I took a look around at them and noticed their distaste for us.

Thorn, Ezra, Cedrick, Xi, and Kiered moved closer to me. I lifted my chin and said, "You took some of my mates away. Haven't you already taken enough, not from me, but from others?"

Some of them laughed. "What are you talking about?" Aaron asked.

Into our link, I asked, *"Cedrick, if the guards approach, are you able to make them believe they're stuck in quicksand?"*

"Kiered and I will work together. They'll believe it."

"Fantastic. I need them held back until I've spoken, and then we can attack."

"Finally," Ezra moaned through the link, while Thorn just smiled.

Taking a step forward, I smiled sadly. "It's hard being queen. So very hard because I not only want to protect my family and my mates, but I want to protect my people. Even the people who aren't my own, but don't have a voice or a say in any matters. Since becoming queen, all I have ever wanted was peace. All I have ever wanted was to live happily knowing that no matter who you are or what you are, or what strength and power you have, that you are safe and happy against those who wish to bully you, who want to corrupt you."

"That's a nice little speech, ghoul, but what is the meaning of it?" Jessica asked, smirking at me like I was about to lose everything I held dear.

"I'm talking about change. It needs to happen, in your life, in everyone's life, but mostly in the people who govern over all of us."

More laughter filled the room. "And why do you think change is needed?" Chryston asked. Was he really so stupid to lead me into subjects that they wouldn't want people to know about? Then again, they thought they had the upper hand since we were surrounded.

"Because all of you are the worst. You're all evil, vile people, and I'm willing here and now to stand up to you all."

"Foolish bitch, you have four. We have many."

I shrugged.

"Why do you call us such things? What is it you think you know exactly?" Samuel questioned, as if he thought he was trapping me into telling them everything, where I wanted to in the first place.

"I'm talking about what you have in the lower levels of the compound. How you kidnap those who are stronger than any of you to drain their power and life source. We know for certain about the lion and tiger alphas being taken. We have footage of it from Gregory's computer before it got deleted." I pointed to one of the guards. "I was sure I saw you on there." Watching him tense told me enough. He was probably one of them involved, even when I wasn't sure myself. But he'd been glaring at us pretty hard.

Gregory coughed and choked on the water he'd inhaled.

"Preposterous." Stephen laughed. He slapped the table with his hand. "All lies."

"I haven't finished. We have proof to show the people. We have proof over all your illegal activities. No council member should be involved in killing and kidnapping people or selling and pimping out women and men. Or taking little girls and boys and using them for their sick games. We have proof of it all, and it's time the people knew exactly who they have ruling over all factors."

Chryston stood. "Even if you had something, do you think we'd allow the people to see it? You are more foolish than I'd heard about."

Jessica also stood. "We're going to destroy you and your people, Paige Alice. I look forward to breaking the bond you have on Asher and claiming him as mine." She made her way to the doorway my men had gone through. "In fact, I might go and try now."

"May I eat her?" Xi asked.

I ignored his question and slowly leaked my power into the room. My claws grew inch by inch, my teeth lengthened, and I knew my eyes glowed.

"You'll not have him. You'll not harm what's mine. And I will protect anyone who wishes for it. This is the last day of the pain and destruction you've delivered on people. As of right now, my allies are infiltrating the compound."

Chryston roared. He pointed to Fiona and Samuel. "Go." He gestured to a guard. "Contact the others. Bring them here."

The guards tried. He called them on their two-way radio, but no one replied. When Fiona and Samuel opened the door we'd entered, we heard the chaos happening on the outside.

"The room must have been spelled silent," Ezra commented and chuckled when they started to look panicked. Fiona and Samuel disappeared out the door. Two gone, now eight to go and the guards.

"What have you done?" screamed Desirae.

"I've brought people with me who have seen the proof, who

know just what type of people you all are, and now they're willing to help put a stop to it."

Jessica started for me, and I welcomed it. I was ready to rip off her head. But Desirae appeared in front of me. Her glowing hand pressed against my chest. I cried out at the sudden onslaught of pain. My mates swung to me, but Ezra was taken to the ground by Quinton. Thorn was thrown up into the air by Aaron, and Cedrick, along with his brother, were busy using their magic against the guards while Xi had shifted and was currently eating the screaming elite enforcers.

I was on my own, and I didn't mind at all.

I grabbed her wrists, and using my strength, I snapped them. She howled in agony and fell to the floor. I spun to Ezra, who was in his hellhound form, just as the wendigo sank its fangs into Ezra's hide. I sprinted over, grabbed the thing around the waist, and held on while it screeched and fought to loosen my grip.

Something hit me in the back of the head. I stumbled forward, dropping Quinton in the process. I glanced at Sapphire. She stood there holding one of the seats in her hands, breathing hard.

"Stop!" Chryston bellowed. "Fellow council members, please come back. Take a seat. We shouldn't have to lift a finger to take down something like her." They moved quickly, all smiling, like they knew what Chryston had planned, which they probably did. "Aaron, if you will."

"My pleasure." Aaron's power choked the room. It wasn't like Alex's. It was smooth and sweet. It stunk and I wanted to get away from it.

"Blood magic," Ezra warned.

A portal opened, and a tall, smiling man stepped through.

"Fuck, that's the demon who worked with Grace. Rebellious," Thorn told us.

Shit just got real.

Rebellious smiled at Thorn. "Ah, the ghoul I was promised. Where is my mage I was also promised?" he asked.

"Capture them all first and we'll give you who you're after," Chryston ordered.

Rebellious glowered at the man. Chryston was smart enough to take a seat. Rebellious sniffed the air. "I want the girl too."

"No," Aaron said. "I am your master. I called you here. You will do as we ask."

Rebellious turned and stared him down, but Aaron looked right back. Xi stalked closer to the demon. I wanted to call him off. I didn't want him hurt. He was a pain, but a part of our family.

Xi leaped. Rebellious turned, grabbed Xi's snake head that was going in for a strike, and ripped it right off.

"Xi," Kiered cried. Cedrick quickly grabbed his brother.

"No, stop," I yelled. Xi dropped to the ground, and Rebellious kicked him hard enough his body went sailing across the floor, slamming into the seats. Xi tried to climb to his feet, but he fell back down.

Rebellious laughed. "Really, Xi. We've fought before, and you've failed. I know your tricks, beast, so don't bother."

Cedrick let Kiered go. He raced over to Xi and knelt over him, whispering things over and over.

Rebellious scoffed. "Pathetic." He turned back to Aaron. "Now, let's get back to business. The girl is mine."

"She's ours. You take the ghoul and the mage."

"You promised me riches and power like I wouldn't believe.

You said I would be stronger than the devil himself. The girl's life will give me the boost I need. I'm taking her."

"I'm the one who controls the portal. I can send you back, and you'll never grace Earth again, neither will your minions."

Rebellious dropped his head back and laughed heartily. In a blink, he was right in front of Aaron with his hand over Aaron's face. Aaron screamed, and we all watched as his body shrank in on itself. Rebellious had drained him of his power in seconds.

"Now I control the portal. Come," he called, and demons crawled, flew, and raced out of the portal. Rebellious faced the other council members. "Shall we talk about a new deal?"

Desirae stood, her hands alight with her powers. "I can still send you back to Hell, demon."

Didn't they know when to shut up and let him think he was getting his own way?

"Alex, Asher, Nate?" I called, using our link.

"We heard, angel," Nate answered. *"We're trying to get back in there."*

That was all I could ask for. I knew they would be dealing with a lot outside those doors.

"You are not strong enough, witch." He waved her off as if she were nothing. To him, I supposed she was. He turned to me, and my heart dropped to my feet. He smiled. "You smell delicious. I have a feeling I could drain your power again and again and you'd just get more back. I'm going to have fun with you."

"You'll not have her," Cedrick said. He moved in front of me. Thorn also stepped in front of me, and then Ezra, back in his human form.

Rebellious paused. He glared at Ezra. "Why do you look familiar?" He drew in a breath. "You smell of home. Who are you?"

"Paige, break the broach," Ezra said through our link, and it was the first time I'd heard him so serious.

Still, I asked, *"What?"*

"Break the broach. Cut off the video, now." His tone scared me.

"Cedrick, can you make yourself look like a guard and grab me?" I asked. *"I don't want people to think I cut off the connection to the live feed."*

"Done."

I could still see Cedrick as himself, but I felt his powers around him. He grabbed the top of my dress, tore off the broach and held it up. "What is this sorcery?" He dropped it and stomped on it. His acting skills could do with some work, but it wasn't too bad.

"Answer me," Rebellious roared. He still hadn't looked away from Ezra. "Who are you?"

I took a step forward. "You don't need to know."

Rebellious's eyes swung to me, and he smiled. "Maybe I don't. You come to me, and I'll forget all about him, little queeny."

"No," all of my mates roared into my mind.

Movement caught my attention. I glanced to the council members who were currently trying to sneak away. "If any of you take another step, you'll be dealing with my mates."

Ezra snarled and shifted his attention their way. I could tell he didn't want to. He wanted to focus on the bigger threat, the demon. *"Don't go near him, Paige,"* Ezra sent me.

I couldn't promise that because I didn't like the demon's attention on Ezra, so I said nothing.

The council members froze; their faces drained.

"I have them," Cedrick said, his voice tight and hard. *"Please be careful, beautiful."*

"I'll keep an eye on the demons," Thorn said.

Pride filled my chest. I knew my mates hated the thought of me in danger, but they still showed me trust by leaving me to deal with the dickhead demon.

However, since Cedrick had the others under an illusion, Ezra shifted his attention back to the demon and me. Now it was my turn to trust him, even when it scared me stupid at the thought of something happening to him again.

"Little queeny," Rebellious sang. I glanced at him and discovered his hand stretched my way, wiggling his fingers.

"Do you really think you'll get away with taking me?"

He laughed. "Who will stop me?"

A form dropped from the roof onto Rebellious. The demon made a grab for Asher, but it was as if Asher was a spider as he crawled over the demon's body. Anywhere my mate touched, blood welled.

Rebellious screamed in anger before he closed his eyes and stilled.

My heart was in my throat; I didn't like it at all. I made a dash forward. A scream built inside of me when I saw Rebellious's eyes flash open. He smiled as his hand whipped out and clamped around Asher's throat.

"Fast little fucker," he growled, and then Asher's neck snapped. His body dropped to the floor, and he was kicked to the side.

I stopped.

I couldn't move.

I couldn't comprehend.

Then it all hit me—the rage, the fury, and the pain of seeing Asher staring up at the roof with no life in his eyes. Even though in the deep crevices of my mind I knew he would heal, I let in all the anguish and used it to fuel myself.

I locked my mind from my mates, shut down the link, and slowly, I pulled my gaze from Asher's body to drill into Rebellious.

The demons around him yelled and cheered. Ezra snarled back.

I pushed them all away from my mind and focused on Rebellious.

Lifting my upper lip, I bit out harshly, "You shouldn't have done that."

Rebellious scoffed, his smile telling me he was amused by me. It was time to show him he shouldn't be.

A growl filled my chest and spilled from my mouth as my teeth grew longer than ever before and my claws extended even more. My body felt thicker, taller. "Asher is mine. You harmed him."

I rolled my head and stopped, my eyes on him again. He opened his mouth to say something, but he paused when I advanced faster than I ever had. In seconds, I was in front of him with my fist jabbed into his gut. He roared in my face when I looked all the way up at him.

He grabbed my arm and tried to pull it free. His eyes widened for the first time, and I saw panic. "You can't be this strong."

"You fucking touched what's *mine*," I yelled up at him.

Chaos descended around us. I could hear fighting, but I didn't move my gaze away from the one in front of me. The one who would pay the most.

Sluggishly, I twisted my hand up in his tight grip and moved my hand upward toward his heart. His body healed as I went, and I grinned, knowing I would be able to inflict more pain since his body repaired itself.

"No," he clipped. His hands around my arm smoked black. It grew upward on my body. His eyes narrowed. Was he trying to work a spell and it wasn't happening? "What are you?"

"I'm Paige fucking Alice, goddamn ghoul queen." I ripped my hand free and easily slashed down through his head. I stepped back and watched him heal.

I laughed. Once he was back to somewhat normal, I asked, "Are you ready for more?"

He said nothing, so I picked for him. I flashed forward, burying my teeth into his shoulder while I grabbed one of his wrists and forced my other hand between his legs. I tore off his balls. Flesh and fabric filled my grip. He screamed and thrashed, but I didn't let go. My teeth stayed in his flesh, my one hand on his wrist as I dropped his balls to the floor. When I pulled my mouth back and moved away once more, shredded skin came with me. I wiped at my face with the back of my arm as I looked at the black smoke circling me.

"Why won't my power work on you?" he puffed out, his voice full of fear and pain chasing his words.

"I'm protected by my mates," I guessed, because I wasn't exactly sure why either.

His hands lifted in front of him. More black smoke poured out and made its way toward me. I stood still and felt its cold touch brush over my skin. I watched it for a moment and then grinned up at Rebellious.

"You fool. She's a ghoul. She can't be controlled or killed by darkness. She's made of it. But our queen is also right. She's protected because of her mates. You didn't think about that, about the other ghoul for her mate, about her vampire, and you didn't know about me," Ezra said from behind me. *"Mi corazón, you've had your fun, but there's only so much your mates can take. He will be dealt with. Come. Step back more."*

"No. He has to pay."

"He will." Ezra's words whispered through my mind.

"Love, I need you." Asher said.

I searched out my vampire to find him propped up leaning against Nate, with Alex at his side also. My heart ached. He was there, gazing back at me with his love shining through.

Rebellious roared. "Who are you?" he asked Ezra once more.

"He's from my own loins, Rebellious" came a voice I knew too well.

"Did he have to say it like that?" Ezra growled through the link.

The other demons all screeched and went straight back into the portal. Back into Hell. I shook my head in shock, not realizing Lucifer was that scary. I just found him annoying.

Lucifer appeared right beside me, causing me to jump. He winked down at me, and I glared up at him. He chuckled and slung an arm over my shoulder. "I'll have to watch myself around you, my dear. Taking his balls was a little harsh, darling."

"Not harsh enough. I would have made him eat them."

"And I believe you, but you have better things to do." He smiled and looked at Rebellious. "You've really fucked up this time, Rebellious. If you had stayed away, this battle would be over. But then you showed your face. Did I hear you want to steal my daughter-in-law?" He shook me slightly at his side.

"Daughter-in-law?"

Lucifer clicked his fingers and pointed at Rebellious. "You got it. Sweet but temperamental, which I'm sure you've noticed by now. Paige Alice is mated to my son, Ezra. Do you want to run right back through that portal and let it be known to any demon who fucks with my family they'll be turned to ashes instantly?"

Rebellious stayed still.

"No? Pity. I'll have someone else spread the word then." Lucifer sighed. "I guess it's time I take care of you, Rebellious."

"Please no, master. I beg you. Please let me live, and I will do anything you want. Anything."

Lucifer straightened. His calm exterior faded and, in its place, stood a hard man who nearly had me fleeing from the look in his eyes.

"It's too late. You harmed my loyal guard. You threatened my family." In a flash, Lucifer was in front of Rebellious. His body glowed red. The heat coming off him swept out around the room. Lucifer wrapped a hand around Rebellious's neck as his body grew brighter and brighter. It traveled up his arm and down over Rebellious, who bellowed in agony. His skin peeled away, revealing flesh, then bones, then nothing.

Lucifer sighed. The heat withdrew with the glow of fire. He walked over to Xi, who was in his human form, leaning against Kiered's chest. He crouched beside them. "See you've found your mate, Xi. Lucky bastard. I guess you're staying with them then?"

Xi nodded.

Lucifer reached out and placed one hand on Kiered's shoulder, the other on Xi's. "I wish you both the best of luck."

The doors behind us opened, and a group of vampires, as well as lion and tiger shifters, entered in a rush.

They all paused.

Lucifer walked back over. He ruffled Ezra's hair on the way.

"Always good to see you, kid." Ezra complained under his breath and shoved him away.

"Dear Paige. Do you want me to take these imbeciles to Hell with me?" He gestured to the council members who didn't seem to be under Cedrick's illusion any longer, but all stared at me as if they saw something scary.

Cedrick's mind touched mine before I heard, *"They witnessed what a fierce, strong, and amazing queen you are, beautiful."*

Pleased they'd witnessed me at my worst—or perhaps my best depending on how you looked at it—it meant they might be more compliant with what I had in mind. *"Thank you, honey."*

I returned my attention to Lucifer, who waited for my response. "No, thank you, Lucifer. They need to stand trial for the people and be punished."

He bopped me on the nose. "Right then, I'm off. See you soon." He vanished right in front of me.

"T-That was the devil," Detroit stammered as he stomped down the stairs.

"Yes, it was."

He whistled. "You are a badass." He made his way over to the remaining council members. "Move and we'll kill you right now in defense." None of them did. I kind of hoped Jessica had. I would have loved to see her dead, and now. Though, it would come.

"Take them all to lockup," I said. "I meant what I said. We'll make it public—their trial and their execution."

"Asher, please. Asher, Nate. I never meant any of it. They forced me into it," Jessica begged.

Waylon stepped into her path and pushed her. "Move, bitch."

Raquel approached me, along with a man who looked like

he was on his death bed at her side. It seemed she held him up. "Paige, thank you."

I smiled. "You found your mate. Was Detroit's brother there?"

Raquel nodded, and I could see, even with the unshed tears, she was happy. The alpha cleared his throat. "I have heard wonderful things about you, Queen Alice. The tigers are in your debt."

"As are the lions," Detroit called.

"No need." I waved them off. "I'm just happy it's over."

"We still have a few things to deal with though, love. Before we can leave," Asher called.

I groaned as I made my way over to him. People laughed. Finnegan was in front of me in seconds. He bowed. "If you will, we will take care of everything here while you all rest."

"That would be amazing, Finnegan. Thank you." He bowed again and then flashed away. Others started out the doors as well.

"Come to me, please," I said as I dropped to my knees beside Asher and took his face in my hands. I studied him, my heart only easing a little seeing him alive. Tears brimmed and blurred my vision. I leaned in and kissed him. Suddenly I was surrounded by all my men in a huddle on the floor.

"We've done it," Thorn said, smiling.

"We have." I grinned, letting Thorn's words sink in.

Finally, the fear evaporated from my body. We actually had a future I looked forward to.

EPILOGUE

PAIGE

"*D*early beloved, we are gathered here in the sight of God—" A throat cleared, and the minister blanched. "—and Lucifer." He nodded. "In the presence of family and friends to join together these men and this woman in holy—" A throat cleared again. The minister wiped at his sweaty brow while I looked over my shoulder and glared at the devil. "—in holy *and* unholy matrimony. Who here gives this bride away?"

"I do," Xi answered and glared at everyone.

"It should have been me," I heard from Lucifer. Thankfully Virginia shushed him.

The minister tipped his head at Xi. "Thank you. You may take a seat now."

"No," Xi clipped.

717

The minister's head jerked back. "No?"

"I'm staying here."

"Xi, I swear I will cut off Kiered's—" Before I could finish my threat, he backed away.

"See what I mean about her temper?" Lucifer whispered, not quiet enough though, of course.

"We should have eloped," I told my mates.

"Relax, sweetheart, it's nearly done." Thorn smiled from around Asher, who was at my side.

"Then we can get to the good part," Ezra commented, causing laughter from the crowd. His father was the loudest.

"Everyone shut the fuck up so we can get married," Nate yelled.

"Nate, really?" Alex snarked.

I glanced up at Cedrick on my other side. "Your mother must think we're all crazy." I was too scared to even glance at Castilina to see her expression, worried it would be a scowl of disgust.

He grinned down at me. "My mother loves you too much to be worried about any of this."

I hoped that was true and stayed that way because I was close to killing Satan.

"Love, it's fine. Now pay attention so we can have you as our wife."

A grin swept over me. I beamed up at Asher. "Okay."

The minister went on, and I was grateful Lucifer didn't open his mouth again. I still couldn't believe my men agreed to do this for me. When I'd brought up the idea of marking them in some way, it hadn't even crossed my mind about having them wear my ring from marriage. When my sister suggested it, I fell in love with the idea but wasn't sure the guys would go for it.

I was wrong. They loved the idea.

Which was how, one month after the battle with the council, after their trials and executions, which all factions could view, we were finally home and getting married. It had taken us what seemed like forever to figure out who would make good council members. People we trusted, people we knew wouldn't lead anyone astray or become corrupted by power and money.

Until Alex suggested the people we already knew.

Aggie, Clyde, and Felnick all moved to the council building. They would be missed dearly, but I knew they were going to do amazing as they worked alongside Raquel, Detroit, and William. They still had two more positions to fill, but there was no rush, and my mates and I were willing to lend a helping hand when needed. Though, from what we'd heard, everyone was happy with the choices, and those who didn't agree either kept silent or lived the way they wanted. Unless it was a way we didn't agree with; then we'd send the enforcers to their doorstep.

Already men and women were coming out of nowhere with complaints of their master, coven leader, or alpha and how they'd been treated poorly. Each case was looked at more thoroughly. We wouldn't blindly believe people until we had hard evidence in our hands.

It would be a long road to a world of peace between all communities, but it would be worth it in the end.

I was just grateful we were finally home. It was amazing to see my family again and it felt like the kids had grown too much since we'd been gone.

Since everyone had viewed what really went on in the meeting room with the council, I had the mages take down the shield protecting us from outsiders. We'd gained more people, even while we'd been away, but I'd made sure to meet them all when I got back. They'd been scared but hopeful for the same future my mates and I were after. Of peace.

The minister broke through my thoughts and said, "I ask you each now to repeat after me."

My men each took their time and repeated the vows. I teared up over each and every one because they said them with such honesty, such conviction, I knew they meant every word.

Then it was my turn. "I, Paige Alice, take you Asher Evans, Nate Felan, Thorn Jones, Alex Smith, Cedrick Nelydriel, and Ezra Morningstar for my wedded husbands. To love and cherish. For better or worse, that means you Nate and Ezra, for richer or poorer. In sickness and in health. From this day and for the rest of our existence."

The minister smiled and nodded. "May the Lord and Underlord—" He winked at Lucifer. "—bless these rings, which you give to each other as your sign of love, devotion, and everlasting peace."

"Also a warning," I added.

"I'm sorry, child?" the minister asked.

"The rings are a warning to those who try and touch what's mine."

The minister cleared his throat and tugged at the neck of his outfit. "Yes, of course. As you place these rings on your partners' fingers, I ask that you repeat these words. This ring is my sacred gift to you. A symbol of my love. A sign that from this day forward, and always, my love will surround you. With this ring, I thee wed." As soon as we were all done, the minister announced, "I now pronounce you, ah, men and wife." He shrugged. "All of you may now kiss your wife."

My men surrounded me, each taking their time kissing the

daylights out of me. Where if I breathed, I would be panting at the end. Hell, I still was.

We faced the room and the cheers of congratulations were deafening.

Ezra stepped forward with his hands out and pushed them toward the ground. The room quieted. "Thank you, everyone. Please enjoy the drinks and snacks in the throne room. Right now, we have somewhere to be."

I let out a squeal when I was picked up over a shoulder. Asher flashed us out of the room, but I still heard the laughter ringing out behind us.

As soon as he had me in our bedroom and the other men joined us, with Thorn closing the door after him, I turned and ordered, "Help me with this dress."

Alex had a better idea, of course. He clicked his fingers and all that was left on my body were my black lacy bra and panties.

"Are you sure about this, angel?" Nate asked as he stalked toward me already naked. My stomach swirled in delight.

"Yes. Double yes, triple yes, forever yes."

A few chuckles went around the room, then Thorn said, "She sounds sure."

"All right, angel. Anything for you." He lunged. His arms wound around my waist and we were airborne for a moment, while I felt Nate shift into his half form, before we dropped to the bed. He was getting faster and faster at shifting; it amazed me. He pulled back enough that I saw his snout, the extra hair, and his sharp teeth. He licked at my neck before he latched his teeth into my flesh and bit down hard. I wrapped my legs around his waist and gripped his shoulders, holding him tightly against me.

He growled against my skin when he realized my panties were in the way and he couldn't push inside me.

"Alex," I moaned and felt the bed dip. He was beside us as Nate let out another growl of frustration. Alex clicked his fingers and I felt the cool breeze over my most heated part.

"He's more wolf at the moment," Alex said. I could tell since he wasn't already inside me like Nate, if he was in his human form, would have been. Instead, he was holding me while using his hips to try and find where he desperately needed to go.

Alex reached between us and gripped Nate's length, but Nate didn't want to be pushed back to line up at my entrance; he kept trying to find it himself.

"Asher," Alex called. I caught Asher behind Nate, his eyes glowing green with desire as he stared down at me over Nate's shoulder. He assisted Alex by pulling back Nate's hips. Alex lined Nate up and Nate thrust right inside, ripping a cry from me.

"Paige?" Cedrick called.

"I'm okay. He feels good."

Nate fucked me hard and fast while his teeth stayed embedded into my flesh. The pain and pleasure hissed through me, driving me wild. All I could do was hold on and enjoy the ride.

Nate paused. I opened my eyes and blinked lazily up at Asher where he remained behind Nate. It was then I noticed he was gloriously naked as well.

"I'm going to fuck him and drink from you, love."

"Yes, please." I nodded.

Nate let out a whimper when Asher slid into him. It took a moment to gain the rhythm back, but Nate soon fucked himself on Asher while he entered in and out of me.

"Wrist," Asher demanded. His pinched brows told me he wasn't going to last long. I loved how my men got so aroused by watching me with the others. I lifted my wrist over Nate's back and gasped when Asher sank his fangs into my skin.

My body reacted as well. I moaned long and loudly when my stomach ignited with that sweet swirl before shooting down to my pussy. My orgasm had me seeing stars behind my closed lids. Nate lifted his head and roared into the room as he shot his cum inside me. Asher hissed out a breath, leaned into Nate's back, still with his mouth around my wrist, and groaned through his own release.

Asher dropped to the bed, gently taking Nate with him. His chest rumbled with a purr.

"Alex," he ordered.

"Right here. Turn your head a little, dove." I did and felt Alex's magic fill the room. He laid a hand over Nate's bite and his other hand pressed down on my wrist where Asher had taken from me. It burned, but I gritted my teeth through the pain.

Asher's purr grew closer. I opened my eyes to see Nate had moved and gently rested his head on my stomach while Asher curled into Nate and leaned up to reach me. A finger traced my lips; then he bent and pressed his mouth against mine. I could drink down the purr he continued with when our mouths opened and we deepened the kiss. It helped me take my mind away from the pain, and excitement and lust surfaced once more inside me.

A loud groan had me breaking the kiss, but it didn't stop Asher from kissing, licking, and nipping at my shoulder, while I looked across the room to see Cedrick sitting naked on a couch and an equally naked Ezra between his legs.

My stomach clenched in the best of ways while my clit throbbed. My gaze stayed transfixed on Ezra's head bobbing up and down on Cedrick's erection. I dragged my gaze up to meet his stunning shining eyes.

"I couldn't resist a bit of play while watching you," Cedrick said.

"Play all you like, honey. I like watching you all as well."

"Merde," dropped from Cedrick's parted lips. "He's so fucking good at this."

Nate snorted. Through the pain, I could now feel him tracing his fingers over and around my stomach. *"I'm better."*

"You wish, wolf," Ezra said, only he never stopped sucking Cedrick's cock.

"Christ, you might want to back off. I'm about to—" Cedrick dropped his head back to the couch as he gripped Ezra's hair and held him still while he lifted his hips and finished coming while fucking Ezra's mouth.

I was soaked, and not just from Nate's cum but from seeing that.

Ezra suddenly stood. He pressed a hand to the back of the couch beside Cedrick's head and I knew, even though I couldn't see, his other hand would be stroking himself.

"Can I come on you?" he asked, his voice rough and low.

"Merde, yes." Cedrick ran his hands up and down Ezra's sides. We heard a sharp hissed breath, and then Ezra grunted out his release all over Cedrick's pale, perfect skin.

Alex sat back beside me, drawing my attention away from Cedrick and Ezra. He clicked his fingers, and I heard Cedrick say, "Thank you." Alex must have cleaned him. I grinned up at him before quickly glancing over to see Ezra resting his back against Cedrick's side while Cedrick had his arm wrapped around Ezra's shoulders, holding him close.

The sight thickened my throat. I loved how comfortable my men were with one another. Hell, if I wasn't me, I would be completely jealous of myself. I was a lucky, lucky woman.

"Is it our turn, Alex?" Thorn asked. I turned to find him naked, erect, and leaning against the wall on the other side of the bed, his eyes dark and hooded.

"I believe it is," Alex said. He moved up the bed and laid on his back. "Paige, come here," Alex ordered. Nate lifted off me and Asher moved back. I rolled over and climbed up the bed on my hands and knees.

"Slowly," Thorn demanded. I moved as if I was a lazy cat toward Alex, who was up on his elbows watching me, his cock hard, ready and waiting for me. "Suck Alex." Thorn's hard voice came from beside the bed. He'd moved without my noticing.

When I got to Alex's hips, I kept my ass in the air and bent forward. I cupped Alex's balls and gently rolled them around while I licked up his length slowly, causing him to suck in a shuddering breath.

"Changed my mind. Straddle Alex's hips," Thorn said. He stood there running his hand up and down himself while watching. "Make sure you sink onto him."

"Gladly," I whispered.

"Please," Alex said just as quietly.

I shifted up, lifted a leg over Alex, and leaned forward as I gripped his cock and lined it up. I teased my opening for a little while, until Alex's hands gripped my hips tightly and he pushed me down onto him. We both sighed in pleasure as soon as I was fully embedded on Alex's length.

"We're going to fill you up, sweetheart." Thorn's hand traced down over my back as he climbed onto the bed behind me. His hand stopped at my ass, where he gave my cheek a light tap.

"Yes, God, yes." I nodded.

Thorn kissed my shoulder. "Give me your mouth first," he demanded. I rocked against Alex gently. He moaned under me as he looked over my shoulder. Thorn kissed me hard and yet so damn sweetly, it had my heart racing faster.

He nipped at my lower lip. "Lean down for me, sweetheart. Present your gorgeous ass to me." I did. I leaned down and captured Alex's mouth in a hot, slow kiss as Thorn prepared me for his hardness.

By the time Thorn removed his fingers, I was grinding down on Alex so hard we were lost in the motion, of the feeling of a close release. Then Thorn edged nearer. He pressed a hand to my lower back and I stilled enough for him to push into me slowly.

I was full, absolutely full, but it was wonderful. Thorn, with his hands over Alex's on my waist, controlled our movements. He pulled me back and I withdrew from Alex, only to thrust back into me and I slid back down on Alex.

I rested a hand on Alex's chest and one back on Thorn's hip, all of us slick with sweat. I let myself enjoy the sensation of being thoroughly fucked by two of my mates.

"I'm close," Alex warned.

"Me too," I said.

"Then let's do it now," Thorn clipped, and I felt his power fill the room and mix with Alex's power. His hands on my hips grew claws, but only one scraped across my skin over and over. Alex's hand slid up to under my breast where his power caressed my body, and too soon, I was climaxing. "Alex, Thorn," I screamed their names. Both men swelled inside me, and their cum implanted into me at the same time.

I collapsed against Alex's chest and felt Thorn back gently

out of me. He helped Alex roll me over, and then Alex was there, using his powers on my hip and under my breast again. The same burning had me whimpering.

"Nearly done," Alex promised. I nodded, but kept my eyes closed. "There."

Opening my eyes, I glanced down my body. Alex handed me a mirror he conjured out of thin air. First I looked at Nate's bite mark on my neck. My pulse sped up. I dropped the mirror and drew my wrist up to see the two puncture marks there from Asher's fangs. A smile crept onto my lips. I skimmed my eyes over Ezra's mark while I sat up on the bed. I flattened my breast a little and caught sight of Alex's mark—it was of a purple flower. I bit my bottom lip and tears welled in my eyes. I kept looking and found Thorn's claw marks on my hip. I traced my fingers over them as I sniffed. My heart burst with so much love.

Not only had they been willing to wear my rings so everyone knew they were taken, but they'd agreed to mark my body in their own special way. Alex then used his magic to make sure those marks would always stay on my skin like Cedrick's and Ezra's did.

Lifting my head, I sniffed again. "I love them. I love you all. This is the best day of my life."

I first tackled Alex and hugged him tightly as I cried my happy tears. Thorn was next, taking my embrace with a chuckle. When I got to Nate, he groaned and complained about me leaking again. Asher swept me up into his arms and stood from the bed, hugging me just as close as I did him. He took me to the men on the couch and planted me on Cedrick's lap. I twisted and wrapped my arms around Cedrick and Ezra.

"Thank you. Thank all of you for giving me this day." I sobbed into them.

"Beautiful, we would give you anything."

"He's right, mi corazón. Anything."

"What's that?" Alex asked. We all looked to him as Cedrick moved me around and tucked me into his chest while I held Ezra's hand. He stared at something on the floor near the door. He started to get up, but Nate held him back.

"I'll get it," he stated. Alex rolled his eyes, and we all watched as Nate went to the door, bent and picked up the piece of paper. He unfolded it, read it, and then his eyes became so wide I got scared. His heart also took off in a crazy beat.

"What is it?" Asher demanded. He flashed over to Nate just as Nate's eyes rolled in the back of his head and he dropped to the floor. I cried out his name and rushed over there. Crouching over him, I checked his body for something, anything.

Asher laughed. I looked up glaring, but his radiant smile wiped that glare away.

"He fainted. He actually fainted."

"Why?" Alex asked. I realized all of my mates stood around us. My men had sleep pants on, while Alex had placed me in a thin teddy.

Asher straightened out the note and read from it. "To my lovely family, this is Virginia, Ezra's amazing mom. As a wedding gift, I am now able to tell you all something. Congratulations, you'll all be parents. Paige is nearly two months pregnant with a little ghoul or elf."

I froze. My body turned to stone. Cedrick dropped to his knees beside me. His eyes welled with tears as he dragged me against him and held me while Asher went on. "I've done my research, and I learned elves have healing powers. While Paige's heart beats, it didn't fix her reproductive system. Cedrick did when they bonded. Paige, darling, your body is now in working order. Of course, there is still some advantages to being different, you still won't menstruate or use the bathroom, but you'll be able to reproduce."

I lowered my hands from my throat and pressed them against my belly. I had a baby in there. A little blob of a baby. I'd thought I'd lost that chance. I was going to be a mother. My men, its fathers.

Asher cleared his throat, and I looked up to see Cedrick wasn't the only one with tears in his eyes; they all had them. We were all overwhelmed with happiness from the news. Asher scrubbed at his face and went on, "Congratulations to you all again. You'll make wonderful parents. I just know it. And Paige, if you think they're protective now, you haven't seen anything yet. I wish you luck because now they know their treasure carries another new treasure."

"Pick her up. Carry her slowly to the bed," Thorn ordered.

"Yes!" Alex cried. "I need to check her over. I wish Virginia told us before I used my magic on her."

Cedrick had me in his arms and did as Thorn said. He took me to the bed but sat on it with his back to the headboard and me between his legs. His hands splayed over my belly protectively.

Ezra paced the floor. "Did you guys fuck her too hard? Did we injure the baby? Fucking hell. Fucking motherfucking hell." He ran his hands over his head.

"Stop!" Asher clipped loudly. I was grateful for it. I knew he would be calmer than the rest. "Thorn, run and get a doctor.

Alex, look between her legs. Ezra, go get some warm towels."
They all raced into action.

Groaning, I thumped my head back against Cedrick's chest.

"Paige, my love, what is it? Are you in pain? Is the baby okay?" Asher cradled my hand in both of his.

Cedrick hummed under his breath. "Please, beautiful, talk to us. Tell us everything is okay."

When Alex tried to pry my legs apart, I'd had enough. It was my turn to yell, "Stop! Just stop." I held up my hand and waited for the others to come back. Ezra ran into the room from the bathroom and threw the towels at us. Thorn rushed into the room with the poor doctor over his shoulder. "See to her," he bit out and pointed at me. Nate then moaned and slowly stood, almost swaying on his feet until Thorn reached out to steady him. Nate sucked in a sharp breath, looked to me, and his eyes warmed in a way I had never seen. But then he shifted, causing the doctor to jump back. Wolf Nate trotted to the bed, hopped on it, and stood over me. He sat on my lap and snarled back at the doctor, the only person he didn't really know in the room.

"My queen, are you ill?" the doctor asked, ignoring the vicious-sounding wolf. She had balls. Good, she would need them when it came to dealing with my men and this pregnancy, it seemed.

Rolling my eyes, I shook my head. "Sorry to bother you. They're overreacting. We just found out I'm expecting."

The sweet older lady, whose name I couldn't remember for the life of me, clapped her hands and gushed, "Oh my goodness, this is wonderful news."

"Thank you, but please don't let anyone know yet."

"My lips are sealed. Please come and see me soon and we'll do some tests."

"I will. Thanks again."

She bowed and backed out of the room, closing the door behind her.

"Now," I started. "As you've seen, I don't need a doctor right now." Nate growled. I smacked his rump. He shifted off me, curled into my side, and rested his head on my belly. I melted. It was the sweetest thing to see. All of them were. It may piss me off, but I knew they were doing it out of devotion and love. However, I still had to say, "I'm not hurt. The baby isn't either. The baby and I can't get hurt if we have sex, so don't think any of you are taking that away from me."

"We will try our best not to hover too much," Thorn said, with a small shrug. He almost seemed chastised, but the way his eyes kept flicking from my face to my belly, I knew it would take time for him, for all of them, to understand. Maybe with a few kicks to their shins, they'd get it. Thorn leaned down and kissed me. He pulled back and smiled. "You're having a baby."

Giddiness rushed through me. I grinned back. "I am." Each mate then took their time to kiss me and then my belly. Although Nate stayed in his wolf form, he still lifted to lick me and then drop his head back to rest on my belly. It was going to be tough, but it was a hurdle I would love to jump through because this wasn't dangerous—this was one made from love.

My life couldn't get any better. I had everything my heart desired.

I guessed the Fates weren't bitches after all.

BONUS

W hispers caught my attention through my half-asleep state. I would have ignored them and curled into Cedric more, then pulled Thorn closer to my back, but I registered the words.

"What do you mean you can't find her?" Nate snarled low. "She's supposed to be in bed."

"I mean exactly that. She's vanished again," Asher stated.

"We need to wake them," Alex suggested.

"Paige needs more rest. They gave her a good workout," Ezra put in. The blankets hid my smile, but Ezra spoke the truth. Thorn and Cedric had worked my body over in ways I would be feeling for a while.

Dragging the blanket down, I sat up and caressed my baby bump as I yawned. After rubbing my eyes, I blinked sluggishly at my other men standing around the bed. Nate held our squirming boy Isaac, who was five and in his cub form. He didn't stop moving until Nate lifted him and slung him over his shoulder. Thin-lipped, Asher stared at the others with his hands on his hips. Alex ran a hand through his hair repeatedly, and our little four-year-old mage, Colson, watched his daddy with a grin. He adored his father and followed him everywhere. Except when it was bedtime. Then he was all mine. He loved his mommy's stories and cuddles.

"Why are Colson and Isaac awake?" I asked.

Alex looked everywhere but at me while Ezra stared down at me, grazing his bottom lip with his top teeth.

Tensing, I asked, "What's going on?"

This time they all turned to me, and I read their worry instantly.

I glared. "What's happened?"

"I have everyone looking," Asher said. His hand came out and patted the air like he knew I was about to get riled.

"Not my fault this time," Nate said with a smirk. Isaac suddenly turned and leaped for me. Thankfully, Nate was fast and caught him before he crashed to the floor. Our little pup was a bit clumsy. He raced up the bed, tripping over his paws. Reaching down, I picked him up and cuddled him close as he licked at my face.

Smiling, I tapped his nose. He was a cutie in both forms. His tongue lolled out before he yipped at me. Yes, very adorable. "Why are both of our kids awake when they should be asleep for Santa tomorrow? What's happened?" I repeated.

Isaac whimpered.

I cocked my head to the side and raised a brow. "Isaac?"

He wiggled out of my hold and bounced down on Thorn,

who grunted and woke with a groan. "You little monster," Thorn said, though he didn't sound upset about being woken. He rolled with Isaac in his arm to his back, laughing as Isaac licked at Thorn's face.

Cedric, who was on my other side, stretched before he reached out for me blindly and tried to tug me back down next to him.

"Come back to sleep, beautiful,"

"I can't. We have an audience."

He chuckled, opening his eyes. "That's never stopped you."

Laughing, I leaned down to give him a quick kiss on the cheek. "That's true. But Asher was just about to tell me what was wrong."

Cedric stilled for a beat before he sat up abruptly. "Evangeline?"

Asher nodded. "We have everyone looking for her, but she's transported herself again."

With Isaac in his arms, Thorn rolled and climbed out of bed. He dropped Isaac into Nate's waiting hold and said, "I'll get the brothers onto it as well."

"They already are," Alex stated.

Cedric stood beside the bed and helped me up. As soon as I was on my feet, Ezra was there, rubbing my belly before he leaned down to kiss it. Yes, like all my men, we were excited about another baby. It just happened to be Ezra's this time, my shifter mates could tell.

"Xi and Kenrick are also out helping," Ezra said as he straightened.

"Really, there's only a few places she goes now. She has to be at one of them," I said as I slipped into the robe that Cedric held out.

Asher shook his head, his long hair falling around his shoulders more. "We've looked. She isn't at any of them."

Fear knifed through me. "Cedric?"

"She's blocking me. I can't feel her." Panic laced his tone.

I gripped his arm and took a deep breath. If I calmed down, he would too. I hoped. "It's okay. We've been through this every time she gets an idea and wants to follow through. Like the time she transported herself into the woods because she wanted to see the pack. Or when she transported herself from school to your mom because she missed her. She'll show up and then… then she'd grounded for twenty years."

He sighed and ran a hand over his face. "All right. I won't panic yet. But I agree with you about grounding her for twenty years."

"Good." I started for the door. "I mean, seriously, what is she thinking by doing this on Christmas Eve?" Opening the door, I abruptly stopped when the devil stood in front of me.

He cocked an arrogant brow. "Missing someone?" He bounced the five-year-old mischief in his arms.

"Evangeline, you are in big trouble, young lady."

"But Mommy. I wanted to see Grandpa Lucy."

"You can't just up and leave. You know this. If someone with ill intentions got their hands on you, it could've been bad."

The men around me let out their own noises of complaint.

Even Lucifer's gaze darkened. "No one would touch her without forfeiting their lives."

Closing my eyes, I drew in a deep breath. "I know, Lucy."

"Only Evie can call me that," he clipped.

Reaching out, I patted his arm just as one of our people walked by and squawked before running off after they saw the devil. So many still feared him. To me, he was my father-in-law who I could hassle.

He scowled at me. "You will die a thousand deaths."

Evangeline cackled and snuggled into him.

Lucifer's expression melted into warmth as he stared down at her. Cedric moved forward, holding his hands out. "I'll put her in bed."

Lucifer placed her carefully in his arms with a soft smile while I said, "But Evie, you have to promise us you won't go anywhere without an adult present."

She perked up. "Can I still go to Hell?"

I really wanted to laugh at that sentence, but I refrained.

"Yes. But as I said, not without an adult with you. Promise us."

"I promise. No more trips without someone."

Leaning in, I kissed her cherub cheek. "Thank you. Now, you'd better get to sleep so Santa can come."

"I will!" she cried.

Cedric kissed my forehead before he walked to the next bedroom, where the children slept. Until they were older, they would stay in one room together. I glanced back to see Nate and Alex had disappeared with our other kids. Probably entering their room through our joined bathroom.

Asher stepped close, and I leaned into him while looking at Lucifer. "Thanks for bringing her back straight away. We'll see you in the morning?"

"I'll be here." He reached out and ran a hand over my bump. "How's the grandchild of my lions doing?"

"Dad, hell, he's not one of your loins," Ezra complained from somewhere in the bedroom.

"But you are, which means—"

I shot my hand up in his face. "I don't want to hear it. See you tomorrow, Lucy."

He glared, then disappeared in the next instant.

Asher steered me back into the bedroom. "Come on, love. No doubt it'll be a big and early day tomorrow."

Yawning, I nodded. "It will."

Ezra, already in bed beside Thorn, flung the blanket back. I removed the robe and climbed in with Asher at my other side. I rolled into Asher, and Ezra molded himself to my back. My body hummed, my links to them filled with love.

"Sleep, love. Thorn and I will set everything up for the kids by morning."

"I have the best men."

They chuckled around me.

ALEX, Nate, and I were shaken awake by three toddlers at five-freaking-a.m. Luckily, we'd prepared for it. Alex clicked his fingers to cover me in a nightgown and them in sleep pants just before Colton climbed in between Alex and me.

The other two jumped up and down. Since he was still in his pup form, Isaac yipped, and Evie yelled, "Santa, Santa, Santa."

I sat up, curling Colton in my arms, telling the other two, "Go wake Daddy Asher, Ezra, Cedric, and Thorn. We'll meet in the hallway in a few moments, but wait for all of us before running to the main living room, please."

My men didn't like to crowd me when I was pregnant. If I had my way, they'd all be in bed with me, but now they took turns to be at my side.

"Yes, Mommy," Evie yelled, and raced off. Isaac followed her with a stumble here and there.

Kissing the top of Colton's head, I asked, "You ready to see what Santa brought you?"

He lifted his head, cupped my cheeks, squished them in a bit, and cried, "Yes!"

Laughing, I gave him another kiss. "Come on then. Up to Daddy."

Alex was already out of bed and leaned down to grab him. He didn't shift away until he gave me my morning kiss. Something all of my men did that I loved. When they started for the door, I turned to Nate. His heated gaze was already glued to my lips.

Grinning, I ran my fingers through his hair before tugging it at the nape. "Didn't you get enough at whatever hour you came to bed?"

"Fuck no," he growled. "Never enough of you."

Leaning in, I kissed him until both of us were breathless, and Thorn called from the doorway, "Let's go, you two. We have three eager monsters out here."

After sharing a smile against each other's lips, I scooted out of bed and met Nate at the end, where he took my hand in his.

Outside the bedroom, and after I'd kissed the rest of my men good morning, Nate scooped up Isaac and told him, "You'll have to shift to open presents."

Our boy's body morphed from wolf to child. I would forever be grateful for the spell Alex had placed on our boy, and many other shifter children in the pack on our lands, which eased the pains when they shifted. Alex quickly clicked his fingers, and Isaac was dressed in a cute dinosaur pajama set.

Down the hall, a person stepped out of the living room and

called, "Move it, kids. Santa has been," It was Alma, Lucifer's better half. I waved while she blew me a kiss.

Nate placed Isaac on the floor to stop him from jumping out of his arms as the kids ran wildly down the hallway. My heart filled with happiness when we heard their squeals and gasps.

As I held Nate's hand as we entered through the double doors, Ezra drew close and curled an arm around my shoulders.

Lucifer instructed Evie, Isaac, and Colton to sit in front of their piles, which had suspiciously grown from what we'd brought them. I glanced at Alma, who winked. Of course they'd added to the already spoilt monsters' gifts. They loved them nearly as much as we all did. Thankfully, I'd banned my people from getting them anything. They'd been upset, but it'd settled them somewhat when I explained that I'd told my sister the same thing.

Evie glanced back at me. "Mommy, can we start?"

Smiling, I nodded. "Go for it." I took a seat on the couch and watched Nate sit on the floor beside Isaac, who had just ripped open a present.

"Mommy!" he yelled, holding it up.

"Wow, baby."

He beamed and thrust it at his daddy while grabbing for another. Nate smirked.

Colton was slower in opening his, and I caught Alex's hands twitching from where he sat beside our son, as if he wanted to help Colton tear the paper to see what was inside.

Then there was Evie, who had Cedric and Lucifer helping to put together a large doll house while she worked on opening other things.

After speaking with Alma, Asher sat next to me as Ezra dropped to the floor in front of me, leaning against my legs.

Reaching out, I rested a hand on his shoulder. He turned his head and kissed it. I shifted slightly to press my head against Asher's shoulder while I sensed Thorn step up behind me. He leaned down and kissed the side of my neck.

My men.

My family.

Yes, we'd had our ups and downs over the years, but I wouldn't give any of it up for anything. No doubt there would be more trials to come, but with all the support surrounding us, we'd get through it.

Together.

THE HIDDEN KINGDOM

L. ROSE

Read on for a look inside: Within the Darkness.
A polyamorous, romance fantasy novel.

CHAPTER ONE

AMARA

Twenty-seven years ago, the world changed. The monsters who lived in the dark walked out into the light, and things for humans weren't the same. Actually, that was wrong. Things were the same for the wealthy, but those who didn't have money to back them, their lives altered in a way no one would have seen coming.

Not for me, though, since I was born into the world already changed. It was my parents' existence that had been altered in a blink of an eye, as had the lives of most of the human race.

The vampires, shifters, and enchanters led the uprising before I was conceived. But it was drilled into me from a young age that the monsters were stronger, faster, and deadlier than us. It was inevitable that, after years of war against the humans, they won and took control.

To try and create some semblance of peace in this new world, a council was formed after battles for land control continued, as well as a whole bunch of other dramas that created even more chaos. Leaders were selected to ensure order. The council contained three members of each species, and they oversaw everyone. However, after holding a fifteen-year-long position, the council members were switched out with newer monsters.

The council also appointed house leaders in various parts of the world—those who stood above the rest and governed, policed, and controlled their assigned areas, only seeking the help from the council when needed.

It was the monsters time to reign, and they relished the control.

Equality only existed for humans with money or skills.

Those who didn't have the riches to stand by the monsters and live a regular life were forced into servitude with no rights and a pittance of a wage. The monsters refused to supply us with anything other than a room, uniform, and food. Our contract could be bought and sold without our input, and, like the poor humans we were, we had to obey our masters.

Needless to say, life as I knew it was pretty damn unfair.

"We've stepped up in the world, Amara. Make sure you don't ruin this for us," Mom said from behind me. She was excited because the family who bought us was one of those governing families. They were vampires, and their family ruled over a large clan.

A shudder swept over me, and my fear rose, but I still caught her gaze in the mirror and nodded. Drawing in a calming breath, not that it helped much, I finished braiding my long raven hair and then ran my hands down the front of my uniform. Double-checking there wasn't a weapon in sight, I exhaled, confident my blades were hidden under the god-awful maid outfit.

Mom went on. "If I was glad for anything, it was when that old codger died, and we were bought by the Prince family."

Sorrow stabbed through me. How could she be so crass? Mr. Langley, a wolf shifter who had lost his mate, may have been old, but he was a good master. He was gentle, kind, and had been my friend and teacher. He'd taught at a local school and allowed me to attend there with him as an "assistant," but really, he'd let me sit in class like the other students. He'd taken over the role of father figure when I lost my real father at a very young age.

I missed Mr. Langley terribly.

"Do not use this power around someone, Amara, and never tell anyone what you can do. No one." Words Mr. Langley had used one afternoon a year ago, when he'd caught me using my power to help in the garden, rang through my mind once more. *"People will want to use you if they find out, and believe me when I say it won't be good for you, my dear."* The urgent tone had struck fear within me. Since the day he'd caught me, he had insisted training me to fight with weapons. It was all for "my own protection." Because one day, I would need to use everything I had to keep myself safe. But from whom, he didn't know, and neither did I.

Always have a weapon on you, even when you sleep.

I did. Always.

Everything Mr. Langley told me to do, I did. He didn't have to teach me. He didn't have to give me the chance to continue school or treat us kindly, but he did. Never once did he treat me like a slave.

"Oh, stop looking like that," Mom demanded, bringing me from my thoughts. "Look where we are." She giggled, and I barely contained my eye roll. "You know, Olivia won't believe the luck we've gained. Why, our rooms are enormous compared to the one we shared at that old man's cottage." She hummed under her breath and straightened the bed I had already made.

"Mr. Langley," I said.

Her cool gaze swung to me. "You dare to correct me?"

I ground my teeth together and shook my head. My gaze went to the floor in front of me. Anger burned inside me. I hadn't despised my mom my whole life. Mr. Langley had told me she used to be good and caring when I was younger, when my father had been around, and I remembered glimpses of her smiling face and sweet words. However, now it was hard to recall those moments.

After my father passed and as I grew older, she turned bitter —telling me she wouldn't have become a slave if it wasn't for me. She would have had the money to be seen as an equal if it wasn't for me. Thankfully, whenever she started ranting, Mr. Langley had always been there to distract her or had pulled me out of the situation.

"I wish you had a different mother, Amara. You deserve so much more."

It had been sweet of him to say, but I couldn't change what I had been dealt. I was stuck in this miserable existence with her.

"Come on. We can't be late when they give the job details out," Mom said as she made her way to the door and glanced over her shoulder to make sure I followed. I had no choice but to do so. "If we're lucky, we'll get jobs in the garden or kitchen. Anything is better than cleaning. My hands just can't take it anymore." She was vain. So very vain. To the point that she thought Mr. Langley would have taken her on as a wife if she flirted with him enough.

It didn't work, of course.

But I had a feeling she would try it here as well. She'd be a fool if she did. I didn't think she understood just how dangerous vampires were.

There was also one job she didn't mention.

A blood slave.

A person who sat around and waited to be called to their master to satisfy their thirst. I prayed to the gods above I didn't get that job, even though I wasn't even sure the gods were real. How could they be? Why would they give the monsters control?

"Straighten your shoulders," Mom snapped when she stopped at the end of the hall. She shook her head. "You should have put on makeup." I'd always refused to use the items she'd stolen from the late Mrs. Langley.

Besides that, there was no point. I didn't want to impress anyone. Mom had caked her face in the stuff, hoping to look younger than her forty-eight years.

She made me sick.

"I swear, if you ruin this for me somehow, I will make your life hell."

I bit my tongue to keep the snort at bay. I was already living in hell, more so after Mr. Langley passed away and he could no longer be the filter between Mom and her controlling ways. Nodding, I waited for her to move around the corner. When she did, I started forward, slouching while shooting her a middle finger.

I stopped when my bottom lip trembled, and hopelessness washed through me. Closing my eyes, I took a deep breath and quickly opened my eyes again. Resting my hand against my uneasy stomach, I drew in another breath.

I was stronger than this. I could do this. I could live and hope to one day have a time in life when I wouldn't have to follow.

I am strong.

A noise escaped my lips when I saw someone standing in the shadows at the other end of the hall. Had the person seen what I did behind my mom's back?

Maybe I wasn't so strong after all, because dread pumped through my veins, causing my hands to shake. I tucked them behind me and gripped them together. With a frantic heart, I thought of the dagger at my thigh, and I swiftly made my way down the hall, then into the room Mom had just walked through.

Mom smiled coldly at me. Anger only I was able to see burned in her eyes. She put on the show for the other new slaves and the head butler who stood off to the side where another door lay. Mom…. Actually, I was sick of calling her my mom. She hadn't been one for many years. In my head I could at least fight back. *Charlotte* pointed to the spot beside her. I shifted over there, and as soon as I stopped next to her, she gave the room a fake smile but pinched my side hard.

"Where did you go?"

I pointed toward the door. "Nowhere. A painting caught my attention outside the room."

She laughed. "You were always easily distracted by things. Simpleminded."

I didn't respond, but I did thank my luck that I remembered the hallway we'd come from had been lined with paintings. The mansion was something like a museum with plates of armor, cased documents, sculptures, and such placed all over. They were mainly in the Prince family's living quarters; the servant's quarters weren't so extravagant. Not that it bothered me. I didn't see the need to show things off for other people's sake. Unless Mrs. Prince enjoyed seeing those things herself.

As I adjusted from one foot to the other, Charlotte pinched me again. I ground my teeth together and busied my mind with the people around us. There were two women my age, or a little older, who giggled with each other; the fools were excited. A man and his son, from what I gathered by the way he had a hand on the young boy's shoulder. The boy, who looked about twelve, seemed scared, the father uneasy. There were two other men. One appeared close to twenty-five and glancing around the room as if waiting for someone to jump out. He was ready to take them on, judging by the way his fists were clenched at his sides. The other seemed to be in his thirties. He stood in a military pose, like nothing fazed him. I'd wondered how they'd come to be bought or why there were so many positions available, but knew I probably wouldn't find the answers.

Then there was one other woman, around the same age as Charlotte, with a weird polite smile on her face. I didn't know this group's story, but they all would have been in the same boat as Charlotte and me.

Poor. Destined for a life of servitude.

All of the women were dressed in black-and-white maids' outfits that went from collarbone to ankle. The men and the boy wore black trousers and shirts with gold ties.

The twentysomething man bounced on his feet, obviously hating waiting for the Prince family to give us details on our assignments.

The Prince family.

Everyone knew who they were.

The head of the family, Kane, was the clan leader, age unknown, but old enough to rule over a thousand vampires and a large part of the city we resided in. I'd heard he was cruel and would kill anyone who went against him. The wife, Crista, was beautiful and cherished among her people. But everyone knew not to cross her or she'd be just as mean as her husband. Then there was—

"Attention. Line up into one line," Bennet, the butler we'd previously met, called. The others scuttled to stand on either side of Charlotte and me. Bennett's head tilted toward the door, and he cleared his throat. "The Prince family has arrived."

The doors behind him opened, and in glided our masters, Kane and Crista Prince.

Their son was Kincaid. He was twenty-three, a couple of years older than myself, and I'd known of him from high school when Mr. Langley had taken a new position there, bringing me with him.

There was no way Kincaid knew who I was, since I was younger and beneath his status. Also, I'd only ever seen him from afar. I made sure to keep out of any alpha's sight and off their radar. Their power intimidated me. Usually, a vampire with Mr. Prince's status would be classed as a master vampire, but the title had changed over time, and all family heads were now referred to as alphas. It simply meant they were more dominant than others. Though, from what Mom had told me, we were only allowed to call our owners "master." The alpha title was used when or *if* a servant had to greet another alpha of a different line, and the monsters also utilized the title among themselves.

I hadn't needed to worry about any type of title with Mr.

Langley. He had preferred for us to use his first name, but I had always called him Mr. Langley to show the respect I had for him.

Charlotte tugged on my dress. I quickly slipped into a curtsey and stayed down until either the people around me stood or someone said something. My knees shook as time went by. I wanted to yell for them to hurry up but would only be punished for it.

"Rise," Mr. Prince ordered crisply.

We straightened, but I kept my eyes downcast. The less attention I got, the better chance I had at a half-decent job within the house. I would even take cleaning. *Please, anything but blood donor.*

"You understand that your servitude is with this house, and you will follow the rules?"

"Yes, master," everyone echoed.

"Everyone, stand tall," Bennett called. "The master will walk the line, stop in front of you, and bestow on you a position within the family."

I wanted to gag, but I quickly swallowed and lifted my gaze to stare straight ahead. My body tingled with an urge to run, and I fought the need by digging my nails into my palms behind my back. I could feel eyes on me, but I didn't dare look away from the wall. I worried who it might be, since the only others off to my right were the Prince family. They were speaking so low that no one could have heard them, and I was surprised they heard each other, but then again, they had abilities they could use.

I sensed movement and heard Bennett say, "This is Camila and Zoe. Both are twenty-three. They worked as housekeepers for the Solaris family."

Mr. Prince hummed. "They would have sold them because of their money situation." When no one said anything, Mr. Prince ordered, "Blood donors."

My stomach bottomed out for the two of them.

"This is Lyall and his son, Elliot. Lyall is forty-one, his son twelve. They were grounds assistants, also with the Solaris family."

"Keep the same positions here."

"We have here Charlotte and her daughter, Amara. Charlotte is forty-eight, Amara twenty-one. They were with Waylon Langley until he passed on."

Mr. Prince grunted. "Waylon was a well-respected man even from within our faction. Previous positions?"

Mom preened beside me.

"Cooking and housekeeping," Bennett informed him.

Mr. Prince stepped closer my way. The sensation of him studying me made my skin crawl.

"The older woman in the kitchens, cleaning when she's not," Mr. Prince announced. Charlotte made a noise in the back of her throat. She thought her looks would have impressed him in some way. When my lips twitched, I quickly thinned them, holding back the laughter desperate to escape.

"Amara will be servant to Kincaid."

No!

My eyes widened, but I quickly blanked my expression and clenched my teeth so hard, I was surprised they didn't shatter.

I would have taken a position as a blood donor over being servant to Kincaid. He scared me, and I wasn't sure why that was. Maybe his hard expression, his cold, dark eyes. Maybe his snappish tone, or the hatred he had in his heart, which bled out through his words and actions.

It didn't matter that our paths had never crossed. I knew all of that to be true.

Whatever it was that terrified me, I feared him more than the father. Quite a feat, since I'd heard terrible things about Mr. Prince.

Mr. Prince stepped along the line, while Bennett stopped in front of me. "Do you understand your position?"

Nodding, I bit on the inside of my lip so I didn't beg for something, anything else. If I did, there was no doubt I would be killed for insolence.

"Are you sure?" Bennett asked.

"Yes," I uttered. I had heard everything about a servant's role. Mr. Langley had informed me of many things in case I was ever in need. Maybe he knew he wouldn't always be around. A servant was to be at their master's beck and call, day and night. I would have to follow Kincaid around like a lost puppy and do anything he wished for me to do.

My stomach rolled, and I swallowed, taking a shuddering breath. Bennett saw my reaction and offered a sad smile before he moved back to Mr. Prince's side. I didn't hear where the others were assigned; the blood rushed to my head too much and my ears started to ring.

What I needed was to calm down. I needed to stop my racing heart, or I would gain the attention of all the Princes. I dug my nails into my palms again, the pain lessening the panic attack. I dropped my gaze to the floor and emptied my mind.

Rolling back my shoulders, I straightened again.

"Someone will be along to take you to your new positions shortly. Thank your masters," Bennett said.

I dipped into a curtsey like the other women as the men bowed. Even Elliot, the youngest. We always had to show respect for the masters, no matter who had control over us within the family.

As soon as the Prince family left with Bennett following and closing the door after them, the two giggling idiots approached me. I tried to recall their names, but I couldn't remember.

"Oh my God, you are so lucky to serve Kincaid. I wish I was working so close to him. Then again, we're just as excited to be blood donors for any of them." She beamed.

The other nodded beside her. "I wouldn't worry about the rumors, though. I'm sure that's all they are."

Confusion dipped my brows. "Rumors?"

"That Kincaid killed his last few servants."

Blood drained from my face.

Charlotte stepped closer. "Please excuse us for a moment." She gripped my arm and dragged me to a corner. Once there, she got in my face and snarled, "How did you get a job like that over me?"

Did she not hear what that woman said about Kincaid? Yet, she was still peeved I got a better-standing position than her. I shook my head, appalled. "I don't know."

Her hold tightened. Nails dug into my skin as she shook my arm. "Don't fucking lie to me."

"I had nothing to do with *their* choice."

"Tell them you won't do it. Tell them you want me to."

They would kill me.

As I stared at her, I saw she knew this, yet she didn't care.

She didn't care about her own daughter's safety. My life.

How utterly disgusting. The knowledge had my stomach churning, hatred rising, and I snapped in a low tone, "No."

Her eyes widened, then quickly narrowed. "No?"

I tugged my arm from her grasp and shook my head. I

couldn't hold back any longer. Not when I now knew that what she felt for me was beyond hatred. I was at a loss with the woman who birthed me.

Shaking my head again, I said, "I knew you hated me, but to sentence me to death because you want to… what? Be known as a Prince servant? So you can brag? Or is it because you find the young Prince handsome and want to—"

My head rocked to the side from the slap she delivered. The noise echoed around the room.

Rage uncurled inside me, and I slowly turned my head back and caught her gaze. Whatever she saw in my expression had her stepping back. For the first time, I wanted to ignore Mr. Langley's warning.

I wanted to hurt her.

Bennett appeared beside us. I hadn't even heard him enter the room again. "What is the meaning of this?"

Charlotte straightened and smiled sweetly. "Oh, just a misunderstanding. But my daughter wishes to ask you something."

Bennett faced me. I glared at Charlotte and said nothing.

Bennett sniffed and hummed under his breath. "Amara?"

"I can't seem to remember what it was, sir. Sorry."

"*Amara*," Charlotte scolded.

"Yes?"

"You wanted to ask him if you could switch—"

"No, *Mother*, it was you who wanted to switch positions with me. But when I refused, you hit me." She gaped like a fish as I turned to Bennett. "I am honored to be a servant to Master Kincaid." The lie tasted disgusting, but I would not follow the woman before me ever again.

"Amara." Fake tears clouded her eyes.

It wouldn't work, not when I had seen the wolf behind the sheep's clothing. I was done.

"Very well, Amara." Bennett nodded. "Please follow me, and I will take you to your new room."

"She gets a new room?" Charlotte cried, only to quickly clamp her lips closed.

Bennett sneered at her before spinning and walking away. "Come, Amara. The rest of you, stay until someone else arrives to show you where to go."

I didn't look back as I followed Bennett, closing the door behind me. Even if I was walking into a new danger, I was glad to see the end of Charlotte, my so-called mother.

L. ROSE

WITHIN THE DARKNESS

INFINITE BOND

L. ROSE

ACKNOWLEDGMENTS

The biggest thanks and appreciation goes to Jay at Covers by Juan. His outstanding talent for the cover work on the trilogy has blown me away. He's been an absolute pleasure to work with and I look forward to working with him again in the future!!

Becky, Donna, and V, from Hot Tree Editing, thank you all so much for your love and support on this endeavour.
Lee Ching, thank you for formatting these books and making them look beautiful!

To all readers, thank you for taking a chance on my work. Not only do I appreciate it, but Paige, Asher, Thorn, Cedrick, Ezra, Nate, and Alex do as well. If it hadn't been for you reading and falling in love with their stories, I wouldn't have had the strength to keep going because it takes a big leap for an author to try something different and believe it could work out. I'm so bloody grateful to you all for boosting my confidence with this series.

Lindsey, Rachel, Amanda, Susan, and Sarez, thank you for reading it early and helping me believe ghouls can find love… and a lot of it!

ALSO BY THE AUTHOR

Titles under L. Rose

Infinite Bond
(m/m/m/m fantasy standalone)

Within the Darkness
(m/f/m/m fantasy standalone)

Titles under Lila Rose

Hawks MC: Ballarat Charter

Holding Out (Free)

Outplayed (standalone related to the Hawks MC)

Climbing Out

Finding Out (novella)

Black Out

No Way Out

Coming Out (m/m novella)

Out to Find Freedom (standalone related to the Hawks MC)

Hawks MC: Caroline Springs Charter

The Secret's Out

Hiding Out

Down and Out

Living Without

Walkout (novella)

Hear Me Out (m/m)

Break Out (novella)

Fallout

Out of the Blue (standalone related to the Hawks MC: m/m/m)

Out Gamed (standalone related to the Hawks MC: novella)

Hawks MC: Next Generation

Coyote

Ruin (m/m)

Texas

Polished P & P Series (m/m romance)

Wreck Me Forever

Never a Saint

Working Out West

Diamond MC

Country

State (novella)

Death

Romantic Comedies

Making Changes

Making Sense

***

Fumbled Love

Bumbled Love